Gregor Piatigorsky

Gregor Piatigorsky

*The Life and Career
of the Virtuoso Cellist*

Terry King

McFarland & Company, Inc., Publishers
Jefferson, North Carolina, and London

All photographs are from the author's collection
unless otherwise noted.

LIBRARY OF CONGRESS CATALOGUING-IN-PUBLICATION DATA

King, Terry.
Gregor Piatigorsky : the life and career
of the virtuoso cellist / Terry King.
p.   cm.
Includes bibliographical references and index.

ISBN 978-0-7864-4635-3
softcover : 50# alkaline paper ∞

1. Piatigorsky, Gregor, 1903–1976.
2. Violoncellists — Biography.   I. Title.
ML418.P63K56   2010   787.4092 — dc22   2010020505
[B]

British Library cataloguing data are available

©2010 Terry King. All rights reserved

*No part of this book may be reproduced or transmitted in any form
or by any means, electronic or mechanical, including photocopying
or recording, or by any information storage and retrieval system,
without permission in writing from the publisher.*

Front cover: portrait of Gregor Piatigorsky, 1930, courtesy of the author;
background *Double Concerto*, Brahms (International Music Score Library Project)

Manufactured in the United States of America

*McFarland & Company, Inc., Publishers
Box 611, Jefferson, North Carolina 28640
www.mcfarlandpub.com*

To my mother,
and to my wife, Laura — who always believed in me and
valiantly endured many lost vacations. I am so grateful you have
such patience and tolerance, and yet still love me.

Contents

Acknowledgments ix
Preface 1
Introduction 3

PART I : A MUSICAL LEGEND 5
   1. Early Years, 1903–1920 5
   2. New Frontiers, 1921 22
   3. Nomad to Success 40
   4. America, Rachmaninoff, Strauss and Stravinsky 62
   5. Paris, 1932–1933 82
   6. World's Busiest Cellist 96
   7. Jacqueline 115
   8. Prokofiev, Hindemith and Teaching 127
   9. The War Years 145
   10. The 1950s: Los Angeles 169
   11. The 1960s and the Heifetz-Piatigorsky Partnership 186
   12. Academe's Bizarre World 206

PART II : RECALLING PIATIGORSKY 215

PART III : "PHILOSOPHIES AND ADVICES" 249

PART IV : WRITINGS 265

PART V : THE RECORDINGS 283

PART VI : APPENDICES 295
   A Guide to the Discography and Filmography 295
   Appendix A: Discography 296
   Appendix B: Live Performances 312

Appendix C: Performance Filmography   319

Appendix D: Interviews and Miscellaneous Appearances on Radio and Television   321

Appendix E: Publications   323

Appendix F: Piatigorsky's Original Compositions, Arrangements and Transcriptions Recorded by Other Cellists   328

Chapter Notes   333
Bibliography   349
Index   353

Acknowledgments

In the many years this book has gestated, some sources have become almost impossible to recall. I know I will leave out deserving people who have helped significantly, and of them I ask forgiveness.

Russian translators and researchers: A special thanks to Galina Kopytova, who devotedly worked to find many details I thought impossible to find; Lydia Ader, Rex Hughes, Alexsander Rakviashvili, Myrna Dyer, N. Tarakovskaya and the Glinka Museum, Moscow, Prof. Tatiana Gaidamovich, and Irina Dubkova, Moscow Conservatory, Maria N. Shcherbakova, Frank Bacon, Don and Janelle Jarvis, Sergey Antonov, Mischa Veselov, Grigorii and Polina Sedukh, Anya Morozkina, Ksenia Sapozhnikova, Galina Plotnikova, and Jan Guernsey. Others include Anne Prescott (Japan), Melitta Fort (Germany), and Magdalena Richter (Poland).

In addition to those interviewed in the text, I must thank Ralph Berkowitz, Anne Mischakoff Heiles, Margaret Bartley, Adele Siegel, Jacqueline and Joram Piatigorsky, Jephta and Evan Drachman, Gregory Piatigorsky, Mischa Boguslavski, Judith Galamian, Beverly Sills, Jean Pierre Fonda (-Fournier), David Dalton, John Barnett, Peter Bartók, Walter and Mariel Bossert, Nat Brandt, Sophie Feuermann, Harold Bruder, Ivry Gitlis, Simon Morrison, Berneil Mueller, Jascha Nemtsov, Art Stephen, Roman Totenberg, Tamás Varga, John Waxman, Harry Wimmer, Roger Williams, Victor Yuzefovich, James Kreger, Paula Majerfeld, Jennifer Caplado, Gretchen Wade, Ichiro Mitsumoto, Keith Harvey, Nicholas Anderson, John Koenig, Nathaniel Rosen, and Jeffrey Solow.

Institutions and other individuals include the Philadelphia Free Library's Fleisher Collection, Bridget Carson of the Boston Symphony Archives, Frank Villella of the Chicago Symphony Archives, Steve Lacoste of the Los Angeles Philharmonic Archives, Berlin Philharmonic Archives, Christy Bird of the University of Hartford Libraries, Grinnell College, the Longy School of Music, the Walton Trust, the Estate of Lord Menuhin, the Casals Museum, the Hindemith Institute, the Koussevitzky Music Foundation, Inc., the Library of Congress, the British Library, Mirte Berko Mallory, Diane Stine of the Aspen Music Festival, and the UCLA Music Library.

To those regarding recordings: A special thanks to Wolfdieter Jordan, whose quest for perfection clarified many mysteries and revealed much about Piatigorsky's Berlin activities; Michael Gray, Gerald Gibson, Jon Samuels, the BBC Music Library, the Yale Music Library and Sound Recordings Collection (Richard Warren, Suzanne Eggleston Lovejoy, Harold E.

Samuel), Gene Pollioni, Kurt Miller, Fred Maroth, Peter Nothnagle, Keith Harvey, Kevin Mostyn, Dave Hermann, Ed Wilkinson, Aaron Snyder, John Maltese, Jack Pfeiffer, Dr. Christopher Nozawa, Frank Forman, the New York Public Library, Dave, Bob, Esther and Anna Kapell, Martin Klingmeyer, and many more.

Thank you all.

Preface

As a student in the Los Angeles public school system in the 1960s, I was given the opportunity to study a string instrument rather than take the usual music appreciation course. It was there that I stumbled upon the cello, and I was immediately attracted by its size and shape. I was given a cello instruction book and blindly started to make my way through it, guided by the teacher's occasional demonstration of all the string instruments.

The musical world was a mystery to me. But, curious, I went to a local music shop and found a recording that featured the cello: the Brahms Double Concerto with Jascha Heifetz and Gregor Piatigorsky. I saved my money until I could buy the record. At home I played it and was mesmerized. I had never heard anyone else play the cello and I realized how little I knew. Beyond my instruction book, I did not know how to improve. But one day a young cellist enrolled in my school. He was rumored to be quite good, and he played in the advanced orchestra. Awestruck, I followed this unlucky fellow everywhere until he was persuaded that I was harmless.

"May I just see you practice? I'll keep quiet." But I didn't. I kept asking him questions. Watching him maneuver the instrument and produce a beautiful vibrant sound I asked,

"How did you learn to do that?"

Looking at me as if I was an idiot, he replied,

"How? I take lessons with a private teacher!"

"Lessons? Do you think I could take lessons?"

"I don't know," he said, "she is a very tough teacher."

I mustered up the courage to ask my parents for lessons. They agreed and I progressed. One day my friend, the luthier Benjamin Koodlach, urged me to go with him to Piatigorsky's home; Bennie would adjust his cello and I could meet the famous man. But I was too scared to go because I knew I was not good enough. Instead I asked Bennie if Piatigorsky might sign one of his albums for me.

A few years later Bennie came to one of my chamber music concerts, and afterwards came backstage with tears in his eyes. "If Piatigorsky is any friend of mine, you are his next student," he said. This was flattering and frightening. But this time Bennie insisted.

He spoke to Piatigorsky and gave me his phone number to set up an audition. For two weeks I was sick to my stomach with anxiety, so fearful I was of the audition. The day before the audition I called and told Mr. Piatigorsky that was I too sick to come. Somehow he knew I was just scared. "You come tomorrow at 10:00," he said sternly.

Bennie told me that Piatigorsky loved to hear music that he didn't know, so I brought an obscure sonata by Rosenhain, a composer reminiscent of Mendelssohn. Armed with

Duport etudes, Brahms and Rosenhain, I did my best, but what an unwanted down-bow staccato I had! One etude modulated into another, ending in panic. He patiently said, "Doesn't matter. Again." I never really finished; my memory failed entirely. The sonatas went better, as I had a piano to hold onto. After my ordeal, he told me when master classes began. That was it. Piatigorsky seemed to know more about me than I knew about myself.

At the master class I was immediately struck by his openness. He was answering questions I had been afraid to ask; my previous teacher ridiculed my curiosity. Piatigorsky exuded the love of discovery, the joy of creativity, and saw curiosity as its constant drive. I was a bit out of place in the class at first because I was so naïve; I merely wanted to play well. The other students were more advanced, ambitious and focused. I soon became brave; deep down I knew I had a gift.

Piatigorsky was perfect for me; his openness and encouragement were gifts I carry with me every day. His generosity was endless. He paid my tuition and provided a fellowship and stipend when I had nothing. Piatigorsky gave me the courage to become myself and the means by which to do it.

What could I do in return? "Just work, be well, be happy" was his usual answer. However, one day he mentioned that he had recorded many pieces in Berlin in the 1920s, but couldn't remember what they were. That was my cue. From that moment on I became a record collector, and finally, his biographer.

Introduction

Grinnell (IA) Herald Register
January 21, 1930
The Third Great Russian: Gregor Piatigorsky, Cellist,
Rounds Out Trio of Gifted Fellow-Countrymen

A young Russian artist, only twenty-six years old, by name Gregor Piatigorsky, displayed a mastery of the 'cello in his recital here Friday evening which more than repaid his hearers for having ventured out in weather approximating twenty below zero. In spite of the frigid temperature outside the chapel was more than well filled by those who came to hear the third of the gifted trio of youthful Russians brought to Grinnell. They have been an interesting trilogy; Vladimir Horowitz, pianist; Nathan Milstein, violinist and Gregor Piatigorsky, 'cellist. All have been masters of their respective instruments and all have brought a rich measure of pleasure and inspiration to the music lovers of Grinnell. It is impossible to tell which one of the three Grinnell people have liked the most; all have been outstanding. Piatigorsky's style is fluent and his technique is masterful. He gives, perhaps, more than any of the three the impression of talking to his audience. Mr. Piatigorsky was generous with encores, of which Valentin Pavlovsky accompanied him in a Praeludium by Bach, in a deft and sympathetic manner. Grinnell will be glad to welcome Mr. Piatigorsky or any of his brother Russians again, any time.

Grinnell, Iowa—May 1976

"I am older, so I should use the older cello," said the frail master. The elder instrument's dimensions were a bit unusual, which made playing on pitch more challenging. Thinking it might help, he asked to use the modern cello. The newer cello suited him better, but suddenly he cut the rehearsal short. It was obvious to both of us that it was going nowhere. "Meet me at the concert with music," he said. "We will choose then as we like."

For the next several hours I was beside myself. It was May 1976 and I was teaching at Grinnell College in Iowa. I had recommended that an honorary doctorate be granted to my teacher, Gregor Piatigorsky. It certainly wasn't the first degree bestowed upon him; he held dozens of degrees from major institutions worldwide. "It would be good to play a concert of the two cellos," he suggested, before his arrival, in his colorful Russian-English.

When we entered the chapel where concerts were held, he immediately remembered playing there long ago. Later, I checked the college archives and found that Grinnell was indeed one of the venues on his first U.S. tour, 1929–1930. He was the last of three young Russian artists appearing that season, the others being Vladimir Horowitz and Nathan Milstein. Now, 47 years later, Grinnell would be one of his last public performances.

At 4:00 we met in the anteroom and decided on a program: duets by Glière and Kummer. We walked on stage; then he spoke to the audience, a rare event. He was entertaining, charming, totally himself, totally calm. We began playing and amazingly the artist within him reemerged, transported to an earlier time, revisiting his vast experience. He left his failing body, gathering all his powers of concentration and physical strength to once again say something with his constant companion, the cello.

The duos were a joy, and the old master made beautiful, poignant music. After several bows he returned to the stage alone and presented two solos that he had composed, replete with their programmatic tales—homage to his composer friends Prokofiev and Bloch. His power of expression rose as he played these familiar works. After the solos he asked the audience if they might like to take a "ten minute pause," after which we returned to play more duos. The packed audience cheered on and on.

How did he do it? He had not played in many months, the cancer claiming more from him every day. After the concert I asked him how he was able to do it. He paused, looked up and slowly said, "I don't know." This mind over matter fascinated me. How did this man become the unique artist he was?

In the many years of gestation this book has taken, I have always wanted it to be a document of fact and objectivity counterbalanced with his distinctive, colorful voice. In my desire to tell the story authentically, I have quoted from Piatigorsky himself whenever possible. I have used his autobiography, *Cellist*, not in the sense of retelling it, but as one of many primary sources. *Cellist* ends in mid-career, but I have used other writings and drafts that reveal more detail as well as delve into his later life. Over the years I have traveled and researched far and wide to get at the essential artist and have interviewed many musicians associated with Piatigorsky and his students. I am grateful to the Piatigorsky family for making his papers available; without those, I could not present his life with the full richness it deserves.

PART I : A MUSICAL LEGEND

1. Early Years, 1903–1920

Early Years: 1903–1916

Isaac Abramovich Piatigorsky was a frustrated violinist, unhappy to be working in his father's bookshop. At 22, he married the sympathetic Basya [Maria] Amshislavska who bore him six children, four boys and two girls.[1] Isaac especially wanted his sons to love music as much as he did. As soon as they were old enough, he started the boys on the violin and piano, teaching them himself. As each of his sons chose music as a career, he hoped they would surpass his own modest musical achievements. The oldest boy, Leonid, enjoyed the violin; and Gregorii, known to his family as Grisha, turned to the cello, as did younger brother Alexander, who later remembered:

> Our father, a modest orchestra musician (viola), loved music with all his heart, especially quartet music. He was devoted to it until he was very old. You would always hear chamber music at our house. In later life, our father only saw his children as musicians. Thinking that the greatest schooling for an instrumentalist is playing in the orchestra, he wanted his children to specifically become orchestra musicians. Besides, father saw financial stability in that field, and rightfully so. He thought that a good orchestra would always guarantee a piece of bread for dinner. In childhood, we all played parts of quartet music with him. Father knew how incredibly gifted my brothers were; he especially praised Gregor's talent. Of course, father's interest in music, specifically quartet music, had a significant influence on the future cellist. Grisha started studying the cello when he was about six years old. By the age of eight or nine, he already amazed everyone with his charismatic sound and unusual performing skills.[2]

During a concert in their hometown of Yekaterinoslav (now Dnipropetrovs'k), six-year-old Grisha first heard the cello and it made a lasting impression on the boy. Back at home, he imitated the cellist by playing an imaginary instrument made with two sticks while still studying the violin with his father:

> Those magic sticks began to sing, to cry, and to speak, lifting me high into a world of sounds, where every mood could come at will, and every dream, be truth. To be forced from my sublimity back to our noisy, overcrowded house was seldom a welcome descent. More often it was a shock of awakening, a moment which — as though defying the violence of interrupted dreams — lasted dreadfully long. Such awakening began to occur at shorter intervals while the magic of my sticks lessened their power of transformation. I found myself on earth more often, but with my senses sharpened for subtlety, I now keenly searched for my own special place in the realm of everyday normality.[3]

When Isaac finally understood his son's passion for the cello, he bought him a full-sized instrument, for his seventh birthday, in 1910:

> "Do, re, mi, fa, so, la si, get up." Father awakened me.
> "What did I sing?"
> "Do-major scale."
> "How many notes?"
> "Seven."
> "Today you are seven. It's your birthday. Come on, hurry! There is something waiting for you," my father said as he awoke me. I followed him into the living room, where the entire family was assembled. I saw a cello. "It's real, not a quarter or half size as for children." I stood awe-struck, not daring to touch it. It was my first cello, and even before I could pluck the strings it was next to me at all meals and at my bedside at night.[4]

Isaac tried to teach his son, reasoning that the cello and the violin belonged to the same family and thus did not require special training. It quickly became apparent that Isaac's instruction was inadequate, so he enrolled Grisha in the local music school, where he joined his brother Leonid. From then on Gregor Piatigorsky's life and future were inexorably linked to the cello.

Piatigorsky practiced with determination during his early years in Yekaterinoslav. He awoke early each day to practice so that he would not disturb his sleeping family and developed a silent system: fingering the cello while bowing in the air. This helped him conceive the sound he wanted and inspired his imagination.

He attended the local conservatory (Music School for High School and Special Professional School, later called the Yekaterinoslav Conservatory), which was a branch of the government-run All Russia Imperial Musical Society, chaired by composer Alexander Glazunov. Excepting holidays, school met seven days a week.

Piatigorsky's first cello teacher at the conservatory was Mark Illych Yampolsky, a member of a dynasty of well-known violin and cello pedagogues.[5] The boy also studied math, science, Russian, and geography. After some months, Yampolsky left Yekaterinoslav and was replaced by the director of the conservatory, Professor Dimitri Petrovich Gubarev.[6] Piatigorsky thrived under his tutelage, becoming the musical wunderkind of Yekaterinoslav and amazing people with his virtuosity, maturity, and depth of tone.

At the start of the twentieth century, the industrial city of Yekaterinoslav had a population of almost 200,000 and was home to an Advanced Mining School, an Orthodox seminary, dental and railroad schools, one classical and one modern gymnasium, several women's gymnasia, and over thirty elementary schools. The town had three daily newspapers, a theater, twenty libraries, a natural history museum, and the conservatory. Though not actively religious, the Piatigorskys lived in the Jewish sector, not far from the main synagogue.

One third of Yekaterinoslav's growing population was Jewish. At that time, Jews were severely restricted from obtaining a public education, as dictated by the Pale of Settlement. Only 10 percent of all Jewish applicants to government-run schools were accepted, and those were admitted only after surviving rigorous competition. The Jewish students who were allowed to attend achieved remarkable academic success. Since they were motivated, they routinely outperformed the majority of Christian students. This further fueled anti–Semitism, which was tacitly sanctioned by the tsar:

> *By the Authority of Nicholas II, Tsar of all Russia, Lord of the North Countries*
> *and Sovereign of the Caucasus, to all subjects between The Baltic,*
> *The Bosporus, The Caspian, and The Black Seas, and all*
> *others living in and under his domain,*
> *To tolerate no Anarchy, Civil Disobedience, Unrest or Destruction of property*
> *except against those who do not acknowledge the dominion of God*
> *and his son Jesus Christ our Holy Savior.*

> *All Loyal Christians will be protected against seizure, confiscation*
> *or injury by any Infidel, Socialist, Anarchist or Jew.*
> P. Petronovich, Governor
> City of Yekaterinoslav[7]

Isaac Piatigorsky knew that if his children were to have a good education, he and his family would have to convert to Christianity. More important, the deadly pogroms in Yekaterinoslav (1905–1909) left a terrible mark.[8] Thus Isaac converted to the Russian Orthodox Church and wore a large gold cross around his neck, making his faith apparent to all. He changed his name from Isaac Abramovich (son of Abram) to Pavel (Paul) Ivanovich (son of Ivan), so that it would sound gentile.

Before the early 1800s, the vast majority of Jewish people did not have last names. When it was required to have them, they often took a name that reflected their geography. The family name Piatigorsky was in itself neutral, and was also a city and province in the Ukraine. Now, as Russian Orthodox, they could hide their race and religion to survive.

Though the family was not desperately poor, it was large, and the need to offset Pavel's lagging interest in his father's bookstore was becoming problematic. Pavel's heart was only in music. To earn more money, he often rented out the children's rooms and any other space in the home. Pavel was able to squeeze in twelve boarders at a time, leaving the children to sleep on the floor. He placated the family by saying that after the deprivation, a comfortable bed would be a luxury. To keep everyone from boredom with food, Maria would say, "Today the soup is better than yesterday, and will be better still tomorrow."[9] Meals often consisted of borscht or goose fat and dried bread.

While older brother Leonid and Pavel played violin and viola, Maria and the daughters played the piano. Maria could not read or write, but music constantly flowed through the house. Pavel also played in the circus orchestra in Yekaterinoslav on evenings and weekends, struggling to stay focused on the bookstore during the day. Sometimes Gregor accompanied his father on his night jobs, and was allowed to play with the locals in the orchestras.

During the summer, musicians throughout Russia augmented outdoor symphonic concerts, including those in Yekaterinoslav. One of the cellists, Alexei Kinkulkin, a former pupil of the German pedagogue Julius Klengel, consented to hear the boy, then aged eight. His assessment was unflattering to say the least: "While I played, Mr. Kinkulkin tapped his tiny fingers on a table and cleaned his nails with a toothpick. He remained silent until I had put my cello away. 'Listen carefully, my boy. Tell your father that I strongly advise you to choose a profession that will suit you. Keep away from the cello. You have no talent whatsoever.'" Kinkulkin would not know the extent of his lack of insight until he met Piatigorsky again in Leipzig in 1922. "'It is a privilege to meet you,' Kinkulkin said to me, 'we have met before — in Etakerinoslav. I played for you when I was very young.' There was a light of recognition in his eyes.'"[10]

Pavel detested the book business and business in general. His love for music was greater than the need to support his large family. He loved his family, but his desire to undertake a life as a violinist called too loudly. As a result, Pavel decided to leave his family, travel to St. Petersburg, and take violin lessons from the legendary pedagogue Leopold Auer. Pavel's father, Abram, was violently opposed to his son's wishes and threatened to disown him and the rest of the family. Abram was strict and stingy and never visited the family in their home. Pavel's defiant departure, his pursuit of music and similar encouragement to his sons, and his conversion to the Russian Orthodox Church was enough to create a permanent break between Pavel and Abram.

Pavel must have felt that his sons could earn enough money with their musical talents to keep the family afloat. This left Gregor, age eight, and Leonid, age nine, as breadwinners of the family. Perhaps Pavel secretly suspected his prosperous father would rescue the family from financial disaster while he pursued his musical career. The times did get desperate, and Gregor was chosen to approach grandfather Abram to ask for help. Abram angrily dismissed the boy and remained true to his word, refusing to give the family a single kopeck.

During the day, Piatigorsky attended school. He rapidly grew taller and was soon able to pass for a teenager. As a nine year old, he was able to earn money for the family doing night jobs — performing in local orchestras, *traktirs* (stables that also served cheap food and drink), restaurants, and burlesque theatres. During this time, he also worked with a gypsy singer who taught him Russian folksongs, gypsy styles, and improvising. These skills were useful for employment as well as musicianship. He would later credit her for helping him to achieve his singing cello tone.

Age 9, wearing the Ekaterinoslav Music School uniform (courtesy Piatigorsky estate).

The newly completed Coliseum Theatre hired musicians through the *cinema bourse*, an employment center that provided musical accompaniment for the novel entertainment that was sweeping the world, silent film. He braved the mocking of his fellow hopefuls, who told him, "Go home to mother; she's probably waiting for you."[11] But Piatigorsky successfully auditioned, passing for an older player. He was very excited about playing music for films, and his enthusiasm and natural abilities eventually allowed him to take over some of the duties from the leader of the group. He began arranging appropriate music to enhance scenes of romantic love, battles, storms, villains and heroes.[12]

About a year after this switch of family roles, grandfather Abram died. Pavel returned from St. Petersburg, bitter and sad, as he had failed completely. He was not accomplished enough to enter Auer's class, and could do no more than take lessons from an assistant. Upon his return to Yekaterinoslav, Pavel found that his sister Julia and brother-in-law Leonid Agranoff had taken most of the inheritance and departed for America.

By now Piatigorsky was a local celebrity and could play Mendelssohn's Violin Concerto on the cello. But Pavel and Maria did not push him into the role of a prodigy; they opted for further study and decided he should audition for the Moscow Conservatory. After Piatigorsky's last school recital under Gubarev,[13] the family began to make their way to Moscow. Gregor, with his father as manager, performed some of his first solo concerts in a few of the cities along the rail line. Arriving at the Moscow Conservatory, he auditioned for the director, Mikhail Ippolitov-Ivanov,[14] and cellist Alfred von Glehn[15] and was awarded a full scholarship.

With Piatigorsky's further studies assured, the rest of the family followed and moved to the outskirts of Moscow. Pavel, with his meager inheritance, bought a rundown apartment building in which the family could live as well as rent out the other rooms. The neighborhood was rough, due in part to its proximity to a makeshift vodka shed. Desperate women mingled among drunken gangs, begging husbands and fathers to come home, sometimes being beaten for their efforts — especially on paydays.

Still the Piatigorskys faced financial difficulties and once again Gregor, now aged ten, had to earn money. The ever-optimistic Pavel accepted a two-month tour with a local opera troupe traveling to towns along the Volga River. Pavel, Leonid, and Gregor would be the principal string players; the opera was Tchaikovsky's *Eugen Onegin*. The company was ridiculously inept and only managed a few performances before disbanding in Astrakhan, along the banks of the Caspian Sea. Pavel took the demise as an opportunity to have a vacation in Astrakhan, but their fun was cut short due to the usual lack of funds. There was only enough money for two train tickets back to Moscow. One of them would have to stay and earn enough to take the train back to Moscow.

Pavel asked the conductor of an outdoor orchestra in an amusement park if there might be any openings. There was room for a substitute cellist, thus Piatigorsky was elected to stay behind and audition. The audition was successful and he quickly learned to be self reliant in unfamiliar environments.

Shortly after Piatigorsky started his new job, the former cellist returned. Piatigorsky was allowed to stay, only if he agreed to play in the second violin section. Piatigorsky accepted the challenge and was provided a violin. He could manage the slower parts, but when the music became more difficult, the youth reverted to playing between his knees, as if it were a cello. The sight of this "clowning" detracted attention from the conductor and created unwelcome applause. Piatigorsky was fired.

Still lacking enough money to return, the boy found a café chantant in the park and successfully auditioned for its orchestra. So that the underaged cellist would not see the nudes onstage, the conductor had him turn facing the wall of the pit, and provided a mirror so that Piatigorsky could see the conductor. This adventure was cut short as well, but this time it was of his choice.

Piatigorsky became infatuated with a barefoot dancer who hated her job. She resented the general unruliness of her audience and its mockery of dance. Piatigorsky, of course, did not understand that the point of her being onstage was for men to view her body in provocative motion, not for her to display her balletic skill. He naïvely tried to rescue her by designing a routine that he could accompany. He chose *Souvenir* by Drdla. As she danced his choreography, it only created laughs and the fury of the management. Piatigorsky rushed back to her dressing room to find the manager firing her. In sympathy, he quit but was given a week's pay.

With that money he bought a ticket taking him as far north as possible towards Moscow. The rest of the way home became a series of hitching rides on freight trains at night, sleeping during the day, and selling everything but his cello for food. He finally made it back to Moscow about twelve days later.

Piatigorsky's studies at the conservatory were constantly interrupted by odd jobs, though he did his best to attend classes during the day. With his nomadic lifestyle, his academic work was abysmal: "My formal education approaches zero.... I was forced into a kind of self-education. I sought the company of people from whom I could learn something. I was ashamed of my ignorance, of not even knowing elementary geography.... Fortunately, a few wonderful people were not put off by my questions. I was interested in so many things and I never had time for them all."[16]

He attended the conservatory on and off from 1914 through 1920, though there is no record that he actually graduated. The core music curriculum he attempted to fulfill consisted of chamber music with piano taught by Alexander Gedike or Fyodor Koenemann,[17] string quartet with E. Rivkind,[18] and piano with V. Ziring, B. Vishau or D. Veis. The general curriculum included classes in Russian, literature, geography, physics, mathematics, German or French, aesthetics, and mythology. Piatigorsky's limited attendance did not reflect his intellectual curiosity; he studied all his life.

As the family patriarch, Pavel Piatigorsky dictated to everyone. But after Pavel left the family to study the violin in St. Petersburg, his power was eroded. Gregor felt that he had become head of the family, entitling him a say in important matters. In 1915, when his sister Nadja became engaged to Dimitri, a low-class boarder living in the apartment below, Piatigorsky objected. Dimitri and his alcoholic abusive family was no safe place for his beloved sister; Piatigorsky was too young to know about his sister's pregnancy and consequent unspoken shame. Pavel was in favor of the hasty union and when the boy protested, his father struck him and ordered him to leave their home.

Piatigorsky left with what he could carry and his cello. He waited outside, hoping his mother would call him back. Hours went by, and after the lights dimmed he knew he was on his own. Through the January snow he struggled towards the business sector. Exhausted, he stopped to rest and fell asleep. Early the next morning a passerby shook him awake. The experience left his hands and feet frostbitten. Mr. Shutkin, a kindly old shopkeeper, took in the boy and nursed him back to health.

As Piatigorsky healed, he knew he needed to find work. Shutkin was frail and very poor—his junk store barely kept him fed. The old man took Piatigorsky to a local *traktir* hoping the boy might find employment. He was hired to work with an accordionist and eventually their plight improved. One evening, as the accordionist was taking a break, someone asked Piatigorsky to play Bach. Suddenly a drunkard yelled at him to stop playing "that kind of music." Piatigorsky ignored the heckling, but the drunk approached and kicked the cello with his boot, breaking it into pieces. Shutkin was there that night; a fight ensued and Shutkin was critically injured. The man who had requested the Bach helped gather the pieces of the broken cello and they both took Shutkin to the hospital. Dear Shutkin died two days later.

Shutkin's friends helped Piatigorsky find new lodgings, but alone again he needed not

The Piatigorsky family in 1912. Back row left to right, all standing: Leonid and Julia Agranoff (uncle and aunt), Maria and Pavel Piatigorsky; middle row: Grandmother Piatigorsky, a cousin, Grandfather Piatigorsky, a cousin; front row: Gregor, Nadja, Alexander, a cousin, Leonid with his arms around another cousin (courtesy Piatigorsky estate).

only work, but also a cello. With his meager funds, the boy acquired a mud-colored relic of a cello, purchased in an outdoor vegetable market. In later years, Piatigorsky recalled:

> On warm days and in well-heated rooms, its varnish smelled like tar. Till today, I cannot understand how with that smell I was able to secure a position in one of the best restaurants in Moscow.[19] It was a so-called salon ensemble of a leader violinist, second violin, double bass, cello, piano, flute and clarinet. Saxophones were little known and even the dance bands did not use them. Thinking of it now, I realize why my strange cello appealed to the eating and drinking audience. It sounded like saxophone, penetrating and loud enough not to be drowned out by the orchestra or clatter of dishes.[20]

For about six months, this would prove to be Piatigorsky's steadiest employment and all seemed well for the twelve year old. He was able to resume classes at the conservatory in the fall of 1915 and could pay his rent.

A rich patron of the Metropol was known to be generous with tipping the ensemble, and especially to their former cellist for playing the patron's favorite piece — a treacly aria called *Fiameta*.[21] Piatigorsky was encouraged to be ready with it, but when the patron arrived and saw a youngster he became angry and started to leave. He assumed the boy could not satisfy his thirst for his favorite schmaltz; but the leader of the ensemble hurried after him, and after several minutes of persuasion, returned in triumph: "Come on, boys, take your ammunition, we are going to play for him in a private room."[22]

Piatigorsky had heard of incidents of mustard-smearing and other indignities to get a tip, and saw the moment as potential humiliation. Unable to understand his colleague's eagerness, Piatigorsky nevertheless played *Fiameta* repeatedly for the patron. Pleased, the gentleman gave the ensemble 1,000 rubles. He then gave the boy 9,000 rubles and told him to buy a better cello. With his sudden riches, his "friends" at the Metropol swindled Piatigorsky out of the money by insisting he buy a fake "Guarneri" cello. At twelve, he was an easy target for the unscrupulous. They all profited in the ruse, as he later discovered.

Piatigorsky's self-respect and pride cost him his job. On what would be his last night at the Metropol, faculty from the conservatory came and listened as the boy played solos. With their applause, they asked the waiter to deliver a tip and to say, "Buy yourself a cigar." Insulted, Piatigorsky ran to the professors' table and threw the money down. He was immediately thrown out.

Things deteriorated. According to Piatigorsky, "My landlady did not believe in extending credit to her boarders. The day I lost my job, she asked to be paid in advance. Days passed." With no income and no prospects, he paid his rent by selling most of his belongings to a traveling Tatar. Even his cello would be sold:

> Waiting to be paid, the landlady ordered me not to take the cello out of the house. I asked her to accompany me to a place where I could sell my Guarneri. A well-known violinmaker took a quick look at my cello and said, "I wonder who keeps putting new labels inside of this factory-made product. The last time I saw it, it was a Stradivari. Before that, it was a Guadagnini. Now it is a Guarneri."
> "What do you mean?" I asked.
> "This Guarneri is the darndest fake. It has been circulating in town for a long time. My boy, it is worthless. Don't buy it, no matter how cheap. That is my advice."
> "It's he who is a fake!" shrieked the landlady, shaking her finger at me.
> "Put it back in the cover." She snatched it. "I will salvage whatever I can," she said, slamming the door behind her.[23]

Piatigorsky now slept in the classrooms at the conservatory, having befriended the janitor. When word of his troubles reached Director Ippolitov-Ivanov and von Glehn, they gave him money and loaned him an instrument:

> It was made in Tyrol by some secondary maker whose name I forgot. It was rather small and girlish. The sound, matching its appearance, was also small and sweet. Soon I discovered that the cello would not stand my ruggedness, nor that it would yield to composer's ideas of bigness. Therefore, I chose my pieces solely to my cello's likings. It was then that I developed a taste for somewhat lyrical and elegant music. I was lucky always during that period to play in a string quartet [the Moscow Conservatory Quartet] whose dynamics, due to a natural limitation of power by my partners, could never reach over mezzo forte.
> An accident in a streetcar resulting in a hole in the rib put an end to my relation with it and it was taken away from me.[24]

Eventually Piatigorsky rented a room from a kindly lady who did not demand punctual payment. His resumed lessons with the sympathetic von Glehn were apparently of little value. Week after week Piatigorsky brought in an etude and absentmindedly played it. It seems that none of the challenging feats of Davidov, von Glehn's mentor, were entrusted to him. Perhaps von Glehn insisted that everyone, no matter the level, complete a course of etude material before advancing to the works of Davidov.

Von Glehn's cello class performed annual recitals, and Piatigorsky asked to be included.

Von Glehn allowed him to choose a piece, not expecting anything particularly challenging. For the concert, his teacher placed students in order of achievement, whereby the least accomplished started the recital, and the most advanced ended it. Piatigorsky began the recital performing the dazzling *Souvenir de Spa* by Servais, leaving von Glehn totally stunned. When Piatigorsky returned to his next lesson, von Glehn confronted him and dismissed him, saying he could not understand Piatigorsky's dual personality. They reconciled shortly afterwards and developed a warm relationship.

Piatigorsky also took several surreptitious (so as not to offend von Glehn) cello lessons with Anatoly Brandukov.[25] But all the while, he yearned to study the European styles of cello playing.

Piatigorsky was well-liked at the conservatory: "He was very thin, and, even at that time, unusually tall. On the street, the urchins used to shout at him; 'uncle, uncle, won't you pick up a sparrow!' and the little pupils of the Conservatory curtsied and in a sweet voice inquired: 'Gregory Pavlovich, what kind of weather do you have there upstairs?' and Grisha used to demonstrate how he had to double over to greet his tiny admirers."[26]

An important event in 1916 made a huge and lasting impression on Piatigorsky. He was asked to stopgap for the famous basso Fyodor Chaliapin, warming up the audience by performing before concerts and during the singer's breaks. Chaliapin was a celebrity of legendary proportions, and, in awe, Piatigorsky looked forward to performing on the same stage with him. By way of audition, he met the basso for luncheon with instructions to bring his cello:

> When we met he impressed me as a giant from another world — his large head, his dynamic features, carefree dress — I can see him now, his striking face above a strong neck exposed by the unfastened collar!
>
> "Play for me some arias. Yes, I would like you to play some of my favorites."
>
> I played a number from Russian operas, elaborating and making fantasies of them; he expressed his pleasure by rising as I ended each one, embracing me and asking for more! Finally, when I stopped to rest a moment, he said, "You sing too much! Most of you string players sing too much. Why don't you speak more on your instruments?"[27]

The first concert was at the Great Hall of the Moscow Conservatory. To his dismay, when he entered the hall, he was not greeted with applause. Piatigorsky began playing but no one listened, as the audience chatter drowned out his playing. At the next concert he encountered the same reaction. Piatigorsky became angry, and to draw the audience's attention, did all kinds of clowning with his cello. The audience started to listen. They cheered, and Piatigorsky responded with encores, much to Chaliapin's ire at being upstaged. Piatigorsky

Piatigorsky's first teachers, left to right: Mark Illych Yampolsky, Dimitri Petrovich Gubarev, Alfred von Glehn, Anatoly Andreyevich Brandukov.

was immediately fired. Despite the disastrous run-in with the basso, the two artists eventually became friends.[28]

Soviet Style: "The First String Quartet in the Name of Lenin"

By 1916 and 1917, any normal life in Moscow disappeared. It was a time of turmoil; World War I had been raging for over a year, fought on Russia's western doorstep. A completely unprepared Russia suffered horrendous casualties, led by the inept Tsar Nicholas II. By February 1917, internal revolts led to the abdication and execution of the tsar, providing the revolutionaries their first claim to power. They established a provisional government in St. Petersburg (Petrograd) with the hope that the decentralization of wealth would give starving peasants their first hope at filling their stomachs. When decentralization failed, the Bolsheviks overthrew the Provisional Government in October and by November controlled Moscow. On March 3, 1918, the Bolsheviks signed the Treaty of Brest-Litovsk with the Germans and pulled Russian troops out of the war. However, civil war continued between the White and Red factions until 1920, when the Bolsheviks emerged victorious.

H.G. Wells was there in 1914 and 1920 and wrote about the scene — wooden houses demolished for their lumber to burn, leaving gaps between homes made of stone: "Every one is shabby; every one seems to be carrying bundles ... ill-clad figures, all hurrying, all carrying loads ... partly the rations of food that are doled out ... [and] partly [the] results of illicit trade."[29] In spite of decaying infrastructure, severe inflation, food shortages, unheated buildings, and the transportation difficulties that Muscovites faced, the arts flourished. And although the ravages of World War I created mass suffering, the government attempted to bring the arts to the people.

The first commissar of education, Anatoly Lunacharsky, did his part to bring the arts to the people. His first challenge was to educate political leaders to the wisdom of preserving Russia's cultural heritage and the professions connected to it. Formerly a playwright, Lunacharsky had his hands full trying to explain the needs of artists to less sophisticated leaders. One of his first pupils was Comrade Lenin, the first premier of the Soviet Union.

Lenin agreed that art should belong to the people, writing that "It must have its deepest roots in the broad masses of workers. It must be understood and loved by them. It must be rooted in, and grow with, their feelings, thoughts, and desires. It must arouse and develop the artist in them." He reconciled the elitist perception of the arts: "Are we to give cake and sugar to a minority when the mass of workers and peasants still lack bread?" He concluded: "So that art may come to the people, and the people to art, we must first of all raise the general level of education and culture."[30]

Though Premier Lenin had a general appreciation for great music, he felt that its emotional response could be dangerous and not always productive to the discipline of the revolution. Lenin sent a letter revealing his dilemma to writer Maxim Gorky in 1918:

> I know nothing which is greater than the [Beethoven's] Appassionata; I would like to listen to it every day. It is marvelous, superhuman music. I always think with pride — perhaps it is naive of me — what marvelous things human beings can do!... But I can't listen to music too often. It affects your nerves, makes you want to say stupid nice things, and stroke the heads of people who could create such beauty while living in this vile hell. And now you mustn't stroke anyone's head — you might get your hand bitten off. You have to hit them on the head,

without any mercy although our ideal is not to use force on anyone.... [O]ur duty is infernally hard![31]

The human suffering was indiscriminate, and conscription showed no favoritism by taking gifted and educated young men into the Red Army. The composer Sergei Prokofiev was called up for service, but was luckily saved by another recent recruit, Gorky. In writing to Alexander Kerensky, head of the Provisional Government, he made his case: "We can't afford using golden nails on soldier's boots." Great musicians were enlisted into the Red Army nonetheless. Sergei Rachmaninov, who was living in Moscow, was ordered to stand watch in his neighborhood, attend rallies, and participate in meetings. The composer felt that it was the beginning of the end for Russia. Having no confidence in the leadership, he soon left Russia, never to return.

The leveling of class was devastating for those who were successful. Salaries were not paid for months on end, and prosperous composers, such as Alexander Glazunov, were ousted from their spacious apartments. The government usurped what it decided was useful and forced the displaced to live in seedy rooms. H.G. Wells found Glazunov understandably depressed in 1920: "He used to be a very big florid man, but now he is pallid and very much fallen away, so that his clothes hang loosely on him.... He told me he still composed, but that his stock of music paper was almost exhausted. 'Then there will be no more.'"[32]

Meanwhile, the conservatory buildings remained unheated and individual lessons were moved to the professors' homes or apartments. To be able to perform in the icy, unheated halls, Piatigorsky was clad in a big worn fur coat, his hands stuck in thick gloves from which the fingers had been cut off to make it possible to work the strings.

In November 1917, the Moscow Conservatory closed its doors until the following fall semester, and Piatigorsky again faced the all too familiar search for basic necessities. When it reopened, many students and teachers were missing.

> The winter was cold and food was scarce. One of the attractions of our house was a rice pudding with raisins, the greatest delicacy of those days. The clothing situation was no better: we managed to secure for Grisha a pair of shoes, left over at the warehouse because they were so immense; but the question of pants (and Grisha was still growing at that time) was quite acute.
>
> One day soon after his concert, Grisha arrived in very good spirits and told us: "You know, as I walk on the street, everybody seems to recognize me and smile at me. I find it extremely pleasant to be a celebrity." My sister looked him over and said: "You had better put on your dress suit, Grisha, to cover the hole in your seat." For a long time after that he wore his dress suit on the street.[33]

In the meantime, he was fortunate to find a room not far from the conservatory, and doubly fortunate that his landlady was lenient about payment. She knew many musicians in Moscow, one of whom was Professor Lev Zeitlin.[34] She arranged a meeting between Zeitlin and Piatigorsky. When Zeitlin met him, he immediately remembered the boy from that terrible night at the *traktir*. Zeitlin never knew his name and wondered what had become of the cellist and Shutkin, the old gentleman he had helped.

Zeitlin was also the leader of a newly organized string quartet. Their cellist had died suddenly[35] and Zeitlin asked the fifteen year old to audition for the group, the preeminent Soviet ensemble known as the First State String Quartet. Piatigorsky wholly impressed them and was immediately engaged. Zeitlin also arranged for Piatigorsky to play with the Zimin Opera Company where Zeitlin was concertmaster. His quartet colleagues referred to their younger partner with the highest praise and were amazed by his musical maturity. Second violinist Konstantin Mostras wrote: "We all marveled at the musical taste, artistry and exceptional logic of Piatigorsky's musical phrasing, who was back then only 15–16 years old.... At the rehearsals he would show an inventive initiative, surprising creativity and swift orientation in the most complex chamber pieces. He had a perfect feel for the style and character of the music we played, and played precisely by sight."[36]

For over two years the First State Quartet was led by Zeitlin, with Piatigorsky as cellist. During that time other members changed: second violin was filled by both Konstantin Georgievich Mostras[37] and Abram Illyich Yampolsky, and viola by Ferdinand Krisch and Lev Milchaylovich Pulver.[38] By the end of 1918, an article in the newspaper *Izvestiya* defined the goals of the ensemble:

(1) to serve the community with the best examples of chamber music,
(2) to organize chamber concerts in Moscow and across the nation for educational purposes,
(3) to create a free school of chamber music by admitting professional music performers to the rehearsals of the State Quartet and to organize new quartets for educational purposes, and
(4) to collect materials for the State Library of Chamber Music.

With the Quartet's distinguished service, and as committed members of Moscow's concert life, they found their own unique ways of interacting with audiences. The Quartet[39] toured a great deal and organized open rehearsals for music students, professional musicians and teachers, as well as for the public. These programs, launched in March 1919, often took place at the Zograf-Plaskina School of Music. Their repertoire consisted of the classics as well as contemporary works, which included the Debussy Quartet.

A few weeks earlier, as a result of the First State Quartet's success and visibility, a meeting was held with Anatoly Lunacharsky to discuss upcoming events. Lunacharsky was increasingly powerful, having been appointed first commissariat of public education, known as NARKOMPROS (an acronym for Narodnïy Komissariat Prosveshcheniya). Its musical division, MUZO, ran musical institutions, replacing Glazunov's Imperial Russian Musical Society in July 1918.

One of the suggested topics of the meeting was to rename the ensemble the First State String Quartet in the Name of Lenin. It was considered an honor to attach Com-

Moscow, Lenin Quartet, 1919 concert announcement. *Bottom:* Translation of 1919 concert announcement.

On Sunday, April 6th,

CONCERT

at Commercial Institute named of KARL MARKS
(Serpuhovskaya, Stremyannyi Ln.)
AS A GIFT TO RED ARMY
of Zamoskvorezky district

With participation of: Ekaterina Gelzer, O.O. Sadovskaya, M. N. Karakash, M. Meichik (piano), Ya. D. Yujny (own novels), V. F. Lebedev (own novels), K. G. Derjinskaya (artist of State Opera), State Quartet in name of Lenin, with participation of: L. Zeitlin, K. Mostras, K. Krish and G. Pyatigorsky.
Sadovskaya and Lebedev will read a scenes from the plays "It's a Family Affair— We'll Settle It Ourselves"
Starts at 8 PM
Commission of Communication with the Front.

rade Lenin's name to the ensemble. With youthful impulsivity, Piatigorsky voiced agitated objection to the cumbersome and unmusical title, suggesting it be renamed the Beethoven Quartet. Those gathered quickly dismissed Piatigorsky's outburst.

Almost immediately the Quartet in the Name of Lenin played for its namesake, one of the first Soviet ensembles to do so. The occasion was a political rally at the House of the Union (in the Kremlin complex). Lunacharsky, in regular contact with Lenin and one of the speakers that day, must have boasted to Lenin about Piatigorsky and the Quartet's accomplishments, possibly noting the new name of the ensemble, and lightheartedly referring to Piatigorsky's youthful outburst. But as Mostras remembered:

> While getting ready for the concert, we were carrying our instruments from the Round Hall that served as a green room, to the stage. We were surprised to see Vladimir Ilyich [Lenin] sitting on the chair behind the columns next to the stage entrance to the Colonial Hall. The meeting that he attended was already over.
>
> After a little confusion due to an unexpected visitor, Zeitlin came up and greeted him saying "hello." After that, Zeitlin introduced his friends to Lenin, told him about the repertoire of the Quartet, and about the concerts. Then Zeitlin asked him, "Vladimir Ilyich, did you know that there is an ensemble in Moscow that is named after you?" He was very surprised, if not startled, and a little uncomfortable. He said that it was not at all necessary. He mentioned that he did not know much about the field of music and suggested that maybe the quartet should carry the name of a famous musician, for example a composer like Beethoven. However, he really liked the idea of organizing a quartet whose goal was to bring the best music to the masses and to help organize other troupes and ensembles of the same sort.

Mostras also remembered a dialogue between Lenin and Zeitlin during that surprising encounter:

> Vladimir Ilyich said, "What are you going to play today?"
> "Quartet of Grieg."
> "That's good. And then what?"
> "Nothing else. We are in a great hurry. We have to appear at another military assignment where we are also performing today."
> "That is wonderful."[40]

Though Lenin was admittedly uninformed musically, he seems to have been interested in speaking briefly with the talented cellist. Piatigorsky was directed to follow Lenin into a small study:

> "Sit down," said Lenin.
> I kept the cello at my side. He looked at it.
> "Is it a good one?"
> "Not very."
> "The finest instruments used to be in the hands of rich amateurs. Soon they will be in the hands of professional musicians rich only in talent." He spoke with a slight burr. There was nothing of the mighty revolutionist in his appearance. His manner of speaking was simple and mild. His jacket, his shoes were like those of a neighborhood tailor. He looked like a well-meaning provincial uncle, and as he sat in a straight chair and looked at me as if encouraging me to say something, my uneasiness vanished.
> "You are very young, but you have a responsible position. It is strange that only in music and in mathematics can the very young reach prominence. Did you ever hear of a child architect or surgeon?" he said, smiling.
> "No, but I have heard of child chess players."
> "Quite right. Do you play chess?"[41] But, not waiting and as if reminiscing, "Chess has been good for the Russians — checkers too. It gives them occasion in this country to fight to win or lose or come out even, on equal terms and merits." He changed the subject abruptly. "Is it true that you protested at the meeting?"

"I am sorry." There was a slight stutter to my voice.

"At your age, one speaks first and thinks afterward," he said, with no trace of sarcasm. "I am not an expert on music, but I know that there is no more befitting name for a quartet than Beethoven."

"I am so glad. So you are not angry with me?"

"No," he said, smiling again. "But I wanted to speak with you. Only what is logical remains. Time filters impurities and corrects mistakes, particularly if made at such times as these. The Lenin String Quartet will not last; the Beethoven will."

He spoke in parables, not touching big topics. But whatever he said was profoundly human and was said with disarming simplicity.

Later, the Quartet participated in a celebration at which Lenin and Trotsky were the speakers and, for the first time, Lenin's name was not attached to the quartet. Piatigorsky went to see him: "He was surrounded by many people, but the moment he noticed me, he pointed at the line on the program which read, First State String Quartet." He said, 'You see?' It was the last time I saw him."[42]

Playing in the Quartet was an exceptional educational experience for the young Piatigorsky. The Quartet increasingly had a role in important celebrations, meetings, and rallies in cities, factories, and military bases. Celebrations such as the Day of the Red Army and the Day of Red Present in Moscow were occasions that incorporated major and regional musical, operatic, ballet, and theatrical organizations together in marathon style.

The portability of the ensemble made diverse events possible — singers, pianists, and poets performed with the Quartet or shared programs with them. The Quartet's repertoire ranged from the classics through Franck and Debussy and produced Chamber Music Evenings at the Veranda Theater of the October Revolution Palace (in the Kremlin complex). Political propaganda was often the primary role of these concerts, one of which included the marathon festivities for the 150th birthday of Beethoven.

During this prolific period, in addition to playing in the First State String Quartet (otherwise known as the Lenin Quartet), Piatigorsky gave recitals with illustrious pianists Yelena A. Bekman-Shcherbina, Alexander Goldenweiser, Nikolai Orloff, and Konstantin Igumnov.[43] Piatigorsky was very much indebted to the gifted Bekman-Shcherbina, who fostered his success in Moscow. With her, he gave the Russian premiere of Debussy's Sonata, the Moscow premiere of Prokofiev's Ballade op. 15, and, together with Zeitlin, the Russian premiere of the Ravel Trio. He also performed with noted singers including the soprano Antonina Nezhdanova,[44] and he occasionally played in Constantin Stanislavski's Theatre.

The Bolshoi Academic Theatre

In the spring of 1918, Zeitlin alerted Piatigorsky, already a member of the Lenin Quartet, to the upcoming competition for the solo cello position in the Bolshoi Theatre Orchestra. Though only fifteen years old, Piatigorsky had, from time to time, been hired as an extra in the orchestra. Knowing that the orchestra did not accept members under the age of 18, Piatigorsky lied about his age. The Bolshoi's distinguished conductors, Václav Suk and Vasili Safonov, led the judging.[45] At the audition, Piatigorsky made an enormous impression and won the position. Because of his astounding accomplishments, Piatigorsky was nicknamed the Child of Moscow.

Vladimir Lenin, though he agreed that cultural heritage was to be preserved and shared with the masses, wanted to cut funding for the Bolshoi Theatre, arguing that it was "awkward to spend big money on such a luxurious theatre ... when we lack simple schools in the villages." Lunacharsky did his best to demonstrate the new absence of elitism by making admission to events free. To level wages across disciplines, he cut musicians' and actors' salaries, and at the same time increased their workloads. The eminent theatre director, Constantin Stanislavski, wrote about the difficulties that arose by opening the halls to the uninitiated: "Our performances were free to all who received their tickets from factories and institutions where we sent them.... We were forced to teach this new spectator how to sit quietly, how not to talk, how to come into the theatre at the proper time, not to smoke, not to eat nuts in public, not to bring food into the theatre and eat it there."[46]

Part of the Soviet redistribution of cultural riches was the confiscation of first-rate musical instruments. Though these instruments were put in the hands of professionals, it was always made clear that the Party owned them, not the individual. Piatigorsky was given a fine Italian instrument to play, a Bergonzi cello. Nonetheless, supplies of all kinds were difficult to obtain and afford. Strings were no exception. Piatigorsky kept a spare set of strings for special concerts, but used anything else he could manage. Harp strings, much cheaper, were passable in tough times; their length made the bargain all the more sensible by cutting them in two.

With the Bolshevik takeover of Moscow on October 25, 1917, daily shootouts between the Whites and the Reds became the norm. Bombing casualties included the Bolshoi Theater itself, which suffered severe damage to its roof. Windows everywhere shattered with the quaking of bombs in Moscow's core. Moscow became the capital after Trotsky signed the Treaty of Brest-Litovsk conceding Poland, Finland, Belarus, the Baltics and, most painful, the Ukraine to Germany. The Bolsheviks were now officially the Communist Party. The Bolshoi at this time also took on a political role, hosting the terrifying Fifth Party Congress in July 1918. The Left Socialist Revolutionaries denounced Lenin, resulting in the Bolsheviks storming the delegation and holding them prisoners in the theatre. Outside the theatre, revolutionaries protested and the Bolsheviks overpowered them in the streets.

As a member of two government organizations (the Lenin Quartet and the Bolshoi Theatre) and being under age, Piatigorsky's military service was complicated. Though not drafted, he was placed in the music regiment of the army, but in a special youth division. This made his military status difficult to reconcile when the Child of Moscow was to be paid. His ration card was designated for the child's division, and entitled him to compensation in sweets, mostly chocolates. Trading sweets for real food was not easy. His colleagues were often issued raw fish and potato peels along with a little bread, considered a feast during the revolution years.

The Bolshoi was the most prestigious orchestra in Russia and position advancement was difficult and rare. In many of the old guard, seeing a youngster leading the cello section caused resentment; to some it was unacceptable. On occasion his cello part was altered (cued) with wrong entrances and cuts. Orchestral etiquette dictates that the cello section enters only when the solo (principal) cellist enters. The defective part caused Piatigorsky to err, which created some embarrassment — for a short while. When Piatigorsky understood what was happening, he had an idea: "At one performance, having a long rest in my part, I put my bow on the music stand, leaned back in my chair, and rested. Suddenly, I grabbed my bow, pretending to make an entrance. The entire section promptly came in at the wrong time, while I, not having touched a string, glared at them. After a few more no less malicious jokes on my part, wonderful relations with my colleagues were firmly established."[47]

The Bolshoi was host to the world's most illustrious artists even in difficult times. It was here that Piatigorsky first played under Serge Koussevitzky[48] and Glazunov. In 1919, the orchestra was scheduled to present the Russian premiere performance of Strauss's *Don Quixote*. The conductor, Grzegorz Fitelberg, announced to the orchestra:

> "The important cello solo in this piece is very difficult. I don't doubt that your first cellist, though very young, is a capable artist. Yet this work, in Europe, has always been performed with a guest soloist. The cello part needs long preparation, just like a concerto. Even more so. Therefore, I have invited Mr. Giskin."
>
> A gentleman with a cello walked in. He was greeted by silence. I liked his appearance and was delighted with the prospect of listening to him. I offered him my place at once and moved over to the second chair. As Mr. Fitelberg was ready to begin, there were voices of protest.
>
> "Our cellist can play as well as anyone! We don't care what they do in Europe. We are here in the Bolshoi Theatre of Moscow," someone shouted. I was embarrassed to see Mr. Giskin, with whom I had already an agreeable exchange, walk out. Under such circumstances the rehearsal commenced. I was too busy sight-reading to know how I played, but after the conclusion of *Don Quixote*, Fitelberg embraced me and the orchestra played a fanfare.[49]

As composer Vladimir Vlasov years later recalled:

> "He read it with such ease that his orchestra colleagues thought he had studied it all his life. His performance made such an impression that endeared him to most. To this day, Bolshoi Theatre veterans still recall [it]. Sixteen years old at the time of that concert he played the difficult piece with such brilliance and mastery that he immediately became the talk of all musical Moscow."[50]

Muscovites selling possessions, 1919.

Nevertheless, the Theatre could not have a teenager play the much older, noble hero of *Don Quixote*. The Bolshoi quickly engaged a replacement, Viktor Kubatzky,[51] a former solo cellist with the orchestra. Piatigorsky was given a mandatory leave that week. Piatigorsky's celebrity was in constant public view, as he seemed to be always performing: "It was a special joy to listen to Grisha's solos in the ballets. He also played the solo parts in the operas."[52]

Because of his success, the conservatory offered the sixteen year old a teaching position. He was ill at ease having to teach older students and his changing voice made him feel even more awkward. Piatigorsky knew that there was more to learn elsewhere, however, and soon resigned his teaching position. Having exhausted what Moscow had to offer, he longed to learn European styles and traditions. He repeatedly went to Commissar Lunacharsky, with whom he was on good terms, to ask permission to leave; but he was always turned down. He was told he was needed in Moscow. Nonetheless, Piatigorsky warned Lunacharsky he would run away if not allowed to leave. Little did Piatigorsky know his opportunity would come sooner than he imagined or planned.

2. New Frontiers, 1921

New Frontiers 1921: Warsaw

> **Bolshoi Academic Theatre**
> **Moscow May 2nd, 1921 #44**
> **IDENTIFICATION CARD**
> *Given to Mr. Gregori Pavlovich Piatigorsky because he is currently a member of the Orchestra at the Bolshoi Academic Theatre and at the end of the season will be having time off. The Board of Directors does not have any restrictions regarding him leaving Moscow. Date of his return must be August 22, 1921.*
> **Secretary of the Board of Directors**

After attending a performance at the Bolshoi Theatre in September 1920, H.G. Wells wrote: "We heard Chaliapin, greatest of actors and singers, in the *Barber of Seville* and in *Khovanshchina*; the admirable orchestra was variously attired, but the conductor still held out valiantly in swallow tails and white tie." In Petrograd he had noted the unheated hall, the musicians playing in overcoats, and the "underclad town population ... appallingly under-fed"[1] and acknowledged that conditions were similar though less grim in Moscow.

The young Soviet leadership decided that the principal players and singers of the Bolshoi Theatre could reach a more diverse population if they were broken into small groups and sent into the countryside where they could perform for workers—just as the Lenin Quartet had. Piatigorsky had just turned eighteen and was part of one of these groups, which also included concertmaster Mischa Mischakoff,[2] a pianist, a baritone, a tenor, and a manager.

In the spring of 1921, they arrived in Kiev. There Piatigorsky happened to meet his friend Elisabeth Marinel on the street: "[Grisha was] hungry and sick with dysentery, she managed to bring him to my aunt's house to fatten him up and to nurse him to health."[3] Piatigorsky soon left Kiev and rejoined the group as they traveled southwest toward the Polish border performing in ever-smaller towns. A special train car—a cattle car—was provided for the tour. The tenor, Alexander Vesselovsky,[4] planned to escape to Poland when the opportunity arose and made enthusiastic promises to the rest of the group. At Volochisk, a town split by the Zbruch River between Ukraine (Volochisk) and Poland (Podvolochisk), the troupe joined a similar ensemble from the Bolshoi, combining forces for a gala concert at a commercial farm.[5]

The following morning, Vesselovsky made arrangements with smugglers to bribe guards on both sides of the river. The smugglers demanded all of Piatigorsky's and Mischakoff's money. Four of the group — Mr. and Mrs. Vesselovsky, Mischakoff and Piatigorsky — were to escape at night to Podvolochisk, Poland. In a letter to his friend and sometime mentor Lev Zeitlin from the Lenin Quartet, Piatigorsky explained why he took the plunge:

> I decided to leave Russia (the idea to leave Moscow was very spur of the moment) after I met Vesselovsky, who promised me the world and told me that we had to leave in just a few days. Me, being so dumb, I did not even find out where we were going, what we were going to do, etc. All I knew was that Fishberg [Mischa Mischakoff] was coming with us. I knew him as a person who knows how to adapt to different situations. I would never have thought, though, that he would be going with us, not knowing where and why. He, as well as I, actually he probably even more than I, was fooled by Vesselovsky....
>
> I was not only guided by my desire to work with famous professors and listen to well-known foreign musicians, but also my desire to "run away" from a well known to you singer — S. Zorich.... [S]he somehow found out about me leaving with Vesselovsky and threw a huge fit because I did not tell her anything. In the middle of the fight she told me that she was planning to go with us; moreover, her plan was to "get engaged" somewhere overseas. Clearly I was not looking forward to this scenario. I had to get out of this situation, so I came to Vesselovsky and asked him to tell Zorich that our plans have changed and instead of going away, we will return back to Moscow after our tour around Ukraine. She did not want to believe us for a long time, but I was able to "make her" stay at home and wait for my return to Moscow. (As far as I know, she is not one of those who can wait for a long time. I heard she got married.)[6]

Apprehended by Polish border guards, they were promptly arrested and taken to the police and customs station. Mischakoff and Piatigorsky were furious with Vesselovsky for his lies about the safety and guaranteed success of their escape. They were also frightened about their future, especially at the thought of being returned to Russia. They would surely be imprisoned, or worse.

At their arrest hearing, they were asked for immigration papers and documentation. Mischakoff and Piatigorsky had nothing but their identification cards as members of the Bolshoi Theatre. Surprisingly, Vesselovsky presented documentation and Polish passports for himself and his wife, and they were set free. The couple abandoned their colleagues, who were left to fend for themselves. Betrayed and terrified, they tried to talk their way out of the situation. "We are musicians," they proclaimed to the chief of police. "You say you are musicians? Not spies? Prove you are musicians! Play!"[7]

Mischakoff played Kreisler's *Schön Rosmarin*, with Piatigorsky plucking the accompaniment. Not sure the police chief was completely satisfied, they played the Handel-Halvorsen *Passacaglia*. The guards applauded.

Unmoved, the chief still demanded papers and then ordered their return to the Russian border. The police guards directed them onto a farm-cart hauled by an emaciated horse. As they traveled the four or so kilometers back to the Russian border, Piatigorsky saw a rail station ahead and asked if they might rest, have a drink, and play some music for them. Noticing a small waiting room filled with peasants, they entered, along with the guards. As they performed for the crowd, they heard the sound of an arriving train. The duo inched their way closer to the loading platform. The guards did not seem to notice. As the train pulled out of the station, the two refugees jumped onboard and made their escape. To their surprise and relief, the guards did not try to stop them.

Having no money, they hid from the conductor until the train stopped in Lwów, Poland (now Lviv, Ukraine). Safely disembarking the train, they headed towards the center of the town, a ghetto. There, they decided to split up, with Mischa in charge of finding lodgings and Piatigorsky money and food. They agreed to meet at an appointed spot a few hours later. "At that time, I had no sense of geography, of where I was going. I only knew that I had left Russia,"⁸ said Piatigorsky later.

While walking, Piatigorsky, damp and shabby, began to hear familiar salon music coming from a classy café. He lingered a moment too long and the doorman motioned for the bedraggled youth to move along. Piatigorsky waited for the doorman to look away, then slipped inside and climbed the stairs, finding the ballroom where a trio was performing for the clientele. With the doorman hot on his heels, Piatigorsky begged the cellist to let him play. Lunging onstage, he grabbed the cello and began to play, to the great delight of the audience, who thought the whole affair was prearranged for their entertainment. The doorman, stymied at the sight of Piatigorsky performing, returned to his post.

Throughout his life, Piatigorsky was known as a great raconteur, a storyteller par excellence. His capacity to expand true events past their bounds was legend. He, like many in the public eye, did not try to set the record straight regarding certain events, and let stories take on their own lives. In fact, he is wholly responsible for the following enormously entertaining, but hardly accurate report:

> When Bolshevik Revolution breaks out I am a boy; everyone is running away, so I take my cello and with musical companions we go to frontier in a cow's railway carriage. On the way we perform for Red soldiers. We have a hall, packed with soldiers, no room left. We play for them — beautiful Debussy, thing like that. At the end only two of the audience remains. I do not think they understand Debussy.

The fugitives reached a village on the Polish border, which was closely watched by Red guards:

> "One night we go across the border. I carry cello over shoulder. Suddenly bing-bang-bang! Two soldiers shoot to us. My health remains goods, but my poor cello — finished."
>
> "Did the shots hit it?" he was asked.
>
> "No, no. There is with us a lady opera singer. She is very awfully fat. As she hears the bangs, she jumps up on my shoulders and puts her big arms round my neck — cello is no more."⁹

The cello was safe, of course, as they played for the Polish police and made their musical escape in the rail station. But the story is nothing but fun. In his autobiography *Cellist*, Piatigorsky gives yet another account of that crossing. The framework of the tale remains; it is in the details that the fantasy begins: "The instant we set foot on the bridge, there were shots from both sides of the border. I jumped into the river. Mischa followed. So did Madame Vesselovskaya, who clutched at me in panic. I struggled to keep my cello above my head. The river was shallow, but I heard gurgle-like sounds close behind me that came from Mischakoff. We reached the Polish border." Later, he acknowledged the lengths to which the fable expanded, but he enjoyed the game all the more:

> "Piatigorsky, who crossed the Dnieper River on his cello, will appear in our city," I saw often in the press. The absurd "saga" created by publicity needed some explanation. "What did you use as oars? Your bow? Doesn't the cello have holes?" some reporters wanted to know. As I laughed off the absurd story, new ones were created. In one town I found photographers waiting in my room. "It's late, I barely have time to change for the concert." "We just want a picture with your cello. It will just take a second." I quickly took my cello out of the case. "Is that the one you crossed the river on?" "Hm — well" not wasting time in taking a normal pose, I put the cello under my chin.¹⁰

Even as a child, before the cello was a part of him, Piatigorsky was attracted to an audience, entertaining them with stories bursting with imagination and fantasy. These two components became part of his artistry on the cello as well.

The world of musicians is exceedingly small, thus it is not unusual to meet fellow violinists or cellists who have acquaintances, friends, or circumstances in common; musicians are never true strangers. Piatigorsky recalled, "No matter what part of the world you inhabit, if you are a musician, you live in music."[11] Accordingly, the café cellist in Lwów had heard of Piatigorsky, and the other members of the ensemble spoke Russian. As instant colleagues, they all chipped in and lent money to Piatigorsky, advising him to go to Warsaw.

Meeting Mischa back at the agreed upon spot, they were both enthusiastic about their success. Mischa had found them a room for the night on credit in Lwów's ghetto. Exhausted, they made their way to a crowded boardinghouse. Mischa hid their instruments under the bed, and though it was uncomfortable lying head to toe, they quickly fell asleep. Soon afterwards they were awakened by an attack of bedbugs. Brushing the insects off, they fled their quarters dressed only in underwear, Mischa clinging to his violin and satchel as Piatigorsky grabbed his cello and its canvas bag which also held all he owned.

Sometime later, while sitting in a café, they were discussing their next step — to head for London via Warsaw. An old gentleman in the café stared at Mischa, and after hearing them speak Russian, approached and asked:

"Do you have a sister?"
"Yes, but I haven't seen her since I was six or seven years old."
"I think I've just seen her," the old man said. "She's sitting right now in the office of the Hebrew Immigrant Aid Society [HIAS] just down the street."

Mischa hurried off, and though not immediately recognizing each other, the two siblings found one another. After a joyful reunion, Mischa heard news of his family, and learned that five of his brothers had immigrated to New York. All musicians, two of them were already members of the New York Philharmonic Symphony.

Mischa's best hope, he decided, was to obtain travel funds and join his brothers in America. He wrote to his brother Teddy (Tevia, the eldest) an urgent note on a special HIAS of America card, hastily filling in for the gap in their communication:

17 July 1921
Dear Tevia,
You don't expect to receive a letter from me, but, thank God, I had a chance to get out.... I escaped not alone but with a buddy, a wonderful cellist, a young boy of 18, Grigori Piatigorsky. He was soloist of the Opera in the same Theatre where I was, and for 4 years played in the Quartet of the Musical Department. For my sake and his, I ask you to send 500 dollars because we don't have any money. Dad will soon come to Poland, too, but if I can leave earlier, I will not wait for him because I have nothing to live on. I'll stay in Warsaw for two days. I hope you will not refuse in this brotherly help for me and Piatigorsky. We hope to pay you back very soon. I have never asked to borrow money before.
I kiss you all, your brother Mischa.[12]

The duo went to Warsaw and looked up their friend Grzegorz Fitelberg, who had conducted the Bolshoi on many occasions and who was a Polish citizen. Fitelberg suggested they see conductor Emil Mlynarski of the Warsaw Philharmonic and Opera. Fitelberg knew that Mlynarski, as the cofounder of the Warsaw Philharmonic and recently appointed director of the Warsaw Conservatory, had more connections. The two disheveled refugees knocked on the Mlynarskis' door asking for asylum. They conversed with Mlynarski, were given a room and a bath, and then joined the family to introduce themselves: "I'm Mischa Fishberg, and this is my friend, Gregor Piatigorsky."[13]

Mlynarski turned out to be a godsend, obtaining identification papers and work permits

```
SALA KONSERWATORJUM
       Sezon 1921-22

Czwartek d. 13 października r.b. o godz. 8 w.
    I-szy WIECZÓR KAMERALNY
         B E E T H O V E N
      udział w wieczorze przyjmują:
Prof. Henryk MELCER (fortepian)
      Michał FIBER (skrzypce)
   Grzegorz PIATIGORSKI (wiolonoz.)
              PROGRAM
           — Część I. —
1. Sonata op. 102, № 2 D-dur na fortepian i wiolonczelę.
   Allegro con brio.
   Adagio con molto sentimento d'affetto
   Allegro fugato.
   wykona Prof. H. MELCER i G. PIATIGORSKI.
2. Sonata op. 47, A-moll (Kreutzerowska) na fortepian i skrzypce.
   Adagio sostenuto. Presto.
   Andante con variazioni
   Finale. Presto
        wyk. Prof. H. MELCER i M. FIBER.

           — Część II —
3. Trio op. 97, B-dur na fortepian, skrzypce i wiolonczelę.
   Allegro moderato.
   Scherzo. Allegro.
   Andante cantabile.
   Allegro moderato. Presto
      wyk. Prof. H. MELCER, M. FIBER.
          I G. PIATIGORSKI.

            REPERTUAR:
W Czwartek d. 20 Października r. b. w sali Konserwatorjum
o g. 8 w. Recital fortepianowy MAKSYMILJANA
BARACA. Program: Bach, Chopin (Sonata H-moll),
Debussy, Skrjabin.
W Czwartek d. 27 Października r. b. o godz. 8 wiecz. w sali
Konserwatorjum II-gi Wieczór Kameralny Schubert
Melcer-Rachmaninow z udziałem Prof. H. MELCERA
(fortep.) M. FIBERA (skrzypce) i G. PIATI-
GORSKIEGO (wiol.).

      Dyr. Konc. JERZY GURANOWSKI.
```

```
                              Cena 20 m
      FILHARMONJA WARSZAWSKA
               SEZON 1921/22.
       pod kierunkiem ROMANA CHOJNACKIEGO.

          Niedziela 13 listopada 1921 r.
       Popołudniowy koncert symfoniczny
                udział biorą:
      ORKIESTRA FILHARMONICZNA pod dyrekcją
            JÓZEFA OZIMIŃSKIEGO
       MICHAŁ FIEBER (skrzypce)
  GRZEGORZ PIATIGORSKI (wiolonczela)
                  — I —
1. BRAHMS. Uwertura „Akademicka"
2. BRAHMS. Koncert podwójny na skrzypce i wiolonczelę
        a) Allegro
        b) Andante
        c) Vivace non troppo
    z towarz. orkiestry wykonają p.p. FIEBER i PIATIGORSKI.
                  — II —
3. SIBELIUS. Poemat symfoniczny „En Saga"
4. R. STRAUSS. Poemat symfoniczny „Don Juan".

  Fortepian koncertowy C. Bechsteina ze składów firmy RIEGERT i GINTER Jasna 6.

                REPERTUAR
ŚRODA:  16 listopada, Koncert dobroczynny.
PIĄTEK 18 listopada. Wielki koncert symfoniczny. Dyrekcja: WILLY
        STEFFEN; Solista JÓZEF SZIGETI (skrzypce)
```

Top: Warsaw, October 13, 1921. *Bottom:* Warsaw, November 13, 1921.

for them. The lucky pair arrived in time to assume vacancies in the philharmonic—as concertmaster and solo cello.[14] The summer season was upon them and they were kept extremely busy: "I was touring a lot with the orchestra, played a huge amount of concerts, made a lot of friends and got paid very well. I was living a good life. If I did not want to keep mastering the cello and travel around the world, I would probably stay there longer, especially because Mlynarski promised me a place at the Conservatory."[15]

Some years later Piatigorsky remembered his time in Warsaw with fondness:

> Warsaw seemed so attractive and brilliant to me. My service in the Philharmonic began my international career. It was there that I played for the first time—the Haydn Concerto and the Dvořák Concerto, and the Brahms Double Concerto with an orchestra. The soul fills with gratitude when you recall the outlook, the concern and nobleness of certain people. How I would like to show my gratefulness toward Emil Mlynarski,

but he died — I am consoled by the fact that before his death I saw him in Philadelphia, and I was able, I think, to express all my respect for him, and my thanks.[16]

In September 1921, Mischakoff was scheduled to play the Tchaikovsky violin concerto under the orchestra's former director, Zdislaw Birnbaum. Orchestra members had spoken very highly of Birnbaum and both Mischakoff and Piatigorsky were looking forward to working with him. The first performance with him was a children's concert presentation of Rimsky-Korsakov's *Scheherazade*. Without rehearsal, the concert was to begin at eight o'clock, but about five minutes before eight, Birnbaum suddenly appeared on the podium, baton in hand. Mischakoff had not yet entered the stage to tune the orchestra, the usual procedure. As Piatigorsky remembered: "Reaching the platform and tapping the music stand, he gave a downbeat. The musicians, thinly scattered all over the stage, began to play. As Mischakoff was absent, I played the violin solo for him. Hearing the sounds, the rest of the musicians rushed onto the stage. 'You are insolent, all of you,' Birnbaum screamed in a fit of insanity. He threw himself on his knees and stood up again. In tears he dropped his baton, cried, 'Good-by, brothers, forever adieu,' and disappeared."[17] His body was found in a lake near Berlin several weeks later. Birnbaum was just 41.

As the winter of 1921-22 wore on, Mischa and Piatigorsky remained in Warsaw and completed a full season with the orchestra. They played the Brahms Double Concerto on November 13[18] and performed many chamber music concerts. The 18-year-old cellist had considerable success. The following are among his first reviews outside of Russia:

> Piatigorsky from Moscow is a young artist undoubtedly extremely talented and very advanced in technique. His sound is enormously resonant and clean and his interpretation is always musical, sustained by good study. Mr. Piatigorsky is recognized as having the substance of a great virtuoso.[19]
>
> CELLIST FROM WARSAW PHILHARMONIC GREGOR PIATIGORSKY
> PLAYS HAYDN CONCERTO
> He captured our hearts. We value him already and remember all his performances. Either with the Warsaw Philharmonic or in chamber concerts and we listened to him on Sunday with great delight and we can say again that Gregor Piatigorsky is an excellent virtuoso and mature musician. His technique does not overshadow nature and simplicity, directness of singing and musical phrasing. And his temperament is not in the way of his noble balanced interpretation.[20]

Berlin, Take One — Leipzig — Berlin, Take Two: 1922–1924

In spite of his comfort and celebrity, Piatigorsky knew he needed to leave Poland for the chance to observe and study with the important European cello masters. Up until then it was violinists who impressed him most; Bronislaw Huberman and Josef Szigeti stood out as artists who opened up a new world of nuance and color. In the fall of 1921, Piatigorsky was invited to the U.S. to study with Pablo Casals,[21] but the invitation must have been indefinite since Casals was touring rather heavily, though he made annual visits to the U.S. Even so, as a "man without a country," Piatigorsky did not have the necessary documentation to travel outside of Poland.

Perhaps the following review of a "Chamber Music Evening of Beethoven" at the Warsaw Conservatory on October 13 precipitated his desire for further study and the need for sponsorship:

> The individual and technical differences [among the three players] were a hurdle to an ideal fusion into a whole. However, the artists' talent and "routine" made the performance a serious one. The violinist Mr. Fibère[22] plays with great artistry, especially due to his great technique. He follows cultural [stylistic] dictates and livens it up with temperament and a strong sense of rhythm. Mr. Piatigorsky is a cellist of great talent who, after yesterday's performance, deserves — even more than after his performance at the Philharmonic — to get under the tutelage of someone like Casals as soon as possible, even if not for long. Then both his talent would deepen and perhaps he would develop a stronger tone. Piatigorsky also must have a better instrument.[23]

During the season, both musicians played solo concerts in many cities beyond their duties in Warsaw. In early 1922, Mischakoff was reunited with a talented refugee fresh from Russia, pianist André Kostelanetz.[24] Kostelanetz had been pianist for the Petrograd[25] Opera as well as for silent films shown in the same hall. Arriving in Warsaw with only a three-day temporary visa, he desperately needed work to stay in the city legally. Mischakoff was able to have him hired as the pianist for the Philharmonic and Opera. Joining with Piatigorsky, the three performed in chamber music.

Following one Sunday afternoon chamber concert, Mischakoff and Kostelanetz met Mr. and Mrs. Leo Keena. Keena was very taken by their playing and asked if they ever considered settling in the U.S. The musicians were very enthusiastic about the idea, but knew the normal wait for visas was three years. Mischa, eight years older than Grisha, and with his many family ties in the U.S., was anxious to immigrate. Kostelanetz recalled, "And now both Keenas smiled at me, and it was Fortune's smile. *'Je suis le consul américaine!'* M. Keena said. If we would come to the consulate the next morning, he would personally issue us our visas."[26]

A short time later, Piatigorsky also met Adolph Held, an American philanthropist and head of the Hebrew Immigrant Aid Society (HIAS) in Eastern Europe. A Polish immigrant himself, Held was sensitive to an artist's need to travel and was able to help fund their passage as well as assist with their arrival in the U.S.

But sometime before the trio were to leave Poland for America (on September 23, 1922), Held approached Piatigorsky with an astonishing proposal: Held would fund Piatigorsky's education provided he live in Germany. Held, as well as Mischakoff, believed that the finest cello professors lived in Germany and that it was the best place to launch the young cellist's career. America would welcome him just as much a bit later, and he would have satisfied his thirst for European styles. With Held's support, Piatigorsky would be financially free to practice, tour, and live as he wished. Held would also provide German lessons and help him acquire a fine Italian cello. A Russian-speaking trustee would be appointed to handle all the finances and be available for practical advice. While Piatigorsky had never accepted financial assistance, he could not turn down such a generous offer, though his dream of coming to the U.S. always lingered.

It was decided that his teacher should be the venerable Hugo Becker[27] in Berlin. The professor was to be paid in cash — ten American dollars — a huge improvement over the ever-unstable German mark. Life as a student in Berlin was cheap, if you had dollars. Four to six dollars a month was enough for Piatigorsky to pay for rent, food, and clothing. Unfortunately, Piatigorsky found Becker to be less than helpful, and a poor teacher. They had perhaps no more than a half-dozen lessons before parting company:

> I went to Germany and lived in the suburbs of the city. I started working, went to Becker, who gladly accepted me as a student and I began those lessons that I was dreaming of for so long. Oh, God! I was so disappointed when I got to know Becker's character as a professor.

I am not going to tell you much about him. I will only say that he belongs to those idiots who say things like "summers could be hot, and winters could be cold" making it seem like he was the only one who knew that. His lessons were extremely boring and due to his awful personality we got into a huge fight and I quit my lessons with him.[28]

He revealed more specifically in *Cellist*:

Without an introduction or making an appointment, I went to the Hochschule to see the eminent cello professor Hugo Becker. When I entered his large classroom, filled with students, Professor Becker stood up. Impeccably dressed, gray-haired, tall, and straight, he was a remarkable-looking man. He asked what I wanted. I said in Russian, "To have lessons." One of the students [Nicolas Ochi-Albi] interpreted for me.
"It's too late in the term to enter the Hochschule."
"Private lessons."
"Then why did you come here?"
"I wanted to speak to you."
Everyone laughed. "The professor said it's a strange idea for someone who can't speak."
"I want lessons."
"The professor asked if you would play something now."
"I will play *Improvisations* by Goedicke."
"What animal is that? Can't you play something civilized?"
"Goedicke is a great musician," I said.
"The professor wants you to play the Boccherini Concerto."
One of the students lent me a cello and Becker went to the piano. After a few bars he interrupted me and spoke to the students with a serious face, but he must have said something funny, because there was laughter again.
"The professor wants you to the play the Schumann Concerto."
Again I was interrupted by more laughter. I continued to play bits of many other pieces until I could not stand the merriment, and stopped.
"Please ask the professor, will he teach me or not?" I said, irritated.
The next week I had my first lesson. Becker was the first and only teacher I had to pay for lessons. He charged a great deal, but the student could choose the length of the lesson — an hour or a half hour. I wanted to go easy on Mr. Held's purse and chose the half-hour one. A servant led me to the study of the professor's luxurious home. Becker and Ochi-Albi were waiting for me.
"The professor wants you to forget you ever played cello before."
"Yes."
You must start from the very beginning."
"Yes."
"Your right arm is your tongue; your left, your thoughts."
"Yes."
"You have no thoughts whatsoever. Even if you have, you must learn to speak first."
"Yes."
Professor Becker showed me how to hold the bow. He seemed pleased. He let me strike an open string. "Professor is encouraged," said Ochi-Albi. "He thinks you are gifted." Becker glanced at his watch. He stood up. The lesson was over.
Ochi-Albi accompanied me home. He spoke with great admiration of his teacher. "It took the professor more than twenty years to solve the problems of the right arm," he said. "His method is perfect. He is a great man — a scientist and a true artist. I have been with him only two years, but my right arm is improving already."
My German progressed very slowly and my practicing of holding the bow was boring. My second, third, and fourth lessons were quite uneventful except at the end, when I would make a bow and say, "Gott sei Dank." Each time it seemed to throw him into a rage. What did I do wrong? I wondered, wishing that Ochi-Albi had been present.
At the fifth lesson the professor was unusually friendly and I was glad to see Ochi-Albi again. He told me how highly the professor thought of me and how rapid my progress was.

"You learned to hold the bow in four lessons. Some can't master it in years. Your bow arm is in almost perfect position on all four strings. The professor has decided to make a great exception and begin to work with you right now on the finest music for our instrument."

Becker spoke again and Ochi-Albi translated. "The situation is now drastically changed. You are not a pupil any more. You are ready to work on great music and therefore you and I are equals."

"We have to be frank, and I expect you to express your opinions freely." He took his cello and said, "I will play the beginning of the Dvořák Concerto — only the beginning. After I have played, you will do the same. Then we will discuss the merit of each performance."

He began. I saw a gust of resin fly, rise and fall in all directions. Ripping off the hair, his bow knocked on the sides of his cello. The stick hit the strings. After some noisy thumping on the fingerboard with his left hand, he stopped. I did not dare look at him. He asked something. His voice sounded happy. I looked at his face and saw that he *was* happy.

"Herr Professor asked how you liked it," said Ochi-Albi.

"It was terrible," I said. Ochi-Albi was silent.

"What? What?" Becker asked.

Ochi-Albi pleaded, "The professor wants to know. What shall I tell him?"

I hesitated. "Tell him it was just fine." I don't know what Ochi-Albi told him. Becker's face was red. He looked at his watch and said the lesson was over. I bowed and said, "Gott sei Dank."

"Heraus!" Becker screamed. "Out of here, you conceited, ignorant mujik!"

On the street a few minutes later, Ochi-Albi reproached me. "You shouldn't have said, Gott sei Dank. It means Thank God."²⁹

Becker, it seems, did not hold anything against Piatigorsky for long. In a letter to his former trio partner, violinist Carl Flesch, Becker compares Piatigorsky to cellist Emanuel Feuermann: "Piatigorsky's talent lies more in the direction of the emotional, Feuermann in that of dexterity. Last year I heard the latter [Feuermann] play the Schumann Concerto in Munich. Technically excellent, but as unromantic as can be. You simply can't perform Schumann without passion and rapture. I have never heard this work — in parts very poetic — played with less feel-

Recovering on the train in Germany 1922 with a snack and mineral water (courtesy Piatigorsky estate).

ing and spirit, and I consider it a matter of regret that so capable a performer has remained so under-developed in these two directions. If he were a pianist or violinist, the public would never forgive him."[30]

In the fall of 1922 Piatigorsky was adrift and homesick in Germany: "When I was in Berlin the first time I missed my former comrades in Warsaw, especially my conversations with dear old Mateysho, the orchestra watchman."[31]

After reflection, Piatigorsky decided to study with the other major icon of the cello, Julius Klengel, in Leipzig.[32] He contacted Jascha Bernstein, a former classmate from Moscow whom he knew was studying with Klengel, to make the arrangements. Piatigorsky was accepted as a private student rather than officially enrolled at the conservatory, since the semester was well in progress. The few lessons with Klengel were of limited cellistic value, but their relationship was important for the young cellist:

> After spending a little more time in Berlin, I went to see Klengel and tried to find my "happiness" in Leipzig. Leipzig, just as Berlin, did not excite me at all. It also had those unfriendly boarding houses, but I really liked Klengel, at least as a person. After seeing him, I was pretty sure that I will finally learn something new, and started practicing. After I played for him, he was so amazed that he did not want me to study with him. He based his decision on the fact that he thought that I was a complete, grown artist and he could not teach me anything I did not already know. I was very surprised and obviously did not believe him. I kept begging him to teach me. All of our lessons were the same — I would come in every week, play new pieces for him, then he would hug me, and tell me what a great job I have done. Truthfully, I would have liked it a lot more if he criticized me.[33]

Top: D'Albert, Klengel. *Bottom:* Mrs. Klengel and Brahms, Leipzig, 1895 (as the original appears).

Klengel class, 1922. Bottom front row, holding cello, Maurice Eisenberg, Mischa Schneider on right; next row: Piatigorsky is 2nd on left, Klengel is 4th; 3rd row: Alexei Kinkulkin is last on right; others are unidentified (courtesy June Schneider).

Klengel taught in a master class setting as well as individually, as many Europeans did. The classes could last several hours and the students listened and benefited from each other's instruction and repertoire. Piatigorsky admired Klengel's ability to transform a naturally competitive environment into a nurturing one by pairing students with those who "have what they want." One student might have exceptional dexterity, or a lush vibrato, while another an electrifying staccato. This gift of "teaching without teaching" influenced Piatigorsky's future teaching philosophy. Klengel was also a generous personality and fostered Piatigorsky with familial concern.

Piatigorsky remembered those days with fondness, and as a time of real progress on his own:

> Day in, day out, an orgy of scales and exercises. Cello everywhere, everyone a cellist. Schneider, Benar Heifetz, Auber, Jascha Bernstein, Honegger, Bauldauf, and more — all a beehive

on the verge of drowning in its own honey, the honey of music by Volkmann, Lindner, Romberg, Popper, Davidov, Duport, Klengel, and Grützmacher. A relentless drill, a tedium of overhauling and overcoming one weakness, only to have others creep in, to multiply themselves like microbes and form new diseases. I fought them with determination and when in the process I tasted some progress or stumbled on a new idea I gained new courage.[34]

His German lessons made it possible to understand the language well enough that Piatigorsky enrolled to audit a philosophy course at the Leipzig University. Thus began his immersion into the education he never had in Russia.

During the holiday break, Piatigorsky and a fellow classmate, Herbert Bauldauf, traveled to northern Italy where Bauldauf's family lived. While there, Piatigorsky enjoyed a well-deserved vacation and became infatuated with Bauldauf"s sister. (Her death a few years later in an auto accident was such a blow that he could not bring himself to return to the Italian Alps.)

Before Piatigorsky left Germany for Italy, Klengel recommended that he reserve concert halls in some of the large cities (Leipzig, Dresden, and Munich) so that when he returned, he could start concertizing. Klengel wrote warm letters of recommendation to the orchestra intendants and Piatigorsky left deposits for the concert halls knowing that Held would approve the expenditure.

The trip to Italy was joyful and fulfilling; Piatigorsky had two very successful concerts and was able to return to Leipzig with reviews and money in his pockets — his own money. His jubilation was short-lived however:

> I came to Leipzig late at night, very tired from the trip. I went to sleep with the thought that in the morning I will start organizing my concerts — pick dates, give good advertisements, etc. But just my luck, nothing happened the way I planned. In the morning I was awakened by a loud knock on the door. I got up and when I asked, "Who is it?" two male voices said that it was the secret police. I let them in; they searched the whole apartment and of course didn't find anything. They proceeded on telling me that I was arrested and that I had to go to the police station with them. I knew that I was not guilty of anything, so I was not worried. I kept thinking that it was a mistake and that everything will be worked out. They did not even let me wash my face; I put my clothes on in a hurry and they escorted me out of my apartment. At the police station they asked me my name one more time, wrote something down, and called for a guard, who grabbed and dragged me to jail. There, they searched me again, took all of my belongings not answering any of my questions and threw me, like a dog, in a cell.... I cannot even begin to describe how I felt; I thought I was going crazy. I will never forget those 7 or 8 hours that I spent in jail. They let me out of there so that I could pack my bags and get ready to go back to Russia. I was supposed to be escorted to the customs in the jail wagon. When I got out, I was crying.
>
> My intuition told me to go see Klengel, who took the whole ordeal very personally and took care of everything. [Klengel knew the chief of police.] It turned out that the visa that I received to travel from Poland to Germany was only valid for 5 days, after which I was supposed to go back to Warsaw. But when it became obvious that I was not even planning on moving back, the German consul in Poland wrote a letter to the police requesting my arrest and return to the country of my citizenship.[35]

Adolph Held was able to help Piatigorsky obtain a German visa. As life returned to normal, Piatigorsky enthusiastically told his benefactor about Klengel's proposal for concerts in the fall. He was shocked to find that Held refused to support the concerts, even in the face of Klengel's advice and effort. Held felt that performances in those cities were completely unnecessary and that Piatigorsky must only debut in Berlin and with a major orchestra.

Disillusioned that Held was able to call the shots in contradiction to Klengel, and that his carte blanche offer was only tenuous, Piatigorsky began to question the wisdom of accepting Held's patronage. Furthermore, Held made mention of Piatigorsky's high expenses, and though they were very friendly and Held brought the subject up gently, Piatigorsky was taken aback. He considered himself extremely frugal, spending only what he needed, saying, "I would not spend my own money this carefully."

Piatigorsky presented Held with his expense book, as evidence of his strict accounting of every mark and pfennig spent. Piatigorsky ate the cheapest food, stayed in the cheapest room, and registered everything the trustee gave him. Held paid the trustee in dollars and the trustee paid Piatigorsky in marks. Piatigorsky always documented the amount given and the exchange rate that day. A vast discrepancy was discovered, exposing the thievery of Held's trustee. By inflating the expense sheet, he pocketed large sums of inflation-free American dollars, cashed through the black market. The discovery angered and embarrassed Piatigorsky. He decided not to accept any further assistance. "It angered me beyond reason, and, unable to control myself, I spoke of his agent's deception, of my distaste for charity, and of my honor as an artist and a man. I said that someone else was the thief, that I didn't need anyone's help, and that I would pay back the money I regretted ever having accepted. Harsh and with an inexcusable intemperance, I abruptly left the confused and embarrassed Mr. Held."[36] No longer having the money to pay for the concert halls, Piatigorsky had to cancel his concerts. He recalled, "I had a lot of trouble canceling the concerts and by the end of this whole chaos, I left to go to Berlin. My goal was to set up a couple of concerts with the [Berlin] Philharmonic Orchestra."[37]

He arrived in Berlin in the winter of 1922-23, rented a room in the Charlottenburg district and paid two weeks in advance. The landlords seemed kind and said he could practice anytime, so he did not mind signing a lease. Again armed with glowing letters of recommendation from Klengel to both the Berlin Philharmonic and the Gewandhaus Orchestra,[38] he set out to reserve a date with the philharmonic. Piatigorsky was frustrated to discover that the 1923-24 concert season was already completely booked, not only with the orchestras but with all of the concert halls. He would have to aim for the 1924-25 season instead.[39]

At this point, he began rethinking his future in Germany, contemplating a return to Moscow. During this period, Lunacharsky's Office of the Soviet Commissar of Education was wooing professional expatriates to return to their homeland with promises of prominence and respect.[40] They wanted to demonstrate to the world that Russia had not descended to total barbarism. The thought of a warm welcome was tempting to Piatigorsky. Though the offer from Held had been a mixed blessing, he reflected on the positive: "There were a lot of good things that happened. For example, my great progress in playing the cello, experiencing life overseas, meeting and listening to many musicians (although I was not too impressed by any of them), my performance in Rococo [Tchaikovsky] again ... was a performance attended by exclusively Russian crowd (it was a concert for the Russian upper class [in Berlin]), and, finally, the great recommendations that I got from Klengel."[41]

Playing "Wherever"

With little money left, Piatigorsky halfheartedly looked for work. Soon his rent was due and by that time he had no money. He sold his watch (a gift from his father), then his dress suit and books. As strings broke he tied them in knots, saving a fresh set for special occasions. His landlords turned off the heat and he slept in his clothes and soon was turned out. With his cello at his side, he never felt truly poor. "It was like having a substantial check in the pocket during the bank's closed hours. Tomorrow I will cash it."

With a few belongings Piatigorsky set out for the Tiergarten district, contemplating a return to Russia. In despair he wrote to Mischakoff asking for advice and how he could come to the U.S. Weeks passed. Piatigorsky was not aware of the dangers that lurked in the Tiergarten area. He slept on a bench that was usually a place where drug dealers and prostitutes gathered. Luckily, a policeman on the Tiergarten beat befriended Piatigorsky. He warned Piatigorsky of the dangers and did his best to keep his bench free from intruders and allowed him to sleep in the park temporarily. One night, as the cellist remembered:

> The friendly policeman was not on his night duty. My bench in the Tiergarten has not been kept free for me to use. There was no one with authority to shy prostitutes away from it.
> "Must you hang around with your damned bass here?" "You scare customers," said one. "If you wait for that jerk policeman — he's never here on Fridays — come on mothers, let kiddy rest in peace — such a jerk to chase us straight into light. This is the only bloody dark spot in the park."
> I did not see her face but I saw her limping as she walked towards the entrance at the side of the zoo. I walked between my cello on one side and her on the other.
> "I am working here — not promenading with music and all — walk ahead, genius" she said, slowing her pace.
> The clock at the city zoo railroad station showed quarter to eleven. I stood and watched the clock as though at a certain hour someone would be waiting for me. There was no place to go and no one to see save passersby who spoke a language I knew as little as their indifference I felt so much. The hunger did not seem to affect me very much. Already in Russia I knew that there is a deadline to a hunger and after reaching it, it does not really hurt. I pressed my cello against my body — my only companion my faithful friend and now my only belonging.[42]

At one point he found himself reaching for a discarded cigarette on the street, but stopped, realizing the depth of his poverty — and bargained with himself to pick up only used newspapers to read. The public avoided the zoo area at night, but just south of it some of the most significant cultural centers of Europe coexisted in relative calm. Institutions such as the National Gallery, the Philharmonic, the Art Library, the Museum of Arts and Crafts, and the Prussian State Library made Berlin a rich cultural hub.

As the nights grew colder, the Tiergarten became unbearable; he had to find shelter. He made the rounds visiting his more prosperous friends who had enough financial support, spontaneously staying overnight and having meals with them. One cellist from the Klengel class, Mischa Schneider,[43] hosted him, unaware of Piatigorsky's desperate situation. Pride and independence prevented him from imposing himself on anyone for long; the usual excuse of "forgetting his keys" was good only once or twice. Piatigorsky held out as long as he could before asking for help. He looked for his friend, pianist Alexander Zakin,[44] but he was out of town. Finally he found Alexander Koretzki, a violinist he remembered from Warsaw.[45] As luck would have it, Koretzki was looking for Piatigorsky. He wanted to tell him that their mutual friend, Bolshoi violinist Boris Koutzen,[46] was looking for him. Koutzen — himself in Berlin only a few weeks — had landed a job at the Café Ruscho on the Ansbacherstrasse near the Berlin Opera House and needed a cellist for a trio ensemble.

It was good to see Koutzen again and Piatigorsky gladly accepted the offer. Koutzen described their duties, which consisted of performing daily from 4:00 to 6:00 P.M. and from 7:30 P.M. to 12:30 A.M. It was steady work and provided enough income to survive. Koutzen was anxious to begin rehearsing, as he had never played in a café or played salon music.

The café had its own library, which included familiar opera, operetta, and symphonic potpourris along with current popular tunes performed in a quasi-jazz style, or "tango-ized" to the taste of the "ten dollar millionaires"; i.e., black market speculators who became wealthy overnight dealing in the dollar's value each day. The cellist was not happy with the thought of playing the same music he did as a nine-year-old. His pay was supplemented by pastries he loathed, as they reminded him of his child's rations in Moscow.

Finally a letter from Mischakoff arrived. He promised to help Piatigorsky immigrate to the U.S., but Piatigorsky needed to fund the passage himself. Mischa was certain he would find work, but in the meantime he enclosed a five-dollar bill. Piatigorsky felt instantly rich and immediately invited all his friends for sauerbraten and beer at the local *Kneipe* (saloon).

The Ruscho ensemble had a history of distinguished musicians, but none of them lasted for more than a few months. Soon the pianist left their ensemble, which left Kouzten and Piatigorsky to play duets until a new pianist, Leopold Mittman,[47] could join them. Koutzen had applied for a visa to the U.S. to join the Philadelphia Orchestra, and when the visa was finalized, he left Berlin. For a time Mittman and Piatigorsky played their own versions of the light fare along with an occasional sonata on quieter nights. Soon Mittman's brother Bronislaw joined the group as its next violinist.

The Ruscho became a favorite meeting place for tourists and emigrants. Other musicians soon turned up to hear them play. Piatigorsky was especially embarrassed when artists of his age such as cellist Emanuel Feuermann or violinist Max Rostal came to the café, sitting uncomfortably close — no doubt surprised that such a noted artist was without enough means to avoid such commonplace work. It was on one of those evenings that it was decided to play a Mendelssohn trio — amidst the clangor of the clientele. After a few minutes of battle, Piatigorsky stormed out of the café and did not return for two days.

One of the visitors to the Café Ruscho was the prominent Hungarian violinist Géza de Kresz of the Pozniak Trio.[48] The trio was in need of a cellist for their upcoming tour and asked Piatigorsky to join them. Piatigorsky enthusiastically accepted both the offer and the expertise of the well-known impresario Richard Hoppe.[49] Hoppe also booked solo recitals and orchestral appearances as well as trio engagements. The trio performed an eclectic repertoire that included Hans Pfitzner's Trio as well as the premiere of Egon Kornauth's[50] trio. Piatigorsky's first German solo reviews were glowing.

In the fall of 1922, Piatigorsky began teaching at the new Russian Conservatory in Berlin. Unfortunately the salary was impossibly low in the face of inflation and he gradually returned to a Spartan existence. Again, he looked for additional work. His former employer at the Ruscho no longer ran the café and Piatigorsky found himself in dire straits. He took every job possible and would rather have starved than take money from anyone again. In a letter to Zeitlin, Piatigorsky recalled: "The thing is that I am the kind of a person who is used to making my own money and it was really hard for me to keep taking someone else's money. I started doing everything possible to stop taking money from the Americans [the Helds]."[51]

By December 1922, Piatigorsky had played a few concerts in Berlin and Leipzig for Jewish organizations that sponsored new music.[52] It was during these concerts that he first performed with friends with whom he would become increasingly associated: violinist Boris Kroyt and pianist Karol Szreter.[53] Kroyt, who Piatigorsky met at the Ruscho in 1922, had performed twice with the Berlin Philharmonic (1914 and 1920), yet he struggled with his sporadic career, just getting by and living with the family of violist Henry Drobatchevsky.

2. New Frontiers, 1921

```
                                           מאוסף
              Preis: 40 Mark               מנשה רבינא
KONZERT-DIREKTION HERMANN WOLFF & JULES SACHS, BERLIN W 9, LINK-STRASSE 42
```

Berlin, Blüthner-Saal	Leipzig, Städtisches Kaufhaus
Mittwoch den 20. Dezember 1922	Freitag den 29. Dezember 1922
abends 8 Uhr	abends 8 Uhr

Gesellschaft für Jüdische Musik in Moskau
Moderne Jüdische Musik

I.

J. ENGEL, Einleitungswort (Jiddisch)

1. A. KREIN . . . Elegie für Streichquartett
   Mitwirkende: Herren Gusikow (Violine I), Koretzki (Violine II), Stoliarewski (Bratsche), Pjatigorski (Cello)

2. J. ENGEL . . . a) „A Mol is gewen" . . . .
   (für eine Stimme mit Violine, Bratsche, Klavier)
   b) „Osso boiker" . . . . ⎫
   A. KREIN . . . c) „Steih ich oif" . . . . ⎬ F. WACHMAN (Gesang)
   d) „Orem bist" . . . . ⎭

3. M. GNESSIN . a) In memoriam eines jüdischen ⎫
                    Minnesängers a. d. 13. Jahrh. ⎬ E. GUSIKOW (Violine)
   J. ACHRON . . b) Melodie . . . . ⎪
   A. KREIN . . . c) Caprice . . . . ⎭

II.

4. M. MILNER . . a) Wiegenlied . . . . ⎫
   J. ENGEL . . . b) Die Wand . . . . ⎬ F. WACHMAN (Gesang)
   c) „Tawass s'hawi" . . . . ⎪
   d) „Minhag chadasch" . . . . . . ⎭

5. J. ENGEL . . . Suite für 7 Instrumente aus der Musik zum Drama
   „Hadibuk" (Theater „Habimah" in Moskau)
   a) „Um wessen willen?" („Mipnej mah?")
   b) Das Hohe Lied
   c) Bettlertänze
   d) Hochzeitsmarsch
   e) „Bedeckns"
   f) Chassidenlied
   g) Das Hohe Lied
   h) „Um wessen willen

a, b, c: in fortlaufender Folge — d, e, f: einzelne Nummern — g, h: in fortlaufender Folge

Mitwirkende: Herren Gusikow, Koretzki, Stoliarewski, Pjatigorski, Kästli (Kontrabass), Baalnemones (Klarinette), Bölmann (Schlaginstrumente)

Am Flügel: L. MONKO

Konzertflügel: *BLÜTHNER*

Während der Vorträge bleiben die Saaltüren geschlossen

Jewish music concerts in Germany 1922 (courtesy Jascha Nemtsov).

Kroyt nonetheless became active in the recording business in Berlin and made a few solo recordings.

Szreter, a former student of Egon Petri, was a well-known solo pianist and accompanist in Berlin. Szreter and Piatigorsky's compatibility led to an association that lasted from 1923 until Szreter's untimely death from leukemia in 1933.[54]

> Thanks to my large circle of acquaintances, I was able to meet the first conductor of what used to be called the Royal Opera Theater [Königliche Kapelle, now called Staatsoper Unter den Linden]. His name is Leo Blech[55] and he told me that they had a spot open for the first cellist.
>
> They had a competition for the position. Supposedly many cellists participated but no one made it and they were still looking for someone to fill in. I was very excited to come across this opportunity and asked to arrange a hearing for me.
>
> I played so well that most of the conductors and members of the orchestra that sat in the audience, and especially Blech, happily told me that I can start working with them as soon as possible. The first thing I did after I heard that, was I told the Americans [the Helds] that I will not be needing their help anymore and thanked them for everything that they've done for me.[56]

As the 1922-23 season began, Piatigorsky found his cello colleagues in the orchestra behaving less than professionally, and some downright aggressively. This felt eerily similar to his first rehearsals with the Bolshoi, where jealous cellists would do their best to confound him by putting incorrect markings (directions) onto his music, causing him to bring the cello section in at the wrong time. It had bothered some of the older members that a youngster was so far ahead of them, as it took years to earn a promotion. The situation in Berlin was similar in that there was a scarcity of good paying jobs, exacerbated by inflation and the influx of foreign artists — particularly Jewish artists. The competition for employment was fierce, and with smoldering anti–Semitism the environment could get ugly.[57]

Arriving at the orchestra rehearsal one morning, Piatigorsky experienced an outrageous incident:

> I worked at the theater only for a short period of time after which I quit because of awful relationships between the musicians, the cellists of course. All of them were full of anger and jealousy; they did not respond to my greetings and even boycotted against me. There was also an incident when I came to play *Das Rheingold*. After the conductor very nicely said hello and asked me to sit down at my soloist place, a cellist, no, actually a cripple from the back stand, got up from the chair, pushed me out of the way and said, "I am not going to let some foreigner take my seat." Of course, I walked out of there with the decision to never go back. The next morning I realized that I didn't have a single mark (money) in my pocket. I was in the worst frame of mind and I did not leave my apartment for a few days straight. I starved myself the way I could never have thought possible. It was a torture — physically and mentally.[58]

Even as Piatigorsky suffered humiliation, he soon saw prospects for both orchestral work and solo concerts:

> I was starving myself until I decided to go and play wherever. Well, it has already been four months and I am still playing "wherever." Right now, my options are like this: I was offered to go on a tour around Italy, Spain, Poland, Lithuania, as well as the suburbs of Germany, where I have already been once [i.e., with the Pozniak Trio]. Also I've been offered to take a place of the first solo cellist at a different Opera Theater in Berlin.[59] They are promising great benefits and atmosphere. Right now I am in the process of negotiation with them. I think I will sign a contract not for a year, as they would like, but only for 6 months [September 1923 to February 1924]. Actually, I am finally starting to feel better about the whole situation and

no matter what it will take, no matter the amount of money it costs to give a concert, I will definitely do it this year.

(Honestly, 9 out of 10 concerts here are awful. This is all because the performances are given not by people who can play, but by people who can afford it. You can give a concert, spend your last money, and then starve yourself for 3 years. It just doesn't make sense.)

Though considering a return to Moscow, he remained ambivalent. His prospects for work in Russia were certainly not solid:

> After that I am hoping to go to Russia. I miss it so much — the Russian art, the dearest to me people who I can't wait to see and hug and kiss, people who I yearn for so badly. If I could find a good and permanent position, an interesting job, play with you and go everywhere with you, then I would be more than happy to leave everything behind and go back to Moscow. If we, like back in the old days, with members of our old group, came overseas as a Russian Quartet, then I think we could do a lot here.[60]

By the summer of 1923, Koutzen received his visa to the United States to join the Philadelphia Orchestra. The work in Berlin slowed down so much that Piatigorsky accepted the de Kreszes' invitation to join them in Hungary. There they rehearsed the Brahms Double Concerto and played the Debussy Sonata with Geza's wife, Norah.[61] It was the last visit; the de Kreszes sailed to Canada later that summer to join the Toronto Conservatory.

3. Nomad to Success

Nomad in Berlin

Nineteen twenty-three was a busy but unhappy year for Piatigorsky. During the day he taught at the Russian Conservatory or rehearsed with the opera. When not performing with the opera at night, he sometimes worked as a freelance cellist in ensembles such as those at the Adlon or Kaiserhof hotels. Since German currency had become almost worthless, accepting food from hotels was a welcome bonus. It was a good evening's work when black market speculators and tourists with dollars tipped the ensembles.

The prominent Russian contingent of artists in Berlin must have helped assuage his longing for home. There were Russian newspapers, meeting places, football teams, and publishing houses. Transplanted actors from Stanislavski's Theatre, painters such as Wassily Kandinsky, celebrated writers Maxim Gorky and Vladimir Nabokov, and talented musicians had settled in Berlin and were flourishing to a remarkable degree. Piatigorsky may have reunited with one such friend in October, pianist and conductor Issay Dobrowen,[1] who performed with the Berlin Philharmonic.

In the aftermath of the Great War, Germany enjoyed an atmosphere of moral, intellectual and artistic freedom that made Berlin a worldwide capital for the arts and sciences. The Weimar Kultur tolerated an atmosphere of openness, and there was the impression that the incredible could happen at any second. Berlin was a city where decadence flourished side by side with genius — an unlikely place for the avant-garde to thrive, amidst economic chaos and the menacing cloud of Nazism. Hedonism grew unimpeded in an environment that saw work and wealth in a futile race to stabilize currency. Astoundingly, the city boasted three opera houses, four music schools, and several professional orchestras. Arts organizations grew phenomenally in the early 1920s, with orchestras and singing societies in nearly every town.[2]

Throughout 1923 Piatigorsky continued to work in Berlin doing, as he wrote, "whatever" even after his tour of Italy, Spain, Poland, Lithuania, and the German suburbs. Even without steady management representation, his reputation spread by word of mouth. A concert in Riga was particularly triumphant:

> We saw a tall, slender, very handsome young man come on stage and elegantly acknowledge the applause. He started his program with the Locatelli Sonata. His staccato runs, lightness of technique, beauty of sound, artistry and virtuosity combined to provide an exposition of cello playing and music never heard before. It seemed as though the roof of the Opera House would come off as the people went wild with applause that they did not want to cease. Then he played the Dvořák Concerto with Ivan Suchov as pianist. He conquered everybody with

the first couple of notes. People were yelling and carrying on like I had never seen before. The enthusiasm and excitement in the hall was fantastic.

Piatigorsky recalled the concert and it resulted in an abrupt end to the tour:

> It was quite a successful concert and I got good reviews. The man who engaged me, Serachevsky, was supposed to come to my hotel the morning after the concert to pay me. I desperately needed the money because I didn't have anything in my pocket. As I waited for Serachevsky that morning, I ate all the lobster necks[3] that I had bought the night before. Hours passed and it was time for me to go to the railroad station. I went to the hotel lobby to see if Mr. Serachevsky had been looking for me and was told, "Oh, he came here and left this envelope for you." I was so happy to get the envelope, but when I opened it, I found only a third class ticket from Riga to Berlin — no money. I walked to the station with my cello and boarded the train. As we began to move I saw Serachevsky looking out from behind a column and waving goodbye to me.[4]

Back in Berlin, he resumed working in the recording studios of German Parlophon, where he had briefly started in January as a freelance player. Very soon he began recording for Vox, a subsidiary of its larger complex, Voxhaus, which became the first radio broadcaster in Berlin. In both cases he worked as

Pierrot Lunaire announcement, December 1923.

an anonymous solo cellist in orchestras and in salon chamber music. The orchestral recordings were chiefly made with violinists-conductors Edith Lorand, Tino Valeria (AKA Boris Kroyt)[5] and the celebrated Romanian violinist Georges Boulanger. On many of these recordings one can hear Piatigorsky's tasteful solos.

The income from this work was minimal, but even so, it was employment and meant working with good musicians, some of whom were friends from Moscow, Warsaw, or Leipzig. As violinists, Lorand, Boulanger, and Kroyt/Valeria recorded many salon trios as well as a few standard works. Karol Szreter, Boris Kroyt, and Piatigorsky preferred anonymity in salon repertoire, and did not allow their names printed on the discs. The association with the Boulanger Trio[6] was primarily featured with the violinist's stock-in-trade of his own prolific compositions. Miss Lorand's offerings as the Edith Lorand Trio were the ubiquitous bonbons that every record label competed to offer as well as some unusual rarities.[7]

With each freelance job, Piatigorsky hoped to meet his weekly rent, but as frugal as he was, times could get desperate. When he could not manage to pay for his unheated attic room, his few possessions were held in ransom, and the Tiergarten bench became his home again.

Berlin, 1924 (note gut strings).

One cold, damp November day, while Piatigorsky was on his way to the Zoo Station, a tall gentleman approached: "Mr. Piatigorsky? I am a musician from the Berlin Philharmonic."[8] Principal flutist Paul Bose explained that Boris Kroyt had sent him to invite the young cellist to join them in an upcoming performance of Arnold Schonberg's *Pierrot Lunaire*. Some of the other musicians included the celebrated pianist Artur Schnabel, conductor Fritz Stiedry of the Staatsoper Berlin, and soprano Marie Gutheil-Schoder of the Vienna Opera (and formerly under Gustav Mahler).

Bose explained that cellist Evel Stegman pulled out of the performance and that Piatigorsky's name came up immediately. Piatigorsky agreed to the performance — twenty rehearsals without pay — and Bose asked him to come to Schnabel's home the following afternoon for a rehearsal. Schnabel remembered his first meeting with Piatigorsky at his home: "Kroyt had told us of a young Russian 'cellist who had just come to Berlin; he was absolutely unknown, was living in an unheated attic in the cold winter, and was undernourished. He said, 'He is a very remarkable artist, most promising,' and recommended him as 'cellist for our ensemble. So this tall young man, Gregor Piatigorsky, was brought to my house. He played one solo piece for us and we were all very much impressed by his music as well as by his charming personality."[9] After Piatigorsky's "audition" they began to rehearse *Pierrot Lunaire*, a piece he had not yet seen. The cello part was missing so Piatigorsky read from the full score. Piatigorsky remembered:

> I was soon completely absorbed in the music. Its originality delighted me, and despite the hunger that gnawed at me mercilessly I think I played well. Everyone seemed pleased, most of all Schnabel.
> "Shall we rest a while? Tea is served in the other room."
> No one except me was in a hurry to have tea. I waited, listening with the others to Schnabel discoursing on *Pierrot Lunaire*, communism, and other interesting topics. However, sensing a rather prolonged dissertation, I slowly moved into the other room. There I saw sandwiches and a variety of cakes displayed on a table. I was alone.
> It was like leaving baby lambs with a wolf. I devoured the sandwiches one by one. I worked fast. When there were no sandwiches left I began the devastation of the sweeter and less satisfying material. These also disappeared with fabulous speed, and only when nothing edible whatever remained on the table did I rejoin the group, who still listened to Schnabel. My absence had not been noticed.
> "Well, gentlemen, tea is waiting for us." All followed Schnabel.
> The moment he entered the room he called the maid.
> "Where are the sandwiches?" he demanded indignantly. I saw her eyes widen with fear.[10]

Later, Piatigorsky made his way back to the Zoo Station. It began to rain, but waiting for it to end, he had an uncontrollable urge to hear music, an urge that went beyond cold and hunger. Walking to the philharmonic, he easily slipped in through the stage entrance with his cello. He found the musicians' dressing room and left his cello there, then located an empty seat in the hall. Ferruccio Busoni was conducting the philharmonic in Beethoven's Eighth Symphony. Piatigorsky was fascinated with Busoni's appearance and his conducting "insanely fast tempi" but he was happy to hear great music again.

That night, as he was leaving the concert hall, the brisk icy wind convinced him to stay inside a bit longer. He retreated to the loge area [known as the Landecker Loge], hid and rested. After the lights went off, he placed his still damp clothes over the seats to dry; suddenly he had an overwhelming compulsion to play. Making his naked way to the stage, he found a chair and played at length, savoring the full resonance he could make in the hall of the philharmonic. Exhausted, he went back to the loge and slept. In the morning, awakened by the Berlin Philharmonic rehearsing a Schumann symphony, Piatigorsky prepared himself for the day in the dressing room. He always kept a toothbrush, toothpaste and a razor in his cello bag.

After twenty rehearsals, and with the afternoon teas as his only sustenance, Piatigorsky felt they had mastered Schonberg's score. The concert was sponsored by *Melos*, a journal devoted to contemporary music and founded by conductor Hermann Scherchen. Its aim was to explore the problem of the breakdown of tonality, the relationship between music and words, and the relationship between music and the other arts, as well as music's sociological foundations. However, its editor, Fritz-Fridolin Windisch, had just been replaced and, in bitter resentment of his ouster, he created a scandal with a group of malcontents. Piatigorsky recalled:

> We knew *Pierrot Lunaire* perhaps more thoroughly than any piece of standard repertoire. Yet, because we were not certain how the composition would be received, we were anxious about the premiere. We were greeted by a large audience and after taking our places we waited for quiet to settle over the auditorium.
>
> Stiedry raised his baton to begin, but suddenly froze in the air.... [W]e heard a sudden

Pianist Karol Szreter.

Left to right: Kreutzer-Wolfsthal-Piatigorsky Trio, 1925.

loud shriek, followed by a series of boos, and a commotion on one side of the hall punctuated by speeches and outcries.

Windisch also jumped on the stage protesting the concert, but was forcibly seized and taken away.

According to Piatigorsky, "Schnabel was equal to the occasion. With great gusto he launched into a circus polka, and Kroyt and I followed him. 'Come on,' he encouraged, 'this is a fish market.' The audience's laughter overcame the confusion, and the atmosphere of vaudeville stopped as abruptly as it had begun."[11] The Berlin performance on January 5, 1924, was a big success, notwithstanding the anti-modernist histrionics.[12] With Piatigorsky's performance in *Pierrot Lunaire*, his true entrée into Berlin's musical elite began.

Success and Love

The weeks following the concert were lonely, as Piatigorsky missed his *Pierrot* partners who had almost become family. He continued to accept any and all jobs that came his way. By February 1924 he had made his first solo recordings for the Vox company. Then, once again, flutist Paul Bose presented Piatigorsky with an opportunity. Bose had made an appointment for him to bring his cello to the philharmonic auditorium within a few days. When Piatigorsky arrived, Bose excitedly described the situation. Since Bose and his colleagues had repeatedly mentioned the young cellist's remarkable gifts and experience to their conductor, Wilhelm Furtwängler, an impromptu audition was arranged. Even though a solo position was not announced and the concert season was well underway, Bose persuaded Furtwängler and his colleagues to listen to Piatigorsky during the rehearsal break.

With almost no time to warm up, Piatigorsky found himself entering the stage he had only experienced as a nude interloper. The strangeness of the moment was intensified by the fact that the entire Berlin Philharmonic sat en masse in the auditorium. Stunned, he hesitated and looked up at the Landecker Loge, remembering that fateful night. His hesitation was long enough to be noticed by Furtwängler, who asked Bose, "What's wrong with him?" Furtwängler's voice brought him back to focus and he played portions of concertos by Schumann and Dvořák, Strauss's *Don Quixote*, Bach, and orchestral excerpts.

The reception by Furtwängler and the orchestra was unforgettable, nearly moving Piatigorsky to tears as Furtwängler embraced him and pronounced him the new solo cellist with the Berlin Philharmonic. The appointment was not unusual for the orchestra in that it traditionally had two solo cellists as well as two concertmasters. Piatigorsky's employment was immediate and demanding. At that time, the orchestra was then owned by the musicians, and was supported only in a limited way by the city of Berlin and the German government. As a result, along with performing the regular season, the cooperative orchestra played concerts in other venues. The orchestra was in financial trouble and offered itself up for hire. For a few thousand marks, anyone could conduct or solo with the orchestra. In Piatigorsky's first weeks in the orchestra, they began touring in Germany and by the summer were also touring Switzerland.

Upcoming on one of the Volkskonzerts was Sarasate's *Zigeunerweisen* — one of the most popular violin showpieces — but this time scheduled to be performed as a cello solo. Surprised, Piatigorsky asked the orchestra's manager and harpist, Otto Müller,[13] if there was a mistake. Müller insisted it was true and that programs could not be reprinted, and further

Konzert-Direktion Hermann Wolff und Jules Sachs Berlin W 9, Linkstrasse 42

Bernburger Str. 22 **PHILHARMONIE** Bernburger Str. 22

Montag, den 19. April 1926, abends 7¹/₂ Uhr

9. Philharmonisches Konzert

Dirigent: **Wilhelm Furtwängler**

Solist: **Gregor Piatigorsky**

I.
Concerto grosso D-dur Nr. V . . . . . . G. F. Händel
für 2 Solo-Violinen, Solo-Violoncell und Streichorchester
Solovioline: Konzertmeister H. Holst
           „ T. Spiwakowsky
Solo-Violoncell Prof. N. Graudan

I. Introduction — Allegro
II. Presto
III. Largo
IV. Menuetto
V. Allegro

II.
Cello-Konzert H-moll op. 104 . . . . A. Dvorak
Allegro
Andante ma non troppo
Finale

III.
Symphonie Nr. IV F-moll op. 36 . . . . P. Tschaikowsky
Andante sostenuto, moderato con anima
Andantino in modo di canzona
Scherzo
Finale: Allegro con fuoco

PHILHARMONIE, Montag, den 26. April 1926, abends 7¹/₂ Uhr
10. (letztes) PHILHARMONISCHES KONZERT
Dirigent: **Wilhelm Furtwängler**
Beethoven: IV. Symphonie B-dur / **Brahms:** I. Symphonie C-moll

Berlin Philharmonic, April 19, 1926.

that former solo cellist, Arnold Földesy,[14] had played it with great success ten years earlier. This was only one of the surprises in store for Piatigorsky and he had to adapt very quickly.

The German mark was finally stabilized in November 1923 (though its recovery took years), and Piatigorsky's financial life was vastly improving. People were no longer paid in huge bundles of cash, and soon the currency became comparable with those of other countries. With the changeover, however, ticket prices were raised, and audiences began to shrink somewhat. Still, decadence and the arts thrived in Berlin.

Piatigorsky's first subscription concert with the Berlin Philharmonic as a soloist was on January 19, 1925, in the Dvořák Concerto. The reviews were ecstatic. In the following review, he was compared to Popper:

> One has to reach back to impressions of David Popper,[15] whom I had the opportunity to hear, or of Casals and the young Gérardy, in order to find a standard for Piatigorsky's unusual maturity. We now know why the Berlin Philharmonic is naming him one of the greatest cellists of the present time! Beauty and power of tones were one with an elemental musical performance. The technical, for instance, an incredibly bold and accurate bowing technique; an unprecedented energy multiple playing of endless pleasure and amazement. The realization of Piatigorsky's youthful mastery and therefore a promising future, is one of the most beautiful experiences of this musical season. His place is absolutely as soloist of a Philharmonic concert. We are going to lose him soon enough to America.[16]

Piatigorsky soon developed a privileged relationship with Furtwängler, stretching beyond the confines of his orchestral position. The two consulted on the selection of programs as well as concepts of string playing of which Furtwängler, a pianist, was not keenly aware. The conductor wanted a better understanding and Piatigorsky was happy to help. One particular phrase in Tchaikovsky's *Pathétique* Symphony bothered Furtwängler, who complained that it never sounded right. The following was Piatigorsky's suggestion for the famous unison melody for the strings:

Tchaikovsky *Pathétique* bowing.

Furtwängler's unique conducting style has often been written about,[17] but Piatigorsky liked to illustrate the contrasts between Furtwängler and Bruno Walter in performances of the Schumann Concerto. The transition from the slow movement to the finale is comprised of a solo cello passage to be played faster and faster. Furtwängler's emotional preparation for the upcoming orchestral downbeat consisted of his notorious quivering of the right hand, ever increasing with the soloist's forward momentum. The anticipation further led to Furtwängler's shaking and stomping that finally erupted in the massive entrance of a triumphant orchestra. In contrast, Piatigorsky played the work shortly afterwards with Bruno Walter in Vienna. As the cellist pushed forward, he awaited the passionate explosion. Instead, the conductor provided a well-poised and proper downbeat.

Furtwängler best conveyed his wishes nonverbally. He would plead to the orchestra: "'Gentlemen, this phrase must be — it must — it must — you know what I mean — please try it again — please,' [and] said to me at the intermission, 'You see how important it is for a conductor to convey his wishes clearly?' Strangely, the orchestra knew what he wanted."[18] Piatigorsky recalled in an interview: "He addressed them like equal artists. He demanded from them as much as he would demand from himself—with great sincerity. In other words, he lifted them up, very often making them greater than they really were. That was his ability, his personal magnetism. Of course of such a richness, fantastic, creative — truly creative — not only re-creative ability that I find quite unique — that human element of spontaneity was always there. There was something of a child in him, a great naiveté, and the orchestra just adored him."

The cellist's respect for Furtwängler's piano playing was no less positive: "I loved to play chamber music with him. I loved his piano playing. I thought he was one of the finest chamber music performers on the piano." In contrast to future recital partners Horowitz and Schnabel, "at no time did he overpower his string-playing partner, who had no advantages of a pedal or open lid."[19] Beyond music, Piatigorsky and Furtwängler also socialized. During a conversation on the subject of dance, they both confessed their inability, and they decided to learn. The awkward duo enrolled in a dance class under assumed names. It was hopeless. "After the third lesson the teacher said that we were exceptional cases and, being unmusical, had better have the special course. We gave it up altogether."[20]

With the day-to-day tussle of a new life, Piatigorsky was not aware of politics or Adolf Hitler to any significant degree until Furtwängler mentioned him. Piatigorsky quickly became educated. Yet, Furtwängler, like so many Germans, proved to be naïve, not able to fully perceive that the ludicrous psychosis of Nazi philosophy would envelop not only Germany but also Europe. Furtwängler's opportunism would reap the temporary rewards of power, but his often-reluctant collaboration with the Third Reich would plague him after the war, even though his intervention saved many Jews, including violinist Carl Flesch.

Concert engagements began to multiply, and Piatigorsky easily made friends with the cultural leaders of Berlin. Late in 1924, at a recital of pianist Ossip Gabrilowitsch, he was introduced to a very attractive lady, Lida Antik. Piatigorsky fell in love, caught up in her worldly charms and cultured manner.[21] Lida, a pianist, came from a wealthy Russian family. She had studied in St. Petersburg with composer Alexander Glazunov who was complimentary of her talent, declaring she was more a musician than a pianist and thought she was better suited to composition.[22]

Lida arrived in Berlin with her family in 1919. Her father was a prominent lawyer and her mother was also a pianist and would soon become a rehearsal pianist for the Berlin Staatsoper. Lida enrolled in the Berlin Hochschule and studied the piano with fellow Russian Leonid Kreutzer. She also spoke many languages and was quickly on familiar terms with Berlin's upper echelon.

Lida had suffered a disastrous first marriage, as a sixteen-year-old, which was fortunately brief. In 1923 she was briefly engaged to Jascha Heifetz and even traveled to New York to meet his parents. Though the romantic relationship with Heifetz fizzled, they remained good friends.

Piatigorsky and Lida were married in April 1925. With her ambition and elegant attainments, and Piatigorsky's thirst for knowledge and inclusion, the union seemed a perfect match. Piatigorsky's nearly nonexistent education was at odds with his intellectual curiosity, and he could feel insecure among the well-educated. Lida sought to introduce her attractive new husband to people who could help move him forward in his career. Because of their friendship, Lida relied on Heifetz to open social and musical doors for her husband. Once the two men met, their regard for each other was immediate and became life-long.

The first need of the newlyweds was to find an apartment, but they were not yet able to buy what they wanted. They took rooms with the von Heeringen family in order to save money — Piatigorsky's pride prevented him from accepting any help from his in-laws. The cellist continued to accept all the work he could beyond the philharmonic and teaching. It was most convenient to continue working anonymously for the Berlin recording studios.[23]

Soon the couple was able to afford a suitable apartment on Südwestkorso, which quickly became a gathering place for Berlin's intelligentsia. When in Berlin, Heifetz spent much of his time with the Piatigorskys. Their home hosted Fritz Kreisler, Artur Schnabel, Edwin Fischer, Bronislaw Huberman, and Josef Szigeti, as well as writers and painters. The celebrities of Berlin regularly attended Piatigorsky's solo concerts.

Excited to share her new beau with Glazunov, Lida sent Glazunov a letter and review describing Piatigorsky's success. She also asked the composer to write a concerto for him:

> Now I have an *enormous* favor to ask you, which for God's sake I hope you will not refuse, since it would be the greatest joy of my husband's musical life. My husband and I beg you to write a concerto, even a short one (however it is more convenient for you in view of your full schedule) for cello with orchestra, which my husband would play with delight, and for which he would be eternally grateful. He *adores* your music and "out of despair" he plays snippets of your violin concerto on the cello. He recently played some of your small pieces at a recital, after which he and I talked about you for a long time and he asked me, since I know you, to make the enormous request of you to write a cello concerto, since no music speaks to the soul and the sound of my husband on the cello like yours, and he will do it all technically perfectly, of that you can be sure.
>
> I just want to have good hope that you will not consider this impudence and will believe the sincerity of my husband's and my passionate request. I will tremblingly await an answer from you, even just a couple of lines, and I hope that you will only send your consent to this, as that will be our very happiest day.
>
> My husband has been performing a lot, as a soloist with the orchestra and in various cities. He has already played almost all of the cello concertos over these two seasons, and he is dreaming of a new concerto written by you, my own dear Aleksandr Konstantinovich.
>
> I again ask your forgiveness for my audacity; please don't leave us both without an answer. We tremblingly await your answer. I send you a thousand heartfelt greetings from us both and from our mutual friends, including Kreutzer....
>
> P.S. My husband will be playing for Furtwängler next winter as a soloist and his dream is to be playing a Glazunov concerto by then![24]

The orchestra toured every spring throughout Europe. Though the tours were taxing, they were exciting. "There was something of the spirit of conquest, with Furtwängler, the poet of conductors, leading his army to victory." The philharmonic spent most of the time on the train, and evenings without concerts were rare. Whenever Piatigorsky had the time, he took walks, curious about unfamiliar cities and their languages. It was during these walks that he began to collect art. From the very beginning, Piatigorsky had an unerring intuitive eye for talent, buying many Expressionist masterworks for a song, long before their creators became famous. Works by Russians such as Kandinsky, Marc, Kirchner, and Gluckmann captivated him, but the Lithuanian Chaim Soutine held a special place. Piatigorsky later recalled, "Without any background or ability ... I roamed in France, Germany, and the Scandinavian countries in search of paintings. I spent more time and more money than I could afford in acquiring them. And when I met an artist whose work I admired, there was no limit to my delight."[25]

Though now well established and secure, Piatigorsky continued to work incessantly beyond his normal duties. One wonders if this Herculean push was driven more by his

Piatigorsky with Furtwängler (right, rear) on tour. The third man is unidentified.

desire to keep Lida in a style to which she was accustomed, or to satisfy his new-found passion for art collecting. In any event, Lida eventually grew annoyed with his hobby.

A Tale of Two Trios

In 1925 the illustrious Wolfsthal-Kreutzer-Piatigorsky Trio was formed. Along with Piatigorsky the trio comprised violinist Joseph Wolfsthal and fellow Muscovite pianist Leonid Kreutzer (Lida Piatigorsky's former teacher); both were celebrated artists as well as professors at the Berlin Hochschule. The trio presented an annual series from 1925 to 1928[26] in Berlin. They explored a comprehensive repertoire, including the Beethoven *Triple* concerto, which they presented with the Berlin Philharmonic in 1927.[27]

By 1924 concert and recording artist Leonid Kreutzer (1881–1953) was also a prominent piano pedagogue in Berlin, instructing many well-known pianists, including Wladyslaw Szpilman, the subject of Roman Polanski's 2002 film *The Pianist.*[28]

Wolfsthal (1899–1931) was the youngest violin professor to teach at the Hochschule and was a favorite of Richard Strauss.[29] Presumably Piatigorsky and Wolfsthal first met as fellow members of the Berlin State Opera [Staatsoper] in 1923, where Wolfsthal was concertmaster. Wolfsthal's premature death at the age of thirty-one was a great blow to the musical community.

The trio toured primarily in Germany and received wonderful reviews.[30] They made only three recordings, all in 1925, of trio movements by Schubert, Brahms and Beethoven. Soon Piatigorsky joined another stellar trio with Artur Schnabel and Carl Flesch, reconstituting the Schnabel-Flesch-Becker Trio. Schnabel's trio had languished after a hiatus taken by Schnabel and the subsequent retirement of Hugo Becker in 1921. The addition of Piatigorsky to the ensemble must have been invigorating to his senior colleagues and it was certainly ironic for Piatigorsky to take his former "teacher's" place.

The Schnabel-Flesch-Piatigorsky Trio was a big success. Beyond the basic repertoire, they premiered Ernst Krenek's *Trio-Phantasie*, op. 63 in 1930.[31] Commissioned by Schnabel for the trio, it was received with harsh criticism, in spite of a superb performance, which called the work "cacophonous."[32] This was Schnabel's last public performance of a new work, even though the pianist was also a daring composer himself.[33] The trio performed in the winter months, while pianists Carl Friedberg or Kreutzer joined Piatigorsky and Flesch for the summer festivals.

Successful ensembles enjoy a sense of humor — a necessary counterbalance to the serious and exacting preparation of programs. It was certainly true with the Schnabel-Flesch-Piatigorsky Trio. Early in their association, Schnabel invented nicknames for each member of the trio. Schnabel was known as Arti, Flesch, the oldest, as Vati [lit. Father/Dad], and Piatigorsky as "Piati" or "Piaty." According to the violinist's son, Carl F. Flesch, "I recall a get-together of musicians who decided to play quartets with instruments exchanged. My father failed miserably with the cello, whereas Piatigorsky acquitted himself well by means of playing the violin like a viola da gamba."[34] Schnabel's reputation for verbal virtuosity can be seen in a letter to Flesch, where he makes an amusing remark about the Schubert Trio's lengthy last movement: "We should try to present its finale so exciting and lively, that its reputation for being excessively long will prove to be slander."[35]

Piatigorsky prided himself on punctuality, but admitted his sloppiness in keeping track of his music. While on tour, he sometimes left his part at the hotel but was always rescued by his partners, who kept copies of the cello parts in their briefcases. Once, his erudite but fun-loving partners wanted to teach him a lesson, and they substituted the cello part to Wagner's *Meistersinger* Overture for a Schubert trio. Piatigorsky knew the Schubert from memory and pretended to read *Meistersinger*, turning the page after some minutes. They could barely finish the first movement without falling apart with laughter.

In 1927 the cities of Berlin and Hamburg celebrated the bicentennial of Beethoven's birth with a festival of chamber music concerts featuring the celebrated Polish violinist Bronislaw Huberman, as well as Schnabel and Piatigorsky. Flesch, who had a long-standing partnership with Schnabel going back to 1911, was not included and was understandably annoyed. It was especially bothersome since Flesch had a pointed dislike for Huberman, whom he regarded as a sloppy, undisciplined violinist. Schnabel's lack of loyalty eventually led to the demise of the trio.

In the 1920s Berlin was not short of talented cellists — Joseph Schuster[36] worked and studied there, soon to join the orchestra himself, and Arnold Földesy still performed regularly, sometimes returning to solo with the philharmonic. Visits by Casals, Cassadó, Marechal, and Mainardi kept the atmosphere cello-conscious. Emanuel Feuermann's career was well established as a soloist and recording artist, and he was also teaching at the Hochschule.[37] At first Feuermann and Piatigorsky appeared to get along and brought their classes to each other's recitals. But in a short time, Piatigorsky's rapid ascent brought out an unfortunate quality in Feuermann: jealousy.

Feuermann, with his fabulous technical facility, had no reason to feel intimidated, but he saw Piatigorsky as a threat. Once, Piatigorsky played the Schumann Concerto for Feuermann, who coldly responded, "Why do you play like that?" At one recital, Feuermann sat

Berlin Philharmonic on tour in England, 1927. Piatigorsky is in front of Furtwängler on left, Nikolai Graudan is on right; concertmaster is Henry Holst.

in the front row and made faces at Piatigorsky while he played, hoping to distract him. Perhaps naïvely, Piatigorsky was unaware of the depth of Feuermann's hostility. Piatigorsky's friend, Földesy, advised him not to be so kind and supportive towards Feuermann "because he does nothing but criticize you behind your back."[38] Piatigorsky heard that Feuermann told people that Piatigorsky had no technique. Frustrated, Piatigorsky finally confronted Feuermann and suggested they have a contest to see who was the weaker player — the first to make an error would be the loser. A passage in the Haydn D Major Concerto was proposed, but the duel never took place.

Later, when Feuermann went to Russia in 1932, Piatigorsky asked him to look up his brother Alexander (Shura), a professional cellist. Piatigorsky had only known his brother as an infant, well before Shura could even hold a cello. When Feuermann returned, Piatigorsky asked if he had met him and heard him play:

> "Yes, I heard him."
> "How does he play?"
> "Like you. Only worse."[39]

Sophie Feuermann recalled attending a Piatigorsky recital in Cologne with her brother: "Munio [Emanuel] and I were a little late. During the intermission we went to say hello. He said, 'Sophie and Munio. I give you my fee, but leave!'" Though their relationship remained strained, they managed to appear friendly. Feuermann wrote to his wife on tour in 1937: "Imagine, the day after tomorrow Piatigorsky is also playing in Torino, both of us on the same evening. I am looking forward to seeing him and am curious what he has to tell." And in March 1940 he wrote to Wilhem Kux: "I stand as the first in my line.... [T]here only remains Piatigorsky, who, talented as he is, in many respects is lacking in quality"[40]

Problems can take place when two musicians share the same last name and profession — writers Alexandre Dumas, father and son, and composers of the Bach dynasty are two examples. The conductor Serge Koussevizky began his career as a bassist, as did his nephew, Fabien, who was in the Bolshoi Theatre with Piatigorsky. When Fabien elected to follow in his uncle's footsteps as a conductor, he changed his name to Sevitzky. By doing so he avoided the comparisons. The Piastro brothers, basically the same age, were both excellent violinists. The older brother went by Joseph Piastro Borisoff, while the younger went by the shortened Mishel Piastro.

Gregor and Alexander Piatigorsky were very different cellists, and it unavoidably caused confusion, especially for Gregor. Since Gregor was older and his career was well established, he suggested that Alexander change his name. The suggestion was not particularly welcome, but Gregor won him over. Perhaps to make a point, Alexander changed his name to Stogorsky — meaning One Hundred Mountains, while Piatigorsky means Five Mountains.

The excellent cellist, pianist and composer Enrico Mainardi also performed in Berlin and once accompanied Piatigorsky in the Debussy Sonata. On another occasion they had fun playing Popper's *Elfentanz*— with Piatigorsky standing behind Mainardi fingering the piece while Mainardi bowed.

When Alfred von Glehn, Piatigorsky's former teacher from the Moscow Conservatory, arrived in Berlin in 1925, it was cause for celebration. The venerable professor had decided to retire, but unfortunately he still needed employment. Piatigorsky was able to arrange for him to teach at the Klindworth-Scharwenka Conservatory.[41] But, several months into his work, he became very ill and could no longer teach. Von Glehn's frightened wife, Käthe, came to Piatigorsky and reported that the director had threatened to withdraw her husband's salary. Piatigorsky took over von Glehn's class, insuring his old professor's salary would continue, and worked without payment for the remaining eighteen months of von Glehn's life. Von Glehn never knew of the financial arrangement. So that he could fulfill his obligation, the conservatory remained open for Piatigorsky to teach at odd hours, evenings, and weekends.

Piatigorsky's first day of work at the conservatory was challenging. A class of about 16 students, including several Klengel students from Leipzig, greeted him. Some who knew him addressed him as Grisha. He paused for a moment and said,

> "This is a school and I am the professor of cello. Whoever does not want to study is free to leave immediately — the faster the better. Our relationship as former colleagues doesn't have any bearing on this situation. We are colleagues and friends after class, as always, but right here and now — I am the professor and you are the students. If you don't want to study you can leave. I will leave the classroom so that you can make your decision. I will be back in ten minutes, and I want to have a different atmosphere in this class. Goodbye."
>
> As soon as Piatigorsky left the room, the young men burst out talking alternately in Russian and German. As I listened to their comments and watched some of them leave, I thought, "My God, what authority this man has!"
>
> When Piatigorsky returned he said, "I'm glad there is a different atmosphere in the room now. Let's go to work."[42]

After von Glehn's death on December 12, 1927, it was obvious Piatigorsky could not keep up the huge demands on his time, and by the following spring, he resigned from the conservatory.[43] Von Glehn's students played Klengel's *Hymnus* at his funeral. "There was a big wreath with a ribbon on it that read, 'To my beloved teacher from his humble student, Gregor Piatigorsky.'"[44]

Von Glehn's class may have had a few veterans of World War I and the October Revolution with various wounds to the hands. Piatigorsky, with comic aplomb, relates a series of increasingly improbable hand deformities found in von Glehn's studio. It is not surprising that Piatigorsky, the storyteller, found humor in exaggerating the extent. The absurdity culminated with a description of one student who supposedly had two thumbs.[45]

Piatigorsky's relationship with Furtwängler made it likely for him to have met composers Hindemith, Stravinsky, Milhaud, Strauss, Schonberg, Korngold, Bartók, Respighi, Honegger, Casella, and Toch during his tenure with the Berlin Philharmonic, as all of them had premieres, conducted, or soloed with the orchestra.[46] However, one of his first meetings with Rachmaninoff was the result of the keen interest impresario Louise Wolff had in Piatigorsky. "Queen Louise" as she was nicknamed, was sovereign in Europe's concert life through the venerable Wolff and Sachs concert bureau.[47] Besides Rachmaninoff, she represented many important artists, including the Kreutzer-Wolfsthal-Piatigorsky Trio, as well as the Berlin Philharmonic and other orchestras.

With Piatigorsky's success, the urge to move to the U.S. intensified. Heifetz and Flesch made inquiries on his behalf— Heifetz approached impresario Arthur Judson hoping he could arrange solo concerts for Piatigorsky in the next year or two. And though the gesture did not produce concerts, it planted a seed. Flesch, who taught at the new Curtis Institute in Philadelphia for several weeks each year, thought Piatigorsky might launch his American career in the Philadelphia Orchestra as principal cellist. Boris Koutzen, by then a member of the Philadelphia Orchestra, disagreed and easily convinced Piatigorsky to come to the U.S. only as a soloist. Agreeing, the cellist echoed, "Everybody likes me as a soloist,"[48] and felt he could have a better career there. Piatigorsky's solo engagements up to 1926 had consisted of separate contracts from various concert bureaus.

By 1927 Piatigorsky had all the concerts he could handle, but the pay was modest, only 1000–1500 Deutsche Marks per concert.[49] From this point in his career, Piatigorsky tried to downplay his orchestral past, wanting no confusion in the future direction of his career. Word of Piatigorsky's restlessness reached the philharmonic's benefactors, and in a move to keep him there, they purchased an Amati cello for him. Up to this point the cellist had always borrowed instruments for his solo concerts.

However, in a few short months he would give up life in an orchestra entirely and focus on a solo career. The timing for the decision came about unexpectedly.

The Soloist

On November 7 and 8, 1926, Artur Schnabel performed Brahms' Second Piano Concerto with the Berlin Philharmonic and Furtwängler. Piatigorsky's extended solo in the slow movement was memorable. Touched and impressed by Piatigorsky's playing, Alexander (Sasha) Merovitch, an eccentric concert manager, approached the cellist and proposed that he join his small concert bureau. Merovitch needed another artist to add to his roster of two: pianist Vladimir Horowitz and violinist Nathan Milstein. Excited, Merovitch went on to describe his plans for the three of them. Piatigorsky, however, had misgivings about the

SALLE MAJESTIC, 19, AVENUE KLÉBER

ASSOCIATION DES CONCERT
DE LA
REVUE MUSICALE

Directeur Fondateur : Henry PRUNIÈRES. — Secrétaire-Trésorier : Raymond PETIT

IIe ANNÉE -- DERNIER CONCERT
LE LUNDI 20 JUIN 1927, A 21 HEURES
AVEC LE CONCOURS DE
Vladimir HOROWITZ
ET DE
Grégoire PIATIGORSKY

SONATE pour piano et violoncelle	Richard STRAUSS
Vladimir Horowitz et G. Piatigorsky.	
SUITE en ré mineur	BACH
GOYESCAS (Intermezzo)	GRANADOS
APRÈS UN RÊVE	G. FAURE
AU BORD D'UNE SOURCE	DAVIDOFF
G. Piatigorsky.	
SONATE en mi bémol	MOZART
Adagio - Menuetto - Allegro Molto.	
6 PRÉLUDES	CHOPIN
Sol mineur - Do mineur - La bémol majeur - Do dièze mineur - La majeur - Ré mineur.	
DOCTOR GRADUS AD PARNASSUM	DEBUSSY
SÉRÉNADE A LA POUPÉE (Children's corner)	—
VALSE OUBLIÉE	LISZT
AU BORD D'UNE SOURCE	—
CAMPANELLA	—
Vladimir Horowitz.	

Les Membres de l'Association peuvent se procurer pour ce Concert des cartes d'amis au prix de **10** francs en les retirant, **à l'avance,** à la REVUE MUSICALE, 132, Boulevard Montparnasse; chez DURAND, 4, Place de la Madeleine et à l'HOTEL MAJESTIC.

IMP. UNION, PARIS

Piatigorsky's Paris debut, June 20, 1927, with Horowitz.

PHILHARMONISCHE GESELLSCHAFT IN HAMBURG

Montag, den 23. Januar 1928, abends 8 Uhr
Musikhalle, großer Saal

NEUNTES PHILHARMONISCHES KONZERT

LEITUNG:

DR. KARL MUCK

Solist: **Gregor Piatigorsky**

VORTRAGSFOLGE:

FELIX MENDELSSOHN-BARTHOLDY:
(1809–1847)
 Ouvertüre zu Shakespeare's „Sommernachtstraum", op. 21

JOSEPH HAYDN: Cellokonzert D-dur
(1732–1809)
 Allegro moderato
 Adagio
 Rondo — Allegro

FRANZ SCHUBERT: Symphonie C-dur, Nr. 7
(1797–1828)
 Andante, Allegro ma non troppo
 Andante con moto
 Scherzo (Allegro vivace)
 Allegro vivace

WÄHREND DER VORTRÄGE BLEIBEN DIE SAALTÜREN GESCHLOSSEN
Das Einnehmen anderer Plätze, als die Eintrittskarten ausweisen, ist strengstens verboten
KONZERT-AGENTUR JOH. AUG. BÖHME, HAMBURG, ALTERWALL 44

Wendet

Concert program with Karl Muck, January 23, 1928.

Dritte Festaufführung

Sonntag, den 3. Juni 1928, abends 6 Uhr

*

Dirigent:
Dr. Wilhelm Furtwängler

*

1. Don Juan, Tondichtung
   (nach Nicolaus Lenau*), für
   großes Orchester, op. 20 *Richard Strauß*

2. Konzert für Violine und
   Violoncell mit Orchester
   in A-Moll, op. 102 . . . . *Johannes Brahms*
   Allegro – Andante – Vivace non troppo
   Solisten: Prof. Karl Flesch (Violine)
   Gregor Piatigorsky (Cello)

   P A U S E

3. Symphonie Nr. 7, C-Dur *Franz Schubert*
   Andante, Allegro ma non troppo –
   Andante con moto – Scherzo: Allegro
   vivace – Allegro vivace

4. Das große Halleluja aus
   dem „Messias" . . . *Georg Friedrich Händel*

*) Siehe Seite 32.

Concert with Carl Flesch, June 3, 1928.

proposal and told Merovitch that while he was flattered, he was not interested. Merovitch assured him that he was completely serious about promoting Piatigorsky as a soloist.

After considering the offer, the cellist realized that the prospect of a solo career might actually be possible. At first he was cautious about abandoning a secure position in Berlin, a place that for the first time in his life gave him a feeling of security. It had been easier to leave Warsaw, having sponsorship and the thirst to learn; still, the idea of venturing into the world conjured up memories of hunger and homelessness. But, as solo opportunities with orchestras increased, he realized he would have to leave the security of Berlin.[50]

Piatigorsky probably met Vladimir Horowitz a few weeks earlier when the pianist played Liszt's A Major Concerto with the orchestra. But after meeting him and Milstein socially, playing together and talking about the direction of their careers — including Merovitch's role in particular — Piatigorsky decided to sign the contract. With Horowitz (Volodya) and Milstein (Nathanchik), the three of them became the closest of friends. Later in the U.S., they were dubbed the Three Musketeers. Of those days, Piatigorsky recalled:

> The long meetings with Sasha [Merovitch] revealed the drastic change I was to expect in my professional life. There would not be a headquarters, no salary, no guarantee, no concentration of activity in one given city or land. I had to be available for concert engagements everywhere. I had to acquire my almost-forgotten uprootedness all over again and to make the wide world my home.
>
> And yet Sasha's gift for outlining the strategy for my future turned the vagueness and insecurity into an exciting daring and a sense of rightness. He spoke of the urgency of humanizing managers, of changing the unhealthy pattern of the concert "business," and of finding the methods of achieving more creativity in the performer's life. Before leaving Berlin he said that there were pending engagements in Europe, and he mentioned the possibility of concerts in South America, Africa, and the United States.[51]

Under contract with the philharmonic, Piatigorsky also performed with Furtwängler in the orchestra's summer festivals, and particularly enjoyed those in Baden-Baden and Heidelberg. There he played many solo works with the orchestra and performed in chamber music ensembles. During the 1920s, Piatigorsky appeared with several of the greats of the time — violinists Bronislaw Huberman, Carl Flesch,[52] Georg Kulenkampf, Erika Morini, and Henry Holst — in the Brahms Double Concerto, and gave recitals with notable pianists including Schnabel, Michael Raucheisen, Szreter, Friedberg, Kreutzer and Alexander Zakin.[53] The cellist also gave the Berlin premieres of Ernst Bloch's *Schelomo* and Anton von Webern's *Three Little Pieces*, op. 11,[54] during which the latter's two-minute pointillistic minimalism caused laughter, even when he repeated it for them. Webern was not surprised when he heard about the reaction, declaring that his music was not ready to be heard, that it was for the future.

In May each year the Berlin Philharmonic made continental tours and in 1927 Piatigorsky experienced his first tour of England. That same year he also embarked on a series of recital appearances with Horowitz in Paris (probably Piatigorsky's debut there) and Hamburg. Their recitals were met with mixed reviews, acknowledging their instrumental mastery, yet noting Horowitz's sound at times overpowering the cello, a complaint also lodged in his recitals with Schnabel. Influential musicologist, publisher and critic Henry Prunières gave Piatigorsky an outstanding review: "Heard in a joint recital at the Théâtre des Champs Elysées ... played in a style perhaps equaled only by Pablo Casals."[55]

Horowitz and Piatigorsky looked forward to hearing two giants in their field play a joint recital in Berlin: Pablo Casals and Alfred Cortot. "We sat in the first row. It was too much for me to see the man at such close range — I was so overwhelmed by that alone."

Meeting Casals some months later was a cherished moment for Piatigorsky, as well as for pianist Rudolf Serkin:

> Casals was staying in the Mendelssohn mansion in Berlin. Rudolph Serkin was also there. I played something with Serkin. It was not a good performance, but Casals was always interested in hearing talented young artists and he was enthusiastic. He asked me to play something alone and it was even worse, but he praised me and complimented me and asked me to play still more. And the more I played, the worse it got — but his enthusiasm increased! I was very unhappy knowing that I had played badly and disturbed because I took his compliments for a lack of sincerity. Shortly afterward, we met again in Paris and I couldn't help telling him my feelings. How could he have complimented me after such a poor performance? He got very angry. He took the cello and said, "You remember, you played this phrase with the third finger — it came right from the heart. It was so musical — and the bowing, you did it upbow. Most cellists play it down-bow, but the way you did it fit the phrase so perfectly. I wasn't false; I was being sincere. Only bad people live for and remember bad things." I was very much impressed.[56]

After playing for Casals, Piatigorsky and Serkin attended his recital. Although the hall was only half full, their enthusiasm soared. After Casals played an encore, Faure's *Sicilienne*, Piatigorsky tearfully responded, "This is not to be equaled."[57]

Piatigorsky's solo engagements were coming in faster than he could manage. In Berlin, Piatigorsky was known as the Wonder Cellist and the Russian Casals. In 1928, during one of the Berlin Philharmonic tours to Paris, Piatigorsky and Furtwängler took time off to perform a program of Beethoven Sonatas at the German Embassy. Afterwards, Piatigorsky was surprised to hear one audience member's remarks:

> [M]any guests expressed their appreciation and some of their views on music. Not particularly fond of such discourses, I felt almost glad at not knowing French. The more sensitive people left me quickly, but one individual, wiry and slightly built, was very persistent. I did not know what he was speaking about, but looking at his expressive face, I was curious to know what he was saying. Monsieur Painleve, member of the French Cabinet, whom I knew and who spoke German, joined us. The thin man continued talking, and after his last sentence, which sounded like a question, shook my hand and abruptly disappeared.
> "Who was it? What did he say?"
> "From what I heard," said Painleve, "Maurice Ravel liked your playing."
> "Ravel!" I exclaimed.
> "Yes, our great composer."
> "What was his question? Didn't he ask something before he left?" I was eager to know.
> "Yes, it was a question," said Painleve, smiling. "Ravel asked why you waste your talent on such abominable music as you played tonight."
> "Abominable? It was Beethoven!"
> Disturbed, I pondered how Ravel could say this. Yet, had he worshiped Beethoven, could he compose like Ravel?[58]

In the fall of 1928, Piatigorsky and violinist Joseph Szigeti played "piano-less" recitals of solos and duos in Germany, performing the Kodály Duo and the new Ravel Duo. Completed in 1927, the work gave Ravel some difficulty as it did for Szigeti who described it as "this devil of a Duo."[59] The duo also posed another problem for the violinist: "Our rehearsals were pleasant but somewhat tense because Szigeti, unaccustomed to playing from music, was troubled by fast page turning in the Ravel. I must admit that those turnings were in the most inconvenient spots.... At the concert, however, he solved this difficulty in an astonishingly practical manner. The large edition of Ravel he augmented by several more copies. He placed them all on a row of music stands, and, instead of turning the pages, he simply 'walked his way' through the work."[60] Very fond of Szigeti, Piatigorsky enjoyed

Gregor with Lida in Heidelberg, 1928.

describing the violinist's unusual way of drawing the bow close to his body, which prompted his joke that "Szigeti is the only violinist who can perform in a phone booth." Their programs also included Reger's D Minor Suite for cello, while Szigeti played Bach. Their performances were very successful as the following review reveals:

> With gratitude we heard a most fitting evening of duets performed by Joseph Szigeti and Gregor Piatigorsky, both masters of their instruments, both fusing the highest level of mastery and musical feeling. The Duo by Kodály in which the musical language speaks so satisfyingly from the composer's mother tongue, without talking in dialect, in which real melody and arabesque alternate so finely, was presented as well as the great masterworks of the solo sonatas of Bach (Szigeti) and Reger (Piatigorsky).[61]

With his orchestra contract ending in May 1928, Piatigorsky expected to make his first tour of America. However, Sasha Merovitch was grooming Piatigorsky for a wider audience. Merovitch chose to take only Horowitz to New York in the 1928-29 season, while arranging for Piatigorsky and Milstein to further accrue foreign concerts and reviews. Sasha planned to use his new American contacts to bring Piatigorsky and Milstein the following season. The desire to come to the U.S. was intensified by friends in Berlin — Kreutzer, Schnabel, Flesch, and now Horowitz — who had already toured there and shared their intriguing stories. Flesch taught at the Curtis Institute in Philadelphia for several weeks each year. Even Lida had visited New York.

The philharmonic was extremely understanding of his needs and gave the cellist time off for his solo concerts. Since his American debut would not be until the 1929-30 season, Piatigorsky agreed to one last season with the philharmonic (1928-29), but limited it to the basic ten pairs of subscription concerts with Furtwängler.[62]

For the spring of 1929, Merovitch purchased full-page portrait advertisements in several American music publications announcing their availability for concert appearances. Ads were placed both individually and collectively for his three stars, with Merovitch humbly designating himself their "General Representative for the World." The gala U.S. tour of his Three Musketeers in the 1929-30 season would be his crowning achievement.

For Piatigorsky, the United States became a kind of Promised Land, a land of opportunity, and a country that seemed to tolerate disparate peoples. He left from Hamburg on October 18, 1929, aboard the American liner *Reliance*, eager to discover the New World.

4. America, Rachmaninoff, Strauss and Stravinsky

First Tour, USA

In order to gain a foothold in the United States, Merovitch contracted with Concert Management Arthur Judson as the trio's American agent. Judson was the most important impresario in America; he managed the New York Philharmonic and the Philadelphia Orchestra and introduced many great artists, including Heifetz, Szigeti, Cortot, and Serkin, to the U.S. market.

As the *Reliance* approached land, excitement and activity burst out; a pilot boat brought immigration officers, reporters, mail and newspapers. Welcoming messages from a few friends and Judson's Concert Management arrived, followed by Piatigorsky's first interview:

> "Are you the Russian cellist?" asked a man with camera, approaching me. Instantly others encircled me with cameras and notebooks. They asked questions and their cameras clicked. The most repeated question was,
> "How do you like America?"
> "It's my first visit and I have no impressions yet."
> The next day at Columbia Concerts, Arthur Judson showed me newspaper clippings. RUSSIAN CELLIST NOT SURE IF HE LIKES AMERICA. "A fine beginning," he said.[1]

Piatigorsky landed in the New York on Sunday, October 27, 1929, two days before the infamous Black Tuesday stock market crash that led to the Great Depression.[2] Unaware of the crisis that loomed, Piatigorsky focused only on his need to find a pianist for his upcoming tour, which was to begin the following week. After several unimpressive candidates auditioned for him at the Judson offices in New York, a new arrival from Russia, pianist Valentin Pavlovsky, made an impact. Right away Pavlovsky and Piatigorsky made music effortlessly, which led to an association of many years. The pianist also worked with other artists including Milstein and soprano Geraldine Farrar.

Their first recital was in Oberlin, Ohio, on November 5. From there, they traveled across the country, performing recitals en route to Chicago, San Francisco and Los Angeles where Piatigorsky also debuted with orchestras. In each city enthusiastic audiences and the press responded to Piatigorsky's brilliant and poetic playing:

> *He gave a performance so excelling that Casals at his greatest might despair of surpassing it.* H.F. Peyser, *New York Telegram*
> *A giant firebrand musical genius. Undoubtedly Paganini at his best was not a whit more heavenly on his violin than is Piatigorsky on his heavenly voiced cello. To describe him as the Liszt*

Schnabel-Flesch-Piatigorsky Trio.

of the 'cello might give some faint idea of the sensations which thrilled those who heard him. Carl Bronson, *Los Angeles Herald*

To praise Piatigorsky's technique would be as trying to measure great love with gold. His technique is a great wonder and the greater wonder is that the message is even greater. He is Orpheus incarnate. David Bruno Ussher, *Los Angeles Express*

Shattering one of the sacrosanct rules of the Philharmonic concerts Piatigorsky played an encore in response to thunderous, undying applause which followed his breathtaking playing of Dvořák's Concerto. Herbert Klein, *Los Angeles Record*

A sensation. To the inner ear there was the same effect as Horowitz creates on the piano — extraordinary beauty of tone, extraordinary feats of agility, extraordinary breadth and warmth of interpretation. Edward Moore, *Chicago Tribune*

His tone is as thrilling, as personal as Kreisler's; as "buttery" as Casals. He phrases with super taste. S. Chotzinoff, *New York World*

Shouts, cheers, cries of "bis" and deafening applause testified to the completeness of his triumph. Not since Casals has a 'cellist given us so fine a concert. Marjorie Fisher, *San Francisco News*

Piatigorsky played the 'cello and a capacity audience lost all reserves and went delightfully mad. They screamed and stamped. No artist that I have heard here has met with a reception even approximating this one.... When Mme. Curie discovered radium she doubtless had a hard time explaining it. Its newness blocked comparison. Such is the case with Piatigorsky's tone. It is ineffable, disembodied, radiant, of a piercing beauty that hurts. Patterson Greene, *Los Angeles Examiner*

In that first season, all three of Merovitch's stars played the same recital venues, following each other across the country by a few weeks. First to appear was Horowitz, then a few weeks later Milstein, and finally Piatigorsky. They performed almost daily, with concert

Friedberg-Flesch-Piatigorsky Trio.

stops along the railroad routes between major cities and college towns. For nearly a decade these Community Concert tours became each musician's bread and butter. Piatigorsky recalled:

> The New York office [Judson] was quite different from those of my European managers, who had only one or two rooms. Here were departments of transportation, sales, field representatives, recital, program, auditing, publicity, and Community Concerts. There were secretaries and receptionists everywhere, offices of vice-presidents, and of course, the office of Mr. Judson, the president. Walking from room to room, I met many men and women with whom I was to be associated for twenty years to come. Everyone was friendly, yet there was something impersonal about the place, just as Merovitch told me it would be. This was one of his reasons for wanting to serve as a personal representative to his three artists.

However, with the trio's phenomenal success, Merovitch turned into a megalomaniac. Billing himself "General Representative to the World," he channeled his own fanatical ambition. He presided as the absolute, infallible authority in fashioning their careers, even cross-examining repertoire. He insisted on "effective" pieces — light, short virtuosic works — and cautioned against the use of "thankless" standard repertoire — sonatas and extended works. Piatigorsky remembered their impassioned discussions: "We listened to his advice, and when alone we secretly scrutinized and criticized his suggestions, only to accept them in the end."

Piatigorsky's fellow Musketeers had been groomed as soloists from childhood, but the cellist was raised in the callous school of survival with the cello as his sole security. Though he enjoyed virtuosic gymnastics as a student, he was somewhat embarrassed to present them as a finished artist. It had only been a few years since he had relied on flashy light repertoire to make a living in the non-concert locales of his youth. As Piatigorsky saw it, "Professionally, I had lived many lives, while since childhood their field and destination had been solely that of the virtuoso. Without the experience of playing in orchestras, operas, operettas, chamber music, teaching, playing in restaurants, movies, and weddings, they could not be expected to understand my concern about embarking upon a strictly soloistic career. In this I was the youngest."[3]

Milstein was not very interested in feeding the public what Merovitch wanted, but was pleased to include Paganini Caprices and began making his own transcriptions. Horowitz, in particular, was recognized for his famous transcriptions of popular pieces. Late in life he admitted, "The audience identified with my transcriptions and that's what I played. That's the only reason I did it. I made lots of money and I'm very glad!"[4]

Perhaps it was Horowitz's success that spurred Piatigorsky to develop his own transcriptions, many of which became standard cello repertoire. He also remembered how fascinated he had been by the great juggler Enrico Rastelli. He likened his unique wizardry with balls and sticks to the dazzling of fingers and bow — the complete freedom and comfort of the body to express itself. Eventually Piatigorsky's "bonbons" became part of his signature repertoire and acquired "a fine collection of bugs—*Bee* by François Schubert, *Mosquitoes* by Fairchild, *Bumblebee* by Rimsky-Korsakov, *Butterfly* by Fauré, and lots of tarantellas."[5] Coincidentally, all three played recitals in succession in Vienna, where each one performed their version of Rimsky Korsakov's *Flight of the Bumblebee*." A Viennese critic remarked, "I was rather at a loss in comparing three kinds of bumblebees. Milstein's fiddle bee was more like a mosquito. Piatigorsky's cello bee had a more threatening droning quality, while Horowitz's was the elegant, playful kind, reminding those who know the story of the Tsar Sultan that the bumblebee is really a prince in disguise."[6]

On this first U.S. tour, Piatigorsky was happily surprised to meet former friends occupying the orchestras with which he appeared. One friend was now in the Los Angeles Philharmonic: cellist Nicolas Ochi-Albi, the helpful Hugo Becker student who translated for him at those few awkward lessons in Berlin in 1922. His biggest surprise was the reception he received from the entire philharmonic. A reporter's account of the excitement generated with his first rehearsal illustrates the moment:

> I must tell you of someone I have helped to discover. He's a 'cellist, named Gregor Piatigorsky, comparatively unknown in this country, I think. They call him the Russian Casals, but he's the Russian Piatigorsky. There's only one.
> Did you ever attend an orchestral rehearsal? As soon as the conductor lays down his baton, the musicians dash for the door and their lunch. Tuesday I happened to stop in just as rehearsal closed. Imagine my surprise when the conductor laid down his baton and the orchestra turned loose a flock of bravos and dashed, not for the door, but for the 'cellist. It looked like the gang on the bench surrounding the fullback after he had run ninety-five yards to the winning touchdown. So I stuck around. They wouldn't let that Bolshevik out of there until 2 o'clock, and there wasn't a musician left the stage while he sat and played and played and played as Orpheus never played.
> The next day I snuck in the stage door and hid for another rehearsal, and the next day the musicians demanded and got another free recital. So you can imagine he's good, regardless of what I might say. Remember the name and hear him when he goes to New York.[7]

On the way back to the East Coast, on November 8, Piatigorsky made his first solo appearance, with Leopold Stokowski and the Philadelphia Orchestra with the Dvořák concerto. It was a huge success noted by the *Public Ledger*: "Gregor Piatigorsky proved a cellist of unusual gifts and equipment, both technical and artistic.... Mr. Piatigorsky revealed a tone of the most exquisite quality and an artistic interpretation which left nothing to be desired. The technical difficulties were played with the greatest ease and fluency."[8]

Several weeks later he returned to New York for his debut with Willem Mengelberg and the New York Philharmonic[9] on December 26. Piatigorsky was especially anxious to play with the great orchestra and the legendary conductor. Unfortunately, Piatigorsky's debut occurred during what proved to be Mengelberg's last season with the orchestra. The conductor would soon resign, as the orchestra and administration had become unhappy with his undistinguished leadership of recent years. Mengelberg's discomfort, anger, and perhaps a large dose of ego, put the conductor in a foul mood. The rehearsal of the Dvořák concerto went badly:

> It was my first performance in New York with the Orchestra and I was nervous, as I didn't know the orchestra, the director or the acoustics of the hall. I strongly felt the curiosity of the orchestra and of all those present, which felt like an examination. The feeling was anxious and joyless and had nothing in common with art.
>
> Mengelberg's secretary introduced me to him. There was a cold nod of the head and the rehearsal began. The Dvořák concerto's long orchestral introduction that morning seemed like it would never end. Not only because of the tempo Mengelberg chose, which was almost twice as slow as the tempo marked in the score which I am used to, but also due to the interminable repetitions, stopping, explanation, and such pedantic minutia. In practice this always brings more harm than an efficient, exact, clear and economical use of time.
>
> Mengelberg talked a lot and his loud voice often drowned out the orchestra, but it seemed that no one was listening to him. It created a strained and unpleasant atmosphere. Making use of the rehearsal break, I tried to tell the director that the tempo seemed too slow to me. He ungraciously interrupted, "Young man! I went through this concerto with the composer and therefore I know the correct tempo better than you."
>
> Defeated by his tone I did not answer. I was certain of his error and of my own rightness. Another half an hour passed and I still had not started to play. Finding the tempo unbearably slow for the second time, and in a more definite tone, I declared that it is impossible to play at this tempo, that in order to make music we must be in agreement, and that only such cooperation can lead to a good performance. He did not listen to me, and when at last, when my solo came, I, emphasizing my disagreement with him, took up the tempo that I considered correct and natural. After several measures he stopped me.
>
> "You are playing twice as fast."
>
> "No," I answered irritably. "It was you who played twice as slow. We must come to an agreement, otherwise I don't see any thought or possibility of making music together."
>
> The orchestra — and this is a phenomenon in America with no known precedent — upheld me, and voices rang out from all sides. "The soloist is right, right...."
>
> I felt uncomfortable. Mengelberg was angry but he gave in. The rehearsal was psychologically and physically agonizing. The concert that evening was not bad, although it was far from ideal. Relations with Mengelberg were strained. The next concert was much worse than the first and finally a few minutes before the third performance someone entered the dressing room and announced that Mengelberg would not be directing the concert and that Hans Lange would be replacing him with no rehearsals. How could this be?! The overture ended and I walked out onto the stage, and only then did I see the man with whom I would be playing. This concert was the only one of the three that I truly enjoyed — full of musicality, goodwill and intuition triumphed, which is indispensable in music.[10]

Cellist Orlando Cole was in the audience at Piatigorsky's debut with the New Yorkers and remembered the impact he made:

> His personality was immediately striking and he had an easy facility that, in those days, was astonishing. He was the first to show an almost violinistic technical flashiness on the cello. And, of course, he played in a very romantic way that was appealing to everyone. Piatigorsky, more than anyone else — including Casals — popularised the cello, and he was the first to

show us what was possible on the instrument — like running the four-minute mile. When Feuermann came along a little later he offered real competition because he, too, was an incredible player. There is no doubt that these two were the fathers of present day playing.[11]

Piatigorsky did not look forward to the additional concerts that had been booked later in the season with Mengelberg, especially those taking place on his home turf with the Concertgebouw Orchestra in Amsterdam, The Hague, and Haarlem, but more immediately concert dates with the London Symphony in his Royal Albert Hall debut performing the Haydn Concerto. Despite their terrible first impression of each other, all was forgiven on their first rehearsal without further discussion; Mengelberg and Piatigorsky went on to play many concerts together through the 1930s.[12] The elder critic Robin Legge reviewed their London concert for the *Daily Telegraph*: "One's mind goes back to the great days of Carl Davidoff for the memory of a precisely similar tone as that of Piatigorsky…. [I]n the lovely Adagio and in the amusing Rondo, the playing was resonant and of a very high order, and the tone most melting."[13]

Perhaps frustrated with temperamental conductors, Piatigorsky may have briefly considered conducting himself, though the thought did not bear fruit.[14] One incident related by Milstein again demonstrated how childish gifted conductors could become:

> I well remember when Toscanini took the New York Philharmonic to Berlin in 1930. It was part of their European tour, which was an incredible success. I was witness to the public's excited anticipation. In the auditorium were Bruno Walter, Otto Klemperer, and Erich Kleiber. Piatigorsky, Horowitz and myself were in a box. Toscanini was in the middle of conducting a Beethoven Symphony (the Eroica) when Furtwängler, who was in the box next door, suddenly stood up and leant towards us exclaiming: "Isn't this a dreadful acoustic!" What he meant by "acoustic" was only too clear![15]

And Piatigorsky recalled Furtwängler's tortured reaction to Toscanini's conducting of the Berlin Philharmonic: "He spoke as to himself, 'It's not just an audience — just another concert hall — it's my — my — I gave all I have and I wanted to give more — I thought I finally conquered my desired and difficult mistress. Tonight I watched her giving herself to another — passionately and totally — and there will be no shame to face me at my next concert. It is I who will be on the defense.'"[16]

During Piatigorsky's monumental first American season, he also appeared with the Detroit Symphony[17] and was surprised to see that Alexander Glazunov was guest conductor on the same concert. The principal conductor, Ossip Gabrilowitsch, led Piatigorsky in the Saint-Saëns Concerto, while Glazunov conducted one of his symphonies. Piatigorsky had first met the composer when, at the age of twelve, he worked in the Metropol Restaurant in Moscow. Piatigorsky knew his two popular cello works, *Chant du Minestrel* and *Serenade Espagnole*, and played them for him. The composer was dining alone and asked Piatigorsky to join him. He spoke kindly to Piatigorsky, and showed an interest in his future. The composer, now aged, also suffered the cruel effects of alcoholism: "Old and flabby, Glazunov had a touching affection for people that seemed even more apparent here than in Russia. Although he was an unimposing conductor, phlegmatic and vague, the orchestras as in Russia, loving and respecting him, did not spare themselves. There, as now in Detroit, the musicians gave him their best, which was more than he was capable of demanding."

Pleased with the concert, Glazunov, Gabrilowitsch, and Piatigorsky visited late into the night. No doubt Glazunov remembered Lida Antik-Piatigorsky, his former student in St. Petersburg, and her proud letter as a newlywed asking for a cello concerto for her talented husband. This time however, Piatigorsky asked Glazunov directly about writing a cello concerto for him. The composer enthusiastically responded, "After what I heard today at the concert, I cannot *not* write a concerto for you."

Glazunov did write a work for cello and orchestra, and had by the summer of 1931 shown his new work, the *Concerto Ballata*, op. 108, to Prokofiev when they met in southern France. Piatigorsky was unaware that the concerto had been written: "Suddenly I receive a telegram from Furtwängler with an invitation to play the premiere performance of the Concerto-Ballade of Glazunov at one of the Berlin Philharmonic's concerts."

Piatigorsky eagerly awaited the music, but his heart sank as he read on the title page "Dedicated to Pablo Casals." The composer knew that the Soviets would not allow him to dedicate a work to a defector, namely Piatigorsky. Even so, Casals was a logical choice since they knew each other from the prerevolutionary era, and Casals' name might draw additional attention. Piatigorsky later commented: "Having looked through the music attentively and having played it through several times, I decided not to include it in my repertoire. I have not, to this day regretted this decision, for the music did not present any interest in any respect, like a dull and mediocre work. It's a pity! How could this great master not have written something better and more meaningful for us poor cellists!"[18] Casals never performed the work either.

Piatigorsky always made time for his audience following concerts, signing autographs and attending receptions. Despite his limited English, he did his best to give interviews, even to school newspapers.[19] The relentless schedule, often with six concerts a week with many between long distances, soon affected his health. Immediately after his American tour he returned to Europe for concerts in Germany, Holland, Austria and Hungary and back to Germany again. He was beset with illnesses nearly every year, some of which were life-threatening. By the end of the 1930-31 season, Piatigorsky was hospitalized with pneumonia in Boston. Concerts were cancelled. He was X-rayed (then only a newly developed technique), and was found to have lung inflammation.[20] He recuperated at the home of friends Alexander and Sylvia Steinert[21] and was cared for by Lida, who had accompanied him on tour that season.

The medical bills accumulated, causing concern to the young artist, since his income was tied up in Merovitch's control. Serge Koussevitzky, conductor of the Boston Symphony, who had remembered him from Moscow and had already engaged him as a soloist for the following season, quietly paid the medical expenses.

Concerned friends, like violinist Albert Spalding, inquired about him. Spalding had recommended Piatigorsky to conductors who were uncertain of the new Russian. The violinist was very fond of Piatigorsky's playing and commented: "The way that Piatigorsky plays the slow movement [of the Schumann Concerto] is one of the finest things I can recall."[22] Piatigorsky eventually completed an abbreviated U.S. tour and returned to Switzerland to continue his recuperation for the next several weeks. "I can't bear the Boston climate. I lay there for 6 weeks with pneumonia and only by some small miracle did I stay alive."[23]

Schnabel-Flesch-Piatigorsky Trio

By 1930, Piatigorsky's celebrated trio — Schnabel-Flesch-Piatigorsky — was in transition. Schnabel had made hints to Flesch of wanting to end the trio, but the discord finally became apparent in April, when Piatigorsky belatedly informed the ensemble that he could not attend a rehearsal. As Flesch wrote to Schnabel: "I would have answered your letter immediately after its arrival if that threat to our trio concert had not surfaced.... It was actually thoughtless of Piatigorsky to accept a concert on the 13th in Vienna; obviously he forgot that you have to come here especially for the rehearsals."[24] Schnabel replied on May 24:

> I too have not heard anything about our concert, and the little I have comes from sources, that are the most fastidious and most able to differentiate.... So, how does it stand with our trio? I love to play, and you know that. But Mr. Merovitch, Piaty's owner let us say, does not seem do have an interest in the union and will chase our young friend around, and mislead and possibly also degrade him. He is not going to see any need for rehearsals, but they are the greatest pleasure.... I am going to talk to Piaty seriously in the next few days, and will then be able to judge what will be possible.

Schnabel's attitude seems to have shifted soon afterwards and Piatigorsky was surprised to hear of Schnabel's threat to end the trio:

> Did you mean me personally when you warned about [having] the last trio concert, or did you mean all three of us! I am going to take the triple concerto with me to Baden-Baden. I also find that we have to be very well prepared for the London concerts, and I am ready and willing to set aside a lot of time for rehearsals. I deem the concerts in London as extraordinarily important in every respect.[25]

Flesch wrote to Schnabel on September 9:

> On the occasion of Piati's stay in Baden-Baden, we did discuss our Berlin rehearsals for the London concerts and compared.... [P]lease let me know right away, which times you decided on so that I may inform Piati to not accept any concerts for those days.
>
> Incidentally, I have had already two pre-rehearsals with P[iatigorsky] for the triple concerto and settled all purely instrumental details. One short rehearsal for the double concerto is enough, because we have played it already often enough.
>
> In reference to our trio work, I have to comment that Piati absolutely denies that he was not interested, and maintains that this disinterest is on your side. Frankly, I have to admit, dear Artur, you are a great enigma to me in this matter. Anyway, one thing is sure, you do not seem to have much enthusiasm to continue playing as a trio with us. The reasons, which are based in your mentality, naturally are your business. I have to tell you honestly that Piati and I have a different point of view. This type of activity is a necessity for us and we do take into consideration whether it is more or less profitable.
>
> You have to come to realize eventually, what you are going to do about it in the future. You see, I am going to give concerts only for a few more years and then would like to play chamber music. When I asked you in the spring of 1929 on a walk to decide about this question, you answered me with a clear "yes," and subsequently set up the dates for the past season. Now, you said no again. Well, how does the matter stand?

Flesch was dismayed to hear of Schnabel's decision to end the trio, but accepted it, responding to him on September 22: "To my greatest regret did I learn of your refusal to play with Piati and me.... I have tried my very best to understand the reasons that had you take this step, but I did not succeed."

Soon afterwards, Schnabel had second thoughts, and the trio seems to have functioned for one last season. In October 1930, the Schnabel-Flesch-Piatigorsky Trio arrived in London to participate in the newly established Courtauld-Sargent concert series. They performed recitals, as well as the Beethoven *Triple Concerto* and the Brahms *Double Concerto*. The Courtauld-Sargent series was started by the wife of wealthy industrialist Samuel Courtauld, with guidance and assistance from Artur Schnabel. The artistic director and conductor was Malcolm Sargent, who led the London Symphony Orchestra. The intent of the concerts

Merovitch's first announcement of Horowitz-Milstein-Piatigorsky to the United States, 1929.

Second U.S. season publicity, 1930.

was, as Schnabel stated, to present "a series of symphony concerts to those music lovers who were not in a position to pay the high prices for tickets to subscription concerts." This was especially popular after the economic crash of October 1929.

Blocks of tickets were distributed by large businesses and given to their employees. The best musicians were hired and Courtauld covered the cost of any rehearsals. Schnabel

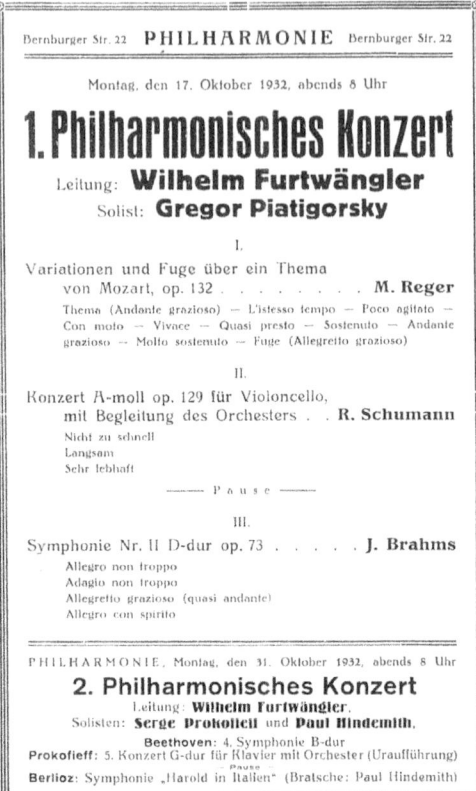

Last appearance in Berlin, 1932.

recalled that Hindemith and Stravinsky could even have seven or eight rehearsals — an unheard of number for London concerts during this period. The demand for tickets was so strong that repeat performances were produced. The concerts also represented a balance of social and artistic prestige with inherent educational merit.

The journal *Musical Record* (November 1, 1930), reported the following regarding the trio's concerts; the familiar piano balance criticism remained:

> The Courtauld-Sargent Concert Club evenings began on October 16 with a programme of double and triple concertos (Bach, Beethoven, Brahms) — an unusual programme, like all of this series. The concert was repeated on the next night.... [T]he return of the violinist, long a stranger to our scene, was welcomed. The violoncellist, a fine artist, had struck us all before by his leadership with the Berlin Philharmonic Orchestra. Their playing Brahms's concerto was seriously beautiful, and Dr. Sargent showed much skill in accompanying. This was the real experience of the evening ... and the Beethoven triple-concerto, though worth hearing as a curiosity, lacks from end to end a single spark of the genuine fire.
>
> An evening of piano trios given by Artur Schnabel, Carl Flesch and Gregor Piatigorsky presented Mendelssohn in D minor, Brahms in C and Schubert in E flat. Mendelssohn's trios are not often heard in the concert room, so that this performance by eminent hands touched the hearts of many who had at some time tried to make music out of the accessible D minor. The critic should not allow his heart to be touched by outside considerations.

Of course, Schnabel is a masterful pianist, and Flesch a sound and worthy violinist, and Piatigorsky a faultless cellist; but all that did not make of them a trio. Take away the touching appeal of that music and its associations with one's youthful enthusiasms — then — the violinist was obviously a dull routineer, the pianist overbearing, and the cellist, for all his talent, without charm. If Brahms's trio seemed thick and stuffy the fault was partly the composer's and partly Schnabel's. The latter was so taken up by a faith in his own significant eloquence that he refused to allow the cello a fair chance.[26]

Piatigorsky was already known in England, having played there with the Berlin Philharmonic, and he returned yearly as a soloist. Even so, England was still a rigidly class-conscious country that did not easily welcome foreigners. His Nansen[27] passport too was a steady reminder of his stateless existence. No matter how often he toured there — sometimes several times in a season — he was never allowed to stay more than two weeks.

Nansen headaches were only one concern with touring. Early in his career the cellist had several discussions with Flesch regarding the profitability of concert life. Flesch was thinking of retiring from heavy concertizing himself: "The other day [Piatigorsky and I] discussed in detail the present-day material conditions of the concert artist's profession. The conclusions were shattering [there follows a list of expenses, and discomforts].... In the USA especially, expenses amount to 60%–70% of the fees … and finally having to listen, in the artist's room, to the remarks of 'musical' people."[28]

Rachmaninoff, Strauss, and Stravinsky

SERGEI RACHMANINOFF

Berlin, November 1928:
I looked forward to my next concert at the Philharmonic. Rachmaninoff was scheduled to appear. Before his arrival Furtwängler worked with the orchestra on Rachmaninoff's Third Concerto, mostly trying to clarify the many little cuts in the score, apparently made by the composer.

On the day of the performance Rachmaninoff sat in the first row of the hall and listened to the rehearsal. His furrowed face looked tired and troubled. His long fingers rubbed his short-cropped hair and his face, as if to refresh himself or to wipe out something tormenting him. Not once did he look at the orchestra, but often at his watch.

He rose. Lean and very tall, he walked to the stage. Not paying attention to Furtwängler, who was rehearsing a symphony, Rachmaninoff sat at the piano, looked at his watch, and thunderously struck a few chords. Perplexed, Furtwängler stopped. He looked at Rachmaninoff, who showed his watch and said, "My rehearsal time was ten-thirty."

With no further exchange, the rehearsal of the concerto commenced. After five minutes or so Rachmaninoff walked to the conductor's stand and began to conduct. The orchestra had two conductors — Furtwängler, bewildered, and Rachmaninoff, swearing in Russian. Even after he returned to the piano, the tension held on until the end of the long and unpleasant rehearsal. Still at odds at the concert, the two extraordinary artists nevertheless brought forth an exciting performance of a peculiar unity.

Mrs. Louise Wolff, preparing a reception to honor the visit of Rachmaninoff, asked me to play his sonata. My friend, the pianist Karol Szreter, practiced fervently. No wonder: Rachmaninoff was his idol. Well prepared and eager, we watched the musical elite of Berlin assembling in Mrs. Wolff's house. Rachmaninoff took a seat a few paces from Szreter and me. He [Rachmaninoff] looked as though trapped or forced to go through an ordeal.[29]

The American writer Geraldine de Courcy[30] had made "American" cocktails for the guests, a novelty. The maids however, served the drinks in tiny shot glasses. Madame de Courcy whispered to Mrs. Wolff, "This drink must be served in glasses for port wine." Mrs. Wolff laughed: "That's enough. They shouldn't drink more of this stuff." Mrs. Wolff's daughter was there and said that the room was absolutely silent before Piatigorsky played, and that he performed "wonderfully masterly, with passion and intimacy."[31] Piatigorsky recalled, "The sonata went well. It had a spontaneous reception."[32]

Despite the enthusiastic applause, the dour composer sat motionless and appeared apathetic. Mrs. Wolff rushed to Mme de Courcy and said: "Quick, give Rachmaninoff two port wine glasses full of the cocktail. Maybe this will loosen his tongue!"[33] Apparently the composer was somewhat perturbed that the performers had made a few unauthorized cuts in the work; but with liquid assistance, he promptly showed his appreciation. Piatigorsky said, "Rachmaninoff shook my hand and said a few complimentary words in his aristocratic brand of Russian (strangely, with the same guttural *r* as Lenin's). Szreter, completely ignored, stood at my side."[34]

Nathan Milstein was there and recalled the following:

> After the performance Szreter wanted to approach Rachmaninoff to ask for his impressions. Piatigorsky warned, "I don't recommend it, Rachmaninoff might tell you the truth." Piatigorsky knew Rachmaninoff was not overly generous with praise. A simple "good" was about the highest encomium one could expect from his lips, but Szreter simply had to find out Rachmaninoff's opinion. Trembling, he approached him and said "Sergei Vassilievich, how did I play?" The reply was brief and to the point: "Very badly!"
>
> Then Rachmaninoff said to Piatigorsky, "I will be three days more in Berlin. Please come and see me," and, pointing at Szreter, "but not with him."[35]

Piatigorsky also remembered:

> I did not see Rachmaninoff, but I spent many hours with Szreter to help him recover from the incident. Several years later, meeting Rachmaninoff in New York, I said with a shade of reproach, that Szreter had died. Sergei Vassilievich, as though receiving good news, said, "Good, I wish him a kingdom in heaven."
>
> Inexplicably the word "good" did not sound cynical, and the "kingdom of heaven" had a religious note and sincerity. As I became better acquainted with his complex nature, I came to understand his forbidding austerity, suspiciousness, prejudices, and dryness on the surface as scars from hard-fought struggles deep within him.
>
> His attitude may have been caused by an unwillingness to expose his innermost self, which was reserved for music alone. I heard from others that he rarely laughed, but once, after I told him a joke, he burst into such violent laughter that I was frightened.
>
> He frightened me once more in his speedboat in Lucerne, when at the steering wheel, in rain hood and phantom-like, he raced, zigzagged and transformed the peaceful lake into a churning whirlpool. As if challenging the trust of his guest, he headed straight for the shore, avoiding it by a sharp turn at the very last moment. He had a smile on his wet face. "You are not easily scared," he said. "You should have seen some other musicians. I like you." I more than liked him. I deeply admired him and he never ceased to fascinate me. But I never took another ride in his boat.[36]

But it was the musical meetings with the composer that remained most cherished. Milstein's reminiscence follows:

> The moments when I played with Rachmaninoff or for him are unforgettable. And Rachmaninoff himself, I think, derived some pleasure from his meetings with us. When he invited us — Volodya Horowitz, Grisha Piatigorsky, and me — he usually wanted us to play for him, and as a rule he did not have other guests.

Once Piatigorsky and I arrived in Hertenstein to see him — as usual, around four in the afternoon but without an appointment. Piatigorsky had his cello, I had my violin. A servant opened the door, "Quiet, quiet, the master is sleeping...." Rachmaninoff usually took a nap after his Russian lunch. The house was completely still then.

Piatigorsky and I tiptoed into the living room. On the music stand we saw the sheet music for Rachmaninoff's *Vocalise*, which we both knew well. Without discussing it, we took out our instruments and began playing the *Vocalise*, standing up, very quietly, in unison, an octave apart.

Suddenly Rachmaninoff came into the room. Sleepy, he looked like a prisoner with his crew cut and striped pajamas with raised collar. Without a word he went to the piano and, also standing, accompanied us — and so beautifully! When we got to the end, Rachmaninoff left the room still without a word, but with tears in his eyes.

We never spoke about that episode with him: we were afraid. But later, In New York, Alexander Greiner of Steinway told me, "Milstein, what have you done to Rachmaninoff? He can't forget how you and Piatigorsky played his *Vocalise*. He says it was marvelous." Coming from Rachmaninoff, even indirectly, this was incredible, wild praise.[37]

Pianist Ivor Newton remembered a curious incident concerning the close circle around Rachmaninoff:

Somehow or other, I discovered, Rachmaninoff's compatriots seemed to be aware of everything that happened to him. One day, as I was walking along a quiet street near Central Park, in New York, I saw his tall, aloof, fur-coated figure approaching and could not resist the temptation to speak to him. "May I wish you good morning, Mr. Rachmaninoff?" I asked, and received in reply a non-committal grunt. "Why are you in New York?" he asked.

"I'm in America touring with Piatigorsky," I replied.

"That must be very interesting," he said, and we parted without another word.

Months later, in a middle-western town, Piatigorsky suddenly fixed me with an inquisitorial stare. "What did you and Rachmaninoff find to say to each other when you met in New York?" he asked sternly.[38]

Trio Elegiac, op. 9

As the Horowitz-Milstein-Piatigorsky Trio debut approached (March 1932), Merovitch was busy promoting their genius. He boasted about them to the *Musical Courier* magazine, maintaining that they often played together for their own pleasure and had the same musical understanding and were able to play together in complete sympathy.[39] Merovitch intended to develop chamber music series with them "in all centers of the world.... We will present the best of music in all forms, and we will invite other virtuosos of our own choice, who later, will become our successors!"[40]

The trio's debut was slated as a benefit for the Musicians Unemployment Workers Fund. Their program included the Brahms Trio in C Major, op. 87, the Beethoven Trio in B-flat Major, op. 11, and the Rachmaninoff *Trio Elegiac* op. 9. The Rachmaninoff *Trio* was their favorite since all three considered Rachmaninoff the reigning Russian musician. (Piatigorsky remembered that after some of their rehearsals, Horowitz shared his own compositions, written during his student days: "music for the piano, a sonata for violin, an unfinished piece for cello ... all had the mark of a true gift for composing.")[41]

By the end of February, the trio met in New York and set about rehearsing their program. Since they knew Rachmaninoff and he lived nearby, they anxiously wanted to play his trio for him. Piatigorsky wrote about the encounter:

Horowitz, shyly advancing many excuses, begged the composer to play it with us instead. Nathan declared that there were no critics present and no risk whatsoever involved, which

An Art Deco photograph, 1932.

made Rachmaninoff laugh, but he categorically declined. We proceeded with the performance. I think it was a good one, and the only listeners, consisting of Rachmaninoff, his wife and two daughters, reacted more than approvingly.

"What pretty music!" the ladies exclaimed. "Who wrote it?"

"I," said Rachmaninoff guiltily.

"Sergei Vassilievich," Milstein began, "why don't you write anything for the violin?"

"Why should I, when there is the cello?" he said.[42]

Rachmaninoff edited his *Trio Elegiac* for their performance, making cuts and adjustments. Milstein wrote of the rehearsals: "The composition [*Trio Elegiac*] has its divine

HOROWITZ
MILSTEIN
PIATIGORSKY

in their

First Chamber Music Appearance

CARNEGIE HALL

WEDNESDAY EVENING, MARCH 30, 1932

at 8:30

For Musicians Emergency Aid

Steinway Piano   Tickets: $2.50 to $1.00

CONCERT MANAGEMENT ARTHUR JUDSON, Inc.
Division of Columbia Concerts Corporation of Columbia Broadcasting System, Inc.
Representative: ALEXANDER MEROVITCH

Steinway Hall   113 West 57th Street   New York City

Horowitz-Milstein-Piatigorsky program, March 30, 1932.

moments, but it also has its longuers. Rachmaninoff himself came to our rescue, cutting about twenty minutes of music. He was delighted that his trio would be on the same program with Beethoven and Brahms, and he attended our rehearsals regularly. Listening to Brahms at our rehearsals, Rachmaninoff would exclaim, 'I don't like Brahms! Too bad!' and then would try to explain, 'Brahms knew how to compose.'"[43]

The public enthusiastically received the long-awaited debut of the Horowitz-Milstein-Piatigorsky Trio, but the ensemble received mixed reviews in the press. The Rachmaninoff *Trio Elegiac* turned out to be the most successful, as their musical sympathies easily merged into his milieu.

The *New York Times* commented that the playing of the Beethoven was "presented with the utmost finesse of detail and a profile always clean and vitally etched, if untouched by those impalpable veils of emotion which attend a performance less immaculately and more poetically conceived." But it was of the Brahms that he pointed out, "Brahms' masterful and highly integrated work unrolled with swinging and elastic tempos.... [It] was whirled along on a wind of spectacular bravura and immense fortes that distended its outlines and ignored the content. With the Scherzo: presto, however, some alchemy of fusion occurred, dimensions were reduced, color became varied and subtle, and the gifts of the three players united in a reading of such brilliance and beauty that it drew quick and vehement applause."[44] This would be the trio's only public performance. (Piatigorsky, however, continually performed chamber music in public, especially with Jascha Heifetz years later.)

Richard Strauss

The 1931–32 season was memorable for Piatigorsky — tours in Holland, England, South America, and particularly Germany. Artur Rubinstein first heard the cellist in Warsaw that season: "Piatigorsky played very beautifully; he was certainly the best cellist I had heard since Casals."[45] In Frankfurt in October 1931, Piatigorsky was soloist under Richard Strauss. The composer conducted him in his own *Don Quixote* and accompanied the cellist in the Haydn Concerto. Piatigorsky probably first met Strauss at the end of 1925 when the composer's "Parergon" from *Sinfonia Domestica* was premiered with the Berlin Philharmonic.[46] The significance of the Frankfurt concerts would stay with him forever.

The rehearsal with Strauss began with the Haydn Concerto; the composer was in a humorous mood:

> After a few bars he stopped and said, "The tutti is too long. It's a concerto, not a symphony. We will make a cut." He counted the number of bars to be left out. "Let's try it." I listened to this impossible cut, but did not dare to protest. At the end of the first movement he asked me to play the entire cadenza. I did.
> "Who wrote it?" he asked.
> I said, "It's mine."
> He murmured something that sounded like a compliment. After the cadenza of the second movement he asked with disgust, "Who wrote that?" This cadenza was also mine, but in my embarrassment I invented "Emil Schmorg."
> "Schmorg? It's awful. I will write one for you right now. Gentlemen — intermission." It was a long one. Strauss wrote with a pencil in my orchestra score (I still have it). When we were on the stage again he put the music in front of me, and after a few bars of the orchestra leading to the cadenza, I began to play it. There was a recitative after which, not believing my eyes, I saw the famous theme of *Till Eulenspiegel*. I played it. There was a roar of laughter. When it subsided, Strauss said, "I prefer the Schmorg."

Following the Haydn, everyone except me was in a fine mood for *Don Quixote*. I was very nervous. I had played it before, but was it the way the composer wanted it to be? After the big solo variation in D minor there was a heavy silence. I didn't dare to look up at Strauss. "Why doesn't he go on into the next variation?" I thought anxiously. Finally he said, "I have heard my *Don Quixote* as I thought him to be." It was a supreme moment, which lasted even when at our concerts he looked at his watch during my long cadenzas of the Haydn Concerto.[47]

Piatigorsky recalled that Strauss had a tendency to conduct a bit too fast and indifferently,[48] but with *Don Quixote*, he conducted with an intensity, so much so that Strauss broke into an uncharacteristic sweat. Strauss requested the solo violist, as Sancho Panza, to play less "beautifully" and to scratch and stutter, which prompted the violist to complain: "I have never been asked to play ugly and funny." The composer responded, "Humor is a great art." Piatigorsky also remembered that Strauss took an unusually long pause after the love declaration for Dulcinea before going on.[49]

After their successes in Frankfurt, the composer wrote to him with his deep appreciation:

> I thank you once again most cordially for your wonderful Don Quixote: technically, musically, and in expression a sheer model. I wished us that you could play wherever the work is performed under a good conductor.
> Your
> sincerely devoted
> Richard Strauss[50]

Richard Strauss's note of thanks after their concerts together.

Strauss nicknamed Piatigorsky *Mein Lieber Don* and they frequently socialized by playing the card game Skat — especially because Strauss always won.[51] Piatigorsky, now on excellent terms with the composer off the podium, urged him to write a solo work for cello and orchestra. Strauss, intrigued, spoke of his ideal in Edouard Lalo's concerto, and promised that he would tackle a work for him. They kept in touch and Strauss attended one of Piatigorsky's performances of *Don Quixote* conducted by Sir Malcolm Sargent and the London Philharmonic while the composer was in London guest conducting the BBC Symphony.[52] They last saw each other in Vienna, where Strauss reassured Piatigorsky of his intentions to compose a work along Lalo's proportions. Alas, the venture did not succeed, as Hitler by then had become der Führer and Strauss' involvement with political opportunism spoiled any thought of pursuing it further.[53]

Igor Stravinsky

Piatigorsky's friendship with composer Igor Stravinsky probably began in late 1924 when he premiered his Piano Concerto as soloist with the Berlin Philharmonic. In 1931 Piatigorsky began performing his own arrangement of Stravinsky's ballet *Pulcinella*, a work based on the music of Pergolesi, initially composed for orchestra followed by a transcription for violin and piano. This work would become a frequent part of Piatigorsky's repertoire, but not in its present state. He tells of its metamorphosis:

> Many times I asked Stravinsky to write for the cello, but to no avail. Finally, impatient of waiting longer, I, myself, transcribed Pulcinella for my instrument.
> Stravinsky greeted me one day: "Considering that I never wrote anything for the cello, I am enormously interested to hear that you play a piece by Stravinsky everywhere."
> "I do," I admitted somewhat self-consciously.
> Soon afterwards we played it together and, spurred by enthusiasm, Stravinsky decided to add the Aria missing in the suite for the violin. We began to meet at the Pleyel Studio in Paris[54] and to work on the piece.
> "Let's christen it *Suite Italienne*," proposed Stravinsky.[55]

The two continued working on the piece while traveling from Italy to New York on board the SS *Rex* in 1933. Milstein, who was also a passenger, recalled their collaboration:

> After lunch I would accompany Piatigorsky to Stravinsky's cabin, where they fussed with the cello part of *Suite Italienne*. Piatigorsky was very daring and persistent in his suggestions, and Stravinsky listened to him. It was fascinating to see them work.
> One of the most daring innovations in the suite is the stunning moment when the cellist tosses the bow behind the bridge, creating a special sound — unforgettable, fantastic effect! That brilliant idea came out quite accidentally.
> Tea was served at 4:45 on the ship. Lovely young women joined Piatigorsky and me for tea. (To tell the truth, he was the main attraction. I was the dummy.) That day, I remember, we were expecting a particularly beautiful young woman. And Stravinsky, of all the rotten luck, was engrossed in the work, with no sign of ending the session. Piatigorsky was beside himself. He was afraid he'd be late for our date but didn't have the nerve to tell Stravinsky about it. And because he was so nervous, the bow jumped out of his hand and slid behind the bridge of the cello! An unusual, whistling sound resulted. Stravinsky literally jumped up. "That's it! Marvelous! I like it! How did you do it?"
> After a few tries they decided to use and write down the accidental discovery. I have to give Stravinsky his due here: his wit, his speedy reaction, his readiness to experiment. Clearly, Stravinsky was delighted. And so were we: at last we could go off to have tea with the beauty.[56]

Another spontaneous experiment made it to the printed edition, though Piatigorsky was never totally convinced of its appropriateness. Stravinsky originally wrote the dynamic of the ending in the Tarantella *pianissimo*. Piatigorsky asked to try it *fortissimo*. Stravinsky loved it and changed it on the spot, though Piatigorsky sometimes played it *pianissimo* to assuage his doubt.

The cello version became more virtuosic than the violin adaptation and bears Piatigorsky's heavy influence; the 21 page pencil draft is in the cellist's hand "with occasional sketches for the piano part added by Igor Stravinsky," indicating their considerable teamwork.[57]

The teamwork was rewarding, and to relax, they played poker. Piatigorsky was surprised by Stravinsky's biting sarcasm and dry wit and objected to Stravinsky continually calling the cello a big guitar. In the end, Piatigorsky was disappointed that their collaboration came to a conclusion:

> I enjoyed our meetings so much that I felt sorry to see the work completed. Before the manuscript was sent to print, Stravinsky came to see me in New York. He produced a paper and said,
>
> "Here is the contract for you to sign. But before you do so, I want to explain the conditions."
>
> "Conditions? But dear Igor Feodorovitch, I did not count on anything. I was happy to collaborate, and I am glad that the Italian Suite will be published."
>
> "No, my friend, you are entitled to royalties. I insist. The question is, if you would agree to the proposition, which is fifty-fifty. To be sure, half for you, half for me."
>
> "But really!" I protested, not wanting to hear of such a thing.
>
> "I am not convinced you understand. May I repeat again: fifty-fifty, half for you, half for me. You see, it's like this: I am the composer of the music, of which we both are the transcribers. As a composer I get ninety per cent, and as the arrangers we divide the remaining ten per cent into equal parts. In toto, ninety-five per cent for me, five per cent for you, which makes fifty-fifty."
>
> Chuckling, I signed the contract.[58]

Piatigorsky shared many of Stravinsky's witticisms to illustrate points with his students. Stravinsky had his own definitions of beautiful — "pretty" was not part of it. He quoted the composer regarding a pianist's performance: "The man is a bore; he plays so beautifully." And speaking to an ambitious young composer who asked the master's opinion of his new composition, Stravinsky called it both "beautiful and new." The young man was in rapture and wanted to hear more. "Yes, yes," said Stravinsky, playing a few more bars. "It is beautiful and new. But what is beautiful is not new, and what is new is not beautiful."[59] The Stravinsky adage most shared by Piatigorsky was "I have no time to be in a hurry," meaning that nothing of value in art is created in fear or haste — that one must consider every note and "own" it.[60]

In 1975, NBC television nationally broadcasted the Lifetime Achievement Awards ceremonies. Piatigorsky accepted posthumously for Stravinsky and gave a short speech.

5. Paris, 1932–1933

1932–1933: Paris, Flesch, and Friedberg

Piatigorsky arrived in New York from Europe in January as usual, and immediately began his U.S. tour. On January 14, he performed at the White House for the first time — for President Hoover.[1] These White House recitals generally featured light repertoire, and paired soloists with other artists, usually a singer, in this case, Grace Moore. However, Piatigorsky's 1959 recital during the Eisenhower administration was the first full recital given by a cellist.

By the summer of 1932 the Piatigorskys were preparing to leave Berlin, as the political situation deteriorated. "Life in Germany, for any musician, let alone a Jewish musician, became impossible under Hitler.... It was barbaric. Artists were stifled."[2] They wanted to move to Paris where Lida's parents lived, but obtaining a visa for Piatigorsky was no easy matter. While the stateless Nansen passport enabled Piatigorsky to tour, problems with the document dogged him wherever he went. Border officials were loath to allow refugees to enter without an exit strategy, since a stateless person could not be deported, becoming de facto permanent citizens. The visa process was time-consuming and worrisome. As he recalled, "Being met by the police upon arriving in a city, marching through the streets with them to headquarters, and seeing one's name on posters plastered on the walls became a habit. To be a fugitive in the morning and the government's guest of honor that night after the concert made the procedure amusing."[3]

In August, a stomach ailment returned and he decided to enter an anthroposophic clinic, which emphasized a strict natural diet and plenty of rest. During his illnesses, he read books on the classics and philosophy as well as studied new music. While recovering, he sent back the corrected cello part to Stravinsky's *Suite Italienne*, and studied Glazunov's new *Concerto-Ballata*. Piatigorsky received a welcome gift from Jascha Heifetz — an arrangement of Heifetz's signature encore, *Dinicu's Hora Staccato*,[4] especially to showcase Piatigorsky's remarkable staccato technique. His staccato had not always been so. On one of Heifetz's visits to the Piatigorskys' home in Berlin, the cellist mentioned his frustration with the flying staccato. Heifetz insisted they drop everything and immediately work on it. A few minutes later Piatigorsky emerged victorious that day, happy to have finally mastered it, and yelling to his pianist Karol Szreter in the next room, "Karolchik! I made it!"[5]

By October the Piatigorskys vacated their Berlin residence and moved to Paris, settling into Villa Majestic (part of the Hotel Majestic on Avenue Kléber), not far from Horowitz's apartment. Since their assets were modest, they did not lose too much money selling the Berlin apartment. Leaving was bittersweet, since Berlin had been very good to them, but with the rising Nazi presence, they both had genuine concern for Germany's future. The decision to move to Paris was timely, as demonstrated by violinist Samuel Dushkin in a letter to Stravinsky from August 22: "In the last two weeks Milstein and Piatigorsky have had fifteen concerts cancelled in Germany, and, for the same reason (Hitler), Horowitz does not play at all."[6]

As new Parisians and at Rachmaninoff's request, Piatigorsky and Horowitz played an unofficial recital for poor Russian students at the Russian Consulate. Piatigorsky forged ahead and toured Scandinavia, Holland, Italy, Switzerland, Austria and Poland that fall. He performed Felix Weingartner's own Cello Concerto with the legendary conductor in Basel in November. Piatigorsky's last concert in Berlin was the Schumann Concerto with Furtwängler and the Berlin Philharmonic in October 1932. The philharmonic was celebrating their fiftieth anniversary year as well as the conductor's first decade with them. A gold medal was presented to Furtwängler on behalf of President von Hindenburg, and the city of Berlin awarded a municipal subsidy to insure the orchestra's future.

That same autumn, the city of Berlin made plans for a Brahms Festival at the Singakademie in honor of the composer's upcoming centennial for the spring of 1933. The plan was to perform all the composer's chamber music with piano, to be played by Schnabel, Bronislaw Huberman, Piatigorsky and Hindemith. Piatigorsky recalled Schnabel's clever, creative, yet "democratic" arithmetic concerning the fees:

> We agreed smoothly upon the programs and dates, and even the question as to how to divide the fees seemed simple, at first. There was no doubt in my mind that it would be in equal parts, but Huberman and Schnabel were silent. Finally Huberman suggested that the matter of money should be left to the managers. (Undoubtedly he was certain that if this procedure were adopted he would come out best.) Irritated, Schnabel came with a winning trump:
> "Gentlemen, we waste our time. The fee should be divided into thirty-five equal parts."
> "Why thirty-five?" exclaimed Huberman.
> "It's simple," said Schnabel. "We will play thirteen works for the piano and strings: three trios, three quartets, three violin sonatas, two viola sonatas, and two cello sonatas — thirty-five parts in all. As all thirteen works are with piano, I should receive thirteen thirty-fifths of the fee. The violin will be minus two cello and two viola sonatas, and will thus get nine thirty-fifths. The cello will get eight thirty-fifths, and the viola five thirty-fifths."
> With mouths agape we all had to agree. It was lucky that Schnabel's ingenuity did not extend to counting the notes, in which case I would have come out much worse."[7]

Before the official contracts were signed with the city government, Carl Flesch heard about the upcoming series from Piatigorsky. Flesch felt betrayed by both Schnabel and Piatigorsky for establishing another trio with Bronislaw Huberman. The situation reopened the wound he had felt during the Beethoven Festival of 1927 under the same circumstances. Though Flesch asked for candor when he questioned Schnabel about his reasons to end their trio, Schnabel's reply was nonresponsive. Schnabel and Flesch had been partners in duos and trios for 24 years, and Flesch, obviously suffering, wrote to him with considerable indignation. He decided it best to end their friendship:

> I was very surprised by your letter, where you assured me of the immutability of your friendship.... Piati informed me officially the other day, also on your behalf, about your project of a Brahms-cycle with Huberman in the spring, as you apparently wanted to avoid a personal discussion.... You, I have to reproach because you declined since 1929 — for totally unclear reasons ... to play chamber music; but then — during my farewell year — you took the first opportunity to work with someone else.
> Although our paths are parting from now on, I remain artistically as near to you as ever. This way, the best of you, your art will remain with me.[8]

On vacation with Horowitz (left), Milstein (in dark suit), and Merovitch (right) in Switzerland.

Schnabel's response claimed steadfast friendship for Carl, but still did not acknowledge the hurt or the way events transpired: "Your letter saddened me very much. You are severing the friendship; you are leaving it.... I am not going to force myself on you. If you like to see me, I am at hand, and you will meet a friend. Your old Artur."[9]

After Hitler's appointment as Chancellor, the Nazi boycott of Jewish businesses and professions was in effect by April 1, and participation in the series was impossible. Schnabel wrote that "it was no surprise when, also on my last morning in Germany, this man telephoned me and said: 'Mr. Schnabel, I have to tell you that I am no longer in charge of the Brahms Festival and plans have been changed. If you want to negotiate with the new man in charge, it would be—' I interrupted him, saying: 'I expected that.' And I think these were about the last words I spoke in Germany: 'Though I may not be pureblooded, I am fortunately cold-blooded. Good luck to you.'"[10]

Later in April the Brahms celebrations were banned under orders from the Prussian minister of culture. However, the centennial went ahead in May in Vienna, since Austria's autonomy had not yet been usurped by Germany. Furtwängler tried to persuade his Jewish cohort to play in Vienna, as well as return to Berlin the next season as soloists. Schnabel, Piatigorsky, and Huberman had all been soloists in 1932, but they refused to appear with Furtwängler again. Piatigorsky even declined to perform on the Vienna series, and Casals was enlisted to replace him.

Nonetheless, the summer trio with Flesch, pianist Carl Friedberg, and Piatigorsky continued to perform together through 1932, though it was becoming apparent that any Jew's days in Germany were numbered — even those as celebrated as Piatigorsky, who was by then almost considered German patrimony in the press.

Milstein (left) and Piatigorsky in drag.

Though Jewish, Flesch was still living in Baden-Baden, seemingly unconcerned about the anti–Semitic atmosphere — perhaps dependent on the income of festival concerts, but more personally, to live near one of his sons, who was born with a severe mental handicap and was living in a facility nearby.[11] As usual, Flesch helped arrange trio and solo orchestral concerts for the Baden-Baden festival with its conductor and director, Ernst Mehlich.

By the summer of 1933, the exhaustion, which was the result of so many concerts, as well as the overwhelming troubles in his marriage took their toll and Piatigorsky's stomach distress returned. To return to Switzerland with his closest friends, Horowitz and Milstein, was all he wanted. Musically, all Piatigorsky looked forward to was a recital with Horowitz in London and rehearsing the Brahms Double Concerto with Milstein for an upcoming winter appearance. It was the violinist's first performance of the work, and the first of many with the cellist.

Piatigorsky still had obligations with Flesch and Friedberg in Baden-Baden, but suddenly decided to cancel the concerts, citing exhaustion. He may not have shared news of his failed marriage with his older colleagues, and since the Piatigorskys still lived together, their split was not obvious. Piatigorsky tried to placate Flesch:

> To my greatest regret did I hear that you are angry with me because Lida and I wrote to you about [canceling] the Baden-Baden concerts. But my dear Vati [Flesch's nickname] ... had I only thought about it for one minute that you would be offended by it, I would not just have written a letter, but a whole "Piatiade"! Surely, I am sorrier than you or Carl [Friedberg] that the concerts are not going to be held — but I really could not do anything about it — my nerves were so shattered in Paris, and I was so tired, I had to think of my health and a real vacation....
>
> [Y]ou as my true friend will understand.... I came here to Horowitz [Sils Maria, near St. Moritz, Switzerland] because it is quieter and the air is better.... Yesterday, I saw Mrs. Furtwängler — soon he will be also arriving here. The little Menuchin [Menuhin] is also here — Milsteins are also near here. As you can see the world is not without artists.
>
> Please, my dearest Vati, write to me how your health is and if you are still angry with me.[12]

Evidently Flesch wrote to Piatigorsky, chastising him for his lack of courtesy. Lida (with Gregor) wrote to Flesch on August 19, which exacerbated the crisis. The old wounds with Huberman also reappeared, and the quotes from the Piatigorskys' letter are surprising and rather brutal. This marks the end of their association with Flesch. Flesch responded on the 20th:

> I think it important to correct some of your assertions which are in contradiction of the truth.
>
> You write: "For years now, I can not reproach myself in the least to have behaved in an un-cooperative or unfriendly manner toward you."
>
> In contrast, I discovered that after you spent about 14 days in August — September in Baden-Baden, and were treated by us like a child in our home, you left for Berlin immediately, where you, behind my back, determined with Schnabel the details for your planned Trio with Huberman as well as the concerts to be performed.... I do not think that this behavior fits the concept of cooperation and friendship toward me of which you pride yourself.
>
> You write: "However, I have come to the firm conviction that your friendship toward me was never sincere and serious.... The rudeness of style of your letter is undignified of every cultured person."
>
> Aside from you obviously not being the right personality, dear Piaty, to give me a lecture about the concept of culture, you might be partially right insofar that I used the word "*Schweinerei*" [lit. "pig's mess"] to characterize your behavior toward me. Although, I admit that this is an unparliamentary expression, nevertheless, quite frankly no better one comes to mind in order to describe the atrocious impression your letter had on me where your wife informed me of your cancellation. Therein it says literally "Piaty is lying in bed and finds it too hot to write himself," etc. Apparently, you do not include in the concept of culture the sense of tact, which one should expect from a "friend."
>
> You would have to tell yourself that such a cancellation had to have a tremendously hurtful effect toward an almost doubly older colleague. Even though I always took care of all administrative matters over the last 5 years for you and Friedberg, it does not mean that I was your concert agent, to whom such a cancellation would have been appropriate....

I got the impression that there was no friendship whatsoever on your part, and that you regarded your connections with me purely from the standpoint of usefulness.[13]

Attempts at recovering the friendship must have made some headway, as Piatigorsky recommended that violinist Ivry Gitlis study with Flesch in 1937 and provided tuition directly to Flesch.

Divorces: Lida and Merovitch

Lida dedicated herself to furthering Piatigorsky's career and helped him in many ways. Intermittently they played recitals together, and toured in the United States and Cuba. However, her piano skills were not virtuosic, so they avoided some of the more demanding sonata repertoire. But touring together was the exception, not the rule, and with Piatigorsky's career skyrocketing, the time spent apart from Lida caused irreconcilable problems.

Piatigorsky wanted a family and envied his friend Boris Koutzen, who proudly announced the birth of his son. "That is my dream,"[14] the cellist wrote back, sending his congratulations. But Lida did not want children, which must have contributed to their growing marital problems. Rumors of Lida's extramarital affairs also turned out to be true, and the final collapse happened at the very end of 1932. There were charges of cruelty on both sides, but they tried to mend the rift as Lida still accompanied him on several U.S. recitals during the 1932-33 season. Though the divorce was finalized in October 1933, the couple still maintained an apartment together through the winter of 1933-34. While on tour, Piatigorsky kept clothes, an extra cello and received his mail there for several months.

Word of their breakup reached the Koussevitzkys, and being loyal to Piatigorsky, they shunned Lida. Piatigorsky tried to take the blame for the divorce, as can be seen in the following letter to Koussevitzky from January 12, 1933:

> For God's sake, forgive me that I am just now writing to you, but you understand — you know how difficult it is to write when your soul is full of suffering, and how difficult it is to say in a letter everything that you're feeling. Lida was really shaken up that you didn't want to talk to her.... Lida is not to blame for anything regarding me, she is a pure and great person and she loved, and loves, me with all her heart. Right now we are going through a big crisis, and that's understandable — in her life with me, Lida has not had much happiness, she hasn't had even the smallest share of what she deserved. I am to blame for a lot regarding her, and of all people I should know. I am not justifying her — she doesn't need that, and those who truly know her cannot not love and respect her. Poor thing, she is really suffering now, and I *beg of you*, please treat her well — she does not deserve different, and I am despairing only at the thought that you are judging her....
>
> Our crisis will pass, and I have faith in my happy life with her — and I believe in our true and sincere love. Help Lida and me to get through this difficult time quickly and painlessly, and I will be eternally grateful to you — just as now, I will never forget your parental relationship to me and the support that you have wanted to give me! Sergey Aleksandrovich was right when he said that internal injuries do heal — therefore this one will heal also. Write me a good letter, I beg of you! Say about my letter, write what you will, but don't force her and me to suffer more tormentedly. We can't get by without each other!

And in another letter to Koussevitzky from October 1933, Piatigorsky writes about the divorce:

> There have been a lot of changes in my life. The main one, of course, is my formal and official divorce from Lida.... [I]t's still too painful for me to talk about it. But I am truly happy about one thing, and that's my friendship with Lida — we have parted the greatest of friends, and I hope and believe that we will always remain so. Lida is living with her mother in Paris; I nowhere.[15] Because my health still wasn't good enough at the beginning of the season, I had to keep the number of concerts in October to a minimum — at this point I have played only three concerts, of which the two in Vienna went exceptionally well — then I played here in Czechoslovakia, and on the 21st I was supposed to play in Paris, but I caught a bad cold and had to cancel that concert. Now my fever is gone, and tomorrow or the day after I will head to Warsaw.[16]

After their divorce, Lida became involved with cellist Pierre Fournier, whom she would later marry. During their courtship, Piatigorsky happened to return to the apartment to retrieve his mail, and noticed a telegram addressed to "Piatigorsky." Assuming it was for him, he opened it and was shocked to read: BARCELONA PLAYING WITH CASALS AND HIS ORCHESTRA. THINKING OF YOU. PIERRE. When Lida happened to return, an exasperated Piatigorsky waved the telegram and shouted: "Isn't one career on this damned instrument enough for you without starting all over again?"[17]

After the divorce, Piatigorsky relied on friends to keep his spirits positive. His friends from Moscow, the Marinel sisters, lived in Paris and had just formed the Marinel Harp Trio. They lived on the Rue d'Orleans and Piatigorsky nicknamed them "The Maidens of Orleans." Inna Marinel remembered a particular visit with Piatigorsky and a mystery guest:

> One afternoon the telephone rang; it was Grisha — he told us that he wanted to see us, and bring a friend of his. An hour later he arrived with a slim, dark-haired young man in tow.
> "Please meet my friend, Haim Ziperovich!" said Grisha in the foyer, and, as he entered the room where the harps stood, he exclaimed mischievously: "Haim, let's play!" Both of them immediately inverted the harps on their columns, and started uproariously pulling the strings.
> We were interrupted by dinner. Over dinner, Grisha, always amusing company, was telling American stories. The guest kept very quiet.
> Towards the end of the meal, my sister said, very casually, to our guest: "You know, I heard your graduation recital in Kiev a few years ago," and enumerated the works on the program. Vladimir Horowitz, since it was he, seemed quite astonished at being thus recognized, and his program remembered. Next, both Horowitz and Grisha insisted on hearing the Trio, but there were strings missing on the harps, and my sister refused to play. Horowitz had just presented the new Ravel Concerto, and musical Paris was buzzing about it. He offered to trade the Ravel Concerto for a few of our numbers, but since our upright piano was old and shabby, with a few keys stuck, my sister told him that nobody could play on that piano anyway. Thereupon, our two gentlemen callers seated themselves at the harps again, this time holding them correctly, and begged to be admitted to the Trio, promising to put on pink dresses, as we were then wearing, and play every note faithfully — and I have no doubt that with their immense talents they would have succeeded to do so very shortly.
> The end of the story is that Horowitz sat at the broken piano, and gave us the most astounding rendition of the Ravel Concerto from beginning to end, with Grisha humming the accompaniment.[18]

The year 1933 was full of significant events for Horowitz and Milstein as well. Merovitch expected to have a lifelong association with his trio of stars, but by late 1933 both Horowitz and Milstein parted ways with him. Piatigorsky had already left by the spring, but due to his contract, remained associated through Judson's management in the U.S. market. Publicity materials listed Merovitch as his representative under the Judson banner until 1935. Afterwards Piatigorsky was represented exclusively through the Judson office, though not by Merovitch. He wrote to the British concert agency Ibbs and Tillet explaining: "As you no doubt know by this time, I have severed all connections with my former representative Mr.

Alexander Merovitch. I understand [he] has made some arrangements for Horowitz and myself to play in a joint recital known as the Aeolus Concert Series. I would appreciate knowing all the details of this concert as regards programme, date etc.... I also want to inform you that all matters will be handled by me direct in the future."[19]

His friends voiced stinging criticism of their manager. They were dissatisfied with his financial arrangements as well as redundancies in representation. Since Horowitz and Milstein had enough momentum in their careers, they did not need to pay Merovitch's 20 percent commission over and above Judson's fees, especially during the depression. Milstein mistrusted Merovitch from the beginning and had the least amount of patience with him, though the violinist may have been a bit unfair when late in life he remarked, "He didn't take us under his wing; in 1925, he didn't have any wings. He only talked big. We didn't know anything, we were naive, so we followed his advice. At first, we did need someone who would be with us, and he adopted us and treated us like [he was] some kind of ministration nurse. If he thought of himself as our father, we didn't feel like his sons." He added further: "The man had no great artistic vision. He didn't know anything, he didn't do anything, he spoiled everything. He didn't plan anything, didn't foresee anything, and made loads of mistakes."

Milstein's unhappiness with Merovitch extended to the personal level, as he considered the man a womanizer and mentally unstable. He recalled being backstage at a Horowitz concert when Merovitch said to the pianist, "'You know, Volodya, you have many enemies who will try to spoil the concert. I will hypnotize them.' Can you imagine telling that to a pianist before he goes on stage?" But even Horowitz had to admit that Merovitch personally shared in their early struggles on Horowitz's first European tour in 1926, during which Merovitch traveled with the pianist. Their finances were extremely inadequate, as Horowitz recalled: "We always had to borrow money. When we traveled, it was third class because we could not afford the best accommodations. I ate cheese sandwiches, believe me, not truffles or caviar."

Apparently Merovitch had gained a reputation for shenanigans. Alexander Greiner, artist representative of the Steinway piano company, kept a black book of individuals that the company sponsored. His entry on Merovitch is telling:

> MEROVITCH, Alexander: Manager of Horowitz and other artists. When in Paris, summer of 1929, Merovitch told me that he was in very bad financial straits so I spoke to Mr. Paul Schmidt who advanced him $1000. This money was advanced with a view to helping him out, firstly, and secondly in order to insure his cooperation with us, stopping further demands with regard to the artists under his management. In 1930 joined Concert Management Arthur Judson as Vice President and Director but his attitude toward other gentlemen in the office became so overbearing that he was asked to resign. Refused and withheld $6,000 worth of checks belonging to Judson. Later took legal action and Merovitch turned the checks over to them in court. Notified us officially of his resignation April 25, 1930. One should be careful in dealing with him.[20]

The trio no longer needed him, but unfortunately Merovitch needed them. He viewed their actions as betrayal. He took his loss very badly. His sister-in-law, Maria Merovitch, remembered his anguish regarding Horowitz: "It was something that he relived from the time they separated until he died. Milstein and Horowitz exploited him, not the other way around. They gave him nothing and Sasha [Merovitch] was the one who paid and sacrificed everything during their first years in Europe."[21]

Though he launched his own agency in New York, he never regained the success he had with his three stars.[22] Failed business ventures and bouts with depression resulted in

Transatlantic passengers, L-R: Milstein, Lida, Piatigorsky, Horowitz, Wanda Toscanini, Bernardo Molinari (behind Wanda), Toscanini. The four women on the right are unidentified.

his suffering two nervous breakdowns. One spouse of an artist whom Merovitch managed during this time recalled that "He became a strange, psychopathic personality. He would get into fits of rage and start screaming, eyes inflamed, for no apparent reason, and it was absolutely impossible for anybody to work with him."[23] Alexander Merovitch died in 1965.

By December 1933, Piatigorsky entered into a recording contract with the Gramophone Company, Ltd., London [AKA "His Master's Voice" (HMV)], inaugurating an era of distinguished recordings that are among his best. The following May he recorded the Schumann Concerto with John Barbirolli and the London Philharmonic. This landmark recording was the first to be made as a continuous performance — rather than broken into the usual four-minute segments dictated by the length of a single side of a 78 rpm record.[24]

On December 21, he attended Horowitz's wedding to Wanda Toscanini in Milan. It was a civil ceremony as Volodya was Jewish, Wanda was Catholic, and Maestro Toscanini had an aversion for celebrations. Though the marriage was announced in October, the ceremony was rather spontaneous, as desired by the maestro. The free-spirited Horowitz had planned to wear a light-colored suit, but Piatigorsky persuaded the groom to wear a more respectable black.[25]

The Need to Leave: National Socialism and Musical Censorship

After President Hindenburg appointed Hitler as chancellor of Germany on January 30, 1933, the official and rapid systematic expulsion of Jews from Germany began. The first concentration camp, Dachau (near Munich), was already in use by March, and on April 1 the Nazi boycott of Jewish businesses and professions was initiated. By September 29 German Jews were banned from all public activities and from owning land.

After Hindenburg's death (August 7, 1934) Hitler declared himself Führer.[26] On September 15, 1935, the Nuremberg Laws were passed, removing Jewish equality and prohibiting "mixed" marriages.[27] By November 1, German citizenship of all Jews was revoked. On October 28, 1938, more than 17,000 Polish-born Jews were expelled, and in November the first widespread pogrom against the Jews of Germany, *Kristallnacht*, signaled imminent and complete eradication.

On January 24, 1939, Hermann Goering ordered the removal of all Jews from Germany through emigration, and six days later Hitler threatened to annihilate the Jews. By March 15, German troops entered Prague, absorbing the provinces of Bohemia and Moravia into Germany, and on September 1, German troops invaded Poland, ushering in World War II.

Jewish musicians at first defied the new order in 1933 by creating the Jewish Kulturbund (cultural federation), which remarkably survived into 1938. The Kulturbund's membership application described its purpose:

> We call upon you! Join the Cultural League of German Jews (an officially approved organization with the goal of encouraging spiritual and cultural life within Judaism). What we want! To give work, life, optimism and focus to hundreds of dismissed people who are about to give up! To make manifest the religious and ethnic solidarity of Jews! To build a proud consciousness for better times on the basis of an affirmation of Judaism in times of plight! To see and experience works of art! To hear and comprehend music! To fortify one's spirit with the spirit of greater ones! To strive to be an appreciative and modest part of a greater whole, bound to the community by conviction and action! One League — One Community — One Will — One Religion.

As head of symphonic concerts, conductor Michael Taube created a new Jewish orchestra with performances in the Neue Synagogue on Prinzregenten-Strasse, while codirector Leonid Kreutzer dealt with other musical entities. Two new string quartets were also formed: the Partos and the Neue Streichquartet in Berlin. In September 1933 the Nazis established the Reich Chamber of Culture, which excluded Jews from the arts. This made the Kulturbund a beacon for Jews and by 1935, the Reich actually made Jewish cultural unions mandatory.

Though the Berlin Philharmonic was taken over by the Reich on October 26, 1933, it was momentarily spared Aryan cleansing.[28] Immediately after President Hindenburg's death the inevitable purging moved inexorably forward. As a prime example of the juggernaut, conductor Otto Klemperer had just been awarded the Goethe Gold Medal from Hindenburg accompanied by a flattering letter as recognition of his work in propagating German musical art and culture through his leadership of the innovative Kroll Opera as well as the Berlin State Opera. In a few short weeks following Hindenburg's death, Klemperer was officially dismissed from the Berlin State Opera.

During the 1920s and 30s, blatant anti–Semitism was promulgated through several publications, one of which, *Handbuch der Judenfrage: die wichtigsten Tatsachen zur Beurteilung des jüdischen Volkes* [*Handbook of the Jew Question: The Most Important Facts for the Judgment of the Jewish People*] by Theodor Fritsch, aimed at the general public and beyond. In it, Fritsch laid out the Jewish infiltration of Germany in all forms of commerce, education, politics, and the arts. By focusing attention on Jewish lineage, the Aryan faithful condemned a significant number of musical icons, both living and dead. For example, Schnabel, Kreisler, Mendelssohn and Mahler, were listed under their categories (i.e., pianists, string players, and composers). Germans were encouraged to eliminate these "undesirables" in their dealings, be it in the concert hall, recording studio[29] or publishing house. Prominent publisher C.F. Peters was among those mentioned, as well as the powerful Wolff and Sachs concert bureau. The book was published yearly and sold in the millions. Piatigorsky, Feuermann, Grünfeld, and Popper were among the cellists mentioned.

Fritsch's work was exclusively extended to music through Hans Brückner's *Judentum und Musik: mit dem ABC jüdischer und nichtarischer Musikbeflissener* [*The ABCs of Judaism and Music, Jewish and Non-Aryan Music Performers*] and musicologists Herbert Gerigk and Theo Stengel's *Lexikon der juden in der Musik* [*Encyclopedia of Jews in Music*]. The latter was published with the added weight of direct sponsorship from the Nazi party (NSDAP)[30] and Hitler's personal appointment of Gerigk.[31] With these added texts one's identity was easily stigmatized and by 1939 those Jewish musicians who could find a way out were long gone.

Piatigorsky's appearance with Furtwängler earlier in the 1932-33 season would mark the end of their great professional association. Piatigorsky repeatedly wrote to the conductor begging him to leave Germany, assuring him that he could probably have his choice of the world's stages. However, Furtwängler chose to stay and his reasoning is still a topic of discussion, debated in several biographies on the conductor.[32] Furtwängler, though certainly not alone, was a key personality in the elevation of official power of the National Socialists in musical realms. For example, London's *Musical Times* quietly noted his ascension in an unconcerned report:

> Dr Furtwängler has not only been appointed first "Staatskapellmeister" at the State Opera, but has been honoured by designation to the high post of "Staatsrat," or Councilor of State, by the Government. He is thus visibly marked out as the official leader of the musical profession in Germany. A new, very characteristic, and significant musical institution in Germany is the officially designated programme committee, whose duty will be to control the programmes of public concerts and to see that they are in keeping with the new cultural spirit of the present time. Furtwängler will be chairman of this committee, its other members being well-known musicians.[33]

Furtwängler, Hitler's favorite conductor, of course knew that Jews were ubiquitous in German musical life and that the prohibition could not completely succeed. He personally negotiated with the propaganda minister, Joseph Goebbels, to obtain exemptions for particular Jewish musicians. Consequently, on June 29, 1933, the following Nazi decree was issued:

> In the centre of our musical life, must be the cultivation of great German music. But that does not mean that the music of the world outside Germany is not to continue to be represented and enabled to exercise the productive value of its suggestiveness for us, Germans.... [T]he same principle is to apply to artists. First, must come German artists, but, in music as in every art, the achievement must always remain the deciding factor. Every true artist must perform in Germany and must be able to be judged by the measure of his capacity. The commission set up by this Decree is the only authority entrusted with the decision in questions of programmes in the musical life of Prussia.

With Erica Morini. Royal Hungarian family in balcony (courtesy Piatigorsky estate).

With Furtwängler's new position, he was anxious to show the world that Germany had not descended into barbarism, and asked all his soloists from the previous season (which included Piatigorsky, Huberman, and Schnabel) to return to Berlin. All refused. That Huberman stayed and performed in the Vienna Brahms Festival in May[34] perhaps gave Furtwängler hope that the violinist might be his Pied Piper. The conductor wrote to Huberman: "Someone must make the first move to break down the barrier."[35] Schnabel, who was at the festival with the violinist, noted:

> Performances went very well and we had great fun and pleasure at our rehearsals, with plenty of time. After one of our concerts we went to a very popular restaurant in the basement of a hotel. There were about fifty people there besides us. Around midnight, Furtwängler came, with two friends, and his behavior seemed planned and prepared. In the presence of these fifty or more people, he addressed Huberman and me, asking us once more if we would not change our minds and come back the following winter to play in Berlin with him. We had been asked before and refused, of course, to do so, for reasons you can easily guess. Huberman asked me to answer first. I made it very simple and said that if all the musicians were called back and reinstated in their former positions, then I would agree to come back. But if they were not called back, I would have to stick to my refusal. To my great amazement Furtwängler replied — and this was obviously not prepared — that I was mixing art and politics. And that was that.

In the weeks following the festival most Jewish artists saw through the charade and spontaneously refused Furtwängler. Above all, the conductor regarded Piatigorsky as a son and could not understand why he did not come to his rescue.[36]

Huberman observed, "It will be recalled that Dr. Furtwängler endeavored to prevent me from publishing my refusal of his invitation to play with his orchestra in Germany. His astonishing argument was that such a publication would close Germany for me for many years, and perhaps forever." Fed up with the lack of outrage from world citizenry, especially Germany, Huberman boldly continued:

> Before the whole world I accuse you, German intellectuals, you non–Nazis, as those truly guilty of all these Nazi crimes, all this lamentable breakdown of a great people — a destruction which shames the whole white race. It is not the first time in history that the gutter has reached out for power, but it remained for the German intellectuals to assist the gutter to achieve success. It is a horrifying drama, which an astonished world is invited to witness:
> German spiritual leaders with world citizenship who until but yesterday represented German conscience and German genius, men called to lead their nation by their precept and example, seemed incapable from the beginning of any other reaction to this assault upon the most sacred possessions of mankind than to coquet, co-operate, and condone. And when, to cap it all, demagogical usurpation and ignorance rob them of their innermost conceptions from their own spiritual workshop, in order thereby to disguise the embodiment of terror, cowardice, immorality, falsification of history in a mantle of freedom, heroism, ethics, science, and mysticism, the German intellectuals reach the pinnacle of their treachery: they bow down and remain silent....
> Germany, you people of poets and thinkers, the whole world, not only the world of your enemies, but the world of your friends, waits in amazed anxiety for your word of liberation.[37]

In November 1933 the SS *Rex* arrived in New York with Toscanini, Piatigorsky, Horowitz, and the sixteen-year-old violinist Yehudi Menuhin. The young man was interviewed about his refusal to perform in Germany, recalling that during August and September 1933 Furtwängler repeatedly asked him to perform in Berlin. Menuhin insisted he would not play, which prompted Furtwängler's outrageous remark that the violinist "would be blamed in the future for Germany's descent 'to the dogs' musically." The conductor had appealed to the teenager to mend "the broken threads that have torn away Germany from the rest of the world.... Help me divorce art from politics even if the politicians don't always make it easy to do so." Menuhin shook his head in disbelief: "You see, they are blaming the artists instead of themselves for a condition which they have brought about."[38]

Piatigorsky took notice of conductors who condemned the Reich, and was especially happy to hear of Furtwängler's sudden resignation from the Philharmonic in protest.[39] The cellist wrote: "What's this with the conductors? Besides Sergey Aleksandrovich [Koussevitzky] and Toscanini, it seems that they have all [finally] rebelled.... True, for Furtwängler it was time! Too bad they didn't do all of that sooner."[40] Furtwängler's resignation was only temporary; he was reappointed the following year, whereupon a good deal of the world presses applauded his return to his post.

Part of the world's collective procrastination was that it had its own rising anti–Semitism fueled by a long and desperate depression. A majority of Americans feared that an influx of needy immigrants would only aggravate the frail hope of an end to the deprivation. The U.S. government on many levels hid information, churches were silent, and the press was far from vigorous in signaling the alarm. At the end of 1939 Piatigorsky reflected on the situation:

> American newspapers again [prior to the Polish invasion on September 1, 1939] were sounding the alarm — the headlines cried out and predicted war in Europe, and everywhere one was impressed by the menacing faces of Hitler and Mussolini. The Germans ate up Czechoslovakia [March 15, 1939] just as they had eaten up Austria before [March 12, 1938].
> But I do believe in the kinship between Hitler and many hundreds of thousands of people in so far as one can identify a rapidly spreading bacillus in connection with the soul ... and the very fact that Germany is infected by it demonstrates the presence of [it in] the soil that

is necessary for such an infection—a weakening if not of the soul, then of the mind and morals.

People who are calm and do not find any immediate danger are saying "Hitler will give in to this" or "He won't swallow these countries" or "These countries will not swallow him." But one always senses in the intentions, desires and hopes of these types of people, a sense if not of helplessness, but of indifference.... One hears the question, "Who will be the next victim of this insatiable animal?".... [A]ll these countless blackmailings and the gangster ways and principals of the politics of a totalitarian country are not only alien, but deeply repulsive.

The large democracies have not yet found a successful antidote to such politics—in any case, all that has been undertaken up until now has not only *not* been an antidote, but rather the opposite—an incentive. The fate of Czechoslovakia will always be a tragic example.[41]

6. World's Busiest Cellist

Castelnuovo-Tedesco, Toscanini and Berezowski

The decade of the 1930s was Piatigorsky's most arduous. Though he had achieved success, he realized that he needed a purpose beyond the path of a wandering virtuoso. He wanted the cello to emerge as a more popular instrument, and accepted engagements wherever possible. Consequently, his mission brought him to remote regions in China, India, and small towns across America. Constantly rethinking the idea of giving recitals, Piatigorsky fashioned varied programs in an attempt to bring listeners a fulfilling afternoon or evening. He experimented with using a chamber ensemble to accompany him in concertos and concert works[1] on the first half of programs. Sometimes he arranged a movement from a Corelli, Handel, or some obscure composer's sonata with a string quintet accompaniment as an opener.

He kept his programs on the Community Concert circuit full of programmatic curiosity, with short contrasting works counterbalanced with more lengthy sonatas or suites. His arrangements of accessible short pieces met the needs of less sophisticated audiences and expanded the cello repertoire. His commanding stage personality incorporated his gregarious character, but without theatrics; behind the musician dwelled the unmatched raconteur. As violinist Itzhak Perlman remarked, "He didn't play, but told a story."

The 1934-35 season was densely filled with work, which, after his divorce, became a refuge. The number of concert engagements surpassed those of his colleagues Fournier, Cassadó, and Feuermann, the latter about to debut in the U.S. that season. By then, Casals was pulling away from solo concert life, increasingly devoting himself to his orchestra in Barcelona. Eventually, work did not fulfill the emotional void and Piatigorsky felt like a weary nomad. His loneliness is apparent in the following excerpt from a letter to the Koussevitzkys:

> My dear ones!
> It's hard to wander the world alone — I'm very tired. The past three weeks I have played almost every day in a different city. I myself am astonished at the miracle by which I am physically enduring such a life. I will spend Christmas completely alone in Portugal.[2]

The cellist had high hopes of a return visit to Russia in late September, but negotiations with the Soviet government failed. The 1934-35 season began with the added task of learning two new concertos while on tour. Both were written for Piatigorsky and would be premiered that season: Mario Castelnuovo-Tedesco's Concerto, with Toscanini and the New York Philharmonic, and Nicolai Berezowski's Concerto *Lirico* with Serge Koussevitzky and the Boston Symphony.

Mario Castelnuovo-Tedesco and Arturo Toscanini

Many Jewish émigré composers came to America to escape Fascism and discrimination. Their presence significantly contributed to a growing artistic diversity, producing music that maintained its roots, yet explored American idioms. Many musicians worked for the Hollywood film industry, others taught. Several were personally associated with Piatigorsky and wrote for him: Milhaud, Foss, Toch, Tansman, Tcherepnin, Zeisl, and Mario Castelnuovo-Tedesco.

Castelnuovo-Tedesco left Italy in 1938, his music having been banned on radio by the Fascists. He eventually moved to Los Angeles and joined MGM's music department; he also taught privately. Though his film credits were unexceptional, his teaching was unforgettable. Musicians such as Nelson Riddle, Andre Previn, and Henry Mancini owe much to his masterful training.

The Tedescos lived in a modest home in Beverly Hills. Like Dvořák, he preferred to compose in the morning, walk in the afternoon, and later mingle with locals, artists, and intellectuals. This routine would prove to be challenging in cosmopolitan Los Angeles. James Wesby wrote: "He went to an International House of Pancakes, and it wasn't busy in the afternoon, so the waitresses would talk to him."[3]

Film *Andante et Rondo* with Joseph Benvenuti, 1936.

Castelnuovo-Tedesco was the oldest of the Jewish émigré composers to write for Piatigorsky. They first met in 1932 in the composer's hometown of Florence, Italy, on one of the cellist's tours. Piatigorsky's accompanist became ill, and Castelnuovo offered to play in his place. Piatigorsky was already familiar with some of Castelnuovo's music, and they quickly became friends. The composer wrote of their first meeting:

> The occasion was simple but charming. Gregor Piatigorsky, the great Russian cellist, came to me at our first meeting: "Castelnuovo, a great many cellists play your works as well as I do, but nobody loves them as much. Write a concerto for me!"
> I was so touched by this declaration that a year later, in 1933, I wrote the concerto....[4]
> I had "great moments" in my artistic career ... when I heard Toscanini conduct my music, and Heifetz playing my Violin Concerto, and Piatigorsky playing my Cello Concerto, and Segovia the Guitar Concerto.[5]

The following article describes how Toscanini got to know the concerto:

> In the spring of 1933, on the SS *Rex* en route to Italy, were two travelers—the greatest of all conductors, Arturo Toscanini, and the most famous cellist of his generation, Gregor Piatigorsky. The small silver-haired maestro, in his middle sixties, and the tall dark cellist, just nearing his thirties, were fast friends. Night after night the dawn would come up over the water as they sat talking of music. The champagne flowed as fast as the talk and the conversation bubbled like the stories of Wagner, remembrances of Verdi, illuminating and unforgettable comments on Beethoven and Brahms, gossip of premiers and prima donnas, and technical discussion of instrumental problems because Toscanini had been a cellist. Until finally his eyes sinking in spite of himself would make a move to go to bed, only to be shamed and stopped by Toscanini's taunt, "You call yourself a young man and you are already tired. When I was young I was different." Finally at three or four or five Piatigorsky would descend to his cabin, fall into a deep sleep only to be awakened a few hours later by an imperious knock at the door. There the maestro stood, vital and immaculate as always, scornful at finding the cellist in the spell of Morpheus.
> It was during one of those long sessions that Piatigorsky mentioned a new concerto by Castelnuovo-Tedesco. Toscanini immediately demanded the score, retired with it for the night, returned with it at seven the next morning. He stormed through the door of Piatigorsky's cabin, waving the manuscript in his face. "The double-stops in the second movement must go and in one place the winds are too thickly orchestrated. But it is good—good," he muttered excitedly, pouring out a stream of minute analysis and comment.[6] The cellist recalled the scene with awe. "Only a few hours before he had set his eyes on the music for the first time and there he was, with the entire score at his fingertips. While I, who had worked on it the entire trip knew little more than my part."[7]

The cellist was still fighting a recurring illness while trying to learn the new compositions, leaving no time to recuperate before his first rehearsal with Toscanini:

> I looked forward to the [Atlantic] crossing, not only because I needed rest, but because it would give me an opportunity to practice. But, as luck would have it, a crippling cold and fever, crowned by seasickness, put me into bed and kept me there with the manuscript of the Castelnuovo-Tedesco Concerto throughout the long voyage.
> Still shaky, the instant I entered my hotel room in New York I received a telephone call from Maestro Toscanini.
> "What have you been doing all this time?" he said impatiently. "Your boat landed hours ago. Hurry, I am waiting for you."
> Soon I faced Maestro at the Astor Hotel, where he lived. Rosy-cheeked, he hurried me to take the cello out of the case and to start rehearsing. He spoke with agitation of the stupidity of conductors and soloists and their habit of playing everything in a wrong tempo. This was his favorite topic and I did not expect him to stop so abruptly. He moved toward me, closer and closer, until his face almost touched mine. He stared at me scrutinizingly with his near-

blind eyes, as if I were a terrible misprint in a score. He twisted his mustache, shook his head, and said, "Bad, very bad. Hemorrhoids again? Didn't you try the medicine I gave you in Milano? It helped Puccini. Your face is green," he concluded gravely.

Maestro at the piano, we began the concerto. Glancing at his score, I noticed that the cello part was virtually covered with penciled fingerings and bowings. No cellist except me had seen the concerto. Surprised, I asked who had made the markings.

"I did," said Maestro.

"Why?"

"Did you forget I was a cellist?" he said, smiling.

"One does hear fingerings and bowings, and I wanted to know if yours would be the same as mine."

Maestro banged on the piano in a true Kapellmeister manner. He spoke and he sang, and his spontaneity and vigor carried me away. By the end of our long and exhilarating session I had miraculously regained my strength, and I returned to the hotel in an exuberant frame of mind.

Piatigorsky recalled sharing the green room with the maestro before a performance. The conductor quickly paced the room, cursing and mumbling to himself. It was impossible for Piatigorsky to warm up and concentrate, and he stopped practicing. Toscanini looked at him and said, "You are no good, I am no good" and continued to pace. Piatigorsky, at wit's end, finally begged, "Please Maestro, I will be a complete wreck." At that moment Toscanini was called to begin the overture. Piatigorsky tried to ignore the conductor's assessment. Maestro returned to the wings, about to walk out with Piatigorsky, who said, "We *are* no good. But the others are worse. Come on, *caro*, let's go."[8]

The following is an anecdote regarding the dedication of the concerto:

> Last Spring Arturo Toscanini and Gregor Piatigorsky, noted Russian 'cellist, were discussing Mario Castelnuovo-Tedesco's 'cello concerto. The white-haired Philharmonic-Symphony conductor asked the Russian musician if he knew whom the composer had authorized to play the new concerto. The 'cellist, who firmly disapproves of the practice of giving one performer exclusive rights to a piece of music, deliberately replied that anyone could perform it.
>
> Just to be certain, Toscanini wrote the 40-year-old Italian composer. He got a vigorous answer: Castelnuovo-Tedesco wrote the concerto specifically for Piatigorsky; would allow no one but the Russian to play it. Promptly Toscanini summoned Piatigorsky.
>
> "You," the conductor chuckled, "are a bad liar."

The anecdote went on to describe the new work's reception and the rest of his tour:

> Consequently at the world premiere of the concerto last week, Mr. Piatigorsky appeared as soloist with the New York Philharmonic-Symphony under Toscanini. New Yorkers, pleased by the Russian's virtuosity, rejoiced that Piatigorsky had to give in.
>
> Critics varied in their reaction. Some dismissed the tuneful concerto as cheap. Others claimed it possessed a delightful lyric value. The slow movement won the greatest praise.
>
> The 'cellist leads an active life. Since early fall he has performed in most of the European capitals. During his present American coast-to-coast tour which ends in April, he will present three new 'cello compositions [in addition to Castelnuovo-Tedesco and Berezowski]. Later in the tour, the 'cellist will present "Italian Suite" by Igor Stravinsky and himself.[9]

Piatigorsky and Toscanini met many times on Atlantic crossings. Once Piatigorsky lured the conductor into his cabin and persuaded him to play his cello, but Toscanini did nothing but tune repeatedly "until it was time for lunch, so I never heard him play the cello. I wonder if there's anyone who heard him." Toscanini on the other hand was the accompanist for his teacher, Professor Carini in Palma, and remembered all the standard material by Romberg, Grutzmacher and Goltermann. He loved to play it and would command Piatigorsky, "Now let's play!"

The cellist performed the concerto several times in Europe where its second movement was singled out as particularly beautiful. Castelnuovo-Tedesco wrote many other works for Piatigorsky. One of those published is the delightful *Greeting Card*, Op.170/3, based upon the name Gregor Piatigorsky.[10] Another outstanding piece is the *Toccata* from 1935,[11] which was presented during several seasons. Piatigorsky recalled the *Toccata*'s premiere with pianist Pierre Luboshutz:

> I called Pierre from Boston.
> "As you know," I said, "the only new piece we play in Cleveland is the Toccata by Castelnuovo-Tedesco. You have the manuscript. There will be very little time for rehearsals. Please work on it."
> "What do you mean?" cried Pierre. "I know the piece — do you know it?"
> In New York I went to Luboshutz's without delay. We had not seen each other for a long time, and there was much to tell to bring us up to date. Eventually we began to rehearse. We worried about not having enough time to work on the new piece. But after we played the Toccata through and, encouraged, were in the mood to work, Genia[12] announced that dinner was ready.
> The view on the table was breathtaking. All thoughts of the toccata vanished. "Our train leaves at ten — we have sleeping accommodations — arriving tomorrow early in the morning. We have nothing to do there until the concert in the evening — right?" We drank a toast to a long rehearsal in Cleveland and a successful tour.
> The first half of the program went very well, and an atmosphere of great warmth awaited us for the first performance of the Toccata in the United States. We began with vigor, and the first fifty bars promised a good performance, when my memory suddenly went astray. I invented as I went along, trying to stay in the style of the music. Pierre turned his pages back and forth, but, realizing that what I was playing was not in the score, he finally discarded the music and, like myself, played by heart. Meanwhile, absorbed with many interesting ideas and harmonies, I saw an opportunity for a fugato. Pierre's talent, or fear, made him match my inventions. The fugato led us gradually to the first theme, but this time, instead of "energico," it was in a lyrical mood. We elaborated on it, using some new material. We must have liked it very much, for we clung to it for a long while. It was a charming dialogue between the two instruments, and it was hard for us to part from it, but we had to. We gradually built up to a great climax that led straight back to the beginning of the piece. Oh, what a joy — after the fiftieth bar I knew exactly the continuation. But now it was Pierre who did not! There was no choice. We had to improvise. The perspiration ran down my face and dropped on the fingerboard and on my cello.
> Pierre shook his head. His hair fell over his forehead and his eyes. He swayed and groaned and encouraged me to still-greater efforts. It was something of a coda now, a great lead to the triumphal conclusion. Faster, stronger, still faster we stormed, until breathtakingly the composition was brought to a finish.
> Exhausted, we responded to the applause. Artur Rodzinski[13] came to see us after the concert. He and Mr. Eyle, the concertmaster of the Cleveland Symphony, took us to the station. "The Toccata," they said, "was very impressive."[14]

Piatigorsky and Luboshutz performed many times together, and later that season appeared in a shared recital with Andres Segovia at Town Hall in New York, sponsored by the Beethoven Association.[15]

Nikolai Berezowski

Nikolai ("Kolya") Berezowski was one of Piatigorsky's oldest friends, having been one of the Bolshoi Theatre's concertmasters. In 1928, the two musicians were reunited briefly in Berlin. The composer's wife recalled the moment: "The two men embraced and kissed each other with Russian warmth and gusto.... His exuberant temperament, vivid imagination and innate sense of 'theatre' make him a lively companion.... I was impressed by the complete frankness with which both Grisha and Nicky discussed the vicissitudes of their careers; neither showed the slightest reluctance in relating the less glamorous periods."[16]

Like many of his Russian countrymen, Berezowski established himself in New York. There, he studied composition with Rubin Goldmark, and became a member of the New York Philharmonic. His talent for composition was soon recognized, and beginning in 1930 his compositions enjoyed steady attention.[17] Koussevitzky became interested in the gifted young Russian composer, and he presented several of his works. With Koussevitzky's attention to his music and Piatigorsky's closeness to both musicians, a cello concerto was inevitable. The piece, *Concerto Lirico*, was completed in 1934 and premiered on February 22, 1935, in Boston.

Piatigorsky had some concern about mastering both the Berezowski and Castelnuovo-Tedesco concertos simultaneously, but Berezowski's piece caused extra stress. Letters to Koussevitzky reveal a worried Piatigorsky: "Regarding Kolya's Concerto, the situation is getting considerably more serious! I don't have the score yet, and I will undoubtedly need to work on it (on the trains!!!) so that it will be ready in such a short time!! I hope that I will learn it, the more so that the music is wonderful!! I will try — I hope that my attempts will meet with success!!"[18]

Piatigorsky wrote to the composer on November 8 1934: "So I still don't know the piece at all. I am hoping to receive the music around November 20th from [Gavriil] Paichadze![19] No matter what, I really want to play that concerto. But will I be able to learn it??!! When?? In order for you to understand my worries about this whole thing, I am attaching a schedule of my concerts before Boston's performance."[20] The cellist wrote the following to Koussevitzky on December 16 1934: "Kolya's concerto really worries me.... I still don't know it by heart.... I'm afraid to perform it!! The Castelnuovo-Tedesco concerto I also don't know by heart, but it concerns me much less, despite the fact that there will be almost no time to practice!"

A further letter to Koussevitzky was written while Piatigorsky was onboard the S.S. *Manhattan*, January 25 1935:

> My near and dear Sergei Aleksandrovich,
>   I was counting on not only getting some rest after such incredible work in Europe, but also hoped to have time to learn the Berezowski Concerto. Here is how it turned out: Right before departure, I got a cold, and here I have been lying for six days with a high fever and a headache! I am alone and in complete despair! Will I be in any shape to play Kolya's concerto? By sweat, yes! But I want to, and I must, play it by heart.

Koussevitzky, undaunted, reminds Piatigorsky of his obligation: "As far as the Berezowski Concerto goes, Kolya wrote it for you and was planning on you performing it. Dozens of cellists have asked him if they could premiere it and he refused them all because he had you in mind."[21]

The cellist had cause to be worried about the premiere, not in terms of his own playing, but because of the composer's sloppy preparation of the performance materials. As Piatigorsky remembered it:

> At noon I was on my way to Grand Central Terminal. I confess that to leave New York and enter the old Pullman car was a relief. It felt good to unload myself from Castelnuovo-Tedesco and to leave the Berezowski Concerto for a while at the bottom of my suitcase. There were several engagements to fulfill, and by the time I came to Boston I had learned the Concerto

Lirico and looked forward to hearing it with the orchestra. I was happy to be with the Koussevitzkys and to stay in the room they always kept ready for me in their house.

At the first rehearsal, confusion ran amok, and, with no composer present, the result was dismal:

> What a morning! Mistakes in the parts and in the score seemed unsolvable. So were the tempi and the dynamics.... The long rehearsal was like swimming in muddy waters. I finally lost my tact and control of myself. It is painful to recall my behavior and my rage and my walking off the stage, swearing and insulting everyone. But above all, I am ashamed of having hurt Sergei Alexandrovich. This was a black morning of my career, and only Koussevitzky's forgiveness and understanding made it possible to go on with the rehearsals and concerts.[22]

The concerts were successful, but the experience left the cellist unwilling to play it beyond 1935. The following review was representative:

> The concert given by the Boston Symphony Orchestra, Serge Koussevitzky conductor, offered as a novelty the concerto for violoncello by Nicholai Berezowski, with Gregor Piatigorsky as soloist....
>
> Mr. Berezowski's concerto grew from a kind of Passacaglia[23] for 'cello and orchestra to a concerto in one movement. The work has admirable continence of proportion and effect. With a finely wrought orchestral score it remains a concerto for the 'cello, with the proper balances. Only once is the orchestra fully released and this passage occurs as an inevitable development of the music thought and not as a flashy interlude between display passages for the solo instrument. Mr. Piatigorsky gave his best to the music, which was heard with great attention and interest.[24]

1935–1937: Tours, Ravel and Bartók, Publishing, Film, Radio and Early Television

While touring Europe, Piatigorsky observed firsthand the growing Nazi threat and became anxious to return to the United States. Despite his Jewish origin, travel was not entirely restricted in 1935. However, knowledge of the Nuremburg Laws no doubt signaled disaster; those who could, left Germany. When German citizenship of Jews was revoked in November,[25] travel became increasingly difficult. On November 12, 1935, Piatigorsky wrote to Koussevitzky:

> Up to this point I have played 16 concerts. I was in England, Holland, Switzerland, Austria, Hungary, Rumania, and Czechoslovakia. Tomorrow I'm playing here; then I'll go to Göteborg, Copenhagen, England, France, and Italy. But whether there will be Spain is unknown ... just as it is unknown whether I will be able to go to America on the *Rex*, they say the Italians are planning to convert the passenger steamship to a military one.
>
> Everywhere in Europe there is a sense of alarm, and the preparations for war can be felt. And in Germany (I had to cross practically all of Germany several times), everything simply positively reminds one of a military camp! Rifles, soldiers, sailors everywhere — their faces are savage and resolute. You can't get butter in the restaurants, and in general the products are "ersatz," like in wartime. Lovely! I would like to already be in America, there it's at least peaceful and people complain less. But the main thing, of course, is that you are there!
>
> I am so tired of being homeless and missing my family [the Koussevitzkys], would that at least Drolbka [their dog] were with me! I would take care of him and cover him up and take him out for walks! I will get to America only in early January — where and when my first concert will be, I still don't know, but I hope that as soon as I arrive I will be able to see you.

> I can't tell you anything interesting about musical life in Europe, since beside myself I haven't heard anybody or anything.
>
> In Berlin the following "heroes" will be performing in November: Thomas Beecham, Cassadó, Gieseking, and ... Chaliapin!!! Toscanini is evidently conducting, besides Vienna and Paris, in Monte Carlo.[26]

Piatigorsky played approximately one hundred concerts in the 1935-36 season, but one concert stood out as a sentimental favorite. Prior to Piatigorsky's annual Chicago Symphony appearance (March 19 and 20, 1936), he asked conductor Frederick Stock to change the program order for personal reasons:

> Mr. Piatigorsky is always a favorite here and his playing on this occasion quite surpassed all his previous records. His account of the solo in Strauss' *Don Quixote* was in the loftiest imaginable vein of poetry and whimsicality. Supported by Mr. Stock's best efforts, the interpretation was one long to be remembered. An equally superb account of the Saint-Saëns Concerto concluded the program.
>
> It had been Mr. Stock's original intention to end with Liszt's *Tasso*, but after the intermission he announced that Mr. Piatigorsky would play the concerto last for reasons he himself would reveal. Silencing the applause which followed the concerto, Mr. Piatigorsky told the audience that this day was the [fifteenth] anniversary of his and Mischa Mischakoff's escape from revolution-torn Russia and that they wished properly to observe the event. Whereupon Mr. Mischakoff arose from the concertmaster's desk and joined Mr. Piatigorsky in a Handel *Chaconne* [i.e., Handel-Halvorsen's *Passacaglia*] for violin and cello, one of the works which enabled them to earn their living as street musicians after they had escaped from their homeland.[27]

Piatigorsky also gave a series of Grotrian Hall recitals in the fall of 1935 which included the London premiere of the Shostakovich Sonata on October 5. The Reich's official emblem was repeatedly stamped throughout his Nansen passport, indicating the inefficient crisscrossing his tours required. He sometimes gave concerts just weeks apart in the same city, making travel even more complex with the endless restrictions his Nansen created.

A notable concert took place on one of his returns to Budapest when he joined violinist Erica Morini and composer-pianist Ernst von Dohnanyi to perform the Beethoven Triple Concerto. The composer had recently been appointed director of the Budapest Academy, and for this concert conducted from the keyboard.[28] Dohnanyi and Piatigorsky played recitals together in the 1930s as well.

Piatigorsky appeared with all of the knighted British conductors, some of whom now almost seem to be from the ancient past: Sir Henry Wood, Sir Hamilton Hardy, Sir Landon Ronald, but most often, Sir Thomas Beecham. With the latter the cellist met his match at verbal ability, and remembered: "I played with Beecham a great many times. It was always very gay ... a very witty man—always made me laugh. They used to say, "I understand that Sir Thomas Beecham is going to conduct as well as talk." Yes, in London we used to call him Sir Thomas Speecham."[29] Beecham championed the works of Frederick Delius and did all he could to promote his music. He brought Piatigorsky into the fold:

> I found in my hotel room an urgent message from Sir Thomas Beecham to meet with him. Resplendent in his dressing gown, he met me warmly at the entrance of his attractive flat. Caressing his beard, he led me to the music room and offered me a glass of Bristol milk [a Spanish blend of sherry]. When I said I did not know what it was, I saw shock in his eyes. I thought the drink was delicious. He drank it extremely slowly, explaining that it gives him time when pressed for time. "We lead awfully crowded lives," he said, probably incorporating me and other musicians. He got up, still nursing his drink and casually walking to the piano, reached to the middle heap of music spread on the top and handed it to me. I saw the

TELEVISION PROGRAMMES

FRIDAY MAY 28 AND **SATURDAY** MAY 29 : VISION 45 Mc/s SOUND 41.5 Mc/s

GREER GARSON will be seen with Campbell Gullan in scenes from *The School for Scandal* on Friday

Friday

3.0 STARLIGHT
BILLIE HOUSTON
and
NINA DEVITT

Both these artists have appeared in television programmes before, but last Tuesday was the first time they had appeared together. Billie Houston, the 'boy' of the famous Houston Sisters, teamed up with Nina Devitt early this year, and wherever they have performed they have been given a tremendous reception. Radio listeners will remember their amusing patter and songs in a Music-Hall programme on April 24.

3.5 POLO
PONIES AND PLAYERS
from the Hurlingham Club
Introduced by Colonel J. Gannon

3.20 BRITISH MOVIETONEWS

3.30 PLAY PARADE
GREER GARSON
and
CAMPBELL GULLAN
in scenes from
'The School for Scandal'
by Richard Brinsley Sheridan
with
Denis Blakelock and Earle Grey
Produced by
George More O'Ferrall

4.0 CLOSE

9.0 STARLIGHT
HILDEGARDE

9.15 PIATIGORSKY
(violoncello)
with
The BBC Television Orchestra
Leader, Boris Pecker
Conductor, Hyam Greenbaum

Gregor Piatigorsky was born about thirty years ago at Ekaterinoslav, Russia. He studied first the violin and then the 'cello at Moscow Conservatoire; his progress was so extraordinary that at the age of fifteen he had risen to the rank of first 'cellist of the Imperial Opera in Moscow. A year or two later he was in Berlin competing for the post of first 'cellist with the Berlin Philharmonic Orchestra, conducted by Furtwängler. He secured this post; a most extraordinary achievement for a youth of twenty. It was not long, however, before he decided to devote himself entirely to solo work, and since that time has appeared with almost every orchestra of distinction in Europe and America.

9.35 GAUMONT BRITISH NEWS

9.45 FRIENDS FROM THE ZOO
introduced by
David Seth-Smith and their Keepers

Today the Zoological Society is holding a Coronation Party. Television sets have been installed so that the guests, who come from the Dominions, can enjoy this programme.

10.0 CLOSE

Saturday

3.0 OLIVER WAKEFIELD
The Voice of Inexperience

Once again the rather incoherent but very debonair Oliver Wakefield will give a speech before the television camera. This is probably his last appearance at Alexandra Palace before leaving for New York to broadcast and perform at the Rainbow Room. He will be back in England, however, before the autumn.

Henry Hall first introduced him to radio listeners in 'Henry Hall's Hour'. He was born in Mahlbatini, Zululand, and came to England to join Ben Greet's company. Then followed nine months with the Lena Ashwell Players; a year at the Royal Academy of Dramatic Art (at which he won a scholarship); work with Matheson Lang; work with Gladys Cooper's company in *The Sacred Flame*; a part in *On the Spot*; a job as understudy to Frank Lawton in *Michael and Mary*; and non-stop Variety. He began broadcasting in America in 1932, appearing with celebrities like Rudy Vallée, Paul Whiteman, Leo Reismann, Ray Noble, and Guy Lombardo. It was Rudy Vallée, he says, who gave him his first big chance in America.

3.10 FILM CARTOON
This ten-minute item will be a Walt Disney production—either a Mickey Mouse or a Silly Symphony cartoon.

PIATIGORSKY, the famous Russian 'cellist, will give a recital with the BBC Television Orchestra on Friday night

JUNE CLYDE, the American film actress, takes part in the second edition of *Pasquinade* on Saturday afternoon

3.20 PASQUINADE
No. 2
Lyrics and sketches by John Cousins and Stephen Clarkson
Music by John Gardner
The cast includes:
June Clyde
Richard Ainley
Antonia Brough
Peter Bull
The BBC Television Orchestra
Conductor, Hyam Greenbaum
Produced by Dallas Bower

3.45 NATIONAL CYCLING FESTIVAL
The start of the Cycle Road Race in Alexandra Park

The Cycle Road Race is one of the main events of the National Cycling Festival. Competitors, made up of four separate ranks of eight, will be seen pedalling furiously round the carriage-way surrounding the building. Many circuits are made, each one taking about four minutes to complete by fast-moving racing cyclists.

4.0 CLOSE

9.0 MR. GILLIE POTTER
Punch and Judex
Mr. Potter's Joyous Judicial Joke

9.15 BRITISH MOVIETONEWS

9.25 DARTS AND SHOVE-HA'PENNY
A competition between rival teams of two well-known hostelries

9.35 LITTLE SHOW

10.0 CLOSE

First appearance on television, BBC, May 1937.

orchestral score of the Delius Double Concerto for violin and cello, and underneath it, the Cello Concerto.

"It's a beautiful mess," he said, "but a promise is a promise, and we had better do something with it worthy of the composer and a man I love so much. We must hurry with all changes and editing while poor sick and blind Delius is still alive."

Just a minute ago two casual people as if by some sudden jolt began looking for a stand —

Bartók Béla Piatigorsky Gregor
szonátaestje
Pénteken, 1937. dec. 10.-én.
este fél 9 órakor a Vigadóban
(Zongorabérlet III. est.)
Műsoron :
Beethoven: (C-dur). *Brahms:*
(e-moll). *Debussy* szonáták és
Bartók: Rapszódia
Jegyek 1—8 pengőig.

Recital with Bartók in Budapest, December 10, 1937.

undressing the cello before I had time to tune the cello and rosin my bow — to join him with furious sounds — Beecham banging on his piano and I squeaking on the cello.

Despite all that, I thought a few ideas of ours were valid and necessary. After a few hours of playing, discussing and writing, and making plans to meet again, we were both ready to have separate lunches.

With the door open and with the last handshake, never able to resist saying something witty or amusing said, "Never play for Delius the C Major prelude of Bach. The last time I saw him he had a visitor about whose fame he no idea [Casals], but who, wishing to make Delius pleasure, took his cello and played for him that prelude. Delius, bewildered, told me the story, 'Just imagine,' he said, 'the fellow came to play C major scales for me!'"

That evening I spent with Ivor Newton and with Delius' music again, whose sonata Ivor insisted to be on our program. He knew it well and his devotion, as the love of Beecham for him, I found quite contagious.[30]

A performance of Bloch's *Schelomo* with the Royal Philharmonic and Beecham was especially noted: "[O]n this occasion it was played as never before by Piatigorsky.... The rest of the program was pale by comparison."[31]

Premieres were usually featured on programs in larger cities, but he often gave a "premiere" on the road if he needed to get used to it. New recital works with piano were continually written for the cellist, and many were published, including those by Louis Vierne, Tibor Harsanyi, Castelnuovo-Tedesco, Isidor Achron and Alexander Tansman. He discovered Debussy's early *Intermezzo* (1882) in a music shop,[32] as well as baroque manuscripts, especially anonymous manuscripts tantalizingly presented, such as "An Unknown Sonata from the Court of Saxony."

The 1930s also saw the first publications of Piatigorsky's own transcriptions, arrangements, and compositions. The German firm Schott published a substantial series that included works by Bach, Scriabin, Lully, and Liadov. Though they were widely performed, his arrangements of Chopin's posthumous *Nocturne* in C# Minor and various movements

10th American season.

from Weber's Violin Sonatas, op. 10a, were particularly popular. He recorded them, as did other colleagues during the 78 rpm era (e.g., Fournier, Mainardi, Tortelier, and Nelsova). The so-called *Adagio and Rondo* is still standard cello repertoire, performed and recorded by many of the major soloists of the twentieth century, and is dedicated to Casals.

Soon after the Schott series appeared, the British firm of Chester brought out a succession of works by Mozart, Valensin and de Falla that Piatigorsky arranged, as well as the cellist's own composition, *Scherzo*. The de Falla pieces from *El Amor Brujo* are now basic repertoire and have also been extensively recorded.

Piatigorsky believed that miniature masterpieces relegated to obscurity, such as those for obsolete instruments or piano four-hands were candidates for resurrection (music "with a little dust on it"). He felt that the job of a transcriber should be straightforward, with little, if any, recomposing.

Since Mozart never completed anything for the cello, Piatigorsky appropriated several divertimenti by Mozart (written for two basset horns and bassoon), transcribed isolated movements, and retitled them "sonatinas."

Back in the United States, Piatigorsky stopped in Hollywood and visited the MGM studios and had at least one date with Joan Crawford.[33] With his good looks, he was given a successful screen test in 1935, but after the experience decided not to pursue it further.[34] He did, however, make several short concert films at the Paramount studios near Paris at this time. The films were produced by the writer-critic-composer Emile Vuillermoz[35] and distributed by the short-lived, Lyon-based Compagnie des Grands Artistes Internationaux (CGAI).[36] Only one of the shorts has survived and was issued: *Andante et Rondo*.[37] The production was uneven, and the editing inferior, yet it reveals Piatigorsky in youthful brilliance. Other artists also participating in the series were pianists Alfred Cortot and Alexander Brailowski, sopranos Elisabeth Schumann and Ninon Vallin, violinist Jacques Thibaud, and Serge Lifar with the ballet of the Paris Opera. Their productions fared much better,[38] while Piatigorsky's films were made at the end of the series run, during the decline of CGAI's financial base. Only Brailowski was paid for the filming, as he insisted on it before filming began. Piatigorsky, along with the rest of the participants, agreed to wait and share in the profits — which never materialized.

CGAI produced the shorts as alternative preludes to major films, rather than the usual newsreels or cartoons. In this regard, CGAI hoped to compete with Warner Brothers' Vitaphone series[39] in the U.S. In 1939 the producers released a compilation film, *The First Film Concert*, in which Piatigorsky and seven others were presented. The *New York Times* reviewer predictably attacked the concept: "As a musical program it is quite acceptable; as a screen musical program it is, with one or two exceptions, a singularly stilted and unimaginative film.... [P]arts of the program range in cinematic dullness from the posed concert-staged shots of Piatigorsky behind his cello and of Thibaud."[40] Another review was enthusiastic: "A fascinatingly fresh approach on the screen is revealed in "First Film Concert" ... [and] this French release is exactly what its title says, a "First Film Concert." Noted artists appear before the cameras unhampered by story details, photographed with close-ups not possible in the concert halls, or else enhanced by imaginative illustration of what the music seeks to convey."[41]

As a permanent resident of Paris by 1932, Piatigorsky again met Ravel. The composer knew of his performances of his Duo for violin and cello in 1928 with Szigeti[42] when the work was absolutely new, and of the Piano Trio's premiere in Moscow with Bekman-Shcherbina in 1920. Piatigorsky wanted to transcribe the composer's famous violin showpiece *Tzigane* and was happy that Ravel was receptive to the idea. The cellist completed his arrangement in 1935, and anxious for the composer's opinion, played it for him. Ravel was delighted with it, and was particularly complimentary of the opening cadenza. Surprised at such a remark, Piatigorsky asked him why he had not made a cello transcription himself. His response was typically droll: "Because I never saw a gypsy in the woods carrying a cello!"[43]

In October 1936, the cellist and Pavlovsky embarked on an intense world tour that began in Genoa and ended in Honolulu by way of Sumatra, Java, Celebes, Borneo, Manila, Hong Kong, Shanghai, and Japan. In Tokyo, he offered an impressive five-recital series that featured unusual repertoire. They included his transcription of Ravel's *Tzigane*, Bach's Sixth Suite, Schubert's *Arpeggione* Sonata, and his dazzling transcription of Paganini's *La Campanella*. The public warmly welcomed him: "The audiences were remarkably attentive and among the most receptive I have played for anywhere."[44]

Since Prince Kuni and the royal family were his hosts in Tokyo, Piatigorsky had little opportunity to meet many Japanese musicians. However, he did make a special effort to meet the celebrated blind composer and master koto player, Michio Miyagi (1894–1956), known as the "Father of Modern Koto Music." The composer fondly recalled the cellist's visit and later wrote of it:

> Learning that he [Piatigorsky] was looking for an Oriental musical composition, and particularly something purely Japanese which he could take back to Europe as a souvenir of his visit, I invited him to my house one day.
>
> While I was conducting him to my studio he suddenly halted before a gakudaiko (Japanese drum) and began to tap it as if to study its sound. Then he fingered a koto, a strange instrument that fascinated him.
>
> He seemed to be highly elated when I played two selections on the koto one of which was my own composition, *Haru no Umi* [The Sea in the Spring]. (I had given him the scores beforehand so that he followed my playing with keen interest.) After I had finished he said that he wanted to try the two compositions on his cello and that he wished to take them back to Europe to play for his audiences there. I felt extremely grateful and happy....
>
> Piatigorsky suddenly went to the corner of the studio ... [and] spotted my contrabass and began to play parts of the music I had given him. I rarely used the instrument and it even had a broken string, but when Piatigorsky began to play it, it produced a marvelous new

With the blind koto master, Michio Miyagi, 1936.

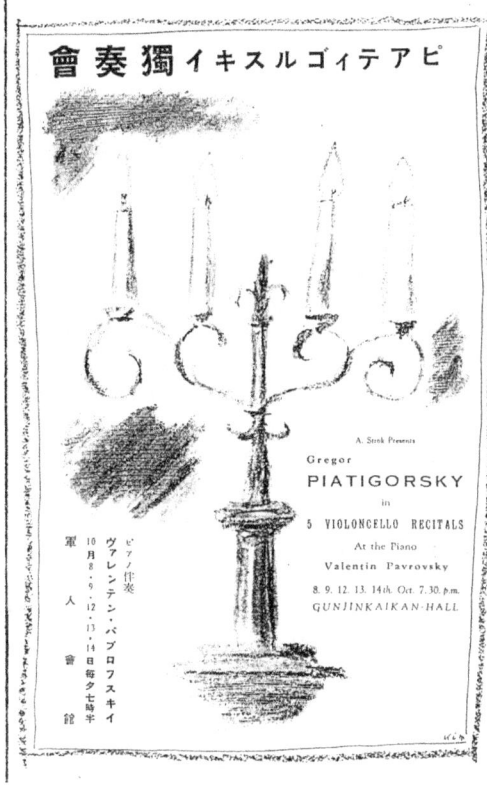

This page and the following two pages: Five recital series in Tokyo, 1936.

sound. And I began to wonder whether his mood when playing the instrument was not similar to that of the painters of old who, during their travels, had the habit of painting on the fusuma (paper sliding door) and the screens of the various inns in which they stayed to satisfy their spontaneous urge to draw.

I was once told that in olden times the masters of the Japanese art of fencing (kendo) considered every object around him as a weapon, and it seemed to me that Piatigorsky regarded all the musical instruments in my studio in a similar spirit. As I had devoted all my life to the koto, just one stroke of the bow by Piatigorsky enabled me to understand him.

Then I heard a scratching sound — somebody was writing. I asked the cellist's manager what it was, and he told me that Piatigorsky was [also] a poet and that he had the habit of writing his travel impressions in verse.

Before leaving, Piatigorsky told me the he was going to play my *Haru no Umi* at his farewell recital soon and asked me to be sure to attend. And just as he was about to leave, he again stopped in front of the drum and began to study its sound by trying to locate the corresponding one on the piano. The Japanese drum has a variety of pitches mixed together and they cannot be distinguished as easily as those of the Western timpani. Even Piatigorsky couldn't pin them down, and with a "tut-tut" he gave up and left.

Some days later I went to his farewell recital at the Hibya Public Hall to hear him for the first time. And he so surprised me with his marvelous skill and even now I can still feel his masterfulness. Just before my *Haru no Umi* he played the *Dance of Terror* by de Falla and it was such an interesting piece and so beautifully played that the audience applauded him enthusiastically. I began to feel worried because his next number, my composition, would

SECOND EVENING PROGRAMME

Fri. 9th. Oct.

1. Sonata in D minor .... Andrea Caporale
   Largo—Allegro—Adagio—Allegro deciso
2. Suite in C major (for violoncello alone) .... B a c h
   Prelude
   Allemande
   Courante
   Sarabande
   Bourrée I
   Bourrée II
   Gigue
3. Sonatine in A major .... W e b e r
   Siciliano—Theme with variations

— *Intermission* —

4. Toccata .... Castelnuovo-Tedesco
   Introduzione—Aria and Finale (First Performance)
5. Sicilienne .... M. T. De Paradis
   Allegretto grazioso .... Schubert
   Prélude .... Debussy
   Zapateado .... Sarasate

THIRD EVENING PROGRAMME

Mon. 12th. Oct.

1. Sonata .... Tessarini
   Largo—Allegro vivace
2. Sonata Op. 102 .... Beethoven
   Andante
   Allegro vivace
   Adagio
   Allegro vivace
3. "Arpeggione" Sonata, in A minor .... S c h u b e r t
   Allegro moderato
   Adagio
   Allegretto

— *Intermission* —

4. Fantasie—Stuecke .... Schumann
   Habanera .... R a v e l
   Papillons .... F a u r é
   Valse sentimentale .... Tschaikowsky
   Russian Dance .... L i a d o f f

第 二 夜 曲 目
10月9日（金）

1. 奏 鳴 曲 ニ短調 .... カポラール
   ラルゴ－アレグロ－アダヂオ－アレグロ デシソ
2. 組 曲 ハ長調 .... バッハ
   プレリュード
   アルマンド
   クーランテ
   サラバンド
   ブレー I
   ブレー II
   ジーグ
3. 奏鳴曲 イ長調 .... ウエバア
   シシリアー 主題に據る變奏曲

— 休 憩 —

4. トッカータ .... カステルヌオーヴオ・テデスコ
   イントロデユヨン－アリア ビ フィナーレ（初演）
5. ④ シシリアンヌ .... パラデイス
   ⑥ アレグレット・グラツイオーソ .... シューベート
   ⓒ 前 奏 曲 .... デビユッシイ
   ⓓ サパテアード .... サラサーテ

曲目多少の御變擾め御承知下さい

第 三 夜 曲 目
10月12日（月）

1. 奏 鳴 曲 .... テッサリーニ
   ラルゴ アレグロ ヴィヴアチエ
2. 奏 鳴 曲 作品一〇二 .... ベートーヴエン
   アンダンテ
   アレグロ ヴィヴアチエ
   アダヂオ
   アレグロ ヴィヴアチエ
3. 奏鳴曲 "アルペヂオネ" イ短調 .... シューバート
   アレグロ モデラート
   アダヂオ
   アレグレット

— 休 憩 —

4. ④ 幻 想 曲 .... シューマン
   ⑥ ハバネラ .... ラヴエル
   ⓒ 胡 蝶 .... フォーレ
   ⓓ 感傷的圓舞曲 .... チヤイコフスキイ
   ⓔ 露西亞舞曲 .... リヤドフ

曲目多少の御變擾め御承知下さい

offer no comparison. But my fears were unfounded, for Piatigorsky played it well and beautifully. In his skilled hands my humble composition became pregnant with life.

When the performance ended I went backstage to thank him, but when I reached his dressing room, there was great turmoil outside the door. It was congested with autograph seekers, and if the door was opened even a little, people shoved their way in like an avalanche. I was finally able to work my way through the crowd, and when the door was opened to allow me in, tens of other people also slipped in and barraged Piatigorsky, and I wasn't able to properly greet him. Though we were unable to speak to each other, I nevertheless am exceedingly happy because through music our hearts understood.[45]

As an encore to his appearance with the NHK Symphony of the Japan Broadcasting Corporation, Piatigorsky again performed Miyagi's signature composition, accompanied by the orchestra and its new conductor fresh from Berlin and the Kulturbund, Joseph Rosenstock. The work had been especially orchestrated for the occasion.[46]

Before his Asian tour, Chaliapin insisted that Piatigorsky accept any recording contracts offered by the Japanese, as they were remarkably lucrative.[47] The well over six-foot singer was also adamant that Piatigorsky have a suit made by his Japanese tailor. Upon seeing Piatigorsky's six foot three and a half inch height, the tailor cried out, "All Russians must be giants!" as he reached for a ladder.[48]

FOURTH EVENING PROGRAMME

Tues. 13th. Oct.

1. Toccata .... Frescobaldi
2. Variations on Theme of Mozart .... Beethoven
3. Concert No. 1. in A minor Op. 33 .... St. Saens
   Allegro non troppo
   Allegretto con moto
   Come prima

— *Intermission* —

4. Sonata in C major .... Weber
   Allegro—Largo—Polacca
5. Nocturne .... Lily Boulanger
   Minuette .... Debussy
   Poème .... Skriabin
   Hopak .... Moussorgsky

FIFTH EVENING PROGRAMME

Wednes. 14th. Oct.

1. Sonata in A major .... Boccherini
   Adagio—Allegro
2. Suite in D major (for Violoncello alone) ..... Bach
   Prelude
   Allemande
   Courante
   Sarabande
   Gavotte I
   Gavotte II
   Gigue
3. Sonatina .... Mozart
   Andante—Minuette—Rondo

— *Intermission* —

4. Suite Italienne .... Stravinsky
   Aria—Tarantella—Serenate e Finale
5. Etude .... Skriabin
   Plaisanterie .... Karjansky
   En Sourdine .... Debussy
   Dance de Feu .... De Falla

第 四 夜 曲 目
10 月 13 日（火）

1. トッカータ .... フレスコバルデイ
2. 變奏曲 モーツアルトの主題歌による ...... ベートーヴエン
3. 協奏曲 第一 イ短調 作品三三 .... サン・サーンス
   アレグロ ノン トロツポ
   アレグレット コン モト
   コム プリマ

— 休 憩 —

4. 奏鳴曲 ハ長調 .... ウエバア
   アレグロ—ラルゴ—ポリカ
5. ㋑ 夜 想 曲 .... リリー・ブランジエ
   ㋺ ミヌエット .... デビュッシイ
   ㋩ 詩 .... スクリアビン
   ㋥ ゴパック .... ムソルグスキイ

曲目多少の御變更豫め御承知下さい

第 五 夜 曲 目
10 月 14 日（木）

1. 奏 鳴 曲 イ長調 .... ボツケリーニ
   アダジオ—アレグロ （無伴奏）
2. 組 曲 ニ長調 .... バ ッ ハ
   プレリュード
   アルマンド
   クーランテ
   サラバンド
   ガボット I
   ガボット II
   ヂーグ
3. 小奏鳴曲 .... モツアルト
   アンダンテ ミヌエット ロンド

— 休 憩 —

4. 伊太利組曲 .... ストラビンスキイ
   アリア—タランテラ—セレナーテ エ フイナーレ
5. ㋑ 練 習 曲 .... スクリアビン
   ㋺ プレザントリ .... カルヴアンスキイ
   ㋩ エンソールデイン .... デビュッシイ
   ㋥ 火 の 踊 り .... デ・フアラ

曲目多少の御變更豫め御承知下さい

On his way back to the United States, Piatigorsky stopped in Honolulu for a concert. An interviewer later commented about his thoughtful policy towards concert organizations during the Depression: "Although Piatigorsky is one of the most successful artists in the profession, his first consideration is that no one who has worked for his concerts shall suffer any pecuniary loss. It is a credo, which he has adopted and maintained throughout the nine years he has been before the public. This is in marked contrast to many who enjoy prosperity at the expense of the producers, demanding and receiving their pound of flesh." When asked his opinion of their concert hall, Piatigorsky gave the only politically correct answer: "There are only two kinds of concert halls. Full and empty. When full, the acoustics are always good. When empty, they are bad."[49]

Piatigorsky regularly performed on the radio in symphonic and recital broadcasts, but apparently first spoke with host Bing Crosby on the *Kraft Music Hall* program in its first season. Scripts prepared for the cellist had to be scrapped because his English was limited and difficult to understand with his thick Russian accent. Piatigorsky was also uncomfortable because of the show's lowbrow humor, and the "selling" of great music through commercial sponsorship. Still, he knew that millions of listeners would hear the cello for the first time — and spreading the beauty of music and the cello to as many people as possible was his fundamental goal.

Little did Piatigorsky know that Crosby did more for classical music than anyone else in the media at that time. By presenting its stars in an informal, imaginary living room, Crosby easily mingled the icons of cinema, along with many elusive concert artists one would not associate with radio, including basso Chaliapin, and pianists Mischa Levitski and Josef Lhevinne. As the *New York Post* noted, "Mr. Crosby presents them not as something that the audience ought to like but as something the audience will like."[50] Piatigorsky remembered:

> When the "artistic" directors from the radio approached me to discuss the program, I was so naive that I suggested to them to play a Bach Suite, or a Haydn concerto with a chamber orchestra. The "artistic" directors looked at me with bewilderment and asked me to explain to them who these gentlemen were, whose composition I planned to perform, and how long the pieces would last.
>
> After my conscientious reply I heard loud, sidesplitting laughter. "Ha Ha Ha! That's a good one! He's going to play Bach for a half-hour! Ha Ha!"
>
> When they were convinced that I was not joking at all [they] began to explain — I should play no more than 3 to 4 minutes [at a time], and more important is the conversation with the star.[51]

He participated on the Kraft program with limited banter. The show consisted of the usual hodgepodge, with Piatigorsky appearing after hillbilly comic Bob Burns performed a bazooka[52] solo entitled "You've Got to Quit Kickin' My Dog Around — in G." The chitchat began:

> CROSBY: Pat, as he is known to some of his colleagues, is perhaps the top seeded cello player of the world today.... [H]e has played with nearly every ace symphony orchestra in the music industry and is here direct from New York via Europe, India and Japan....
> [*Piatigorsky performs Tchaikovsky's Valse Sentimentale*]
> CROSBY: Bravo, Piatigorsky. You can be captain of my cello team any time you want to put on the uniform.
> PIATIGORSKY: All I understood of what you said was "bravo." Thank you.
> CROSBY: I doubt if any of our clients have attended cello recitals in Japan or India lately. How does the audience dress in, let's say, Japan?
> PIATIGORSKY: Kimonos.
> CROSBY: How about in India?
> PIATIGORSKY: Towels.
> CROSBY: Sounds like very décolleté audiences.
> PIATIGORSKY: They are great lovers of music.
> CROSBY: And so are we. As an encore Gregor Piatigorsky plays "Zapateado" by Sarasate. Incidentally, "Zapateado" or "The Shoemaker" was originally written as a violin showpiece. And when you can locate a fellow who's willing to swing it on the cello, you're a sucker not to have him do it."[53]

Piatigorsky received a parting gift, a substantial block of Kraft cheese, which proved difficult to carry back to the hotel.

As the 1937 season's tour resumed in Europe, the 40th anniversary commemorating Brahms' death was observed, especially in Vienna. As part of the observance, Piatigorsky and Erica Morini performed the Double Concerto over Austrian radio with Oswald Kabasta and the Vienna Symphony in April.

Several years before commercial television transmission was launched in the U.S., the BBC in London was well on their way with the experiment. Among the very first BBC Television broadcasts was the coronation of King George VI, on May 12, 1937. Two weeks later a concert was transmitted from Alexandria Palace on May 28 with Piatigorsky performing the Haydn Concerto. This was among the first concerts ever broadcasted. "I volunteered to perform on it without fee. I had to wear a bright jacket, as did everyone in the orchestra, and we played under such a bright and hot light that we all almost melted away. I tried to locate someone in London who had watched the performance, but no one had. No wonder — there were no television sets!"[54] Most Londoners watched at various "Radiolympia," i.e., broadcast centers placed in public areas for viewing the exciting new technology. Those early telecasts ran for two hours a day: 3:00–4:00 P.M. and 9:00–10:00 P.M. Legendary artists participated in those early years and included Schnabel, Cortot, Neveu, Spalding, Primrose, and Tertis.

BARTÓK

When Piatigorsky was asked what his favorite recital was, his answer came without hesitation: "the one with Bartók." In that performance he felt joy and completeness with the composer, an experience that was unforgettable:

> I completed an International Celebrity tour in England, gave three recitals in London with Ivor Newton and a concert with orchestra with Sir Landon Ronald, and then went to Budapest for a concert with Bela Bartók. Having little time for rehearsal, he asked me to come straight from the station to his home.
>
> What a relief and pleasure it was to see him. He asked about my journey and my tour and wanted to know if I would like to rehearse first and rest later. He spoke of Hungarian folk music and of a composition he was working on, and played a few excerpts on the piano from the manuscript. His soft hands made music as strong as his face, as penetrating as his eyes, and yet as delicate as his frail body. We rehearsed, and during lunch we agreed that we had really not rehearsed at all but just played, and when we repeated anything it was merely to give us the pleasure of playing once more. In the afternoon we went through the program, which consisted of the E Minor Brahms Sonata, Beethoven's Sonata in C Major, the D Major Cello Suite by Bach, the Sonata by Debussy, and the Rhapsody by Bartók. It was wonderful to play and to be with him.[55]

Musical America magazine, 1939.

The *Chesterian* reviewed their appearance in Budapest, December 10, 1937:

> It surely is an unparalled case, this Bartók who is now one of the finest pianists of our time. For he has recently brought his technique up to every requirement, and does not as one could expect from so eminent and individual composer, specialize on his own works, but played at a Sonata recital with Piatigorsky where his own marvelous Rhapsody was placed between Beethoven and Debussy, only the highest admiration can be expressed.[56]

Another review was rather devotional of Bartók as the musical hero of Budapest. It is significant that they encored the Brahms rather than the Bartók *Rhapsody*:

> Bela Bartók and Gregor Piatigorski right in the opening piece of their piano-cello recital, in Beethoven's last sonata in C major, lead [sic] the audience of music connoisseurs crowding the Vigado to the highest pinnacle of Beethoven-playing and generally speaking of musical interpretation.
>
> When we talk about pinnacle, we obviously mean Bartók's piano playing, though Piatigorski, who is a cellist with virtuosic technique and a grand tone ... nicely adapted to the grand concept of Bartók, by voicing the cello part with brilliant instrumental mastery.
>
> In the Rhapsody that followed, the internally boiling, free forces of impulse, passion and emotion were built into a strictly contained union. What other work could not be better observed than in the Rhapsody?! The composer casts a musical bronze of poetic concept in a folksy, instrumental style that reflects improvisation, freshness, capricious changeability and sudden inspiration.
>
> If these two "modern" interpretations of Bartók surpassed all imagination with their emotional fullness, overheated fantasy, unprecedented intensity of expression and noble economy, than the same can be said again of the Brahms Sonata in E-minor, which closed the recital. No wonder, that the audience hardly let the artists leave the stage until they repeated the middle movement of the sonata. For what Bartók displayed especially in the purest, most gentle and moving lyricism, indeed, had the effect of a revelation ... almost with the purity of a child.[57]

7. Jacqueline

Jacqueline, Marriage, and Fatherhood

After their divorce in 1933, Lida and Piatigorsky remained friends; but when he found out her involvement with cellist Pierre Fournier, they parted company for good. Piatigorsky's concert schedule increased markedly each season, and the opportunity to explore a serious romantic relationship became increasingly difficult.

It was not until 1935 that Piatigorsky first met his future wife, Jacqueline de Rothschild. There were significant similarities between Lida and Jacqueline. Both played the piano, though Lida's skills were more advanced. Both were victims of an abusive first marriage, and both came from successful and prosperous families. On the other hand, Lida's ambition and joie d' vivre dramatically contrasted with Jacqueline's quiet, shy demeanor.

Jacqueline, raised in a powerful, wealthy family, was prevented from entering into the usual activities of a young woman. In matters of the heart, Jacqueline had been completely controlled by her parents, and so had no opportunity to exercise her instincts. As a naïve single woman, her view of the world was jolted into reality when she left the security of home: "Until the age of eighteen I had never been alone in the street or in a store, and even after that I was driven everywhere by a private chauffeur. I had never been in a market or even seen the kitchen. I had never dialed a phone, made a call myself or even seen a public phone."

Edouard de Rothschild, the benevolent patriarch, dominated the family, and as a result, Jacqueline remained naïve, unaware of their fabulous wealth. Talking about money was absolutely taboo, a subject only discussed by the Rothschild men. Her parents' only desire was for Jacqueline to be cultured and socially adept for marriage. Jacqueline remembered her father's dictum: "Girls need not work; girls need not learn."[1] Instead, she excelled in riding, golf, piano, and, especially, chess.

At twenty-two, Jacqueline seriously studied the piano and was hopelessly infatuated with pianist Alfred Cortot. Though he paid scant attention to her, she followed him throughout Europe, listening to his recitals, master classes, and lectures. She was more successful at her other passions, tennis and chess, talents she later excelled at in world-class competition.[2]

One of her friends, the distinguished pianist Anja Dorfmann, invited Jacqueline and a few friends to a party that Gregor Piatigorsky also attended. Piatigorsky, gregarious and open, was attracted and asked the shy Jacqueline for a date. She agreed and suggested they play golf, a game he had never played but braved in order to seal the date:

> In brand-new shoes he had bought for the occasion (which unfortunately were too small) he fumbled the ball. Years later he told me how much he had suffered on that first date, as each step was painful. And in spite of sore feet and my offending suggestion that he improve his golf, he wanted to join me for the summer!
> When I told my mother she warned, "Be careful."
> "What do you mean?" I asked. "He's very nice."
> "But you don't know him."
> I wanted Grisha to drive down with me to Meautry so he could see the horses with their fillies, but I was still insecure. The disaster of my first marriage was not yet erased. Though I was annoyed at my mother for creating doubts in me, I thought she was right. I had encouraged a stranger. My old fears rushed back. How will I manage? I wondered. Will I know what to say? I looked at my mother and said,
> "I told him he could come." She sensed my worries.
> "You are going too fast," she said. "Don't do it."
> "But we already agreed; I can't get out of it."
> "It's easy," my mother said. "Just write and tell him your plans have changed."
> Unhappy and yet partly relieved, I composed a letter telling Grisha that something had come up and I wasn't sure which day I could leave, but that maybe I could still see him in Meautry. Grisha never answered my letter. I had defeated myself, killed what I wanted most. And I spent a lonely summer.[3]

That summer led to a year without contact. Partly to reach out to Piatigorsky, and partly to give young musicians an opportunity to perform and make a little money, Jacqueline began a series of soirees she called Davidsbündler, named after composer Robert Schumann's club of believers interested in only the best in art. Before the second evening's concert, Anja called to say that Gregor was in town and asked if she could bring him along. Jacqueline quickly agreed, but when Anja arrived without him, Jacqueline knew he was still upset with her for the brush-off from a year ago. Luckily, Piatigorsky had second thoughts, arrived later that night, and stayed after all the guests had left.

Jacqueline felt that the year in between had made it possible for her to open up to Grisha. She suggested he and Ivor Newton, Piatigorsky's accompanist, rehearse at her residence the following week. The week mended the fence somewhat, but Jacqueline was not ready to sever her ties with the past, especially with those people whom Piatigorsky thought did not have her best interest in mind. The summer of 1936 was pivotal for their relationship and led to a confrontation:

> At twenty-four, on the verge of entering a new life, I was still hanging on to the past. It seemed difficult to face a total break. Piatigorsky and I had been close for only a few weeks. Somehow my daily hour at the psychiatrist's created a wedge between us.
> "We could go out tomorrow afternoon."
> "No, I can't. I have to be at Dr. Loewenstein's at three o'clock."
> "You don't need him anymore. It's ridiculous. When are you going to get out of that?"
> He was annoyed. Pointing to Cortot's picture, he added,
> "And get rid of that ugly face."
> "I don't want to."
> He picked up his own photo, tore it up.
> "Then you don't need me."
> He reached for his coat and hat.
> "Where are you going?"
> I was distressed. He didn't answer. He just walked out.[4]

Hours turned into days and she felt she would lose him forever. It shocked her into breaking away from the chains of false security. But though she threw the picture of Cortot away, it did not bring Piatigorsky back. Finally Grisha called and they were able to patch up their discord. The relationship took hold; this time it was for keeps. Soon he joined her at Château de Ferrières, the Rothschilds' estate near Paris. With Cortot no longer hovering above Jacqueline's world, the reality of her piano playing was exposed. She could not even manage a simple piece Piatigorsky had given her to play with him:

> "I can't," I told him.
> "Try anyhow," he said, and sat with his cello, waiting to play. I tried; I fumbled and stuttered on the piano.
> "Your rhythm," he said. "Count one, two, three, four."
> I couldn't sight-read, I couldn't keep time. I had practiced endless hours. The piano had been the entire focus of my drive to break out of three worlds which imprisoned me — my childhood with Nanny, my parents' world, and my inner thundering world of despair. Several years of effort were crumbling to nothing. I was falling into a dark abyss.
> "Your teacher is criminal," he finally said as I sat very silently, my arms hanging. But I knew it wasn't my teacher's fault if I wasn't capable.
> "She kept leading you on but never taught you music."

Piatigorsky was concerned about Jacqueline's musical outlet, knowing how devastated she was about the piano. He wanted her to enjoy making music and decided she should try something new. So before Piatigorsky left on his next tour, he presented Jacqueline with a bassoon. "This is better suited for you than the piano. It is the same register as the cello. There are less notes to play so there is no need to play fast."[5] Relieved, she taught herself how to play and soon achieved an enjoyable level of playing. Arthur Rubinstein recalled a visit: "Jacqueline entered their drawing room with a bassoon in her hand and, after greeting us, began to play a tune on it. 'In case the Rothschilds lose all their fortunes, I decided to make my living playing the bassoon. I found that this is the instrument most in demand in America.' We laughed but had to admit that she already played it rather well."[6]

By the winter of 1936 it was obvious to them that they were going to be together forever. Jacqueline met Piatigorsky in San Francisco in November after his world tour, and traveled with him as he continued the tour in the U.S.:

> The question was not "Will you marry me?" or even "Shall we get married?" but "How will we squeeze a marriage between two concerts?"
> After each concert someone gives a party for the artist, and after Piatigorsky played at the University of Michigan in Ann Arbor, Mr. and Mrs. [Charles A.] Sink, the local managers [University Musical Society], gave the traditional party. I signed Jacqueline de Rothschild in their guest book. The next morning we got married in a private civil ceremony in Mr. Sink's home. Thus, on the same page in the guest book I was proud to sign Jacqueline Piatigorsky. We had a glass of champagne and immediately left for a different town, another concert.[7]

Months later, they returned to France where Jacqueline's parents held a small religious ceremony for them. The only demand Edouard de Rothschild had made on his daughter was that she marry a Jew; wealth was not a concern.[8] Piatigorsky established a close relationship with his in-laws, especially Germaine.[9] Beyond the love that melted their differences away, their marriage balanced two basic needs: "Contrary to Grisha's childhood, our relationship was based on a bond of solidity. I gave him the much-needed security of a home, and he protected me. When, without any reason, residual fear from my childhood reappeared, he said, 'As long as I am here nothing bad will ever happen to you,' and I believed him."[10]

On October 5, 1937, their daughter Jephta was born in Paris, but Piatigorsky needed to leave for concerts in America the following morning. The separation was difficult for both parents. Ignoring the approaching Nazi threat, Jacqueline hired a Jewish nurse, and after months of bureaucratic difficulties, received papers allowing the nurse to travel to the

United States. While Piatigorsky toured, Jacqueline, a nursemaid, and Jephta stayed at the Pierre Hotel in New York.

Last Escape and Sanctuary

Piatigorsky had faced danger for much of his life. Home was not safe — he had encountered the pogroms, dodging the drunks and derelicts who frequented the lowly watering holes he worked in Yekaterinoslav, and the expulsion from his home at the age of twelve. His perilous crossing into Poland and the escape from Polish police weathered the youth into a savvy adult. He now (1938–1939) routinely zigzagged across Nazi-occupied lands aware that his safety was tenuous. Writing to his brother Shura, Piatigorsky lamented: "Soon I will have to return to Europe. It is not fun there; you can always feel the fascist hand everywhere."[11] The Nansen passport he carried was a persistent reminder of his phantom nationality and exacerbated dangerous situations that were beyond his control. The cellist observed: "France is literally filled to overflowing with refugees and émigrés. Of these, the Russians should be numbered among the émigré 'aristocrats.' These oldest of post war martyrs have gone through all the refugee schools of thought and wisdom — the most resourceful have quickly become Frenchified (as in Germany they have become Germanized and in America, they have become Americanized, etc.) The weakest of them long ago lost their most valuable possessions — their health and their hope. They live a pitiful existence."[12]

After his marriage to Jacqueline, Piatigorsky began to feel more secure, not entirely because of the wealth of his in-laws, but also because of the warm reception he received from a strong and supportive family. Jacqueline's parents loved Piatigorsky. Knowing he wanted to settle in the United States, Piatigorsky applied for citizenship in 1937. Though Jacqueline learned Russian and Piatigorsky spoke poor French, the couple decided to learn English together.

After the 1938–39 season in the United States, the Piatigorskys looked forward to returning to France for the summer. Before their departure, Piatigorsky's friend Boris Koutzen[13] visited them, full of excitement. He described a country estate in the Adirondacks with 115 acres and a large furnished stone house near a river. He knew the realtor and suggested that they all take a drive to see the property near the village of Elizabethtown, New York. The estate was magnificent, with a view beyond Piatigorsky's imagination. When he saw the tall birch trees of the Adirondacks, he fell in love; the wilderness and the terrain reminded him of Russia. He told the realtor that he had only five thousand dollars to spend, and that he was sorry to waste their time; the property had be worth over twenty times that. Nonetheless he bid the amount and gave it no further thought.

The Piatigorskys returned to France in June and spent the summer on idyllic Lac d'Annecy near the Swiss border. The area's peacefulness lulled them into a false sense of security. Piatigorsky read the newspapers and listened to Hitler's speeches and the daily broadcasts describing the deterioration between Germany and the rest of Europe. Though worried, he did not think war was imminent. Piatigorsky's Nansen passport had been issued by the French police, and had to be renewed and defended with each excursion. Its value was little more than official identity, and represented no nationality or right to work. However, if France declared war, Piatigorsky would be conscripted and sent to the Maginot Line, even though he was thirty-six years old and not a French citizen.

lez/Rußl. 8. 1. 1873, V-Virt, ML., früher ordentl. Prof. der Akademie der Tonkunst in München — Berlin.
Petuchowski, Dr. Ernst, * Berlin 26. 3. 1905, KM — Berlin.
Peyser, Hans Heinrich, * Berlin 1. 2. 1903, KM — Berlin.
Philip, Philipp, * Hamburg 21. 3. 1867, ML (V, K), ChM — Hamburg.
Philipp, Eugen (Ps. Philippi, Eugen), * Lübeck 14. 10. 1856, † Berlin 21. 5. 1920; KM, Komp (u. a. Rixdorfer Polka: „In Rixdorf ist Musike").
✢ **Philipp,** Isidore, * Pest 2. 9. 1863, KVirt, ML, Komp. Seit 1934 in Amerika.
Philipp, Josef, * Lemberg 14. 6. 1895, KLtr (V) — Berlin.
Philipp, Rudolf, * Hamburg 13. 11. 1858, † das. 3. 3. 1936, MSchr, Komp.
Philippi, Eugen, Ps. für Philipp, Eugen.
Philippi, Fritz, * Berlin 9. 5. 1893, KM, ChDgt, KLtr (K, Harm) — Berlin.
Philippsborn, Fritz, * Berlin 24. 2. 1915, OrchM (V, Fag) — Berlin.
Philippson, Moses (Vornamen später abgeändert in Max und Louis; Ps. Cramer, H.), * Lübeck 13. 12. 1864, † Hamburg 10. 10. 1929,. Operetten-Komp.
Philips, Rosette, geb. Loewenthal-Rheinberg, * Frankfurt/M. 3. 3. 1868, MLn (K) — Frankfurt/M.
Philipsky, Margarethe, geb. Rosner, * Wien 10. 3. 1900, Sgrn — Berlin.
✢ **Piatigorski,** Gregor, * Jekaterinoslaw 20. 4. 1903, VcVirt — Berlin.
Pick, Alfred (Ps. Postary, Alfred), * Forst/L. 5. 1. 1872, UntM (K, G) — Berlin.
Pick, Gustav (Ps. Aurach, Th.), * Rechnitz (Ung.) 10. 12. 1832, † Wien 29. 4. 1921, Komp (u. a. „Wiener Fiakerlied").
Piechler, Arthur (H) (Ps. Paulus, E.), * Magdeburg 31. 3. 1896, Studienrat, Org, Komp, ML — Augsburg.
Piete, Guido, * Orsova 4. 5. 1905, KM, Komp u. kaufmännischer Vertreter — Sofia (Bulg.).
Pietruschka, Mayer, * Opatow i. Rußl., 17. 2. 1901, UntM (V) — Berlin.
Pincus, Johanna (Ps. Linde, Anna), * Bromberg 17. 11. 1880, Cembn, Pian, MSchrn — Berlin.
Pincus, Heinz, * Berlin 1. 8. 1904, UntM (Trp, V) — Berlin.
Pinczower, Herta (Ps. Ower, Rita), * Obornik/Pos. 29. 10. 1904, Sgrn — Breslau.
Ping-Pong, Ps. für Weißmann, Samuel Friedrich.
Pinkus, Alwin Oskar, s. Alwin, Oskar.
Pinkus, Gertrud, geb. Hoffnung, * Berlin 9. 5. 1893, MLn (K) — Berlin.
Pinner, Valentin (Ps. Waldau, Harry), * Liegnitz 7. 4. 1876, KM, Pian, Komp (Opern und Schlager), Textdichter — Berlin.
Pinozzi, Carlo, Ps. für Rothstein, James.
Pirani, Eugenio, * Ferrara 8. 9. 1852, † Berlin 12. 1. 1939, Pian, Komp, ML.
Pisk, Paul Amadeus, * Wien 16. 5. 1893, Dr. phil., Komp, MSchr, Mitarbeiter der „Musikblätter des Anbruch" und größerer Zeitungen — Wien.
✢ **Pisling - Boas,** Nora, * Den Haag 19. 11. 1886, Sgrn u. Ref, u. a. am „8-Uhr-Abendblatt" in Berlin.
Pisling, Sigmund, * Wien 22. 6. 1869, † Zuckmantel (Ostsudetenland) 1. 9. 1926, MSchr, Ref, Kritiker am „8 - Uhr - Abendblatt" in Berlin.
Pistol, Friedrich (H), * Wien 1. 8. 1908, UntM — Wien.
Pitsch, Manfred (H), * Niederschönhausen 15. 5. 1906, UntM (K, Akk) — Berlin.

Lexikon der juden in der Musik [*Encyclopedia of Jews in Music*], the Nazis' official listing of Jews to boycott.

```
Sonderstab Musik                    Paris, den 19.2.1941
                                    Vg.



                    Notiz über Bezeichnung von Kisten
                    ════════════════════════════════


Gregor P i a t i g o r s k i ,  Avenue Foch 19-21


    MR  1               Bücher und Noten
    MR  2               Schöng. frz. Literatur
    MR  3               Bücher
    MR  4                "
    MR  5                "
    MR  6                " (Prachtbände in Goldschnitt)
    MR  7               Keramik
    MR  8                "
    MR  9                "
    MR 10                "
    MR 11                "
    MR 12               Schallplatten und Bilder
    MR 13               Keramik
    MR 14                "
    MR 15               Bilder
    MR 16               Bücher
    MR 30               Alte Elfenbeinschnitzereien
    MR 31               Gold- und Silbergeschirre
    MR 32               Gold und Silber
    MR 33                "    "    "
    MR 34                "    "    "
    MR 35 (Lederkoffer)  "    "    "
    MR 36 (Lederkoffer)  "    "    "
```

Manifest representing 3 out of 23 crates of Piatigorsky's possessions taken by Sonderstab Musik, registered on February 19, 1941 © Mémorial de la Shoah/CDJC, Paris, France).

Later that summer, a telegram arrived notifying Piatigorsky that his offer for the Adirondack estate, called Windy Cliff, had been accepted. The happy news made Piatigorsky anxious to return to the United States and finally experience owning his own piece of mother earth. Their joy quickly faded as Jacqueline became increasingly uneasy with the news of Hitler's August 23 pact of nonaggression with Russia. On September 1, when Hitler invaded Poland, her intuition dramatically turned to panic and she insisted the family leave France immediately. Piatigorsky balked, but Jacqueline demanded and telephoned to reserve a cabin on the next ship leaving for New York. Within an hour they left for Le Havre and boarded the *Ile de France.* They were lucky to have gotten a cabin, as the ship was completely sold out when they arrived.[14] Within two hours France declared war: "The ship was frozen. No one was allowed on or off as we stood in the harbor. September 3, 1939, was a hot and muggy day. People were crowding the deck, walking aimlessly back and forth. The heat increased and breathing became hard as we waited." The tension mounted further when a rumor that a submarine had been sighted: "For two days and two nights we stayed in the harbor, full of anxiety, silent, hoping for news that did not come. Then suddenly the ship was released and we sailed. The crossing was rough as we went up and down with the swelling of each wave. I was pregnant again and my daughter was twenty-three months old."

Very soon after they arrived in New York City, Piatigorsky traveled north to the Adirondacks, eager to see his new home. Looking from the front of Windy Cliff, down to the Boquet River's valley, and up behind, he felt settled for the first time:

> Our new home was actually a summer resort, a lovely charming house at the top of a hill. Behind it the mountain, heavily wooded and alive with animals, went up for acres. In the winter the temperature reached 40 degrees below zero, which would freeze the water pipes, which were above the ground. We were three miles from the closest village of twelve hundred inhabitants, which had no movie house and no real hospital, but only a community house and one country doctor. At the foot of the hill an abandoned caretaker's house stood, and across the only road in the woods the Boquet River ran on a very rocky terrain. The river had deep-spots for swimming and was fed by ice-cold little springs. We often swam with piglets from the neighboring farm.[15]

With the spread of war in Europe, the Rothschilds were keenly aware of the increasing anti–Semitism around them. They made efforts to blunt the trend. Germaine was insistent that Jewish refugees be employed at the Rothschild properties, and by March 1939, she created a hostel for approximately 150 refugee children. Immediately following the German invasion in May 1940, the new Vichy regime severely restricted the rights of French Jewry. The decree that all Frenchmen who left the country after May 10 would face confiscation and sale of property (with proceeds going to the Vichy state) was the last straw.

The Rothschilds stubbornly remained in France a few more months, with objets d'art hidden among the properties, away from the main estate; Edouard's famous collection of paintings was moved to Brittany. Since the bulk of Rothschild wealth was only passed down to sons, Edouard saw to his daughter's needs by depositing ten thousand dollars in a London bank in September. (As far as the Piatigorskys knew, this was the extent of her inheritance, and they did not discuss it further. Piatigorsky's earnings paid all the bills.)

The Rothschilds left for the United States in July, but since immigration did not accept refugees directly from France, they were forced to drive over the Pyrenees through Spain to Portugal. There they flew from Lisbon to New York on Pan Am's *Yankee Clipper,* arriving on July 10, exhausted and terrified by their first air travel. Since they were only able to take a few belongings, Edouard arrived in New York with $1,000,000 in precious stones. It was reportedly the largest sum yet brought by a war refugee.

On July 31, radio reports announced that Marshal Pétain's Vichy government had confiscated the Rothschilds' estate along with those of the four wealthiest families in France. Edouard's art collection was eventually discovered, and Reichsmarschall Göring, as Hitler's "buyer" of artworks, took several Dutch and French paintings for himself. Masterpieces by Vermeer and Boucher and portraits by Hals and Rembrandt were set aside for Der Führer. The prices paid were ridiculously low, with the proceeds, it was announced, going to French orphans. The Rothschilds were the major single source of plunder, with 3,978 items taken.[16] Though most items were returned after the war, several priceless works have not yet been found. Edouard spent his remaining years in search of his lost treasures.

Also among the pillage was a Stradivari cello Piatigorsky purchased in Berlin from cellist Arnold Földesy. Piatigorsky left the instrument with the Rothschilds in September 1939, and after the war gave up hope that the instrument would ever be recovered. Unexpectedly, in 1953 he received word that the cello may have been found. An anonymous individual had offered the Strad to Mathias Niessen, a violin dealer in Aachen, Germany, for less than $200. Suspecting the instrument was Piatigorsky's, Niessen bought it. Where it had been in the intervening years remains a mystery. After confirming its identity, Niessen sold the cello to Germaine Rothschild for the sum he paid, whereby the Baroness flew to Los Angeles to personally deliver it to her son-in-law.

The Nazi plundering of private homes in France spared no one. Its music division, Sonderstab Musik, headed by Herbert Gerigk, systematically devoured all forms of art. In August 1940, Gerigk opened the Paris office of Sonderstab Musik on Boulevard Haussmann, claiming that his primary mission was the repossession of German manuscripts in France. But Gerigk soon gave directives to confiscate material owned by political adversaries of the Reich, as well as to force record companies and music publishers to remove their stock of Jewish music (i.e., composed or performed by Jews). The effort to expunge even included the removal of the large sculpted relief of Mendelssohn near the ceiling of Berlin's Philharmonic, which revealed a conspicuous gap between the other "pure" German composers Beethoven and Bach.

In September 1940, the first in a series of individual confiscations from important Jewish musicians and composers took place: Harpsichordist Wanda Landowska's collection of historic musical instruments and library of 10,000 music books were packed in crates and transported to Berlin. In February 1941, Piatigorsky's apartment was completely emptied, as were those of composer Darius Milhaud and pianist Arthur Rubinstein. Piatigorsky's losses were significant: Correspondence with Richard Strauss, his Jewish librettist Stefan Zweig and Furtwängler; artworks, composer's manuscripts, and recordings were among the casualties. A partial list of its contents reflects typical Nazi officialism (see illustration).[17]

The arrival of Baron and Baroness Rothschild at Windy Cliff in July 1940 proved challenging for the Piatigorskys. Though Gregor was proud to offer his home to them, the Rothschilds, especially Germaine, expected their needs to be met in the manner to which they were accustomed. But without servants and attendants to take care of every detail, the Rothschilds decided it was best to move to the Windsor Hotel in Elizabethtown, where they managed to endure the remainder of the summer.

The Rothschilds immediately drew attention in Elizabethtown, but were adaptable enough to be a valuable force rather than a mere curiosity. They attended fundraisers and functions to aid the Community House Hospital and the baroness helped organize fundraising concerts and card games for the Red Cross.

Windy Cliff was built in 1896 as a summer residence and was not winterized. As the winter of 1940 approached, the Piatigorskys moved into a home in Elizabethtown, and spent the following winter in Stamford, Connecticut. Meanwhile, the Rothschilds moved to New York City, where they remained throughout the war. For the next eight years the Piatigorskys spent summers and holidays at Windy Cliff.

Soon townspeople grew to accept the strange-sounding giant and his odd visitors. In time, violinist Louis Persinger, Valentin Pavlovsky, and Fredric Mann[18] bought summer homes close by. Conductor Artur Rodzinski and Bela Bartók rented cabins in the nearby town of Lake Placid.

One Russian visitor to the Piatigorsky home was violinist Ivan Galamian, a former member of the Bolshoi Theater Orchestra[19] with Piatigorsky. Galamian had recently moved to the United States, hoping to become its foremost violin teacher. Leopold Auer, the reigning pedagogue, spent his last years in the United States; and after his death in 1930, Galamian felt that the U.S. would welcome another Russian in that role. Galamian's visit to Windy Cliff in September 1940 convinced him that a summer music conservatory in the area could be successful.

This visit and many more led to the establishment of the Meadowmount School of Music where Galamian was to enjoy his greatest fame.[20] In those early years as cofounder, Piatigorsky offered spiritual, musical and financial fuel to give it impetus. The school still thrives today, even after the deaths of Galamian in 1981 and his widow, Judith, who ran the school until 2005. The Gregor Piatigorsky Memorial Fellowship continues to support deserving students.

Each summer Piatigorsky played benefit recitals for the Elizabethtown Community House, which also served as its only hospital and clinic. His son Joram was born there on February 4, 1940. (Remarkably, that very morning Jacqueline had been ice-skating with daughter Jephta, and simply walked from the rink to the Community House where she gave birth.) That winter Piatigorsky joined the local Kiwanis Club, sang along with its members at the Deer's Head Inn, and soon performed and spoke at meetings and fundraisers. At Windy Cliff, Piatigorsky made his first attempts at learning to drive, a skill that he never really mastered. There are tales of his nearly running down townspeople when his car jumped the curb. (Later, in Los Angeles, he avoided left turns at all costs.)

Groundskeeper Leonard Duntley, though barely literate, helped solidify Piatigorsky's philosophy that all people have a gift for something. On first impression, one could easily assume that an uneducated person was not accomplished, but Piatigorsky was delighted to learn that Duntley was an expert on all the plants and animals in the area. On walks together, Duntley spouted off meticulous details about the flora and fauna, including their Latin names, their characteristics, and their relationships to other forms of life in the Adirondacks.

The Raccoon Rap

The Piatigorskys' first summer at Windy Cliff was an adventure. Wildlife often made unwelcome appearances, especially a family of raccoons that liked to visit the kitchen and the long winding porch that wrapped around the house. Jacqueline used the porch for the children's naps and naturally feared for their safety. Even after the Piatigorskys put up chicken wire around the porch, the raccoons still managed to find their way in. One animal crawled into Jephta's crib. The Piatigorskys' handyman, Johnny Hooper, suggested they trap the raccoon. The trap worked, but broke the animal's leg. After Piatigorsky saw it suffering, he had Hooper take it to the local veterinarian. The instructions were to save the creature at all costs, let Piatigorsky know how it was doing, and then release it.

Piatigorsky resumed his concert season in October, and by November was in New York to play the Elgar Concerto with Sir John Barbirolli and the Philharmonic at Carnegie Hall. After Piatigorsky took his first bow and walked off the stage, the orchestra's manager, Bruno Zirato, met him in panic. While the audience was still applauding, Zirato told Piatigorsky that the state police were there to arrest him. Piatigorsky, with the music lingering in his mind and the applause still sounding, did not grasp the situation. After more bows, when the applause subsided Piatigorsky returned to his dressing room where an excited Zirato met him again and whispered: "Don't you understand? He is here to arrest you. It was all I could do to stop him before your concert." Piatigorsky, putting his cello in the case, was still confused. "What is all this about? What does he want to arrest me for?"

The manager had no idea. Piatigorsky met the officers, who informed him that an arrest warrant had been issued for hunting raccoons out of season, a criminal offense. It turned out that someone in Elizabethtown heard that Piatigorsky trapped one and decided to report him. The cellist had many concerts in quick succession — a repeat performance the next day, and a recital in Chicago the following day — and there was no time for any delays. Asked how he could avoid imprisonment, they suggested that he plead guilty, sign a document and pay a $25 fine at once. Piatigorsky gladly handed over the cash before the unsuspecting public greeted him in the greenroom.[21]

Piatigorsky annually toured the West Coast, and in the 1939-40 season he looked forward to appearing again with the famed Polish-German conductor Otto Klemperer in Los Angeles. Klemperer, who arrived there in 1933, a victim of Nazi persecution, needed a new post; Germany's loss was Los Angeles' gain. But at the rehearsal the conductor seemed not himself; manic-depression and the early signs of the brain tumor were about to change his life forever. Piatigorsky remembered the day:

> At 8:30 in the morning we arrived in Los Angeles and a rehearsal was scheduled for 10:00 A.M. The rehearsals with the orchestra are almost always more tiring than the concerts themselves, and the harder it is to calm one's nerves, the less one is prepared for them. At times you don't manage to have time for breakfast and you have to go straight from the train station, after an exhausting trip, filthy with cold hands and you appear on the stage before an orchestra, with musicians who expect a lot from you and who are usually either unforgiving critics or true worshipers.
>
> Klemperer had asked me to play the Haydn concerto, but I refused and requested to replace it with Schumann. Klemperer agreed to this very unwillingly. It is strange how such wonderful musicians, as Klemperer and Toscanini dislike this concerto.
>
> Poor Klemperer, what's with him? How he has changed! I am used to seeing this fanatical musician, powerful and despotic, a giant who bends to no one, true to his will and awkward in his handling of both orchestra and soloist, as well as of his own conductors baton.
>
> Where has the categorical and unreserved Klemperer disappeared to? He has turned from a lion to a Saint Bernard, huge weak-sighted and helpless. He was clearly not in agreement with the tempo that I requested at the rehearsal but he didn't protest and didn't argue as he used to before — in Berlin, in New York or even the last two years in Los Angeles.
>
> It was as if his great height had diminished. He conducted in an unauthoritative and preoccupied manner, hunched over, not tearing his eyes from the score. I had expected the complete opposite from him, and there was no end to my surprise. I had to continually stop the orchestra in order to request something from him. Like a guilty child, he tried to fulfill all my requests. There were many of my old colleagues in the orchestra — I knew several from Moscow, others from Europe, but the majority I knew from the concerts I played with them

Elizabethtown, 1941: (left to right) Jacqueline, Joram, Gregor, Jephta, Edouard and Germaine de Rothschild (courtesy Piatigorsky estate).

in Los Angeles 10 years ago, which apparently left an impression not only on my own memory but also on theirs. After the rehearsal the orchestra gave me an ovation, which did not coincide, neither with my own mood nor with Klemperer's condition.

    Klemperer requested that we rehearse once more tomorrow morning. After this rehearsal I was definitely convinced that Klemperer was ill. He heard poorly and seemed to see poorly as well. I was filled with pity for him but I didn't know how or with what to console him, or how to bring him happiness. Both concerts went very successfully but I was poisoned by Klemperer's unhappiness. It was even worse that he tried with all his might to conceal his illness. The poor man — I imagine his suffering and shudder with horror. My respect for him as a musician has increased still further. How solid must be the foundation on which his musical edifice stands if in the presence of such an illness he is still able to perform beautifully Shostakovich's First Symphony and Mussorgsky's "Pictures from an Exhibition." It was not so long ago that he would work with fanatical persistence on something, be it an opera or a symphony. He would put the Klemperer stamp on everything with his firm hand. At rehearsals he was capable of setting the driest orchestra or chorus member ablaze with his enthusiasm, but also of completely wearing down the most hardy and patient of his colleagues. He belonged to art with all of his being and did not give a thought to his own personal laurels. It seemed now that he was rehearsing for himself, he was afraid of himself and this diffidence led him to endless repetitions of one passage or another. By the tired faces of the orchestra members I understood that they did his for him and withstood it out of pity for him.[22]

Klemperer's problems persisted and led to operations and bizarre behavior and humiliation. Though he lost his post in Los Angeles he was eventually able to gain back his conducting reputation.

8. Prokofiev, Hindemith and Teaching

Sergei Prokofiev and the 1939–40 Season

Though there was only a 12-year difference in age between them, Prokofiev and Piatigorsky had fascinating contrasts. Where they both left post–Revolutionary Russia to pursue careers in the West, Prokofiev was given the blessing to leave by Anatoly Lunacharsky, the Soviet People's Commissar for Enlightenment, while Piatigorsky was denied. The government viewed Piatigorsky as a defector, Prokofiev as a cultural emissary. Piatigorsky eventually received invitations to return, and in 1934 agreed to a homecoming performance. Levon Atovmyan, a Soviet cultural official and musician, made the offer but it did not work out. Prokofiev, however, returned to the Soviet Union as a permanent citizen in 1936.

Piatigorsky was an early champion of Prokofiev's music, performing the early *Ballada* with the renowned pianist Bekmann-Shcherbina on several recitals in Moscow. The *Ballada* was premiered with the composer and Piatigorsky's friend and former von Glehn student Yevsei Belousov, at the Moscow Conservatory in 1914 (just a few months before Prokofiev's graduation). Opportunities such as these, as well as his local ascendancy with the Lenin Quartet and Solo Cellist with the Bolshoi, may have brought the teenager to Prokofiev's attention. However, the premiere of Prokofiev's suite from the ballet *Le Chout* (*The Buffoon*), op. 21a, with the Berlin Philharmonic in 1927 offered a better opportunity to know the composer personally. At least by 1932, Piatigorsky had played many things for the composer (including the *Ballada*), and urged the composer to write a cello concerto. The cellist made a persistent effort in spite of Prokofiev's initial protestations: "I don't know your crazy instrument," Prokofiev said. I played for him and, demonstrating all possibilities of the cello, saw him from time to time jump from his chair. "It is slashing! Play it again!" He made notes in the little notebook he always carried with him. He asked me to show him some of the typical music for cello, but when I did, he glanced through it and said, "You should not keep it in the house. It smells."[1]

Their correspondence seems to be lost, and their contact was intermittent, confined to direct and indirect encounters in Europe (Berlin and Paris) and the United States (Boston and New York) in the 1920s and 1930s. Prokofiev's diary entry for May 22, 1932, recalled an important meeting in Paris:

> Piatigorsky, a good cellist, came over. Koussevitzky can't praise him enough. Piatigorsky very much wishes for me to compose a concerto for him, vows to play it everywhere. I already have an outline (and themes) for a fantasy for cello and orchestra. If Piatigorsky can come up with the money I'll do it. Though he boasts of admirers, where will he get it? He brought his cello and played my Ballade with me very well.[2]

Prokofiev only started to sketch the concerto in the summer of 1933 in Paris, where Piatigorsky was then living. The work eventually receded into the background until he returned to the sketches in early 1934, telling composer and dearest friend Nikolai Miaskovsky that it was still in a "somnolent" state.

The concerto basically remained dormant until 1937, at which point Prokofiev, now in Moscow, slowly resumed work on it. The composer later clarified his impasse: "The first sketches did not satisfy me, I clearly felt 'seams' between the various episodes, and not all the music was of equal value. After the long interruption I revised the concerto, adding some new material."[3] Despite being substantially drafted, the concerto languished as he scrambled to finish the music for Sergei Eisenstein's film *Alexander Nevsky* in 1938; the composer complained of being "up to my ears" with the film. Prokofiev finished the concerto outside Moscow in the artist's enclave of Nikolina Gora in October.[4]

Prokofiev's whirlwind tours of France, England and the United States in 1938 — his last out of the Soviet Union — did not afford Piatigorsky much opportunity to communicate with him:

> We corresponded about the concerto. Prokofiev's letters were astonishing. They would read, "dr gr," (dear grisha) and so on, his signature being sr pr (sergei prokofiev). Proud of his consonant abbreviation system, he ignored the difficulties it presented to his correspondent. Finally he completed the first movement. I received the music and soon we began to discuss the other movements to come. The beginning of the second, which followed shortly, appeared as excitingly promising as the first. "Even so, it will lead to nothing. I cannot compose away from Russia. I will go home." I thought that the decision had come to him not lightly. Soon, with his wife and two little children, he was set for departure.

On the *Normandy* crossing from New York to France, the composer apologetically, and with some embarrassment, announced to Piatigorsky that the concerto was nearly finished, but that he could not dedicate it to Piatigorsky or give him the right of first performance. As a Soviet citizen, the composer could not allow the premiere performed by a famous expatriate, one who had been erased from the public record; it could be interpreted as an act of defiance that might endanger his family. The work needed to be presented in the Soviet Union first. The news initially depressed Piatigorsky, but Prokofiev urged him to give the American premiere, ensuring that the music would reach him as soon as possible. Piatigorsky was afforded modest consolation knowing that the concerto would be published, and that he would not be prohibited from touring with it in Europe.

By the time the completed manuscript arrived, Prokofiev was in southern Russia, which made further communication about the concerto difficult. Piatigorsky wrote, "In my letters, sent through the courtesy of the Soviet Embassy, I asked Prokofiev to make changes, pointing out certain weaknesses of the work. He thanked me for the suggestions and said that he would take them into consideration."[5] Doubtless responding to Piatigorsky's proposals, Prokofiev added a cadenza and adjusted some of the passagework.[6] Pianist Ivor Newton remembered touring with Piatigorsky when the manuscript arrived:

> Although the tour was in any case going to be strenuous, Piatigorsky agreed to prepare two new concertos — that of Prokofiev, to be conducted by Koussevitzky, and the other by Frederick Stock, conductor of the Chicago Symphony Orchestra.
>
> As we set off on our tour, the Prokofiev arrived as a manuscript copy with a piano accompaniment, but there was only the cello part of the Stock concerto available for Piatigorsky to study during our tour and I was impressed with his application in the difficult circumstances of our exhausting journeys. As soon as we went through the Prokofiev work together, Piatigorsky seemed to absorb both the cello solo and the orchestral parts immediately.

> Wherever we went in the United States, the two new concertos were so much on his mind that, as soon as he reached his hotel bedroom he would take out his cello and, sitting on the edge of the bed, would begin to work at any passages about which he felt uncertain when mentally studying the music on the train. He was not able to see or hear the orchestra parts of Stock's concerto but as soon as he arrived in Chicago and began to rehearse it, he was quick to grasp its total shape and sound.[7]

Immersed in the concerto in the summer of 1939, Piatigorsky wrote to Koussevitzky:

> I finally received the Prokofiev concerto.... [T]he concerto is superb, and it gives me great pleasure to work on it. I have not yet seen the score, but I am sure that the concerto has been orchestrated with Prokofiev's usual mastery. The cello part is uncomfortable and difficult, but I hope to successfully overcome these difficulties.
>
> Where and when should the premiere of this concerto be? As I have no directive from you, I have not given Prokofiev to a single orchestra in Europe. The ideal could be only one thing — and that is the Boston orchestra! But I was a soloist with you just last summer, and of course I don't even dream of being one this summer! Be so kind, Sergey Aleksandrovich, as to let me know of your decision. We are going to America in December and will stay there probably five or six months. I have a lot of work ahead of me in Europe. Concerts in all of the Scandinavian countries, England, Holland, France, and in all of the countries that are accessible and not barbaric "for now."[8]

The U.S. premiere was scheduled in Boston with Koussevitzky on March 8, 1940. As the date of the premiere neared, Piatigorsky and Koussevitzky found themselves increasingly unclear about certain details: "The many problems we faced with the composition were hardly solved by a word from Prokofiev." And, as Prokofiev wrote to the cellist: "Do whatever you find necessary. You have *carte blanche*."[9]

The tone of resignation discerned in the composer's remark was no doubt due to the concerto's ruinous premiere in Moscow on November 26, 1938. According to pianist Sviatoslav Richter, who rehearsed it with the soloist, cellist Leonid Berezovsky, the performance was an unmitigated disaster. Unfortunately the conductor and soloist were not up to the task either musically and technically. Richter declared that "the music was foreign to his [Berezovsky's] nature. He shrugged his shoulders and sighed, groaning at the difficulties and becoming terribly upset." Richter and Berezovsky went to the composer's apartment to play through the concerto for him: "Berezovsky looked terribly confused. And it was no doubt because of this that Prokofiev, clearly in no mood for compromise, immediately sat down at the piano himself and began to say things like: 'Here it should be like this, there it should be like that.' I stood in a corner out of harm's way. Prokofiev was businesslike, but not pleasant. Berezovsky's questions clearly annoyed him.... He wanted to hear what was in the score — nothing more. Berezovsky had a tendency towards sentimentality...." Richter never played a note.

To be accepted for public performance, the concerto needed to receive official approval from the Union of Soviet Composers. Richter was surprised when the audition, which occurred in a smoke-filled room in the union's headquarters, was met with enthusiasm from the cultural bureaucrats: "'A real event! Every bit as fine as the Second Violin Concerto!' There was a lively and positive discussion, and everyone present wished Berezovsky well. No one doubted that the work would be a tremendous success. 'This is a new page in our history.'" The concerto was assigned a prominent place in the second *dekada* (ten-day festival) of Soviet music.

Hopes ran high until the orchestral rehearsals began. The conductor, Alexandr Melik-Pashayev, found the score difficult to interpret, confusing the musicians. Richter recalled that the "tempi were as impossible as they were wrong. It seemed to me that [Melik-Pashayev] utterly failed to grasp the work's inner essence. It was a total fiasco."[10] Prokofiev's reaction to the premiere performance was terse and gruff: "When the composer came backstage to salute the artists, Melik-Pashayev the conductor tried to break an awkward silence. 'Well, Sergey Sergeyevich, what did you think?' Prokofiev replied with an ingenuous smile: 'Nothing could have been worse.'"[11]

The reviews were discouraging, and the composer received little response from his colleagues. Prokofiev himself answered the critics angrily, defending the concerto and declaring, "The concerto is very much like the [very successful] Second Violin Concerto!" But even Miaskovsky pointed out some of the problems in the form, noting in his diary, "First-rate music but somehow it doesn't quite come off."[12] Critical reaction to the American premiere on March 8, 1940, was certainly more positive, albeit consistently mixed. As Piatigorsky recalled, "The performance in Boston went well and the response of the audience was gratifying. A few days later in New York, where we repeated the work, the affair turned for me into a mild nightmare. At one point in the second movement, through some inexplicable mishap, the orchestra took a tempo four times faster than indicated. There was no time to reflect as I, as if by a jolt of lightning, attacked passages that even at the right tempo were extremely rapid. I don't know if anyone of the press or the audience noticed what happened, but how I came through it alive remains a mystery to me to this day."[13]

Alexander Williams's review in the *Boston Herald* the following day was characteristic:

> The new work is very interesting on more than one count but that it by no means as attractive as the 2nd Violin Concerto ... or the piano concertos. The first movement makes its way easily and at once to the ear. A charming lyrical melody is heard against a varying ostinato background. You can't miss the effect of this or fail to take pleasure in it.... With the second movement ... there also is not much difficulty in becoming acclimatized ... though we may feel that he has elsewhere done the same thing better. At first bat we should say that Prokofiev became so interested in the cello as a virtuoso instrument that he was content with that aspect alone.... [I]n the middle variations of the finale it bogs him down.
>
> We should reflect though, that it would be presumptuous to condemn the concerto on the ground that we were unable to assimilate easily some of the last movement.

Grateful as it was in itself, the typically bustling Prokofiev finish seemed, again, strangely out of place.

> This is, moreover, much too interesting a work to be shelved, even if cello concertos were as common as daisies. Mr. Piatigorsky played it with that overwhelming technique of which he is master and which he needed here in full measure.

The concerto mainly suffered from the last movement's considerable length. As Warren Story Smith of the *Boston Post* tersely added, "The first movement is charming; the second, slightly less persuasive and the third, though full of ingenuity, seems to get nowhere."[14] Despite the plans he had reported to Koussevitzky, the onset of World War II prevented Piatigorsky from touring in Europe. The concerto was not heard again until December 1945, with cellist Maurice Gendron and the London Philharmonic under Walter Susskind.

The concerto's long and bruised journey somewhat improved after Mstislav Rostropovich performed it with piano accompaniment in a recital on December 21, 1947, which was dedicated to the 30th anniversary of the revolution and fell on Joseph Stalin's birthday. Prokofiev was in attendance — only his second hearing of the work — and later asked Rostropovich to help revise it, explaining that "Although there is some good material in the piece, the structure is not compact enough."[15] Eventually the Concerto was reworked, morphing into the *Sinfonia-Concertante*, op. 125 (1952).

Prokofiev (left), Koussevitzky (second from left), and Piatigorsky (far right), 1938. Others unidentified (courtesy Piatigorsky estate).

The passive dismissal of the original concerto, especially by performers, is not justified. In fact, it is a unique example of its time, full of invention. Its 18th century scope, high spirits, and vibrant colors recall the composer's *Classical* Symphony. The orchestration is often very light, sparkling, and unusually chamber-like, but Prokofiev's unique use of tuba and percussion gives the impression of weightier symphonic proportions.[16] The massive, sprawling finale of the concerto could certainly benefit from a few thoughtful cuts to tighten its shape. Indeed, when Piatigorsky and Koussevitzky performed it in New York on March 14 and 16, 1940, they omitted a variation and an interlude in the finale, reducing the concerto's length to just under a half hour. Though the *Sinfonia-Concertante* remains the best known, the original version is slowly gaining attention. As Piatigorsky concluded, "I am grateful that there are now two major works for the cello by this great composer and unforgettable man."[17]

Prokofiev often stayed with the Koussevitzkys in Boston on his U.S. tours in the 1930s. The Piatigorskys also stayed with them, and to unwind, they all played bridge. Prokofiev's musical wit and sarcasm seemed to extend to his personality. He thought out loud as he played, and when Piatigorsky and Prokofiev partnered, his remarks became more personal and cutting with each of Piatigorsky's poor bids: "Playing bridge, he was even more blunt. Through some unfortunate circumstances a few times I happened to be his partner. Although a weak player, I was not entirely insensitive to his remarks, uttered under his breath. 'Why is the idiot bidding spades?' he would say, or, 'Should I let the cripple play his three no trumps?' One day it led to a clash that ended, however, with an affectionate embrace."[18] Prokofiev's criticism was silently directed to himself, however, when playing chess with

Jacqueline Piatigorsky, a champion player who represented the United States in international tournaments, including the women's Chess Olympiad. Though the composer was himself a champion who had defeated several world-class masters, here he was humbled. The first game they played ended in a draw, but the second game went to Jacqueline. Prokofiev quit after that.

Piatigorsky himself composed and contributed many worthwhile works, as did many of his predecessors and contemporaries, including Marechal, Bazelaire, Cassadó, Mainardi, Casals, and later, Tortelier and Rostropovich. Piatigorsky began composing in his youth and often performed his own pieces in recitals. One such work was *Promenade*,[19] a Prokofievian march for solo cello written in homage to the composer. The occasion was a farewell party that Piatigorsky hosted for Prokofiev at the end of his last tour of the United States in 1938. Piatigorsky played the piece to the delight of the composer, the two men unwittingly parting company for the last time.

The other new work Piatigorsky presented in the 1939-40 season was the Concerto in D Minor by Frederick Stock, conductor of the Chicago Symphony. Stock and Piatigorsky had played about thirty concerts with the orchestra when the cellist wrote the following: "He is one of those rare people and musicians who is not steeped through with the love of money, nor vanity and narcissism. I am touched by the loyalty, constancy and goodness of this musician."[20] Their camaraderie was one of great trust, as is evident in the following recollection from a member of the orchestra:

> I will never forget one Monday morning — it is still so clear in my memory.... There was a Monday morning rehearsal ... and we had a concert in Milwaukee that night.... [T]he Old Man [Stock] started out announcing as follows: "The program for tonight is Brahms third ... now I want a little more from the third horn, and etc., etc. Now the program for tomorrow — Tuesday —" Now about here Piatigorsky walks out and starts to rehearse the Dvořák Cello Concerto. He plays the introduction and then Piatigorsky plays a few bars and then he stopped and asked Stock what he thought and Stock said, "it's okay so I will see you tomorrow afternoon" and that was that.... [I]f I had looked at my watch I would have guessed less than ten minutes of rehearsal time had passed."[21]

Knowing that Stock was also a composer and arranger,[22] Piatigorsky had inquired about his cello concerto for years. By 1939, ten years after its premiere, the conductor voiced his reservations about the piece. Piatigorsky wrote:

> The concerto is complex and difficult. The manuscript is unclear and indecipherable. I worked on it all summer. I didn't have the score. The piano part didn't coordinate with the cello. And there were many mistakes in both ... [yet] I recognized and fell in love with the concerto. I regretted that it hadn't been played anywhere in Europe before Chicago. Such was my amazement when before my very departure for America I received the following telegram: "Stock finds his own concerto to be tasteless and outdated and requests that you play the Schumann Concerto in Chicago."

Stock eventually gave in and agreed to schedule it for the following season, on April 4 and 5, 1940, one month after the Prokofiev Concerto premiere. The *Chicago Daily Tribune* reported:

> [Piatigorsky] ... play[ed] Frederick Stock's concerto under the composer's own direction ... in a manner which emphasized once again his phenomenal technique and his ability to make the cello on occasion, sing with a heart storming intensity and beauty of tone but which did not render the concerto completely comprehensible to an Elmo Dullard like the writer of this review. Perhaps this is recondite music which requires several hearings before its mysteries stand revealed — or perhaps last night's performance was of an unusually static quaint, and

failed to exploit to the full the musical and emotional momentum which the concerto doubtless possesses.

At any rate, only the second movement, with its gently curving lyric themes shone with a steady, lovely light of its own. The first and third (to change the metaphor, once again) sounded labored and difficult in spots.[23]

Piatigorsky thought that Stock was the best orchestral accompanist. One reason was his unusual position while accompanying, standing deeper into the orchestra and sometimes without a raised platform. He directed with the sensitivity of a chamber musician, easily balancing the soloist. They would perform the new Hindemith Concerto the following season, and with the concerto's weighty orchestration, the balance between cello and orchestra was particularly challenging. Of all the performances of this work, those with Stock were most satisfying for the cellist.[24]

Paul Hindemith

Piatigorsky probably met Paul Hindemith for the first time in 1925 when the Berlin Philharmonic premiered the composer's *Concerto for Orchestra*, op. 38. From then on, Piatigorsky held the composer in the highest regard: "I have played with him many times. A great mind — he knows everything there is to know about music, and all instruments. He is the direct link to Brahms."[25]

In the late spring of 1933, both men were scheduled to play a cycle of chamber music for the Brahms centenary, sponsored by Furtwängler, the new Reichskammermusik Director. The programs were to include Bronislaw Huberman and Artur Schnabel as well, but because of Nazi anti–Semitism, Piatigorsky and Schnabel refused to participate, and left Germany. The concerts still took place, but with Casals replacing Piatigorsky and Harold Bauer substituting for Schnabel. Hindemith remained for the festival, and even though his wife had Jewish blood, Hindemith stayed in Germany until exiled to Switzerland in 1938. Hindemith was invited to teach at Yale and at Tanglewood, Serge Koussevitzky's new summer school in Lenox, Massachusetts. He arrived in February 1940, his fourth trip to the U.S.

CELLO CONCERTO (1940)

Hindemith's first visit to the Berkshires (Tanglewood) in the summer of 1940, two weeks before the beginning of classes, was very peaceful. He was able to take long walks in the country and felt for the first time " a sort of love for this country" and began to compose the cello concerto, his first work composed in the U.S. That summer the composer and Piatigorsky were reunited at Tanglewood, where the cellist was on the faculty as well as appearing as a soloist: "When I had finished the first pages of the score and when Koussevitzky saw them, he seized the work immediately. Piatigorsky happened to also come by that day and the both of them arranged for the work to be in one of the programs in Boston with following performances in New York and elsewhere."[26] Their excitement led to the premiere the following season. As Hindemith continued work on the concerto, Piatigorsky noticed that he could compose whenever and wherever he wanted, even in a room filled with chattering people, seemingly without distraction.

Inspired by the peacefulness and long walks Hindemith delved into the Cello Concerto and was able to report to his wife that the work was nearly finished by July 14. However, Hindemith was a bit optimistic about the completion. On July 28 he wrote again to his wife: "The cello concerto is still not finished as yet. I have had too much work to do over the last ten days so I could not write. Furthermore, the heat was so intense that even moving a pen caused continual perspiration." Frustrated, on August 6 he wrote to her a third time: "The cello concerto still is not completed. It is no wonder, because I haven't had time since school started, and I threw away the almost completed last movement, because I did not like it anymore. Now I don't have any great ideas."

With Hindemith (right), Tanglewood, ca. 1941 (courtesy Piatigorsky estate).

A new third movement was completed on September 9. Immediately Hindemith began to work on the production of the orchestra parts for Associated Music Publishers (AMP). The making of the orchestral materials (score and parts) took undue time, which Hindemith found annoying. Trouble with the parts plagued the composer for months. At first he met the delays with humor, writing to editor Ernest Voigt in January 1941:

> Sir, it really has become a cross to carry with this cello concerto. First this almost illegible score, then the impossible cello part—and now I receive complaints from Boston that the material is full of mistakes.... Is there really no better copier in New York, the city of millions, than this moon calf, and no better corrector than the sloppy Dessau!?[27] I can hardly face going to the rehearsal....
>
> I found the corrections made by Dessau; nevertheless, he left more than 400 mistakes uncorrected. All in one an admirable worker whom we want to show for money at the next world fair together with the moon calf.

While the composer was writing the concerto, Gertrude Hindemith wrote to her husband asking if he had any particular cellist in mind. He replied: "I wasn't thinking of Munio [Emanuel Feuermann] when I composed it, actually, I wasn't thinking of anyone. I was only interested in trying something similar with the cello after having composed the violin concerto." Perhaps sensing that Feuermann was miffed by his choice of Piatigorsky as soloist, Hindemith continued: "Feuermann could have let me know he was interested after I told his wife when I met her at the New York concert that I was going to write a cello concerto.... [T]he only thing I have heard relating to Feuermann was in a letter from [Fritz] Stiedry, who wrote that in case I have a concerto he would like to have Feuermann play it

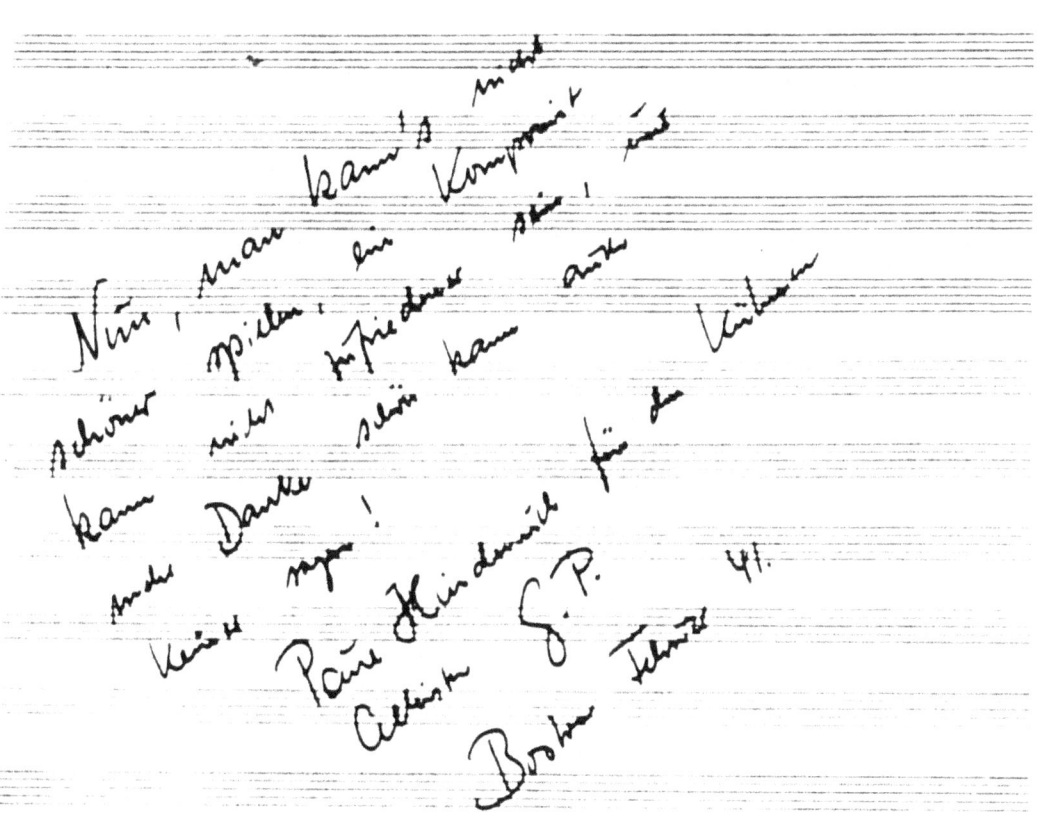

Hindemith's dedication of the Cello Concerto.

on one of his 'New Friends of Music' concerts. This is decidedly a second-rate group, like the ensembles we had in Europe. I definitely prefer the Boston Symphony."

Hindemith and Piatigorsky had a warm and humor-filled friendship, which is evident in their correspondence. Piatigorsky repeatedly asked the publisher for the solo part to study to no avail, which shocked the composer when he heard about it in October. Hindemith's barely containable anger towards his publisher spills over in frustration:

> Where in the world is the score of the cello concerto?... The poor Piattist Cellogorsky writes in despair how he should study the concerto, if he doesn't receive it now.... And also Koussevitzky is crying. The delay (five weeks instead of four days!) could cost us the entire season and that would really be a shame. I want you to send a photocopy to Piatigorsky as soon as possible, and since he must rehearse it with a pianist send him a piano reduction also — it is high time!

A few days later on October 7 Piatigorsky wrote to Hindemith with excitement: "Everything is clear in the cello voice and I am excited about it!! I am more than curious to play it at least once with the piano reduction! My expectations are very high, because I believe (after having seen the first two movements in Lenox and the cello voice of the whole concerto) that your concerto is the greatest and most ingenious that has been composed for the cello so far. I only hope and wish to play it well."

Still, the irritated composer continues to worry about the parts, complaining again to

With Galamian (right) at Meadowmount, 1942.

Voigt that "the writer of the cello concerto copy is a "Mondkalb" ["mooncalf"].... [L]ook at all the mistakes from page 15 on! You should never hire such a sloppy worker." By January Hindemith's hope for problem-free rehearsals and concerts of the new concerto turned to anxiety: "Koussevitzky tells me that my cello concerto will be performed on the first Friday and Saturday of February. I am afraid our Mondkalb will not have the parts ready by then. Since he does not work well under pressure, I would like very much to know what you propose.... I could do the brass and percussion parts here and that would save time." And finally, after the first wave of concerts was completed, Hindemith wrote to Willy Strecker, lifelong friend and head of the publishing firm Schott that "there was again much distress at the rehearsal, and it was even thought they might have to cancel it. Only the pleas of the composer prevented this from happening! After the main rehearsal I got the corrections which had been in Boston during the rehearsal — again several hundred. Finally I got all the material sent to me after the New York performance and still found 400 errors. The solo cello part was rewritten three times and corrected six times!"[28]

Hindemith and Piatigorsky had no problems working out details of the concerto, and in spite of all of the difficulties in the production of the score and parts, the first performances of the cello concerto were a resounding success. The premiere took place February 7, 1941, in Boston with Piatigorsky and the Boston Symphony Orchestra, Serge Koussevitzky conducting. Later in 1943 Piatigorsky still poured effusive praise on Hindemith: "I can hardly tell you — how much I love this work!! The genius is in every note." Hindemith was present at the premiere and wrote with pleasure to Strecker: "The premiere was last week in Cambridge and Boston, with the great Gregor behind his cello—wonderfully played and with great success. Three days ago it went to Brooklyn and yesterday it was in New York, I heard the performance yesterday, the best of all so far, but the audience there is abnormally dull and only made a mediocre success out of it. Nevertheless, the work will be played extensively. It is already on the program for the next winter in New York—with Mitropoulos."

Of the many favorable reviews, the following by the young composer John Cage, who heard the concerto at Tanglewood in 1941, may suffice:

> One of the most moving experiences we made this spring we owe to Piatigorsky and Hindemith's "Concerto for Violoncello and Orchestra." It was played beautifully, Frederick Stock directed. This is not only a concerto where a soloist unfolds his virtuosity, but where the musical relationships are also relationships between people. This is particularly clear in the last movement, where the orchestra plays martially, while the cello stays by itself, marginally, poetic, and not marching, because it has another opinion. The cello professes the standpoint of the individual with growing intensity, and this until the last possible moment. After that it is clear that one has to choose between madness and conformity. The latter course is taken and the cello becomes a subordinate part of the triumphant orchestra.[29]

Composer Paul Hindemith gave Piatigorsky a grateful dedication on the manuscript of the piano score:

> *Well, one cannot play it more beautifully,*
> *A composer cannot be more content,*
> *And more thanks cannot be said by anyone!*
> *Paul Hindemith to the daring cellist G.P.*
> *Boston, February '41*

Despite the great success of the performances in the United States, no commercial recording was made with Hindemith and Piatigorsky. Writing to Hindemith in 1957 Piatigorsky said, "I was very sad that we couldn't make a recording together because we 'belong' to different [recording] companies." Fortunately there is a remarkable radio broadcast from 1943 with Piatigorsky and the composer conducting the CBS Symphony.

VARIATIONS ON AN OLD ENGLISH NURSERY SONG "A FROG HE WENT A-COURTING"

The meetings with Hindemith at Tanglewood led to two more works commissioned by Piatigorsky: *A Frog He Went A-Courting:* Variations on an Old-English Nursery Song (1941), and the *Sonata* (1948), one of Hindemith's finest works. Piatigorsky first asked Hindemith to write something short for the cello, complaining of the lack of shorter recital works. The cellist played Hindemith's early *Phantasiestuck* and *Capriccio*, but wanted something new. The composer surprised Piatigorsky with a humorous setting of Variations on an Old-English Nursery Song, *A frog he went a-courting*. The work was completed in November 1941 in New Haven. The music is vivid and full of fun. The nursery rhyme is about a frog on the hunt for a bride—he proposes not to a frog, but to a mouse. The wedding guests include a tomcat that puts *"an end to all of this,"* incongruously depicted by a serious *fugato*.

On November 30, 1941, Piatigorsky thanked the composer for the cello variations, which were brought to him in Elizabethtown by Jacqueline Piatigorsky: "Your Frog Variations are great!! I am excited—of course I didn't expect any less to come from you. You couldn't have made anyone happier! Where did you get the story from? Wonderful!!"[30] After asking if he could visit the Hindemiths in January 1942 in New Haven, he added: "Of course I will take the cello with me to show you how a tenor can transform itself into a fly and a frog! ... I thank you from the bottom of my heart for your music and words! With many greetings to the two of you, your ol' boy G. 'Frogagorsky.'" In 1941 Hindemith asked AMP if they wanted to publish the work. It was rejected, but was eventually published by them in 1952. Despite Piatigorsky's enthusiasm, the piece remained unplayed for two years. On March 18, 1943, Piatigorsky replied to a letter from Hindemith:

> It has been a long time since I have written you. Maybe it was because I felt so guilty!! I rushed you so much with the Frog variations, and then when it was finished, and after I had been so excited about it, I didn't play it! ... My reasons to explain are dumm [sic]. I had trouble memorizing it! It is much harder than your concerto! Maybe I also didn't feel so well health-wise — maybe I was also just a little lazy.... Since I didn't give a cello recital in New York this winter, and since my accompanist had problems with his voice — I just postponed the performance until next winter. Well, however it may be, I am excited to play the piece and I ask you not to be angry with me that I haven't played it yet!

Piatigorsky and pianist Ralph Berkowitz premiered the work in June 1944.[31] Hindemith enjoyed drawing and painting and sent the Piatigorskys a lovely portrait of a frog playing the cello as a greeting in spite of the delayed premiere.

Sonata (1948)

The *Sonata* (1948) has gained a distinguished place in the cello repertoire, and is considered one of the composer's most heartfelt works. It was written in February and March of 1948 when the composer was living in New Haven, Connecticut. Piatigorsky wrote to Koussevitzky with the exciting news: "When I played in New Haven, I saw Hindemith, who promised to write me a sonata. Today he sent two parts, and in a week he'll send the third, and already on March 19th I'll play it at Carnegie Hall. It's wonderful music! He's becoming more and more a 'romantic,' and it seems to me, is moving away from German scholastics."[32] The premiere was scheduled for March 1948 in New York, but it had to be postponed as Hindemith had difficulty in completing the last movement, "Passacaglia."

Piatigorsky telegrammed Hindemith on March 30, 1948, saying the music arrived too late for a premiere: THANK YOU FOR MAGNIFICENT THIRD MOVEMENT WHICH UNFORTUNATELY ARRIVED TOO LATE EVEN FOR COLUMBIA UNIVERSITY. Piatigorsky finally premiered the new sonata on August 14, 1948, at Tanglewood, with pianist Ralph Berkowitz. A few days later, Piatigorsky wrote to the composer:

> Dear Paul! I finally performed your sonata. Not only I, but the whole world will forever be thankful to you for this work! We played it well and it was a great success. Even the rascals and the brainless newspaper idiots [must] have felt the grandeur of the sonata! I love the work, and I only regret that you haven't heard it. Gertrude would have been right to call me "conceited," but she did not know that my conceit and pride results from the fact that I am friends with you!! ... I thank you for everything and I embrace both of you. Always your Grisha (Piatigorsky).

Hindemith had a good sense of humor but his music could sound severe and Teutonic. Although the composer eschewed romantic excess, he never wanted his music performed literally, without sentiment or personality. When Hindemith conducted Piatigorsky with

TENTH SEASON   FOURTH CONCERT
1943-1944

The Denver Symphony Orchestra

Horace E. Tureman, Conductor
GREGOR PIATIGORSKY, Guest Conductor

**Friday Evening, February 4,
at 8:30 o'Clock, Denver Auditorium**

Soloist—GREGOR PIATIGORSKY, 'Cellist

PROGRAM

OVERTURE TO THE OPERA "EURYANTHE"...............Weber
CONCERTO FOR VIOLONCELLO AND ORCHESTRA
   in D major, Op. 101..Haydn
    1. Allegro   2. Adagio   3. Allegro

INTERMISSION

RUSSIAN FOLK SONGS FOR ORCHESTRA, Op. 58............Laidov
    Chant religieuse   Chant comique   Rondo
    Chant de Noel   Berceuse   Choeur danse
    Complainte

SOLO GROUP
    Pezzo Capriccioso, Op. 68..Tchaikovsky
    Three pieces from "Music for Children," arranged
       by Piatigorsky ....Prokofieff
            Regrets   Valtz   March

MARCH SLAV ....Tchaikovsky

Ralph Berkowitz, Accompanist for Mr. Piatigorsky

The Piano is a BALDWIN

Late arrivals will be seated only during the intervals between numbers.

First and only conducting appearance, 1944.

the CBS Symphony in 1943, the "interpretation" was very free, Hindemith bending as Piatigorsky rounds out phrases in his own inimitable way. The composer even treated the orchestral tuttis with expanse, going "against" the score. For a composer whose works seem written in stone, this freedom is revealing.

    Piatigorsky recalled the premiere (May 5, 1946) of Hindemith's *When Lilacs Last in the Door-Yard Bloom'd, A Requiem "For Those We Loved,"* written in memory of FDR and

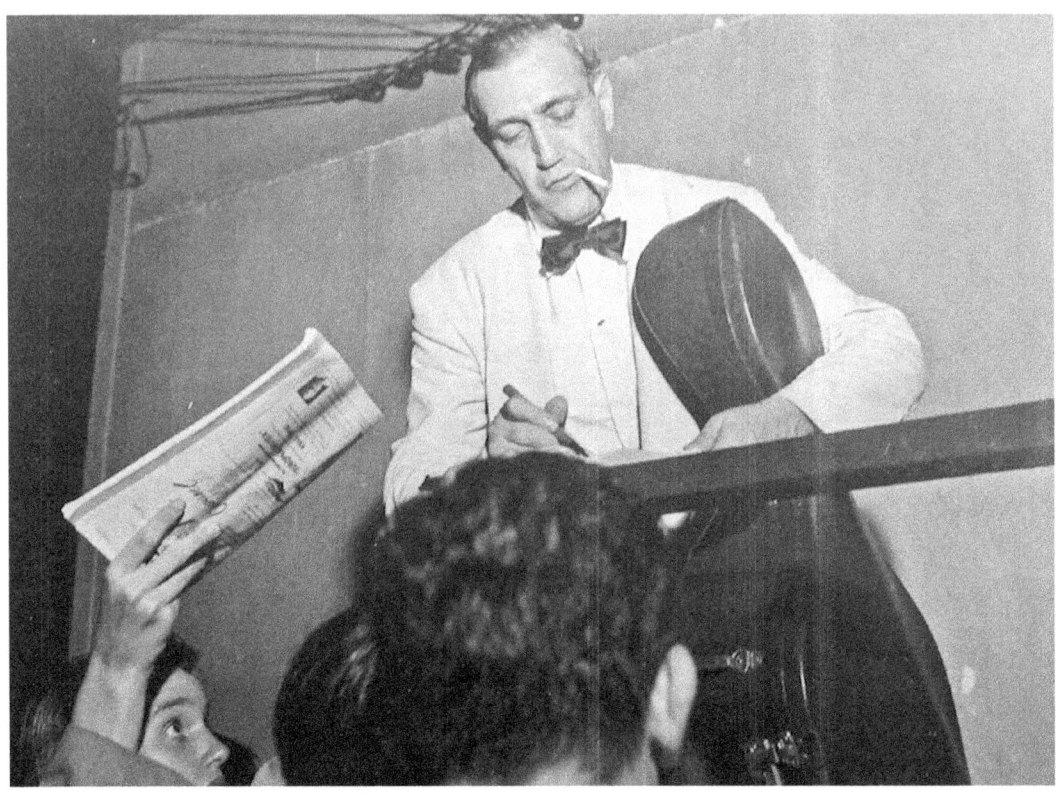

Signing programs on tour.

the Americans fallen in World War II. The text was secular, based on the poem by Walt Whitman on the death of Abraham Lincoln. Piatigorsky sat in the audience with Leonard Bernstein, Aaron Copland, and other American composers, and afterwards asked them what they thought of the music. They were unmoved. Bernstein said it was nothing but "a chip off the old workbench."

Piatigorsky was dumbfounded that they could not feel the soul in this music. But, he knew one part of the problem could have been Hindemith's seemingly businesslike approach to conducting his own music. After the concert Piatigorsky stepped into the Russian Tea Room near Carnegie Hall and saw Hindemith at a table alone, looking withdrawn. Piatigorsky joined him and found that he was disappointed by the lukewarm response. He wondered why musicians did not respond more to his music, especially this work, which he felt would become a standard commemorative American composition. (Hindemith had become a U.S. citizen a few months earlier in January 1946.) He acknowledged the cellist's emotional interpretations, and asked why others did not respond in similar ways. Piatigorsky suggested that someone else might conduct his works with more fantasy, particularly works steeped in emotion such as the *Requiem*, because they are removed from it enough to feel its emotional freshness.

Hindemith lamented that his conducting engagements were most often of his own works, and wanted to conduct programs with or without his music as a guest conductor, not as a composer. His readings of the basic orchestral repertoire reveal an expressive performer, though his performances on the viola, his primary instrument, are rather dry.[33]

There is an interesting postscript concerning the cello concerto and composer William Walton. In 1963, Walton completed one of his most successful orchestral works, *Variations on a Theme by Hindemith*, the theme being from the second movement of Hindemith's Cello Concerto. Hindemith was delighted and wrote to Walton:

> Egregio Amico:
> Finally our criss-cross journeys came to an end and we could sit down in front of the exhaust of our gramophone and play your piece, score before us. Well, we had a half hour of sheer enjoyment. You wrote a beautiful score and we are extremely honored to find the red carpet rolled out even on the steps to the back door of fame. I am particularly fond of the honest solidity of workmanship in the score.... I also shall put it on my programs as soon as possible ... and I shall do my best to become a worthy interpreter of WW.[34]

Alas, Hindemith did not live long enough to perform it; he died in December.

The Curtis Institute

With the tragic death of Emanuel Feuermann in May 1942, the Curtis Institute of Music in Philadelphia lost its only cello faculty member. Feuermann had been at the school for just a year. Efrem Zimbalist, eminent violinist and president of Curtis, asked Piatigorsky to join the faculty, and he accepted at the end of May. Despite tension between the two cellists, Piatigorsky dedicated a number of concerts in 1942 to Feuermann's memory. The Piatigorskys eventually took an apartment on Rittenhouse Square in downtown Philadelphia, near Curtis. Several colleagues were neighbors, including conductor Eugene Ormandy, who lived one floor above.

Piatigorsky was interested in resuming his teaching career, and his summer work at the Berkshire Music Center at Tanglewood had attracted new students. It also provided an early opportunity for Feuermann's students to become familiar with their new teacher. Piatigorsky knew how to handle the delicate transition between teachers. Lorne Munroe, a former student of Felix Salmond[35] at Curtis, remembered the delicate transition:

> I will always remember my first lesson, with Piatigorsky. I had the bent thumb on the bow from the Salmond days, which means everyone had to do that. (I remember looking at Salmond's hands and he had long fingers; he had to do it that way. There was no way he could put his thumb on the bow without bending it. But why teach everybody like that?)
> I was in torture, I was in pain. Piatigorsky saw that and realized it, and didn't say a word about Salmond. But he made up a joke and said, "If you go to New York and you find an idiot on the street — you'll see the idiot because he has a sign on his back that says "idiot," I-D-I-O-T — and you hand him the bow and he takes it and he "shakes hands" with the bow. You tell him to hit you with the bow. Will he have his bent thumb to hit you with it? Of course not."
> Piatigorsky grabbed the bow in his hand and said that was my first lesson. The next time I came back in the fall, I played entirely differently; he didn't have to say anything else.[36]

At Tanglewood, Gordon Epperson remembered his advice about discipline: "Piatigorsky would give little sermons. He would say things like, 'I've had all kinds of students since I first came to this country. I've had depressed students, and I've had conceited students who wanted to be famous and give concerts. But I've seldom had an enthusiastic worker.' And then he would look around at us to let the lesson sink in."

The number of future principal cellists that passed through Piatigorsky's class at Curtis is impressive. Besides Lorne Monroe (Philadelphia Orchestra, New York Philharmonic) there was Paul Olevsky (Philadelphia Orchestra — its youngest principal, St. Louis Symphony), Robert Sayre (San Francisco Symphony), Robert LaMarchina (Los Angeles Philharmonic, Chicago Symphony), Shirley Trepel (Houston Symphony), John Martin (National Symphony), and William Stokking (Philadelphia Orchestra). Notable cellists who worked with Piatigorsky during the summers were Zara Nelsova (who spent three summers in Elizabethtown and Stamford, Connecticut), Samuel Mayes, and Raya Garbousova. The distinguished Danish cellist Erling Bengtsson studied extensively with Piatigorsky and later became his assistant.

Though Piatigorsky was head of chamber music at Tanglewood, he was less effective as a coach than as a teacher of cellists at that time: "He coached our group in the Schubert cello quintet, which was a great experience. He was quite affable and was very, very sure of himself. He would enter the room, moving slowly like a big cat, usually a little bit late, and would talk casually about one thing or another. He would then slowly pull his pipe out of his pocket, go through the pipe maneuverings and light it, all the while still talking. And then we'd begin to play. He would say things like, 'Careful with the intonation,' or 'You must look at each other.' And that's almost as specific as it got."[37]

The Curtis faculty often collaborated. Composer Gian Carlo Menotti wrote an entertaining parody for the Curtis Institute's annual Christmas party in 1943 in anticipation of the institute's upcoming twentieth anniversary year. As the pièce de résistance, Menotti wrote a *Terzetto* for three baritone voices and piano (with bassoon ad libitum), which was

With Fritz Reiner, conducting.

performed for faculty and guests. The singers were Piatigorsky, William Primrose and Menotti, with Zimbalist at the piano. Piatigorsky described it:

> The text of that Terzetto was the Curtis Institute catalogue. I don't think it was a very inspiring text, but it was a text. They chose me as their great star. I began to study, driving crazy everybody at home with my voice. But my voice — I don't know how beautiful it was — it was big, very big. The walls were shattering when I would sing. I was really practicing, like seldom I would practice.
>
> The great day came; the house was full. There were a lot of singers there. I remember Elisabeth Schumann and some others. Zimbalist played his introduction and I was prepared to fill the hall with my shellacking ability. After a little

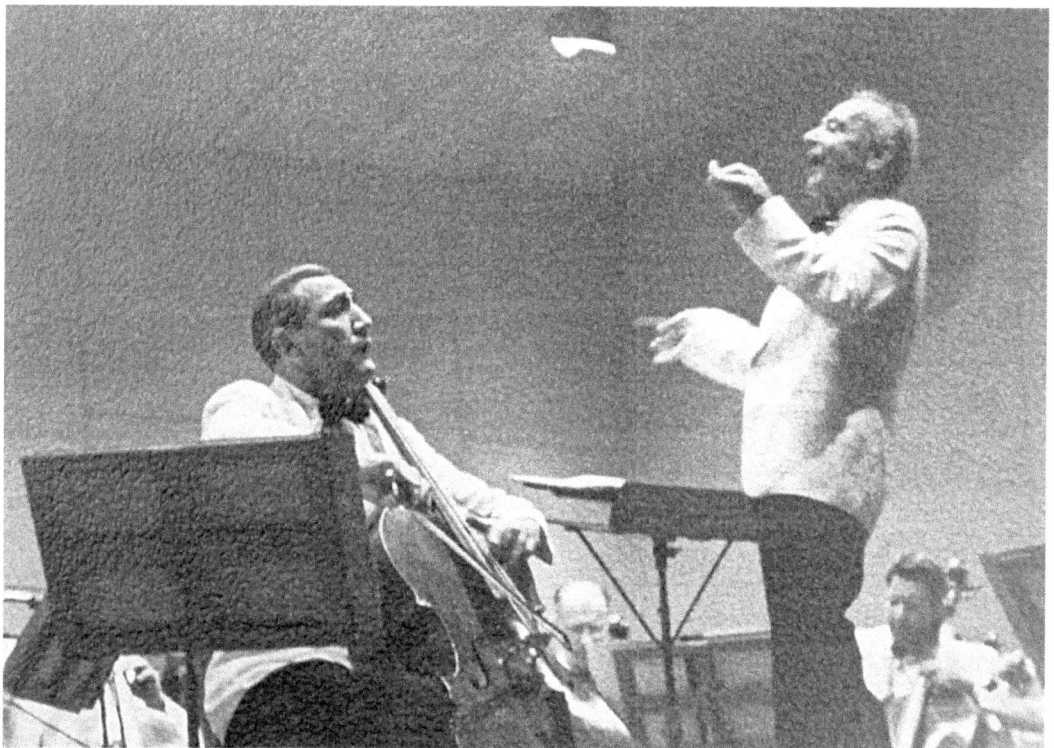

Top: With Albert Spalding (right). *Bottom:* With Koussevitzky, Tanglewood (courtesy Piatigorsky estate).

introduction there was my big solo recitative that began: The Curtis Institute of Music, Rittenhouse Square, Philadelphia, Pennsylvania.... I started. Nothing came out, nothing. Now, they thought that it's a trick to make them laugh. But I was never "this close" to crying and more than that, I start to have more respect for singers.[38]

Piatigorsky's relationship with Zimbalist was never warm. Zimbalist, as director of Curtis, did not offer contracts that met the cellist's demands, and Piatigorsky resigned in 1944. Press releases claimed that the resignation was the result of the increasing pressure of concert work, citing 54 appearances with the major U.S. orchestras for the upcoming season. Zimbalist begged him to return, and offered a three-year contract, which he reluctantly accepted. But contracts continued to cause problems and his salary stagnated.[39] Despite conflict, they continued to perform trios with pianist Isabelle Vengerova, and Piatigorsky gave yearly recitals.

Pianist Vladimir Sokoloff was concerned about his salary at Curtis and spoke with friend Ralph Berkowitz: "Ralph would ask, 'What's Zimmie like?' and I would ask, 'What's Piat like?'" But when they got down to the nuts and bolts of salaries Sokoloff discovered a huge gap between them. Ralph told Piatigorsky, who then talked to Zimbalist, "'You know, Efrem, things have gone up.' Next month I got a big raise."[40]

Zimbalist and Piatigorsky's last appearance together was at the 25th anniversary of the founding of Curtis in 1949. At that gala concert, they performed the Brahms Double Concerto with the Curtis orchestra.[41]

Though living on Rittenhouse Square with Curtis nearby was a big plus, in the fall of 1949, the family moved to Los Angeles, seeking a drier climate for the children's health. Piatigorsky remained head of Curtis's Chamber Music Department, and though willing to make trips back to Philadelphia, the commute became a serious concern. After failing to agree on a new contract with Zimbalist, Piatigorsky resigned for good in March 1951.

9. The War Years

Citizenship and Service

Gregor Piatigorsky had arrived in New York for his first American tour on October 27, 1929, just as the U.S. stock market crashed and the U.S. economy spiraled down into the Great Depression. Remembering his own experience with poverty and destitution, he was keenly aware of the plight of the "starving artist" and never forgot the kindness of those who assisted him during those less fortunate years. Generosity was one of Piatigorsky's most memorable traits, and he found ways to repay the country that had welcomed him so completely. First among the civic causes he helped was the Musician's Emergency Fund (MEF), which provided aid to needy musicians through the dark days of the depression and World War II. (The Horowitz, Milstein, Piatigorsky trio concert in 1932 was a benefit for the MEF.)

The cellist personally assisted talented musicians by funding scholarships, commissions, and outright gifts of much-needed cash. One such gift went to fifteen-year-old violin student Ivry Gitlis, which made his study with Georges Enesco, Jacques Thibaud, and Carl Flesch possible. Before America's entry into World War II, Piatigorsky also helped raise thousands of dollars for the Allied Relief Fund in England through his concerts.

During the war years, Piatigorsky's service took the form of concerts and fundraisers, with New York City's "Monday Morning Musicales" series as a frequent performing venue. Later, as a member of the Artists Committee of the MEF, he also worked with the Hospitalized Veterans Music Service to bring entertainment to servicemen, and made tickets available to service men and women for his recitals.[1]

Piatigorsky participated in patriotic radio programs that featured foreign-born Americans, such as *America Preferred* and *Russia Fights*. He also played for the National War Fund Drive, and with the New York Philharmonic at an anniversary celebration of the founding of the Czechoslovak Republic. He served on numerous committees such as the Foster Parents for War Children with celebrities such as Thomas Mann and Billy Rose, as well. Piatigorsky and Milstein performed the Brahms Double Concerto several times to promote the sale of war bonds and stamps, including the New York City's Works Progress Administration (WPA) Symphony Orchestra.[2] In 1944 Piatigorsky helped sponsor the new American Youth Orchestra conducted by Dean Dixon. The orchestra performed at soldiers' hospitals, debarkation centers, and military clubhouses.

Four months before he was granted U.S. citizenship, Piatigorsky registered for the draft and received a hardship deferment. On August 29, 1942, he swore his allegiance to the

United States in the Elizabethtown courtroom. On his first day as an American, he celebrated by giving a free concert for the community in the same courtroom. (Receipts were given to the local Community House, where his son had been born six months earlier.) The day he became a U.S. citizen marked the end of twenty-one years of phantom nationality, and his home at Windy Cliff epitomized the momentous journey home.

That same month he wrote to the U.S. War Department recommending the establishment of an Army Symphony Orchestra. Piatigorsky's support of the war effort was continuous and selfless. He played for servicemen and women wherever and whenever he was asked. During the war, Piatigorsky's three brothers served in the Soviet army. Alexander (Shura) reported to Gregor: "We musicians are prepared at any moment to exchange our bows for rifles for the fight against the damned Fascist Nazis." Piatigorsky helped his former homeland with concerts to benefit Russian War Relief as a member of the American-Russian Committee for Medical Aid to the USSR. He sent financial donations through the Soviet embassy and provided musical supplies, instruments and medical equipment. The war years saw a tightening of the availability of metal products in order to serve the military machine both in the U.S. and in the USSR. Strings were difficult to get, but in 1943 Piatigorsky made an arrangement with the Super-Sensitive String Company to ship strings to the Soviet embassy. Piatigorsky was also a member of the Jewish Council for Russian War Relief, and many other organizations that helped relieve suffering in occupied countries.

Replying to Shura, he confessed, "No enemy can break our souls! I work very hard and try to help as much as I can to fight the enemy. I know that my trying does not even compare to what the other men have to go through on the battlefields. I work much and am trying with all my might to be of use in the fight against the enemy. More than anything, I would like to play for the Red Army."[3]

Through the U.S.'s information radio service's Voice of America, he broadcasted greetings to Russian allies, hoping to reach his former countrymen. Andrei Gromyko, the new Soviet ambassador to the U.S., invited Piatigorsky to the commemoration of the 27th anniversary of the October Revolution in 1944. As an American citizen, it must have felt ironic to be acknowledged by a representative of the regime from which he had escaped.

The War Department issued several series of transcription discs containing excerpted rebroadcasts of mainstream radio programs, often introduced to the troops by celebrities. (It was thought that rebroadcasting programs in their entirety, with familiar theme songs and commercials, would only make the troops more homesick.) These programs were made available to all military entities foreign and domestic. The War Department also issued a series of V-Discs ("Victory" discs with distinctive red, white and blue labels) of which Piatigorsky recorded a spoken greeting to the troops and performed two short works.

The War Department routinely commandeered radio programs, many of which featured Piatigorsky, such as the *Bell Telephone Hour*, *The Pause That Refreshes*, the *Ford Evening Hour*, and *Invitation to Music*. Broadcasts of symphonic concerts by the leading orchestras, such as the New York Philharmonic, the Philadelphia Orchestra, and the Detroit Symphony were presented through the Armed Forces Radio Service, a subsidiary of the War Department. In addition, Piatigorsky donated funds to Armed Forces Master Records, Inc., designated to establish record libraries "for good music."

On May 17, 1943, Piatigorsky's Russian ancestry was heralded when he performed for the "I Am an American Day" celebration in New York's Central Park, which was broadcasted worldwide and captured in newsreels. Many celebrities performed at the event, which attracted over a million people. At the end of the program Piatigorsky was mobbed by

Playing for the USO.

bobby-soxers, shocked that he was so well-known to teens. After taking a bow, he discovered that the furor was "for a skinny, little fellow sitting next to me whose name was Frank Sinatra. They didn't even see me!"[4]

Ironically that same ancestry and his wartime contributions to Russia, then an American ally, came under the FBI's scrutiny. Piatigorsky was investigated as a possible communist sympathizer for his performances supporting foreign countries. Those occasions, even for groups as innocuous as the Friends of Czechoslovakia, were labeled possible communist fronts by J. Edgar Hoover. At one such function, Piatigorsky and Vice President Henry A. Wallace were under suspicion of supporting a communist-front organization. When the war ended he continued working with celebrities to petition the U.S. government for support of public music projects.

With no European tours during the war years, Piatigorsky's travel in North America increased. The summers at Windy Cliff were a welcome respite, and the cellist became ever more involved with local activity. (Nearby artist Wayman Adams painted Piatigorsky's portrait in 1942, which won first prize at the Carnegie Institute Exhibition the following year.) The war also required a few sacrifices to save resources. Sharing a taxi was common, which prompted his joke that he was going to change to the piccolo as he was asked to "travel light." He sometimes was refused taxi service while carrying "that machine" and used buses while holding the cello over his head. Even in the best of circumstances, traveling with an instrument and luggage can be a problem, and every touring performer experiences mishaps.

Performing for the Navy. Fellow cellist Frank Miller is looking on.

Clowning for the Waves, c. 1943.

Piatigorsky described an amusing confrontation he had with Canadian customs authorities. An obscure law called for the deposit of 40 percent of an instrument's value while it was in the country. When asked what value he placed upon the cello, Piatigorsky shrugged, "It is like a part of me," he said. "Would you ask me, for example, to place a value on my head?"[5] The border authorities went into discussion. Finally they emerged with the decision that the market for cellos was glutted and a good one could not be worth more than $100. Piatigorsky smiled and paid the required $40 deposit. His instrument was the magnificent *Sleeping Beauty* Montagnana made in 1739, and conservatively valued at $30,000 (1940s value — today easily over one million dollars).

Later, another encounter with Canadian officials tested his patience. Deciding he was tired of lying, Piatigorsky gave an honest estimation of the value of his cello at $40,000. At 40 percent that meant a deposit of $16,000; he told them neither he, nor anyone else for that matter, would carry that much cash with them. In haste, the officials put a value of $200 on the cello and Piatigorsky was asked to pay $80. The cellist refused. Other passengers waiting to cross were getting impatient. Piatigorsky had an appointment with the governor-general and concerts to play, and he let them know that he would personally hold the officials responsible for any delay.

As the guards huddled in conference again, they decided to call Ottawa, the capital of Canada. The governor-general's office verified the appointment, and he was passed through. After Piatigorsky brought the matter up to his host, the law was soon dropped.

Piatigorsky, like most professional cellists, always bought a second seat to insure the safety of his cello for air travel. His usual name for his inanimate passenger was Miss Cellogorsky. Buying "her" a ticket was particularly irritating when the plane was empty, which still irritates any cellist today: "I was furious. They strapped it into the seat alongside me. I got even. I ate two lunches, smoked two cigarettes, and asked the stewardesses twice as many questions."[6] Ivan Galamian often told of one of Piatigorsky's run-ins with airline personnel:

> On a tour in a smaller city, he encountered trouble at the airport when he was ready to depart. The official in charge was insisting that the cello be placed "in with the other baggage."
> Piatigorsky remonstrated, "But I have purchased as extra ticket for it. I always do. I keep it in the seat next to me on the planes."
> "But you cannot take it on the plane. It must be consigned to the baggage section."
> "Look it up in your rule book."
> The official began thumbing through the section on musical instruments.
> "What kind of instrument is it?"
> "An oboe."
> Oboe was permitted.[7]

Martinů, Foss and Dukelsky

Piatigorsky's summer activities at Tanglewood consisted of heading the chamber music department and coaching groups, as well as soloing with the Boston Symphony. Piatigorsky often read chamber music with students and faculty and while BSO personnel provided cello instruction, he offered advice to talented young musicians and entertained them with his extraordinary story telling — sometimes at the local pub. His enthusiasm for the young led to his sponsorship of annual monetary awards.

Chamber music was a constant source of community all his life, especially during the war. One joyful evening at conductor Antal Dorati's home however, was brought to an unceremonious end:

> One evening a particularly illustrious company assembled at our house in Forest Hills, Long Island: Yehudi Menuhin, William Primrose and Grisha Piatigorsky. After some food and talk we sat down and played a piano quartet by Brahms; it went so well that we decided to play it again there and then. The second performance was even better. Excited and overjoyed, we embarked upon a third. When we were about halfway through, a police car drove up to the house, and an enormous policeman appeared in the doorway, shouting at us in a furious voice: "Shut off that radio!"[8]

In 1942 Koussevitzky invited the prominent Czech composer Bohuslav Martinů to be the Berkshire Music Center's composer-in-residence. He arrived in the United States in 1941, having fled his homeland after the Nazi takeover in 1938. His arrival was only possible through the generous friends who responded to an article in the Swiss magazine *Dissonances*[9] asking for financial assistance for him. Conductor Paul Sacher paid for his passage as well as commissioned the Violin Concerto, which Mischa Elman premiered in 1943.

Martinů's five years of exile in America were very fruitful: He composed twenty-six works. Koussevitzky commissioned orchestral works, and Piatigorsky commissioned the *Variations on a Theme by Rossini*, a standard in cello repertoire. The composer and cellist had a very creative collaboration, and Piatigorsky admitted to an extraordinary input in the

Left to right: Composer Bohuslav Martinů, violinist Richard Burgin, Charlotte Martinů, Piatigorsky, c. 1943 (courtesy Diana L. Burgin).

solo part himself. The work was premiered in Philadelphia on November 8, 1942, and was the first of a projected series for the cellist. Following the success of the violin concerto, a cello concerto was commissioned, and though it was mentioned several times in the press as a work in progress for Piatigorsky, it did not come about.[10]

Tanglewood had a rich and creative atmosphere, drawing many of the world's great talents, one of whom was Lukas Foss. A wunderkind composer, pianist and conductor, Foss came to the United States from Berlin in 1937 to continue his musical education at the Curtis Institute. He also studied with Hindemith and Koussevitzky at Tanglewood, and was soon appointed pianist with the Boston Symphony. During the mid–1940s Foss wrote his *Capriccio* for cello and piano for Piatigorsky. The work has immediate appeal through its American characteristics, and has since become a staple in cello repertory.[11] Foss stated that the music is "as American as many of my native American colleagues' music and perhaps less self-consciously so, since love and discovery prompted this expression rather than the dutiful nationalism of the period."[12]

Foss could not have written his American period music without the pioneering work of Roy Harris, Virgil Thomson, and especially Aaron Copland. Copland was a longtime faculty member at the Berkshire Music Center at Tanglewood. The composer arranged two movements (*Waltz and Celebration*) from his very popular ballet *Billy the Kid* for Piatigorsky, probably in 1949.[13] The movements are a guitar-impressioned waltz portraying Billy and his sweetheart, and a wild dance after Billy's capture.

Composer Vladimir Dukelsky was a friend and colleague of both Serge Koussevitzky and Gregor Piatigorsky. Like Piatigorsky, he escaped Russia during the civil war and eventually made it to New York. There he met George Gershwin (born Jacob Gershovitz) who suggested he also Americanize his own name to Vernon Duke. Best known as a songwriter of popular songs such as "April in Paris," "Autumn in New York," and "I Can't Get Started," Duke retained his given name for his classical works for most of his life and had a successful career in concert music, film, Broadway, ballet, and he was a close friend of Prokofiev. Piatigorsky commissioned a concerto from Dukelsky in 1942. Up until then the composer had written a piano concerto for Arthur Rubinstein and a violin concerto for Ruth Posselt. Dukelsky completed the orchestral materials to the cello concerto just before joining the military.

As the concerto was being studied, Piatigorsky suggested an alternate ending to the first movement. At first the composer balked but after the premiere on January 4, 1946, he wrote to Koussevitzky: "I owe you and Grisha another vote of thanks for the new ending of the 1st movement which he proposed and which you enthusiastically endorsed. It is not easy for a composer to agree to so drastic a change but I must admit that both musically and formally the curtailment of the coda is a miraculous improvement. The change has been incorporated in the printed piano & cello version."[14]

The critics did not always welcome Dukelsky's music. The composer was relieved that there was at least some praise for the concerto in Boston and New York. This was the first time both cities' critics had some degree of agreement on a new Dukelsky work.

> The Boston Symphony and Serge Koussevitzky brought to Carnegie Hall a new cello concerto composed by Vladimir Dukelsky for Gregor Piatigorsky, who appeared as soloist and played it brilliantly. The orchestral parts were equally sparkling. Mr. Dukelsky's concerto is alert and imaginative music, in which broad, songlike melody keeps company with brisk doings that are occasionally astringent in harmony. Sometimes, I thought, things were happening too rapidly for completely comfortable listening, but what was happening was interesting, and, altogether, the concerto was a welcome visitor.[15]
>
> ... original and arresting music ... brilliantly performed by Mr. Piatigorsky.[16]
>
> [I]t might be said that it is interesting in details, but not sufficiently impressive as a whole. The music exaggerates color at the expense of structure thus repeating once more a pattern recurring in most of Dukelsky's symphonic scores. There is no lack, however, of brilliant episodes, stretches of romantic lyricism, and in the finale one is reminded of Tchaikovsky's exuberant and almost aggressive march rhythms. Piatigorsky's eminent virtuosity presented the pretentious piece to the best possible advantage.[17]
>
> Although the work was directed with sincerity and authority ... even such a combination could not rescue it from dullness and monotony.[18]

> [T]he concerto is undeniably effective for an astonishing magician of the cello like Mr. Piatigorsky.[19]

However, with less than absolute rave notices, a bitter and frustrated Duke wrote: "Grisha had a resounding success with the concerto in Montreal, but I suspect that he would have created an even greater sensation had he played a set of virtuoso variations on *Chopsticks*; the representative music lovers of the town, whom I met at supper afterwards, were all politely noncommittal about my work. The critics the next morning, while praising Grisha to the skies, tore me to bits."[20]

Conducting

In 1943 the Denver Symphony was searching for a new conductor and asked Piatigorsky to take part in a fundraiser for the orchestra. They proposed that he conduct as well as play in order to create as much publicity as possible for the event. At first he refused, but after their persistent requests, he finally asked his manager, Arthur Judson, what he should do. Judson strongly urged him to accept, even though the cellist had never conducted. Acquiescing, Piatigorsky enlisted his neighbor, Eugene Ormandy, to give him a few pointers. Piatigorsky conducted works by Weber, Liadov, and Tchaikovsky, and played the Haydn Concerto and short works as soloist. The concert was a huge success and was followed by many offers to guest conduct elsewhere. Convinced that the cello was enough of a challenge, he refused. He recounted the experience in *Cellist*:

> Ready to start with the *Euryanthe* Overture by Weber, the concertmaster whispered, "The Star-Spangled Banner." I had not rehearsed it, and, somewhat bewildered, I gave a sign to the drummer and let him go on for an unreasonably long time. Majestically I raised my hand for a crescendo, and only when it reached its peak did I recall the national anthem. The capacity audience sang and the sound of the orchestra was impressive. The performance of the *Euryanthe* Overture which followed drew enthusiastic applause.
>
> Next on the program was the Haydn Cello Concerto. I faced my instrument in the backstage room almost in confusion, as if it were a piece of furniture I had never seen before. I frantically ran over passages I had played all my life. Although the concerto went very well, its impact seemed pale in comparison to the reception of my conducting during the entire program.
>
> The little baton had such an easy victory over my Stradivari. But it felt more bitter than sweet, and when offers for guest conducting began to come in from all over the country, I swore never to touch the baton again.[21]

In the summer of 1944, the Piatigorskys vacationed in Rockport, Maine. There Grisha composed his *Variations on a Paganini Theme*, based on Paganini's popular 24th Caprice for solo violin. Many composers, including Brahms, Liszt, and Rachmaninoff, used the theme for their sets of variations. Piatigorsky composed fourteen variations, each of which portrayed characteristics of performers he revered. Among those included were Casals, Heifetz, Milstein, Hindemith as a viola player, Kreisler, and Koussevitzky as a double-bass player. Rather than list the artists seriatim, he left it to audiences to guess their identities. The work is a cellistic tour de force and it became a favorite on his recital programs. His concerts usually included his own transcriptions, many of which have been published and have become part of the standard cello repertoire.

The *Variations* was orchestrated[22] and premiered on the *Bell Telephone Hour* in 1945. Piatigorsky also played it with several orchestras, always coupled with another solo work.

In 1946, he was scheduled to perform it with Dimitri Mitropoulos in Minneapolis. Piatigorsky was surprised to discover that the conductor had not seen the score until the night before the rehearsal. Mitropoulos, with his legendary photographic recall, had memorized it. Piatigorsky, modest about his compositional activities, recalled, "I heard many compliments after the performance but was glad the only composer present, Mr. Křenek, shook my hand and did not utter a word."[23]

In 1945 publisher Carl Fischer proposed many projects that unfortunately were never completed. One was in conjunction with pianist Artur Schnabel, who replied to the publisher: "To edit Beethoven's piano and cello sonatas for Carl Fischer, with Piatigorsky as co-editor, is certainly a most attractive proposition. Unfortunately I shall not have the time required for such a noble task (which, believe me, I resign with much hesitation)."[24] Other proposed projects were editions of the Boccherini, Dvořák, and Schumann concertos as well as a "Tchaikovsky Concerto" that Piatigorsky was to create from various non-cello works by the composer.

In April 1948, Piatigorsky and Horowitz publicly performed together after an absence of sixteen years. The occasion was the Chaliapin Memorial, commemorating the tenth anniversary of the passing of the singer, and took place at Hunter College in New York. The organizer of the event was none other than Michel Kachouk, Chaliapin's longtime manager, who in 1916 hired Piatigorsky to perform with the basso in Moscow. After the war, Piatigorsky resumed touring outside the United States, and aided the rebuilding of Europe through benefit concerts. In 1948 he traveled to England, Scotland, Finland, Scandinavia, Switzerland, the Netherlands, Belgium, and Paris. Of special interest was the Edinburgh Festival where he gave recitals and performed with the Concertgebouw (under Van Beinum) in the Dvořák Concerto, and with Menuhin and the London Philharmonic (under Sir Adrian Boult) in the Brahms Concerto (it was Menuhin's first essay with the work). Piatigorsky's old friend Furtwängler appeared at the festival one week before Piatigorsky's arrival. They last saw each other in Paris in 1939. At that time, Piatigorsky begged the conductor once more to come to the United States or accept any position offered to him away from Germany and Austria. He assured him that he would be welcome in any country. Piatigorsky himself never returned to either country and lamented that it was Furtwängler's stubborn naïveté and weak character that prevented his decision to leave.[25] They did not meet in 1948. Elisabeth Furtwängler described it as "two ships passing at night."[26]

At the end of 1948, the controversial conductor accepted an offer to conduct the Chicago Symphony. Rubinstein and Horowitz refused to ever appear with the orchestra if Furtwängler was appointed director. Furtwängler had been cleared by three denazification courts in Berlin and Vienna and also by a German jury of musicians and stated, "The Interallied Court in Berlin acquitted me of all charges in June 1947, and I have a letter of exoneration from the U.S. Military Government."[27] Jascha Heifetz is quoted from the *New York Times* on January 7, 1949: "Mr. Furtwängler had ample opportunity to get out of Germany before and even during the war and that he chose to remain, thus serving the cause of Nazism." Hurok's roster of artists followed (including Milstein, Brailowsky, Pons and Kostelanetz), even if some of them did not actively lobby against the conductor, as was the case with Piatigorsky and Milstein. Milstein defended the conductor:

> I remember Furtwängler openly displaying his opposition to Hitler. "I am German but what is happening in Germany at the moment is truly filthy."
> Some Americans have never forgiven Furtwängler for staying in Nazi Germany and conducting there. A rather disagreeable incident, in which certain critics have tried to involve

THÉATRE DES CHAMPS-ÉLYSÉES
Directeur : ROGER EUDES
Mardi 9 Novembre 1948

*Au bénéfice exclusif
des Orphelins et des Blessés de la Division Leclerc*

Sous la présidence de
Monsieur VINCENT AURIOL
Président de la République

UNIQUE RÉCITAL
PIATIGORSKY
au piano
IVOR NEWTON

PIANO GAVEAU   DISQUES "VICTOR"

" OFFICE ARTISTIQUE CONTINENTAL "
Mme N. BOUCHONNET, 45, RUE LA BOÉTIE,
PARIS-8ᵉ - TÉL. : BAL. 42-51 - R. C. Seine 726-181

Recital for war orphans, Paris, 1948.

Aspen Festival's first season: Milstein (left) and Mitropoulos, July 6, 1949 (courtesy Berko Photo, ferencberko.com).

me, happened when Furtwängler was invited to direct the Chicago Symphony Orchestra in 1948. Several famous American musicians announced that they would boycott the Chicago Orchestra if he accepted the post. I didn't join the protest despite the fact that some of my best friends had signed the anti–Furtwängler declaration.

Soon after this incident I was performing in Chicago and a journalist came backstage to find me. "Have you signed the protest against Furtwängler?" "No, and why should I have done? Furtwängler is a great musician, he is absolutely not a Nazi, and if the protest succeeds it is the Chicago orchestra that will lose out."[28]

With (left to right) Walter Paepcke (with cigarette), Albert Schweitzer and Barker Fairley, 1949 (courtesy Berko Photo, ferencberko.com).

Piatigorsky's perceived protest particularly hurt Furtwängler. Critic Claudia Cassidy later met Furtwängler in Salzburg and he asked her only one question: "Did Piatigorsky really sign the declaration?" She said, "I [am] afraid so." The conductor shook his head in disbelief and said, "I can't believe it. He was like my own son."[29] Furtwängler found out much later of Piatigorsky's automatic inclusion.[30] In a letter to Gilbert Back from late 1949, the conductor pondered: "It is possible, of course, that the same thing happened to Piatigorsky as to Milstein, who himself explained this to me here, and also apparently to Busch — namely that without their permission, protests against me were made up and published by certain interested parties."

The confusion is resolved in Daniel Gillis' book, *Furtwängler and America*: "Back replied on December 14, 1950, that he had recently seen Piatigorsky and that Piatigorsky denied ever having taken part in any action against Furtwängler."[31] The conductor remained unrepentant to the end: "Until this very day I am convinced that staying in Germany was the thing to do. I had great difficulty to decide whether to go or to stay, and it would have been much easier to emigrate. But there had to be a spiritual center of integrity for all the good and real Germans who had to stay behind. I felt that a really great work of music was a stronger and more essential contradiction of the spirit of Buchenwald and Auschwitz than words could be."[32]

Sabbatical, Writing and Film

Throughout his life, Piatigorsky had a strong desire to write. He regularly wrote poetry in Russian, and often quoted Pushkin in letters to his brother Shura. He had written several (unpublished) volumes, but showed them only to friends. In 1939 Piatigorsky considered writing his life story and began a journal, lasting for about a year. The journal reflected little on his past, but it demonstrated the constant strain of concert life — awful hotels, bad food, and fighting the weather while carrying a suitcase and cello.

Writing eventually became an outlet for his abundant fantasies and his formidable ability as storyteller. For him, this became tangible evidence of an educated and cultured man — skills he did not acquire as a youth. In the 1940s he began writing stories and limericks in English, and joked about his limited grasp of the language: "For years there was a competition of whose grammar and pronunciation [of] English had been worse between myself, Dr. Koussevitzky, Gregory Ratoff[33] and some others. I don't know who was the winner, but judging from the fun and laughter and imitations people made of my English, I must have ranked pretty high."[34]

He simultaneously began writing both a philosophical novel and his autobiography during the 1940s. By 1947 the scheme of his novel, *Mr. Blok*, took shape. Piatigorsky wrote the title of the book first, before he actually established Blok's character. He knew other "Blocks"— the composer Ernst Bloch, and the Russian poet, Alexander Blok, but neither inspired the subject of his novel. By the late 1940s, writing began to consume his spare time. He wrote whenever he could while on tour, using scraps of paper of any kind, be it a napkin or a used envelope, and refused anyone's help. He vowed he would not translate from Russian.

Piatigorsky announced he was taking a sabbatical beginning the fall of 1949, but it was only a slowdown; contracts had already been signed far ahead for concerts. His first solo and trio sessions at RCA were scattered throughout 1950, but he was able to slow down enough to finish *Mr. Blok*. He is quoted in the *Chicago Tribune*: "In the beginning, it was not easy. Not everybody wanted to hear the cello! But I kept on playing…. I have lived in trains and hotel rooms, I have carried my big cello from city to city. I have never refused an interview, even to a school paper. I have seen everybody after a performance who wanted to see me. Today, when the cello is a loved instrument, like the violin or piano, I feel I have helped a little. For a while, I can stop."[35]

In a 1952 interview he explained his slowdown:

> Since I was 7, I have been playing the cello. After 40 years, it is only natural for me to be my own severest critic. When the amateur plays, he is in heaven; the professional sweats blood as he is in the other place. It is the same in any field of creative endeavor.
>
> I decided 4 years ago that it was time I took a holiday. I wanted to enjoy myself as an ama-

teur. So I looked around me and asked myself what did I know least about? The answer was easy. My English.

My English is terrible. I cannot write a decent letter. My two children make fun of my English. I decided this was a fertile field for me. My spelling is terrible and I cannot even type. But I was fortunate in finding a secretary who would transcribe my longhand.... By the time I received the typewritten copy, I was too far ahead with the plot to read back.[36]

His writing took on a more serious tone after he met a real writer:

Then one day while I was in Minneapolis for a concert, Mr. and Mrs. Robert Penn Warren, the author of *All the King's Men* and professor of literature, invited me to lunch. I had fallen in the habit of carrying my manuscript in a briefcase so that whenever I had a free moment, I would write. As I sat down, Warren asked me what I had in the briefcase. I told him and he asked to see the manuscript. I was terribly embarrassed because I know what a chore it becomes for me when I am tired and have to audition youngsters. Now I am the youngster and I wait anxiously while Warren reads.

Hours must have passed before finally Mr. Warren returned. "It's the best darned thing I've read in a long time." Probably seeing me dumbfounded, he had to repeat. Now it was my turn for laughter. I could not stop. Not paying much attention and dead serious, he asked to keep the script with him and to make a telephone call to his publisher, Random House. Still dumbfounded I can't recall what I said until he spoke to Mr. Haas and Mr. Erskin and said that the script must be sent to them at once. I tore off a few last pages so that I could continue from where I stopped; I thanked my hosts and departed. My concert schedule was tremendous.

I was sure he was joking until I reached New York where I found several letters waiting for me — from book publishers. They wanted my book! I was flabbergasted. I decided to try myself and sent parts of the manuscript to several publishers. They all offered contracts. So I signed with Random House.

Now I have finished the book. I have enjoyed every minute of it. But suddenly I am devastated. I realize I am no longer an amateur. I have a contract. My joy as a novice is gone. I must work more and rewrite and delete. As a professional, you see, I am highly critical.[37]

Mr. Blok was also perused by the nearly blind Aldous Huxley, who also encouraged Piatigorsky to have it published. Huxley was an old friend that he first met in the 1920s in Berlin with James Joyce; they both attended Schnabel-Flesch-Piatigorsky trio rehearsals. Nevertheless, Piatigorsky was not confident about publishing it and never submitted a final draft — even after publicly announcing its completion to *Time* magazine. He thought there would only be interest in his memoirs. Piatigorsky described the book: "It is a philosophical satire which I will probably just call *Mr. Blok*, the name of the hero. He is a good man, not old or young, rich or poor, free yet chained, an artist and an intellectual, successful but not famous, a man who comes from some foreign country, a human being who loves people but who has no personal attachments, to whom everything happens and nothing." The following is from the book's preface: "*Blok* is as much myth as reality, a prayer and a satire, as ageless as a genius and a common man. He is the world in which he does not quite belong, and I could not say more than that he is unique, like you and like me — just perhaps more obscure and a little more lovable."

Piatigorsky was, however, persuaded to write his autobiography, but he took to the task with hesitation. He had started taking notes in 1939 and wrote in Russian. Though he signed a contract with Doubleday in 1947, his autobiography was not published until 1965. The book limped along for years despite the publisher supplying Piatigorsky with a typist and editorial help. The head editor, Ken McCormick, was patient and cajoled Piatigorsky to keep the pages coming. Even so, by 1956 he was considering returning his advance payment as he felt he could not complete the book. His creative energies were spread thin with his heavy schedule, and he also became sidetracked with composing a symphony. He braved sharing the work with the perfectionist Hindemith, who was complimentary. Nonetheless, the symphony as well as *Mr. Blok* were never published. Portions of the autobiography, however, were published in the *Atlantic Monthly* before the work appeared in book form as *Cellist*.[38]

Film

By the end of the 1930s, Piatigorsky had become increasingly wary of the virtuoso life. He would complain to friends that he "loved the music" but "hated the profession." Harry Ellis Dickson recalled: Whenever he came to Boston and I would ask: "Grisha, how are you?" his answer was always the same: "Lousy! Goddamn profession, always traveling, always worried, always nervous. Lousy profession!"[39]

He began to think of other things and briefly considered a second career in Hollywood, as it had lured pianist José Iturbi, Heifetz, and many singers. Rudolph Polk, a promoter and professional violinist who became increasingly involved in the film industry, principally spurred the idea on.[40] After his solo career fizzled, Polk moved to California and became a secretary and personal representative to Heifetz in the 1930s.[41]

"Rudy" Polk became Piatigorsky's agent for radio appearances in Hollywood and tried his hand as an independent music manager.[42] They read chamber music at the home of Konstantin Bakaleinikoff, a friend of Piatigorsky's from the Moscow Conservatory. A former cellist, Bakaleinikoff made hundreds of films in Hollywood as a music director.

Hollywood took notice of Piatigorsky, who had been named one of the ten most handsome men in the United States and was the subject of many artists.[43] The flirtation went so far as Piatigorsky taking a screen test in 1939. Dorle Soria wrote of the crossroads: "Grisha, who was to play in Los Angeles, said out of his despair that he wanted to get into the movies. We said he was too gloomy. Hollywood liked cheerful people. Grisha pondered the impasse and solved it. 'I will change into violinist to make happy ending.'"[44]

In 1940, Howard Hawks and Samuel Goldwyn thought Piatigorsky would be a good candidate for the role of psychology Professor Magenbruch in *Ball of Fire*. The comedy is based on a story Billy Wilder fashioned from *Snow White and the Seven Dwarfs*, featuring eight encyclopedists on a quest to complete the book of human knowledge. The producers thought Piatigorsky's personality and thick accent might prove cinematic, but he declined after another screen test, unimpressed with the whole process.

The cellist's friendship with Danny Kaye led to another effort to appear in film, this time in a remake of *Ball of Fire*, called *A Song Is Born*, in 1947. Kaye was to star and producer Samuel Goldwyn offered the part of Professor Magenbruch to Piatigorsky. Though picked up by limousine and given the royal treatment, Piatigorsky was not comfortable with the prospect of acting rather than performing. The part went to Benny Goodman, and the film became a jazz showcase.

Piatigorsky once attended a Danny Kaye performance at New York's Roxy Theatre. The vast movie house was packed and Piatigorsky stood in the wings, listening to one of Kaye's famous patter songs, Cab Calloway's "Minnie the Moocher," during which the audience repeated the comedian's chorus of nonsense syllables. Kaye suddenly sang out, "Piatigorsky" and the 5,000 people in the auditorium sang the name back, then, "Next Wednesday night," and finally, "Carnegie Hall"—the audience repeated every word in unison. "All my life," Piatigorsky told Kaye, "I've been trying to get people to pronounce my name, but they never could get it right. You sing it once, and you get it back right 5000 times!"[45]

A film that Piatigorsky did appear in was *Carnegie Hall*. The movie attempts to please everyone with a storyline that creates an excuse to showcase major artists. At its best it is a historical document of superlative artistry, featuring Lily Pons, Bruno Walter, Heifetz, Rubinstein, Jan Peerce, Stokowski, Rodzinski, and Reiner. The coproducer of *Carnegie Hall*, Boris Morros, claimed among his many accomplishments to be a cello wunderkind, and Piatigorsky's first teacher.[46] The latter is, of course, not true, as Morros grew up in St. Petersburg, while Piatigorsky lived in Yekaterinoslav and Moscow. Piatigorsky recalled:

> I did not see the script, but I was told that it would be an authentic history of the famous hall. The list of performers in the picture was formidable [including] someone impersonating Tchaikovsky inaugurating Carnegie Hall, and heaven knows who else. My query as to what I should perform was answered, "Anything you wish." The contract signed, I asked again, but the identical answer had a slight modification: "Anything you wish, providing it's not over two minutes long."
>
> I played *The Swan*. Well, it's not something unusual for a cellist to live in the company of this bird. There is nothing wrong with it: the music is fine, the bird is noble, as is the legend of its death; but there is hardly anything worth while that cannot with some effort be transformed into a travesty. In Carnegie Hall I recorded the piece with a harp. Finding the sound satisfactory, the next day I came for the shooting of the picture. To my bewilderment, instead of being photographed with the one harpist with whom I made the recording, I found myself surrounded by half a dozen or so ladies with harps. They all were alike, wearing identical flowers, gowns, and expressions.
>
> "Can they play the harp?" I asked Mr. Morros.
>
> He said, "No."
>
> "What are they doing here?"
>
> "I need them for the background." The busy producer had no time for further conversation. He was arranging the position of the group, giving orders to cameramen, and hurrying me to the make-up room. Unaccustomed to theatrical beautification, I disbelievingly watched my face undergo drastic changes. With "voluptuous" lines around my eyes and with my face coated with something like pink stucco, I returned to Mr. Morros. "You look gorgeous," he said. "Just gorgeous," he repeated after my sequence of Carnegie Hall had been completed.
>
> I attended the "premiere" of the picture and stormed out of the theater after *The Swan*. The sight of the cellist wrapped in a bouquet of harpists was devastating, but my post-mortem cries did not last, and this experience became a souvenir not unlike one of the comical or sad snapshots one finds in an old family album.[47]

A publicity photo exists which suggests that there may have been a further role for Piatigorsky at some point. Rubinstein, who also appeared in the film, wrote about his experience:

> Mr. Morros welcomed me at the New York airport and drove me in his Rolls-Royce limousine to my hotel. During the long drive the verbose Mr. Morros treated me to a big avalanche of names he had obtained for his film, even resorting to a good deal of lying.
>
> "I'll get Toscanini, Kreisler, the whole bunch of them," he shouted. At that point, I lost my patience.
>
> "Boris," I said severely, "I can bet that before your film is over, Harry James will play the trumpet and win the day."
>
> "Only for three minutes" Boris said.
>
> I was only guessing at random but fell on the right name![48]

In early 1949 the ambitious Rudy Polk pitched an idea for a film series to include Arthur Rubinstein, Heifetz and Piatigorsky, capitalizing on the trio's upcoming summer concert series at Ravinia. The centerpiece would be called "The Trio," surrounded by solo film profiles for each member. The trio agreed to film the television programs for his new production company, Artist Films, Inc. The impressive venture expanded to include several other artists, such as guitarist Andres Segovia and tenor Jan Peerce.

Though the trio were apprehensive — not expecting any market success — they agreed to a share of profits rather than a fee. The series unfortunately did not make money and folded.[49] Piatigorsky and Rubinstein accepted the loss, but Heifetz would not let the matter die. The ever-enigmatic violinist wanted his projected profits and suspected Polk of swindling him, as well as Heifetz's trio partners. He came up with a scheme. Invite Polk over for dinner and a game of cards; let the police know ahead of time so they could raid Polk's home in search of evidence. The police "took hold of his belongings and bank account. Ironically, nothing unethical on Polk's part was later discovered."[50]

Only a few of the "signed contracts" were realized — aimed at the mass television audience, garbed within superfluous plots. Television was then in its infancy and finding a national sponsor or network was not easy. The films were televised several times and they were eventually sold to the educational film market. (The films are now commercially available on DVD.) The Trio is seen in abridged versions of Mendelssohn's Trio, Op. 49, and Schubert's Trio in B-flat.[51] The playing is spectacular, especially the artful, virtuosic bowing in the Mendelssohn Scherzo. The trio also had an enjoyable time of it, hamming it up in a fake argument, laced with harsh words for the camera, albeit in Russian, adding comic relief to an otherwise dreadful script.[52]

Piatigorsky's solo film is a stunning example of his artistry at the height of his career, demonstrating total command of his instrument and poetically nuanced turns of phrase. The performances took place in a television studio with pianist Ralph Berkowitz, as part of a silly story attempting to carry the masses through great music by personalizing the performer. The applause was provided by an unseen audience made up of Heifetz, Segovia, Rubinstein, the producers and any of the crew with free hands.[53]

There are several later films with Piatigorsky as subject. One was by Tim Whalen Jr. (*Gregor Piatigorsky*, 1966) and another was by Steven Grumette (*An Afternoon with Gregor Piatigorsky*, 1975). Both films see him in performance and teaching at home and at USC. A short documentary, *Choose Life*, was produced by the Jewish Chautauqua Society in 1973 where he plays portions from Bruch's *Kol Nidrei* interspersed within a historical backdrop.

Television appearances are rare beyond the Polk films, but fortunately those, as well as the *Bell Telephone Hour* and *Producer's Showcase*, are available on DVD. The European premiere of the Walton Concerto over the BBC has been released by EMI. A two-hour documentary, *The Master and His Class* (1972), is an in-depth view into his teaching style, and a seven-hour series for German television features Piatigorsky reading from *Cellist* in German (1970).

By the 1940s, Los Angeles was beginning to boast an artistic population that dramatically contrasted the Hollywood image of movie stars and vanity. Bruno Walter, Thomas Mann, Igor Stravinsky, Arnold Schonberg and others established residences there, contributing to the change in public perception. Residents as well, the trio attended occasional private evening musicales in Los Angeles. On one such evening, the guests also included Stravinsky and a reporter. The latter overheard a conversation that revealed Rubinstein's wit as he made small talk:

> "This is the most extraordinary experience I shall ever have!" said a gushing admirer.
> "I think I understand what you mean," Rubinstein replied.
> "We do make pretty good music together, considering we have to use local talent."[54]

The Rubinstein-Heifetz-Piatigorsky Trio Or Should That Read: The Heifetz-Rubinstein-Piatigorsky Trio

Jascha Heifetz was well known in Russia, even before the 1917 Bolshevik Revolution. Leopold Auer's violin wunderkind in St. Petersburg was already soloing outside of Russia by the age of twelve. Heifetz's reputation did not go unnoticed in Moscow, where the musical contest between the two cities was intense. St. Petersburg, modern, extroverted and European, challenged Moscow, traditional and introverted. The rivalry formed a great divide in the Russian musical world.

The young Piatigorsky heard a performance by the sixteen-year-old Heifetz in Moscow in late 1916. By then Heifetz and his controlling father had recognized the necessity of leaving the chaos of Russia and departed for America in 1917. While Heifetz's career took a direct path to international stardom, Piatigorsky's meandered, performing in cafés and nightclubs — something young Heifetz never experienced.

After Heifetz and Piatigorsky met in 1925, their friendship was sealed. There were many informal chamber music gatherings at the Piatigorsky apartment in Berlin that included many of the era's leading musicians: violinists Kreisler, Elman, Kulenkampf, Spalding, Wolfsthal, and Szigeti; cellists Feuermann, and Mainardi; and pianists Schnabel, Szreter, Serkin, Gieseking, Raucheisen, and Edwin Fischer. During one of Heifetz's visits, Piatigorsky complained about his difficulty with staccato bowing. Heifetz said, "come in the next room and we shall see." Twenty minutes later the problem was solved and Piatigorsky yelled to his friend and accompanist Karol Szreter, "Karolchik! I made it!"[55]

Piatigorsky developed a staccato technique with the bow that became the envy of string players and perhaps Heifetz himself. Though Heifetz had a fine staccato, he admired violinist Erica Morini's, and asked her how she achieved it. Heifetz's admiration of Piatigorsky's playing (and of his elegant staccato) is reflected in the violinist's special arrangement for him of one of his signature encores, *Hora Staccato*, by Dinicu.[56]

In July 1937 Arthur Rubinstein and Piatigorsky recorded the Brahms E Minor Sonata. Rubinstein and Heifetz were scheduled to record the Franck Sonata the following year. Since RCA (then in contract with EMI/HMV in Europe) "owned" the artists, they also proposed to record Rubinstein-Heifetz-Piatigorsky as a trio in 1937. But RCA found it impossible to pull together all three artists at that time due to their hectic schedules. (After Heifetz and Rubinstein moved to Los Angeles, cellist Emanuel Feuermann, also a RCA artist, followed in 1939. RCA was able to bring its three Angelinos together to record three works in 1941— RCA's answer to the illustrious trio of Alfred Cortot, Jacques Thibaud, and Pablo Casals. Feuermann's death in 1942 ended the ensemble; they never performed together publicly.)

Piatigorsky's relationship with his manager, Arthur Judson, of Columbia Concerts, had always been professional, but the cellist's repeated requests for higher fees came to a head in early 1949. Piatigorsky made an appointment with Judson to clear up the matter. He once again asked for a better fee, suggesting it be the same as, for instance, the soprano Lily Pons. Judson said, "But you are not Lily Pons!" which sent the cellist into a rage. Piatigorsky shouted, "I am not Lily Pons! I am Piatigorsky!" He then asked Judson if he had ever attended one of his concerts. Judson said he didn't need to; he knew Piatigorsky's playing from his many years of fame, recordings, and broadcasts. The cellist responded, "Then I

VIOLIN
Efrem Zimbalist

Ivan Galamian   Veda Reynolds

VIOLA and *Chamber Music*

William Primrose   Karen Tuttle

VIOLONCELLO
Gregor Piatigorsky

Woodwind and String Ensembles
Marcel Tabuteau

Brass Ensemble
Charles Gusikoff

ORCHESTRA
Alexander Hilsberg, *Conductor*

FLUTE	**OBOE**
William Kincaid	Marcel Tabuteau
CLARINET	**BASSOON**
Ralph McLane	Sol Schoenbach
HORN	**DOUBLE BASS**
Mason Jones	Roger Scott
TRUMPET	**TROMBONE, TUBA**
Samuel Krauss	Charles Gusikoff

PERCUSSION
David Grupp

ACCOMPANISTS

Vladimir Sokoloff   Martha Halbwachs Masséna

· 8 ·

The Curtis instrumental faculty.

The Faculty

SERGE KOUSSEVITZKY, *Director*
AARON COPLAND, *Assistant Director*
RALPH BERKOWITZ, *Executive Assistant to the Director*

Orchestral Conducting and Orchestra
SERGE KOUSSEVITZKY
Assisted by:

LEONARD BERNSTEIN	RICHARD BURGIN
ELEAZAR DE CARVALHO	HOWARD SHANET

LUKAS FOSS
Members of the Boston Symphony Orchestra

Chamber Music
GREGOR PIATIGORSKY, *Head*   WILLIAM KROLL, *Associate Head*
Assisted by:

JEAN BEDETTI	FERNAND GILLET
SIMEON BELLISON	RUTH POSSELT
RALPH BERKOWITZ	ZVI ZEITLIN

Members of the Boston Symphony Orchestra

Composition
AARON COPLAND   JACQUES IBERT
Assisted by IRVING FINE

Opera
BORIS GOLDOVSKY, *Head (on leave of absence)*
JAN POPPER, *Acting Head*
Assisted by:

SARAH CALDWELL	FELIX WOLFES
LEO VAN WITSEN	And others, to be announced

Choral Conducting and Chorus
HUGH ROSS   ROBERT SHAW (*on leave of absence*)
Assisted by EDWARD BARRET

Solfège
KATHARINE WOLFF

Analysis
JULIUS HERFORD

The Tanglewood instrumental faculty.

quit. You cannot represent someone you don't know!" Impresario Sol Hurok was contacted and quickly offered Piatigorsky a contract with Hurok Attractions.

It required five years of planning before the Rubinstein-Heifetz-Piatigorsky Trio took to the stage in July 1949. The Trio presented a series of four concerts at Ravinia, the summer home of the Chicago Symphony. They performed several trios, including Beethoven's *Arch-*

duke, Brahms's op. 8 and Schubert's op. 99, as well as three others that they would record for RCA the following year (Tchaikovsky, Ravel and Mendelssohn). Rubinstein also played duo sonatas with them.

But the Ravinia concerts almost did not take place. On May 14, 1949, Ravinia's 1400-seat wooden pavilion burned to the ground. A short six weeks later the 14th Ravinia Festival opened on schedule under a 33-ton canvas originally constructed to shelter B-29 bombers. The unusual canopy posed no problem for its legendary musicians. Piatigorsky remembered: "Luckily this architectural emergency brought by accident acoustics superior to those of some new halls built by expert acousticians and architects."[57]

Another near disaster occurred during a rehearsal the day before one of the concerts. Piatigorsky accidentally knocked his cello against a chair and broke a corner off the *Baudiot* Stradivarius. After a shocked silence, all three musicians fell to their hands and knees and began a frantic search for the tiny fragments, passing their hands over the floor of the stage in order to gather every shred. When it seemed that all the pieces had been recovered, Piatigorsky dashed via train and taxi to a well-known luthier in Winnetka where the repair was done perfectly, to the cellist's relief. The experience reminded him that his signature stride while entering the stage—with cello held up high above music stands—was for practical reasons.

Rehearsals began in mid–June in Beverly Hills and were intense and lively, lasting ten hours a day. The musicians did not allow any visitors; Rubinstein remarked, "That was the kitchen work, and you don't cook in public." When the trio rehearsed in Chicago, they allowed Ravinia to amplify the musicians. With nearly 10,000 listeners crowding under the huge tent, Rubinstein was unhappy with the results: "With this mic, I play what is fortissimo and drown Jascha. But what should I do? Play mouse? I go crazy if I hold back and go nibble-nibble; fortissimo is not like a mouse." In a review of the concert series, *Time* magazine quoted the cellist: "If you have one man who is very meticulous and precise [Heifetz], one who is more general [Rubinstein] and one who is ... ah ... melancholy [Piatigorsky], you must work very hard until you all feel [the music] together."[58]

That remarkable summer, the trio was awarded honorary doctorates on August 10 at Northwestern University, an unusual gesture for three artists in one discipline. *Life* published an article about the trio and dubbed them the Million Dollar Trio, though the tag annoyed them. The trio also filmed a television portrayal, replete with corny narration—but their playing of Schubert and Mendelssohn trios is nothing short of spectacular. Television was then in its infancy, but in spite of its flaws, gave all three exposure to a vast audience.

Besides Ravinia, the summer of 1949 was busy. Piatigorsky's annual obligations at Tanglewood with performing and heading the chamber music program were augmented with the inaugural season of the Aspen Music Festival. Basically, Aspen had been a mining ghost town, and was only recently transformed into a resort. The Festival started as the bicentennial celebration of the German poet-philosopher Goethe, where many notables attended, performed or lectured, including Albert Schweitzer, who, among his many other amazing accomplishments, was also a Goethe scholar. Conductor Dimitri Mitropoulos and the Minneapolis Symphony were Aspen's orchestra in residence, and featured Piatigorsky, Rubinstein and Milstein as soloists (who also gave recitals).

By October 1949 the Piatigorskys had moved to Los Angeles. This made it convenient for the Rubinstein-Heifetz-Piatigorsky trio to record in the summer of 1950 for RCA, the exclusive recording venue for each of them.[59] These recordings were hugely successful and are still among the handful of recordings that have never been out of print in the RCA catalog.

Though their rapport in rehearsal was fully functional, further collaboration as a piano trio did not take place after the recording sessions of 1950. Heifetz and Rubinstein feuded. The difficult history between them stemmed from the recording sessions of the Franck Sonata in 1937, and continued through the trio's work with Feuermann in 1941; all three had sufficient egos to drive recording engineers to distraction, as each wanted their part featured as they saw fit. Both Rubinstein and Feuermann noted Heifetz's predomination with the balance and microphone placement. The residual strain emerged eight years later into the new trio with Piatigorsky. Ivor Newton, one of Piatigorsky's favorite pianists, recalled: "When I asked him how he had enjoyed this episode in his career, he simply replied, 'They wanted me to play like a mouse!' On one occasion, I understood from Piatigorsky, they were rehearsing [for a balance check during the recording sessions] together when Heifetz stopped playing. 'The balance is all wrong,' he said, 'I can hear the cello.'"[60] On a musical level, Heifetz preferred forward motion, while Rubinstein preferred less. This caused the expected arguments, but Rubinstein may have had another underlying grudge. By chance, the pianist discovered that Heifetz's concert fees were double those of Rubinstein. Artur Weschler-Vered reported:

> [Rubinstein] walked in to the office of Sol Hurok, who at the time also served as Heifetz's [and Piatigorsky's] agent, and said: "You will give me a thousand dollars for a concert, I'll do for you twenty concerts per month, and you'll take care of all the arrangements around." When his huge success began to be translated into serious money, Hurok came to Rubinstein one day and told him: "Listen, I can't pay Mr. Heifetz twice as much as I pay you, while you keep filling up the concert halls for me all the time."[61]

Their war escalated to include publicity materials; Heifetz bitterly resented that publicity bore the names Rubinstein, Heifetz, Piatigorsky — always in the same order. Rubinstein wrote:

> "Why can't we change it and give each one of us a chance to be the first-named?" said Jascha.
> "I couldn't care less," I answered indifferently, "but as far as I know, all trios are published for piano, violin and violoncello, and it is the tradition to publicize the players in this order."
> Jascha didn't want to give in so soon.
> "I have seen some trios printed for violin and violoncello, accompanied by the piano," he said.
> "They must have been printed by yourself, Jascha."
> "What do you mean?" he said indignantly. "I've really seen them."
> I began to see red.
> "Jascha," I shouted, "if God played the violin, it would still be printed Rubinstein, God and Piatigorsky."
> No reply from Jascha.[62]

As more publicity and record jacket design was planned, the old argument intensified. Rubinstein was the victor, but the battle killed the ensemble's future. Years later, the sting of the incident still lingered for Rubinstein:

> I know every violinist worth knowing and Heifetz is the worst man I ever met. He's a great musician, but absolutely awful as a person. I cut myself away from this horrible person 20 or 30 years ago and I haven't heard from him since ... nor do I want to.
> I remember the difficult times we had when we recorded together. He always wanted his name first, before mine. He was completely uncompromising and this caused us to discontinue our cooperation.
> The world should know what kind of a man Heifetz really is.[63]

Throughout the battle, Piatigorsky remained insulated: "Everyone agreed upon dates, programs, fees, and even on what order the names should be printed on the program and who should walk on stage first. This, of course, was not my problem, for everyone knows that the cellist is always the last."[64]

Boston Symphony violinist and conductor Harry Ellis Dickson thought he could bring the trio together once again, and proposed that they become the centerpiece of the 10th anniversary of Brandeis University. The trio would receive honorary doctorates and perform the Beethoven Triple Concerto with the Boston Symphony. Brandeis and the Boston Symphony approved the project; conductor Charles Munch sent personal letters to each musician with the proposal. Piatigorsky replied that he was pleased about the idea and would participate. Dickson remembered: "For a long time nothing was heard from the other two, until I met Rubinstein at a concert in New York. He informed me that he wouldn't be caught dead on the same stage with Heifetz. A short while later, a letter came from Heifetz saying he was too busy."[65]

10. The 1950s: Los Angeles

In the 1950s, Piatigorsky's publicity material boasted that he had been heard by more people than any other living cellist. With the advent of television, he quickly became the most visible cellist as well. Initially Piatigorsky was hesitant about appearing on TV and joked: "A friend explained that it would take over one hundred years for that many people to hear me in concert. He failed to tell me how many seconds it would take them to forget."[1]

Other than the syndication of the solo and trio films, his television appearances were rare in the United States. Among them were performances on the *Bell Telephone Hour* and *Producer's Showcase*. The latter was sponsored by RCA and impresario Sol Hurok with a viewing audience estimated at 23 million people. Hurok boasted: "The show went over with such a bang, it created such a revolution, that it proved to everybody that the American people are not morons. They can accept the greatest in music and in opera. NBC and Hurok will give it to them."[2] Piatigorsky also appeared on the BBC and CBC (Canada) in recitals and orchestral concerts, including the European premiere of Walton's Cello Concerto with the Royal Philharmonic.[3]

The 1954-55 season was a heavy one. Piatigorsky arrived in London in October and recorded the Beethoven sonatas with Solomon, then played a recital with Ivor Newton on BBC Television, followed by a tour of Europe and Israel, after which he had a visit with Toscanini in Parma, Italy. Though it had been years since the two had seen each other, they felt that no time had passed. The energetic maestro and the cellist stayed up talking until the early morning, pausing only to play the maestro's records at a deafening volume:

> All day we were together, yes and most of the time we spent talking all the time.... [H]e was almost 90 I believe at that time.... [H]e was his usual enormous vigor and he listened to his records, hundreds of them. He liked to listen to them very loud, you know, you could hear two miles away, and so we discussed things and so on. Finally when 3:00 in the morning, just before leaving, and with his wonderful smile, tender smile, said to me "I want to give you something.... I want to give you a present. Please tell me what can I give you." So of course I suggested, "Maestro — stay well, be healthy, be happy, that's what I want." "No, no, no, I want to give you something!" I said, "well I think it was about 25 or 30 years ago I asked you for your photo," and he said "What? All these years you waited and I did not give you?" And he started screaming in a tremendous excitement, and finally wanted to give a huge photo of his which was hung on the wall. His daughter Wally said, "Now look. Grisha can't travel with his cello and this huge photo of yours. No, you must give something else." "No, that is the best I have and that what he going to have!" and he tried to tear it from the wall. Finally he didn't get it, but the next morning, before I left the hotel, which was before 7, the man at the reception desk said, "Maestro Toscanini just left and here is an envelope

for you." In this envelope were two photos, one written in Italian in red ink and the other in English. Later on the train when I read it, I must say, I just burst in tears because such a dedication I never received from anyone.[4]

Celibidache, Schippers and Koussevitzky

In La Scala, Piatigorsky performed with conductor Sergiu Celibidache in what the cellist thought were the best Dvořák concerto performances of his career. The conductor demanded an unheard of four rehearsals rather than the usual single run-through for the concerto. Their collaboration created an inner connectedness usually found only in chamber music. In an interview Piatigorsky recalled: "His accompaniment was unforgettable. I played a concerto I had played hundreds of times before, but with Celibidache it seemed like a completely new work. I never understood why a conductor so absolutely marvelous was as little known and as little in demand."[5] Late in life Celibidache recounted that the two greatest soloists he worked with were Piatigorsky and violinist David Oistrakh: "Piatigorsky's sound was incomparable ... it was the warm and melancholic sound of a real man with a huge musical soul, but without any sentimentality.... [H]e never played in a mechanical way, but always in the way of "symphonic spirit."[6] Piatigorsky performed again that season with Celibidache in Israel, and donated his fee on this occasion — as well as the fees from his seventeen remaining concerts — to the Israel Philharmonic's pension fund.

The cellist's support of Israel was notable, and over the years he gave numerous benefit concerts, including fundraising events to endow the American Fund for Israel Institutions and the American Fund for Palestinian Institutions. In Paris he was awarded the Legion of Honor, not only for his artistry, but also for his aid to war-orphaned children. In May 1955, he also played Faure's Elegy for the Albert Einstein Memorial at UCLA.

After World War II, Piatigorsky began to acquire a large "collection" (as he would say) of honorary degrees bestowed on him from American colleges and universities, as well as honorary membership in the Royal Philharmonic Society and Royal Academy of Music in London. These tokens of recognition meant something real for him, especially since he had not received any degree as a student.

Piatigorsky was a regular presence at annual summer festival concerts with the major orchestras at Ravinia (Chicago), Tanglewood (Boston), Robin Hood Dell (Philadelphia), Hollywood Bowl (Los Angeles) and Lewisohn Stadium (New York). Outdoor concerts posed their own set of problems to plague soloists. Noises — natural or human — can occur at the most awkward moments. Airplanes, crying babies, or thunderstorms can test the concentration of any performer. Once, annoyed by people eating popcorn during his performance of *Don Quixote*, he complained to conductor Fritz Reiner. The conductor had little sympathy, wryly suggesting: "Do as we conductors do — turn your back towards them." At another Ravinia concert, Piatigorsky performed the Dvořák Concerto and asked conductor Pierre Monteux,

> "You remember we played it in Amsterdam 28 years ago?" He's 79 years old and for him to name 28 years does not mean much — but what about me? It made me feel his age and even older when I think of knowing Tchaikovsky's brother, and several very intimate friends of Schumann and Brahms.
>
> Our concert was a happy one and the weather was just right. The audience was very receptive and enjoyed the music almost as much as their picnics on the lawn. Our second concert

I would like to skip on account of unfavorable weather and half a dozen noisy trains which chose to pass exclusively during pianissimo passages.

Working with unknown conductors could hold surprises:

Just before I left Chicago there was a telephone call.

"My name is Schippers"[7] the voice said, "How do you do? I am your conductor in New York," he said. "You see I never conducted all these concertos. Can I see you?"

"I am sorry. I am leaving," I said.

"Can I see you in New York?" he asked.

I said "Positively. At the concert."

Well, it was my first blind date, and very agreeable one, for though only 22 years old, I found him a true artist with a fine intuition — which can never be replaced by knowledge in the world.[8]

Piatigorsky tried to make his guest appearances more valuable in the 1950s and suggested he stay in towns for longer periods of time to integrate into the musical life of a community. One such occasion was unintentional but memorable for Gerhard Herz, an administrator for the Louisville Chamber Society:

Among my memories, none is more vivid than an evening in 1956. Cellist Gregor Piatigorsky, in town to appear as soloist with the Louisville Orchestra, attended a concert by the Budapest Quartet and at intermission, went back stage to greet his old friends.

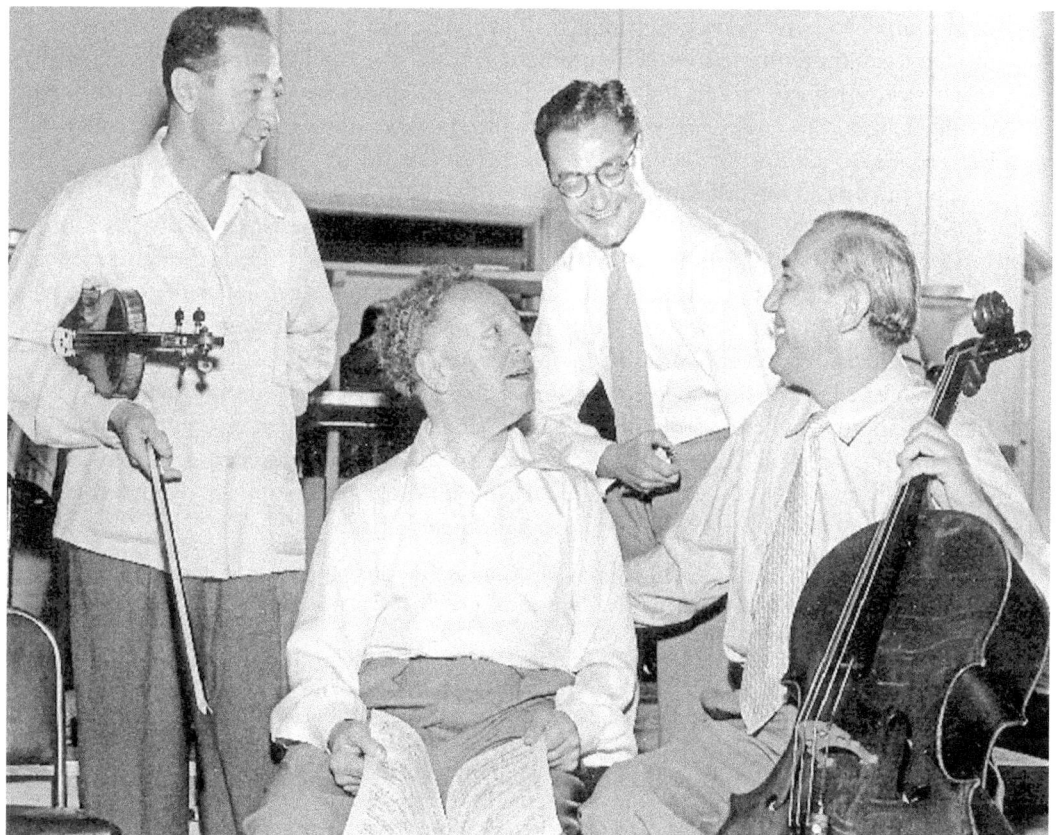

Left to right: **Rubinstein-Heifetz-Piatigorsky Trio with recording engineer Richard Mohr (wearing glasses), 1950.**

>   A great Russian embrace, with everyone shouting "Misha!" "Grisha!" "Sasha!" Kisses left, kisses right.
>   I turned to Sasha and said, "The Schubert C Major!" [Schubert's Quintet in C major for two violins, viola and two cellos].
>   The Budapest, as fate would have it, had played Schubert's quintet the night before in Indianapolis with a talented local cellist, and the music for it lay in the trunk of Sasha's car. A hasty conference was called, with Piatigorsky agreeing to play if he could perform the first part, since he had never played the second. A courier was dispatched to Piatigorsky's hotel to get his cello, while Fanny Brandeis, the Society's secretary, and Schneider went before the audience to announce "a lengthy intermission."
>   About an hour later, Piatigorsky joined the Budas on the stage of the University of Louisville Playhouse.... I still remember the Schubert Quintet as one of the society's absolute high points; it was sheer heaven.[9]

In the 1950s Piatigorsky also began to explore other interests beyond his life in music. Since childhood he had been fascinated by snakes and fish, and he began more serious study of herpetology and oceanography. An eager student, he traveled to the California deserts with noted scientists to see animal life firsthand. At home he also collected stamps and continued his writing.

Living in Los Angeles, a rapidly expanding city crisscrossed with new highways, required driving a car. His first attempt at driving had been in Elizabethtown but had been a disaster — one sidewalk excursion convinced him to give up. In Los Angeles, his children teased him: "Mother can do everything, you can only play the cello." So, for the second time, he tackled driving lessons. An automatic transmission and bribing the official with concert tickets helped him finally obtain a driver's license. Never really comfortable with driving, Piatigorsky could easily get lost on the freeways of Los Angeles. He remained extremely fearful of left turns and would go to great lengths to avoid them.

Despite his driving difficulties, Piatigorsky emerged as one of Los Angeles' first citizens of culture in the 1950s. He sponsored and assisted many organizations, especially the Young Musician's Foundation (YMF), later becoming its president. YMF's "Debut" Orchestra was a preprofessional orchestral program that trained gifted musicians, such as conductor Michael Tilson Thomas (who also served as accompanist in Piatigorsky's classes). Piatigorsky was also musical advisor and supporter of the Music Academy of the West in Santa Barbara.[10] Its distinguished faculty included conductors Richard Lert, Fritz Zweig and Maurice Abravanel, soprano Lotte Lehmann, violinist Sascha Jacobsen, and pianist Gyorgy Sandor.

After the death of Serge Koussevitzky in 1951, Piatigorsky began to pull away from Tanglewood, choosing to stay closer to Los Angeles during the summer. Koussevitzky's spirit, however, remained intact:

>   I cannot think of Sergei Alexandrovich Koussevitzky in the past tense because he is and because he will be, just as his dreams became reality and just as his vision is still at work, is bound to be realized in the future.
>   "I dream only the dreams which promise to come true," he said. Indeed, he had the gift to dream at will. He always looked forward; he would take a look back only to see how much had been already achieved, to gain strength to move upward again — but he never climbed alone.
>   Greatness in art is something one cannot learn. Greatness in man is something one cannot imitate, but only learn from and be inspired by. The rules were never dictated by a country where Koussevitzky resided. The obstacles to his ideas were swept away and rendered helpless by his overwhelming will to build monuments of music which in his lifetime became testimony of himself.
>   His enthusiasm and unfailing intuition paved the road for the young, encouraged even the

masters, and inflamed the masses to spur him to go on building. He taught even cynics to see inner values and not to despise a cry from the heart. He discovered composers, he performed them and published their works. He created orchestras, publishing houses, foundations, schools and festivals. He fought for Americans in America, for Frenchmen in France, for Russians in Russia.

One saw him in a rage and in tenderness, in outbursts of enthusiasm, in happiness and in tears, but no one saw him in indifference. He demanded only the extraordinary, and no one could give him less. He had a magical gift for transferring even trifles into an event of urgency because to him there were no trifles in matters of art.

Everything about him seemed elevated and important, and his every day was a festival.[11]

Koussevitzky was tireless in his support and development of composers through commissions and publication; major works by Bartók, Hindemith, Copland and others were made possible through his devoted efforts. Even though by 1949 he had retired from the Boston Symphony and spent his final years guest conducting, Koussevitzky continued to commission works with the establishment of the Koussevitzky Music Foundation. His generosity also extended beyond music. In his final weeks Koussevitzky asked Piatigorsky to gather a group of donors in order to establish a fund to support the elderly writer and poet Ivan Bunin (1870–1953). Bunin was the first Russian to receive the Pulitzer Prize for Literature (1933).

In his last letter to Koussevitzky, Piatigorsky, as a director of the Koussevitzky Foundation, referenced a commission he was charged to offer Arnold Schoenberg for a special psalm celebrating the new state of Israel. Schoenberg had already embarked on a series of "modern psalms" that became his final efforts. Piatigorsky knew Schoenberg from the 1920s, beginning with the celebrated Berlin performance of *Pierrot Lunaire* as well as the premiere of the composer's arrangement of Bach's *Choralvorspiele* in 1925 with the Berlin Philharmonic. Piatigorsky, however, never performed Schoenberg's arrangement of Monn's Cello Concerto. When Schoenberg asked Piatigorsky why, he honestly told him that he did not like it. Schoenberg was angry with him for years.

Piatigorsky's last letter also reveals Koussevitzky's effervescent plans for the immediate future:

Dear Sergei Aleksandrovich,
 I hope that your flight to New York has not tired you out and that the change in climate will not negatively affect you.
 I have carried out your instructions. I spoke with Arnold Schoenberg and Jascha Heifetz. Jascha had "mixed up" Bunin and Yesenin [a pro–Soviet poet] ... and started to refuse, but when I calmed him down, explaining that Yesenin hung himself long ago, he agreed to participate in the aid to Bunin and to give a hundred dollars. He requests that his name not be mentioned, also he is not taking on an obligation to contribute regularly but prefers to help out from year to year. In principle, he is interested in the David ceremonies but requests details before he accepts a place on the committee.
 It would be good to write to him, but on May 8 he will already be leaving for England (not for long, it seems).
 Schoenberg sounded very bad on the phone. Poor man, he is very weak and complained a lot about his health and about the fact that he can't work. But despite that, when I started to talk about your proposal to write the Psalms, he perked right up and was *happy* that you thought of him. By the way, he has almost finished three Psalms (*not* King David) that he was writing for the Vinaver choir and intends to dedicate to Israel. The text of Schoenberg's psalms is in Hebrew. Any day now I will go inform him — he asks that we *force* him to work and says that he needs a strong jab.... I am certain (and he agreed in principle) that he will write a new Psalm *especially* for the ceremony in Israel.
 I am constantly thinking of you and pray to God that you soon get all your strength back.
 A big kiss to you and Olga. Jacqueline also sends kisses. Always your loving Grisha.[12]

Koussevitzky and Schoenberg were not particularly close, though they were born and died within days of each other; both died a few weeks later.

Commissions

Due to crippling deficits, the Hollywood Bowl cancelled the 1951 season shortly before its scheduled opening. To help put the organization back on track, Piatigorsky gave a benefit concert at the Bowl with the Los Angeles Philharmonic and conductor Alfred Wallenstein.

The New York Philharmonic also faced a similar financial crisis. Bruno Walter appealed to Piatigorsky and other soloists for help. Piatigorsky responded by making a contribution to the orchestra as well as appearing the following season in a Pension Fund concert for the orchestra under George Szell in Tchaikovsky's *Rococo Variations*. Benefit performances for pension funds were becoming more frequent as musicians demanded financial security in their retirements.

Piatigorsky continued to fund several cello scholarships. In 1957 he joined the faculty of Boston University, mostly in an advisory capacity, bolstering their new string program to combat the declining enrollment of string students in the United States. Samuel Mayes, principal cellist of the Boston Symphony Orchestra, was closely associated with Piatigorsky in his role as cello department head. As part of the string development program, Piatigorsky donated his university salary to a scholarship fund for cello students.

He also continued supporting composers with the hope of broadening the cello repertoire, and sponsored various competitions for composers at the University of Chicago and the Peabody Institute. After giving the U.S. premiere of Darius Milhaud's *Cello Concerto no. 1*[13] in 1949, Piatigorsky kept it in his repertoire for several seasons. By 1954 he commissioned Milhaud for another work for cello and orchestra — *Suite Cisalpine sur des Airs Populaires Piédmontais*, op. 332.[14] The commission evolved from their work at Tanglewood and the Music Academy of the West. Piatigorsky granted the opportunity to premiere the *Suite* to Reine Flachot,[15] the Piatigorsky Prize winner of 1954. The prominent Polish composer Alexandre Tcherepnin wrote an engaging suite for Piatigorsky in 1953 based on folk material from Georgia, Russia, and Ukraine — *Songs and Dances*, op. 84 — which concludes with a spirited Kazakh dance.

Piatigorsky's connections with Hollywood composers netted several works by Castelnuovo-Tedesco, Eric Zeisl, Richard Hageman, Miklós Rózsa, and others. But it is the background behind Erich Korngold's autographed dedication of his *Cello Concerto* to Piatigorsky that is unclear. Perhaps there was an initial plan for a concert work for Piatigorsky, which developed into the composition that was used in the film *Deception*. Piatigorsky was offered to record the soundtrack to the film, but apparently asked too much. The inscription reads:

> *To Gregor Piatigorsky*
> *(for whom this concerto was originally written!)*
> *in admiration*
> *sincerely:*
> *Hollywood, 1953*

After viewing Franz Waxman's film — *The Story of Ruth* (1956) — Piatigorsky asked the composer to write a concert work using Ruth's theme. Although Waxman never completed

Konzert in C-dur
in einem Satz
für Violoncello und Orchester
von

Concerto in C-major
in one movement
for Cello and orchestra
by

Erich Wolfgang Korngold
Opus 37

❋

Klavierauszug | Piano score

Edition Schott 4117

Orchestermaterial nach Vereinbarung | Orchestral score and parts on hire

B. SCHOTT'S SÖHNE
MAINZ: Weihergarten 5
Paris: Editions Max Eschig
48 Rue de Rome

SCHOTT & Co. Ltd.
London W.1: 48 Great Marlborough Str.
New-York: 25 West 45th Street
Associated Music Publishers Inc.

Printed in Germany — Imprimé en Allemagne

Erich Korngold's inscription to the Cello Concerto.

the piece, the composer's son hoped something could be utilized from the many pages of sketches of the arrangement left after his death and asked composer Angela Morely to arrange and develop the sketches into a viable work for cello.[16]

Another Waxman work, *Auld Lang Syne Variations* for piano quartet, was composed in 1947 as a party piece to help bring in the New Year with his musical friends. The setting was probably at Heifetz's home, where he hosted an annual New Year's party in Los Angeles. The local performers were Heifetz, Piatigorsky, and Primrose, with Waxman at the piano. *Auld Lang Syne* weaves parody quotations by Mozart, Beethoven, Bach, Shostakovich, and Prokofiev.[17]

Viennese composer Eric Zeisl was one of the younger émigrés who eventually landed in Hollywood following the Anschluss. He and his wife narrowly escaped the *Kristallnacht* pogrom of November 9, 1938. Zeisl settled in Los Angeles and tried his hand at film music, but never landed a screen credit. He ended up successfully teaching at Los Angeles City College where his most notable student was the Oscar-winning composer Jerry Goldsmith. His contemporaries, including Korngold, Milhaud and Stravinsky, praised Zeisl's "expressive melody, rich harmonies, strong dance-derived rhythms, and imaginative scoring."[18]

Zeisl composed his Cello Sonata for Piatigorsky in 1951, but was commissioned in an unusual manner. Zeisl's widow, Gertrude, remembered that

> from time to time we saw in the paper certain organizations that seemed to help the artist. And there was this New York Art Foundation, and we wrote to the Foundation, and surprisingly enough, Piatigorsky answered. We had an interview with him, and Piatigorsky immediately loved Eric, so we got from this Foundation support, which was, however, very small. But it enabled Eric to do the Cello Sonata, which was dedicated to Piatigorsky.[19]

The inspiration for the piece came from Zeisl's study of Jewish musical sources compiled by composer and camp survivor Solomon Rosowsky. The expressive, slow movement incorporates biblical cantillation formulas that Rosowsky discovered.

Though Piatigorsky did not perform the sonata, he was still interested in Zeisl's work and commissioned a cello concerto in 1955. The concerto was completed in 1956 and was given the title *Concerto Grosso*. Though dedicated to Piatigorsky, he did not perform this work either, in part because he did not think it was sufficiently soloistic. The solo part was on such an equal footing with the ensemble that the cello could not emerge dramatically enough. Piatigorsky suggested that the composer create a characteristic and idiosyncratic setting for the soloist, but Zeisl would not change any part of the piece. This prompted Piatigorsky to say, "You are very selfish. You are thinking only of what pleases you and not what you should do to please me."[20] Gertrude Zeisl recalled: "[Zeisl] worked with great care and really took, sometimes, maybe two or three days for a few bars. And so the idea of changing something that was so carefully laid out and worked out was unthinkable to him."[21]

Piatigorsky also suggested to Zeisl that if the work was to be performed in a large hall, the cello should be amplified. Gertrude Zeisl agreed: "I could see that he [Piatigorsky] was right—that there were passages that were very difficult for the cellist to [be heard]. And yet he would appear as a[n] [elusive] figure, and you could not really distinguish it as a solo instrument should be; [I am] sure that he never thought of this when he was composing. He was composing the things that were dictated by something to him. And he did not really think of the performer."[22]

Unfortunately, several other projects in the 1950s were never completed. Piatigorsky was interested in works where the cello could portray a symbolic hero with limited programmatic content (such as Bloch's *Schelomo*). In early 1951, John Alden Carpenter began a large work titled *Song of David* for Piatigorsky. Only a few pages were written before the composer's sudden death. In 1959 the cellist commissioned Roy Harris to write a large-scale work, tentatively titled *The Life of Christ*, scored for large orchestra, women's voices and children's choir; only the "Kyrie" was completed.[23]

Sir William Walton

Piatigorsky greatly admired William Walton's concertos for violin and viola written for Heifetz and Primrose. The cellist sent an inquiry to impresario Ian Hunter,[24] proposing a cello concerto on December 1, 1954. A fee was suggested, and Hunter was confident that the premiere could be given at the Edinburgh Festival in August 1956, with a later performance in October in London, on one of his concert series. Hunter suggested he write directly to Walton outlining his ideas for the work, including its length and form. However, in early 1955 Piatigorsky chose his friend and recital partner, the eminent British pianist Ivor Newton, to approach Walton directly with the cello concerto commission. Newton wrote:

> I was deputed to discuss the possibility with Sir William, a coolly elegant and at the same time entirely professional and business-like composer who prefers to keep profundities of feeling for his compositions and not waste them in conversation.
>
> "Would you consider writing a cello concerto for Piatigorsky?" I asked him. Walton's reply to Newton:
>
> "I'm a professional composer. I'll write anything for anybody, if he pays me." In a moment came an afterthought in which Sir William's impishness, one of the qualities that audiences have learned to recognize in his music, won a minor victory. "I write much better if they pay me in dollars."[25]

Piatigorsky was thrilled with the commission and when Walton came to the U.S. to supervise the San Francisco and New York City Opera productions of his *Troilus* in October, Walton flew to Los Angeles to confer with the cellist. After they deliberated on the concerto's concept, Piatigorsky felt that he had "never met such a rare combination of greatness and simplicity."[26] From this point forward, a comprehensive correspondence documents every phase of the concerto's creation. This extraordinary collaboration includes home recordings Walton made speaking to Piatigorsky about general tempi and ideas for cadenzas. Walton even sings the cello line as he plays the piano reduction. But, there were problems, delays, and doubts from both sides throughout the process. Walton began sketching the concerto in August 1955,[27] but it was primarily composed between February and October 1956: "...have got the vc cto under way but that is only that. Rather a good opening."[28] Susana Walton wrote of her husband's attraction to the concerto: "[William] thought of the cello as a melancholy instrument, full of soul; accordingly he wrote a rather sad tune in the opening.... He certainly had a special affection for the cello concerto as it had come very spontaneously, and he felt it was the closest to his personality."[29]

It was not difficult to find venues for the launching of the concerto. The premiere of the work was fixed with the Boston Symphony and conductor Charles Munch for December 7 and 8, 1956, with rehearsals on December 4 and 6. The recording was also scheduled with them for December 10 for RCA. The British premiere was set for February 13, 1957, and four New York Philharmonic concerts were scheduled for May 2, 3, 4, and 5 with Dimitri Mitropoulos conducting.

In 1956 the U.S. State Department selected Piatigorsky as its first foreign-born artist to represent the United States overseas. Piatigorsky toured seven Asian countries from August 21, returning to Los Angeles on October 11. He created quite an effect: "[Piatigorsky] described as "incomparable" the musical appetite and responsiveness of the peoples of the Orient, adding that the American compositions he scheduled on each program — and which were generally unfamiliar to the native audiences — were among the most enthusiastically received.

Even in Korea, where he gave one of the first cello recitals ever presented, almost 2000 people had to be turned away."[30]

Piatigorsky knew his 1956 State Department tour of Asia would be demanding. He wanted to learn the concerto as soon as possible beforehand and on April 24 urged the composer to send the first two movements. Piatigorsky was relieved when he received the first movement on May 10, exclaiming it to be "magnificent ... with only one note to change." A week later Piatigorsky wrote to the composer:

> I cannot tell you how enchanted I am with the first movement — so much so that no other music seems to be able to penetrate my head, which is filled with your concerto.
>
> I played it with the piano, and from the scanty indications of the instruments I well believe you, that finally there is a piece for the cello where the cellist does not have to force and fight to death to be heard.
>
> If I am not wrong, you have in this movement a vibraphone. Is it so? I don't know why, but I always had a certain allergy to this instrument. I assure you that is the only thing that is of a slight question, though if you do like it, I am all yours.
>
> My new Stradivari [the *Batta*] is of such glorious quality that as a special request for his genius, I would love to have some spot for it in your concerto, *unmixed* with any other instruments, in whatever form it be.
>
> I am awaiting every note, every bar, of the second movement, with the anxiousness of a desperate lover.[31]

The following week Piatigorsky began to show concern about the pace of the composition, and by July he seems desperate:

> My concert schedule for the next winter is extremely heavy ... beginning in September in Japan I will not stop until May. Only now I have time to practice.... [P]lease be an angel and send me anything new, so that I can learn the continuation of the Concerto by sections. Is it possible? Or you hate to do it before a movement is completed?
>
> I am waiting for the continuation of the Concerto desperately. Oh please please send me something!!!
>
> I know how terrible it must be for you to write under such a pressure.
>
> I pray for both of us.[32]

Finally, by August 2 the long anticipated second movement arrived, and provoked two comments: "A part of the second movement has just arrived. My god, if there ever was a masterwork for the Cello and Orchestra — yours certainly is!! But how difficult! And what a challenge!

On August 10th I am going to Hong Kong–Manila–Saigon–Singapore and Japan.[33]

Both enthusiastic for the concerto and anxious for the finale, Piatigorsky reminds the composer about his desire for a heroic ending on September 4 from Saigon:

> I practiced your Concerto in Hong Kong — Manila and now here. The more I know it the more I love it — It is wonderful!!! ... It is hot and filthy here — but Manila was worse. I am tired — but yet pleased with an extraordinary reception everywhere.... Do you hate me for making you work?!!! Now that there are two magnificent movements (almost two!) I just can't wait for the Finale!! I hope it will have a real exciting and grandiose ending — unlike the too short coda of Hindemith — Schumann or Prokofiev — Yours will be *the* concerto![34]

Walton was at the finish line by October 21 and wrote to Walter Legge: "I shall finish the Vlc. Con. in a couple of days or so as it is on the whole fairly satisfactory which from me is saying a lot. It is in fact the best of the three concerti."[35]

Piatigorsky returned from the Asian tour quite spent:

> I came home in a state of complete exhaustion, but instead of having rest I had to go on tour again. Now I have a second movement and a part of the third of your Concerto. I love it!!

With Fredric Mann and Jack Benny (right), 1955.

Although I am still very much concerned about a quite [quiet] ending of the concerto.... But we will see!... Before the Premiere on Dec. 7th in Boston — I must play 2 concerts in Pittsburgh, 6 concerts with the Philad. Orch (In Washington — Philad. and New York) then — Toronto — Detroit — Winnipeg. 4 more concerts in Canada and one in Connecticut. Besides the great fatigue I will work with enthusiasm on your Concerto — There is no Cello Concerto as beautiful as yours. I pray it will have a grandioso ending — not a bravura — nor calm like so many other works."[36]

When Piatigorsky cabled his acceptance of the completed work, Walton responded boastfully on November 4:

... so happy that you think the whole work wonderful. It is to my mind the best of my, now three, concertos. But don't say so to Jascha [Heifetz, who commissioned the Violin Concerto].... I must thank you in the first place for having commissioned the work, but more for the patience with me in my darker moments, and some were very dark indeed.... I only hope it will come up to your expectations when you come to play it with the orchestra. If anything in the orchestration — that vibraphone, for instance — should irk you, just cut it out, because it's not absolutely essential (though I might miss it).[37]

On November 9 Piatigorsky enthusiastically responded about the completed work:

I can't thank you enough for the wonderful concerto you gave to the world and I also want to assure you that it will have a glorious and everlasting life — *independent* of the quality of

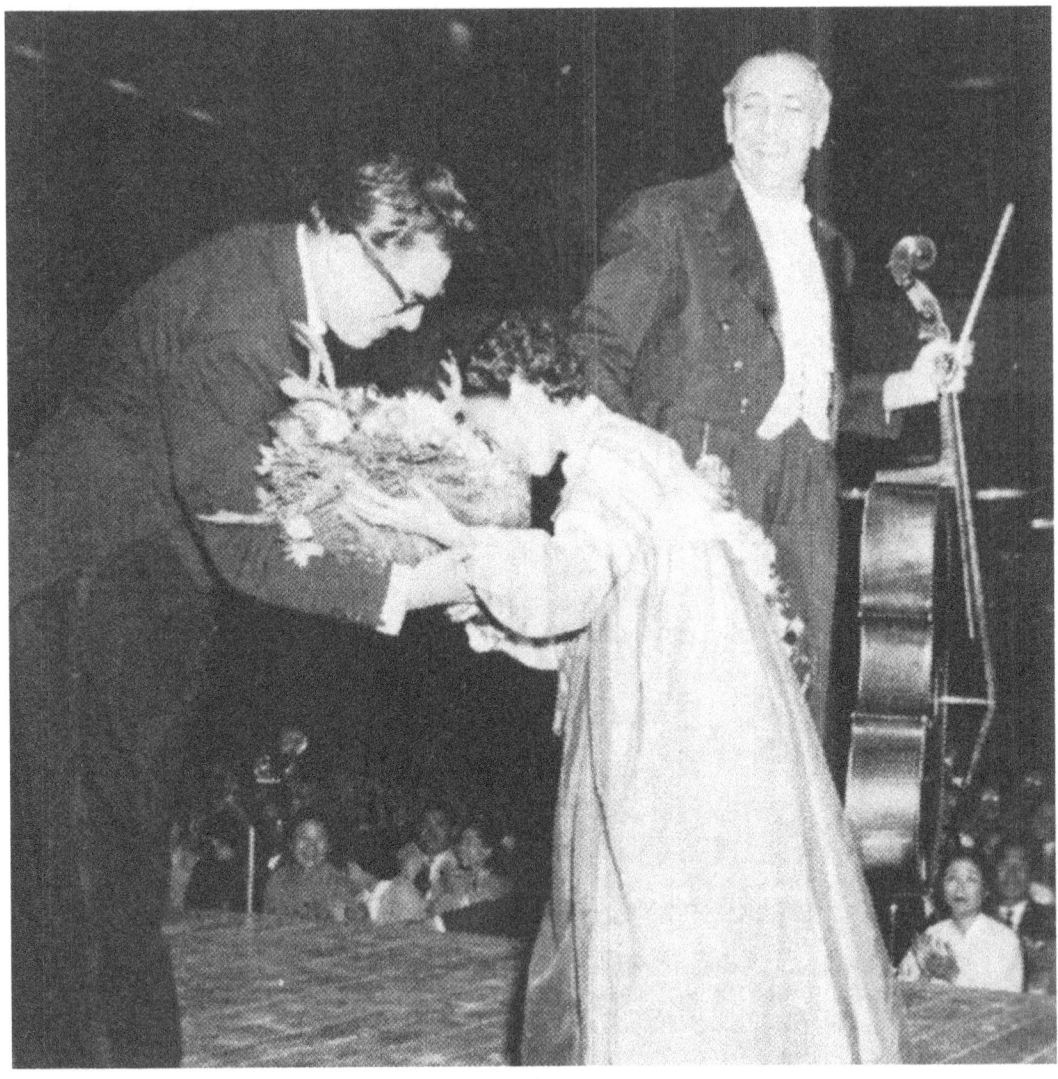

With Ralph Berkowitz in Korea, 1956.

the performers for nothing can kill real beauty. I will play the concerto with great love and admiration I have for it and you and I only pray that God will help me to do justice to this noble music."[38]

Not surprisingly, Piatigorsky developed a painful incapacitating ulcer and the premiere was postponed a few weeks later to January 25, 1957. A concerned Walton responded: "I only hope that you do not feel that my being behind-hand with the concerto has been a contributing factor."[39] Though resting at home, Piatigorsky continued working on the piece, and even after acceptance the ending was still a matter of concern: "A few weeks ago I played the concerto for Jascha. He was *very impressed*. When I asked if he has any remarks to make he said — that he would like to end the concerto on the high G instead of going down. He also thought the 2nd solo improvisation is somewhat too long. As he is the first person to hear the concerto I thought to pass his reaction to you will interest you."[40] Walton

Walton Concerto with Sir Malcolm Sargent and the Royal Philharmonic, 1957.

took the comment to heart and composed a new ending and sent it to the cellist. Piatigorsky responded on January 7: "Upon receiving your new ending I wrote you at once but did not mail it waiting for Jascha's return (He was in Arizona for Christmas). I was glad I waited for now I shall tell you what we both think of the changes. Without any hesitation we preferred your *original* version of the ending."[41]

The premiere however, was very gratifying:

> I know you could not help but be proud of yourself as we all were — if you would be present yesterday afternoon at the world premiere of your Concerto! It was a huge success and one felt the deep impression the music made on the audience. I never before played with more love nor felt more keenly the inspiration of the orchestra and the conductor. This concerto as I predicted before will live forever as a true and noble music. It has everything to make the cello sparkle and sing in a direct simplicity and logic so characteristic of a great work.
>
> It is sincere and lovable and it does not depend on opinions, for the beauty is indestructible. I told you before of the stupidity of the Boston critics — well, where are the intelligent ones? With reluctance I am sending two — One said — as you will read it; too difficult for him to judge on first hearing, [so] why didn't he attend the rehearsals with the orchestra?
>
> It seems that only musicians have time for music & the critics are too busy to learn anything about it.[42]

The first London performance was less than three weeks later, at a Royal Philharmonic Society (RPS) concert on February 13, 1957, with Sir Malcolm Sargent conducting. Queen

Elizabeth, the Queen Mother, attended and the BBC televised the concert.[43] Piatigorsky was elected an Honorary Member of the RPS and also waived his fee from the Society. Walton planned to attend the London premiere, but on his way he and his wife were severely injured when their car crashed into a cement truck near Rome. Walton broke a hip and was hospitalized for many weeks. Lady Walton suffered broken ribs.

Prior to the concert (February 11), Roy Douglas, Oxford University Press's editor and arranger of several Walton scores, met with Piatigorsky at the Savoy Hotel to discuss further alterations to the cello part. Walton's approval was needed that night and was confirmed by telephone from the hospital. Douglas also wrote the piano reduction of the concerto for publication.

After tapes of the Boston and London performances were sent to Walton, he wrote to Piatigorsky with some suggestions regarding the solo improvisations where the cello is without orchestra: "I do so hate asking you to do this, and I know you won't think it is because I don't appreciate your playing of the work as a whole; but it is just in these parts that the performance could be tightened up. While I, of course, don't expect you to adhere rigidly to my tempi, I do feel the discrepancy of your timings and mine is a little too much." The composer wanted the interpretation "altogether more tough and rhythmical."[44] Piatigorsky took his suggestions and incorporated them quickly, and rerecorded the solos. Even so, he lamented: "I am only sorry to have recorded the concerto at such an early stage."[45]

When Piatigorsky's recording was issued in 1958, Walton thanked him for "an absolutely superb interpretation and performance. Everything about it is just as it should be, and your playing magnificent!"[46] Walton also wrote to Alan Frank, head of the music division at Oxford University Press, on July 10, 1958: "I must say the recording is pretty superb both as a performance and as a work — and I say it who shouldn't — and to hell with Messrs. Heyworth and Mitchell. They should, by the way, both be blacklisted so don't send them *any* scores of my works!"[47]

The only snag with the composition stemmed from Piatigorsky's lingering concern about the very end of the piece: "There was only one question in the entire concerto — the ending of it. I felt that it should kind of [end] ... triumphantly, very organ-like and large, and it didn't feel like that."[48] In Piatigorsky's original suggestion to Walton in 1955, he had asked that: "the ending should be brilliant and the coda fairly long; all the existing concertos end abruptly, even the Dvořák."[49] And Walton wrote to Alan Frank on Christmas 1956: "Piatigorsky wrote that he was not happy about the end, or rather Heifetz to whom he had been playing the concerto wasn't. Accordingly, as I always do what I'm told, I've written two new endings and leave them to choose. Both are I think better than the original."[50] In spite of Walton's attempts at conciliation, Piatigorsky performed only the original ending. The last movement (*tema e improvisandi*) was Walton's favorite theme and variations — its ending did not bother the composer at all.

With the success of Walton's three concerti, impresario Ian Hunter suggested a double concerto be written for Heifetz and Piatigorsky in 1957. The composer was not immediately taken with the idea, as both he and Piatigorsky had recently survived serious physical challenges. "Ian Hunter has suggested I write a double concerto for you & Jascha! Not just yet I feel!"[51] And afterwards writing to Alan Frank he said, "Of course a double concerto, however spectacular the kick-off might be with such stars, has not much of a chance in the ordinary way. How often is the Brahms played? Not very often and one could hardly expect to equal that. However if the spirit was moved and the dollars jingled who knows?"[52]

Piatigorsky and Heifetz instantly pressed the idea to Walton, and even planned performances hoping to entice him. Piatigorsky wrote to the composer on February 1 1967:

> I was so pleased to hear from Jascha that you are well. I will think of you wishing you from all my heart to pass with colors the forthcoming examination in.... You will. After that (and who knows perhaps even before the one act opera!) you will start the piece for violin and cello. It does not have to be a concerto. Perhaps a Fantasy — Poem or Rhapsody — Jascha and I shall be delighted with anything you choose.
>
> However it is important that the orchestration does not demand extra instruments — other than let's say arc in the Brahms Double Concerto. (This was the reason why I had to play Haydn instead of your concerto last October in New York.)
>
> Our next concert with orchestra is planned for October 1967. It is needless to tell you how eager we are to play your new composition.
>
> Of course it should be a commission, though I feel that [a] — dedication — looks warmer on paper! But this little thing of course is up to you.[53]

They then rescheduled it six months later hoping to spur him on.

> I have not heard from you in such a long time!...
>
> Both Jascha and I are longing for a good news! Our concerto in Los Angeles is definitely set for March 1968 and it *can not* be without a piece for violin and cello and orchestra by W. Walton.
>
> We want it so badly! I would very much like to come to see you sometime in September. Will you be in Ischia?
>
> Jascha sends you and Lady Walton his best love, so do I.[54]

Backstage: touring showing its strain (courtesy Piatigorsky estate).

Months passed and Walton, as guest conductor of the Houston Symphony Orchestra in January 1969, told the *Houston Chronicle* that "six projects near to his heart" were "urgently pending."[55] The Double Concerto was mentioned in the group, though sadly it remained unfulfilled. By 1974 Walton thought he would compose a work along the lines of Chausson's Poème. "Perhaps for the moment not to tell Jascha.... I've been asked to write so many pieces, but I think I shall chuck the lot & concentrate on the piece, whatever it may be, for you both."[56] There seems to be some misunderstanding as to the commission's impasse. Walton took the blame as Piatigorsky reiterated the commission: "But now having your letter before me I know that your feelings are mostly of doubts.... Please don't! Whatever you write is of great importance to music. It is only that at this time a Double Concerto is of a particular urgent need. Who after Brahms could give it to the world?! *You.* And in this can not be a doubt. If the cellist would be good enough, there would not be a Double Concerto — Brahms would have composed a cello concerto."[57]

In summer of 1974, Piatigorsky returned to England to perform with Barenboim, Perlman and Zukerman in recital and chamber music appearances at the City of London celebrations. After a seventeen-year absence he felt he was not forgotten; enthusiastic responses confirmed the British affection for him. He felt energized and eager to return the following year to perform Walton's concerto several times. The subject of the ending crept up again, and Walton objected to it, saying that it was "like adding a new hem to an old skirt!"[58] Piatigorsky disagreed and ten weeks later made a specific suggestion, writing on December 3, 1974:

> I am planning to start with the Walton Concerto with the L.A. Philharmonic and Zubin Mehta Oct. 23, 24 and 26 — Nov. 1st in San Diego, Nov. 12 at Iowa Festival and Nov. 24 in New York, all with the same orch. and conductor. I also plan to play the concerto in London perhaps this spring.
>   At the same time I could not help wishing that the very conclusion of the concerto, instead of resembling the mood of the ending of the first movement would transform by your adding only a few bars to the touching reminiscence mood, to a bright and ringing conclusion. Please think on it again!! It is terribly vital for me at this time when everyone is waiting for my confirmation of the proposed engagements. You can do so much with so little! For example if after 8½ bars after 18 the orchestra would take over the cello line — upwards — upwards — cresc. poco a poco — orchestra bigger and bigger and me sitting and enjoying the slow rising to the sky — noble and majestic.
>   I pray you are not angry with me but it is only my love for the piece and you and our friendship that makes me dare to make any suggestions at all.[59]

Around Christmas 1974, Walton wrote another new (twenty-three-bar) ending for the concerto.[60] The composer suggested an ending akin to the slow movement of his Symphony No. 2. Walton told Piatigorsky that he (Piatigorsky) was the only one who had doubts about the ending, but that he would try once more. This was his fourth attempt to please his dedicatee and Piatigorsky approved it in February: "Perhaps it was foolish of me to make any suggestions at all — for it is so beautiful as it is. It's only that the idea of a strong chord like full orchestra ending excited me and I had to share my thought with you. I am planning to play your concerto in London on June 24 (with Barenboim)."[61] Walton ruminated over the fuss: "I don't know why it bothered me so much. I'm losing confidence in my powers and find composing increasingly difficult. I never found it easy but now it is the very devil." And, in conversation with Arthur Jacobs, Walton recalled Piatigorsky's original doubts about the ending: "[B]ut I didn't have any [doubts] until many years later. Then I thought, 'Perhaps he's right.'"[62]

The loss of a double concerto by Walton notwithstanding, the Cello Concerto is now a standard work, having been recorded by most eminent cellists. Upon Piatigorsky's triumphant first performances, *Time*, on May 13, 1957, reported it was "a marvel of taste and tone. Under his sensitive hands, the cello sang like a deep-throated bell, soared melodically, sank to a velvety whisper; in the more rhapsodic passages it seemed to shiver with musical delight. Cellist Piatigorsky, 54, had never seemed in better form."[63]

After the 1956-57 season, Piatigorsky suffered bursitis that caused the cancellation of several concerts, including an appearance with Bernstein in Israel.[64] Exhausted, Piatigorsky decided to take a limited sabbatical to recover for the 1958-59 season. A sentimental highlight of the following season (1959-60) was a return visit to the White House, hosted by President and Mrs. Eisenhower. Piatigorsky and one of his oldest friends, pianist Alexander Zakin, presented the first full recital by a cellist at the White House.[65] Piatigorsky had performed for each administration since Herbert Hoover, but always in mixed programs shared with other artists.[66]

11. The 1960s and the Heifetz-Piatigorsky Partnership

The Heifetz-Piatigorsky Partnership

Piatigorsky started to pull away from a heavy concert schedule after his world tours of 1956-57. Illness and general weariness of concert life began to take its toll and writing became increasingly time consuming. "The sacrifice which I make through my work as a virtuoso lies very heavily on my soul, and makes me think seriously about continuing that sacrifice."[1] His manager, Sol Hurok, frustrated with his pullback — along with two eccentric pianists in his care — jokingly threatened to advertise:

HOROWITZ
GOULD
PIATIGORSKY
Available for a limited number of cancellations

Over forty years of traveling had taken its toll on both Piatigorsky and Heifetz. Independently, they decided not to resume the life of a traveling soloist. Heifetz summed it up: "It requires the nerves of a bullfighter, the vitality of a woman who runs a nightclub, and the concentration of a Buddhist monk."[2] "My sweating days are over."[3] Heifetz further complained: "It is not like the piano, whose tone is kept in tune by the tuner. Playing the violin is all guesswork; you cannot even scratch a mark on the wood so you can tell where to put your fingers to repeat the right note."[4]

Living only a few miles apart, Piatigorsky and Heifetz regularly played chamber music with friends and colleagues at their homes. Los Angeles was ripe with talent. Other musicians also hosted evenings of chamber music with them, including violinist Henri Temianka of the Paganini Quartet, as well as music lovers of high standing in the arts. Members of the Los Angeles Philharmonic, visiting soloists and world-class players in the recording industry filled out those extraordinary reading sessions.

In 1954 RCA proposed that Heifetz, Piatigorsky and violist William Primrose record the five Beethoven String Trios. Primrose was no stranger to Piatigorsky or Heifetz, and he had already recorded with Heifetz. However, scheduling problems and illnesses delayed the project; it took three years before the series was launched in March 1957. On the second day of recording, they began the longest of the five works, the *Trio in E-flat*, op. 3. The recording sessions were high spirited and playful, as the music often suggests. During the

Gregor Piatigorsky

first movement Heifetz made an uncharacteristic left hand "plunk" repeatedly on the E string during the passage from measure 248 to 251.

After the take, Piatigorsky asked, "What was that noise you were making? Shouldn't we retake?" Heifetz replied with his, as Piatigorsky described, "gefilte fish face": "What noise?" The little "in" joke remains for all to hear, although one has to listen very carefully. Piatigorsky, not to be outdone, responded with a very subtle ricochet of two notes in the Finale at measure 348.[5] A Primrose contribution to the high jinks has yet to be discovered.

Piatigorsky enjoyed Heifetz's recording philosophy: "We often played a work through as a whole, preferring the spontaneity of spirit to technical detail." But the trio was surprised and saddened to hear their producer, Jack Pfeiffer, say after the Beethoven *E-Flat Trio*, op.3 session, "What a dreadful pity it is that the record we just made is obsolete." Piatigorsky asked, "What do you mean?" He stated that stereophonic equipment would be exclusively used very soon.[6]

Primrose remembered that the trio "worked amicably for the succeeding half-dozen years. In all the association I had with Heifetz, he never tried to dominate any musical situation. I never had the feeling that he was trying to impose his way and only his way. He would listen very carefully to Grisha, because he had the greatest respect for him [and] his closest relationship was with Piatigorsky. He listened to other people's opinions as well, and in every case if he didn't approve he expressed himself to that extent." Primrose recalled an exceptional moment of Heifetz's playing from one of those sessions — the third movement of Beethoven's *Trio in G*, op. 9 no. 1: "This is an incredibly touching piece of playing — among his most moving."

A few years earlier Heifetz had made a secret recording of a parody of bad playing. He played it for Piatigorsky and Primrose after one of the trio sessions, pretending that it had been sent to him for approval. Primrose remembered: "We just stared at each other with a wild surmise. But, mark you, we kept remarking: This fellow is talented! No doubt about it. He must have been very badly taught, yet he is talented. His fingers are remarkable in certain passages, but when he comes to a scale he misses part of it and ends up a half tone too high."[7]

Years later, after finding out the truth, Primrose decided to tease his colleagues at Indiana University during their hearings of taped auditions. After he anonymously played the Heifetz tape, they hesitatingly agreed that the player might have some talent, but when it came to place admittance into a professor's studio, they all balked. When Primrose told them it was Heifetz, quite a hullabaloo ensued.[8]

In May 1960, Heifetz and Piatigorsky began a series of recordings together lasting until 1968. The first was Brahms' *Double Concerto*. The conductor was Alfred Wallenstein, a former cellist himself, leading what in essence was the Los Angeles Philharmonic (his former orchestra). Contractual issues no doubt allowed members of the orchestra to be hired individually as a "pick-up" group, calling it the RCA Symphony Orchestra. RCA had on many occasions used other major orchestras as "The RCA Symphony." This memorable recording captures some of the fabulous bass in Piatigorsky's *Batta* Stradivarius, especially the fourth note in the opening cadenza, landing on the low D-sharp.

Later that year Piatigorsky and Heifetz recorded the Kodály *Duo* and wrapped up the Beethoven String Trios (opp. 8 and 9, no. 2), this time in stereo sound. (Unfortunately the Beethoven sessions from 1957 were still monophonic.) The Kodály *Duo* and the Beethoven *Serenade*, op. 8, won a Grammy in 1962.

In 1961 the two friends launched the famous Heifetz-Piatigorsky Concerts series. The musicians who collaborated with the duo were both world-renowned artists of the concert stage, and preeminent recording musicians in Los Angeles. These artists demonstrated their talent through private readings with Heifetz and Piatigorsky, which served as auditions. Besides William Primrose, the group included pianists Leonard Pennario, Leon Fleischer, Jacob Lateiner; violinists Israel Baker, Arnold Belnick, Paul Rosenthal, Pierre Amoyal, Christiaan Bor; violists Joseph de Pasquale and Sol Schonbach; cellists Gabor Rejto and Laurence Lesser. Following many of the concerts, the repertoire was recorded by RCA in Los Angeles.

The first Heifetz-Piatigorsky concert series took place in the Hollywood hills at the outdoor Pilgrimage Theater in August 1961. As Heifetz, Piatigorsky and Primrose were about to start their dress rehearsal, Heifetz shuddered as a jet whistled over, provoking a tense demand:

"Who's in charge of the lights?"
"Hey, Joe," yelled a sport-shirted technician, "the fella wants you."
Joe, the lighting man, fidgeted with the dome lights.
"How's that, Mr. Heifetz?" he asked triumphantly.
"The lights are wonderful," rejoined Heifetz, "but we can't see the music."
"I can't see Mr. Piatigorsky," called Heifetz's cheerful, young-looking wife, Frances, from a back-row seat.
"It's a great loss," rumbled the bearish, white-haired cellist. "A great loss."[9]

In 1962 pianist Leon Fleisher was invited to join the first Heifetz-Piatigorsky Concerts later that season at San Francisco's War Memorial Opera House. Wanting to stay close to home, the trio rehearsed in Los Angeles. The repertoire was the Brahms *Piano Quartet in C Minor*, op. 60, with Primrose, followed by the Schubert *Trio in E-flat*, op. 100. Heifetz and Fleisher played ping-pong during breaks, but Fleisher was not impressed with Heifetz's game. He noted that though Heifetz usually won, he never sweat. At that time Heifetz was going through a difficult separation from his second wife, Frances. Piatigorsky and impresario Bill Judd warned Fleisher not to question Heifetz or even look at him cross-eyed. However, when they were reading the Schubert, Heifetz began flipping through the pages in the last movement looking for places to cut. Heifetz said, "The worst thing is to bore the audience." Whereupon Fleisher, shocked by such a remark, replied, "No, the worse thing is for the performer to be bored." This caused Piatigorsky to cringe and Heifetz, who was completely taken aback by the remark, to stare at the young upstart.

Nevertheless, the music making was joyous and the rehearsals democratic. Heifetz was not always in the mood to work, but two or three sessions were sufficient to prepare for what Fleisher described as a great concert. Before the concert Fleisher complained to Piatigorsky that there was no warm up piano. Piatigorsky replied with one of his legendary witticisms: "Practicing before a concert is like giving breathing lessons to a dying man."[10] The line has been repeated to innumerable students and colleagues plagued with the same problem.

The recordings of the Heifetz-Piatigorsky Concerts series are high-powered performances, vital and artful. There is much to glean from each artist, though the actual composition sometimes fared less well than its superb performers might suggest. Heifetz, who was not known for sluggishness, predominantly led the tempi. His headlong approach works for most pieces, but the Schubert C Major Quintet's *Adagio* movement suffers from Heifetz's restlessness with Schubert's broad expanse, sustained melodic lines and generous pauses. The tempo is a convincing one, but not fast enough for Heifetz, and he plays his pizzicati with a noticeable degree of haste.

The same haste is true in Schubert's *Piano Trio in E-flat*, op. 100. As pianist Jacob Lateiner remarked, "He just didn't have the patience for such things."[11] One can quibble about other matters, but — as with Pablo Casals' chamber music recordings from his festivals — one hears the leadership of tempo, with Casals' the reverse of that of Heifetz. Casals tugs at his colleagues to play slower, giving room to the phrase and the beat.

An interesting moment in Beethoven's *Piano Trio in E-flat*, op. 1 no. 1, occurs in the Finale at measure 455. Here Heifetz played one of his artfully nuanced shifts of a tenth during the motive's last statement. It was clearly flubbed. Heifetz refused to retake. Lateiner recalled Heifetz saying, "Everyone knows I can play it. Leave it in."[12]

In October and November 1963, Piatigorsky spent intense weeks of recording with Heifetz: six piano trios, two duos, and concertos by Vivaldi, Haydn, Mozart, and Rózsa. Piatigorsky had commissioned Miklós Rózsa's *Sinfonia Concertante*, op. 29, for him and Heifetz. However, the duo recorded only the second movement, *Tema con variazioni*, during the first of three sessions that week (October 7, 1963). (Its intriguing incubation is discussed later in this chapter.) Rózsa described the events leading up to the recording:

> That autumn Heifetz wanted to perform the slow movement alone at one of his concerts with Piatigorsky. The orchestra for that concert consisted only of strings, two oboes and two horns — the orchestra of Mozart's violin concertos. After much argument I agreed to rescore the movement for this tiny combination, although of course many important orchestral colors

went missing as a result. Then to my surprise I learned from one of the players that all the concerts were to be recorded, including my piece. Heifetz had established the custom of giving the concerts without a conductor, which may have looked impressive, but the orchestra was unable to keep together. I was not invited to the recording, and Heifetz forgot to conduct with his bow during Piatigorsky's solo, so that the pizzicati cello and basses didn't know precisely when to play. Not a happy experience for anyone, least of all the absent composer.[13]

Two days later, Piatigorsky recorded his own arrangement of the Haydn *Divertimento* with the RCA Chamber Orchestra, using local studio musicians and a few members of the Heifetz-Piatigorsky classes. The *Divertimento* was usually heard with piano, but USC colleague and composer Ingolf Dahl orchestrated the work for a classical era orchestra. Uncharacteristically, Heifetz was concertmaster of the orchestra for the session — his only recording as an orchestral player.

Piatigorsky, in turn, was principal cello in the orchestra the following day for Heifetz's recording of the Mozart *Concerto* No. 5 "Turkish." The two occasions are a notable example of their regard for one another professionally and to their lasting friendship.[14]

Heifetz and Piatigorsky performed and recorded several duos ranging from Boccherini to Toch. The choice of Ernst Toch's *Divertimento* began with a misunderstanding on Heifetz's part. Heifetz knew the *Divertimento* for violin and viola and assumed it was the same work transcribed for violin and cello.[15] When they met to rehearse the work, Heifetz exclaimed, "What's this piece? I don't know this." After showing Piatigorsky his violin part, Heifetz made the embarrassing discovery. The cellist came back a few days later, having learned the viola version, whereupon they performed and recorded it almost immediately. Piatigorsky's experience with reading violin and viola music — substituting missing parts at home and at the Coliseum Theatre in his youth — served him well.

Another unusual recording was Martinů's *Duo* no. 1. This was not really a recording in the sense of takes and retakes, but of a complete play-through in the studio, including tuning between the movements. The performance sparkles with electricity and spontaneity.

Piatigorsky felt that Heifetz's best chamber playing was in the slow movement of the Mendelssohn *Trio in C Minor*, op. 66. He also mentioned that one particular recording of a chamber work for RCA was frustrating. Piatigorsky protested the speed of a specific movement and asked for a retake at a slower pace. Probably no one else in the world could suggest to Heifetz that he was playing too fast. Heifetz agreed to try a slower take, but at the next attempt stubbornly kept the same tempo. Piatigorsky was upset and considered leaving. Heifetz, taken aback, reassured him that he could have any tempo he wanted. They tried again. All was forgiven. Moments later the recording engineer, Jack Pfeiffer, announced that they had a problem with the equipment and would they please try it once more. The earlier quick tempo promptly crept back.

An amusing moment occurred during the Brahms *Quintet*, op. 111, from 1968. There was a problem with the start of the scherzo movement where the cello has to catch a lightning fast viola entrance. After a few failed attempts, violist Milton Thomas suggested that he cue the start, but Piatigorsky, angry with himself, shouted, "Just play!" It was the end of a very long day of recording.[16]

Primrose's penultimate recording in the series was the Dvořák *Piano Quintet* from March 1964, which has remained unissued.[17] It is reported to be a fine recording, but rumor has it that Heifetz rejected it because of Primrose's faulty intonation. The Mozart C Major *Quintet* was recorded two days later and yet was released. One is aware of Primrose's slight hearing lapse during his solo in the slow movement, but the rest of the ensemble work is

Left to right: Heifetz, producer Jack Pfeiffer, and Piatigorsky as stagehands.

lovely and has been issued both on LP and CD. The Dvořák *Quintet* was rerecorded later that year with violist Joseph de Pasquale.

That year Heifetz abruptly severed his performing and recording relationship with William Primrose, a working relationship of some twenty-five years. In his autobiography, *Walk on the North Side*, Primrose recalled that the trio "disbanded after some dozen recordings.... I would say this was mainly due to my hearing problem [the result of a major heart attack]. Over the last couple of years of our collaboration Heifetz was very helpful, very considerate. But the time came when my ability to hear a particular section of the scale accurately became a matter of considerable moment to the ensemble. The actual break in our personal relationship I never could fathom."[18]

Heifetz, Primrose and Piatigorsky were touted as the royal triumvirate of the string world, reigning from USC (Institute for Special Musical Studies). But after a year at USC, Primrose's teaching load was almost nonexistent. In the intervening time the violist accepted a position at Indiana University where he hoped to be busier with talented students. Heifetz resented his departure, wanting him to stay in Los Angeles and establish their visible nucleus with Piatigorsky, confident that the world would come to them in due time. Heifetz, however, never let Primrose know his true feelings about departing USC, leaving Primrose unaware of his resentment. Primrose did not discuss the meeting or share the problem with Piatigorsky.

A year later Primrose returned to California. Quite by accident he ran into Heifetz on the street: "He made it clear in no uncertain terms that he was considerably upset by my behavior. He 'thanked' me for all the letters I had written to him. The irony wasn't very subtle, since in our long association I don't think we exchanged more than three or four letters. He felt that we had started something together at USC and I shouldn't have quit."[19]

After the sabbatical (1949–1950), Piatigorsky began to pull back from his relentless concert tours, as shoulder inflammation and other illnesses caused him to cancel concerts. Following the extensive tours of the 1954-55 and 1956-57 seasons, he began to limit concert appearances. By the mid–1960s he was in semiretirement.

As the years passed, Piatigorsky and Heifetz became closer, each helping the other to stay active and healthy. Piatigorsky used to say that without Heifetz's fiddle, the violinist would self-destruct. Heifetz, conversely, by planning concerts, kept Piatigorsky in form. Without a definite commitment to a performance, Piatigorsky would not practice, choosing rather to read with friends. So, the Heifetz-Piatigorsky connection evolved into an important extension of their retirement, and gave the world another glimpse of their instrumental mastery.

In the final years of the Heifetz-Piatigorsky concerts, a few of their students were asked to join them in concerts and recordings. These students were already accomplished virtuosi, and their association with the masters gave them a push in their concert careers. Laurence Lesser relates his experience with the Tchaikovsky Sextet *Souvenir de Florence*:

> We played from a photocopy of the first edition, which Heifetz had obtained, and in the rehearsals there were frequent discussions about details in the score. One of the most instructive moments, though, came in a rehearsal of the slow movement. Its outer sections are essentially a *pas de deux* for the first violin and the first cello, with the other players providing a respectfully murmuring accompaniment. Naturally, the solo lines spun out and intertwined with a great deal of freedom. The rest of us struggled to follow their every nuance and subtle shift of rhythm, but with increasing inaccuracy and discomfort. Heifetz finally stopped us and jokingly said he felt like he was trying to hit a moving target—if we would play the rhythm "straight" it would be his job to figure out how to bend his line around our regular rhythm. While we did eventually need to relax ends of phrases, his general practice advice truly solved the problem.[20]

By 1968, the Heifetz-Piatigorsky recording series ended, and their last "official" Heifetz-Piatigorsky concert was in April 1972. However, they would on rare occasion play on USC's campus as "guests" on student recitals, where their last performance was in 1974 in Handel-Halvorsen's *Passacaglia*. Heifetz's shoulder surgery in 1975 prevented further public performances.[21]

Musically the two artists could be polar opposites, yet together they were well matched. Artful compromises reflected their sensitivity and respect for each other. Piatigorsky had a way with timing that could make a musical moment relax amid Heifetz's highly charged phrases. These magical moments are more evident in live concerts than in their recordings.[22] Together Heifetz and Piatigorsky performed over 70 works and recorded nearly 50 of them. Several of their recordings received Grammy awards.

Piatigorsky was perhaps Heifetz's best friend. They lightheartedly referred to each other as Admiral Piatigorsky and General Heifetz, played cards, swam, enjoyed the beach, talked, compared their stamp collections, and in earlier times, played passages for each other. When Piatigorsky died, Heifetz called Jacqueline, saying he was too broken up to attend the memorial service, and gave his condolences. Piatigorsky had been a stabilizing influence on Heifetz and after his death, Heifetz became more reclusive and eccentric.[23] Miklós Rózsa affectionately wrote about Piatigorsky's relationship with Heifetz: "Grisha absolutely adored Jascha;

11. The 1960s and the Heifetz-Piatigorsky Partnership

With Heifetz in Malibu.

Jascha was his god. Piatigorsky was a huge man, but in the presence of Heifetz he was like a little child. He had played with everyone, and used to say simply that no one played the violin like Heifetz. Everyone wanted something from Heifetz, but not Grisha; all he wanted was his love, and this he had. Which is why, when Piatigorsky died, I felt terribly sorry for Jascha; for I knew he had lost his only real friend."[24]

1960s: Budapest Quartet, Casals, Moscow

The beginning of the 1960-61 season found Piatigorsky very happily involved in a concert series at the Library of Congress with the Budapest Quartet. Together they performed the sextets of Brahms and Tchaikovsky, the C Major *Quintet* of Schubert and several Boccherini quintets, along with a sampling of standard quartet repertoire. Piatigorsky had last appeared there in 1947 in a recital with Reginald Stewart. The Budapests were all good friends with Piatigorsky, especially the Schneider brothers. Mischa Schneider was a fellow Klengel student in 1922 and always kept in touch with Piatigorsky. Violinist Sascha (Alexander) Schneider was also developing a conducting career besides the Budapest Quartet tours. The Schneider brothers, especially Sascha, were behind the establishment of the Casals Festivals in Prades and later in Puerto Rico, where Sascha was a codirector.

Piatigorsky was invited to inaugurate the 1967 Casals Festival in Puerto Rico. The older master and Piatigorsky had not worked together in over 30 years. Back in 1931 Casals had written to Piatigorsky offering to conduct two concerts with him as soloist in any piece he liked with his orchestra in Barcelona—precisely on the dates that Piatigorsky was scheduled to play with Richard Strauss. Piatigorsky was frustrated but had to turn Casals down, and needlessly worried that he would be angry with him. They did play several concerts soon after. His first performance with Casals was the Schumann Concerto. Sascha Schneider recalled the occasion (as Piatigorsky told him):

> Piatigorsky was getting more and more nervous, with many sleepless nights worrying about how he would play.... The nearer the day came the worse it got. He lost weight, he couldn't keep any food down, he threw up and, finally he couldn't even shave himself anymore without cutting himself. So he gave up shaving and went to a barber. At last, he arrived in Barcelona for the rehearsal a day in advance so as to get a good night's sleep with a sleeping pill. It didn't help very much and he still couldn't swallow any food. He practiced from 6:00 A.M. until 9:00 A.M. and finally went to rehearsal.
>
> While he was sitting in the artists' room warming up, Casals' brother, Enrique, came in, introduced himself, apologized that his brother Pau had a horrible cold with a temperature and couldn't possibly get out of bed, and said that he had asked him (Enrique) to conduct in his place. "This was the happiest moment of my life," Piatigorsky said, "Suddenly I felt great saying, of course how badly I felt that Pablo Casals couldn't conduct and that I hoped he would get well soon and, at that rehearsal, I think I played the Schumann Cello Concerto better than I ever played it in all my life." The orchestra applauded and he went back to the hotel, ordered a big steak with lots of vegetables, a salad, cheese, fruit, cake and a good bottle of Spanish wine and finally went to sleep—his first real, deep, enjoyable sleep in a year's time.
>
> He was really looking forward to playing the Schumann.... [V]ery happy, he went to the concert hall and before walking out to play, who comes in but Pablo Casals, wrapped up in a woolen scarf, nose and eyes running. Casals embraced him and said, "I simply couldn't stay in bed and disappoint you and so I just had to come to conduct the Schumann Concerto for you." "Imagine what happened to me" Piatigorsky told me, "Suddenly the whole world collapsed and I have no idea how I played. But received as a present from Casals' embrace, the most horrible cold I have ever had—a wonderful souvenir of playing the Schumann Concerto in Barcelona."
>
> When Casals and I engaged Piatigorsky to play the Schumann Concerto in Puerto Rico ... I wanted to be sure the story was not an invented one and so Casals verified to both of us that it was absolutely true and that he had gotten out of bed to conduct for him. Of course this time Casals conducted again, without a cold, and it was a wonderful reunion of this small and very tall man.[25]

However, it was not certain that Casals, then over 90, would be able to conduct, as he had been gravely ill after a prostate operation that winter. But, he happily announced at the first orchestra rehearsal, "I didn't think I would be here with you this time. But, thank God, we are together again, and we can make lovely music."[26] There was no evidence of any diminished vigor, and the concert was warmly received. (The orchestra also had many Piatigorsky students filling out the cello section.)

Zubin Mehta was a guest conductor that season. While Mehta and Piatigorsky were swimming together at the Caribe Hilton, the conductor suggested he drop the scheduled work on his concert — Bruckner's Fourth Symphony — and perform *Don Quixote* instead. Casals was very happy with the change. The music was obtained in time, and the orchestration was covered — save for the wind machine that Strauss used to heighten the illusion of flight. It was a favorite performance for Piatigorsky, one where he felt the spirit of Strauss through Mehta. "Don Pablo was sitting in the wings on the evening of the concert to see his two friends perform.... At one point, during the F-sharp Major variation, which depicts Quixote lost in reverie, Mehta turned to cue the basses and saw a movement of white in the wings, a handkerchief. The Old Man was weeping."[27] Sascha Schneider remarked on the performance: "I don't think any cellist has ever played the *Don Quixote* as beautifully as Piatigorsky, nor will it ever be played as well again. He simply was Don Quixote when he played. His performance in Puerto Rico was extraordinary."

Sascha Schneider, concertmaster in the orchestral works, was the conductor for Piatigorsky in the Haydn D Major Concerto. Schneider, Isidor Cohen, Milton Thomas, Casals and Piatigorsky played the Schubert Quintet. It was Piatigorsky's first time playing the second cello part.[28]

Piatigorsky was invited to judge the 1962 and 1966 International Tchaikovsky Cello Competitions. But his arrival in Moscow in May 1962 was an important occasion, not only because it was his first return to his homeland, but also because it was the first time he had seen his father and brothers in 41 years, one of whom, Anatoly, was born after Piatigorsky's ouster from home. (Piatigorsky's beloved mother died in 1956.) Pavel was now in his mid-eighties and frail; it was a last visit, as he died in July. Communication with his family had been difficult. Gregor was shocked to hear that all his shipments of food, money and gifts had been confiscated for years. Without knowing, his goodwill eventually placed the family under suspicion of spying (especially brother Leonid).

After World War II, Piatigorsky asked violinist Yehudi Menuhin if he might find time to meet with his father on his visit to Moscow. Menuhin was shocked to meet Pavel, who launched a violent tirade:

> "You bring me messages of my son?" He shouted. "What kind of a son do I have? What kind of a son is it that forgets his father?"
>
> "He hasn't forgotten you; he's worried about you: that's why I asked to see you," I managed to interpose.
>
> "Why doesn't he ever write? Why does he never send me anything? Not so much as a word!"
>
> "But he does! All the time! Letters money, parcels. They can't have got through."
>
> Far from softening his wrath and distress, my explanation served only to deflect him to a new target.
>
> "This cursed miserable regime! It doesn't care about its old people. It leaves them to rot. It has no heart, no pity!"
>
> He made not the slightest attempt to muffle his rage, but declaimed it for all the world to hear. The musicians around were terrified. Addressing him by first name and patronymic, they implored him to stop:

"Be quiet! Please be quiet!" And when these appeals failed, dragged him, still shouting, away. I did not see him again. It was the only ominous crack in the happy surface of my Moscow days.[29]

Leonid Piatigorsky (1902–1974) became known as a successful conductor of light music and operetta for the Moscow Radio in the 1940s, and presented a weekly program (Pavel was in the viola section). For Stalin's birthday broadcast, his ruthless concertmaster gave Leonid a new score from a Georgian composer, suggesting it was a marvelous nationalistic piece, the perfect vehicle for such an occasion. Though Leonid could not read Georgian, he agreed to program it, ignorant of its title — "Overture for the Death of a Hero."

Envious of Leonid's job, the concertmaster contacted the KGB and accused him of spying for the Americans, and, as further proof of his disloyalty, presented the music to the KGB. Leonid was already under watch as the intended recipient of Gregor's confiscated gifts. He was shipped off to Siberia and the ruthless concertmaster was promoted. In spite of long, vehement protests of his innocence, Leonid was given the choice: "either sign a confession and admit you are a spy, or you will be killed."[30]

The Stalin era wielded absolute power, but after Stalin's death in 1953, cases were reopened. Since there was no evidence, Leonid was released. While at the gulag, Leonid organized a symphony orchestra made up of prisoners from a consortium of gulags. The orchestra presented musical "evenings" for local officers and the enlisted. After his release, Leonid had a very difficult time finding work; but true to his industrious initiative, he created a very fine "scientist" orchestra in Moscow made up of semiprofessional players. A modest salary was attached to the organization, but he was able to supplement it through guest conducting appearances.

Following the infamous McCarthy-Hoover paranoia during and after World War II, guilt-by-association not only fueled the racial internment of Japanese-Americans, it was also the case that many foreign-born American artists had a difficult time defending themselves against allegations of communist associations. Piatigorsky's FBI file reveals his presence at "subversive" fund-raisers that were "communist fronts," some of which were attended by members of the current administration. Fortunately Piatigorsky's file was cleared of any questionable activity, and he was, in fact, invited by the State Department to represent the United States as its first foreign-born artist in 1956. He joked about the cold war, commenting, "I think I had better change my name to Pat O'Gorsky."[31]

Piatigorsky's return to Moscow in 1962 left a deep impression. Not only did he connect with family, but he was also able to see many important musicians from his youth, including Sergei Shirinsky of the Beethoven Quartet and Konstantin Mostras of the Lenin Quartet. He visited the Bolshoi Theatre, but was sad to see that little improvement had taken place, noting that the same orchestral parts he had played from were still in use.

A meeting with Moscow's musicians and competition participants was arranged with Piatigorsky at the small hall in the conservatory. After he spoke, many friends asked him to play. Sviatoslav Knushevitsky gave him a cello — Piatigorsky's old *Bergonzi* cello from his Bolshoi days. He played his own humorous *Prokofiev Meets Shostakovich in Moscow*[32] to great applause. The impression upon his colleagues led Shostakovich, Khrennikov, Kabalevsky, and Khachaturian to propose to compose variations upon a theme for Piatigorsky, with each composer contributing a variation; but it was never completed.[33] The enthusiasm for Piatigorsky's composition prompted his cellist brother, Alexander (Shura) Stogorsky, to ask for a copy. Piatigorsky had never written out the piece, but sketched it out for him. Stogorsky subsequently published it in the music journal *Soviet Music*.[34]

Piatigorsky's presence in the competition led to a few changes. One controversial change concerned the universally accepted rule that a member of the jury may not vote on his or her own student. His brother Shura recounted the following: "'I protested against that tradition,' Gregori Pavlovich told me, 'I would be so offended if anyone thought that I might be cheating. I would vote against my own mother, if she played out of tune. My colleagues agreed with me.'"[35]

Another suggestion that took hold was the inclusion of Beethoven, Brahms and Bach in the repertoire of the competition. Piatigorsky thought that prizes or diplomas were not necessarily the most important aspect of the competition, that comments and suggestions from masters could be helpful. "I hope," said Gregori Pavlovich, "that in the future, we will have real forums for solving and discussing performance problems. I, for example, would love to know which forum I can go to in order to discuss technical questions, talk about it openly with one another, hear different views."[36]

He also brought an air of tolerance regarding talented performers who might falter under the unusual strain of the competition: "The cellist was very nervous; he forgot the text of the piece, got confused and was forced to leave the stage. Some members of the jury wanted to eliminate the musician from further competition. However, Gregori made sure that the contestant repeated his performance in the second round. He talked to the performer and told him that he believed in him. As a result, the contestant played wonderfully, passed through to the next round, and got one of the first places."[37]

Piatigorsky was very impressed with the Soviet level of playing, and they won all the prizes in the string areas in 1962:

> Preparation of Soviet musicians made a big impression on me. Many things became clear for me. Clear that young people in your country treat music competition much more seriously.

Moscow, 1962. *Left to right:* Leslie Parnas, Natalia Shakovskaya, GP, Natalia Gutman.

And not only young people, not only people who organize the competition (it is amazingly organized, with unusual tact, with unusual hospitality and cordiality) treat it seriously, but everybody — without exception.

I saw how Soviet participants, these young girls and boys, worked with such serious thinking of each note. Unfortunately, in other countries, particularly in my country, there wasn't serious preparation for competition. Everyone has a right to present his country at the competition, if he has enough money for one-way trip. When I will get back home, first thing I will say — we have to work, to

Top: Playing duos with David Oistrakh, Moscow 1962 (courtesy Eduard Schmieder). *Bottom:* Moscow, 1966. *Left to right:* Piatigorsky, Stogorsky, Cassadó, Fournier, Shafran, Rostropovich.

work more seriously. We need careful preparation for competitions such as the Moscow one. Not everyone has a right to present his country.

General level of competition was high; I was deeply touched by many musicians as true cello talents.

Definitely, Tchaikovsky competitions, including cello competition, will exist and its representation will get wider and wider from time to time. I would like very much if such a beloved by everybody Dmitry Dmitrievich Shostakovich would stay as a chairman of this international competition.[38]

During the second competition in 1966, *Izvestia* reported on June 16:

I do not know of any other international competition that could compare with the Tchaikovsky Competition in scale and in the care taken in its organization. One must salute a government for whom art is a staple, not just a luxury. Art needs attention from government and the people.

Speaking of competitions in general, I hope that there will come a time when musicians find a real approach, a true means for assessing human gifts. Throughout my life — and I am a very old artist, although not such an old man — I have been constantly asked: Who is the No. 1 violinist on earth, the No. 1 cellist, and the No. 1 conductor? Such questions have seemed and still seem as ridiculous as the questions: Who is the best composer, writer, artist?

In the world of performing arts, determining who is the most famous is not so difficult. For this, one does not need to be a musician. But who is the most interesting? That is more complicated to determine. In general, an artist becomes interesting only when it becomes impossible to compare him. I find similarity very frightening.

While listening to the young people at the competition here, I have felt a certain heaviness. I love young musicians. And I have yet to meet one — whether old or young — who did not go out onto the stage wanting with all of his soul to give listeners the best he had. It's difficult for me to sit in the jury and penalize a person with such a sincere, burning desire to give his very best.

In my opinion, this Tchaikovsky Competition is at least as high caliber as the last, and perhaps higher. This is due mainly to the inclusion of Beethoven and Brahms compositions in the compulsory program. These composers make it much easier to determine which of the competitors has gone deeper into the music, has made the more decisive approach to real art, truth and nobility.

Today — by this, I mean a very prolonged extension into the recent past, not a year or two — cellists are experiencing a renaissance period. The level of cello playing as an art and cellists themselves have risen extraordinarily, their breadth has expanded. Just 20, 25 [32 actually] years ago, the fact that I had recorded the Schumann Concerto in London under the conductor Barbirolli was unbelievable even to Pablo Casals.

Every epoch brings something of its own to an art. Of course, we want to feel like we are the most progressive. And that may very well be. Discussions of contemporary performance trends are quite frequent and probably justified. Nevertheless, it is difficult to substantiate that the cello is played better today than during Boccherini's time — at least, I'm not so certain it is.

Young musicians are often in a rush. This is their primary shortcoming. Every talented boy or girl is trying to conquer the world as fast as they can. But in art, there are no shortcuts, corners can't be cut, nothing can be skipped over. Many musicians still have to reach into the depths of the music, to comprehend its higher meaning and learn not to capsulate it into separate categories: chamber music, virtuoso…. There is only one, indivisible "music" in the world.

What I call "total balance" is always the most important thing for me. What does this mean?

I wish enthusiasm for the young musicians, because music without enthusiasm is like life without oxygen. I would also tell them to make a proper study of themselves, of their own personal qualities.

Let young musicians understand and always remember that those who give their lives to something bigger than themselves are the ones who live well.

Piatigorsky students won Silver Medals in both competitions. Stephen Kates spoke about winning a silver in the 1966 competition:

> That was like landing on the moon for the United States. For an American in 1966 to get that far in a competition in the Soviet Union was a great accomplishment in itself. There was a Cold War raging at the time. In a way, I considered it to be a Gold Medal. Leslie Parnas had won the Silver Medal four years before me, and knowing his wonderful playing, I felt good about getting the same honor as he. No non–Russian had ever won Gold at that point in the Tchaikovsky Competition except for Van Cliburn. It took another twelve years before that glass ceiling was broken again by Nathaniel Rosen in 1978. The majority of judges were from Eastern Bloc countries. There were only four Western judges out of eighteen: Piatigorsky, Cassadó, Fournier, and a Finnish judge. I wouldn't say it was "rigged," it was just the climate of the times. I realized as I walked out on stage for the first round at the tender age of 23 ... that that was "my" moment to present myself on my own terms to those historic musicians. Part of my mental preparation for the competition was to imagine ... myself walking out in front of twelve people that I idolized to the point of hero-worship, who had, in a sense, molded me as I was growing up through their performances, master classes, recordings, and legendary performances. Now I had the chance to show them who "I" was, and what in essence they had helped to create.[39]

Boccherini, Rózsa, and Schifrin

LUIGI BOCCHERINI

One of the works that made Kates' repertoire stand out in the competition was the Sonata in C by Boccherini, a work unknown to the jury. The sonata was basically an arrangement Piatigorsky made from an early edition that he had performed and recorded many years before. For Piatigorsky, the greatest cellist-composer was Luigi Boccherini (1743–1805); and though some of his music was printed, most of the composer's output was unknown. Best remembered for his Cello Concerto in B-flat and the familiar minuet and rondo from two of his 119 quintets (for 2 violins, viola and 2 cellos, an ensemble combination he may have invented), Boccherini was an unjustly neglected major composer whose life and works were in dire need of discovery.

Just as Piatigorsky was the catalyst for Jacqueline Piatigorsky's self-discovery of hidden gifts, he was similarly inspiring to his mother-in-law, Germaine de Rothschild. Though Germaine was not particularly well-educated in music, Piatigorsky persuaded her to tackle the monumental task of writing Boccherini's biography. Piatigorsky knew that Germaine had the wherewithal to search the world for documents regarding Boccherini's life and music — be it antiquarian printed editions, manuscripts, or letters. During her research she enlisted the help of French musicologist Yves Gérard, who guided the research that resulted in a 700-page catalog of nearly 600 works. Germaine's biography was published in 1962 and the catalog in 1969, both lasting testaments to one woman's strength and courage.

Piatigorsky received many accolades for his 60th birthday. Composer Ernst Toch composed *Three Impromptus* for solo cello,[40] and the America-Israel Cultural Foundation sponsored a gala tribute. Jack Benny was the master of ceremonies. Knowing that the cellist had lent his name and effort to dozens of causes, including those close to home — the Hollywood Bowl and the Young Musicians Foundation — he tossed off the occasion:

Above: With Rubinstein, 1966. *Below:* With Casals, 1967.

The honoring thing is very embarrassing; on the one hand you don't consider yourself deserving; on the other, by accepting, you contradict yourself.

Today, there are so many good causes. Look at your mail — not one bad cause! ... Serge Koussevitzky used to say yes to anyone who ever asked him anything. Then one day someone criticized him for not doing what he said he would. "I'm weak," claimed Koussevitzky, "and so I promise everybody everything. But I'm strong enough not to keep my promises."[41]

In 1968 Piatigorsky received several tributes that pleased him in his 65th year. One was the "Outstanding String Teacher of the Year" bestowed by the American String Teacher's Association and the other was being honored at Indiana University. At Indiana he was hosted by Janos

With Zubin Mehta (pianist Doris Stevenson in background), about 1968.

Starker, who remembered Piatigorsky's characteristic humor: "I drove Piatigorsky from Indianapolis in the company of Bernard Greenhouse and Aldo Parisot, and at one point Grisha said, 'Be careful, Janos.' I asked, 'Why?' 'Imagine four famous cellists died. What a celebration the cello world would have.'"[42]

The Chamber Society of California paid tribute to the cellist on March 29, 1968. Performers included soprano Marni Nixon and eight of Piatigorsky's students conducted by Henri Temianka. Actors Gregory Peck and Robert Stack cochaired the event with honorary patrons Leonard Bernstein, Ray Bradbury, Pablo Casals, Jascha Heifetz, Zubin Mehta, Isaac Stern and Andres Segovia.

Miklós Rózsa

Miklós Rózsa was one of Hollywood's greatest composers, with Oscar-winning scores such as *Double Indemnity, Ben Hur*, and *Lost Weekend*. He was also a composer of concert

With Prime Minister Golda Meir, 1970.

music, and, in fact, never stopped writing concert music. Through a fluke meeting with the Korda brothers, both fellow Hungarians, he began his other career in Hollywood. His autobiography, *Double Life*, explores his years in two worlds of music.

Piatigorsky had the idea of commissioning a double concerto for him and Heifetz. The violinist had already commissioned the Violin Concerto, and by 1963 Rózsa completed the *Sinfonia Concertante* for violin, cello and orchestra. The composer wrote about the events leading to the completion of the work:

> I had known the cellist Piatigorsky for years. He was an incomparable raconteur and his book *Cellist* is full of these anecdotes, charmingly written, but with little of the flavor of his own telling of them. He ought to have recorded the book in his excellent English swamped by an absurd stage–Russian accent. Now Piatigorsky was a close friend of Heifetz, and one day he telephoned me to say he would like to have a talk with me professionally. He had a "vonderful plan." I was to write a concerto for him and Heifetz, a double concerto.
>
> I went to my beloved Rapallo [the composer's Italian refuge] with my family and finished the work in my three months, calling it *Sinfonia Concertante*. When I got back I called Piatigorsky and told him the first draft was finished, and I thought we should all try it through. The first movement began with a long passage for the cello alone before the violin entered. Heifetz pulled a face. "I can't wait as long as that. Give him about four bars and then I'll take over." The whole of the first movement went on like that. If one had a long solo, the other insisted on a solo of equal length; if one had a brilliant passage and the other a lyrical tune there was a squabble again, and so on. I made note of the required changes and saw the movement getting longer and longer.
>
> The second movement was a theme and variations. Now it is well known that the solo

With Perlman, Zukerman and Barenboim, Denmark, 1971 (courtesy Erling and Merete Blöndal Bengtsson).

cello can easily be overpowered when violin and orchestra are playing together, so I gave the long main theme to the cello to establish it. Then the violin joins in and begins the variations. Heifetz hated it.

"Do you expect me to stand there like an idiot all that time?"

Piatigorsky would reply, "Yes, Jascha, we expect you to stand there like an idiot!" But Heifetz was so adamant that I agreed to write something completely different. We didn't even try the last movement.

A month later we met again to try the slow movement. Piatigorsky said I reminded him of Toscanini.

"But how, Grisha? You've never seen me conduct."

"No, but your piano playing's just as lousy as his!"

As for my new offering, Heifetz pronounced it lacking in inspiration. Then we tried the last movement. Heifetz complained that it wasn't brilliant enough. We tried the revised first movement, with all its modifications, now more than twenty minutes long. Finally Heifetz agreed that the original second movement, the variations, was better, provided that he could play the theme at the end, very high, with some cello pizzicati, very low.

The actual premiere of the complete concerto took place later in Chicago, conducted by Jean Martinon; Victor Aitay and Frank Miller were the soloists. It was a fine performance, but I realized, sitting there, that the piece was overlong by a good ten minutes. We made cuts for the later performances, but unfortunately too late for the critics, who all complained of the same thing. I applied myself severely to tightening the piece up, and it is now published in its definitive form.

Violinist Manuel Compinsky and cellist Nathaniel Rosen first performed *Sinfonia Concertante* in its printed, revised form. Rózsa, who was conducting, recalled a rehearsal that Piatigorsky attended: "Stoppp!" he shouted at one point when we were apparently getting carried away. "Jascha and I couldn't play it this fast!" We slowed down.

Following Piatigorsky's death, Rózsa wrote a loving tribute in the form of an unaccompanied cello work, *Toccata Capricciosa*: "*Toccata Capricciosa* is not an elegy: rather it reflects something of Piatigorsky's incomparable vitality, open-heartedness, buoyancy and bravado, qualities which he shared with his teacher, Julius Klengel (to whom my Cello Duo is dedicated), and which are sadly missing in many performing artists today."[43]

With Du Pré and Barenboim, 1970 (courtesy Violoncello Society, Inc., New York).

LALO SCHIFRIN

Piatigorsky proposed another double concerto after the Rózsa commission to another well-known composer associated with Hollywood, Lalo Schifrin. The composer recalled the genesis:

I was asked by Gregor Piatigorsky on behalf of Heifetz and himself to write a double concerto which they were planning to record, I believe, for RCA and perform the world premiere at the Dorothy Chandler Pavilion in Los Angeles. I had frequent meetings with Mr. Piatigorsky who was conveying his suggestions as well as Mr. Heifetz's ideas.

We were using these meetings also to play chess (you probably know Mr. Piatigorsky was a great chess master). Unfortunately, Mr. Heifetz fell ill and we were unable to pursue the project to the end.[44]

The concerto was completed in 1968, but having come at the end of the soloists' active performing careers, lay dormant. The work is now called *Sinfonia Concertante*, and is a tour de force, with many cadenzas and bravura passagework. A theme and variations finale transforms through many styles, including a jazz episode. Its rollicking coda was extended at Heifetz's request, and brings the work to a dramatic close.

12. Academe's Bizarre World

The Teaching Saga

By 1959 Piatigorsky and Heifetz were well-established residents of Los Angeles, and as their careers were slowing down, they both had the urge to teach. Piatigorsky had taught during two periods in his career: the Russian and Klindworth-Scharwenka conservatories in Berlin in the 1920s, and the Curtis Institute of Music and Tanglewood (at the Berkshire Music Center) in the 1940s.

After resigning from Curtis (1951) and the Berkshire Music Center as head of the chamber music department (1954), Piatigorsky continued to support several youth organizations: Peter Meremblum's California Youth Symphony,[1] the Young Musicians Foundation, and the Music Academy of the West in Santa Barbara, where he became Musical Advisor and a regular fixture in the summers.[2] He briefly joined the faculty of Boston University for 1957-58 (mostly in a peripheral role), launching their new string development program with BSO principal cellist Samuel Mayes. (Piatigorsky donated his fee to the scholarship fund for cellists.)

Heifetz, though not nearly as experienced in teaching as Piatigorsky, remembered Leopold Auer's pronouncement to the young violinist: "someday you will be good enough to teach." Both Heifetz and Piatigorsky believed string playing was, as Auer said, "a perishable art. It must be passed on as a personal skill. Otherwise, it is lost."[3]

In 1959 Heifetz—and some months later, Piatigorsky—were briefly associated with the University of California, Los Angeles (UCLA), a major university very near their homes. But two insurmountable obstacles marred their short stay. The music department was not vibrant enough to sustain their master classes since it emphasized the academic aspects of music rather than performance. But more disappointing was the department's lack of enthusiasm. Purportedly, internal faculty jealousy blocked further contracts due to complaints that the duo did not possess advanced academic degrees. In fact, neither had graduated from any institution.

Fortunately, in 1962, the University of Southern California (USC), a private institution, offered Piatigorsky and Heifetz a much better situation within its school of music. USC created the Institute for Special Musical Studies especially for them. The institute's faculty also included violist William Primrose. Together the three were the reigning masters of their instruments. They were also the West Coast's beacons to the world, and USC expected immediate success. But the institute had a sluggish beginning; Primrose was unhappy that he had so few students, and a year later he accepted an offer to teach at Indiana University.

However, Heifetz and Piatigorsky remained and cultivated astonishing studios. The establishment of the Heifetz-Piatigorsky concert series and recordings added to their ever-widening allure.

Without warning, after four years, the institute was closed and their contracts were unceremoniously terminated. The dean at the time, Raymond Kendall, resigned in protest. A year later (1967), Kendall, Heifetz, Piatigorsky, and other faculty joined forces to inaugurate the Performing Arts Academy of the Music Center, a creation of Ralph and Dorothy "Buffy" Chandler, owners of the *Los Angeles Times*. The Chandlers wanted Los Angeles to become a musical hub and enthusiastically used their influence to make it happen.[4] The Los Angeles Music Center had been inaugurated in 1966 with the Los Angeles Philharmonic's new conductor, Zubin Mehta. The academy was the West Coast answer to New York's Lincoln Center with the Juilliard School nearby. All the performing arts were included, from ballet and dance to composition. Within a year, it became apparent that the academy was too cumbersome and isolated. Its facilities were nonexistent, as the school was basically an office building. There was no orchestra, practice rooms or concert hall, and no dormitories — strictly a commuter school. The idea to merge in some fashion with nearby USC seemed logical.

USC had since changed the name of the music school and merged it with the film and the drama schools to create the School of Performing Arts. Ambitious plans for new buildings were made. (Clark House, a spacious but inadequate mansion on campus, was its main music building.) USC's board of directors asked composer Grant Beglarian to become its new dean. As a prominent officer in the Ford Foundation, pulling him away from New York was difficult. He said he would consider the job later if they kept the position open for a year, and they did. Faculty pianist John Crown was appointed interim dean.

After several months, Beglarian received a surprising call from Crown saying that Mr. Heifetz and Mrs. Chandler would like to talk with him. "Mrs. Chandler was Mrs. Chandler, but Mr. Heifetz? Being a violinist in my day, that was really something!"[5] Chandler and Heifetz knew that if Beglarian went to USC he would be more involved in music than in the other arts, and wondered if there might be a way of combining forces and creating a whole new institution. Conversations and documents went back and forth for five or six months.

USC's board chairman and Chandler agreed to finance the merger, with USC continuing its music school. The academy would exist for visiting professors, namely Heifetz and Piatigorsky, all under the same administrative umbrella. The two artists would continue teaching at the academy at their present salaries.[6] With that understanding, Beglarian accepted the job and was appointed dean of the School of Performing Arts in March 1969 by USC president Norman Topping. (Topping had been president during the institute's era as well.)

But Beglarian received a shocking call in April. At the final board of trustees meeting, some questioned the plan, claiming that they did not have enough money to build a school of music. According to Beglarian, when it was pointed out that Mrs. Chandler supported it, and it could succeed, one of the board members who was "to the right of Genghis Khan in terms of politics" claimed that Mrs. Chandler was a communist and said, "we don't want to be associated with someone like that." Film tycoon Jack Warner, a board member, said, "Well look, if all you need is some money to build a music school, we'll give you the money. Why are we going to bed with Ralph Chandler?"[7] The board then made the astonishing commitment of five million dollars to build the school of music but did not include the academy component.

Mrs. Chandler had by this time already made the decision to close the academy. Piatigorsky was not "in the loop," and received word of the academy's closing in May after he and Heifetz had already signed contracts for the fall semester. Piatigorsky was anxious about his student "orphans." "One does not have to die" he wrote, "to be buried."[8] Heifetz, however, looked at the cancellation as a breach of contract and initiated a lawsuit against the academy, even though he knew that he would likely be returning to USC's nest in the fall.[9]

Having already accepted the deanship, Beglarian made an appointment with President Topping to get to the bottom of the impasse. Beglarian remembered the conversation:

> "Well that's very nice [about the new building], but what do we do with Heifetz and Piatigorsky? I mean, we've made a deal."
> Topping replied, "I don't know, it's up to you. What do you want to do?"
> "I want them back at USC."
> "Why would you want them back?"
> "It would be as if the business school was offered Bernard Baruch[10] to come and teach. Would you say, 'I don't know, do you want them?' Of course I want them! Aside from their teaching, they bring a whole aura to the school, it gives the international stature that we need, especially if you're going to be doing all kinds of other things."
> Topping interjected, "Except that we haven't got any money. What kind of salaries are you talking about?"
> "Well, I want them to get basically what you pay your football coach."
> "Are you crazy?"
> "No, that's what I want, that's what I think they're worth."
> "I can't do that."
> "OK, I'll tell you what. I'll work for a dollar a year as a dean. Put my salary and whatever other monies you have towards these salaries.[11] Look, I've just moved here, you're paying me a lousy salary — I'll put it in the papers: 'Incoming Dean Works for a Dollar a Year in Order to Hire Heifetz and Piatigorsky to USC.' How would you like that?"
> He looked at me scrutinizingly — he never heard any dean say anything like that.
> Topping gave in, "OK; I'll give you the money."

When Beglarian asked Heifetz and Piatigorsky to return to USC, they instantly replied, "When do we start?" Heifetz loved Beglarian's demand that the violinist become the highest paid faculty member, and was thrilled to learn that he made as much as the president of the university. Piatigorsky on the other hand, did not view salary as such an important issue (neither of them needed the money). Beglarian recalled: "I didn't tell that [Heifetz's exact salary] to Piatigorsky because I couldn't do it for both. But I knew he [Topping] would [pay it] to Heifetz, because he [Heifetz] was very well connected to the press and could make trouble. Piatigorsky wasn't like that. No. He would say to hell with it, and walk away. Not with Heifetz. Heifetz was a union organizer."[12]

To "seal the deal" the three met at Beglarian's home on July 23, 1969. Heifetz brought 24 glasses and a bottle of chilled vodka. Born in Russia, Beglarian remembered an old tradition and prepared black bread and salt. Both musicians were, to quote Beglarian, "Absolutely bowled over by that; they found a soul mate in me. We drank and smashed the glasses in the fireplace. My seven-year-old son Spencer was horrified, wondering, what kind of people are these barbarians?"

Heifetz and Piatigorsky were very happy at Clark House and both told Beglarian that he could use them in an effort to persuade the university to fully support the arts — for publicity, funding, or politics. The three men became united. USC was also the recipient of many performances with Heifetz, Piatigorsky and their students. Some were rather spontaneous, and were without the slightest advertisement. Word spread like wildfire. Every seat

was filled for these recitals. Either or both would appear without fanfare to support their students in chamber works as "guests." Piatigorsky also had class recitals where several students performed.

But by 1972, USC had failed to complete necessary building projects or even deliver on budgets for Heifetz and Piatigorsky's master classes. Both artists wanted nothing to do with tuition matters. That year, the Eastman School of Music invited Beglarian to interview as its new director and offered a salary twice that of what USC paid. Beglarian met with USC's president and threatened to leave unless they committed enough money to endow the Heifetz and Piatigorsky chairs.

The president presented the proposal to the board and it was approved, but the school never funded them even though Heifetz

Top: A last concert with Heifetz at USC, 1972. *Bottom:* A last photograph with Heifetz, USC, 1974.

A last photograph with the family, April 1976. *Left to right:* Jephta Drachman, Joram, Gregor and Jacqueline Piatigorsky (courtesy Piatigorsky estate).

and Piatigorsky agreed to give benefit concerts to help raise money. Heifetz gave his last recital in October 1972, and Piatigorsky and Heifetz gave two final Heifetz-Piatigorsky concerts, demonstrating their commitment to the school. "I think we charged in those days astronomical amounts of money — like $100 a ticket, but the idea was to create a kind of a public awareness more than the money."

USC awarded Piatigorsky an honorary doctorate in 1974, and the establishment of his chair followed — Piatigorsky jokingly called it the "wheel chair." Funding his chair (at one million dollars) was, according to Beglarian, "a snap." In early 1975 President Hubbard announced grants of one million dollars each from the USC trustees "to honor these two men, who are the greatest in their fields, inaugurate a new style of giving to the arts in Los Angeles."[13] The reality was that the Heifetz chair was not funded for many years despite Beglarian's efforts. Piatigorsky wanted the performing arts on the same level as creative arts: "As a cellist and teacher, I used to play everywhere in the world, each time sitting in a different chair — never carrying with me a chair.... I am happy now to have a permanent one."[14]

As part of the Piatigorsky Chair in Violoncello, the Gregor Piatigorsky Seminar for Cellists was inaugurated in 1977 and has featured the world's most well-known cellists. No institution has had such a broad representation over such a long period of time devoted to a performer. The first holder of the chair was Lynn Harrell, followed by Ronald Leonard. The Piatigorsky Prize was also established, awarded to an outstanding cellist. Hamilton Cheifetz, William de Rosa, and Stephen Isserlis are among the recipients.

Valediction Too Soon

Piatigorsky's generosity was increasingly evident in his semiretirement. Benefits became a common activity. One took place in Los Angeles in a benefit for Wellesley College, which his daughter Jephta had attended. Comedians Jack Benny and Bob Hope[15] did a few skits with Piatigorsky. Another was Piatigorsky's return to Israel in 1970, with Jascha Heifetz for a series of benefit concerts, and again in 1974, with Zubin Mehta and the Israel Philharmonic. Both times he visited with Israel's leaders, President Zalman Shazar and Prime Minister Golda Meir.

Above all else, Piatigorsky's last years were consumed with teaching; still the desire to perform beckoned him. On the 40th anniversary of his arrival in the U.S. he celebrated with several successful concerts in Los Angeles and New York. In 1973 the Chamber Music Society of Lincoln Center sponsored a 70th birthday celebration both at the Kennedy Center in Washington, D.C., and Alice Tully Hall in New York. The galas featured the cellist with pianist John Browning and soprano Beverly Sills as well as several of his students. To top it off, composer Gian Carlo Menotti was commissioned to write a suite for two cellos and piano.

Knowing Piatigorsky's interest in Anton Webern's music, Hans Moldenauer, the distinguished musicologist and collector, brought three unpublished early works to Piatigorsky's attention. Discovered in 1965, they represented Webern's first compositions as well as the transitional period before his studies with Arnold Schonberg. Webern was also a cellist of modest accomplishment, and certainly played his two early pieces, *Zwei Stücke* (1899). Almost Wagnerian in intent, these elemental snippets tell little of his future path, while the terse, mature Cello Sonata (1914) telegraphs the logical line to serialism. Piatigorsky premiered the three unpublished works, and performed the Op. 11 on June 3, 1970, with Victor Babin at the Cleveland Institute of Music. While there, he also received an honorary doctorate.

In the summer of 1974, he participated in the City of London Festival with Daniel Barenboim, Pinchas Zukerman and Itzhak Perlman in chamber music and a recital with Barenboim. Jacqueline du Pré could not appear at the festival due to her battle with multiple sclerosis, but Piatigorsky visited her every day and they played duets.

But by 1975 Piatigorsky was diagnosed with lung cancer, not surprising after almost a lifetime of smoking. An operation to remove a portion of the affected tissue was successful. He stopped smoking and expected that his convalescence would promise a new life. He made plans to perform the Walton concerto with Mehta and the Los Angeles Philharmonic. The composer had written a new ending for the work in response to Piatigorsky's many pleas for a more dramatic conclusion. At the same time, he kept encouraging Walton to write a double concerto — anything he wanted and of any length — for himself and Heifetz. Unfortunately the composer never made a start.[16]

A year later, a spot was discovered in Piatigorsky's other lung, signaling that the cancer had spread. In typical Old World fashion, dying was never discussed or even mentioned, either by his doctor or his family. Piatigorsky accepted invitations from several universities where honorary doctorates were conferred upon him, including one at Columbia University and another at Grinnell College where I was on the music faculty. While at Grinnell, Piatigorsky and the author performed a duo recital where he also played two solo compositions that he had written years earlier: *Prayer in Homage to Ernest Bloch*, and *Stroll: Prokofiev Meets*

With Milstein and unidentified students in Zurich, July 1976. Gary Hoffman is second from right (behind Piatigorsky) and Steven Isserlis is on the far right (courtesy Gary Hoffman).

Shostakovich in Moscow. In June 1976, despite failing health, he also agreed to open the new Robin Hood Dell series with the Philadelphia Orchestra and Eugene Ormandy in *Don Quixote* and the Brahms Double Concerto with Isaac Stern. By the accounts of those who were present, this was an unfortunate decision, for he was too ill and weak to perform at his best.

Piatigorsky accepted an offer to give master classes in Zurich in July and was delighted that Milstein would also be there. As ill as he was, he gathered all his strength to teach many up and coming cellists. I was touring with the Mirecourt Trio then and we rendezvoused with Piatigorsky in Zurich. While there, I took Piatigorsky to hear Milstein's recital, but by the intermission he asked that we leave, as he was so weak and needed rest. However, he and Milstein shared a few teaching sessions, where they coached both the Double Concerto and the C Major Trio by Brahms with the Mirecourt Trio.[17] Following our performance, Piatigorsky and Milstein entertained all of us by walking around the studio playing a Kreislerian waltz, Piatigorsky strumming my cello. We all laughed at the sight, which remains a vivid memory. It was the last time he played.

That night he became very ill with a high fever and began spitting up blood. The Piatigorskys left the following morning on the Concorde and flew to the United States, where they stayed several days in Maryland with their son and daughter before returning to Los Angeles. He died at his home a few weeks later.

Serenity in the '70s (courtesy Ryan Selberg).

I visited him on his last day. He lay in bed with an oxygen mask covering his face. When I entered the room, he pulled the mask off and said, "Ah, Terry. My best friend!" I asked him if he needed the device, and he replied, "No," and laid it aside as we visited. He spoke to me for some minutes, giving me heartfelt advice as he had done so often over the past eight years. He also spoke about wanting to live to be 80 so he could finish his work, including his desire to work with me on a book on cello fundamentals. The flexing pupils of his brown eyes told me that his life was slipping away. I asked him how he felt about dying. He said he saw himself from above, hovering: "I just wake up and see myself above me." I kissed his hand as we talked, but I knew he needed to rest. When his doctor arrived I left the room and sat at the top of the stairs to weep quietly. Then I heard him ask the doctor about his breathing difficulty: "What do I do when I panic?" "Move into another position" she said. The end was never expressed in words.

I met Jacqueline and her sister Bethsabée downstairs. I wanted so much to give him hope to live, to keep on fighting. I told them that I would get his recordings republished. "How soon?" asked Jacqueline. "A few weeks," I said, though I knew I could not control the timing of such a project. She said it was too late. He died early the following morning, on August 6. I returned to their home and went upstairs, cried and said good-bye. His open mouth made me hope he hadn't struggled at the end.

The following day, the Los Angeles Philharmonic dedicated their performance of the Verdi *Requiem* to him. A memorial was given at USC and was attended by many caring people whom he had touched in life. Rabbi Edgar F. Magnin, Zubin Mehta, G. Peter Fleck, and Anna Bing Arnold spoke. Dean Beglarian gave the eulogy, a poignant message that Piatigorsky would surely have loved and been humbled by. Itzhak Perlman performed Rachmaninoff's *Vocalise*, and several students played Villa Lobos' *Bachianas Brasilieras no. 5*. Finally Jeffrey Solow, Daniel Rothmuller, and I performed the Popper *Requiem* with pianist Doris Stevenson.

Earlier that year, Beglarian had been talking with Piatigorsky about Native American literature. Its sentiment and simplicity touched Piatigorsky. Beglarian shared part of it at the memorial that ended with a Sioux quote, "[E]ven the eagle dies."

It is a mark of the Piatigorsky legacy that many of Piatigorsky's students have remained good friends over the years. The collective process of our shared vulnerabilities, the wisdom imparted from our lessons and the supportive environment he provided brought us together for life. The bond that comes from work, dedication and the pursuit of beauty is a timeless measure of life as good "servants of music." It was he who taught us to spend our energies on "something greater than ourselves."

PART II : RECALLING PIATIGORSKY

Accompanists

> *He's not a romantic Gitano*
> *The fellow who sits at the piano*
> *His life is not light and dark is his sorrow*
> *He is on the watch[,] he always must follow*
> *No matter who's singing or playing in front*
> *He often must track them as though in a hunt[.]*
> *And seldom the critic has tired his wrist*
> *Reviewing and praising the accompanist*
> *They may be stupendous in Mozart and Brahms*
> *Prokofieff, Hindemith[,] Bach or Saint-Saëns*
> *No matter his efforts enormous or small*
> *The man at the piano can not change his role*
> *Oh poor man of art, so short is your story*
> *Hard work, little cash, servitude and no glory*

Piatigorsky's little poem of empathy demonstrates his awareness of the injustice most accompanists suffer. He wrote in *Cellist*:

> His position in the world of music is peculiar, and although the life of a soloist is unthinkable without him, his immense importance rarely receives due recognition. Good recital programs for the bow instruments consist of ensemble music with a piano part of equal importance — equality that the accompanist is not permitted to enjoy. His piano lid is closed. He must be discreet. He uses music, and for a scant fee plays by far more notes than the soloist. His name on the program is not prominent and in the reviews he is scarcely mentioned. It is to be expected that sooner or later, on or off the stage or most likely both, he will resent his celebrated employer. However, old professional accompanists in time develop an extraordinary defense mechanism, and in discharging their duties are as unperturbed as a fakir on a bed of nails.
>
> Once, on the subject of my piano collaborators, it is difficult to be swayed away from it. Were I to speak of Ralph Berkowitz, it would encompass more than [thirty] years of activity. Thoughts of Ivor Newton and [Valentin] Pavlovsky bring many heart-warming episodes to mind; and images of Van der Pas, whom I saw without a cigar in his mouth only on the stage, of Otto Herz of Budapest, who practiced black magic in addition to his accompanying, Arpad Sandor, Emanuel Bay and others — all pass vividly through my mind.
>
> One day in Paris a young man came to audition for a position as my accompanist. He was frail-looking and very eager. He played for hours, but, enchanted, I asked for more. Finally he asked, "Will you engage me?" His voice was anxious. My answer was "No." His color changed.
>
> "You don't understand. You are so young. You are a master. You must not spoil the wonderful career that is awaiting you." I embraced him. It was Dinu Lipatti, a name that speaks so fully of beautiful achievements and recalls the tragedy of his premature death.
>
> One of the reasons that influenced me in advising Lipatti is the stigma the word accompanist carries, a prejudice that can hinder a solo career. This feeling is even exemplified by the refusal

of a world-famous pianist to record sonatas with an equally prominent string player for fear of being thought an accompanist, and so falling down into the gutter.[1]

The following are recollections of two of Piatigorsky's long-time pianists. The first is Ivor Newton, who was, along with Gerald Moore, one of Britain's leading accompanists. Newton worked and recorded with the great artists of his time, and was one of the first pianists to bring a distinct personality to the accompanist's role. It was Newton who in 1926 persuaded the then violinist William Primrose to study with Eugène Ysaÿe. Ysaÿe, in turn, persuaded him to take up the viola, and he soon emerged as the premiere violist of the mid–20th century. Newton was also a philanthropist and willed his estate to the Musician's Benevolent Fund, an organization supporting retired musicians. His estate enabled the fund to create the Ivor Newton House in Bromley, a home for 21 residents who are cared for by a staff of over 30. The nonprofit organization allows the residents to pay reasonable fees according to their circumstances.

Ivor Newton

When I visited Casals at his retreat in Prades on the French side of the Pyrenees, he talked of his younger colleagues. Of one distinguished cellist Casals said, "He is a born musician." Of another he said, "He is a born virtuoso." When I mentioned Piatigorsky, Casals declared, "He is rarest of them all. He is a born artist."

A question was once put to me; if as an accompanist, I had to spend my entire career working with only one artist, whom would I choose? After much thought, I decided that I would be quite happy to travel round the world and make music interminably with Piatigorsky. I have known a great many musicians and have been happy to count a number of them among my friends, so that whoever I chose I should miss much that is delightful and memorable to me, but Piatigorsky has many of the qualities that most appeal to me.

Piatigorsky is a born artist, one of that very rare breed in whom art and personality are so combined as to put him among the giants of music. Both on and off the platform, his companionship is entirely absorbing. Musically, he has everything — a wonderful command of the cello, from which he produces strong, beautiful tone, a keen musical intelligence and an adventurous taste in music of all kinds. His art has always dominated his life, and apart from his love for his family, is the one thing that completely absorbs him. But for all his devotion to music, Piatigorsky still has room for great generosity in friendship — he always appears to me to prefer people to places and, when invited to dinner, to be far more interested in talking with a fantastic, sometimes almost surrealist wit than food and drink.

Now that Piatigorsky is dead, one wonders which half of the dual personality who seemed to inhabit this tall, handsome physique (as he carried his cello on to the platform, he made it seem not much larger than a viola) will be missed most. He was first of all an entirely dedicated musician, to whom the cello was sacred and music an art to be served with religious fervor.

The other Piatigorsky was a compulsive talker, never silent, preferring, as it seemed, people to places and talking to eating. Much of his talk was verbal clowning governed by a wildly active fantasy. On one occasion, when he had arrived after an overnight flight, an interviewer hoped that Piatigorsky had slept well on the plane. "Sleep!" he said tragically, "haven't slept for years!"

However wild the stories he tells, there is a quality of fantasy about his character that makes it possible to believe they might really have happened. I was often surprised to hear of the exotic adventures he imagined for me. "I must tell you of an extremely extraordinary thing which happened to Ivor recently. Tell me, Ivor, was it in Rio? No, it must have been Budapest, or, perhaps, Venice. No, I'm wrong. It was in Manchester." Only those with no sense of humor took his inexhaustible flow of witty nonsense seriously or failed to be delighted.

Whenever he had a cello in his hands, Piatigorsky had no time for anything but music; he became at once an intensely serious, dedicated musician. But between concerts he was always his lively, witty self, and the wit was always that of a keenly intelligent man with a fundamentally serious outlook. A tour of the United States with him provides not only memories of places and people, and of works he played gloriously, but also of his percipience as well as his high spirits.

In the United States, artists' fees are no secret from the world, and it is important that they never decline. "How is so and so playing?" Someone will ask, and the reply will be, "Oh, he (or she) is slipping. This season, he (or she) is only getting two thousand dollars a concert." After a recital as we drove away from the hall Piatigorsky would say, "Tell me, was the concert a sensation or a flop? In this country there is nothing in between." When I had replied, he would say, "Yes, but did I play like a thousand dollar, two thousand dollar or three thousand dollar artist?"

At many of our concerts in the United States, Piatigorsky ended the program with his own brilliant transcription of Paganini's *La Campanella*, and although we were constantly together, I never heard him practice this taxing virtuoso work, though he always played it at the recital impeccably and easily. The wonderful musicality of his performances, I often thought, could only be the result of a great deal of reflection and mental study, while his impeccable technique must have come from the early development of his natural gifts.

I remember rehearsing Debussy's Cello Sonata with him. "To play this well," he said, "you'll have to forget that you're a sound, clean-living Englishman. You have to be a neurotic, highly-strung, over-sensitive Frenchman, who lives on the Left Bank, drinks absinthe and maybe takes drugs. But don't forget, a Frenchman sees to it that every thirty-second note, every demi-semi quaver, is precisely in place."[2]

The cellist refused to rehearse slow movements for a second time, saying "Either one can play a slow movement or one can't; a rehearsal won't do it."[3] A typical example of the good-humored cellist was during one of their English tours when they performed for one of London's great music lovers, Lady Ludlow. She established a concert series for her intimate friends consisting of a mix of royalty and upper class, never more than fifty guests. She called the concerts Musicales, and always invited three major artists. One such event included Piatigorsky and the famed tenor Beniamino Gigli. Ivor Newton recalled:

Lady Ludlow would escort such royalty as were present to the supper room, while her son, Sir Harold Wernher, escorted the other guests. Our artists' room was one of the smaller drawing-rooms which contained some of the incomparable Wernher collection of renaissance jewels, Limoges enamels, and rare English porcelain. After the music, we would make our way to this retreat and, when the guests were already assembled in the supper room, be invited by Lady Ludlow to join them at supper (she once came to the artists' room for this purpose and was astonished to find the short, portly Gigli and the tall slim Piatigorsky dancing a minuet with proper stateliness). After our formal entrance into the supper room, we would be presented to the Royals.[4]

Shortly before Piatigorsky died, he wrote to Newton and enclosed a check for 500 pounds for Newton's Musician Benevolent Fund. Newton summed up his association with the cellist: "That I played for Piatigorsky throughout Europe and America will always be one of my most happy memories. He served with love and reverence the profession he adored. To be his friend was a joy; to be his colleague was a privilege."[5]

RALPH BERKOWITZ

Ralph Berkowitz enrolled at the Curtis Institute in Philadelphia in 1928, a fellow piano student with Samuel Barber and Gian Carlo Menotti. He later became a staff member at

Curtis, taught form and analysis, directed the Historical Series concerts, and coached vocal students. He performed with many of the Curtis faculty, including a Beethoven series with cellist Felix Salmond.

In 1940 he resigned to become accompanist for Piatigorsky. From 1946 to 1951 Berkowitz was executive assistant to Serge Koussevitzky at Tanglewood and from 1951 to 1964 he was Dean of the Berkshire Music Center at Tanglewood. He recorded with many artists, especially with members of the Boston Symphony.

In 1953 he also became executive director and principal pianist of the June Music Festival in Albuquerque (where he moved), and five years later business manager of the Albuquerque Symphony Orchestra until his resignation in 1969. In addition to teaching, lecturing, composing and performing, Berkowitz was an artist. His paintings, pastels, woodcuts, and drawings are in numerous private collections in New York, Philadelphia, Boston, Los Angeles and Albuquerque.

Berkowitz recalled his initial meeting with Piatigorsky:

> I met Piatigorsky for the first time in 1940 in Philadelphia. He had been playing with Valentin Pavlovsky who became very sick, so he asked me if I could join him for a few concerts. Those few concerts turned in to thirty years of playing together in many parts of the world. I had heard Piatigorsky in his debut concerts with the Philadelphia Orchestra in 1929 when he first came to the United States, but at that time I never thought that he would become a very close friend, collaborator, and life-long companion.
>
> We never argued; you can play with some people and have no chemistry or musical contact, but not with Grisha. I still remember our first few concerts. The third or fourth one was in Orchestra Hall in Chicago. It was a program which included the Brahms E Minor Sonata. We had not played this sonata at previous concerts. The days went by and I finally said, "You know, we really ought to rehearse that piece." Piatigorsky said, "Yes, of course we have to." But it never happened. And I give my word that we sat on the stage of Chicago's Orchestra Hall and played that work together for the first time! Of course he had to have more confidence in me than I had.
>
> His interest in young people was really very special. Once when we played in Seoul, a young family, a father and mother, with their three little children came to the hotel to meet Piatigorsky. The children were perhaps four, five and six years old. One played the cello, one the violin, and the other played the piano. Piatigorsky was so taken with the talent of these children that he gave the family money to come to America. Years later Grisha and I went to a high school in Beverly Hills and heard those children who were by then teenagers. One of the girls was Kyung-Wha Chung, who is now one of the great violinists of the world, and the pianist-brother has just been named director of the Bastille Opera in Paris. [Myung-Wha Chung studied cello with Piatigorsky at USC.] Piatigorsky was kind to many young people giving them bows, helping them acquire cellos and so forth. He was not only interested in them as musicians but as human beings.
>
> Sometimes on tour Piatigorsky would be met by his mother-in-law, the Baroness de Rothschild who traveled a great deal. She and her husband, Baron Edouard, were very close to Grisha. Once in Florence we were joined by the Baroness. She had received an invitation to the home of Bernard Berenson, the legendary art critic. Later in the afternoon I had tea with the Baroness, and I asked her if it had been a large lunch party. She replied, "Oh, a very small one, just myself and the Berensons." And then she hesitated and said, "No, wait a minute. The King and Queen of Sweden were also with us."

Berkowitz followed Piatigorsky's advice regarding a new association with the Boston Symphony, Koussevitzky and Tanglewood:

> The assistant manager of the Boston Symphony was Thomas Perry, a former pupil of mine. He asked me to become dean of Tanglewood, but I told him I'd never worked behind a desk and wouldn't know what to do. But many months later he sent me a telegram while I was in

Caracas on tour with Piatigorsky telling me the job was still open. I discussed it with Piatigorsky who said, "What do you have to lose? You'll have a nice summer and your family will enjoy it." So I became Koussevitzky's assistant until his death in 1951, and was named dean of what is now called the Tanglewood Music Center.

Piatigorsky adored Koussevitzky. Koussevitzky was like his father. Koussie loved Piatigorsky for many years previous to Tanglewood and Piatigorsky could do no wrong as far as Koussie was concerned. That relationship was extremely warm until his dying day. Koussevitzky's valet and chauffeur/butler — a man called Victor — was engaged by Piatigorsky when Koussevitzky died. You know, he kept Victor and his wife as housekeepers for many years after Koussevitzky died."[6]

Reminiscences of Friends and Colleagues[7]

JASCHA BERNSTEIN

[There was an amusing] story concerning his ego. In several of the German papers he was constantly being referred to as the "Russian Casals." Once, when Casals came to Berlin, Grisha decided to get even. The host for a party to which both cellists had been invited happened to be a friend of Grisha's, so he asked him to announce to his guests that there would be a reception to honor Pablo Casals, the "Spanish Piatigorsky."[8]

IVAN GALAMIAN

Piatigorsky was great inspiration for me. I think he was the greatest string player generally. He had the imagination, the tone, the way of phrasing. Very uneven; sometimes he played badly. When he played well, I didn't think anyone played that well.[9]

LYNN HARRELL

In 1956, when I was 12 years old, I was taken to hear Gregor Piatigorsky play with the Dallas Symphony Orchestra. Onto the stage came this immense figure, cello held high radiating energy and seriousness. Everything was there; the lean and intense tone, the imaginative use of rhythm as though the music was just speaking, a technique that was quite awesome and almost thrown away somehow. All the terrible rigors of playing this "big box," this large and obstinate enemy, all the details of frustration known to all of us from the practice room — had been erased. If they still existed for him, too, they were his business not ours. Smooth, certainly, but with an edgy kind of intensity that seethed, that burned — there was always great life to his music, And, as I discovered later, as was the playing, so was the man.

Did he really leave his home in the Ukraine when he was 10 years old, work in a nightclub to help support the family before then? Could he truly have been principal cellist of the Imperial Opera in Moscow at only 15 years old? Imagine between-the-wars Berlin in which this striking, handsome young man earned his living while taking lessons with Julius Klengel, an almost mythical figure to us now. For those, two and more generations later, who went to his master classes, it was as if we were being rooted in the very heart of music. What he was passing on stretched back into a time when Brahms, Wagner, and Dvorak were living men.

I first played for him in 1962. He was such a great performer that he could always make criticisms in a way so entertaining that the sting was always soothed away — and the lessons always incredibly clear. I still cherish the image of him sitting opposite me, the smoke of his cigarette getting in his eyes, his voice so full of colors and shading, accent, and meaning, He was truly like a great Russian bear.

In some ways, we live now in a smaller time, in days of smaller men. How lucky we are that Grisha's own playing, so full of life, hope and giving, reaches out across that darkness through his recordings and students. I am especially fortunate — in my time I was able to hear and to meet the fathers of our instrument: Casals, Piatigorsky, Rostropovich, Rose — to try to pass on a little of what he gave to us all.[10]

Allan Harshman

I met Piatigorsky first at Heifetz's home. Heifetz called me to play some chamber music and Mr. Piatigorsky was there and Leonard Pennario; it was around the time of the concerts in Los Angeles and San Francisco. I didn't study with Heifetz like most people who say they did. I enjoyed playing with him very much. Heifetz had something he wanted to read through, and I don't remember what it was, but I didn't know the composition either. He gave me the music a couple of days ahead of time and I didn't have too much time because I was working extensively. When I was practicing the music a little bit, looking it over, there was a phrase that repeated itself exactly. Instead of playing it the same way, I played it on a lower string, which made a difference, even if it was just the same phrase. Nobody ever made fingerings or bowings and things like that, but I did put down very lightly a fingering that I wanted to do. I did so after we got through, nobody except Mr. Piatigorsky noticed. He said that he knew with a wink, that it was a nice phrase. I was very impressed with how he noticed exactly what I did, even though we were all so-called sight-reading. I guess that was part of his personality — to make people feel good.

I was really sight-reading. I played all of what we call "section position" in picture studios. There's no time to read or practice. You just play it through and record it. I had a lot of experience with that, and it came in very handy many times. Heifetz was very covetous about his own phrases. It was praise enough if he called you.

All the way through, the attitude from rehearsal to recording session was the same with Piatigorsky and Heifetz. You had fun on the beach, but your music is one thing. You do the best you can; you don't play around with it. You don't joke with it.

We recorded the Spohr Double Quartet. We played it in Hollywood, then three weeks later we went to RCA and recorded it. We played it partly through to get balance; the people recording it were very experienced. They got the balance and mike placement and we just sat down and played it. They played it back, and I don't think we did any changing. Heifetz wanted to make a note of it [being recorded live] on the record.

I didn't think it was a very interesting piece of music. I did not venture any opinion on interpretation. If Heifetz didn't catch it, it shouldn't be caught. So it was not up to me except Mr. Piatigorsky would go in the booth with him. Mostly the decisions on interpretation were already done and we played it as it was played in the concert. It was one of the high points in my life.[11]

JACOB LATEINER

My close friendship with Piatigorsky started in my early teens, when I was a student at the Curtis Institute of Music in Philadelphia (1941–1948). He became a big brother, father and friend to me. We maintained our friendship when I actively started concertizing and after he moved to California. For a number of years he was most anxious to introduce me to Heifetz and kept asking me to stop off in Los Angeles during one of my tours. In 1961 I was finally able to do so.

I shall never forget the evening at the Piatigorskys when, after dinner, we waited Heifetz's arrival. He came — with violin.... It turned out that we were to play trios that evening. I had not prepared anything and was caught completely by surprise. The question arose as to what we should play. On the piano was a volume of Beethoven trios. Heifetz said, "Let's start with that." I asked, "Which one?" "Well, let's start at the beginning of the book," he answered. I had never played op. 1 no. 1, and don't consider myself a good sight-reader.

I must admit I recall little about that evening. My main memory is of having thought, "here I am, 33-years-old and a very junior member of this group, playing with one of the great legends of the century" (I had often played and talked about music with Piatigorsky and was used to him).

The next day during lunch Piatigorsky seemed rather fidgety. Mrs. Piatigorsky finally asked him whether he was anxious because Heifetz had not yet telephoned. "Yes," he replied. Eventually the phone rang; Piatigorsky went to take the call and came back with a huge grin on his face: "Heifetz liked you very much."

It was then that I learned I had been auditioned the previous evening to participate in the projected Heifetz-Piatigorsky series of concerts. And it seemed I had passed with flying colors; I played in four series of concerts.

One of the greatest satisfactions was the utter professionalism in our work. We would start to rehearse on Monday mornings at 10 o'clock. We stopped at 1 o'clock for lunch and then went on until we were so tired we couldn't concentrate any longer. The schedule was repeated on Tuesday, Wednesday, Thursday and Friday. The next Monday the routine would start all over again. The rehearsal process was democratic; we all spoke freely and openly about our perceptions both for the concerts and in listening to playbacks of the recordings. By the time we performed, we were so used to each other that any one of us could do something we had never done before and the others adjusted immediately. We felt a spontaneous re-creation of the music at that moment. It was so integrated yet so fresh. These are among the most precious memories of an association I was fortunate enough to have experienced, and they will remain with me for the rest of my life.[12]

ZUBIN MEHTA

Having grown up in a part of the world where visits by the great artists were a rare phenomenon, I used to regard names like Heifetz, Piatigorsky or Rubinstein to be as formidable and inaccessible as the remote peaks of the high Himalayas.

It was therefore with the greatest awe that I looked forward to my first meeting with Gregor Piatigorsky. At dinner after one of his celebrated chamber-music concerts in 1961 with Jascha Heifetz, I asked him just one question regarding his recollections of Richard

Strauss' conducting of *Don Quixote*. His reply took over the rest of the evening. As a matter of fact, it continued for the next 15 years through endless hours of conversations and quite a few of concerts.

I cannot forget the first of these performances. It was born out of a talk while we were swimming off Puerto Rico in 1967. We both had been invited by Pablo Casals to perform at his festival. Piatigorsky's *Don Quixote* was one of such beauty that during the great F-sharp-major variation I turned for a glimpse of Casals, who always sat in the wings. He was weeping. I think at one point or another all of us were weeping.

For my part, I had joined a colleague with whom I breathed musically with such complete oneness that after a performance of a work that took just over 30 minutes, we found ourselves closer than six previous years of discussing that same work had brought us. Communication between two musicians on a spiritual level is a phenomenon that cannot be defined accurately — it is more the unspoken word — the meaning that lies between the notes that draws us closer to one another.

Gregor Piatigorsky has on many an occasion put me on the right path. For all his valuable advice and above all, his friendship — I thank him.

Gregor Piatigorsky is a type of man and musician in equal parts that I would like to be like. I'd like to be his kind of musician, just all embracing, universal in his taste, very generous and very warm in his outpouring of the art of making music. And as a man, not just another one of those stereotype musicians who don't know about anything but music either. He was a man who was deeply involved in everything he undertook. He had interests outside of music that ranged from the study of snakes to gerontology to writing books on philosophy. He was working on a novel just before he died.

He was also an equally good performer and a teacher, which is a very rare combination. Sometimes you have the great teachers of the world who cannot perform everything they want to or they profess to teach or there are those incredibly gifted instrumentalists who just do it naturally and don't know how to impart it to others. Piatigorsky had both these gifts and practiced them.

You can go to any great orchestra in the United States and you will find pupils of Piatigorsky playing. You can go to almost all the schools of music where you will have a man who has been either very close to him or is directly his pupil. Then, his dedication to contemporary music was exemplary. He played nearly every concerto that was written for cello.... When we would sometimes do a world premiere or an American premiere at the [Los Angeles] Philharmonic, he would call me and say, "Now, how did it go? Did it interest you and did you think it would last? And, what are the characteristics, etc." He would be vitally interested. Also he was some sort of a recluse, because he spent most of his time, most of his last years with his students and then some of us, his friends. But yet he knew everything that was going on in the world of music. He had a correspondence with people all over the world. He was also intensely interested in the propagation of the cello itself. Not only for the music for the cello, but in the upkeep of the great cellos, the instruments of the world.

Piatigorsky was a great raconteur and we musicians knew that the same sense of storytelling seeped into his music-making. Sound to him was like conversation; the cello was just part of his body. One had to hear him play a cadenza from Bloch's *Schelomo* or an eight-bar phrase from Haydn's D-Major Concerto to realize that every note was just in its right place and always supremely logical. On the other hand, his love and respect for music of his time always found him ready to perform works by 20th-century composers. When we played a premiere at the Philharmonic, he was extremely interested in the results.

My dearest Grisha, how we will all miss you. Who is going to tell me all those little stories about Furtwängler and Toscanini? Talking to you was like going back to the late 1920s and '30s in Berlin and New York. My dear friend, I feel a giant has crossed my life's path. Thank you for all that you have given us faltering musicians. It is the full circle which you so gloriously achieved that we must strive for.[13]

Zara Nelsova

It was not until 1942 that I first went to study with Piatigorsky. I had heard him as a very young child in London when he first came over from Germany; he absolutely overwhelmed everybody with his magnificent playing and his fabulous personality. But I didn't meet him until years later, when I was in my early 20s. When he performed in Toronto, I yearned to play for him, but I didn't quite know how to arrange it. Finally, I found the courage to ask him if he would listen to me play. He said that he was terribly sorry, but that he had to leave the next morning at the crack of dawn to catch the train to the next city on his concert tour. His departure from the hotel was supposed to be at something like 8 o'clock, so I got myself up around five in the morning and quietly took my cello out of its case and tried to get my fingers moving. Then I packed up my cello and I went to his hotel room and knocked at the door. He opened the door, absolutely astonished to see me. I said, "Oh, Mr. Piatigorsky, I just happened to be passing by, and I hoped that you might be able to hear me." He invited me in and I played for him. Then I went to study with him a year later, which was a wonderful experience. I studied three summers with him, going through the repertoire, concerto after concerto. We talked about musical, not technical, ideas since my technique was already well established.[14]

Joseph de Pasquale

My initial meeting with Piatigorsky was just wonderful. He was a great cellist. Piatigorsky was so complimentary of my playing with the recording of *Don Quixote* I made with him in 1953. During the playbacks he said, "Joe, you are wonderful," and things like that. I said, "Likewise, you're fantastic!" So we had a mutual admiration society. The *Don Quixote* was outstanding. I played it with him during the season at Symphony Hall. It was really memorable.

He was delightful and I loved his accent, it was a joy to hear. We played with Piatigorsky and Heifetz on two occasions at Carnegie Hall. I recorded two concerts one year and the other the following year. When I went out to California to record, I naturally spent a lot of time with Piatigorsky, and Heifetz was there all the time. He was sociable, but not like Grisha. He was much more jovial and sometimes he would be too jovial and Heifetz would give him "the look." Then he said, "Grisha, pipe down." I enjoyed those times so much. To play with those men ... it was a great honor. Heifetz was the greatest violinist who ever lived; I would say that about Piatigorsky too, but there were other cellists; no other violinists came up to Heifetz; he was unique. I have memorable feelings of the concerts and recordings.

As far as the sessions, you had to follow Heifetz; he was the first violinist. On playbacks Heifetz would say, "a little more viola there," or "a little less viola there," and "I want to hear more of myself." Things like that, he would balance it very well, but he liked to be the prima donna. I think it was always musical. After the New York concert in 1966, we talked a bit after the concert. Piatigorsky had his usual scotch, which he loved, and we always said he had a hollow leg; he could put down a few. Heifetz was the opposite. He had one vodka, and that was it.

There was no difference of attitude between rehearsals and recording sessions. If you made one major mistake Heifetz would not splice. We would go back to the beginning; he liked the continuity of the thing. He did not like to splice, one note here and there. Grisha was that way too. He was a very modest and wonderful man, and funny. Especially after a few scotches. A delightful man. The memories of him will live forever.[15]

Leonard Pennario

My first meeting with Piatigorsky was at a concert at Tanglewood in 1949. I played chamber music there with members of the Boston Symphony early that summer in 1949, and some of those pieces I would later do with Grisha and Heifetz. I had no idea that someday I would be playing and recording with that great man. I had the realization of a life long dream playing with them. It was a fantasy dream come true.

We met again in the spring of 1961, at the first reading of the trios with Heifetz, a few months before the concert. Everyone could put in their thoughts in the rehearsals, the same as in the recording sessions.

I was hoping, of course, there would be other things. I especially wanted so much to do the Rachmaninoff Sonata with Piatigorsky, because that was something we had played in recital. It was a work very meaningful to both of us. I'm just sorry we never recorded it.

The working relationship with Piatigorsky was ideal. There was much give and take; it was very harmonious. It was such a joy to me, especially since we were friends. There were other occasions we played together. We had evenings here and evenings at Heifetz's and at Grisha's house. We played with a special group of friends. They were all special because they had different repertoires. There were several works I wanted to do, especially the B Major Brahms, but Heifetz didn't want to do it because it began with the cello. He resented the thing. It didn't take much for him not to want to do something. There were other things we did too, the Faure Piano Quartet with Primrose, the Mozart trios too. There were many felicitous touches and things that happened in those evenings.

The next time we were all going to meet at Primrose's place. Primrose said to Heifetz that when they meet at Pennario's home, he should get to choose the music. Primrose thought Heifetz would never allow anyone else to choose music![16]

Janos Scholz

The passing of Gregor Piatigorsky, in my estimation, marks the end of an era, comprising as it does the earlier decades of our twentieth century, which witnessed such very important changes in the evolution and art of violoncello playing. I, myself, while active as a cellist, lived through those heroic years, all the time observing and admiring what was being accomplished by four superlative artists in particular — in their establishing new high standards of performance as well as introducing a novel approach to technique [i.e., Casals,

Cassadó, Feuermann, Piatigorsky]. I knew them personally; I was proud to have considered two of them my friends.

Considered as a performer, he was what in German one would call an *Urtalent*, constantly bubbling like a fountain, giving us with both his hands lovely music, most happily and beautifully interpreted. On stage he was a supreme performer with an unsurpassed presence and sense of projection. Nobody who saw him will ever forget how he carried his instrument on high — like a fiddle — while pointing his bow like a rapier.

Grisha was a true child of Russia. He brought with him to the West a good deal of the great Russian musical heritage, and he then absorbed here and there many other impressions, all of which served to develop him into the towering, potent artist he remained to the conclusion of his life.

But there was still another side to his personality which placed him apart from the other three artists I mentioned before. In him there was an inborn sense of generosity and empathy for the younger generation, which I found to be altogether unique among artists of our age. From the beginning of our Violoncello Society, he expressed the keenest interest in our work, in our aims. He came to us with his advice; he played for us; he spoke to us and he encouraged us to be in constant touch with him. As a teacher he trained more of our successful young artists than had any other cello pedagogue. His students carry the stamp of genuineness in their approach and performance, besides displaying an elegance and beauty of warm sound![17]

DANIIL SHAFRAN

I remember Gregorii Pavlovich Piatigorsky not only as a great artist, but also as a chapter in history of cello music performance. Even next to such a giant as Casals, Piatigorsky was a musician, professor, a person who inspired composers in the field of instrumental music — he is an important epoch in the history of our art.

Everyone knows the brilliant "start" of Piatigorsky's career. The artist himself did an amazing job of writing about it in "Cellist," a book that was published by us [in Russia]. Unfortunately, fewer and fewer people are still alive who can remember his early years, people who played with "Grisha" in the Bolshoi Theater Orchestra, and then listened to his first solo performances. I had a chance to meet Gregorii Pavlovich in the last period of his artistic life. Even before I got to listen to his recordings, I knew a lot about him from other musicians and magazines. After World War II, *Musical America* [magazine] was filled with Piatigorsky's portraits and reports on his concerts. I was interested in everything about him — his repertoire, intensity of his life on tour, and his thoughts about the performing arts. In the photographs, I saw an extremely elegant middle-aged man with eyes that delivered kindness, which came though his whole persona.

When I finally heard Piatigorsky's recordings for the first time, my impressions of him proved to be true. He performed the Concerto by Schumann with flourishing sound of the cello, softness of the main contours and interpretations, and flourishing — I purposely repeat this word — communication with an instrument. Later I heard his recordings of all Sonatas by Beethoven for the cello along side pianist Solomon. They made a huge artistic impression on me. The Sonatas were introduced in a strict, I would even say aristocratic manner. I wanted to listen to them over and over again. As I got more and more acquainted with them, I discovered an amazing flow to Piatigorsky's instrumental art, the fine structure of musical phrase, and deep comprehension of the character of Beethoven's music. I will not even mention the sound of his instrument, and the "golden" shade of Piatigorsky's instrumental palette....

Music interpretation — that is probably the most important thing that you can take away again and again from Piatigorsky's variations of different pieces. It doesn't matter whether he is playing the concerto by Dvorak, where his style is so sensitive yet masculine, or whether he is playing a little "dry" Sonata by Hindemith of 1948; whether he is fiercely synchronizing in passion and rhythm of music with Milstein while playing the Double Concerto by Brahms, or with Heifetz in order to create Passacaglia by Handel or Italian Suite by Stravinsky — you always get amazed by his managing the performance as an art. His intellectual ways of creating musical phrases, freedom of rubato that never shreds his musical flow, forever full vibrato that does not even for a second slow down the intensity of the sound, all of those elements naturally develop into perfect form.

And, finally, my personal encounter with Gregorii Pavlovich. Year 1960, New York, my first American tour. On one of the few nights free from performances, suddenly, the phone rings in my small hotel room. I pick it up. On the other end of the line I hear a deep, velvety voice speaking perfectly clean Russian. Introduction: Gregorii Piatigorsky... Tells me that he wants to meet, get acquainted, and talk a little.... In half an hour, came in a person who I was dying to meet for so long. My first impression of him did not differ from the one I already had by looking at the photographs in various magazines. It almost seemed like Piatigorsky did not age at all. He had a grand presence; it appeared as if he filled all the space around him. And even though he was 57 years old, he kept himself physically fit and very dynamic. He was at least a head taller than all the people he spoke to, but he never looked at them from above — this was my later impression of him.

I listened to Piatigorsky, holding my breath. He was a great storyteller and could hold anybody's full attention; he retained great memories and stories about musicians. His own life, as a person and as an artist, was also full of adventures. He talked for a long time and we didn't notice how the evening flew by. After midnight, when all the lights outside of my window started to dim, Piatigorsky got up to leave. Before saying good night he asked me if he could play my cello. I must admit that I do not like letting strangers play my instrument — to touch my Amati. With Piatigorsky's charming personally was so wonderful, that I could not say no.

And I never regretted it: I have never heard my instrument sound so malleable and so natural. Just as the lightning illuminates enormous territories, spreads the horizon, clearly outlining everything around you; those few minutes that Piatigorsky was playing gave me an opportunity to infiltrate the heart and soul of this remarkable musician. And now, while listening to his recordings, I take them in through the prism of that enlightening experience; I can almost see and feel a living artist.

In the next few years I met Piatigorsky only two more times. One encounter happened at the Tchaikovsky's Competition in Moscow. It was wonderful to observe his interest in the young talented performers. Piatigorsky belonged to those artists who had similar warm feeling towards his own students as well as other members of talented youth. I remember his interest in the participants of the competition: Natalia Shakovskaya, Natalia Gutman, Valentin Feigin, and Michael Khomitzer. Piatigorsky hated the list of ratings; he mentioned many times that it is uncalled for in art. One of his favorite phrases was "The beauty of the bouquet lies in how well different flowers go together." Piatigorsky's feelings toward performing arts came though everything he did — in his own performances, and in relations he had with his young colleagues, in all of their triumphs and failures. He never put pressure on his students, although they could not help but get influenced by such a remarkable artist. He never tried to make his students become like him; he had a rare teaching ability of seeing a performing style of a young artist. He worked and developed it, making it complete. It's just enough to remember Piatigorsky's students that we have heard at the competition in Moscow, students such as L. Lesser and S. Kates. The first one is firm and even a little "mathematical," the second — very temperamental. But both of them are wonderful musicians, genuine artists. Overseas, I got to meet many of Piatigorsky's students. They all praised him as an artist, a professor and a person.

I regret the fact that I never had a chance to listen to Piatigorsky in concert. In 1964, during my second tour in America, Piatigorsky invited me to visit him. We talked for only about an hour. Piatigorsky was clearly not feeling well. His Stradivari cello sat silently on the piano. Later, Lesser told me, with a smile on his face, that that instrument is so sensitive and light that it almost seems like it can play by itself. Piatigorsky asked about his friends from Moscow, and I kept switching my gaze from the piano to the wall where there hung authentic Matisse, Lautrec, and Modigliani. "Maestro, you forgot your Amati in the back yard," I suddenly heard the voice of Piatigorsky's wife, "but don't worry, I picked up your cello; it's in the other room, and you may continue your conversation...." You can only imagine my shock!

Apparently, even though I have already met Piatigorsky a few times in the past, every encounter was so exciting and nerve-racking for me that I let go of my cello for just a minute to hold my camera and take a picture; I was able to drop my instrument and forget about it. To do that with all the love that I have for my Amati!

Today, when Piatigorsky is no longer with us, I am thinking of his role in the history of cello art. I could never see him better as a cellist and a perfect example of a member of Russian cello school. With his music, whose characteristics always included singing, ease of his technique, amazing instrumental mastery, that never turned into his only goal, he developed the best traditions of that school on the American soil, which gave rich profits. I will always remember my encounters with Gregorii Piatigorsky as very precious moments in my life.[18]

Isaac Stern

For Gregor Piatigorsky's last birthday, Isaac Stern and a good portion of the world of music were invited to participate in a book of letters honoring Gregor Piatigorsky, whom I regarded as an artist of legendary accomplishment and a great teacher who had inspired young cellists for decades — and I said precisely that, and more, in the letter I wrote. He was one of the great cellists of the second half of the twentieth century — the first names to come to mind when one spoke of cellists were Casals and Piatigorsky.

I had met him in Los Angeles soon after Alexander Zakin joined me as my regular partner at the piano in 1940. Zakin had known him in Berlin back in the mid-twenties.... Piatigorsky was ... someone for whom I had the greatest respect and affection — for his talent, his humor, his urbane knowledge of the world.... Whenever Zakin and I were in Los Angeles, we would visit him. We were able to use his studio as a rehearsal space — it had a wonderful piano and extraordinary paintings by Soutine, Leger, Dufy, Matisse, Picasso, to name only a few, as well as vodka and sandwiches. There was also a chess table, because his wife, a member of the Rothschild family, had been women's chess champion in the United States and went on playing chess all her life.

There were many moments of musical happiness with Grisha, as we called him. We would play chamber music in California and, in later years, we gave concerts together, playing the Brahms Double Concerto for violin, cello and orchestra. At one time we played a tour with the major orchestras of the United States. His natural talent was so enormous; he didn't especially like to practice a great deal. Arriving to play a concert in Seattle, he was asked by the organizers when he wanted the rehearsal with the conductor and if he would need a room to practice in before the rehearsal. He said, "Practice? What do you mean, practice?"

One particular memory strikes me at this moment. Many members of the audiences who have heard me over the years might remember that sometimes I come out from the wings through the violin section to take my place as soloist at the center of the stage, and I hold my violin up, my left hand practically at eye level so as to clear all the music stands and the backs of the players in the violin section. I learned that from Piatigorsky, who, when we walked onstage together, was worried about his cello because of the size of the instrument and the need to maneuver it through a narrow corridor of orchestral musicians. He would hold it at shoulder height, straight ahead, as he walked — a magnificent gesture and a lesson to me in the need to establish a certain character of one's own when coming onstage.[19]

The Students Remember[20]

ERLING BENGTSSON

The sentence, "Do you need anything?" will always be associated with my years of studying with Piatigorsky many years ago. He has shown us how "to serve," as the most important thing in life and art, that the artist and the human being are inseparable.

Never a day passes without in some way, directly or indirectly, referring to Piatigorsky. He has given us and the world a treasure, which makes life richer and better.[21]

MYUNG-WHA CHUNG

It was an auspicious start. The first time I met Mr. P was in 1966 right after my graduation from Juilliard. And instead of going through the usual audition routine, I was accepted to his master class at the recommendation of one of his then students — the late Stephen Kates. His decision showed the trust he places in his students, a gift I inherited from him which would serve me well as a teacher myself in later stages of my life.

Quite often during my three years of studying with him in Los Angeles (1965–1968), it was my good fortune to get to drive him from his home to school once or sometimes twice a week. I lived with a host family, not far from Mr. P's house in Brentwood, so it became my pleasant routine to pick him up and take a 45-minute drive to school in my old Chevy. The conversation with him and even the silence we managed during the ride gave me special joy and a feeling of privilege. I do not remember any serious, lengthy conversation with him, but the occasional vignettes and nostalgic stories of his life in old Russia, his music and his friends were not only entertaining and educational but made me understand and love him a great deal more.

I was the only woman in the class throughout the three-year period. Mr. P had trouble pronouncing my name and decided to give me a Russian name: "Muong-Va-nishika." At other times, he simply called me Princess. He was a great teacher throughout, but what I remember most was that he was always there when I was down and discouraged. He drew out the best from each of his students and encouraged them to learn from each other. He made each of us feel special. No set formula, nor any trace of "you've seen one, you've seen them all" stuff in his teaching. No wonder I sometimes felt I was his only student and I really mattered to him.

One important lesson which stayed with me all these years, constantly adding meaning and value, was what he told me at our very first meeting at his house. After pleasantries, his talk turned to the art of ball juggling. His point? That I should strive to become as comfortable with the bow as the juggler is with his balls, to the point where I can use it as a natural extension of my right arm. An arm good enough to convey my emotion, my passion and all I have not unlike the writer's pen in delivering everything the writer wants.

Mr. P is always with me as I now teach students here in Korea, all very talented, all very different, and I constantly strive to inject a dose of Mr. P in my relationship with each student of mine.[22]

Gary Hoffman

In spite of the fact that the only personal contact I had with Piatigorsky was in 1976 he was before, and to this day, remains a primary influence in my life — cellistically, musically, and personally. As a kid learning how to play, I discovered his recordings and read his autobiography, and immediately and forever fell under the spell of his vivid and humane personality. He became a model as to what a cellist can aspire to, in every way. I believe, even then, that I was as much attracted to his vision of how life can be for a musician as I was to his musical/cellistic aura. I think it was and remains to be this totality, a complete musician and complete life, which strikes me the most. And above all, complete honesty, sincerity, and humility toward music, always presented with dignity and self-respect.

The two weeks in Zurich were revelatory and a dream come true — to actually meet, talk with, and play for this man I revered for years. It is all the more poignant for me in that he passed away within the two months following. I could point to certain details or ideas articulated in those master classes, but that would be disguising, at least for me, the true value of those experiences. They had so much more to do with the larger picture — of life, of music, and, of course, the cello, but in the context of one's life, personal as well as musical. It wasn't ever about fingerings or bowings, but of things ultimately much more valuable in the long term.

A few years ago at a cello festival in Kronberg, Germany a man approached me with an envelope. Upon opening it I realized I was seeing for the first time photographs I had searched for 23 years, taken on the last day of the master class in Zurich, outside on the steps with the hopeful 20 year old and Piatigorsky, whose presence looms large, at it still does today.[23]

STEVEN ISSERLIS

I met Piatigorsky for the first time in 1974 when he gave a series of concerts; a recital with Daniel Barenboim, and chamber music with Barenboim, Pinchas Zukerman and Itzhak Perlman at the City of London Festival. I went to his recital, which I *loved*. It was so different from any other cello recital I'd heard; everything was so free, so imaginative. It was the first time I'd heard anyone make the Chopin sonata sound like great music.

A few days later, I went to play to him at his hotel. (Raphael Wallfisch was there too, which was reassuring.) I didn't play very well, as I remember, but Piatigorsky didn't seem to mind. He was so wonderful — his accent, what he said, the atmosphere he created. He talked about a few things cellistic — suggested a different fingering in the 1st Bach prelude (to continue the barriolage so that it didn't seem as if I'd "run out of gas," as he put it), and about how one had to imagine under what limitations a composer was writing. He used as an example a place in the Mendelssohn D major sonata, which he was sure that Mendelssohn would have written an octave higher if he hadn't been worried that it'd have been too difficult.

After that, he was my hero of heroes and he accepted me as a student — though with the proviso that I must be able to drive a car (I was only 15 in 1974). I didn't see him again till 1976, in Zurich. By then — although I didn't know it, and it was difficult to tell — he was very ill. I'd arranged by then to go out to Los Angeles to start studying with him that September. In Zurich he greeted me warmly, in that amazing voice of his; it was great to see him again. In retrospect, I can see that he wasn't feeling well; some of his lessons were quite brief. But then there were wonderful moments when he would get inspired and start playing — again I remember the Chopin sonata particularly, but there were also memorable excerpts from the Schumann concerto, the Debussy sonata, etc. Everything he played was so aristocratic.

One day he and Milstein gave a joint class on the Brahms Double Concerto, which was great fun. Milstein made serious points, but Piatigorsky was more interested at that lesson in telling funny stories. At one point he and Milstein played an impromptu duet, playing gypsy music, both standing and walking around. It was hilarious. It was only much later that Jacqueline Piatigorsky told me that sometimes before those classes it would take Piatigorsky two hours to get dressed — he hid his illness brilliantly.

I parted from him easily, excited that I would see him far more extendedly just a couple of months later. And then came the news....

When I think of him, I suppose the main word would be "warmth." There was such a genuinely caring aura about him; I remember him being so distressed when a young boy burst into tears about the blisters he'd developed on his fingers. Piatigorsky didn't know what to do — in desperation, he took out his handkerchief and stroked the offending fingers with it. His warmth spread to everyone around him; and one can see the after-effects in his family, who are some of the most lovely people on this rather crowded planet of ours. And one can hear it through every note of his playing — as I said, he was a true musical aristocrat.[24]

STEPHEN KATES

Piatigorsky did not just dwell on technical elements. He had a great deal to say in other areas and the technical things were usually dealt with on other levels. After all, we had eight or more students to observe in each class. We were often able to solve technical problems by observation and inquiry. We bounced off each other like ping-pong balls.

He took his teaching very seriously. He also did a fair share of demonstrating. Simply watching his incredibly natural bow arm was an education in itself, not to mention the way he produced sound. His sound seemed to come from everywhere and virtually fill the room to the bursting point. Both Mischa Schneider and Jascha Bernstein, who were with him in Leipzig as students with Klengel, thought that he was the most natural cello talent they had ever known.

His cello students normally studied with him in a master class format, but I found myself at his house for five or six hours every week for private lessons. I'd come over at ten in the morning and leave at four in the afternoon. We'd play duets, take walks on the beach in Santa Monica, or go outside and pick plums and oranges from his garden. When not discussing music, he'd talk a lot about his philosophies and his feelings about the world and life and what I needed to be aware of as I built a career in music. In other words, he gave me an education, not just a cello lesson.

His approach to teaching was absolutely unique and he was exactly the right teacher for me at the time. He provided a rare combination. I was musically and technically ready to meet him head-on and he poured his heart and soul into me as though I were his own son. (He did this with all of his students, so I was no exception.) He was an extremely devoted teacher and I believe that he exerted the greatest influence on me, as I think back on all the teachers I've had. It certainly took me years to get out from under his shadow, which is a must for those of us who have been highly influenced by one person or another, if we are ever to discover who we are.

In some ways he was not the greatest stickler for details. After I left California, I went back to Juilliard to complete my degree, where I studied with Claus Adam. Claus was the cellist of the Juilliard Quartet at the time and his influence on me as a chamber musician was profound. Claus immediately expressed concern about how I held the bow. Note that this was after I had won the Silver Medal at the Tchaikovsky Competition and had already soloed with the Chicago and Boston Symphony Orchestras and the New York Philharmonic. Claus noticed that I played in such a way that the third finger and the thumb were virtually opposite each other when I held the bow. He wanted me to be more conscious of the center of contact being between my first and second fingers and my thumb. I then went back to an old photograph that had been taken during a performance at a Young People's Concert in 1967 with Leonard Bernstein conducting. The photographer had shot a close-up of my bow-hand, which showed the bow being held between my third finger and thumb. After some thoughtful consideration and an obvious improvement in control, I adopted the new bow position.

A year or two later I was talking to Piatigorsky about how Claus Adam had made a radical change in my bow hold, that my second finger and thumb were now pretty much opposite each other. He looked at me and said, "What do you mean? You've always held the bow like that." I then showed him the photograph, which had been taken when I was still studying with him, and there it was, 1 against 3. He looked at me in shock and a little embarrassment and said, "I never realized it. How was it possible that you held the bow like that? It's all wrong!" That was the way he was. Obviously as long as you had the agility and were able to produce a sound he approved of, he didn't care how it was done. He was more interested in other things that were not done to his satisfaction and focused his attention on them instead. He clearly did not deem that my bow grip was injurious to my being able to bounce, sustain, or cross strings, so it was a non-issue. And yet Claus saw it in the first lesson and brought it to my attention; that was one of his specialties. I have never regretted changing. We must always be willing to accept new ideas in order to grow and improve.

Piatigorsky wasn't obsessed with technical details. Instead, he was obsessed with making music, communicating, and creating tonal variety, as well as opening his students up to their inner selves and to the music being performed. This was his real specialty as a teacher. He was also very concerned about rhythm and shifting without unintended slides. Despite the fact that he was known for his incredible slides, he wouldn't allow his students the luxury of audible shifts unless they could justify them musically. He was the only teacher in my training who discussed the difference between a slide and a shift and turned it into an art form. He would say that a slide is a decoration and a shift is a motion that gets you from point A to point B. If you don't consider adjusting the pressure when done on a continuous bow, the shift will be audible, and you will be responsible for the result if it has nothing to do with the music.

I always had a tendency to complicate things. He would often say, "Just play simple. Be simple. Go directly for the meaning of something. Don't look for answers in high places." In a sense, he streamlined my playing tremendously and was extraordinarily successful in getting me to cut to the chase when I'd play. My temperament often got in my way because I would become so emotionally involved in a piece that I would not notice how I actually sounded.

Piatigorsky helped put this into perspective for me. He said that I should use my temperament to enhance the power and delivery of my concepts, but that I should take care to not get lost in it. Piatigorsky taught me to look directly into the eye of the music and to become physically unencumbered by emotional considerations, though without eliminating a drop of emotion, which is a neat Zen-like trick that took years to master.

There are many former students of Piatigorsky that have maintained contact with each other, creating what the late Dimitry Markevitch, also a former Piatigorsky student, once facetiously referred to as the "Piatigorsky Mafia."

He spent hours in the teaching studio and in his home, giving us every conceivable piece of information that would help us to climb to the top of the ladder of cellistic excellence. But it was his genuine love for his students and the cello that forged a common bond between us that is undeniable.

But he would give us "advices" (as he would call them) as to what lay in front of us in terms of dealing with management and conductors and the problems that face all musicians, whether orchestral, solo, and so on. He was extraordinarily conscientious about telling us what the pitfalls were when dealing with the music business, how easy it is to fall into certain traps, and how to avoid them.

He did not want to afford his students premature success because he felt that success had to be earned through time and grade and hard work. As a matter of fact, he was somewhat critical of success as he saw it in certain young "artists." He felt that success, if it came at the wrong time and for the wrong reasons, would be a curse. As a result, he was extremely guarded with the use of his personal power to promote even the people that he loved and believed in. He desperately wanted all of us to find personal fulfillment in our lives and in music from which professional success would usually follow.[25]

PAUL KATZ

Just as Piatigorsky, Primrose, and Heifetz joined the USC faculty. I auditioned for Piatigorsky and became one of the students in his very first class at USC. I studied twice with Piatigorsky, actually. I studied with him in my senior year when Rejto went on sabbatical. Though I loved Piatigorsky and the classes, I had never yet been away from home and I dreamt of going to New York. So I left for two years to study with Greenhouse and got a Masters degree, and then returned to Piatigorsky for a second time.

I don't recall it being particularly competitive. We were all good cellists, and Piatigorsky, consciously or not, seemed to appreciate each of us for our own uniqueness. The atmosphere was supportive and Piatigorsky was a father figure to us all.

Having said this, I must admit that those years were extraordinarily stressful for me because I found it difficult to please Piatigorsky. All lessons were in a master class format which meant that all criticism, even that which most teachers would save for private moments, was done publicly. Those classes could be very trying and some suffered more than others. The classes were held every Monday and Thursday from ten in the morning to three in the afternoon, which could be a *long* five hours.

He wanted to help everybody find their own personality and to be strong communicators. I thought of myself as being musically communicative at the time, but I was still shy as a person and he was such an immense extrovert that he could intimidate me. It wasn't easy, but in the end he was very helpful in getting me to throw off my inhibitions and to absolutely go for the jugular when I performed.

Piatigorsky was a larger-than-life personality and he had an enormous sense of humor, but the way I remember it was that his students were often the butt of his jokes. It was all in good fun and most of the stories and the jokes that he told had a pedagogical purpose, but he was tough, and he liked being the center of attention. Making fun of the person in the hot seat was part of the arrangement. Actually, I doubt that everyone in the class would characterize it in this same way — probably at 19, I was just a little too fragile. Some of us seemed traumatized, but others, particularly Steve [Kates] and Larry [Lesser], at least on the outside, appeared unbothered. I think we all enjoyed it when somebody *else* was up there.

He would try to stimulate our imagination in every way possible and was more interested in hearing a statement of conviction than whether what was being done was interpretively good or bad. It could feel quite liberating. Imagination also meant writing our own cadenzas and even improvising in class. Being on the shy side, I found it extremely difficult to improvise in front of anyone, not to mention Piatigorsky and all my exceptionally talented colleagues.

He gave us lots of exercises, like 3+1 bowings, where we might play a rapid three-octave scale at the frog, three notes slurred, one note separate, and then repeat it, three notes slurred, one note separate, but over the course of the scale, gradually and evenly move the bow out to the tip. Then we'd do the same thing while staying at the tip, and repeat 3+1 one more time while moving back to the frog. We would then repeat the whole three octaves ×3 again with the same patterns, but starting up-bow.

He also focused on expanding our dynamic range. He talked about playing softer and softer and softer, or louder and louder and louder, which he said was the equivalent of "a painter with more colors on his palette." He was brilliant when it came to playing and teaching bow distribution and painting colors with bow speed.

Piatigorsky was interested in everything that had to do with performance, including things that we might laugh at now. I remember when I first joined Piatigorsky's class I was excited that I was going to be studying with the "Great Grisha," so like a good Californian, I went out and bought a new orange short-sleeved shirt. The shirt was made from a material called Ban-Lon, which is like a golf shirt. When I entered the room for our very first class, he immediately threw me out, telling me to come back in a suit and tie. He didn't act angry or offended, he just ridiculed me for not knowing how to present myself. This was the first of many times when being the butt of his humor wasn't fun. I was humiliated, actually.

I returned three days later and he threw me out *again*, this time because my suit was not properly tailored! The sleeves were a bit long for high fashion and hung slightly over my hands. He gave me a lesson in how the shirt cuffs needed to be 2" longer than the jacket sleeves, so that the cuff (and the cuff links) were visible when in playing position. Then he told me to go have my suit properly tailored. That is actually the very first thing Piatigorsky taught me! But this was an important pedagogical lesson as far as he was concerned, because how we walk and how we bow, how we sit at the instrument, how we dress, and how we carry ourselves on stage was an important part of what he taught us. And while some of this seems outdated and extreme, I think that the visual side of performing does count, and what he taught me in principle helped me in my performing career.[26]

Terry King

For Piatigorsky, a student's inherent qualities were the starting points of development; through those qualities the process of reevaluation, exploration and discipline began. Trust and confidence were established between student and teacher and rapport grew. The order of the specific tasks that needed to be mastered was individualized. Piatigorsky used to say that no one could hide from his or her shortcomings; sooner or later their problems had to be confronted.

This confused me at first. Later on when I became an assistant, we discussed new students and evaluated them. I would never suggest to Piatigorsky what I thought the student needed, but was surprised to see him bypass what I felt was a noticeable fault. Sure enough, it was tackled in time, after trust was established. Not all students needed a period of adjustment; many were so well-equipped and experienced that they were ready for anything. However, one thing he insisted upon was to do whatever he suggested, whether it was technical or musical. A student had to show him that the challenge was understood — after that one was free to make any personal choice.

Our classes met twice a week for several hours. We always had excellent pianists to work with and we arranged rehearsals as needed.[27] Piatigorsky disliked using or depending on what he called a crutch. He wanted us to be able to survive in less than ideal situations — for example, the height or slope of a chair, heat, or cold. He always spoke from his own experience saying, "I only tell you this because it has happened to me" or "I won't sell you a 'bum' steer" to quote old western films. Though not a recommended daily diet, he would expect us to be able to play without a warm-up. He might point to one of us and say, "Play."

He often made his points by telling a story or experience and its vividness made the characteristic last. It enlarged an aspect of preparedness, strength, or as he often said, "you must develop a thick skin." He expected memory as a means of "getting it in your blood" and fearless delivery. Piatigorsky believed the greatest gift was intuition, and when counterbalanced with work and devotion, it had deeper meaning.

Piatigorsky had few dogmas. Certain principles of left and right hand function were made clear, but he rejected most methodology that sounded absolute. He emphasized flexibility of the right hand, especially the fingers on the bow, and a flat wrist for strength. The fingers were used to express infinite shadings, weights, and inflection. The hand was balanced for lifting the bow as well as for power. The left hand was poised to play rapidly with minimal motion with "prepared" fingers in descending runs (i.e., the next note completely ready before its sounding moment) as well as diagonally for vibrato.

Our technical studies included those by Duport, Popper, and Piatti. But his pleasure was seeing us tackle the concerti by lesser composers: Volkmann, Molique, De Swert, and Herbert and cellists Davidoff, Popper, Romberg, and Servais. He believed that the role of a solo persona is intrinsic in all music and that the technical demands of these works were presented in a valid dramatic setting. It was here that we could fully assert our personalities; he suggested we cross-out Romberg's name and pretend it was a lost Beethoven concerto thereby treating it with utmost care, style, and attention. The lack of a specific performance tradition of the piece also freed the player to find oneself. But it was exercising and imitating our singing that most shaped the individual. Fingerings that reflected our singing were part and parcel of our training. Piatigorsky always encouraged individuality through gaining inner strength. He said many times that anybody who is conceited and pompous in life is a fool, but anybody who is modest and retiring at the cello is a criminal.

Piatigorsky always urged us to use "urtext" (unedited) editions of printed music and was always happy to see a manuscript or sketch as a means of connecting with the composer's intent. Piatigorsky had a marvelous way with music that was new to him. Occasionally I played new pieces written for me. He digested the works easily and even gave composers wonderful suggestions. He complained that if a new work was written with the assistance of a cellist, he knew exactly where the intrusion occurred. Once I brought the composer Roy Harris with me to play the new duo I commissioned from him. Piatigorsky was very pleased and complimentary, but his only hesitation was about a passage I had suggested to the composer!

He said many times that he loved his students. And, we loved him.

John Koenig

I began studying the cello at age twenty while I was a senior at UCLA majoring in music composition. I met Piatigorsky in the spring of 1971 after I'd been playing only about six weeks. Terry King, my first teacher, arranged for me to play in the master class, mainly to demonstrate his ability as a teacher. Even as a rank beginner, I considered it my responsibility as a musician — and my duty to Terry to make a good showing — to play to the limits of my ability, so I made every effort to prepare well.

But once I was actually in Piatigorsky's studio hearing the "real" students play, I began to feel uneasy about how it was going to go. From my perspective, the class members played at a level that seemed utterly unattainable. Even though I was out of my element (I had to borrow a jacket and tie to come to the class, as there was a dress code and I didn't own a sport coat), I did appreciate the seriousness of the occasion — being invited to occupy the time and attention of such a great master even for a few minutes. And this feeling was intensified by the rarefied atmosphere, the amazing force of Piatigorsky's personality and his unusual, but compelling way of expressing himself. As I listened to him focus on "problems" in the students' playing — playing that already seemed perfect to me — I became more and more intimidated.

Eventually, after several impressive performances by members of the class of mainstays of the repertoire, Piatigorsky asked me to play. Somehow I summoned up my courage and played the piece I had prepared, a simplified arrangement of a little march by Bach. When I finished, Piatigorsky praised me warmly and asked me to play it again. He gave me some advice and, aware that I played the guitar, asked me to try some pizzicatos and told me that perhaps I should develop pizzicato as a specialty as his friend, Ennio Bolognini, had done. He then invited me to visit the class whenever I wanted.

Over the next four years, I continued to study with Terry, but when he accepted a post at Grinnell College in Iowa, I had to make other arrangements for continuing my studies. Before Terry left town, he talked to Piatigorsky about my being in the class for the upcoming year and Piatigorsky said I should come. It was an incredible stroke of good fortune.

The Piatigorsky master class was one of the greatest and most intense musical experiences of my life. In the class, I was confronted with the most profound questions about how we, as performers, should approach creating art and because of my time with Piatigorsky, I was guided toward being able to answer those questions.

Piatigorsky was a gigantic figure. His personality was larger than life. He told incredible stories; often personal accounts of musicians we students knew only as figures from history. The very way he spoke commanded attention. These things, as well as his own exalted place in the pantheon of our art would have been sufficient to provide a memorable experience for any student. But these things were not why the class was so valuable. What Piatigorsky offered us was a direct conduit to the essential secrets of our craft: the hows and whys of true musical expression; what was important to strive for and what — whether or not commonly practiced by musicians — should be rejected, and why. His insights derived from a long career as a performer in a wide range of settings and his convictions were always based on the manifest intentions of the composers as expressed in their scores and other writings, on Piatigorsky's experiences working with composers themselves and with other legendary performers, and, of course, on logic. His command of these matters was profound and his ability to convey them was unmatched.

It was clear to me that I was being exposed to something extraordinary and I did my best to assimilate as much of what he imparted as it was within my power to absorb. And, although Piatigorsky had nagging physical ailments by this time, and had long since stopped concertizing, when he would take a student's cello and demonstrate a passage in class, it was like magic. I have rarely experienced anything as moving as his breathtaking expressive perfection when he played even a simple phrase.

I experienced another stroke of luck due to an accident of geography. I lived only a few blocks from Piatigorsky, so I was selected as his driver to and from class twice a week. These trips took forty-five minutes to an hour each way, so he was my captive audience — and I his — for several hours a week. This allowed us to develop what became an abiding friendship.

From then on, it happened regularly that my phone would ring and when I answered, I would hear his distinctive voice on the line saying something like, "Hello John (my name somehow rendered in 2 syllables), tell me, are you interested on [sic] boxing?" (He wanted to know if I wanted to watch an Ali fight on TV with him.) Or "Hello John, tell me, would you like to come over, maybe play a little duos?" Sometimes he would invite me over to watch a basketball game or go to lunch or dinner together with Mrs. Piatigorsky or others. Sometimes he'd just ask me to play for him and I'd have a lesson. Other times, he just wanted to talk about whatever was on his mind.

After the class ended for the summer, I would go to Piatigorsky's house almost daily and play for and with him. He was preparing for a two-week master class that he was giving in Zurich and two performances of the Brahms Double Concerto with Isaac Stern in Philadelphia and he was noticeably out of shape, which I believe was largely the result of his ongoing treatment for lung cancer, the gravity of which none of us students really understood, since he had taken pains to shield it from us.

One morning my phone rang and when I answered, I heard him bellow, without ceremony or introduction, "Oowell, dis ees da lazy BUM," by which he meant that although he should have been practicing, he wasn't. I felt terrible later when the thought came to me that he was probably relying on our duo playing (which was punctuated by several long breaks and other diversions during the course of a day) as his means of trying to resuscitate his technique sufficiently to be able to play the concerts with Stern; no small thing since the Brahms Double is not a walk in the park. In retrospect, I wish I could have provided him with more of a challenge but it was not in the cards for me to be anything other than the student, good friend and companion I tried to be, because, above all, I sensed what he really wanted to was to talk and be with a kindred soul; someone to whom he could impart the things that were meaningful to him.

In late June of 1976, I drove him and Mrs. Piatigorsky to the airport and helped get them and his cello on the plane. He blanched when the security officer started to handle his cello, the Baudiot Stradivarius. But almost immediately, we made her understand how rare and valuable it was and she backed off, but not without first asking him patronizingly, "Oh, you play this?" He handed me a few dollars for parking, and after I told him I was going to practice hard while he was gone and that I'd have a lot to play for him when he returned, he grinned broadly and said, "Well, you'd bettah!" Then he told me not to forget to pick some plums from his favorite plum tree in his garden and he and Mrs. Piatigorsky boarded the plane. That was the last time I saw him alive.

Not long after Piatigorsky's death, I became the co-principal cellist of the Jerusalem Symphony and the next year, I moved to Stockholm to play in the Swedish Radio Symphony. Later on, I produced many jazz and popular recordings featuring some of the world's top performers in those genres—figures ranging from Wynton Marsalis to Mick Jagger and many others of like stature. I have applied the essential secrets of musical expression that Piatigorsky conveyed to me in virtually every musical setting I've found myself in since those glorious days with him and I'm sure that as is the case with every other student with whom he felt a connection—and there were many of us—I feel him with me every day.[28]

ROBERT LAMARCHINA

I first met Piatigorsky when I was eight years old at the Curtis Institute, in about 1938. I had several teachers; when I was seven, my teacher was Felix Salmond and his assistant was Leonard Rose. [Later LaMarchina worked briefly with Feuermann, then Piatigorsky.]

I have little sense of what Feuermann and Piatigorsky gave me. My dad was there with me all the time. He was the one who would remind me about my lessons. He took the lessons seriously and pounded them into my mind. I've forgotten more than I remember! But getting the aura of the man, being in his presence was powerful and inspiring.

A remembrance of Piatigorsky was the time I was playing something in Haydn and I had to go from the C on the A string to high D on the third octave. It was with a good *glissando* and he thought it would be nice not to do it. He stopped me and said, "'Booby, if drug store is two blocks away, and one drug store is five blocks away, which one do you go to?" I picked the one that is two blocks away. "Same thing in cello. Put your thumb down on D string and cross over and play D."

I went to all of the concerts in those days — we all used to go as a group. His class would go to the concert, and the same with Feuermann. It's quite different today.

He bought me a suit while I was at Curtis. He took me out shopping one day and decided that I needed one. Studying with him wasn't an "ABC" kind of arrangement; I don't remember a lot of lesson points. I never thought he was a great teacher, but a great performer. He was still a young man in his 30s. There must have been a big difference in the way he taught then and the way he taught later.[29]

Laurence Lesser

From an article in the *Boston Globe*:

> By the time Lesser was 12 or 13, he reached the "moment of rebellion" most child musicians feel. "I didn't want to practice any more. [His teacher] Gregory Aller belonged to a chess club that Mme. Piatigorsky belonged to, and Piatigorsky often came along to kibitz. Aller asked Piatigorsky to listen to me. I didn't want to go play for him at all; in my childish mind it seemed equivalent to sentencing myself to a life in music. I went in with an enormous chip on my shoulder, and Piatigorsky totally disarmed me. 'What can I do for you?' he asked. I told him I wasn't sure I wanted to be a professional musician. He said, 'What makes you think you could become one?'" That was the challenge that sent Lesser off on his way.

From Piatigorsky I learned how to think about music. He was more effective as a psychologist. He would never give us bowings and fingerings; instead he would urge us to sing. He wanted for us to become his friends, not his students; his teaching was always in the old master/apprentice mode. He was a marvelous raconteur, and he always had useful advice for us. He had no respect for music critics; "nobody walks onstage trying to do his worst," he would remind us.

As a teacher, Piatigorsky often gave the impression of being purposely vague. He was wary of offering too much in the way of specific "technical" information, although he certainly had a clear notion about how the instrument should be played. He gave his pupils few technical exercises, but managed to convey his notions to them by actual demonstration or sometimes through psychological methods. I remember quite well one occasion when a certain student was asked to "look out the window" while playing (the student was so hypnotized by the visual aspect of his playing that he neglected to listen to himself), and the entire class sat amazed at the immediate radical improvement which became apparent in the player's sonority.

So far as bowings and fingerings were concerned, Piatigorsky hated to provide them, although here too, he had quite definite ideas about when our choices were bad. But he wanted his students to learn to think for themselves and not be mimics, thus, if we chose poorly, he showed us why. He constantly urged his students to "sing out loud," so that in this way they might learn to copy their own ideas about the music.

Although playing in his class was almost always more difficult than playing on stage, I never felt at any time that Piatigorsky tried to "'put down" his students. Rather, it was the high standard that playing for him represented that made us all nervous. His advice was consistently so imaginative and practical that as a consequence every one of us kept coming back to him long after we had left the class.[30]

Mischa Maisky

I am very lucky; I am the only cellist in the world who took lessons with both Rostropovich and Piatigorsky. It was Piatigorsky who first noticed this, actually, not me. There were plenty of Rostropovich students and there were plenty of Piatigorsky students, but somehow I managed to be the only one to have studied with both of them, not only two of the greatest cellists of all time, but with two of the great cellist personalities.

Even though my Professors were very different as individuals, in general they were very much alike. There were things Piatigorsky said that Rostropovich said as well. They even used exactly the same expressions at times. Neither Piatigorsky nor Rostropovich tried to create copies of themselves. Fortunately, both Piatigorsky and Rostropovich had the same goal for me. Both were amazing at encouraging their students to develop their own personalities in a very creative way. Both rarely demonstrated on the cello and both believed strongly that, as important as the cello is, it is just a tool for conveying the music's message, for communication. These days, many young people seem to prioritize the instrumental aspects of playing over the music they play. They believe that in order to succeed they must play louder, faster, and cleaner than anybody else. The danger of this approach is that the music becomes secondary, since a performance becomes more about how well somebody plays instrumentally instead of about the music.

Both Piatigorsky and Rostropovich helped their students open up and develop their imagination. Both also helped their students figure out what a composer wanted to say, how the music affected them personally, and what their musical goals were. Once a musical vision was clarified, then each student was free to find his or her own path to this goal. There are many ways to one's musical goal and it didn't matter which one was taken as long as the end result was what a student was striving for. Studying with him was extra special because I hardly spoke a word of English and he spoke beautiful Russian, in a style that is no longer heard. I ended up being his last chance to pass on his experience and ideas in his native language. Fortunately, I was incredibly anxious to absorb whatever he had to say. I was like a sponge. As a result, we had an incredibly intense relationship.

I went to his USC masterclass twice a week and I played for him at his house almost every day, each time playing a different piece. My studies were very different than his other students, like Raphael Wallfisch, who studied with him longer and in a more traditional way, concentrating on particular pieces for many months. I had a very different experience because I tried to play everything I could for him, even pieces I couldn't quite play, so that he could give me a general idea of what he strived for. I must have played at least a hundred different works for him in four months.

After our private lessons we would play chess, since we were both passionate about the game. Then we went for long walks and talked about all sorts of things, and not just music.

Then we would have lunch together, usually at Hamburger Hamlet, which was one of his favorite restaurants.

He was such an incredible gentleman that he would find ways of giving me very important advice in a very subtle and indirect manner. For instance, he once quoted something Stravinsky told him at the end of Stravinsky's life, "I feel like I don't have time to be in a hurry anymore." At the time I thought more about how clever the quote was rather than what Piatigorsky was actually trying to tell me. I figured out later that he was trying to say that I needed to slow down and be more patient. He was right, of course. I was 26 years old and I felt like I had to make up for lost time, since I had to start over in so many aspects of my life. I was in a new country, I didn't speak the native language, I hadn't played the cello for two years, nobody knew me, and I didn't have my own cello. I felt like I was way behind, especially after watching so many wunderkinds in the West who were developing major careers. I was in a hurry and I was trying to do things too fast. It has been over thirty years since Piatigorsky died, and I still feel his presence in the sense that I am still digesting his ideas and feeding on the positive energy he directed my way. Regardless, I ended up spending what was in many ways the best four months of my life when I went to Piatigorsky. I don't mean to imply that he was a better teacher than Rostropovich, since to rank them would be as silly saying that Mozart was a better composer than Beethoven. But I was definitely a better student while I was with Piatigorsky. I was older and I had much more life experience, since the last two years of my life in Russia were like twenty years.

The four months with Piatigorsky probably involved more total "face time" than I had in the four years I studied with Rostropovich. Rostropovich was on tour so much that he would be gone for a few months at a time. But when he returned, he was like a tornado, and he radiated with such intensity and energy that we would remain inspired until he returned from his next tour. My time with Piatigorsky was very different, since he was nearing the end of his career and he performed much less. Piatigorsky was nearing the end of his own life and he knew it. When it was time for me to leave Los Angeles, Piatigorsky told me that he didn't want me to go. I ended up spending a very late night at his house on my last day and as he walked me to my car he said, "You know, Mischa, I don't think I'll ever see you again." I replied, "What are you talking about? I'm coming back next year!" He said, "Yes, but I'm very ill." He knew his time was near. For some reason that I now forget, I never did go back the next year and he died. He was right.

I feel lucky that I had a very special relationship with both Rostropovich and Piatigorsky. Rostropovich became my father in my first life and Piatigorsky became my father in my second life.

My impression is that their approach is very unique, since many teachers seem to dictate bowings and fingerings to their students and work relentlessly on technical mastery. They treated the cello as a middleman between the music, the performer and the audience. It was an object used to show off your genius. I will be forever thankful to them; they were able to teach me that the technique is just a tool to convey what is most important — music. Again, it is vital to find a balance here: no matter how pure your instrumental beginning (talent) is; it's just a "work" tool. However, at this day and age, "design," "packaging" and flawless ("perfect") performance, are very important. Sometimes the tools may even unconsciously replace the goal. Music becomes a method of showing how "fantastically" — how quickly, how loudly, how extensively, how beautifully — you can play your instrument. The exact purpose of playing music gets lost. Because I am very afraid of that and remember that at all times, I prefer to "under practice" than "over practice." I come to a dead end when people ask me how many hours a day I spend with my cello.

Piatigorsky taught me that strength comes from being able to slow down. When I moved to the West, I constantly thought that I was falling behind, that I had to hurry. But with Piatigorsky.... We had a "ritual": every day I played a new piece for him (we went through more than one hundred pieces together), then we would work on it, then we played chess, and then take a walk while talking about everything and anything.[31]

DIMITRY MARKEVITCH

I was very fortunate. I first started to study with Piatigorsky in 1930 when I was seven. I was his only student then. I had the benefit of two schools—first the Casals school through Eisenberg and then the Russian school through Piatigorsky. I moved to America in 1940 to follow Piatigorsky. At the time I thought I would soon return to Europe, which was at the beginning of what was then called the "Funny" war. I ended up staying for the duration of the war and I went to Tanglewood, where I played one of Copland's trios with Leonard Bernstein on the piano and Jacob Krachmalnick on violin.

If you haven't heard Piatigorsky perform live you don't know what the cello can sound like. Today we have Rostropovich and Yo-Yo Ma, but I still have in my ear Piatigorsky's sound, which was very warm, generous, and powerful. He also had a fantastic technique, which nobody has matched to this day. As an example, nobody can do flying staccato the way he did. He could do it up and down bow with no difficulty at all. If you listen to some of Piatigorsky's old records you will hear his phenomenal technique. He was a very gifted and instinctive player and always played from his heart, but he was also very interested in finding original editions and manuscripts. He strove to play in an "authentic" manner, way before it became fashionable. Thanks to Piatigorsky and his desire to go back to original editions and manuscripts, the historian, Yves Gérard, thoroughly researched Boccherini and his music and wrote a large volume on the composer, just as Köchel did for Mozart. People forget Piatigorsky's deep commitment to trying to understand the composers' original intentions.

Search out his recording of the Schumann concerto, which he did in the early 30s. It has never been topped and is absolutely fabulous. I hope young musicians will discover his unique artistry. Seek out the wonderful films he did with Ralph Berkowitz and the trio with Heifetz and Rubinstein done in the 1940s. You will see it as well. Piatigorsky was not just a great performer and teacher, but my dearest lifelong friend.[32]

NATHANIEL ROSEN

When I try to organize my thoughts about Piatigorsky, I am hindered by the magnitude of the subject. His presence in my life was a constant; from the age of thirteen I was a member of his master class. I feel like he is my musical father, and I use the word "is" because he seems to be present in my life to this day, almost thirty-five years after his death.

When Piatigorsky began his master class at USC, it was one week after the death of Fritz Kreisler. Piatigorsky noted this milestone event in several monologues in those early classes. However, I missed most of the content of these talks because of the master's grotesque pronunciation of so many common English words. My main focus in these early classes was the "deal" he made with me, his youngest student. "If you don't get bored playing these two pieces (Goltermann Concerto No. 1 in a minor and Piatti Caprice No. 8), I will not get tired listening to them." This is what he said and he was as good as his word. I stayed on those pieces for the entire semester and let them open a whole new world of cello playing.

A few years later, in 1966, I was a part of the Piatigorsky Team at the Third International Tchaikovsky Competition in Moscow. I use the word "team" advisedly, and he was our coach. Steve Kates, Larry Lesser and I were the members of this team. In those days, it was not unusual for competitors in international competitions to have their teachers on the jury, and so it was in this case. Steve won the silver medal, Larry won fourth prize and I was a finalist diplomat.

For several reasons I was pleased that my teacher was there. It was encouraging just to know that he was there and there was the possibility of using the experience as lesson material for the future, which indeed happened. Moreover, in between flights on my way to Moscow, I had the privilege of staying overnight at Mr. Piatigorsky's mother-in-law's home in Paris on the Avenue Foch near l'Etoile.

The home of Baroness Germaine de Rothschild was filled with treasures and I enjoyed a tour given by the hostess. Mr. Piatigorsky gave me a lot of money to go out and have dinner because he, Mrs. Piatigorsky and the Baroness Rothschild had an engagement for the evening. As instructed, I walked to the famous Prunier restaurant but was too intimidated to enter. Instead, I walked around Paris and ate spaghetti in a humble bistro. Upon returning to my lodgings, I was met by a uniformed footman who was waiting for me in order to lock the gate after my return. It dawned on me that this person's job was to wait for me so that I wouldn't have to ring the bell to be let in. In the middle of the night, I half awakened to the sounds of my teacher and his wife whispering softly in my bedroom. I felt the addition of another blanket and immediately resumed my dreams. In the morning, I found Mr. Piatigorsky's navy blue cashmere topcoat on top of the bed, keeping me warm.

In Moscow, I made the acquaintance of the world's greatest cellists from the older generation: Cassadó, Fournier, Shafran and Rostropovich, to name just a few members of the illustrious jury. I was pleased to be invited to have lunch with Mr. and Mrs. Pierre Fournier and their son, Jean-Pierre. Mrs. Fournier, who had been married to Piatigorsky once upon a time, embarrassed me with rhapsodic praise of her first husband in the presence of her second. In her ardent voice, she exclaimed, "There was *nobody* like Grisha!" I was embarrassed for Mr. Fournier and also, I didn't like the word "was," since Piatigorsky was very much alive. But Mr. Fournier was a model of grace and kindness.

There were great cellists of the younger generation too, not all of them participating in the contest. I became friendly with Jacqueline du Pré, who was studying in Moscow at the time, and came to hear me play the difficult first round of the contest. She told me that she admired my performance of the required Popper etude and confessed that she never felt herself able to play such etudes well. Be that as it may, I was thrilled to hear her graduation performance of the Haydn C Major Concerto with her teacher, Rostropovich, conducting.

While I was having a grand time, Piatigorsky was not. His stomach was bothering him enough to cause him some absences from his juridical duties. He was disgusted that the only medical attention given him was a handful of smelly blue-veined cheese. I was quite disturbed at the quality of his hotel lodging, which was low. The contestants were housed in another hotel, which had all the amenities that youthful spirits required—dancing at dinner, drinking, and conviviality. It was twelve years later that I returned to take the gold medal in a much more serious atmosphere. Although Piatigorsky was no longer alive, I felt his presence even more this time.

JEFFREY SOLOW

One July day in 1966, during my third summer at the Music Academy of the West in Santa Barbara, California, where I was studying with Gabor Rejto, we had a distinguished visitor, Gregor Piatigorsky. To entertain Piatigorsky and to provide several cello students with an opportunity to play for him, Rejto arranged a special concert in which I played Tchaikovsky's Rococo Variations. I didn't know it at the time, but this was my audition for Piatigorsky.

It was two years later that I finally joined Piatigorsky's master class at the University of Southern California. He wanted his students to help and learn from each other, and by the time someone started a new piece it was likely that he or she had already heard other students' lessons on it and perhaps even played it for them. Piatigorsky strongly encouraged us to find out what was to be performed in each class and bring our copy of the music and make notes, so he didn't have to repeat things over and over. He was consistently supportive, kind, generous and often very entertaining. He held that we were not his pupils, a word he disliked, but that he was an older, more experienced colleague and together we were all "students of art."

The year before I joined, Piatigorsky had considered retiring from teaching and he had greatly reduced the class's size, so in 1968 there were only two continuing students, Nathaniel Rosen and Myung-Wha Chung. Over the next few years the class grew until it usually had about eight members (including at various times Raphael Wallfisch, Paul Tobias, Godfried Hoogeveen, Terry King, Emanuel Gruber, Susan Moses, Denis Brott, Leopoldo Tellez, Karen Buranskas, Elemer Lavotha, Peter Rejto and Mischa Maisky). Laurence Lesser, Piatigorsky's teaching assistant, worked with newer students on specific technical issues and would sometimes hear repertoire before it was brought to class. There was also always a class pianist, first Gerald Robbins and then Doris Stevenson.

Piatigorsky wanted the men to wear a jacket and tie to class, ostensibly because in concert we perform in these restrictive clothes. But I think he felt that, more importantly, if we had to dress up for class we would take it more seriously and learn better. The student whose turn it was to play sat in the "hot seat" in the middle of the room while Piatigorsky sat behind a small table with the score and a pencil. The rest of us would be scattered around the sides of the room (with packed lunches!). He never brought his cello but instead would demonstrate things on the students' instruments. He liked us to watch his playing carefully from all angles and we learnt a lot from hearing how our cellos could really sound. Those who were ready to do so moved rapidly through repertoire, but sometimes he would have a student work on the same piece for a very long time. I studied the Davidov Concerto no. 2 for almost my entire first year in the class.

Famous as a raconteur, Piatigorsky didn't disappoint us. He had an inexhaustible fund of anecdotes, which he told with great animation and charm in his personal and unmistakable Russian accented English. Some of his stories were merely humorous but most had some musical or professional point. His creative mind came up with multitudes of wonderful descriptions: he knew how to find just the right word or turn of phrase. Evaluating a prospective instrument: "You know, Jeffrey, this is first-rate second-rate cello"; expressing his philosophy of music: "There are two kinds of music: music that is better than you are and music that you can play better than it is." After Lesser and Michael (not-yet-Tilson) Thomas attempted to resurrect the almost never performed Concertino by Roussel, Piatigorsky remarked: "You know Larry, there are some pieces ... (pauses, turns several pages) ... is like doctor trying to revive a corpse."

Piatigorsky felt that personal expression was crucial both in playing and in learning to play: "First you must have something to say, then you will develop the technique to say it." He appreciated and cultivated virtuosity but eschewed thinking of technique as merely a collection of gadgets. To him it was "the ability to express what you want to say on the cello" and included controlling a large palette of instrumental colors, inflections, nuances, articulations, glissandos and dynamics. In fact, to Piatigorsky, music and technique were inseparable. His goal was to transcend the cello and communicate through it to the audience, and he wanted to teach his students to do the same. The greatest musical sin was to be boring.

The great Russian bass Feodor Chaliapin, with whom the young Piatigorsky had toured as the entr'acte for Chaliapin's recitals, taught him one of the most important things he ever learnt: "Grisha, you sing too much on the cello. You must learn to speak on the cello." This led Piatigorsky to the understanding of real bow technique — in particular, the use of the vertical aspect of the bow and not just the horizontal. "Your thoughts are your vibrato," he said, "the bow is your tongue." He taught us to flex the stick into the string to shape notes and phrases (referring to Kreisler's bow technique in this regard) and also stressed lifting the bow off the string, which he felt many cellists couldn't or didn't do well.

It may be surprising to those who think of Piatigorsky as the great Romantic cellist that he emphasized musical discipline. He often admonished us to have the character not to do something we were inclined to do musically or cellistically ("I have this pencil but I don't eat it!"). He was the first teacher I had who even mentioned getting a good edition, let alone insisted on it. The most frequent words I heard him say in class were, "Read the music! What did the composer put there?" But he didn't want us just to follow the letter of the text, he wanted us to read between the notes and find the composer's real meaning. For example, he pointed out that there are many kinds of accents, even though they all look the same on paper, and each must be played differently to express different things. He often railed against "dot-itis"—the disease of playing a note short because it has a dot over it—and explained that a dot doesn't mean short, it means putting a space after a note, before it or both. We had to think about why the composer put that dot there and how to play it so it conveyed their intention. The other "disease" he warned us against was "black note disease"—rushing through fast pieces or fast passages.

Piatigorsky hardly ever gave his students bowings and fingerings. He allowed us, or rather made us, think up our own. A frequent assignment was to find all the possible fingerings for a given passage so we could discuss the merits and drawbacks of each. In general he encouraged us to stay on one string and change positions rather than stay in one position and change strings (an example of the Russian School versus the Franco-Belgian or the German School). This preserves the color and the line, and if the string in question is the A string it also produces greater sonority. He wanted us to seek out opportunities for instrumental creativity in the music rather than just protect ourselves from danger; "safety first" was not his motto. He felt it was better to take a risk for a higher musical goal than simply be secure and in so doing guarantee a lesser result — although he never wanted us to choose a fingering that was musical but suicidal!

Piatigorsky always knew when to be practical and often spoke of the importance of being "normal" as a cellist and musician. If a student were entering a competition with the Dvorak Concerto, for instance, he advised him or her not to play the original version of certain passages as he had advocated in class (Mischa Maisky has recorded the Dvorak with many of these original passages) because it might cause the judges to question their ability to play the standard version and hurt their chances of winning. (Piatigorsky encouraged many of his students to enter competitions, but as he grew older he was less and less a fan of such events, saying they were suitable for sports but not for art.)

As an artist Piatigorsky holds a similar position in the world of the cello as does Kreisler for the violin: although he had a brilliant technique he was more interested in communication than in mechanical perfection. While he acknowledged the importance of perfect intonation ("Every idiot can hear it if you play out of tune") he got bored practicing solely to that end, and probably for that reason his own intonation was not always pristine. Piatigorsky felt that if a cellist had a healthy and natural technique he or she shouldn't have to spend too much time working on sterile instrumental mechanics. His favorite analogy went something like: "If you know how to drive correctly you don't have to learn over and over again in each new city. You just look at a map and you can go wherever you want." He always wanted us to find music in everything we played — even scales.

I worked with Piatigorsky intensively for five years but, with the example of several of Heifetz's students before me, I could see the possibility of being overwhelmed by so strong a musical personality and after 1972 I distanced myself from the class to a certain extent. Over the next few years, during which time I became his teaching assistant, I studied intermittently, sometimes just getting postconcert lessons over the telephone.

Naturally, as I have matured and gained experience as a performer and teacher, I have developed my own ideas about the musical, technical and philosophical aspects of cello playing. Piatigorsky would have wanted and expected this. He frequently said that the most important thing he could help us to learn was "to stand on our own two feet." I am grateful that I had the opportunity of studying with such a great master who was so empathetic toward his students. He genuinely wanted to help us succeed on the instrument he loved so well.[33]

PAUL TOBIAS

A cellist to me could never be a stranger
(From *Cellist*, by Gregor Piatigorsky)

Virtuoso in the studio as he was on stage, Piatigorsky, when teaching, made remarkable use of language, diplomacy and philosophy. As a matter of fact, he was also an outstanding psychologist.

Never at a loss for giving insightful cellistic guidance, he fostered an overall learning environment in which the artist individual in each of us was continuously being stimulated and encouraged. Always full of new ideas, this man above all had a disdain for the fashioning of carbon copies. "You must be able to do it this way," he was fond of saying, "because I want you to be armed to the teeth." All the time, he coaxed and provoked his young colleagues to "chew your own food."

While a marvelous artistic freedom existed in the Master Class, Piatigorsky managed to create his own special kind of discipline. This atmosphere, I must say, differed radically only on the surface when one compared it to the strict demeanor pertaining in the Heifetz Master Class, which met on the other side of the wall of our room. Piatigorsky had high expectations of his students in terms of decorum, and despite the seeming casualness of the four- to five-hour class sessions — with the leisurely monologues and anecdotes intervening — nevertheless, everything served with great focus and success to illustrate some never to be forgotten lesson — be it either in music or life.

"We're not wholesalers" he used to tell us. "We deal in quality, not quantity." His belief in the essential single-note character of the cello, like his sonority, was a common theme running through the classes; i.e., to play one note as if it were destined to last an entire day, so it alone would be "worth the price of admission" — it would catch the ear, and remain forever in one's memory. Piatigorsky possessed the marvelous gift of being able to teach people how to listen to what they were doing.[34]

Raphael Wallfisch

I first met Mr. Piatigorsky in 1973 when I went to study in LA. The first thing that happened when I arrived at Bundy Drive to meet him was that he took my cello and played a part of Elgar's *La Capricieuse* (fabulous down bow staccato) which left me awestruck. Then I played some Bach and he said, "Raphael, we are in business!"

I studied for two wonderful years at USC (officially) and a lot at Bundy Drive between 1973 and 1975. I came having just completed my studies at the Royal Academy of Music in London, and needed that extra time and space to prepare for entry into the musical profession. Mr. Piatigorsky proved to be the best possible teacher I could have chosen. His way of unlocking potential was just what I needed. With his kindness and typical largesse and generosity of spirit he helped me to begin to really express myself on the cello, a process that continues to this day! Not a day goes past in my constant practice and concert giving when his wisdom and great advice doesn't reaffirm itself and also through my own teaching I see the genius of his ideas! Of course, there were times when GP seemed to say less about some pieces and phrasing, reserving an opinion for a more appropriate moment and a later stage in my development. I remember Nick Rosen assuring me that I should keep taking the same work back for more lessons and I would find that more and more would unfold — he was right. I tended to take too much repertoire — GP called me "eager beaver"! However, I loved his way of experimenting with fingerings and bowings, phrasings, dynamics — demonstrating the myriad ways it was possible to interpret a musical moment.

It was clear to me that his way of teaching relied a lot on the student having a solid technique and ability to think for himself. Of course, "to think for yourself" was probably at the root of GP's teaching ethic! His assertion that no two students of his played alike was probably true, although it certainly was difficult not to pick up some typical Piatigorsky ways of doing things.

His picturesque ways of teaching through strong and dramatic analogy was also important to help us teach our private students and ourselves! For instance the story he told of attending Alexanian's class in Paris and having a discussion about "banging" the fingers of the left hand hard on the fingerboard as the ideal way — he was asked his opinion as honored guest and said, "[W]ell, you know — if I bang my hand hard on the door to shut it, it only moves half an inch ... but when I gently push it — it slams shut!" A great truth — demonstrating simply and effectively the unnecessary use of force!

There are hundreds of such moments of teaching genius through humor and truth. Some more that come to mind are (Debussy Sonata, Finale) "Raphael! Debussy writes *delicatissimo* not delicatessen!" Also, mama and papa fingerings—"You paid for the whole bow—use it!" These admonitions and advice coming on his wonderful Russian accent and with the timing which he was master of much powerful impressions!

I also loved his view that he was not prepared to entertain anyone's misguided ambitions—he would only help someone he felt that he could do it.

I did have the chance to appear in public with Mr. Piatigorsky in an extraordinary performance of *Bachianas Brasilieras* no. 5 with Heifetz playing the soprano part on the violin and seven of us students plus Mr. P at Hancock Auditorium! An amazing experience![35] Also at chamber music parties at Bundy Drive and at Heifetz's house—playing the Dvorak Sextet and the Schubert Quintet. Mr. P insisted on playing cello II on the Schubert, because he liked to "watch the scenery go past"! When my spike slipped on the Dvorak Sextet on Heifetz's highly polished parquet floor, GP quickly took off his belt and rigged up a spike holder for me! One day Mrs. P insisted on taking me shopping—she bought me a beautiful tail-suit and sports jacket. The biggest help to my career was the incredible role model that he presented—generous, larger than life, endlessly curious, humorous, ingenious, honest and incredibly demanding![36]

PART III : "PHILOSOPHIES AND ADVICES"

Musician, Teacher and Servant of Art

> *The best thing a musician can possibly do after he has acquired a great deal of experience is to pass it on to younger musicians. So many people are now gone—Kreisler, Toscanini, Rachmaninoff—who never had students. This is a great loss, and we must not repeat the mistake.*
>
> *Many people are too small to teach, but no one is too big.*
>
> *It is not the job of the teacher,*
> *to make an adoring audience of his students.*
>
> *Of all the titles applied to me, I like "teacher" best of all.*
> *I'll stop teaching when I stop learning.*

Gregor Piatigorsky's teaching legacy is palpable today, as it has been for generations. Since the 1940s, his influence has been epitomized worldwide through soloists, great orchestras and chamber ensembles, as well as through the teaching profession. Piatigorsky trained the principal cellists of leading orchestras in Boston, New York, Chicago, Dallas, Houston, San Francisco, Cleveland, Pittsburgh, Minneapolis, Philadelphia, Washington, D.C., Berlin, London, Vancouver, Toronto, Amsterdam, Berlin and many more.[1] Among soloists are Nathaniel Rosen, Leslie Parnas, Steven Isserlis, Raphael Wallfisch, Jeffrey Solow, Paul Tobias, Mischa Maisky, Denis Brott, Erling Blöndal Bengsston, Stephen Kates, William De Rosa, Gert von Bülow, Laurence Lesser, Emanuel Gruber and Gottfried Hoogerveen, who owe much to their study with Piatigorsky. His students also occupy important teaching positions in leading conservatories and universities, perpetuating his example for future generations.

Piatigorsky respected his students and that quality penetrates the overall spirit of learning. He stated in one of his masterclass recital programs at USC:

> All my former and present students did not come to me to acquire talent—they came because they have it. They all started to study cello early in their lives, and I knew most of them only after they had studied with one or several masters. Among them were Casals, Rejto, Starker, Tortelier, Rostropovich, Schoenfeld, Magg, Greenhouse, Klengel, Adam, Rose, Feuermann and others. By no means will I be the last one. For those marvelous young artists, which many of them are, will never stop learning and enriching themselves, and their responsibility towards art will not decrease with the development of their respective careers, for this is the essence of their lives, young or old.
>
> We work hard, spurred by enthusiasm, and more often than not the results are rewarding. We are friends, and I am looking forward with great confidence to their future as the true servants of art. I hope you will love them as I do.

Piatigorsky's teaching style was unique. Gone were the rigid formulae one associates with traditional linear training. There were no preestablished procedures or routines. The student, when accepted, already had a high level of accomplishment and the potential for success. The hands, the head, and the spirit were coordinated into a whole that could then flower into artistic expression. This style radically differed from Casals:

> I once asked him [Casals], point-blank, whether he didn't think that a student might have some good ideas of his own, which should be encouraged so that he could develop his individuality. He jumped up excitedly and went to the wall. "No!" he said, "the student must be like an apprentice. The Master draws the line, and the student re-traces it." He made a gesture with his arm, drawing an imaginary line along the wall. One of the memorable phrases he liked to use was: "A good imitation is better than a bad original."[2]

Piatigorsky's adage was "Originality is better than any imitation," which he expanded upon on film:

> I believe one remains a student of music as long as one lives. I like very much to teach. I like young people; I like to share my experience and, if possible, to help them. I was one of the few concertizing artists in this country to do a lot of teaching as well. Many of my friends, men like Rachmaninoff and Kreisler, never gave a lesson to anybody. Such people were astonished at my teaching, and they asked me, "How can you do it?" To many of them, teaching is somehow a lesser activity, only concerts matter. Certainly the world looks at it in that light. Therefore, an artist gets thousands of dollars for one concert and only a few dollars for one lesson. Furthermore, being a teacher seems to reduce his rank. Now, I find that deplorable. Money, large audiences, standing ovations — they're all false and ridiculous criteria to a true servant of music.
>
> Nobody can really choose music as a profession as you can choose to become a dentist or whatever. It chooses you. So actually from the beginning you have very little to say. You are taken by it. There is the cello, that little box with four strings. Yes, it was made by a genius, but still it is a wooden box and it is amazing how wide, all encompassing, that it does not leave time practically for anything else — so it is constant, never-ending, striving for something that's almost unachievable. The reason for that feeling is that if as a performer, you perform great music but — you can never perform it well enough. The music remains above you. You're just striving to reach it, and the better you become at it, the music moves higher. So it becomes unreachable. You have to give all your life only to discover that it's not enough. You have to live thousands of years maybe to know, and I don't know half of the possibilities.
>
> People who occupy or try to spend their life with beautiful things must have something beautiful in themselves. A person who is occupied with great music must fall in love every day, not with a boy or a girl, but fall in love with a piece of music.
>
> We have many different artistic needs that must be expressed. In olden times a man took great pride in making a chair, and he signed his name on the chair. Today, unfortunately, you find signed chairs only in museums. The point is that an artisan derives great satisfaction from and takes great pride in his work. When you put your mind to it, there is hardly anything in the world that cannot be made lovingly to give pride and pleasure to the one who makes it and to the one who uses it. The search for beauty is endless.[3]
>
> To love the work you are doing, to be lucky enough to find the right outlet for your expression, your contribution, and to love to be fascinated with the work you are doing, I think is the most essential thing. Too many people do the thing they hate instead of love, so it becomes a chore, and then it becomes a purely economical problem — problems of opportunity. But if you are lucky enough to dedicate your life to something you love, to something that is greater than you are, as someone said, then you are a lucky person indeed.
>
> I think it is the most difficult thing on earth to find, to really hit on what responds to your character, your talent; and it is also a question of luck. You can see, for instance, Maestro Toscanini, whom I have a good fortune to know very well. Originally he was a cellist. I don't know how happy he was with the choice of his instrument, but I'm fairly sure about one thing: that we would not know Maestro Toscanini at all. His conducting came quite by accident.
>
> It is very essential from early age; to find the work you're capable of loving. As a matter of

fact you don't have to be an artist. I don't believe people should separate artists from the rest of humanity. One might say, "I'm just working in the office," or, "I have a little shop where I sell things." I do believe that everyone can do something well, and anyone who would do things — even if they were not paid — from pure love or the interest, enthusiasm, fascination of the thing — will become automatically an artist.

Often, professions, which have a great deal of beauty in them, are unfortunately done by machine instead of man. Conversely, all jobs to which it is impossible to attach love and esteem should be replaced by machines. I don't think there should be many factories of whatever we use, of furniture, of things. It should be done by people, by people's hands, so that lives pass in beauty, fascination, and adventure, in dignity.

The most important challenge is to develop something precious that was given by Nature. Only by developing individuality, one's artistic nature — and this is inherent in almost everyone, for each person is capable at something, talented at something. It is the job of education to find that something. But, many people never discover what that gift is. Too often there is nobody there to help them make the discovery.

I assure you there is nothing complex about this matter of music. There are only two sensible things to do about it. The first is this: make music if you can. And the second is this: if you cannot make it, listen to it. This covers the field.

Teaching: The Noblest Art

I believe in lifting people up. You don't have to be a genius to know your faults, but wise enough to recognize and develop your strengths. Yes, I love my students. I couldn't teach them unless I did.

I have been learning and teaching all my life, and slowly over the years I have begun to realize how much is involved in teaching. Take a man who can fall madly in love, have great rages, but when he begins to play a musical instrument he is like a corpse. People say he has no temperament. Of course he has temperament, but it has to be pumped out, like oil. I don't believe there is anything more difficult than to be a good teacher. You have to be a psychologist, a friend, and oil pumper. And you have to feel. There is no one method. You cannot teach everyone in the same way.

My main idea about teaching is to have a good useful influence. My desire is to make them people, artists who are happy in their profession, so that they become real servants of art. I find that that is the most difficult thing, because it goes hand in hand with all the technical and musical development. What really matters is, how they will use their art as human beings in a productive life. It is a very, very honorable occupation to be a good servant of art. I want them never to lose enthusiasm. Never to be apathetic, and actually, to think as little as possible on so-called recognition, success. Some people want to become world-famous overnight and so I am not a good use to them because, here, it is music and how to serve it well. I don't want to be participating in some kind of a business; I want them to be fine artists!

Teaching surpasses everything because it is the most difficult and demanding of professions. It is not like being a mathematician or a chemist. There are no formulae or prescriptions for a teacher to follow, because a teacher must deal with a total human being. There is a great deal of feeling involved. A teacher must make a student perceive certain truths. For example, that he need not be endowed with brilliant insight to know all his shortcomings, because his shortcomings are glaring, and everyone has an abundance of them. If a student plays beautifully, I do not take credit. I didn't give him the talent. I do take credit for being a good friend who has much more experience.... [I have] some extraordinary young people coming from all over, their problems, their weaknesses, the character of their development — I had to think about it. It is a great responsibility, too. Especially because they seem to consider me as their friend. Of course the most important thing is to know that I am their friend, and that I as teacher see their gifts, that I see the positive in them. And actually it gives them, I hope, encouragement to enfold the best of them.

To find [the right teacher] sometimes is difficult; I do not know where he is to be found. But I can tell you what he must be. He must be most of all a good man. Without goodness one cannot be right in any walk of life. The heart must be right, as well as the mind, and if the student ever finds that his teacher is not a good man he should seek another. The teacher must also be a psychologist. He must be able to cause things to grow in a young mind just as the gardener causes things to grow in a garden. Isn't that what psychology is, making the mind grow? [The teacher] must know his and his student's emotional nature. This is also psychology. To know only his instrument is certainly very far from sufficient.

There was a very curious incident, in Berlin where I was teaching and among my students was one who I particularly admired, an extraordinary talent, and I gave him all the time in the world, and all the effort. I just wanted to give him all I had. It was a heavenly talent. And to my disdain, this poor boy, from lesson to lesson, became worse and worse. Because I played for him better and better, as a matter of fact I never played a concert performance as well as for him, until probably he must have lost hope or something. I always give examples, he would play, and then I would play so that he would really hear.

Well, the result was of course the greatest catastrophe. I murdered him; I lost my sleep too. Because I just did not know, why all other students of mine made fine progress, and this one, exceptional student of mine, has such a disastrous result. Well, until I tried to play less well for him, I thought maybe this is the point. And gradually I began to play for him worse and worse, and he was better and better, until when he graduated it was a triumph. Actually, he was magnificent. And as I rushed to congratulate him, he stood with other students having a discussion. But as I approached him, he disappeared. And one of the students said, "This impertinent fellow dared to say that you are a very fine teacher, but certainly a lousy cellist." I considered this the greatest compliment that I ever received from a student.

The student must learn to feel, and he must be taught the ability to portray various emotions. For the entire art, is, after all, an emotional one. Thousands of emotions, subtle, strong, delicate; so many emotions. We know that temperament cannot be instilled or taught. It is easy to say one is, or is not, born with temperament, yet the teacher has a responsibility. He must devote more energy towards the emotional message of the works the student is to play. Even the very advanced player spends more time with technical considerations than with problems of artistry. And that is too bad.

On a string instrument you can't really learn to *know* something. You can show how to hold the bow, but if you teach somebody to hold the bow perfectly, he still will not produce the sound. You cannot learn how to *learn*, you must learn how to *feel*. That is the basis of my teaching where the technical aspects are concerned. Because you don't know where the notes are, you can only feel them. Your hand feels.

For me, the most important part of music is what I call an "overall balance." What does it mean? I judge by three most important "possessions" that a person has:

1. Head: intellect;
2. Heart: emotions, feelings;
3. Technical skills: ability to communicate ideas.

If one of those qualities is overpowering the others, then it results in disproportion. To uphold the balance is the most important task. If the balance is there, then while listening to a musician you would never say something like, "Ah, what wonderful feeling!" or "Ah, look at his technique!" or "Ah, he is so intelligent!" You would simply say, "What a great artist!"

"SUCCESS IN MUSIC DOES NOT COME TO THE PERSON WHO IS INTERESTED IN SUCCESS ALONE."

Piatigorsky's idealism is an uplifting antidote in an era of fading arts.

The child starts out with a dull teacher. Plunk, plunk. What should be a beautiful experience becomes drudgery. Terrible. We must keep them in flames. Each one [student] would like to be a genius, or at least a flashy, very important virtuoso. And, true enough, I am fascinated when I hear extraordinary talent. But at the same time my idea is that every student must be a good servant of art. That is important. I consider myself nothing but a servant of art. I try to serve it well.

I would like to wish young musicians to have more enthusiasm in their art because to live without enthusiasm is the same as living without air. I would also like to wish them success in studying, learning about themselves, about their own abilities. Young musicians should know and always remember that a person lives well only when one gives their life to something that is bigger and better than themselves.

Success in music does not come to the person who is interested in success alone ... if a student concentrates upon himself alone, he ends up with nothing but bitterness, despair and failure. They must have the feeling of being needed to bring music to people. They must be able to play everything, everywhere. When I was very young, I was most anxious to play in New York, London, Paris. But I also played in many places where the cello had never been seen or heard. I think I was the first person to give a cello recital in Oklahoma.

The way of the rat race, that people have to be famous, very quickly, that they have to be successful — this is so much burden on these poor, young wonderful people, so I repeat to them the same thing that Stravinsky used to like to say, "I have no time to hurry." And it is good. Don't hurry. Nothing runs away. Develop yourself. Be good, and everything else comes to you.

If a man truly has something worthwhile to give, there are thousands ready to receive it. And in very many areas of this country there will be hundreds of miles where there is not one fine cellist. One can play, one can organize chamber music groups, one can teach — why should not one serve and at the same time make a living? But always, one must carry the thought of service first. The only students I worry about are those who have tendencies to be depressed, to fear of failure.... If they only knew that a life of concertizing is full of worries for the artist.

I love teaching; I love to see things grow. It's a tremendous pleasure when I travel to see in an orchestra, every part of the world, one of my kids sitting there, as first cellist. It's a wonderful, wonderful feeling.

Piatigorsky's father gave him perhaps his greatest lesson before Grisha left home at the age of twelve, as he often quoted:

> I haven't anything to give you. But take some very important advice: In life you will meet three kinds of people —
>
> 1. Those with whom your relation is indifferent
> 2. Those who try to push you down.
> 3. Those who bolster you up.

The first type is the greatest in number, and they don't matter. From the second type, you must always run away as fast as you can. But the third type, which will be very few in number, you must make your friends, and you must hang on to them no matter what.[4]

Musical "Advices"

Piatigorsky's thick Russian accent remained even after thirty-seven years of living in the United States. He also spoke with a colorful, creative use of the language, and was known to invent words. One such word was "advices"— elegant statements of his core beliefs. Though communication was never a problem, he was sensitive to its misunderstanding. Once Stephen Kates was pressured by Piatigorsky to do his well-known imitation of him. After he performed, Piatigorsky said, "What are you talking about? I don't sound like dat!"

and angrily left without saying goodbye.[5] In giving advice, his "Piatigorskese" converted it to giving "advices."

Here are many such "advices" in his own words taken from interviews, articles, and recollections from the author.

THE INTERPRETER[6]

Art was created by man. Nature wasn't; stars and mountains don't exist for the purpose of me admiring them. But when I hear music that I just cannot believe man has created, then I know I'm confronting something pretty big.

It is impossible for a performing artist to lead an isolated life. A performer must be a man of many loves. With a composer, the less he is influenced by others, the better. But a performer has to understand a large number of composers, every composer he performs. He must be tremendously rich in his ability to penetrate, and that is certainly not an easy task. As a performer, you must be everybody and yet you must be yourself, a different personality. Yet you cannot be a typical Mr. Miller and play well. There is something which must be in you which must penetrate as the composer did. Therefore, you have a many-faced person, just like an actor. One day an actor plays the role of a king, the next time he is a tramp or something. But the musician's job is much more intricate, much less visual. It's not a very easy matter. It is advantageous for you to play and think of what the composer has intended to do and you must respect him. It was helpful for me to be in contact with many composers. You know how a composer reacts and you know what freedom you can take. For instance, it was so easy to work with Igor Stravinsky. I remember working with Stravinsky on the Italian Suite and the ending of the Tarantella. So as we played, we finished pianissimo, and he said, "Well, that's fine." And then I said to him, "Igor Sergevitch, let's try the last two bars fortissimo." "All right let's try." "Oh, that's fine." And he marks, fortissimo. Well, that's quite a drastic change, you know. And yet, it proves that although a piece is published and printed, it still remains alive. It is not something dead, something absolute at all. Wouldn't it be a tragedy if everyone played in exactly the same way?

The composer can only write the shell in which the essential significance of the music is held. The artist must know how the music sounded before it was written down; one must hear it as the composer heard it for the first time.

Interpretation is very creative. The interpreter doesn't lose his personality to the composer. What an absurdity to say, "Here is a performer who excludes himself," or to insist, "A performer plays Beethoven well only if he himself disappears." If he disappears, he is a corpse. No one disappears. The performer is a human being. His judgments might be right or wrong, but through them he is always there.

Of course in the time of Nikisch, the great conductor, in the score happens not to be a ritardando, but one has made one — where no one was particularly unhappy about it, providing there was a mood. That attitude was drastically changed by Maestro Toscanini, who said, "I play as it is printed in the score." Well, it was not quite true because I played with him, and we, both of us, permitted us quite considerable liberties. So, like the beginning of every tradition, it causes misunderstanding. So then it becomes for years, a series of musicians who say, "I play in the way it is written." It is all very relative.

Sure, he plays what's written. But what is written? Very little, actually. The few indications — tempo, dynamics, whatever — what are they? Take "piano "— it means soft, but how soft? That already is a question. There is a difference between a piano of Mozart's and that of Stravinsky. Now let's say there's a hold, a fermata. How long a fermata? It doesn't say. Maybe there's time for you to have lunch, and then to continue. How short the fermata? You decide, and when you do, it is absolutely impossible to hide your personality.

It is too late to think about all this during a performance. You must think about it all your life. You must live with pieces, and try, with all your sincerity, depth, and knowledge to understand what composers really meant, and what their pieces say to you. That's quite a responsibility. How gratifying it is, though, when you reach people, when they respond strongly.

But remember, public or general taste is a complicated matter. I have played for audiences the world over, and have found few differences between one group of listeners and another. I often find the public's intuition remarkably sound. I think the public feels something. It differentiates.

On the other hand, the public likes sensationalism, and pride enters into their judgments. You will find people who like something and are ashamed to admit it, others who hate something and are ashamed to say so. But very few people are truly knowledgeable. I'm afraid that applies even to musicians.

The performers are making enormous physical and technical advances although I don't think much intellectual or spiritual progress. Today the stress is for so-called technical perfection. Sometimes the younger artists, in order not to miss a note, they miss rather a thought. But never a note. So therefore there is a certain restraint, a certain fear.

I have known many composers — Richard Strauss, Hindemith, Stravinsky, Prokofiev. In all the contact I had with composers, I can't remember any quarrel with them. More often than not, they agreed with me. And they were wise to do so [a hearty laugh]. Probably the most exciting of my life as an artist was with works that I've helped bring to life. One has a very special sense of responsibility; they write for you, you work together and then there is the first performance of the work — the desire to bring the music to the public the way the composer told me. I probably would have had the same feeling if I had worked with Mr. Beethoven or Mr. Mozart.

You see, we don't have many important emotions. People fell in love thousands of years ago and today it is still modern. Thoughts like love and hate, fear and joy, tears and laughter — we live in these emotional mainstreams and art has always expressed them.

Art was created by man. Nature wasn't; stars and mountains don't exist for the purpose of me admiring them. But, when I hear music that I just cannot believe man has created, then I know I'm confronting something pretty big. Everybody knows the differences between all material things ... fine cars, not so good cars, the best clothes, the finest restaurants. Why, in art, especially music, are we so convinced that people will always choose something cheaper?

THE VIRTUOSO

Speaking of the work of a virtuoso, one must not, it seems to me, attribute to it the role of a sacred duty or of an all-loving heart, which gives itself up for the happiness of the world. No, the virtuoso thinks of himself about his own pleasure and about his own personal gratification. Ambition and narcissism are the main motivators and key factors of this virtuoso machine. I call him a machine because I can't find a more appropriate definition for a person who is capable in a given season of traveling around the world, giving up to 160 concerts. Only a machine that is in good working order is able to emerge with honor from such a task. To create a name for yourself, and a good market value, to conquer the world marketplace and then to uphold your position — those are the concerns of the virtuoso.

To this end they are prepared to give their all, not stopping before any hardships, throwing their health and life into the gluttonous jaws of career. An established career (although it can never be completely created!) is sacred to the artist, and this is understandable, for he has paid dearly for it.

It's a shame that the students who fill the conservatories know nothing of this thorny path — they work with dreams of a shining future and the bright radiance of praise. Poor things! I would like to tell them, for their own good, everything that I know about myself and about other, older artists. I would do this, not to discourage them, but on the contrary, to better prepare them for this life and work that they dream about. Some might be turned off, but some might take another path, perhaps a more certain one.

I will begin by saying that in order to be an international virtuoso, one must above all be possessed of an athletic health and iron nerves. A student who has the shining talent of a virtuoso, but a weak heart would be prudent not to give himself over to the life of a virtuoso. Besides health, knowledge of the instrument, musical education, talent, intellect, etc., the most important factor is *character*. In whatever way his character is not strong by nature, he must harden and develop it, and only then, when he has become steely and indestructible, then the virtuoso can consider his career to be insured against many things.

But of course it is not insured against everything. An unlucky event, managers, intrigues all undermine the artist, and one awkward move, a careless word, or the smallest ill informed action is sufficient to cause, if not a complete fall, then the slowing of a career or strong unpleasantness.

NEW MUSIC

It is a great pity that Mozart did not write a single work for a solo cello.
It was because there was nobody to interest him sufficiently in it.

Polytonality, atonality — I cannot speak of music in those terms. We hear continually talk of "modern music." To me Beethoven's last quartets are as modern as anything ever written in that they are new. They will always be new for they say that which was never said before and never will be repeated. As Richard Strauss said, "I know only two kinds of music — good, and bad."

There are those who expect music always to be beautiful. How can this be so? Life is not always beautiful. It is sometimes ugly, stupid. If art is an expression of life, must it not contain these elements as well as beauty and nobility? In Strauss' *Don Quixote* the Don, for all the magnificence which he sees himself, is not a glorious figure. He rides a donkey, and not a beautiful charger. And Sancho Panza — surely he is an awkward person. How could the music speak of this and be graceful and lovely? No — the music must contain truth.

Some people refuse to listen to contemporary music denouncing it as harsh, queer, strange. Well, I may not love it as much as I love Beethoven, with whom I've lived all my life, but at the same time I know we require constant rejuvenation. Now that so many composers are writing music for the cello, I cannot but feel optimistic as to its future. It is the duty of the artist to interest the composer as well as the public in his instrument.

To write original music now is more difficult than writing music in Bach's time. People then were more involved in formal structures: madrigals, fugues, and so forth. Today, it's all different. To compose tunes like those which Tchaikovsky wrote would be old hat. People would say that they weren't "original." [But in some ways], composers have it much easier today; there are so many foundations, and all of them are afraid to miss a genius.

So modern composers are always searching desperately for that which has never been done before. They really must be sincere in what they're composing and not worry about whether it's the fashion of the moment. Oscar Wilde said that the best aspect of fashion is that it is the first thing to disappear.

We must remember, Mozart and Beethoven didn't hear all of the sounds we hear. They never heard the sound of a car motor starting, running, grinding, stopping. They never heard a telephone ring, or an airplane roar. It's like painters who didn't see what our astronauts have seen. In every period, there are thousands of new sounds, thousands of new vistas. So how can one be super-conservative and say, "I'm just used to some music that I call classical and it's the only good music."

One time Aldous Huxley came to our house, and saw the television, and he cried out, "Et tu, Brute?" I said, "How did you come to my house — did you ride a donkey?" True, you can reject the auto because it kills people, but it is quite a formidable invention. You can also reject TV programming because it is capable of boring us to death. But it is not the fault of TV. It means only that better programs are needed.

One must play the music you understand, and then you can do justice to it. The worst thing it is to play the music that you don't like. Now, it never happened to me, because at the moment I play it, I love it. What's happened before or after, well, that's my private business. But while I'm playing it, I love it, whatever it is. I have played new music all my life, although people sometimes laughed, especially once in Berlin in 1926.[7] I understood it with no trouble. Maybe my audience had trouble, but I didn't. Now *I* have [trouble]. I just don't understand. They are writing music that is not only different from the conventional way but even their annotation is different! I am sometimes sent scores that look like designs for some new kind of scientific apparatus you have to go to school to understand. Lots of recent pieces are full of gadgets, electronics and too many people are annotating music, just making noise. Often compositions say that the performer can play at certain places anything he wants for any length of time, or he can play upside down or start at the end.

One composer came here in order to bring a piece that he had dedicated to me. I was very flattered. [The work had significant improvised sections.] Suppose I followed that instruction and did something atrocious? Then I would do harm to the piece. Or suppose I played something very good? Then the composer would get totally undeserved credit. So I told him, "Look, if I can do everything myself, it should be my composition — not yours!"

I went to a big gallery in New York and saw a painting. Not really a painting — a frame with nothing inside, just canvas — white canvas. And so I came to the owner of the gallery and said, "Look, you forgot to put a picture there." And he looked at me up and down, and said, "Didn't you read the catalogue?" So I said, "No, but I didn't come to read, I came to see paintings and I see there's no painting there." Well, he thought I was a real ignoramus and so I looked at the catalogue and sure enough, in Number Eighteen for that painting, that canvas, there was written a title: Nothingness —. Nothingness. Well, there's some idea there but certainly not much effort. And to me, effort is always important.

But still I hesitate to say that all this is wrong. So, today one should use new sounds, but their use should have a sonic idea behind it — some perception, some thought. But, certain composers write music mostly for each other because nobody else listens to it. Naturally, I don't know all the composers today; not all of them are quite so "far-out." Still, I am very interested in the "far-out" ones and hope to like and understand their music one day, maybe. Well, I keep trying.

When Marcel Duchamp stopped painting, I asked him why. He said, "Well, each time I do something, I must have to say something completely new. I don't like to repeat myself. I don't want to become a factory." Someone asked me several years ago what would make me stop playing. Only one thing could make me stop — if I would notice that some kind of routine would creep in — if I will stop feeling very acutely.

THE HEALTHY MIND

I think it's just unfortunate cases that great artists be mentally sick, spend life in great misery, have very poor family life, poor health, bad habits, alcoholism or whatever it was. I think it was not the rule. There were quite a few very healthy people among the creative minds.

Boredom still remains the greatest danger of humanity, the enemy of humanity. I remember when I was very young I was in the orchestra, and I noticed that most of the members of the orchestra were bored to death. And the only person who was vibrant and full of enthusiasm was the conductor. Never a rehearsal was long enough for him. All the other musicians were looking at their watches and hoping that the torture would be over. I began also to be bored together with all my colleagues. But I was very fortunate to find a cure for it. I just could not stand to be bored. So I asked myself why is the conductor the only person who is enthusiastic, who is full of vigor, perspires? I found he is just more interested in what he is doing than I.

So I began to study every score that the conductor was conducting. Until to the great astonishment of my colleagues, after a rehearsal, I said, "My goodness, it's all over? Can't we rehearse a little longer?" They thought I was joking. It was absolutely the truth; it's the way I felt. And even once while playing some symphony, I think it was Brahms's First Symphony with Furtwängler. It was a fine performance; I did not play only my cello part, I was tremendously concerned about the entire score. And when the performance was over, and the audience applauded, I stood up; I took a bow, which everyone thought was very funny.

In choral works I used to sing with the chorus. By the way, once I entered too soon, just one bar before the chorus and the poor people heard my horrible voice coming through the air. Well, it was fun you see; I was interested, and I'm terribly grateful for that.[8]

Hobbies

On my travels, mostly in Europe, I spend a great deal of time looking at the galleries of paintings and sculptures and developed quite a passion for plastic art. Once in Paris, I walked by a gallery and I saw in a window a painting of a chicken hanging on a hook and chain. It was not a dead chicken. It was a strangled one. It was a murdered bird. It was something cruel and something infinitely tender. For a long time I did not know the name of that painter, but I always would, of course, recognize the same master. So I would acquire more and more paintings by him until I met, one day. And it was Chaim Soutine, and as an artist, rather fascinated me and then of course he was a very shy man, frightened man. Well then, he is still my very great favorite. I have left here only four of the Soutines, but I love them.

I believe in having hobbies. I find the more good hobbies a person has the more chances there are for a successful life. Some small enjoyment, fishing, climbing mountains, playing chess, of course I'm not very good almost at anything. As far as my hobbies are concerned, I took a special care never to become expert in any of those hobbies because the moment one takes it very seriously, there is a great chance of diminishing the pleasure. It's very good to know a little bit about it. Not to take it too seriously, just enough to think that you are quite good. The less you know, the more chance that you will be pleased with yourself. I try to keep it that way. There are some other domains in my life when I cannot afford that.

Chess

*In the world of music I am known as a cellist. In the world of chess,
I am known as the husband of Mrs. Piatigorsky.*[9]

Jacqueline Piatigorsky was a champion chess player and represented the United States in the Women's Chess Olympiad. In the 1960s she was the highest U.S. Chess Federation–rated female chess player in California and ranked number 2 in the United States.

Dedicated enthusiasts, she and her husband sponsored two important chess tournaments, the Piatigorsky Cup in 1963 and 1966. The 1966 tournament, which was held in Santa Monica, was probably the greatest held in the USA since the New York Tournament of 1927. The Piatigorskys also sponsored the first invitational U.S. Junior Chess Championship in 1966.

A bit of controversy followed the 1963 Cup. During a very tense match between Sammy Reshevsky and Bobby Fischer, Piatigorsky had an evening concert and arbitrarily decided that the game should start in the morning so that he could attend. Bobby said, "No, I want to play during the scheduled time." Piatigorsky replied, "I pay and I decide when you play." Bobby complained, "I signed a contract in which it was stated that we play in the afternoon. That's what I'm going to do."

Fischer forfeited the game, and although the match was tied, Reshevsky was declared the winner.[10]

Cello "Advices"[11]

PRACTICE: "IT'S ALL MENTAL"

I am not a very good disciplinarian. I make them feel quite free, but they deal with beautiful matters and so they must become beautiful themselves. I don't approach them purely mechanically, it would be too simple, it would be like exact science. I never tell them how long to practice, because in music there is nothing mechanical. But I teach them how to practice. Because music requires a combination of spiritual, physical, intellectual and emotional qualities; they have to master all those ingredients.

I do not feel that artists have to spend hours a day to keep their technique efficient. If that were the case one would not be in a position to participate in the other joys of life. Nor could he enrich his art. Of course, mind you, I am not saying that one should not work. But definitely I say that if one has developed a firm technique, it is not necessary to slave over the instrument for the rest of his life in order to keep in good form.

When a person steps out on a platform to play, he may be troubled because of a difficult passage near the beginning, or he may find that his vibrato doesn't function with as much smoothness as always. Or that he cannot draw steady bows. So naturally, he feels that by practicing more and more, he will conquer these difficulties.

But, it is not practicing that will do it. It is all mental! He must train his fingers and his bow arm to work well under tension. He must train the fingers to follow. It is a question of directing his emotions, and the development of his will. I feel that way about the bowings too. Once we have mastered them, they require very little work to maintain. That also goes for the staccato! Do you want to know how I mastered the staccato? All I did was try and vibrate with the right hand. As soon as I felt that I actually was vibrating with the right hand, I knew I had mastered the light staccato bowing.

I am in love with music; in music there is the solution. Without difficulties you would see only idiotic smiling faces. How can you be satisfied with an achievement if it has not been difficult? I can play the same piece for 20 years and never be satisfied with my performance. Each time I discover some new challenge, some new demand that it makes of me. To meet those demands is never easy. But without those demands, life would be dull. And life is anything but dull.

LEARNING A NEW PIECE

More than one angle should be considered prior to learning to play a new piece. Too often, I feel that the performance of musicians indicates that their approach to the study of their solo numbers was via a technical rather than a musical course. We must never forget that a worthwhile piece of music can be made to display emotions, varying moods, sometimes simple, at others complex. It should be the purpose of the performer to express these moods. Yet so often we hear performances with the player absorbed primarily with the exposition of technical problems, making their execution a paramount feature.

The first thing I impress is the need of a thorough understanding of the musical thought to be conveyed: that the work should be memorized and performed mentally. It should be sung. CPE Bach wrote that you must sing; you never sing as unmusical as you play. For instance I had lessons once when I was very, very young with a gypsy singer — her name was Polina. She taught me how to sing on the cello Russian gypsy songs. They were the most wonderful lessons that I had — if you do it sincerely, and try to penetrate the meaning of it.

The structure of the composition should be studied and understood, and each phrase weighed as to its meaning in the whole. I would say to the pupil, "Try to love that piece of music. Allow it to inspire you. Spend much time with it in your thoughts. Following such procedure your eventual performance of it will be ever so much more successful." The value of this advice will be immediately apparent then, when you take your instrument and play it. Marks and fingerings you may then decide would be helpful will be decided by your emotional grasp of the work.

MEMORY

In the past, playing from memory was generally considered short of a miracle and had a certain glamour. Toscanini was thought to have an amazing memory. He said, "You know, everybody say I have such a marvelous memory. Yes, but I am blind, I have no other way. You know, I wish I could conduct from music." Nowadays, it is a common practice by all performers and yet it is not infrequent that I am asked how it is done.

While I cannot speak for my colleagues, from my experience I know that to memorize music with which I am impressed has never been a chore. It went willingly into my fingers and penetrated my heart and blood, to remain. Not so, the music which did not say much to me, but which I had an obligation to perform. This I managed only with great effort to memorize, but even then not lastingly or very securely. There had to be a certain method, a certain dependence upon the visual texture and bowing and fingering, serving for a point of departure, and many more almost mechanical devices one would not dream of applying to music which speaks for itself.

Happily, most of the music I play, I love. Therefore though keeping it ready at almost any given time, the part of memorizing does not create any serious problem. This is true to a certain extent. It never occurred to me to count how many billions of notes, short and long, soft and loud, nor the multitude of thoughts and moods they represent, are stored in me.

In the main, it is my guess that when one does so much of his work from memory, memorizing becomes a natural accomplishment — a matter of unconscious absorption. There are of course various degrees of the quality and difficulties of memorizing music, but above all there is one undisputed factor about good memory and that is a gift of God.

THE LEFT HAND

I wish to stress an important point — important, because of its effect on technical development, and because of the fact that cellists are often handicapped by habits they hold on to from past tradition. I speak of the importance of correct finger action. We still frequently hear the expression, "lift the fingers very high and bring them down on the string in a hammer-like blow." This advice, I fear, is not only incorrect, but quite dangerous. The finger must be brought down on the string with firmness, and must press into the string after it has struck. The hammer-like blows are responsible for much trouble in left-hand technique.

Not only should more be known about shifting, but cellists should constantly listen to each of their shifts while practicing. Of course we know the main problem in connection with the cello is to determine when to shift and how to do it. But when cellists shift from one position to another they concern themselves with the left-hand, without realizing what an important part the bow arm plays in the shift.

The pupil must decide in each specific case whether the shift is to be heard, or whether it is not to be heard. In each instance, the musical phrase must guide the decision. Some shifts should be heard very distinctly. Others not at all.

First consider the shift where we do not wish to hear any slide at all. Here we shift in the usual manner, but at the same instant that we perform the shift we make a careful diminuendo with the bow arm. Thus, the shift becomes inaudible.... [I]t is the bow arm, by crescendo and diminuendo, which determines the nature of the shift. This same process continues when the only shifts which I allow to be heard, I make a slight crescendo with the right hand.

VIBRATO

The job of teaching the vibrato to a young student requires experience, yet I wonder if it can really be taught, after all? I feel that all the teacher can do is guide the position of the pupil's hand so that he oscillates correctly and rhythmically. From then on, the beauty of the vibrato depends upon his own musical personality and his own conception of tone. To me, the vibrato seems more or less like human faces. People are born with a certain type of vibrato, just as they are born with a certain face. Nothing is so characteristic of any player as his vibrato, and nothing so much differentiates one string player from another. The vibrato is the window to the soul. It can be misused, like lipstick ... too much ... well....

But one cannot vibrate successfully without having a definite musical idea behind the vibrato. We vibrate with the fingers, at times with the wrist, at times with the whole arm. He who has only one vibrato for all types of expression is certainly grossly undeveloped. Then there are places where one hardly vibrates at all.

Many use the vibrato as a habit, almost like an "eye-tick." When a person has mastered the fundamentals of the vibrato, he can only improve his tone by improving his whole musical stature! What I do not like to hear is a cellist who will use the wrong vibrato in a certain type of passage.

During one of his trips to Moscow as a member of the jury of the Tchaikovsky Competition, Piatigorsky mentioned to his cellist brother, Alexander, what he felt was an abuse of vibrato:

> One time we were coming back from the competition to the hotel Metropol. Gregori was walking, swaying from side to side. I asked him what was wrong, and he said, "Don't ask. Most of the competitors vibrated too much. They don't understand that vibration is one of the methods used to enrich the sound, it has a lot of styles, you have to know how to use it — it's an art. I am sure that most of the young performers don't even know how to play the scales without vibration!"

FINGERINGS

Fingerings must suit the music. The easiest way to perform a passage may not be the most musical way. My plea to performers is that they should not be affected by the natural tendency to make passages as easy as possible.

We may solve a certain passage and be content, but yet may feel that musically we are not expressing ourselves as we desire to. Our duty is then clear. To think about the passage until we have really "satisfied" its musicality.

Therein, I believe, is one of the great ingredients of my friend, Pablo Casals. The longer I knew him, the more I realized how much he was absorbed with the musical content of music. He would play a passage with technical fluency, but would remain quite unsatisfied. He could play with the most extreme ease, yet was always troubled by passages in many of the important works.

We often played duets together. I was soloist also with his orchestra in Barcelona. One time in Paris, I heard him in a performance of the Beethoven Trio in E-flat major [Op/70/2]. He played with Cortot and Thibaud. After the concert, I went to see him. When he saw me, he ran to me,

"Please, please, have you a piece of paper? You know the last movement — that difficult passage for the cello? Well, I am so excited, please I must write this down! After twenty years of struggle and after twenty years of looking for the right fingering, I have it now! I must write it down!"

I was deeply affected by his joy.

Another angle in connection with fingerings is the matter of their importance with the individual. I can finger a passage to portray great warmth, yet another cellist will find it difficult to elicit warmth with this fingering.

Casals has a very short but very broad hand. And I have long fingers but a hand that is not so broad. It is foolish to say that his fingerings are the best in certain cases, because I could not use them in many instances.

There is another principle of fingering which is more applicable to the cello, and which I consider important. I have heard cellists, whom I know to have wonderful ears and astute accuracy of intonation, play out of tune. Each of our fingers possesses a certain subtle and intuitive feeling of its own. Whatever the reason, or where it emanates from is not our great concern. We know it exists. The shape of the hand, the flexibility of the fingers, contribute to the cause.

In fingering passages we must take into consideration natural feeling. For instance, if we play B in the first position on the G-string, and if we use the third finger, we are doing something very unnatural. For many reasons, this third finger has no feeling for that note. There are certain notes that every finger knows, and these notes must be carefully taken into consideration if we wish to finger passages within that instinctive law.

One of the incorrect steps is to write in fingerings and bowings when beginning the study of a new piece. Following that method one is apt to become a slave to the technical markings. If adhered to persistently, the habit becomes fixed and if the markings are inflexibly bound up with his playing they tend to prevent musical expression.

I must confess, that I have often fingered passages which I later feel, though solving a problem technically, do not allow me to fully express the mood I would convey. So, the course is clear, I keep working and changing until finally I achieve the desired results.

Intonation

Under the most ideal circumstances, playing in tune is a major achievement. The situation gets more complicated when one plays with others and is a constant concern. As Heifetz once remarked: "[It] is all guesswork; you cannot even scratch a mark on the wood so you can tell where to put your fingers to repeat the right note." The cellist made an experiment:

> I gave four concerts with an orchestra. Finally, before the fourth concert, I asked for a rehearsal. Then, when we were all sitting, I asked the men to tune. "Take your time," I said to them. "Take ten minutes. Give your instruments time to adjust to the temperature of the room." They did not know what I was doing; they thought I must be crazy. After that I asked the leader of the first violins and the leader of the second violins to sound an A. They played and they were not in tune together. "Which one of you is in tune?" I asked. This one said, "I am." I said to the other one: "Tune to him." I asked each of the strings to tune, and then the oboe. They were all out of tune. When they played together they did not listen to what they heard from each other. It was all mud.

Holding the Bow

Cellists often struggle to develop a bow grip, which conforms to a particular school of string playing. The theory and tradition that we get from these schools, however, can be dangerous. (One of my early teachers tried to tell me how to use the bow. "It is like the span of a bridge," and proceeded to draw a bridge, with its beams and girders. When he finished we had for our contemplation a very neat drawing of a bridge, probably technically correct, but I still did not know how to hold the bow!)

Why not adopt a natural method of holding the bow? Let us take the right thumb. Cellists would do well to experiment with the thumb. Perhaps, it should be less curved!

In the traditional manner of holding the bow, we do not get enough strength. By adjusting our bow grip to a more natural one, we get fifty percent more volume. You see, if you open your hand and then close it, you do something that is very natural. Now, that same natural impulse should be applied to the bow. The more the fingers touch each other, the better. It is natural, also, for there to be a straight line between the elbow and the wrist, and of course, this natural element should be applied to the cello.

I am not inclined to favor the wrist in going from one bow to another. On the cello I feel the wrist has been very much misused, much more than any other part of the arm. You know, the wrist is a pretty weak joint. Using the wrist also has a way of placing the bow in the wrong direction. Why don't cellists forget about the wrist and develop the knack of bow change with the fingers? It can be done.

TONE

I will tell you something that I think each cellist will say: "Oh, I know this," and yet it is something which few cellists correctly apply. If they did, we would have more beautiful cello playing. And that is the speed of the bow. There is a relationship between the strength of the tone and the speed of the bow. The stronger one wants to play, the faster one must move the bow. It sounds simple, doesn't it? Yet why do we hear so much scratching? Why so many tones are not clear? A cellist will say, "but I press my fingers very firmly!" We all want a big tone at certain times. Of course we do. Press the bow as much as you wish. Press unlimitedly. Fill the auditorium with the gloriousness of tone that only a cello can produce, but move the bow quickly.

I was curious to know why, after attending so many cello recitals; I failed at times to distinguish the low tones on the C string, especially in pianissimo passages. I think many musicians find this a disturbing factor in their performances. Try to develop an astute sense of acoustical timing. In the lower stings, if a fast passage were played a little bit slower, or rather, if the performer would realize that such a passage requires a little longer time to carry, much more clarity would result.

It must also be considered that the piano, used in accompaniment, has an uncanny faculty of covering, or absorbing the low tones of the cello. After all, the cello was originally a chamber instrument, built to be played in intimate surroundings, in small halls, and with light accompaniment, such as provided by the harpsichord. We hear it now in huge auditoriums, with the accompaniment of concert-grand pianos, and against the background of tremendous symphonic orchestras!

I believe this story is attributed to Casals. He was to play a concerto with orchestra accompaniment, and was naturally concerned about tonal balance. Yet, before the orchestra had even started to play, Casals turned around to the conductor and whispered, "I am sorry, but I am afraid it is a little bit too loud."

SOME OBSERVATIONS FROM THE MASTER CLASSES

To a student playing laboriously: "It's very important not to play very 'importantly.' If you begin to play a fairly easy, gay and amusing piece with great importance, then the piece becomes less important than the player. If the piece is simple and gay, then the cellist must be simple and gay."

To a student who flubbed a note: "Ours is a single-note instrument, so we have to play well one note at a time; every note must be good. You must imagine that you are in an auction, and every single note has to be so good that you can sell it without any argument! Every note must have quality, as if all by itself it is some kind of melody."

To a student with a blank expression: "There is a certain absent look in you when you play. You can imagine that it is not important how you look, but I can assure you that it is. I remember once in Kansas City we were rehearsing and an insurance agent interrupted us. He wanted to insure our fingers, but one of the musicians said, 'Why do you talk only about the finger? Why aren't you concerned about the nose? Do you think any of us can give a recital without a nose?' In other words, the total appearance is of great importance."

To a student with a self-effacing manner: "Forget about modesty; be a show-off. There has never been written a modest symphony, a humble rhapsody. You must be able to say with great feeling, 'I hate you' or 'I love you.' Once you are able to say that, you will find you can play the cello."

To a messy student: "Your playing reminds me of an Armenian salad. You don't know what's in it."

Part IV : Writings

Cellos

> *My oldest friend is my beautiful Stradivari cello, created by a 96-year-old genius 251 years ago — and if his hand trembled when he made it, perhaps that gave it more tenderness. Despite its age, I know its future is as noble as its past.*
>
> *My cello has been transported on mules, camels, trucks, rowboats, droshkies, bicycles, gondolas, jeeps, a submarine off Italy, subways, trams, sleds, junks, and on a stretcher in Amalfi. But by far the most nerve-wracking experience of all is when, in full dress, I must transport the cello in my own hands across the stage each time I have to play.*

Most everyone knows that there are four sizes of violoncello. But I probably was not an average child because I did not go through those traditional four seasons. Instead of starting with the ¼ cello, I began with the violin and viola simply because we had them at home. Also I could hold it between my knees as comfortable as any cello. It was not before I reached the age of seven that I got a cello. But it was of such an indefinite shape, color and character that it was difficult to tell not only the size but the kind of an instrument it was supposed to represent.

But I played and practiced on it with such delight that my parents began to hope that I would never ask for another one. Of course they were mistaken for I wanted a better cello — a real one, with dark red varnish and shiny, not like the one my teacher had — a light-blond fat cello with an enormous belly like my Aunt Fanny when she was waiting for my cousin Zodik. I liked my Aunt very much, but I would hate to possess a cello like her.

My father was a musician and he understood my need for a better instrument, but he was also a wise man, and so he knew that by waiting for it longer, it would make me feel more deserving of having it later. Well, I certainly waited for it long enough, and if my father achieved anything by that at all, it was contempt for the monster I had to live with meanwhile.

Finally, the great day arrived and before my eyes there were two instruments to choose from. There was no hesitation on my part, even before playing, I pointed towards the one, darker in color and nicer looking,

"One does not judge upon looks — here — try this one."

"No." I protested meekly. "It looks like Aunt Fanny"

"What? What is this? A joke?" said my father.

I will try not to describe the painful procedure of purchasing the cello on that day; it is needless to say which of the two cellos I brought home with me — But the most offending to my dignity was my father's argument, as though he has just bought a pair of ski shoes for me.

"My son," he said. "You will see that the cello will prove most wear-resistant." He was so right! No matter how hard I would scratch on it, or knock it about, for many dreary years it did not show any damage. It survived two floods, one fire and even the weight of a ninety-five pound bag of potatoes.[1]

Piatigorsky did not own a fine cello until well into his tenure with the Berlin Philharmonic. Several wealthy music lovers heard that Piatigorsky was considering quitting the orchestra to embark on a solo career. In their desire to keep him in Berlin, in 1927 they presented him with a Nicolá Amati cello made in 1670.[2] However, Piatigorsky had shown a greater fondness for Arnold Földesy's 1712 Stradivari, and before retiring to Budapest, Földesy sold it to him for a modest sum.

Piatigorsky used a total of six Stradivaris during his career, and owned four of them. The cellist had reservations about the "Földesy" for his first American tour, and borrowed the *Piatti* Stradivari from Francesco Mendelssohn, a distant relative of the composer. For the 1932-33 season he played another Stradivari[3] lent to him by the violin dealer Emil Heermann in New York. The Amati was reenlisted the following season.

Piatigorsky's next cello came by way of a friendship developed in Boston. He first performed in Boston in 1931, and became a favorite of Serge Koussevitzky, conductor of the Boston Symphony. He returned every season, even if not engaged with the symphony, for public and private recitals. Ernest B. Dane, a wealthy Bostonian and patron of the arts, first engaged Piatigorsky on a purely professional basis, and paid him handsomely to play recitals for a dozen or more of his houseguests. Gradually the cellist and his benefactor became friends, and soon no season was complete without Piatigorsky making music in their home. In 1934, Piatigorsky made an extensive tour of the British Isles.[4] Arriving in London, he ran into Dane, who invited him to dinner that night. The conversation lagged; the cellist's usual expansive flights of fancy were missing, and he seemed distant:

> "You look worried. Are you feeling well?" Dane asked.
> "I'm all right," I said. "It's my cello [the Földesy Stradivari]. It has a cancer." I spoke of the sound-post crack on the back and of hours spent at Hill's, the eminent violin experts in London. "But even they can't do a thing about the crack. No one can."
> Mr. Dane said he had always wanted to visit the famous Hill shop. The next morning we met there, and I introduced him to Alfred Hill. After they looked at several Stradivari and Guarneri violins, Dane asked if Hill had any good cellos. "I not only have a good cello here but a magnificent one, one of the great cellos of the world. It lay unused for over seventy years at Berkeley Castle, owned by the Fitzharding family. And now it is on the market."
> He brought out a magnificent Montagnana from 1739. The instrument was a pristine example—undamaged, uncut,[5] and in its original luminous golden-orange varnish. He handed Piatigorsky a bow. Piatigorsky tentatively drew the bow over the strings. It barely had a sound, but captivated the cellist. Hours passed as he struggled to coax life into it: "I looked at it again and again and played as if possessed, until Alfred Hill returned once more, this time alone. 'Mr. Dane,' he said, 'did not want to interrupt you. He had to catch his boat back to the United States. This Montagnana is his gift to you.'"

Piatigorsky could not believe his good fortune.[6] The cello has since been given the name *Sleeping Beauty*.[7]

After playing the Brahms Double Concerto with Erica Morini in Budapest, Piatigorsky confided to Koussevitzky: "All is well with me—I am playing a lot, and the concerts on the new cello are meeting with double success!" And again in November 1935: "I still can't get used to the thought that I have such a wonderful cello, and I am afraid that this is just a dream and that one terrible morning I will wake up and not have it!!"

But by 1939, despite his luck in obtaining the cello, he had difficulty touring with the instrument. It was about this time when the cellist experimented using a steel A string rather than the customary gut string.

From Gut to Steel[8]

Until now, I have resisted with all my love toward my instrument, with all my feelings of humanity in art and with all my admiration for the great instrumental Italian masters, the use of steel strings.

I have protested against this idea of the "steel age," when practicality and power have defeated ideals and quality. In steel strings one can see the beginning of the fight against ancient instruments, against the genius of forms, the beauty of lacquered woods and of that spirit and wisdom which the great masters invested in them. For in veinous strings there is life, blood flowed through them, and when they were stretched on an instrument, they vibrated and lived under ones fingers. But like anything living and delicate they are very susceptible to changes in climate — they rise and fall, they split and don't remain in a single inanimate state.

In this lay their charm, but also their difficulties. Besides this, there is a quality that dominates veinous strings — the timbre of sound above its strength and brightness. All of this has made me act according to a characterless Russian proverb — "In order to live among wolves, one must howl like a wolf."

Playing in huge halls, and traveling from one end of the country to another, subjecting my instrument to sudden and frequent climate changes, I decided to become practical, i.e. to follow the general rules — to follow the path of least resistance. The first concert was physical and moral torture. In the second concert, I felt the advantage of the brightness, the more true metalicness of the sound, and in the third concert it became clear to me that in this country the import of good French wine will not increase, there are no requirements for more refined or higher tastes — petroleum has replaced blood, steel has replaced wood and quantity has replaced quality. Clear and bright metal has stifled the Stradivarius and Montagnana.

Like a failed love, he described the break-up with the Montagnana in *Cellist*:

We were inseparable for many years, traveling and playing uncounted concerts together — perhaps too many for both of us to endure. But the brave Montagnana, though badly in need of a rest, abused and exposed to all climates and acoustics, stood by me, giving its best. It was I who, though physically fit, tried to lessen my demands upon the cello by accepting fewer engagements and even leaving out of my programs some of the contemporary works which I thought were too brutal and percussive for my Montagnana to bear.

Though I knew I had to have two cellos, it was inconceivable for me even to look at another one, much less hope to find a replacement. I spoke of my problem to Alfred Hill; he had a particular cello in mind for me [the "Lord Aylesford" Stradivari] and furthermore, an exact copy of it made by Vuillaume.

Piatigorsky's affair with the *Aylesford* was brief despite its beauty and attraction:

Though the purpose of any musical instrument is to produce sound, it is conceivable for even the deaf to admire the cello as they would a piece of sculpture. The great luthiers considered ornaments — such as the scroll, purfling, and f-holes — of enough aesthetic value as to give much of their creative efforts to them, despite their having little or no effect on the sound itself. In fact, if only the sound mattered, I could not have fallen so desperately in love with just the scroll of a cello as to purchase it before even hearing its sound. It belonged to the *Aylesford* Stradivari, made in 1696. Though a very impressive instrument, the beauty, power, and grace of its crowning scroll were what I could not resist. Only after the *Aylesford* had been repaired did I finally play on it.[9] But although I found its sound admirable, its very large size put a strain on my fingers and I was forced, reluctantly, to part with it after a year or so.[10]

The *Baudiot*

About two years later [1947] my friend Rembert Wurlitzer, the renowned violin dealer of New York, called me in Philadelphia. He was brief. "It is here. Just arrived from London. Hurry." Sensing what to expect, I dashed to New York. There, facing the *Baudiot*[11] Stradivari, and after striking only a few notes on it, once more I gave free rein to my enthusiastic impulses and bought the cello on the spot. As at first encounter, one feels an immediate rapport with some people, so it was the *Baudiot*. There was no need to get better acquainted — no work, no study required — and I played on it from the first day with joy and complete confidence.[12]

In 1725 Stradivari made only two cellos, but how different they are! One, known as "La Belle Blonde," is light and elegant; while the *Baudiot*, in contrast, is red, dark, and ruggedly masculine. Its head (scroll) is classical and proud. Its f-holes are sharp and its purfling uneven, as if impatiently but determinedly cut by the then eighty-one-year-old master. Judging from its appearance and its extraordinary quality and richness of sound, one would expect a dramatic history and heroic stories of its past.

The *Batta*

Horace Havemeyer was one of the most admirable art collectors I have had the privilege of knowing. With a keen sense for quality, he and his lovely wife surrounded themselves in their Park Avenue apartment in New York with only the choicest examples — were it Vermeer, Stradivari, or Manet. An amateur cellist himself, he owned the two foremost cellos of Stradivari, the *Batta* and the *Duport*.

At my first visit, they stood side by side, like two kings resting in their royal caskets. (My *Baudiot*, too, when I am at home, is kept in a similar wooden case specially made by Hill & Sons.)

"Do you want to see them?" asked Mr. Havemeyer. So much had I heard about these legendary instruments and dreamed to see them one day in the flesh that I felt now like being invited to enter paradise. I waited, watching Mr. Havemeyer take the instruments out and carefully placing them for me to see. Dazzled and as if blinded by some mysterious light emanating from them, I had to close my eyes for a moment. When I opened them again, there was a sight to behold! A glow of colors of all shades from soft to bright transported me into a land of enchantment.

After my first visit, whenever I was in New York I would not miss an opportunity to see the *Batta* and the *Duport*. But no matter how often I was questioned on which of the two cellos I preferred, it was impossible to decide. Only after Mr. Havemeyer lent me the *Duport*, with which I spent almost a year, did I know that I favored the *Batta*. I think that Mr. Havemeyer knew it all along, for he always handed me the *Batta* first to play, and it was the *Batta*, he said, that I played last each time before departing. He also confessed one day that the reason he could not lend me the *Batta* was that it belonged to his son-in-law. Later, it must have been my dear friend Havemeyer who intervened in my behalf and persuaded his son-in-law to sell me his *Batta*. He did, and I shall not stop being grateful for it to both of them.[13]

Stradivari made all in all about 60 cellos. Some of them were oversized, too big. But from 1700 on he began to make the cello as we know it today. Stradivari really showed his great genius more in the cellos than in the violins, because he is the one practically who created the cello as we know it today.

Masters Stradivari, Guarneri, and Montagnana, they all took tremendous care and pride of making the scroll, the head of the instrument. And the very characteristic is almost like the face of a person. Together, you see, woven together, everything that is beautiful is now connected. For the audience it would not make much difference, but it is very important to have a beautiful instrument that inspires the player. Actually he must be in love with his instrument.

For me it is something very much alive. Sometimes an instrument is so sensitive it is unbelievable. The instrument feels the atmosphere. It feels my mood, too. Sometimes it encourages me. Sometimes it tells me, "I don't like that climate, could you put that silk cover over me?"

> I have played the cello for over 65 years and consider myself an extremely young man, but a fairly old musician. But with the cello, not a day passes that I do not look for something new. There is a never-ending search with the cello, and that is the great beauty of it. For me, it is still full of surprises, full of new adventures. When I look at my cello, I think to myself how much less I am who can play only a little while on it; it stays forever young. How marvelously preserved it is, how new it looks, how beautiful it sounds. The times change, and still nobody can build a better cello. It would seem ridiculous in the time of the jet for someone to ride a donkey. But for me, for my music, the donkey is better than the jet. It seems impractical, but the best things in art are not really practical.
>
> Conventionalities such as "out of this world" or "too good to be true" take on real meaning when applied to the *Batta*, which safely can claim to be one of the finest works of art human hands have ever created. I own a letter in which Alfred Hill describes at length the touching history of this great instrument.
>
> I played the *Batta* for a long time before appearing in concert with it.[14] In solitude, as is befitting honeymooners, we avoided interfering company until then. I would dream of it — five days and sleepless nights — thinking I must be deranged. From that day on, when I proudly carried the *Batta* across the stage for all to greet, a new challenge entered into my life.
>
> While all other instruments I had played prior to the *Batta* differed one from the other in character and range, I knew their qualities, shortcomings, or their capriciousness enough to exploit their good capabilities to full advantage. Not so with the *Batta*, whose prowess had no limitations. Bottomless in its resources, it spurred me on to try to reach its depths, and I have never worked harder or desired anything more fervently than to draw out of this superior instrument all it has to give. Only then will I deserve to be its equal.

British violin dealer Charles Beare quoted Piatigorsky's humorous remark regarding the *Batta*:

> He marched on to the stage feeling terrific. Then Piatigorsky said:
> "I heard a little voice in my ear. It came from the scroll. It said:
> 'Who the hell do you think you are?'"[15]

Critics

> *"Did you ever receive a bad review?"*
> *"Certainly! Only, I don't collect them."*

Once, after playing the Dvorak Concerto on tour with the Chicago Symphony in the Midwest, Piatigorsky was ripped to shreds by a local critic. Though he had played the work all his life, the critic accused him of not really knowing the piece. After the second performance the critic brazenly appeared at the reception with a glass of champagne, eager to speak with Piatigorsky. Piatigorsky avoided him, but was cornered. Almost proud, the critic introduced himself, whereupon Piatigorsky said, "Oh yes, you're the gentleman who wrote that lovely review about me. I'll tell you what. I will give you my fee if you can play five bars of that concerto. I will also give you my fee if I can't write the first 500 bars of the concerto." Needless to say, the contest never began.[16]

The following are various quotes from Piatigorsky on the subject of criticism.

> *There was a young man named Olin*
> *Who from concert to concert went strollin'*
> *For so many a day*
> *At such very small pay,*
> *We propose to call him St. Olin.*[17]

About Critics

During my long career as a musician I have received and actually read thousands of reviews among which were many favorable and many adversarial — some belligerent, some enthusiastic, some ignorant and occasionally some insensitive ones.

Critics are human beings, but they don't know it. The performer is also human, but he knows it in excess. The so-called virtuoso is not necessarily a glamorous courtesan or a symbol of vanity and brilliant emptiness. They can be very useful servants of music. A professional performer knows a piece of music he performs always better than the person who gives him a free lesson in the newspaper the next morning. The effort of a performer to penetrate into a composition and to master his instrument is enormous and never ending. To the contrast of effort on the part of the critic — rushing to the next phone booth to let the world know of his impression of the concert — which is still going on. Some even put those spontaneous phone booth creations into the form of a book, obviously thinking of immortality, and probably in defiance of the conception that nothing is as dead as yesterday's newspaper.

The practice of comparing performers and tagging them with titles as, let's say "The Prince of Pianists," "The King of Violinists," etc., is not only nonsensical but too monarchistic, too undemocratic. I would also recommend to abstain, in the name of Heaven and Art, from "The Greatest Dead or Alive!" Those superlatives are comical and only true if speaking of boxers — a knockout is a knockout.

A critic likes to identify himself as a reporter, but he never is. Some are even not instructed in music — just as I am in possession of a glowing review, which I of course cherish, of my recital in Cincinnati written by a sports reporter. A wrestler never played cello. How about suggesting let's say, Mr. Toscanini be a referee in a wrestling match?

To pan an unknown or little known performer, who often goes through hardship to make his appearance possible, is a certain form of sadism. And to blast a famous one is nothing short of vanity. The first is like tearing off the wings of a fly. The second is like making an elephant fall with a single blow.

I agree that some performers ought to be discouraged, but it can be accomplished best by the friendly advice of a teacher, psychoanalyst or a friend in private.

A good performer is not made by a critic. I almost forgot to state that a critic never perspired at a concert, but a performer, always. I would like to add that all who desire to serve art honestly, be it critic or musician, should try to forget their own self-importance. Be more humble and assume greater responsibility towards art and people. To all [we] have the same goal towards a better world that music is capable of making, and as sincere servants of art, we must not betray it with a witty word now and then — or [taking] personal advantage of success in our professions that may tempt the critic, or a flashy show-off passage on the part of the performer. All who love music beyond themselves and try to serve it with all the good knowledge and gifts at their command, are people I love and respect. All the others I would not consider my friends, or for that matter no one else's. As someone once said, "the greatest secret of life is to spend it on something that will outlast it."

Critics and New Music[18]

*All critics are great champions of modern music —
before they hear it performed.*

After the concert I had to really hurry to make the train, but thanks to a fast car, we arrived too early at the station. I sat at the counter, drank apple juice and read the paper. I found the critique of the concert. I read it through and was touched. It seems that for the first time in my entire career I read a critic and thought, how correct, simple and free of dilettantism. An amazing time has come for critic-reviewers, especially for those working in large cities. My god, what a profession; it takes audacious courage to take up this kind of work. In New

York, a critic is known to run several concerts in a single day. What great knowledge and superhuman instincts are needed in order to publicly declare the qualities and shortcomings of a piece performed for the first time at one of these concerts. At the same time the poor artist who is performing the piece requires weeks of concentration simply to understand the new composition and months and years to grow accustomed to it. And even then, you suddenly make changes and you find old mistakes in your performances and new beauty in the composition. And yet the critic listens to it in passing and knows everything — it's superhuman!

I can't think of one clear instance of the "genius" of critics. It was in Berlin, a long time ago, while I was still playing in the Berlin Philharmonic Orchestra. In the program of one of the concerts was mentioned the premiere performance of *Variations* by Schonberg for full orchestra. At the first rehearsal, we simply picked at the notes and barely progressed forward. Because of the great difficulty and intricacy of the *Variations*, Furtwängler fixed an extra rehearsal and hours, which rarely happened with the Philharmonic. I wanted to obtain the score, but in the entire city there was only one, which Furtwängler had, and the other copy was in Vienna with Schonberg.

I spent all day at Furtwängler's, together with him on the score. Then again a rehearsal, endlessly, painstaking work with no clear results, for even the last rehearsal did not resolve many problems and did not make the work completely understandable. The orchestra and the director were nervous before the concert, which rarely happens. The *Variations* was the first piece on the program. The audience became quiet in the hall and the concert began. The first 25–30 measures were going well when suddenly a flute it seems entered one 16th early. This was enough for a small confusion, and Furtwängler tried to correct it through signs and gesticulations, but it was too late. Despite all the intensity of the orchestra, all the attention and effort, it became clear to everyone that the train had become derailed and that the losses would not be minimal. The sounds given forth by the orchestra were inconceivable. Blushing and perspiring, Furtwängler gesticulated his arms in vain, banged his feet and reminded one of a mad man who has just wildly run out of a mental institution. It seemed that only the director was still looking at the notes. The orchestra had evidently lost hope of finding salvation in them, and everyone played from memory, each as if from his own personal repertoire. My neighbor was repeating a passage from the Saint-Saëns Concerto — it was impossible to hear the others individually due to the unbelievable noise.

The chaos continued for a long time, each person feeling it was his holy duty to play something as long as Furtwängler was continuing to gesticulate. And then finally, the last waves of his arms and the orchestra almost simultaneously grew quiet. The audience applauded, (they always applaud) but there were also shy whistles. The next day, the critics came down on these whistlers. How could they not be ashamed not to understand and value such a splendid performance of such a deep and immortal work?

Genial and unpretentious critics (alas, they are few!) bring about less harm through their work than embittered critics with learned pretensions. Although only for the simple reason that true talent has never been destroyed by abusive critics, just as mediocrity has never risen up and held its own due to laudatory critics. It is a shame that managers traditionally reprint or rather cite individual phrases from the critics' pithy ramble in order to advertise the artist. The critic believes in the importance of his own existence and is only cynical towards his victims, but never in reference towards himself.

> *In Chicago there's a lady of letters*
> *Who maligns the work of her betters.*
> *Though she loses the scent*
> *One hundred percent,*
> *For laughs we're always her debtors*[19]

Composers as Critics[20]

Richard Strauss once responded to a lady asking him about music — program music, classical music, and romantic music — "My dear lady, I know of only two kinds of music. Good music and bad music." Even with such an erudite and well-behaved statement from a master, composers can be terrible critics. Strauss told me about a composer he disliked. He was furious about the popular acclaim accorded this man. "He is overrated," Strauss said, "on his feet he has the shoes of a mountain climber; on his head, the cowl of a monk, and here — putting his hand on his heart — he has nothing."

The composer he was panning was Brahms. Strauss was not the only great musician who could not appreciate another composer's music. Tchaikovsky was another creator who did not admire Brahms. Sibelius disliked Wagner and Prokofiev was no devotee of Tchaikovsky, at least he wasn't before his return to Russia. On the other hand, Schumann was an advocate of Chopin and Brahms; Berlioz, a champion of Beethoven; Mendelssohn resurrected Bach, and Liszt encouraged Wagner.

Every performer or composer hates critics, but I know it is not so easy [to be a critic]. On a sabbatical I thought it was time to understand critics. I became an unofficial critic. I went to concerts, rushed to hear all, pieces I did not know, I tried to be as honest as possible. I discovered that it is not possible to know 25%.

One concert I reviewed writing that they did not play together, it was unbalanced, sloppy and a bore. A very nasty review. Before this I thought it was not possible to do. After the concert I got hold of the score. I discovered they are not supposed to play together. It was a very good performance. I was not crazy about the piece. A remarkable performance. The problem was I did not know the piece.

I avoid confrontation with critics especially those who write glowing reviews of my performances. How could I face a man who thought a perfectly lousy concert was divine, or meet a person who tears you to pieces? Those people — it is best to imagine them dead.

Critics can also take on an elite attitude towards their country's idiosyncratic bloodline. The English were known to eschew others as being deficient in the secrets of Elgar. The following is a good example concerning Casals' performances of the cello concerto:

> Experience goes to show that players who are not Elgar's fellow-countrymen find considerable difficulty in catching his peculiar tone of voice.[21]
> Once again a foreign artist did not "get hold" of the very English idiom of Elgar.[22]

The cellist recalled an absurd review he received in a recital with Ivor Newton:[23]

> I remember the dean of [British] critics, Mr. Ernest Newman and his criticism of Beethoven's Handel Variations ... that it should remain somewhere buried in the dust, every note of it bad, that there are greater works and it should not be played.

Piatigorsky played both sides, extending the olive branch: "I never considered critics as enemy — now only to ask more, and perhaps say less."

Jascha Heifetz spoke of Piatigorsky's character: "Essential to his importance as a musician, are his strong likes and dislikes. In a world of yes and no and middle of the road, it's rare to find someone with the courage of his convictions."[24] Apropos, after a performance of *Don Quixote*, the *New York Times* took the cellist to task for his excessive liberties, saying, "He ended with a pianissimo downward-glissando (not in the score)...." Piatigorsky responded, "It *is* written in the score. Maybe it's not in the score the man on the *Times* used."[25]

And finally, Piatigorsky comes full circle to admit that imperfect as it is, the professional critic is still a better choice than a colleague: "If only artists should be allowed to judge fellow artists, it would result in mass murder. Listening to my colleagues' judgments of the their brother musicians, the reviews by critics appear angelic."

KOUSSEVITZKY OVERHEARD AS CRITIC

Koussevitzky was the source of many stories that Piatigorsky recalled from the Tanglewood years. Some of them are quoted below:

> The composer Irving Fine was rehearsing one of his works with the school orchestra and saw Koussevitzky appearing on the stage:
> "Fine, Fine!" — he said — "It is awful!"

> After Aaron Copland conducted the orchestra, Koussevitzky came to see him after the concert,
> "Your composition is *vonderful*!" he said enthusiastically.
> "Thank you," said Copland, "but how did you find my conducting?"
> "Let's speak of your composition...." Again and again Copland wanted to know, but Koussevitzky avoided.
> A few weeks later Copland attended a concert in which Koussevitzky conducted his own composition. After the performance Copland greeted Koussevitzky,
> "Marvelous conducting!"
> "But, how you find my composition?" asked Koussevitzky eagerly.
> "Well, you did not tell me how you liked my conducting" said Copland. "Tell me now, and I will tell you of your composition."
> Koussevitzky hesitated, then exclaimed "That bad is my composition not!"

> Koussevitzky kept repeating a passage in a funeral march at a rehearsal.
> "No, No" — he screamed — "look here — can't you understand?" he pleaded addressing the bassoon player —
> "It is a funeral march — please try it again."
> Finally losing his patience, the bassoon player said — "I know it is a funeral march."
> "Good, good," said Koussevitzky "But it is you who is a corpse!"[26]

An unlikely critic was put to the test at a well publicized trial:

> When Igor Stravinsky was suing the Leeds Music Company for use of his music from "Firebird," Albert Goldberg, music critic of the *Los Angeles Times*, was called as an expert witness. The defense counsel asked him to sing the *Berceuse* [one of the familiar melodies]. Mr. Goldberg demurred, saying, "I'm not a singer." The lawyer insisted and Mr. Goldberg agreed to hum it. When his performance was completed the judge said, "I agree with Mr. Goldberg. He's no singer."[27]

The Reluctant Judge

> *I saw a tennis match yesterday — one man won, the other lost. Some of the strokes of the loser were absolutely immortal, but he was considered a loser. That's not right.*
>
> *It is the obligation of people of art to find some other way to give people of talent some incentive, but it cannot be useful to discourage a hundred merely to encourage one.*

Glenn Gould accused competitions of inflicting "spiritual lobotomy," and pianist and teacher Russell Sherman called them "the anti–Christ."[28] But, the modern reality of competition is in its ubiquity; competition tries to replace the traditional grassroots struggle for recognition.

While Piatigorsky and Heifetz were judging a singer, a flutist, a clarinetist and a composer, they faced a dilemma: "Now, how can one say who is best among different categories? Can you compare an orange with a bicycle? Can one say which is better? They were all good young artists." Piatigorsky insisted that each contestant get a prize. The outcome: he had to pay for two of the prizes himself.[29]

Piatigorsky described his experience judging with Arthur Rubinstein and composer William Grant Still:

> We heard seven musicians, six different instruments and a composer. They were all very good; they played well. I waited for the others to speak. Artur said it was the flutist, a great performer, a great musician. I know that Artur knows nothing about the flute. I said: "Artur, if you think he is the greatest, you should be willing to give him a scholarship." He agreed to do so. Then I said that I would give a scholarship to the young pianist, John Browning. Then I said that I would give another scholarship for the composer [William] Grant Still [to award] (I knew he could not afford it).
>
> So then we called in the committee and asked them whether, since we together would give three scholarships, they could not arrange to give scholarships to all the others. They agreed that they could. Now everyone is afraid to accept when they learn I am to be a judge on a committee. They are afraid it will cost them money.
>
> Ours is a world of champions. Music gets to be like tennis or football. You have to be the best, the biggest, the greatest, the most. In art, that's a catastrophe. Thank goodness I never needed to play in competitions. I have never won an official prize. I am not a boxer. You know, in a fight, one man is laid out half dead on the side, with a broken nose — he's the loser — and the other dances around him — he is the winner. That's prize-fighting, a bloody, competitive, hit and knock area. Why should it interest an artist? Art is not competitive, but, alas, artists are. They're made to be. My students go all over the world in order to compete. In that way, they have hope to gain some recognition; what a misfortune.
>
> Unfortunately, musicians are arranged in ranks. It's worse than the military — there's a general, a lieutenant, a brigadier general — and at the bottom there's a private first class, who plays in the orchestra: For me, this is illusory. I have met so many wonderful musicians who played in orchestras. Look, even Dvorak played viola in the Prague Symphony. Also, many very admirable people do not choose instruments with large solo repertoires. They may prefer the clarinet, the oboe or the horn. They become soloists in the orchestra. No one seems very anxious to know their names or to celebrate them very much. But they have all my admiration.
>
> Though they may play the same instrument, even the same piece, each musician is unique. As soon as people reach a certain level, it's preposterous to make comparisons. I am seldom able, myself, to compare one artist unfavorably with another. The only thing I can say is, "There's a wonderful artist," not, "This fine artist is better than that fine artist." Differences are good. They're interesting. It would kill me to try and say who's "the best." I can say X is good at Beethoven, Y is good at Mozart. But how does anyone number them, one-two-three? It's not possible in music or any other art. You can't say, so-and-so's the greatest poet or writer or painter. Look at the paintings on my wall. That one is Toulouse Lautrec, this one Rouault, this is Fragonard, there's Modigliani. Would you ask me, who is the best of these? Wouldn't you say, to be excellent is enough?[30]

Piatigorsky was persuaded to judge the Tchaikovsky Competitions of 1962 and 1966. He is quoted in *Izvestiya*[31] where the Soviets won in all the string areas in 1962:

> I don't know how to measure the art — with meter, centimeter, or any other way; I didn't find any way. I think that it is quite enough if musician is remarkable. I never in my life could say which composer was the greatest, which performer was the best. Performer is good when you cannot compare him to another one, when performer has a personality.

Piatigorsky was asked to make suggestions for future competitions, some of which were implemented, especially with regard to repertoire:

In the program of next competition would be good to present more classics, for example Beethoven, Brahms. I was thinking how nice it would be if at the end of hard competition judges could stay for a few simple and important days more, for meeting with young musicians — at non-competition atmosphere and to talk honestly. After all, the most important thing in our profession is not medals and diplomas, but knowledge. If a person who came here, learned something, he had a reason to come here. Young musicians should meet with those who went already through fire and water. We have to talk to each other as friends.

I don't want to comment a list of laureates and diplomats by their names. I will only say that I was touched by a little girl with serious face — Natasha Gutman. She is absolutely charming. Talent, a great talent. But I agreed with the judges that first prize was definitely deserved by Natalia Shakovskaya as a more mature musician. The fact that women won first prize is also very good. I feel that women are playing more energetically. [Toby] Saks, for example. She plays like three men, absolutely phenomenal energy. Gutman plays very charming, femininely, but she has the power. I was very interested by her. I kissed her once, such a serious and cute, such a shy and sad girl. And after that I noticed that she suddenly smiled. That was the only one smile that I saw from her during whole competition.

I hope that all wonderful talents, who were remarked by judges of Tchaikovsky Competition, will continue — in our profession are no presidents and generals. You can have a big "rank," but if you play awful, you will lose "name."

I will look forward with all my heart to come here again. Thank you for hospitality. I was happy to be with you in Moscow.

Gerontology: Age — Effect and Myth

Piatigorsky thought about aging and liked to talk about it. His last years were occupied not only with teaching but also with gerontology. He claimed that he was as busy as ever in his seventies, just differently. His family noticed how long he sat at his desk every day and would ask what he was doing: "I'm busy. I am busy thinking."

> I cannot swim long distance or play soccer anymore. But this thing that people automatically expect from an artist if he reaches a certain age — that something happens to technique — that means the ability to say, to express what you want — people get hard of hearing, don't see, but the fingers — they can only do what they are told to do. Transcendence? It's a question of character, not ability.
>
> Aging and the expectation of death — people make too much of that. I just read in the paper where (Field Marshal Bernard Law) Montgomery died. Why, the only trivial thing that happened to him in his lifetime was that he died in his bed. People — artists particularly — want to leave behind something, to be remembered, to leave their mark. They don't realize they can't really do it. One must know that remembrance is not of prime importance. It is natural to be forgotten, and to forget. All those kings and prime ministers we were taught in school — it was boring to memorize. So it is not such a tragedy to be forgotten.

Piatigorsky would also agree with his friend Nathan Milstein, who spoke less seriously about his advancing age: "I don't celebrate anything. Whether it's 10 or 50 years, it doesn't matter. I play…. It only gives me pleasure that I've played so long and nobody has arrested me for it."[32] To Piatigorsky there was one true regret of aging: "missing the friends who I made music with."[33]

THE ARTS: CREATIVITY IN AGING
An address entered into the Congressional Record[34]

MR. CHURCH. Mr. President, during the week of February 12 [1973] the new facilities at the Ethel Percy Andrus Gerontological Center [of the Leonard Davis School of Gerontology] at the University of Southern California were dedicated.

Over the years, the Andrus Center has been an outstanding leader in supporting research in the biological and social sciences as well as graduate training community service program. At the recent dedication, several memorable statements were made. One such example is an address by the renowned cellist, Gregor Piatigorsky.

His remarks — "The Arts: Creativity in Aging" — offer many provocative suggestions for improving the lives of elderly. But his central theme is that a feeling of fulfillment, such as he has achieved through music, is central to the well-being of all individuals, both young and old alike.

Indeed, he said:

The thing that prevented me from observing my own aging was and is music — the passion for which never lessened — and the cello, with which I did not part for the last 63 years.

Mr. President, I commend the remarks of Gregor Piatigorsky to my colleagues, and ask unanimous consent that his statement be printed in the Record.

There being no objection, the statement was ordered to be printed in the Record, as follows:

THE ARTS: CREATIVITY IN AGING

I must begin with praise for old age. The German saying is, "the old wood burns the best," and we all know that the good old wine tastes best as old fiddles sound best, and as a child I loved old people best. Our best aim is to reach the summit. Among many advantages of an older person over a younger one is that, looking back, he can appreciate the distance he has covered already — often a view of magnitude and beauty denied to the young. As long as one keeps climbing and spiritually growing, one will fuse with the nature, which is movement, a symbol of life.

Next April I will be 70 years old, and reaching this age I suppose I should know something of the process of aging, but the fact that I don't or perhaps because I don't, I was asked to speak to you today.

AGING: AN ACHIEVEMENT

The thing that prevented me from observing my own aging was and is music — the passion for which never lessened — and the cello with which I did not part for the last 63 years. I could not part with it even today. I brought it here to show it to you in all its beauty and vigor at the age of about two hundred fifty. There is a glory in old art because we have learned to admire it almost as much as we learned to fear our own old age. I think we should regard our capacity of aging as an achievement rather than defeat. It is true that at the age of 96 when Antonio Stradivari made my cello, his hand trembled a little — only to contribute a special charm and tonal quality to it.

I am not the only worshipper of mature age. As we know, in Japan only men of 60 are free to wear bright lining in their kimonos and are at last free to speak their minds.

"Only fools don't behave according to their age," said Heine, and he is right, although it does not occur too often, and if it does, it's only harmlessly comical.

"Come on, girls," one occasionally hears octogenarian ladies call at the ladies' clubs, and men among themselves occasionally would turn from grandfathers to cute boys.

TEMPO OF LIFE

As I said, the life is movement, and everything has its tempo, but it becomes serious when a person must move with someone else's tempo and become out of step with his own. This all-important factor is often neglected, and people are judged, employed and discharged according to their actual age and not to their physical and mental tempo. Thus compulsory retirement at a given age is often cruel and unwise. Alertness of mind, wisdom, knowledge and enthusiasm do not disappear at a bureaucrat's signal. There are men over 80 and 90 who continue to enrich the world with their extraordinary deeds. Some of them happen to be artists, but isn't everyone who strives for and achieves excellence an artist? I have not yet met a person without talent for something. Why should there be so few who recognize it and start developing it at an early age? You don't have to be a fiddler, poet or painter to be an artist. An artist is a person who loves something he strives to do well and who will do it even if he has a price to pay for doing it.

There was a cobbler in Vienna, a man over 60. Watching him work, he reminded me of one great sculptor. He made a pair of shoes for me, which I wore and admired for 25 years. We became friends. One day a charming young princess noticed my shoes and expressed a desire to meet their creator. I brought her to his workshop. But after thoroughly examining her feet he called me aside and whispered, "I can't do it. I don't like her feet." It was embarrassing, but his drive for artistic achievement seemed worth monetary sacrifice.

A LOVE FOR WORK

A love for one's work I give the highest priority in man's life. More professions inspiring love should be created, and occupations below human dignity and aesthetics should be given to the machine, which in turn is capable to be beautiful and exciting to create and practical to use. I don't think these thoughts are utopian, but rather, realistic and vitally needed. There is nothing more unfortunate than to earn one's living by work one dislikes. Among many evils it breeds boredom, an enemy capable to destroy man.

CREATIVITY

Not unlike many other definitions, the meaning of creativity has a variety of connotations, as, inventiveness, development of something created already, rediscovering or putting to practical use something, though small and prosaic, to the good of humanity. So, speaking once to Mrs. Goldberg of the gigantic creativity of Leonardo da Vinci, she said her late husband's contribution to humanity by inventing the safety pin was as great, and monetarily perhaps more profitable.

There are areas of the past which I feel would be good to transport to our machine age: like artisans who would make a chair on which they sign their name and which later becomes a piece of art the people can see only in the museum.

Primitive people in Africa and elsewhere don't think of themselves as artists carving masks and all ornaments for their festivities and rituals. In highly civilized countries, everything is geared toward professional or commercial perfection, while a source of personal satisfaction could be derived from a compulsion to produce something beautiful with one's own hands. One may call it a hobby. There are not enough of them cultivated. For people, art is something standing totally apart, something they would not dare to be a part of without the assurance they belong to the mysterious clan of geniuses. They should be reminded that working with wood, varnish and primitive tools people centuries ago produced objects no one in our civilization can duplicate.

There should be a search for lasting pleasures. I know a lady in Los Angeles who loved tennis at an early age. I saw her on the tennis court the other day at 87, still playing, smiling, cracking jokes and slightly criticizing herself and her partner. A game of chess or fishing will enhance life continuously. I like amateurs, the true lovers of things, who, though they enjoy listening and watching, like to participate in performance themselves.

OUR OWN SPEED

It's true that the tempo with age does change and in some areas slow down, but precisely those changes of the tempo, which begin to occur from the beginning of life one should not only be aware of, but learn to master. An infant prior to entering school rarely sits still. His tempo is erratic and fast.

Suddenly he finds himself at school and forced to act at someone else's tempo. The same experience he would have to endure throughout his life. If he does not adapt to it, he might lose his own tempo and find himself out of step with the moving world. Music, which consists of many tempos prescribed by the composer, must be executed by performers as indicated. For a good one it will come naturally, for untrained ones it will be a disaster. So it is in daily life. We must adapt ourselves to the tempo of others yet know our own speed, an important factor in aging well. It will teach us how to speak and when to preserve our energy.

Maestro Toscanini, who hated doctors, hospitals and dentists, at the age of 90, was finally persuaded to undergo a complete checkup. There was a whole coterie of them. They pronounced him completely fit.

"You are virtually 90, and you have the heart of a 30 year old man. Could you give us some idea of how you managed to preserve your heart in that wonderful state?"

Toscanini said, "My heart? I never use it."

There was an extraordinary boy who received his doctorate at Yale University in music, (composition and the piano) philosophy and I think in something else at the age of 14. He had to decide which field to pursue. His parents brought the boy one nice summer day to me. Instead to meet a kind of wizard from another planet, I took a long walk along the lake with a somewhat confused, but healthy boy. His choice was leaning toward music, but he expressed great interest in medicine too. It was obvious that he, as other child prodigies, took somewhat prematurely a tempo of intellectuals above his age and skipped the activities of children his own age.

I did not know how strong he was in music or the other fields, but taking a glance at the beautiful lake, I said, "You ought to learn to swim." He seemed astonished but enthusiastic about the idea. I have not seen him for many years, but I have heard he is a successful physician now, and I want to hope that by now his collection of tempos is complete.

THE ARTIST AND LIFE

As a music teacher who deals with exceptionally talented young artists, I feel it's necessary to spend almost as much time discussing problems of life as those of music itself. It all hangs together. I want them to give their lives for something bigger than they are. Those who understand and are able to catch the spark, succeed to become good servants of art and well-balanced people of purpose. The others, even if they succeed in their professional career, might turn frustrated, often envious, and bitter.

There is a story about a dead boy lying in the street and surrounded by people.

"How ugly. Disgusting," muttered the crowd. Then they heard a voice. "Look at his teeth. They are beautiful." It was the voice of Mohammed. The ability and the desire to see and to hear the beautiful whenever one finds it will help the young and old alike to beautify their own lives as well as to desire to encourage the others.

We become increasingly stingy in voicing our approval of others, perhaps out of a fear to appear insincere. We would rather criticize than compliment people while not hesitating to shower generous praises on a fabulous pizza or a great hotdog.

Once a new student, while playing for me, visibly suffered from his poor performance. And poor it was until I heard one beautiful note.

"This note was beautiful," I Interrupted. The student shocked, looked disbelievingly at me. "Please repeat that note," I asked. "Yes, it's good. Now try it a little stronger. Wonderful. Now softer and longer, please. Now you have started," I said, "an exciting collection. Tomorrow there will be a few more fine notes, then a phrase, and finally an entire piece." I am glad to say that it turned out to be true.

The reaction to the negative in a person is infinitely more deeply anchored than that of the positive, and while the self-criticism is of value, it is not effective without a starting point of self-recognition of one's own strong points. A word of reassurance and sincere recognition is a good medicine at any age.

At one time an important and known artist, but now old and forgotten greeted me on the street.

"You don't know me," he mentioned his name. "I just want to shake your hand." Indeed the name was familiar to me. Very impressed, I called a meeting of the society, which consisted of the present leaders and active members in the same field. All colleagues were delighted to present to the old man a plaque with the so well-deserved glowing inscription. The old man, very moved, said that this unexpected honor will give him the courage to lead an active life again. He did become a changed man.

I am not a scientist to dare to offer to this learned assembly some results of my physiological or psychological research on gerontology, simply because there was no research, no remedy, to solve the problems of old age for people who wait for their death and who feel so totally unneeded. And yet because we have arrived at the point where there seems no solution is coming from experts, it is not unlike with the baldness of a man's head. Where there is no stopping of falling hair, one would not hesitate to consult even a barber.

ACCOMPLISHMENTS AND AGING

There is nothing to stop aging, but to slow it down can and should be made easier. It can be, by activating interests, by helping to keep interests all — and by appreciating the accomplishments of the old. The majority of the people, and I think young people at that, are the onlookers, the audience. They can afford to watch others perform. The old ones should perform themselves as much as they can. And in as many areas they can, and they should be involved.

Once I had a weird dream of a war and of an old-people-hating dictator who drafted into the army instead of the young, only men and women over fifty. Instead of indignation, it created tremendous excitement among them.

Live and proud in their uniforms, and trained by good instructors, they won the war and their pride and glory. And with the admiration of all, they lived happily ever after. Should we stupidly stick to wars forever, this could perhaps be the solution. For who would want, after all, to kill old men, and who would not, with so few years left to live, fight more ferociously to save the lives of those destined to live much longer. For such a prospect to become a hero, I would volunteer myself today. But joking aside, I am convinced that to better anyone's existence, and I don't mean necessarily economic conditions, a human being cannot prosper without ideals, genuine interests, love and enthusiasm as well as without recognition for achievements however small.

POWER OF SELF-RESPECT

I can't emphasize enough the power of spirit and self-respect the marvelous qualities, which rise above deprivation, humiliation and physical handicaps. There is a young, world-known violinist with both legs paralyzed. He walks on crutches, but he plays heavenly on his violin everywhere in the world, and there is no one who sees him as a cripple and he is the last one to think so of himself.

During the revolution in Russia five families were cramped together in one small apartment, hungry and deprived of most physical needs, heartily they welcomed me to join them. Even if I would have a choice I would join those wonderful people. The stories they told, the nobility of their minds, their humor and even their lack of appetite at the meals so that someone else eats their miserable portion all remain in my mind as the most wonderful experience. They were intellectuals with many hobbies and above all, professions they loved.

Professor Einstein played the violin, though not very well. But who knows if he would be the same Einstein with no violin at all, or God forbid, if he would play the violin expertly. Once after playing the violin, he wanted to know how he played: confused I said, "relatively well." We had a good laugh.

LEARNING AND EXCITEMENT

The other day I heard a prominent scientist say that the trouble with America is that the students don't want to learn, and the teachers don't want to teach. I don't agree with him. I would say that the students don't know how and what to learn, because the teachers, as if unaware of the many distractions and excitements the present life offers, stick to their subject matter which, though they know very well, they don't present in an exciting and inspiring manner to students. There is no such thing as a dull subject of study, and I knew mathematicians who thought mathematics poetic and magical just as I knew professors of art, philosophy and literature pedantic and dry enough to make it an insufferable bore. So it is with architecture and music as in politics. Things are changing rapidly, and as a politician becomes more a performer, so perhaps should be a teacher. A physicist can easier become something of a performer than an actor something of a physicist.

Because the process of aging is unstoppable, the vital interests can make this process not only undisturbing and little noticeable but even welcome. For as long as tomorrow will remain to be a new day for every man, the process of growing will not differ from the aging world. Only those who take the new day routinely for granted and act and feel that it will make a repetition of yesterday again, will not have to worry about aging because they are dead already.

GROWTH AND FEELINGS

As a musician I am often exposed to ideas on music advanced to me by non-musicians. Perhaps as a compensation or vengeance, I do the same to scientists. After all, according to Oscar Wilde, questions are never indiscreet. Only the answers. One of my ideas about retarding or eliminating aging altogether was to slow down the process of growing to the extreme. As long as something does not stop growing, it can't stop living. My son, who is a biologist, gave me only a nice smile as an answer. But then in a book by Ruth C. Ikerman I found the following statement:

"The human organism has to grow or die. Growth is always blocked in some way when feelings are blocked."

Well, there we are at feelings again — a word almost in disrepute nowadays. At schools a little chap with a feeling for a flower will be a sissy, and a big boy a hippy or something. Musicians will turn to sentimentalists or even to amateurs for feelings supposed to be contrary to intellectuality or scholarship. But I am all for it. I consider "feeling" as a base of all things. Obviously the word itself has many grades of meaning, just as definitions of good and bad. It's like a smile, which is a human prerogative. Cows don't smile. Of course some smiles are unattractive and even ugly, but there are more of the beautiful ones produced naturally and reflecting simple niceness. I like that un-dynamic word. It's unassuming and indisputable, and a nice person seldom disappoints and a nice person does not have to be a mediocrity.

AGING WITH JOY

If someone would take the effort to translate my English into English, he would read the following prescription for aging joyfully:

1. Know your strong points. Enjoy your qualities. Find them. Keep them. Develop them and remember that you don't have to be a genius to know your shortcomings: there are too many of them in every man, but it takes intelligence to recognize your qualities.

2. Look for the qualities in others. You will get along with more people, and they will like you better, too.

3. Don't be afraid to get conceited. There are no truly conceited people — only the stupid who act like one. I heard once a lady approaching a great artist explaining: "You are God." "Yes," he agreed, "but what a responsibility."

4. Everyone is too old for something, and no one is too old for everything. It goes in stages. As in sports, people over 30 are in the last stages of professional activity, in many more professions, people of the same age are at their beginning.

SEASONS OF LIFE

Man has many of the elements of nature, but when I erupt, I try to harm no one. It's possible to master and dominate oneself without being a fakir.

You don't have to consider yourself old, but it is reasonable to classify oneself in one of the four seasons — let's say winter. For even though you could not become spring again, there is nothing wrong with winter, with no mosquitoes, no heat of the summer or wetness of the fall. Of all ages I find babyhood the most hopeless one. One can't recall a thing, even the total dependence on the adults. And if later on in life you are curious about your early childhood, a psychoanalyst will search for a source of damages to confuse you further though one thing could be made clear, that love alone cannot teach or justify parents' actions.

Adolescence can't possibly be of any attraction to a so-called mature person, proof of which is that I still try hard to get out of it. The nice thing is to be what one is, especially because there is no choice. I am too busy to see the reality of things, and I had better see it right if I visit my grandchildren. I know they need my kisses or baby talk as a hole in the head, but I am free to give them something they can play with or something they need. It starts and ends right there not only with children but with the relations with the rest of humanity. Once it is established that you derive pleasure in doing things for others, no one would be disturbed by feelings of obligation and gratitude, which seldom fail to breed resentment.

Men are a herd of animals, but they cannot accept it. They cannot live as a herd of animals, so they had to create human rules, which are also a herd of rules but much more complex. They tried it for centuries in vain. Men never had good government, perfect rules of relationship between themselves; animals do. Man can be forced to obey, and to do or not to do something against his will is an everyday occurrence, but it is quite different to force oneself to do or not to do something because one wants to do it. In the first situation it means a submission and defeat in the second, it is victory.

THE REASONABLE REACTION

However, I know some extraordinary people whose skill in pleasing themselves will make every situation acceptable. In bad times they can always prove that in the past it was worse, and so alone the idea gives them a feeling of comfort. They are good at turning negatives to positives, including their own stupidity which they are clever enough in some instances to apply as self-defense and prevention of minor annoyances. Though the tendency to self-love is seldom attractive, it's more advantageous than self-dislike. I traveled for years with a person whose respect for his own body and soul reached extraordinary proportions. Although we lived in identical conditions, he fared much better than me. My breakfast was poor, his, delicious. My newspaper had bad news, his had promising. My air in the sleeping car was stuffy, his was fresh. My neighbors across the corridor were noisy, causing me sleepless night. The same noise from the same people put my friend peacefully to sleep. Even performing the same program, his concert was a delight, mine short of disaster. Right or wrong — he was the winner.

The right attitude, or let's call it reasonable reaction, to happenings in life can be achieved by self persuasion, and it's a good habit to smile at things or at least take them only relatively seriously. In every comedy one laughs at the misfortunes of others. One can laugh at one's own as well. Of course all this is in a psychological domain. The process of aging deals mostly with the physiological one, and I don't see a drastic separation of the two except for serious illness.

I knew a playwright, Mr. Sheldon, who was completely paralyzed and blind, but who could hear well and had a beautiful, clear voice. Bedridden, he kept his working schedule, dictating to his secretary, and he received friends. I happened to be full of grudges the day I met him, and although young in years, I felt old and depressed. But I left Mr. Sheldon a transformed man. He taught me to rejoice over the riches I possessed, and, through the years, to admire everyone who tries to overcome their weaknesses with the help of recognition of their own strength.

BITTERNESS: THE WORST COMPANY

The bitterness is the worst company an old person can possibly have. Bitterness creeps slowly into one, and it has many disguises, ingredients, and a whole arsenal of justifications, to point to each unfairness committed towards one during a long life. The accumulation of such unfairness and injustices, real and imaginary, is formidable and, unfortunately, easily memorizable. I think that one should forget them instead, but this is more difficult, though it is possible and it is worthwhile. Anything is good that helps to combat bitterness and self-pity.

Even a child could be of help in extreme cases: like one old grandfather whose hands were so shaky that at meals he would break china plates. The family decided to serve his meals at a separate table on a wooden plate. One day the head of the family saw his little son carving a wooden plate.

"Why are you doing it?" he asked.

The boy said, "I am making a plate for you to use when you will be grandfather's age."

The next meal the grandfather joined the family table.

Once I heard a story that might be taken as an example of dissatisfied-with-their-fate people. Everyone, as the story goes, was permitted to put all their sufferings, dissatisfactions and whatever into a bundle and place it in a huge heap among all other people's bundles. This done, everyone could choose any bundle instead of their own and bring it home. Very soon after, people rushed back wanting to get their own bundles back. No one could exist with other people's troubles, which are much worse than one's own.

There is an old joke — "as a cook he is a good astronomer." Perhaps you will say that as a gerontologist I am a good cellist. I would not mind, for vice versa — but it would be a big flop for my career as a musician.

PART V : THE RECORDINGS

One can virtually trace Piatigorsky's entire career — from his early Berlin period[1] to 1972 in Los Angeles — through his recordings. From anonymity in studio orchestras to his first solo recordings, one is aware of a special quality in the artist that penetrates through the primitive recording process before the age of the microphone. Those qualities emerge through a warm vibrato and a vocal approach to shifting. Nineteenth century vibrato tended to be narrow by today's standards, and shifting tended to reflect methodology rather than musical line; shifting was determined more by playing all notes within a position before venturing to another position.

We begin to hear the full richness of his sound in the late 1920s solo pieces done for German Parlophon, and later in the 1930s in London for EMI. His work with Columbia Records in the 1940s is quite variable in its quality, especially with the orchestral recordings; Piatigorsky was never happy with their reproduction. He felt that the solo cello was never focused or balanced properly, which prevented the full range of tone and expression from reaching the microphone. Things vastly improved when he signed with RCA, though little basic solo repertoire was made. This was also the beginning of the collaboration with Heifetz that produced dozens of recordings and is the subject of chapter 11, "The Heifetz-Piatigorsky Partnership: Concerts and Recordings."

From Salon to Solo: The Berlin Years, 1922–1930

The audio evidence of his general playing style dates from the time he was 19, during the acoustical period of recording (prior to 1926) in Berlin. Though the repertoire recorded was insignificant, it nonetheless shows the unique charm Piatigorsky could bring to the most ordinary music or ensemble. Perhaps the most striking feature of the early recordings is that they bring to light a mature artist with an unmistakable identity and a very sensuous approach to sound.

Piatigorsky's first recordings were made anonymously with violinists Edith Lorand, Georges Boulanger and Boris Kroyt, both in piano trios and in the orchestras they conducted. Most of the music they recorded was the light, popular pieces that suited the tastes of Roaring Twenties Germany.

Edith Lorand, Piatigorsky's first recording collaborator, was renowned as a concert soloist, having studied with the celebrated pedagogues Jenö Hubay and Carl Flesch, but her fame was made as the violin soloist and conductor of her own orchestra.[2] Lorand recorded several obscure short salon pieces with Piatigorsky and later in 1926 they recorded standard trio movements by Mendelssohn, Haydn and Goldmark with renowned pianist Michael Raucheisen.[3]

From 1922 to 1923, Piatigorsky's work at the Ruscho cafe led to a meeting with his next two collaborators, violinists Georges Boulanger and Boris Kroyt. Boulanger[4] worked at the competing Russian cafe in town, the Förster, at which Piatigorsky was probably occasionally employed. Both Kroyt and Boulanger had been recently brought on board with the new Vox Recording Company, which was anxious to compete in the lucrative salon and light music market. Piatigorsky, as a fellow refugee, was the natural choice for the "in house" cellist at Vox. The "in house" pianist was most likely Karol Szreter, a musician who frequently performed with both Kroyt and Piatigorsky throughout the decade.

The trio recordings with Boulanger and Piatigorsky are fascinating in their freedom and improvisation. Boulanger's playing is infectious and unpredictable, and its decadence thoroughly beguiling. In contrast, in their first recorded piece, Piatigorsky's playing is stiff and self-conscious.[5] However, later that day in the same recording session, the cellist matches him perfectly in an improvised Russian fantasy displaying the uncanny ability he had throughout his life to quickly assimilate new styles and adapt to different players.[6]

While Boulanger was able to primarily record his own gypsy style compositions, solos and orchestral tidbits, Kroyt's purpose for Vox was to fill the gap with the ubiquitous orchestral light music, all the rage of Weimar-era tastes. At Vox, Kroyt[7] recorded both as a solo violinist and as a conductor under the pseudonym "Tino Valeria." Vox created the Italian appellation, a commonly used gimmick, to increase sales by using exotic identities.[8] This was especially necessary since older established recording companies already had a head start producing endless popular repertoire. Kroyt recorded chamber tidbits with Piatigorsky and Szreter as the "Tino Valeria-Trio" (including an arrangement from Tchaikovsky's ubiquitous *The Seasons*—a work also recorded by Piatigorsky seven times), while the "Kroyt-Trio" presented standard serious repertoire.[9]

By 1924 Piatigorsky also had recorded several short solo works for Vox, but in 1927 he severed his relationship with them; it appeared that Vox had not paid him for his solo discs. Vox was in financial trouble though it kept a regular pace of monthly releases for two more years before bankruptcy. The Vox catalog was one of the most remarkable for its short life span. Artists like D'Albert, Földesy, Korngold, von Sauer, von Vecsey, and Grünfeld were among the historical figures who recorded for Vox.

Throughout the 1920s Piatigorsky continued to record on several labels. He completed six solo discs for Polydor/Polyphon, followed by three discs with the illustrious Wolfsthal-Kreutzer-Piatigorsky Trio from April and May 1925.

Hyperinflation in the 1920s affected everyone, including record companies. Even after the revaluation of the German Mark, Piatigorsky's 1925 Polydor recording of Tchaikovsky's *Rococo Variations* netted him the grand sum of 250 marks, then equal to approximately one U.S. dollar.

After the Polydor sessions of 1925, Piatigorsky continued to record with occasional ensembles in salon and traditional piano trios. After dropping work at Vox, he very often joined the popular bandleader and violinist Dajos Béla.[10] Though the Béla recordings are full of charm and warmth, and are wonderfully spontaneous, Piatigorsky feared that if he was directly associated with salon works he would not be taken seriously. As a rising artist, especially in Berlin, he wanted no confusion as to the direction his career was taking. He was also rather dismayed that he was still performing the café drivel he had played when he was a youngster in Yekaterinoslav and Moscow. Consequently, his recording agreement with German Parlophon and Odeon for the Béla series stipulated that Piatigorsky would remain anonymous, and that the discs could only mention the "Dajos Béla Trio." But as

Piatigorsky became well known, his name helped sell records. With the first issue of the Béla recordings, Parlophon/Odeon used his name on the labels. When he protested, the recording company promised to remove his name on future pressings and re-recorded the entire series. Fortunately Piatigorsky did not suffer being associated with such things as *Extase* and *L'Ideale*.

The distribution practice of the recording industry at that time was to create alternate takes (i.e., different performances) for export. These variables are a telling case study in improvisation by Piatigorsky. With each take, the cellist moves the tempos more freely and lines are altered in subtle ways. The other members in the group chiefly keep to their scripts and respond to his lead. One disc in particular is Massenet's *Meditation*, wherein Piatigorsky completely improvised his part.

During the mid-1920s Piatigorsky, Szreter and violinist Max Rostal occasionally worked for the Tri-Ergon label. They recorded the usual trio fare, and as before, kept their names out of the venture, revealed only as the Tri-Ergon Trio or Instrumental Trio.[11]

The cellist recorded many short pieces for German Parlophon/Odeon with Szreter, and almost all were done in one take. Piatigorsky's recordings continued to sell well into the 1930s, even though German record companies were pressured to eliminate Jewish performers from their catalogs after 1933. Though the economic crash of 1929 caused a 66 percent drop in the production of new records over the next four years, dealers continued to sell Jewish artists "under the counter" (especially to international buyers) even after Goebbels' 1938 ban of non-Aryan records.

England's His Masters Voice (HMV) began a series of memorable recordings with Piatigorsky in late 1933. These recordings are, as a whole, his best studio work. There seems to have been a relaxed atmosphere, no doubt influenced by the experienced Fred Gaisberg, recording pioneer par excellence. Great care was taken to record to the satisfaction of all, which was a rarity with Piatigorsky's recordings.

His usual partner in England was the excellent pianist Ivor Newton (1892–1981). Newton frequently performed and recorded with the finest artists living or touring in England. The two were great friends, and whenever Piatigorsky came to London they always visited no matter what the cellist's commitments might be. Together, they recorded several short pieces that are among his finest and capture the increasing elegance of Piatigorsky's artistry as he reached his thirtieth year.

In early 1934 Gaisberg planned for Piatigorsky to record the Beethoven sonatas with Schnabel. They recorded Beethoven's G Minor *Sonata* twice (in May and December) the second of which was released. Piatigorsky complained that the cello was not heard enough — his only complaint with the EMI series — and he again voiced concern before the release of the LP reissue in 1974. Aware of Piatigorsky's apprehension, the excellent engineer Anthony Griffith made the transfer. After listening to it played on a modern playback system, Piatigorsky was relieved (though he would not have minded more cello). Perhaps he was also sensitive to the criticisms of their recitals together where Schnabel was often accused of overpowering the cello. Nonetheless, this is a powerful, propulsive performance and full of bravura, but unfortunately it was their sole accomplishment together.

During the Schnabel recording session, Piatigorsky telephoned Newton:

> "Please do me a favor. Come to the recording studio and turn pages for Schnabel."
> "Surely Schnabel has a friend or pupil who can help him?" Newton responded.
> "Oh, do please come, and then Schnabel will talk to you. If you don't, he will talk to me all the time. I want to concentrate on playing the cello, not on listening to him." Newton

arrived at the studio in time to hear the pianist berating the piano tuner. "What have you done to this piano? Yesterday it was beautiful, now I cannot play a note on it. What have you done?" Turning to Newton, Schnabel began a discourse on Wagner, whom he thought a poor composer. After the session Newton asked Piatigorsky, "Tell me, why is Schnabel so down on Wagner?" "That is easy to explain. Wagner has never written him any piano sonatas." In listening to their playbacks separately, Piatigorsky remarked, "The only way to record with Schnabel is to put the cello up against the microphone and record the piano from Paris." Then Schnabel's turn, "Of course, with HMV it seems to be a tradition that the piano should never be heard."[12]

Nineteen thirty-four also saw Piatigorsky's benchmark recording of the Schumann Concerto with the London Philharmonic under the baton of former cellist-turned-conductor John Barbirolli. The circumstances of the session are fascinating, since this was the first commercial recording made without breaks, i.e., performed continuously as in a concert performance. In the 78 rpm era (roughly until 1950), recorded lengths were limited to about three to four minutes at a time, depending upon the diameter of the disc (10 or 12 inches). Conductors and soloists had to identify and create breaks in the composition so that one side of the disc could end and the next begin logically and musically. This was disturbing to the performers, since their tempo and dynamics had to remain consistent while waiting between takes for the cue to start. HMV came to the conclusion that it was better to have two recording machines running, one beginning precisely as another ended. Noncommercial radio transcription discs were already being used this way to record concerts and spoken events for rebroadcast. Piatigorsky recalled the following:

> In a busy London season there was no time for rehearsal or even for timing the duration of the sides, so the engineers devised for this occasion their own system of using several turntables, one taking over for another as it faded out at the end of a disc. It enabled us to record the entire concerto without interruption with only a single incident, when Mr. Goossens, the oboist of the orchestra, yelled "bravo" at the end of the concerto with the red light still on. It was the sincerest bravo I ever heard, and I am rather pleased it was impossible to totally erase it. I remember Casals, Feuermann and others were waiting for me in London for tea. I came in late with my cello. "Why?" they asked me. "I just recorded the Schumann Concerto," I said. There was tremendous laughter. They said it was impossible. I was one of the first. And today — every little girl records and plays it. For a long time it was considered practically unplayable.[13]

Goossens recalled the incident with a bit more detail. After the complete play through, Piatigorsky asked for a retake starting from the cadenza which then leads seamlessly to the coda of the concerto:

> Like all artists he was capable of having an off-day, and on this occasion he was dissatisfied with his performance of the cadenza. I felt sympathy for him. After several attempts he finally decided to break and try later. When we had assembled again the recording producer recommended we do a rehearse run before making the recording. The tension was high and Piatigorsky played brilliantly, throwing off the cadenza with superb artistry. I was so carried away that I could not restrain myself from shouting "Bravo" in a very loud voice. All was silent for a brief second. Then the producer came into the studio ashen-faced and full of despair. They had recorded it!

After the initial dismay had passed, Piatigorsky said: "I can't play it again." But he held a simple solution: "Simply put on the label

'CELLO — PIATIGORSKY
BRAVO!— GOOSSENS.'"[14]

Piatigorsky inserts his own cadenza in the concerto, which according to the cellist, is based on a sketch in Schumann's own hand. Writing to his brother Shura, he elaborated:

> The Cadenza for Schumann's Concerto that you transcribed from my record is more Schumann's than Piatigorsky's. I was friendly with some of Schumann's relatives (all old people) who lived in Frankfurt. From them I found some sketches written in pencil of that cadence, which were made by Schumann himself. I followed them, trying to restore his handwriting as closely as I could. I tried to follow his precise idea. I used to have that sketch, but it was taken during the war along with many other things.[15]

The Schumann Concerto has always had a special place in his repertoire, and has left indelible impressions on many. Nathan Milstein recalled a particular performance with Reiner and the New York Philharmonic in 1943:

> Grisha's playing was incredibly emotional. Piatigorsky created an atmosphere, as if he were writing the music before our eyes. Sitting in a box with Fritz Kreisler, Mrs. Kreisler and Raya Garbousova.... It was a reverie, a dream.... We were all spellbound, especially in the slow movement, when one could notice Kreisler's lips twitching. After the performance was over, Kreisler sat a long time immobile. When he turned to me I saw his eyes were red, from tears. He was embarrassed. Like all of us, he had been terribly moved by the playing of Piatigorsky, a great and unique artist. This, with Chaliapin's "Boris Godounov" in St Petersburg in 1916, [was] one of the most profound musical experiences of my life.[16]

In Paris during the summer of 1936, pianist Arthur Rubinstein joined Piatigorsky in recording the Brahms E Minor Sonata. This was an excellent collaboration and the two saw eye to eye on Brahms' organic unity and took a no nonsense approach. It contrasts sharply with their 1966 recording, which is both expansive and regal. The two versions are fascinating in their contrasts and similarities.

From November 1936 until late 1939 Piatigorsky did not record. It was a time of political turmoil and not until after he settled in the United States (September 1939), did he sign an agreement with Columbia Records. With this new venue, he recorded a great deal, though much of his work remained unissued. The cellist was not at home in the studio, and tried to make recordings as true to performance as possible. Piatigorsky viewed retakes as dishonest, and stubbornly resisted doing them. His recordings paid a price for this honesty compared to most artists who made retakes to their content. Minor flaws were often not "corrected" in sessions during the Columbia years, and the cellist simply rejected anything he felt was not up to his standards. Some scheduled sessions were scrapped entirely if he felt it was not good. In May of 1940, Robert Casadesus and Piatigorsky attempted to record the Chopin Sonata but the session was scrapped. Apparently neither Piatigorsky nor Casadesus could agree on the style of playing the work.[17] Another session from October 1941 was dumped that included his arrangement of Paganini's *La Campanella*. This is a particular loss as the piece was one of his most spectacular recital finales.

The Saint-Saëns Concerto was recorded with the Chicago Symphony and Frederick Stock in March 1940, and the Dvorak Concerto was recorded with the Minneapolis Orchestra under Dimitri Mitropoulos in April; but the latter was never issued. Amazingly, Columbia discarded their original discs in 1990, including the Dvorak session. Why the library was not saved or given to a repository is a mystery.

While Ivor Newton recorded a few discs at Columbia Records with Piatigorsky, the cellist had established a regular touring partner for the U.S., Valentin Pavlovsky (1907–1959). Pavlovsky and Piatigorsky began working together in 1929 on their first American tour. They recorded frequently in the 1940s, and Pavlovsky also toured and recorded with many other artists, including Geraldine Farrar and Milstein. Piatigorsky and Pavlovsky's only extended recorded work was the Shostakovich Sonata, a fine example of their partnership. Pavlovsky's poor health and a car accident prevented them from working together much after 1945.

In 1940 Piatigorsky also began working with pianist Ralph Berkowitz. Their association became the longest of all his partners. Berkowitz and Piatigorsky recorded from 1940 to 1956 and played concerts together until 1970, an association of some thirty years. Their work is extensive and notable for its breadth and scope of repertoire.

In 1941 a very beautiful recording of Strauss' *Don Quixote* with Reiner and the Pittsburgh Symphony was made. Henri Temianka and Vladimir Bakaleinikoff played the violin and viola portrayals of Dulcinea and Sancho Panza. Here the solo work is very poetic all around. This Sancho is a unique portrayal of the unsophisticated but good-natured valet, forgoing the usual elegant viola playing. Bakaleinikoff accomplishes some of the "quixotic" shifts of character with limited vibrato. Also, the unison string sections of the orchestra use matching fingerings, which gives the broad melodies a unified personality.

Unfortunately, little of the standard recital works have been issued. Waiting to be heard are the sonatas by Grieg, Debussy, Barber, Brahms, and the E-flat Variations of Beethoven, as well as many short pieces. These performances are vintage Piatigorsky, bursting with largesse, strength, and the fantastic richness of sound for which he was so well known.

In 1946 the cellist again recorded the Dvorak Concerto with Ormandy and the Philadelphia Orchestra. The balance and sound quality on this recording is not flattering to the soloist, and it further suffers from few retakes. The choice of recorded breaks (stopping every four minutes) was also unfortunate; starting a new take in the middle of passagework was certainly erroneous. Nevertheless, this is an interesting performance and still captures some of Piatigorsky's essence.

Piatigorsky and an enthusiastic Samuel Barber approved a 1947 recording of the composer's Sonata for release. It was announced along with Piatigorsky's 1945 recording of the Brahms F Major Sonata, yet neither came out. In the case of the Brahms, when Columbia eventually did want to release it, Piatigorsky felt he would be happier to simply rerecord it. His unreleased recordings of the Saint-Saëns Concerto and Bloch's *Schelomo* still await hearings. To his annoyance, he felt very rushed when he recorded the Saint-Saëns, his final recording with Columbia, in April 1949.

After ten years with Columbia, Piatigorsky wrote to Goddard Lieberson, the soon-to-be vice president of Columbia Records, asking when his contract with the company would expire. Piatigorsky was never happy with Columbia's recording methods, especially with orchestral recordings, and their distant microphone placement. He was also unhappy that much of his effort remained unreleased even after approval. In spite of his warm friendship with Lieberson, he asked to be relieved of another signing.

Upon completing his Columbia contract, Piatigorsky signed with RCA in April of 1950. At the same time he also changed managers, dropping Arthur Judson (Columbia Concerts) for Sol Hurok (Hurok Attractions). His first assignment was the trio recordings with Rubinstein and Heifetz in August. (Details regarding the Heifetz recordings will be found in chapter 11.) By September 1950, he and pianist Ralph Berkowitz began their first sessions at RCA. Piatigorsky remained with RCA for eighteen years, ending with the last of the Heifetz-Piatigorsky series in 1968.

Still in the RCA (now BMG/Sony) vaults are second attempts at the Debussy Sonata and Beethoven's E-flat Variations and short pieces, all from 1950. The G Major Solo Suite of Bach was recorded twice (in 1955 and 1959), in an initial attempt at recording all of the suites, but this was never completed.

Piatigorsky's sensuous 1951 recording of the Saint-Saëns Concerto with Fritz Reiner and the RCA Symphony Orchestra was recorded in Chicago. The orchestra was essentially the Chicago Symphony Orchestra. The cello section on this recording was remarkable in that it included Frank Miller, Janos Starker, and Laszlo Varga. The first stand of viola was none other than William Lincer and Carlton Cooley.

It must have been a joyous moment when Piatigorsky and his close friend Nathan Milstein recorded the Brahms Double Concerto in 1951. Both had frequently played the work together, and as soloists in the concerto at Robin Hood Dell, the summer home of the Philadelphia Orchestra, a recording was planned. The conductor was again Fritz Reiner, a new RCA artist along with Piatigorsky and Milstein. However, the Philadelphia Orchestra had an exclusive contract to record with Eugene Ormandy (a Columbia Records artist). By designating the orchestra as the Robin Hood Dell Symphony Orchestra, it posed no breach. This is a passionate performance of a work Milstein was not always happy to play. "The cello has everything; it starts every tune!" he complained.[18] The three musketeers recorded only twice in ensemble together: Milstein and Piatigorsky in the Brahms concerto, and Milstein and Horowitz in Brahms' Violin Sonata in D Minor.

In the bygone days of recording, singers and instrumentalists frequently recorded together. Among the most enduring were Enrico Caruso with Mischa Elman, John McCormack with Fritz Kreisler, and Alma Gluck with Efrem Zimbalist. Since so many of his artists appeared on RCA, Sol Hurok had the idea of pairing up members of his stable on a recording called *Great Combinations*. He designed instrumentalists to join singers in interesting tidbits: Jan Peerce with Elman, Ezio Pinza with Milstein, Robert Merrill with Menuhin, and top billing going to Marian Anderson and Piatigorsky. The repertoire included Anderson's most familiar numbers, "Carry Me Back to Old Virginy" and "My Old Kentucky Home." Piatigorsky sketched out obbligato parts from the scores and recorded them together with Anderson's usual pianist, Franz Rupp.

A follow up album was released entitled *S. Hurok Presents*, the familiar banner for any artist on his roster. Here RCA lifted short works from previously recorded albums. Tchaikovsky's *Valse Sentimentale* was Piatigorsky's contribution.

Berkowitz and Piatigorsky recorded sonatas by Bach and Prokofiev in the summer of 1953 at Tanglewood. It was an unusual venue in which to record, yet it yielded Piatigorsky's favorite recording thus far in his career, the Prokofiev Sonata. Berkowitz remembered: "RCA spent a lot of money to make the Red Barn at Tanglewood into a recording studio. The very first — and I think the only — record made there was Piatigorsky and myself. Prokofiev and Bach. I remember there were birds that flew in singing when they heard the music, and the producer had to get one of our garden men with a huge, high broom to swish it up in the air to frighten the birds away."[19]

Piatigorsky toured extensively in the fall of 1954, traveling much of Europe. One of his commitments was to record all the Beethoven Sonatas with Solomon in London. This was an amicable partnership, but it suffers from a certain stiffness. "Solomon is a fine man and a great artist. I have great hope that the recordings will satisfy us both."[20] However, Piatigorsky found that Mrs. Solomon hovered over him like a fierce protective mother. She felt that the cello sonata project was a nuisance because it interrupted Solomon's recordings of the complete Beethoven piano sonatas (which he ultimately never finished due to a stroke). Whenever Piatigorsky made a suggestion, she made an unpleasant fuss.[21]

HMV (part of EMI) in England had a long-standing agreement with RCA Victor to produce these performances in the U.S. Shortly after their issue, RCA terminated the association; consequently, the records were not brought into general circulation in the U.S. For years these discs were collector's items and fetched high prices.

In 1955 Piatigorsky completed the Beethoven series, with the three sets of Variations, partnering with pianist-composer Lukas Foss. In June 1958 Foss rejoined Piatigorsky in the recording of the composer's *Capriccio* for cello and piano. The performance of *Capriccio* is exemplary and bounces along infectiously. The remainder of the disc included two works with which the cellist was closely associated: Stravinsky's *Pulcinella* Suite and the Debussy Sonata. The Stravinsky suffers from a lack of editing, and the Debussy seems less interesting compared to Piatigorsky's earlier efforts of 1947 and 1950.

Piatigorsky and Berkowitz recorded the Hindemith Sonata (1948) and the Barber Sonata (once again) in 1956. (Unfortunately, Hindemith's Variations on "A Frog He Went A-Courting" was not recorded, although Piatigorsky had commissioned it as well as the sonata.) The Hindemith Sonata is one of the composer's strongest works. Berkowitz recounts a curious mishap in recording the sonata: "I remember when we recorded the Hindemith Cello Sonata (1948) for RCA (and, by the way, we premiered the work at Tanglewood) to everyone's horror it was discovered that eight bars had been lost in editing the tape. I had to go from Philadelphia to Los Angeles in order to record those eight measures."[22]

Piatigorsky's sonata work from July 1965 with Rudolf Firkusny (Prokofiev and Chopin) is disappointing in that Piatigorsky was not in ideal shape for a recording. He was not quite over a bout with mononucleosis and it had left him weak. It is unfortunate that these sessions were not rescheduled, because just a few months later, back in the studio with Leonard Pennario, the effort is outstanding all around. Peccadilloes aside, the Firkusny recordings won a Grammy for 1966.

The Piatigorsky and Pennario recording of Mendelssohn's D Major Sonata glistens; it is facile yet sings constantly. Pennario's legato is perfectly suited to Piatigorsky's playing. The Strauss Sonata is another triumph, the slow movement being truly one of his most successful recordings. It is an important account not only for the playing, but also for the cellist's connection with Strauss. Piatigorsky and Strauss played the sonata together in informal settings and had been friends for several months before the takeover of Hitler. Piatigorsky stated that Strauss was very fond of the work.

In October of 1966, Piatigorsky and Rubinstein were reunited to record the Brahms Sonatas. Though Rubinstein had never played the F Major sonata, Piatigorsky was unconcerned. *Time* magazine noted: "Artur," he says, "will read the score on the plane to California, and he will make it sink into his mind and into his fingers, and when he arrives, he will know it better than I, who have played it all my life."[23] The second sonata however, is a mixed bag. There are memorable moments to be sure, but the balance is a bit piano heavy and ensemble problems exist in the Adagio movement. However, the recording seems to capture a concert performance rather than a play-through.

A brief return to Columbia Records (now Sony/BMG) in April 1972 consisted of recording Anton von Webern's complete works for cello and piano with Charles Rosen. These were to be Piatigorsky's last recordings. As a young Berliner in the mid–1920s, Piatigorsky was eager to demonstrate his intellectual austerity beyond his brilliant technical and musical accomplishments. Apropos, Piatigorsky premiered Webern's *Drei Kleine Stücke,* op. 11, there in 1926. The German capital was not prepared for Webern's music, which may have seemed like silly, vaporous gestures. Since its remarkable brevity is under three minutes long, Piatigorsky presented it twice. The performance was met with laughter. Webern, though not present, was not surprised to hear about the audience's reaction. He felt his music was not ready to be heard; he thought it belonged to the future.

Knowing Piatigorsky's interest in Webern, Hans Moldenauer, the distinguished musicologist and collector, brought three unpublished early works to Piatigorsky's attention. Discovered in 1965, they represented both Webern's first compositions and the transitional period before his studies with Arnold Schoenberg.

Webern was also a cellist of modest accomplishment, and certainly played his two early pieces, *Zwei Stücke* (1899). Almost Wagnerian in intent, these elemental snippets tell little of his future path, while the terse Cello Sonata (1914) telegraphs the logical line to serialism. Piatigorsky premiered the three unpublished works, and performed the Op. 11 on June 3, 1970, with Victor Babin at the Cleveland Institute of Music.

Charles Rosen recalled their recording session:

> The only time that a recording in which I took part was tampered with — that is, where something on the tape was altered by machinery, was in the second of the four pieces of Anton von Webern for cello and piano that I recorded in Hollywood with Gregor Piatigorsky for the album of Webern's complete works planned by Pierre Boulez [Three Little Pieces, Op. 11]. Piatigorsky was a very grand figure, generous and hospitable, with a wonderful command of both his instrument and the music and he had in fact, given the first performance of these four pieces by Webern (although he confessed to me that at the premiere [in Berlin] he had tried to play from memory and had failed with one of the pieces more or less reinventing it on the spot). He had, however recently suffered a spell of mononucleosis and easily became tired. When we did a couple of takes of the second piece, I told him that he was a little late with one pizzicato sforzando a few bars after the beginning of the piece.
>
> "Perhaps you are early," he suggested amiably.
>
> "In a way," I replied, "because there is an accelerando in the two beats before the pizzicato and you continue in strict time."
>
> "Let us forget about the accelerando," he proposed.
>
> "But the piece is only a few seconds long," I objected. "Without the accelerando not very much is happening."
>
> "All right," he said grudgingly with a resigned smile, and we tried twice more.
>
> The second time the pizzicato was right in place, but somewhat soft and a bit timid. I thought it unnecessary to bother him further, but back in New York where the tape was edited, I made a prudent adjustment. The recording had been produced with two tracks: one microphone on the piano, one on the cello (perhaps there was a third track for room sound). We re-recorded the tape with the cello track alone raised two decibels louder until the pizzicato, and then quickly lowered the volume of sound right after the pizzicato back to the original level. We then spliced the new tape from the pizzicato to the end, producing it fine for the cello on that note — I never told Piatigorsky what we had done, but he seemed pleased with the recording.

What Might Have Been

A fascinating bit of recorded history is demonstrated in Philip Hart's biography of conductor Fritz Reiner. During the Philadelphia Orchestra's 1931-32 season, J.P. Maxfield of the Electrical Research Products division of Western Electric brought sound technicians to the Academy of Music for a series of experimental recordings.

These recordings demonstrated a degree of audio fidelity then unknown in commercial techniques; some were actually in stereophonic sound. Reiner, then assistant to Leopold

Stokowski, was very interested in these experiments and may have had test recordings made with Piatigorsky, Heifetz and Elisabeth Rethberg. These test recordings were to be made before hiring the orchestra, and Reiner inquired about union fees for the orchestra members. The fate of these experiments is unknown. However, a concert was recorded in stereo that included Horowitz in portions of the Tchaikovsky Concerto.[24]

In early 1934 there were plans with Fred Gaisberg at HMV to record the Beethoven trios with Schnabel and Huberman, as well as the Beethoven sonatas with Schnabel. Only one Beethoven sonata was made and the recording of the trios never happened. (It is a pity that the Schnabel-Flesch-Piatigorsky Trio never entered the recording studio as well.)

In 1939, Columbia proposed recordings, including the Brahms Double Concerto, with Piatigorsky, Milstein, Frederick Stock and the Chicago Symphony. Later, in 1946, the same work was proposed with Joseph Szigeti. Lieberson referred to the Szigeti project as the "double hernia" concerto as it suffered from so many negotiations that the project eventually died. A Schumann Concerto with either Ormandy or Rodzinski was planned for 1947 along with Bloch's Schelomo (the latter was recorded with Ormandy but remains unissued).

By the summer of 1952, pianist William Kapell, Heifetz and Piatigorsky had played informally together a number of times and were very happy with their collaboration. At Heifetz and Piatigorsky's request, RCA planned to record a trio series with Kapell. (By then, Rubinstein would have nothing to do with Heifetz.)

In 1953, RCA proposed that Kapell and Piatigorsky record the complete Beethoven Sonatas, the Rachmaninoff and Mendelssohn D Major Sonata, and complete the Brahms sonatas with Heifetz (only one was made). The terrible and untimely death of Kapell in an airplane crash on his way back to the U.S. from a tour of Australia ended what would have been a historic collaboration. According to producer Jack Pfeiffer, "Heifetz loved Willy. He never forgave him for dying young."[25] Kapell loved Piatigorsky and wrote to him that year with gushing praise: "It was a joy and happiness to see you and play with you again.... I was as always deeply touched and moved by your beautiful and passionate playing.... The way you play your cello is one of the most wonderful single things in the whole world.... What a wonderful thing to do, when one can do it so divinely!... [T]here is *no one* who can play the way you do."[26]

In 1957, negotiations were initiated by RCA to record Horowitz and Piatigorsky in the Rachmaninoff Sonata. Piatigorsky agreed to the project, but it was a difficult period for Horowitz, and despite their long-standing camaraderie, Horowitz was unable to commit. This is a particular loss, owing to their friendship and collaboration with Rachmaninoff. Horowitz preferred recording at home for much of the 1950s, and any disturbance of his controlled environment, even by old friends, was not to be. The same was true with Horowitz's oldest recital partner, Milstein; only one recording was made, yet many discussions to record more repertory did not yield results. In addition, a proposal to record sonatas with Heifetz and Horowitz was made, and although they agreed to do so, their war of egos prevented either one from traveling to New York (Heifetz) or to Los Angeles (Horowitz).

Composer Miklós Rózsa remembered an evening that eventually led to a recording, but it failed to persuade Piatigorsky to participate:

> Leonard [Pennario] often gives chamber soirees, and the best musicians in Hollywood are invited to play. Piatigorsky was often there with his cello and invariably had the party for forty or fifty guests laughing with his wonderful stories. On one occasion Pennario gathered a group together to play my Quintet, Op.2, which dated from my conservatory days. We had innumerable rehearsals all those years ago, but these artists, after a single run-through, gave

the most thrilling performance. The head of a recording company was there and wanted to record the piece. Pennario and I both tried to persuade Piatigorsky to take part in the recording, as he had just played so magnificently, but he begged to be excused — he was no longer well, and feared the strain of recording.[27]

PART VI : APPENDICES

A Guide to the Discography and Filmography

The discography is organized into six categories: **Composer**—*Composition*—Performers—*Recording Date or Issue*—Record Label and its catalog number—[Matrix and take number]

Beethoven, Ludwig van (1770–1827)
Sonata no.2 in g, op. 5, no.2. Artur Schnabel, piano *12/6,16/34* HMV DB 2391–93 [2B 5192-3, 6198-3, 6199-3, 6200-4], RCA M 281, Victor JD 486-488 (Jap.) [7201-4, 7202-3], Recital Records 406, Seraphim 60300, EMI C053 3078, Music & Arts CD 674, Pearl GEMM CD 9447, Pavil CD, Naxos Historical 8.110640, Shinseido Classics GGR 7140

After the initial publication, subsequent issues are listed chronologically, including other venues, formats, and reissues. CD issues are listed last.
CD labels: BMG, RCA/BMG, Amadeus BMG, RCA/BVCC, RCA SACD, Pearl, Music & Arts, Naxos, Shinseido, Palladio, Testament, Arlecchino, Maestro History, Coffret Longbox, Andromeda, Biddulph, Cascavelle, Pavil, Sony MHK, Documents, and Quadromania.
Recordings prior to 1950 were first issued in 78 rpm, both in 10 and 12 inch diameter. The 10 and 12 inch Long Playing (LP) 33.3 rpm era began with Columbia in 1948. RCA followed with the introduction of 7 inch 45 rpm discs but soon joined the rest of the industry with 33.3 LPs. The next format was stereo in the mid–1950s, then tape and cassettes in rapid succession. Formats continued to develop reaching the Compact Disc (CD) in the 1980s.
Piatigorsky began recording in the 78 rpm era in Europe with the Berlin labels: Parlophon (prefix P), Odeon (prefix O), Polydor (prefix D), Polyphon, Schallplatte Grammophon, Vox, and Tri-Ergon.
The history of these firms is quite complicated: Parlophon shared some of their catalog with Odeon and Parlophone (prefix R and E) in export; Parlophone was the English version of Parlophon for many of Piatigorsky's discs.
German Odeon also shared some of their catalog with English Parlophone.
From 1933 through 1936 GP recorded in London for HMV/EMI, followed by Columbia (U.S.) from 1940 through 1949. His longest contract was with RCA from 1950 to 1968.
The filmography reads like the discography: **Composer**—*Composition*— date of production — *Title*— Sources ending with DVD availability.

Appendix A: Discography

Dall'Abaco, Evaristo Felice (1675–1742)
Trio-Sonate in e, op. 3 no. 6 (Adagio), Edith Lorand Trio *9/12/23* Parlophon (unissued) [6435]

Arcadelt, Jacques (1504–1568)
Ave Maria (with harmonium and Hammerflügel), Edith Lorand, violin *6/7/23* Parlophon P-1555 [6385], Parlophone E-10217

Arensky, Anton (1861–1906)
Trio no. 1 in d, op. 32. Leonard Pennario, piano Jascha Heifetz, violin *10/17/63* RCA LM/LSC/LSCSD 2867 [PR-A5 4586-89], RCA SB 6661, BMG 61758; (*Elegia, Scherzo* only), Kroyt-Trio: Karol Szreter, piano Boris Kroyt, violin *1924* Vox 06141 [1424A, 1425A]

Bach, Johann Sebastian (1685–1750)
Sinfonia no.3 in D, BWV 789, Jascha Heifetz, violin William Primrose, viola *8/18/60* RCA LM/LSC/LSCSD 2563 [L2-RB-3318], RCA ACL1-4947, GD 87964, RCA FTC 2076(tape), RCA 7964-2-RG(CD), BMG 61768, RCA BVCC 37118 (Jap.)
Sinfonia no.4 in d, BWV 790, Jascha Heifetz, violin William Primrose, viola *8/16/60* RCA LM/LSC/LSCSD 2563 [L2-RB-3316], RCA ACL1-4947, GD 87964, RCA FTC 2076(tape), RCA 7964-2-RG(CD), BMG 61768, RCA BVCC 37118 (Jap.)
Sinfonia no.9 in f, BWV 795, Jascha Heifetz, violin William Primrose, viola *8/15/60* RCA LM/LSC/LSCSD 2563 [L2-RB-3317], RCA ACL1-4947, GD 87964, RCA FTC 2076(tape), RCA 7964-2-RG(CD), BMG 61768, RCA BVCC 37118 (Jap.)
Sonata no.2 in D, BWV 1028, Ralph Berkowitz, piano *8/14,15/53* RCA LM 1792 [E3-RC-3305-1, 3306-1, 3307-1, 3308-1, 3309-1, 3310-1], RCA LVT 1037
Suite no.1 in G, BWV 1007. (mvts 1,2,4,5,6), *11/7/55* RCA (unissued) [F2-RB-5896-99]; (complete), *10/19,20/59* RCA (unissued) [K2-RB-4691-96]
Suite no.3 in C, BWV 1009. (Bourree), *1949* Kultur DVD 1101; (*Gigue*), *c.1934* HMV (unissued)
Suite no.5 in c, BWV 1011(Sarabande), 5/29/47 Columbia (unissued) [XCO 37832]
Suite no. 6 in D, BWV 1012 (Sarabande arr.), Edith Lorand Trio *11/6/23* Parlophon (unissued) [6545]

Bach – arr. Charles Gounod (1818–1893)
Ave Maria (Meditation). Grete Mancke, mezzo soprano, Edith Lorand Trio, Dominator harmonium & Hammerflügel *11/23/23* Parlophon P 1586 [6569], Parlophone E10106; Karol Szreter, piano *6/3/30* Odeon 2990 [Be 9019], Parlophone R862, Odeon (Arg.) 193582, Columbia J5489 (Jap.), Decca 20010, 20019

Bach, Leonhard Emil (1849–1902)
Frühlingserwachen, Orchester Georges Boulanger (GP obb.) *c.1926* Vox 8624 [2511-G]

Bakalainikow, Mischa R. (1890–1960)[1]
Russische Romanze Habe Mitlied mit mir... Karol Szreter? piano, Georges Boulanger, violin *3/24* Vox 01555 [1676-A]

Bänsch, Kurt
Andante religioso, Edith Lorand Trio *11/14/23* Parlophon P 1653 [6559]
Romantique, Edith Lorand Trio *11/16/23* Parlophon P 1653 [6562]

Barber, Samuel (1910–1981)
Sonata, op. 6. Ralph Berkowitz, piano *5/29/47* Columbia (unissued) [XCO 37833-37]; Ralph Berkowitz, piano *1/6/56* RCA LM 2013 [G2RB-408-2]

Beethoven, Ludwig van (1770–1827)
Minuet no.2 in G, Wo010 (arr.Béla). Karol Szreter, piano Dajos Béla, violin *3/8/27* Parlophone E 10618 [xxB 7646]; Karol Szreter, piano Dajos Béla, violin *2/28/28* Odeon O.6608 AA.212004 [xxB 7646²]
Sonata no.1 in F, op. 5, no.1, Solomon, piano *10/5/54* RCA LM 6120 [F2RP-3162], HMV/EMI ALPS 1345 [2XEA 596], La Voix de son Maitre FALP 430-432, EMI/RCA RL 731/RLS 731, EMI 1 C 147-63382/89, Testament SBT 2158, Palladio PD 4194/95
Sonata no.2 in g, op. 5, no.2. Artur Schnabel, piano *5/9/34* HMV (unissued) [2B6192, 6198/200, 7201/2]; Artur Schnabel, piano *12/6,16/34* HMV DB 2391-93 [2B 5192-3, 6198-3], RCA M 281 [6199-3, 6200-4], Victor JD 486-488 (Jap.) [7201-4, 7202-3], Recital Records 406, Seraphim 60300, EMI C053 3078, Music & Arts CD 674, Pearl GEMM CD 9447, Pavil CD, Naxos Historical 8.110640, Shinseido Classics GGR 7140; Solomon, piano *10/11,12/54* RCA LM 6120 [F2RP-3163], HMV/EMI ALPS 1346 [2XEA 597], La Voix de son Maitre FALP 430-432, EMI/RCA RL 731/RLS 731, EMI 1 C 147-63382/89, Testament SBT 2158, Palladio PD 4194/95
Sonata no.3 in A, op. 69, Solomon, piano *10/12,14/54* RCA LM 6120 [F2RP-3164], HMV/EMI ALPS 1346 [2XEA 598], La Voix de son Maitre FALP 430-432, EMI/RCA RL 731/RLS 731, EMI 1 C 147-63382/89, Testament SBT 2158, Palladio PD 4194/95
Sonata no.4 in C, op. 102, no.1, Solomon, piano *10/8,11/54* RCA LM 6120 [F2RP-3166], HMV/EMI ALPS 1347 [2XEA 599], La Voix de son Maitre FALP 430-432, EMI/RCA RL 731/RLS 731, EMI 1 C 147-63382/89, Smithsonian R032LGR-9270, Smithsonian RC 032-4X5L-9265(cassette), Melodiya D17717 (10"), Testament SBT 2158, Palladio PD 4194/95
Sonata no.5 in D, op. 102, no.2. Ralph Berkowitz, piano *6/6/45* Columbia X 258 [XCO 34904-07], Columbia 71709-11, LX 1136-37; Solomon, piano *10/4-5,12/54* RCA LM 6120 [F2RP-3167], HMV ALPS 1347 [2XEA 600], La Voix de son Maitre FALP 430-432, Melodiya D17717 (10"), EMI/RCA RL/RLS 731, EMI 1 C 147-63382/89, Testament SBT 2158, Palladio PD 4194/95
Trio in Eb, op. 1, no.1, Jacob Lateiner, piano Jascha Heifetz, violin *3/23/64* RCA LM/LSC 2770 [RR-A5-3227-30], RCA 645.029 (Fr.), BMG 61761, RCA BVCC 37119-21 (Jap.)
Trio in c, op. 1, no.3 (Minuetto), Leonid Kreutzer, piano Josef Wolfsthal, violin *5-6/25* Polydor 66212 [1954 as], Grammophon B29077
Trio in Bb, op. 11 (Adagio), Leonid Kreutzer, piano Josef Wolfsthal, violin *5-6/25* Polydor 66212 [1950 as], Grammophon B29076
Trio in Eb, op. 70, no.2, Leonard Pennario, piano Jascha Heifetz, violin *10/3,4/63* Vox Cum Laude VCL 9041/VS 6339, RCA/BMG 61759 [PR-A3-4529-4532], RCA BVCC 37119-21 (Jap.)
Trio in Eb, op. 3, Jascha Heifetz, violin William Primrose, viola *3/28,29/57* RCA LM 2180 [H2-RB-2672-75], RCA CRM6-2264, R42474(6), RCA SER 5729/31, RCA 630459, BMG 61741, RCA BVCC 37119-21 (Jap.)
Trio in D, op. 8 Serenade Jascha Heifetz, violin William Primrose, viola *8/15,22/60* RCA LM/LSC/LSCSD 2550 [L2-RB-2509-13], RCA CRM6-2264, R42474(6), BMG 61756, RCA SER 5729/31, RCA A630640, GD87870, RCA 7870-2-RG, RCA BVCC 37119-21 (Jap.)
Trio in G, op. 9, no.1, Jascha Heifetz, violin William Primrose, viola *3/27/57* RCA LM 2186 [H2-RB-2668-71], RCA CRM6-2264, RCA SER 5729/31, BMG 61741, RCA BVCC 37119-21 (Jap.)
Trio in D, op. 9, no.2, Jascha Heifetz, violin William Primrose, viola *8/17,22/60* RCA LM/LSC 2563 [L2-RB-2505-08], GD 87873, RCA ACL1-4947, RCA FTC 2076(tape), RCA SER 5729/31, RCA 7873-2-RG, BMG 61773, RCA CT GK 87873, RCA BVCC 37119-21 (Jap.)
Trio in c, op. 9, no.3, Jascha Heifetz, violin William Primrose, viola *3/29,30/5 /* RCA LM 2186 [H2-RB-2676-79], BMG 61741, RCA CRM6-2264, R42474(6), RCA SER 5729/31, RCA BVCC 37119-21 (Jap.)

7 Variations in Eb from Mozart's the Magic Flute, Wo046. Ralph Berkowitz, piano *6/4/45* Columbia (unissued) [XCO 34886-87]; Ralph Berkowitz, piano *6/7/45* Columbia (unissued) [XCO 34887]; Ralph Berkowitz, piano *10/24/45* Columbia (unissued) [XCO 34886-87]; Ralph Berkowitz, piano *9/19/50* RCA (unissued) [EO-RC-399-1,1A/442-1,1A]; Lukas Foss, piano *6/13/55* RCA LM 6120 [F2-RB-1993-1, F2RP-3165]

12 Variations in G from Handel's Judas Maccabäus, Wo045, Lukas Foss, piano *6/13/55* RCA LM 6120 [F2-RB-1992-1, F2RP-3165]

12 Variations in F from Mozart's the Magic Flute, op. 66, Lukas Foss, piano *6/14/55* RCA LM 6120 [F2-RB-1994-1, F2RP-3165]

Benatzky, Ralph (1884–1957)
Abends in dem kleinen Städtchen(Ungarischer Shimmy), Orchester Georges Boulanger (GP obb.) *11/23* Vox 1529 [1582-A]
Glocken der Liebe (Valse Boston), Orchester Georges Boulanger (GP obb.) *1/24* Vox 1531 [2045-B]

Bíhari, János (1764–1827)
Ungarische Kuruczenlieder: Bercsényi nótája, Edith Lorand Trio (+2nd violin) *1/17/23* Parlophon P 1551 [6167], Parlophone E 10153
Ungarische Kuruczenlieder: Hadik óbester nótája, Edith Lorand Trio (+2nd violin) *2/10/23* Parlophon P 1551 [6199], Parlophone E 10153
Ungarische Kuruczenleider: Primitalis Magyar (arr. Bihari-Kesergöje), Edith Lorand Trio *1/17/23* Parlophon (unissued) [6168]
Ungarische Kuruczenlieder: Requiem fia haláhára, Edith Lorand Trio (+2nd violin) *1/17/23* Parlophon P.1460 [6169]
Ungarische Kuruczenlieder:Szerenad a Tisza-haz elott, Edith Lorand Trio (+2nd violin) *1/17/23* Parlophon P 1460 [6166]

Bizet, Georges
Menutt no.1 L'Arlesienne Suite, Orchester Georges Boulanger (GP obb.) *c.1926* Vox 8634 [2501-G], Kristall 1206

Bland, James (1854–1911)
Carry Me Back to Ol' Virginny (arr. GP), Marian Anderson, contralto Franz Rupp, piano *2/1/51* RCA LM 1703 [E2-RP-4454], WDM 1703, RF 277 (7") (Fr.) [E1-RW-1984-A1, 49-3805A]

Bloch, Ernest (1880–1959)
Prayer, from Jewish Life. with organ accompaniment (Karol Szreter?) *9/3/29* Parlophone E11058 [xxB 8387], Decca 25139, TLC-2587 private LP issue-Thomas Clear; with organ accompaniment (Karol Szreter?) *10/14/29* Parlophon, Odeon 177625 (Arg.) [xxB 8387-2]; Ralph Berkowitz, piano *12/28/47* Columbia (unissued) [XCO 39823 1A]
Schelomo; Artur Rodzinski, New York Philharmonic-Symphony *11/26/44* AS 631 (CD) live broadcast; Eugene Ormandy, Philadelphia Orchestra *12/28/47* Columbia (unissued) [XCO 39800-04 1A]; Charles Munch, Boston Symphony Orchestra *1/30/57* RCA LM/LSC 2109 [H2-RB-1201-03], RCA SB 6676, RB16027, RCA ACL1-4086, RCA LSB 4101, Testament SBT1371

Boccherini, Luigi (1743–1805)
Sonata in C (arr. GP), Valentin Pavlovsky, piano *10/8/45* Columbia 71785D [XCO 31471-1C,31472-1C], Biddulph LAB 117
Sonata in D, Jascha Heifetz, violin *11/18/64* RCA LM/LSC 3009 [RR-A3-4888], BMG 61759

Bohm, Carl (1844–1920)
Still wie die Nacht, Tri-Ergon-Trio: Karol Szreter, piano Max Rostal, violin *c.1927 rel.3/28* Tri-Ergon TE 5118 [01086 or 1086]

Boulanger, Georges (1893–1958)
Atlantic (foxtrot), Karol Szreter? piano Georges Boulanger, violin *3/24* Vox 01554 [1668-A]
Flirtation, Karol Szreter? piano Georges Boulanger, violin *4-5/25* Vox 06246 [2163-A]

Mein Waltzer, Karol Szreter? piano Georges Boulanger, violin *2-3/24* Vox 06166 [1621-A]
Olivier (foxtrot), Karol Szreter? piano Georges Boulanger, violin *2-3/24* Vox 06182 [1645-A]
Olympiade (foxtrot), Karol Szreter? piano Georges Boulanger, violin *2-3/24* Vox 06182 [1655-A]
Oriental (intermezzo), Karol Szreter? piano Georges Boulanger, violin *3/24* Vox 01554 [1669-A]
Potpourri russischer Lieder, Karol Szreter? piano Georges Boulanger, violin *c.11/23* Vox 06167 [1572-A, 1572 A]
Vox-Boston, Karol Szreter? piano Georges Boulanger, violin *c.11/23* Vox 06166 [1569 A]
Zigeuner-Träume, Karol Szreter? piano Georges Boulanger, violin *2-3/24* Vox 06174 [1646-A]

Boulanger, Lili (1893–1918)
Nocturne, (with autograph etched on disc) Valentin Pavlovsky, piano *10/22/36* RCA RL-14-B [VD 925] (Jap.) 8618-2 (Victor Record Lover's Society)

Boyd, Tod
Samoaisches Wiegenlied, Michael Raucheisen? piano Edith Lorand, violin *10/26/23* Parlophon (unissued) [6515]

Braga, Gaetano (1829–1907)
La Serenata [Der Engel Lied] (arr.). Karol Szreter, piano Dajos Béla, violin *3/2/27* Odeon AA 68038 [WxxB 7634 (label 7634-2)], 6611AA, AA212047, Parlophone E 10593, E 15221; Karol Szreter, piano Dajos Béla, violin *2/28/28* Odeon O-6611b [WxxB 7634-2 (label and disc)]; Karol Szreter, piano Dajos Béla, violin *2/28/28* Odeon (Arg.) 177571 [xxB 7634², xxB 7634³]

Brahms, Johannes (1833–1897)
Concerto for Violin and Cello, op. 102. Nathan Milstein, violin Fritz Reiner, Robin Hood Dell Orchestra *6/29/51* RCA LM 1191 [E1-RP-0273-5S, E1-RP-0274-5S], RCA AVM 1-2020, RCA WDM 1609, La Voix de Son Maitre FALP 171, BMG 09026-61485-2, BMG BVCC 37333 (Jap.), BMG BVCC 37052 (Jap.) original edition SRA 2825 (Jap.), RCA TK1-3 (Jap.), Naxos 8.111051; Jascha Heifetz, violin Alfred Wallenstein, RCA Symphony *5/19,20/60* RCA LD/LDS 2513 [L2-RB-2197-99], LSC 9891, RCA LM/LSC 3228, RCA SB 2140, GD 86776 RCA LP RR 6069-S (Ger.), RCA Readers Digest LP RR 6069-S (Ger.), RCA LSC 9891-D (10") (Ger.), RCA Sampler SPS 33-508 (excerpt), RCA SOR. 640.712 (Fr.), LP 630634, RCA Gold Seal P 1988, RCA 640712, RCA 6778-2-RC, BMG 61779, BMG 6778, BMG 63531, BMG 82876-59410-2, BMG 09026-635312, Amadeus/BMG AM 064-2, BMG 09026-61779-2 The Concerto Collection (5 CDs), BMG BVCC 37052 (Jap.), BMG BVCC 37492 SACD (Jap.), Domestic LP(Cisco Music ALSC2513) LCISCO2513 180 gram reissue, RCA 88697-04605-2 SACD, (*Andante*) BMG 9026-63906-2 *Heifetz Adagios*
Piano Quartet no.3 in c, op. 60, Jacob Lateiner, piano Jascha Heifetz, violin Sanford Schonbach, viola *8/17,18/65* RCA LM/LSC 3009 [SR-A3-5868-71], GD 87873, RCA SPS 33-508 (sampler LP excerpt), RCA CT GK 87873, BMG 61773, RCA 7873-2-RG, BVCC-37123-4 (Jap.)
Quintet no.2 in G, op. 111, Jascha Heifetz, Israel Baker, violin Paul Rosenthal, viola Milton Thomas, viola *9/16,17/68* Vox Cum Laude VCL 9041/VS 6338, RCA/BMG 61759 [WR-A3-6717-6720], BVCC-37123-4 (Jap.)
Sextet no.1 in Bb, op. 18, Budapest Quartet, Walter Trampler, viola I GP, cello I *10/6/60* Columbia (unissued) Library of Congress live
Sextet no.2 in G, op. 36, Jascha Heifetz, Israel Baker, violin William Primrose, Virginia Majewski, viola Gabor Rejto, cello II *8/28,29/61* RCA LM/LSC/LSCSD 2739 [M2-RB-3426-29], RCA LD/LDS 6159, GD 87965, SB 6652, RCA 7965-2-RG(CD), Amadeus/BMG AM 064-2, BVCC-37123-4 (Jap.)
Sonata no.1 in e, op. 38. Arthur Rubinstein, piano *7/6/36* HMV DB 2952-54 [2LA-1176-1,1172-2, 1178-1, 1179-1, 1180-1, 1181-1], Disque "Gramophone" DB 2952-54, RCA M 564 15437-39 [032567-72], Victor JD 993-995 (Jap.), RCA LCT 1119, WCT 1119 [E2RP-4271, 15434-36], Recital Records 406, Seraphim 60300, EMI C053 3078, EMI IC 2LP 137 1544561, Electrola[Da Capo IC]137-1544553, La Voix de Son Maitre 2901823, Pearl GEMM CD 9447, Music & Arts CD 674, Biddulph LAB 086CD, Pavil CD, Testament SBT 2158, Fono Enterprise Piano Library PL 233; Reginald Stewart, piano *3/21/47* Music & Arts CD644 Library of Congress; Arthur

Rubinstein, piano *10/11/66* RCA ARL 1-2085 [ARL1-2085A-1], RCA RL 12085 (It.), RCA/ BMG09026-62592-2, BMG 63064, RCA 09026630642 (Jap.), RCA BVCC-37314 (Jap.), RCA RVC-2121

Sonata no.2 in F, op. 99. Ralph Berkowitz, piano *6/5/45* Columbia (unissued) [XCO 34890-96]; Ralph Berkowitz, piano *10/17/46* Columbia (unissued) [XCO 34894-96]; Ralph Berkowitz, piano *10/18/46* Columbia (unissued) [XCO 34890-93]; Ralph Berkowitz, piano *5/28/47* Columbia MM690 (71703-06) [XCO 34890-4B, 34891-4B, 34892-2E, 34893-3O, 34894-2B, 34895-2C, 34896-4B, Columbia ML 2096 [LP 1955-56]; Ralph Berkowitz, piano *5/29/47* Columbia (unissued) [XCO 34896]; Arthur Rubinstein, piano *10/11/66* RCA ARL 1-2085 [ARL1-2085B-1], RCA RL 12085 (It.), BMG 63064, RCA/BMG 09026-62592-2, RCA 09026630642 and RCA BVCC-37314 (Jap.), RCA RVC-2121

Trio in B, op. 8 (Scherzo), Leonid Kreutzer, piano Joséf Wolfsthal, violin *5-6/25* Polydor 66213 [1951 as [?]]

Trio in C, op. 87, Leonard Pennario, piano Jascha Heifetz, violin *10/16/63* RCA/BMG 61769 [PR-A5-4564-4567], BVCC-37123-4 (Jap.)

Bruch, Max (1838–1920)

Kol Nidre, op. 47. with organ and piano accompaniment *9/3/29* Odeon O-6731 [xxB 8389-90], Parlophone R 9273, Parlophone E10961, Decca 25501, Columbia J8572 (Jap.); Eugene Ormandy, Philadelphia Orchestra *12/28/47* Columbia 12882D [XCO 39805-1A,-39806-1O], Columbia LX 1095, Columbia 266573 (Arg.), Sony Classical MHK 62876

Busoni, Ferruccio (1866–1924)

Kleine Suite, op. 23 (Espressivo lamentoso), Lukas Foss, piano *6/3/58* RCA LM/LSC/LSCSD 2293 [J2PB-1214], AFRS C 1151

Chopin, Frédéric (1810–1849)

Introduction and Polonaise Brillante, op. 3 (GP ed.), Valentin Pavlovsky, piano *10/25/40* [XCO 29047-1 *(Introduction)*], *10/8/4* [XCO 29046-3 *(Polonaise)*], Columbia 71889D, Biddulph LAB 117

Nocturne in c#, op. posth. (arr. GP), Ivor Newton, piano *5/10/34* HMV DB 22271 [2B-4740-2], RCA 8419B, Music & Arts CD644

Sonata in g, op. 65. Robert Casadesus, piano *5/10/40* Columbia (session destroyed); Ralph Berkowitz, piano *11/24/47* [XCO 39419 1A, 39420 1C, 39421 1A, 39422 1-C] *12/9/47* [XCO 39584 1-A, 39585 1-D] Columbia M 854 (72843-45), Columbia ML 4215 [XLP 1577]; Rudolf Firkusny, piano *7/22/65* RCA LM/LSC 2875 [SRA3-5739-42], RCA LSCSD 2875, RCA 645 063 (Fr.), Time Life STL 555, Melodiya M10 44841, Testament SBT 1419

Cui, César (1835–1918)

Orientale, op. 50, no.9 (arr.), Ralph Berkowitz, piano *10/24/45* Columbia M 684, 17413D [C0 35352-1A], Columbia RL 3015 [CXLP 2637], Arleccchino A74

Czibulka, Alphons (1842–1894)

Herzen und Blumen, Karol Szreter? piano Georges Boulanger, violin *3/24* Vox 06174 [1675-A]

Danbé, Jules (1840–1905)

Menuett, Karol Szreter, piano *6/10/27* Odeon 0-2410 [Be 5829]. Karol Szreter, piano *9/13/27* Odeon O-2410 [Be 5829-2]

Davidov, Karl (1838–1889)

Romanze, op. 23, Karol Szreter, piano *4-5/25* Polydor 66171 (B28009) [1262av]

Debussy, Claude (1862–1918)

Romance (arr. Gretchaninoff), Valentin Pavlovsky, piano *10/7/41* Columbia MM 501, 17308D [CO 31468-1] Columbia 17447-D, L058, Columbia D 108, C10108 (Can.), Biddulph LAB 117

Sonata no.1 in d. Ralph Berkowitz, piano *12/9/47* Columbia (unissued) [XCO 39586-88]; Ralph Berkowitz, piano *9/20/50* RCA (unissued) [EO-RC-443 1,1A/444 1,1A]; Ralph Berkowitz, piano *1/10/56* RCA (unissued) [G2RB-410] (first mvt); Ralph Berkowitz, piano *5/26/56* RCA (unissued)

[G2RB-503]; Lukas Foss, piano *6/5/58* RCA LM/LSC/LSCSD 2293 [J2PB-1246], Melodiya M10-44841, AFRS C 1151

Drigo, Riccardo (1846–1930)
Serenade from Les Millions d'Arlequin (arr.), Karol Szreter, piano *1924/25* Nordisk Polyphon (Denmark) S 48007 [1719 ax] (Order no. X.S 48007), Polyphon 31483 Kat. Nr. 26465

Dvořák, Antonín (1841–1904)
Concerto in b, op. 101. (first mvt) Nicolai Malko, Danish Radio Orchestra *10/13/32* Danacord DACO 134-38, Danacord DACO CD303 (live broadcast); Dimitri Mitropoulos, Minneapolis. Symphony Orchestra *4/4/42* Columbia (unissued) [XCO 32636-45][2]; Eugene Ormandy, Philadelphia Orchestra *1/17/46* Columbia M 658 (12476-80) [XCO 35643-1C/35644-1A/35645-1A/35646-1A/35647-1B/35648-1A/35649-1E/35650-1A/35652-1A/35657-1A], Sony Classical MHK 62876, Columbia Y 34602, CBS 61778, Columbia ML 4022 [XLP 296-97], Maestro History XXCM 205236-303 (Ger.), Coffret Longbox 222343-354 (Fr.); Charles Munch, Boston Symphony Orchestra *2/22/60* RCA LM/LSC 2490, LSCSD 2940 [L2-RPB-0883 (mvt I), 0884 (mvt II), 0885 (mvt III)], RCA AGL1-3878, AGK1-5265, RCA SB 2114, RB 16245, RCA VICS 2002, RCA VICS 1386 (Ger.), RCA 630 585 (Fr.), RCA "linea tre" GL 142078 (It.), Melodiya M10 44841, RCA RCA 640 673, RCA 09026-61498-2(CD), RCA 64073, RCA CJVC0014 JVC Music LP reissue in 180 gram vinyl, RCA LSC 2490 Classic Records MFSL 45 rpm180 gram vinyl (4 12" discs), RCA CR LSC 2490-200 Classic Records reissue 200 gram Super Vinyl Profile RCA GL 85265 (Ger.) Direct Metal Mastering, BMG 74321 21289 2, RCA Classics 74321 40451, Time-Life Records STL 5542G (mvt 1) 5441H (mvts 2-3), RCA/BMG 09026-61498-4 (cassette), RCA SRC-1014 (74321-87294-2) Shinseido Classics (Jap.), BMG BVCC-7913 (Jap.), BMG BVCC SACD 34432 (Jap.), XRCD JMCXR-0014 (extended resolution) L2RY-0997/0998, New Star Hall Classics, Shinseido Classics CD SRC1014, Victor JVC XRCD JMCXR 0014 (Jap.), Andromeda ANDRCD 5131 (Bel.), RCA SACD Hybrid Multichannel 82876663752, RCA *Living Stereo* CRCA 66375 SA (Hybrid Multichannel SACD), (first movement) RCA/BMG 63665, (*Finale abridged*), RCA/BMG 09026-61567-2 *Living Stereo* Audiophile Sampler (*Finale*), RCA 170128
Quintet in A, op. 81. Jacob Lateiner, piano Jascha Heifetz, violin Israel Baker, violin William Primrose, viola *3/24,25/64* RCA (unissued) [RR-A5-3231-34]; Jacob Lateiner, piano Jascha Heifetz, violin IsraelBaker, violin Joseph de Pasquale, viola *11/9,10/64* RCA LM/LSC 2985 [RR-A3-4883-86], RCA SB 6745, GD 87965, BMG 61772, RCA 7965-2-RG, RCA BVCC 37125 (Jap.)
Trio no.3 in f, op. 65 (I, II movements slightly abridged), Leonard Pennario, piano Jascha Heifetz, violin *11/11/63* Columbia M 33447 [AL 33447, BL 33447], Columbia MP 38781, AS 244 (excerpt), CBS 76421, CBS 60.264 (Ger.), BMG 61770 [PR-A5-5883-86]
Trio no.4 in e, op. 90 Dumky Leonard Pennario, piano Jascha Heifetz, violin *7/1,2/68* RCA LM/LSC 3068, BMG 61764 [WR-A3-1493-97], RCA SRA-2600, RCA BVCC 37126 (Jap.)

Eccles, Henry (1670–1742)
Sonata in g. (Largo and Corrente) Karol Szreter, piano *1/24* Vox 06244 [1643 A]; *(Largo [Larghetto], Corrente, Adagio, Gigue)* Karol Szreter, piano *4-5/25* Polydor 66170 (B28006-07) [1259av, 1260av (?)], Grammophon B28006-07, Odeon U-20 (Jap.)

Fauré, Gabriel-Urbain (1845–1924)
Après un rêve, op. 7 [Nach einem Traum] (arr.), Karol Szreter, piano *6/10/27* Odeon 2224 [WBe 5831 (A)-1], 193180 (Arg.), Columbia J5348 (Jap.)
Elégie, op. 24, Ralph Berkowitz, piano *11/24/47* Columbia MM 808, 72768-69D [XCO 39417-1A, 39418-1A], Columbia ML 4215 [XLP 1578]
Tarentelle, op. 10, no.2 (arr. GP). Valentin Pavlovsky, piano *10/7/41* Columbia (unissued) [CO 31469]; Valentin Pavlovsky, piano *1/8/42* Columbia M501,17308D, L0 58 [CO 31469-2], Columbia 17447-D, D 108, Columbia C10109 (Can.), Biddulph LAB 117

Feltzer, Willem H. (1874–1931)
Scherzo, op. 3, no.2, Karol Szreter, piano *9/3/27* Odeon 11681 [Be 8457], Parlophone R1078, Odeon

Foss, Lukas (1922–2009)
Capriccio, Lukas Foss, piano *6/3/58* RCA LM/LSC/LSCSD 2293 [J2PB-1215], AFRS C 1151, New World NW-281(CD)

Foster, Stephen (1826–1864)
Plantation Songs (arr. Maud Powell) Old Black Joe Edith Lorand Trio *10/27/23* Parlophon P.1632 [6521] [6520 unissued], Parlophone 10113, Odeon 3102
My Old Kentucky Home (arr. GP), Marian Anderson, contralto Franz Rupp, piano *2/1/51* RCA LM 1703 [E2-RP-4455], WDM 1703, RF 277 (7") (Fr.), [E1-RW 1985-A1, 49-3804B]

Françaix, Jean (1912–1997)
Trio in C (1933), Jascha Heifetz, violin Joseph de Pasquale, viola *11/11/64* RCA LM/LSC 2985 [RR-A3-4887], RCA SB 6745, GD 87872, BMG 61774, RCA 7872-2-RG, RCA BVCC 37125 (Jap.)

Franck, César (1822–1890)
Quintet in f, Leonard Pennario, piano Jascha Heifetz, violin Israel Baker, violin William Primrose, viola *8/21,22/61* RCA LM/LSC/LSCSD 2739 [M2-RB-3423-25], RCA LD/LDS 6159, SB 6652, BMG 61764, RCA BVCC 37125 (Jap.)

Francoeur, François (1698–1787)
Sonata in E (arr. Trowell) (Largo and Vivo), Ivor Newton, piano *12/17/34* HMV DB 2539 [2EA-596-2], RCA 8995, Victor RL-8 (Jap.), TLC-2587 private LP issue Thomas Clear, Music & Arts CD644

Ganne, Louis (1862–1923)
Extase. Dajos Béla, violin Karol Szreter, piano *3/2/27* Parlophone E 10618 [xxB 7635], Odeon 6612AA, 68035, Odeon AA 212004, A.170076, U 10014 (Jap.); Dajos Béla, violin Karol Szreter, piano *3/8/27* O-6612 (AA68035a) [xxB 7635²], Odeon AA. 212004; Dajos Béla, violin Karol Szreter, piano *2/23/28* Odeon O 6612 [xxB 7635³]

Gillette, Ernst
Au Village (Dorfgeschicten), Michael Raucheisen? piano Edith Lorand, violin *10/26/23* Parlophon P-1583 [6517], Parlophone E 10113

Glière, Reinhold (1875–1956)
Duo, op. 39 (Prelude), Jascha Heifetz, violin *11/18/64* Columbia M 33447 [23558], MP 38781, BL 33447 and CBS 60.264 (Ger.), CBS 76421, BMG 61762, RR-A3-4890

Glinka, Mikhail (1804–1857)
Elégie (arr.), Karol Szreter? piano Georges Boulanger, violin *3/27* Vox 06349 [1543AA], Kristall

Gluck, Christoph Willibald (1714–1787)
Orpheus und Eurydice (Reigen seliger Geister), Michael Raucheisen? piano Edith Lorand, violin *10/26/23* Parlophon (unissued) [6518]

Godard, Benjamin (1849–1895)
Berceuse, from Jocelyn (arr.). Karol Szreter, piano *1924/25* Polyphon 50441[Kat.Nr.110049] [553 az]; Karol Szreter, piano Dajos Béla, violin *3/2/27* Odeon O 68037 [WxxB 7633 (label = 7633-2)], Odeon O 6611A, Parlophone E 10593, E 15221AA, 212047, Odeon O-6611a [WxxB 7633-2 (label and disc)]; Karol Szreter, piano Dajos Béla, violin *2/28/28* Odeon (Arg.) 177571 [xxB 7633², xxB 7633]
Berceuse Cachés dans cet asile, Tri-Ergon-Trio: Karol Szreter, piano Max Rostal, violin *c.1927* Tri-Ergon TE 5118 [01113 and 1113m1]; Tri-Ergon-Trio: Karol Szreter, piano Max Rostal, violin *rel. 3/28* Tri-Ergon Colorit 3145 [1113m1]

Goens, Daniel van (1858–1904)
Scherzo, op. 12, no.2, Karol Szreter, piano *1/24* Vox 06170 [1642 A]

Goldmark, Karl (1830–1915)
Trio no.2 in e, op. 33 (Andantino grazioso & Scherzo), Michael Raucheisen, piano Edith Lorand, violin *12/14/26* Parlophon P-9078 [W2-20036], Parlophone E10639, Decca 25137

Granados, Enrique (1867–1916)
Intermezzo, from Goyescas, H62 (arr.Cassado-GP), Ralph Berkowitz, piano *9/18/50* RCA LM 1187 [EO-RC-398-1A], RCA Italiana LM 1187, RCA WDM 1578, RCA 45 rpm EP 3045 [49-3524B-2A], Victor SD 200 (45 rpm) (Jap.), RCA ERA 122 (45 rpm extended play) [E3RW-2668 1S A1], La Voix de Son Maitre EP45 RF 7 229 M3-138776, Andromeda ANDRCD 5131 (Bel.)
Orientale, from Spanish Dances, op. 37, no.2 (arr. GP), Valentin Pavlovsky, piano *10/9/41* Columbia (unissued [CO 31466 Fred Plaut, engineer]), Columbia M501 [CO 31466-1], 17307D, L063, Columbia D 108, C10107 (Can.), Biddulph LAB 117

Grazioli, Giovanni Battista (1746–c.1820)
Sonata no.5 in G (Adagio), Karol Szreter, piano *1/24* Vox 06170 [1644 A]

Grieg, Edvard (1843–1907)
Anitras Tanz (from Peer Gynt), Orchester Georges Boulanger (GP obb.) *11/23* Vox 01564 [1590-A]
Ave maris stelle (arr.), Edith Lorand Trio *2/22/24* Parlophon (unissued) [6699]
Sonata in a, op. 36, Ralph Berkowitz, piano *6/8/45* Columbia (unissued) [XCO 34921-27]

Handel, George Frideric (1685–1759)
Kammersonate Nr 14 in D (arr. Seiffert), Edith Lorand Trio *11/6/23* Parlophon (unissued) [6543]
Konzert in g (Sarabande), Edith Lorand Trio, Dominator harmonium *11/6/23* Parlophon (unissued) [6544]
Largo, Ombra mai fu, from Xerxes (arr.), Karol Szreter, piano *1/25, rel.8/25* Vox 6259 [2700 B]
Larghetto (Sonata op. 1, no.9 arr. Hubay). Karol Szreter, piano *6/10/27* Odeon 2410 [Be 5828]; Karol Szreter, piano *9/13/27* Odeon 2410, Odeon 193126 [Be 5828-2]
Prayer from Te Deum in D, HWV 283 (arr. Flesch), Ivor Newton, piano *10/25/40* Columbia (unissued) [XCO 25698]

Handel — arr. Johan Halvorsen (1864–1935)
Passacaglia, Jascha Heifetz, violin *10/12,14/63* Columbia M 33449 [23558], MP 38781, BL 33447 and CBS 60.264 (Ger.), CBS 76421, BMG 61761 [PR-A3-4563 & PR-A5-4540]

Haydn, Joseph (1732–1809)
Divertimento in D, (Hob XI:95,113) (arr. GP). Ivor Newton, piano *10/25/40* Columbia (unissued) [XCO 25682, 25683]; Valentin Pavlovsky, piano *1/8/42* Columbia 11830D, LOX564 [XCO-25682-4, 25683-5], Columbia, LX564, Biddulph LAB 117; Jascha Heifetz, concertmaster, Chamber Orchestra (orchestration by Dahl) *10/9/63* RCA LM/LSC 277 [PR-A5-4537], RCA 645.029 (Fr.)
Sinfonie Nr 100 "Militär" (Minuett), Edith Lorand Trio *2/22/24* Parlophon (unissued) [6700]
Trio in F, XV:2 (Minuetto), Karol Szreter, piano Dajos Béla, violin *3/8/27* Parlophone E10618 [xxB 7646], Odeon O.6608, AA.212004; Karol Szreter, piano Dajos Béla, violin *2/28/28* Odeon O.6608 [xxB 7646²]
Trio in G, XV:25 (Rondo all'Ongarese: Presto), Michael Raucheisen, piano Edith Lorand, violin *12/14/26* Parlophone P 9078, [2-20035], Odeon 3215

Hindemith, Paul (1895–1963)
Sonata (1948), Ralph Berkowitz, piano *1/9,10/56, 5/26/56* RCA LM 2013 [G2RB-409-1, G2RB-503-6 (mvt II)]

Hummel, Johann Nepomuk (1778–1837)
Cello Sonate in A: Romanze (arr.), Edith Lorand Trio *10/26/23* Parlophon (unissued) [6519]

Ippolitov-Ivanov, Mikhail (1859–1935)
Suite Caucasiénne [no.1]. Dans d'aoule Edith Lorand Orchestra (GP obb.) *1/17/24* Parlophon P 1651 [6644]; *Dorfszene* Orchester Georges Boulanger (GP obb.) *c.1926* Vox 8616 [2289-1G], Kristall 1204; *Dans le défilé* (as above) Edith Lorand Orchestra *1/17/24* Parlophon P 1651 [6643-2]; *Aufzug des Serder* Orchester Georges Boulanger (GP obb.) *c.1926* Vox 8616 [2291-G], Kristall 1204; *Cortege di Sardare* (as above) Edith Lorand Orchestra (GP obb.) *1/18/24* Parlophon P 1652 [6645]

Kahl, Victor (1877–1959)
Weihnachtsfantasie, Tino Valeria Trio: Karol Szreter, piano Boris Kroyt, violin *1924* Vox 06316 [943AA, 944-2AA]

Kodály, Zoltán (1882–1967)
Duo, op. 7, Jascha Heifetz, violin *9/20,21/60* RCA LM/LSC/LSCSD 2550 [L2-RB-2535-7], RCA A 630640, 7871-2-RG, BMG 61758

Kun, Läszlo (1869–1939)
Kuruczenlieder:Szerenád a Tisz-ház elött, Edith Lorand Trio (+2nd violin) *1/17/23* Parlophon P.1460 [6166]

Lange, O. H. (1840–1911)
Meditation on a Bach Preludium, Nr. 7 (Der 12 Kleinen Preludien), Edith Lorand, violin +harmonium & Hammerflügel *6/7/23* Parlophon P-1555 [6382], Parlophone E-10217

Leoncavallo, Ruggero (1857–1919)
Mattinata, Edith Lorand Trio *12/11/23* Parlophon (unissued) [6596]

Liadov, Anatol (1855–1914)
Prelude, op. 11 no.1 (arr.), Edith Lorand Trio *9/23/23* Parlophon P.1554 [6437], and as — Edith Lorand "with orchestra" Odeon 3131 [3131B]

Lully, Jean-Baptiste (1632–1687)
Gavotte (arr. GP), Karol Szreter, piano *9/12/27* Odeon 2411 (A45380) [WBe 6100], 193320 (Arg.), Columbia J5447 (Jap.)

Lundvik, Hildor (1885–1951)
Hostsang (Herbstlied), Edith Lorand Trio *2/10/23* Parlophon (unissued) [6198]

Mania, Paul (1883–1935)
Berceuse, Edith Lorand Trio *11/6/23* Parlophon (unissued) [6542]

Martinů, Bohuslav (1890–1959)
Duo no.1 (Rondo abridged), Jascha Heifetz, violin *11/18/64* RCA LM/LSC/LSCSD 2867 [RR-A3-4889], RCA SB 6661, GD 87871, RCA 7871-2-RC(CD), BMG 61775

Massenet, Jules (1842–1912)
Méditation from Thaiis (arr.Béla). Karol Szreter, piano Dajos Béla, violin *3/8/27* Parlophone E 10580 [xxB 7645], Odeon AA.212025, O-68042; Karol Szreter, piano Dajos Béla, violin *2/28/28* not verified as released [xxB 7645^2]

May, Hans (1891–1959)
Natascha (russische Weise), Karol Szreter? piano Georges Boulanger, violin *11/23* Vox 01530 [1583-A]

Mendelssohn, Felix (1809–1847)
Octet in Eb, op. 20, Jascha Heifetz, Israel Baker, Arnold Belnick, Joseph Stepansky, violin William Primrose, Virginia Majewski, viola Gabor Rejto, cello II *8/24,25/61* RCA LM/LSC 2738 [M2-RB-3430-33], RCA LD/LDS 6159, A 640761-3, RCA TP3-5022, BMG 61766, RCA BVCC 37119-21 (Jap.), RMG Records/Melodiya RMG-1445, (Scherzo) BMG 09026-62645-2

Sonata no.2 in D, op. 58, Leonard Pennario, piano *11/15,19/65* RCA LM/LSC/LSCSD 3021 [SRA 3-8316-18, 3-8323], RCA SB 6785, Testamant SBT 1419

Lieder ohne Worte, op. 62, no.1 May Breeze (arr. Kreisler). Karol Szreter, piano *9/3/29* Odeon O 11681 [Be 8456]; Karol Szreter, piano *9/3/29* Odeon O-11681 [Be 8456-2[3]]; Karol Szreter, piano *10/14/29* Odeon O-11681 [Be 8456-3], Odeon (Arg.) 193635,[4] 10103 (It.), O-167895, Columbia J5521 (Jap.), Parlophone R1078, Decca-Odeon 20066, Music & Arts CD674

Trio no.1 in d, op. 49
(Andante con moto (abridged), Scherzo). Michael Raucheisen, piano Edith Lorand, violin *12/14/26* Parlophon P9042 [20033], Parlophone E 10563 [2-20033-2], Odeon 170025; Michael Raucheisen, piano Edith Lorand, violin *12/14/26* Odeon 3212 [(W)2-20033-3]; Michael Raucheisen, piano Edith Lorand, violin *12/14/26* Parlophon P9042 [20034], Parlophon P9042 [20034-2], Parlophone E 10563 [2-20034-2], Odeon 3212 [(W)2-20034-2]; *(I(abridged), II, III)*, Arthur Rubinstein, piano Jascha Heifetz, violin *1949* Concerts on Film Library/ *The Trio* Kultur (video)/DVD 1102; Arthur Rubinstein, piano Jascha Heifetz, violin *8/25/50* RCA DM/WDM 1487, RCA LM 1119 [EO-RC-0380-85 all take 1], RCA CT 7768, RCA A12R0286 (It.), HMV ALP 1009, Melodiya D12479/80 (10"), RCA FALP 111 La Voix de Son Maitre, RCA 7768-2-RG(CD), Melodiya RMG-1445, BMG 63024, RMG Records/ BMG 61767

Trio no.2 in c, op. 66, Leonard Pennario, piano Jascha Heifetz, violin *11/7,8/63* RCA LM/LSC 3048, AGL-4949 [PR-A5-5879-82], BMG 61767, RCA BVCC 37119-21 (Jap.)

de Micheli, F.
Serenata spagnola, Edith Lorand Trio *2/10/23* Parlophon (unissued) [6197]

Moszkowski, Moritz (1854–1925)
Guitarre, op. 45, no.2 (arr. Moszkowski-GP). Karol Szreter, piano *4-5/25* Polydor 66171 (B28008) [1261av]; Karol Szreter, piano *6/10/27* Odeon [Be5627]; Karol Szreter, piano *9/13/27* Parlophone R3543 [Be5827-2], Decca 20043, Odeon 2331 [A45366], Odeon 193126, Columbia J5348, E5482 (Jap.), Music & Arts CD674

Mozart, Wolfgang Amadeus (1756–1791)
Concerto no.5 in A for Violin (Turkish) K.219, Jascha Heifetz, violin, Chamber Orchestra GP, principal cello *10/10/63* RCA LM/LSC 2957, AGL1-5250 [PR-A5-4533-35], RCA AGL1-4931, RCA LM/LSC 3265, RCA CRL6-0720, RCA 7869-2-RG(CD), RCA FRL2 7163, BMG 61757

Divertimento: Menuett [K 563?], Edith Lorand Trio [violin, viola, cello] *11/16/23* Parlophon (unissued) [6561 and 6562]

Quintet in C, K.515, Jascha Heifetz, Israel Baker violin William Primrose, Virginia Majewski, viola *3/26,27/64* RCA LM/LSC 3048 [RR-45-3235-38], RCA AGL1-4949, RCA FRL2 7163, BMG 61765, RCA BVCC 37118 (Jap.)

Quintet in g, K.516, Jascha Heifetz, Israel Baker violin William Primrose, Virginia Majewski, viola *8/29,30/61* RCA LM/LSC 2738 [M2-RB-3438-41], GD 87869, RCA LD/LDS 6159, A 640761-3, RCA TR3-5022, RCA 7869-2-RG (CD), BMG 61757, RCA BVCC 37118 (Jap.)

Serenade no. 13, K 525 Eine kleine Nachtmusik (Romanze), Edith Lorand Trio *2/22/24* Parlophon (unissued) [6701]

Sinfonia[5] in D (arr. GP), Ivor Newton, piano *1/17/40, 10/25/40* Columbia (unissued) [XCO 25686-87]

Sonatina in A, K.439b (arr. GP). Ralph Berkowitz, piano *6/4/45* Columbia (unissued) [XCO 34888-89]; Ralph Berkowitz, piano *6/7/45* Columbia 72827D, Z101 (Jap.) [XCO 34888-2, 34889-2], Columbia 3-249 (LP) [XCO 1193-94 (ZLP 1193-4)]

Nardini, Pietro (1722–1793)
Sonata in C (arr. J. Salmon) (Lento), Ralph Berkowitz, piano *6/5/45* Columbia M 590, 71703D [XCO 34897-1C]

Paganini, Niccolò (1782–1840)
La Campanella (arr. GP) Valentin Pavlovsky, piano *10/9/41* Columbia (destroyed) [Fred Plaut, engineer]

Piatigorsky, Gregor (1903–1976)
Preludio, 12/9/47 Columbia (unissued) [XCO 39589]
Procession (AKA Stroll or Promenade), 5/29/47 Columbia (unissued) [XCO 37838]

Variations on a Paganini Theme, Donald Voorhees, NBC Symphony *5/11/45* (live concert) Pearl GEMM CD9981-3

Plantation Songs (arr. Maud Powell) (1867–1920))
Old Black Joe (Foster)/Shine On (Schoolcraft) Kingdom Coming (Work), Edith Lorand Trio *10/27/23* Parlophon P.1632 [6521 (6520 unissued)], Parlophone E10113, Odeon 3102

Popper, David (1843–1913)
Chanson Villagoise, op. 62, no.2, Karol Szreter, piano *6/10/27* Odeon 2224 [WBe 5830], Odeon 165. 164 (Fr.), Odeon 193180 (Arg.)

Der Schmetterling (The Butterfly), Karol Szreter, piano *1924/25* Nordisk Polyphon (Denmark) S 48006 (Order no. X.S 48006) [1718ax], Polyphon 31483 Kat Nr. 26464

Prokofiev, Sergey (1891–1953)
March, op. 65, from Music for Children (arr. GP). 10/24/45 Columbia (unissued) [XCO 35355]; *9/19/50* RCA (unissued) [EORB 3783 1,1A]

Masques, from Romeo and Juliet, op. 75(arr. GP); Valentin Pavlovsky, piano *10/9/41* Columbia M 50 [CO 31456-1], 17446D, L063, Columbia 17307-D, D 108 and C10106 (Can.), Biddulph LAB 117; Ralph Berkowitz, piano *1949* Concerts on Film Library/*Gregor Piatigorsky* Kultur (video)/ DVD 1101

Sonata, op. 119. Ralph Berkowitz, piano *8/11-13/53* RCA LM 1792 [E3-RC-3301-1, 3302-1, 3303-1, E3-RC 3304-1 (III mvt)], RCA LVT 1037, RCA A 630.224 (Fr.); Rudolf Firkusny, piano *7/21/65* RCA LM/LSC 2875 [SRA3-5736-38], RCA 645 063 (Fr.)

Waltz from Music for Children, op. 65 (arr. GP), Ralph Berkowitz, piano *10/24/45* Columbia (unissued) [XCO 35355]

Rachmaninoff, Sergey (1873–1943)
Vocalise, op. 34, no.14 (transc. GP). Ralph Berkowitz, piano *10/17/46* Columbia (unissued) [CO 37025]; Ralph Berkowitz, piano *10/18/46* M 684 [CO 37025-2A], 17412D, Arleccchino A74, Columbia RL 3015 [CXLP 2637]

Ravel, Maurice (1875–1937)
Pièce en forme de Habanera (transc. Bazelaire), Valentin Pavlovsky, piano *1/9/41* Columbia M/MM501 [(unissued CO 31457 Fred Plaut, engineer) [CO 31457-2]], 17306, D 108, Columbia C10105 (Can.), Biddulph LAB 117

Trio in a, Arthur Rubinstein, piano Jascha Heifetz, violin *8/28/50* DB 21294-96, DB 9620-22 (78 rpm) [EO-RC-386-1A, 387-1A (mvt I), 380-1A (mvt II), 389-1A, 390-1C-(mvtIII, start of IV), 0391-1A (IV)], RCA LM 1119, GD 87871, WDM 1486, RCA DM 1486, HMV ALP 1009, RCA A12R0286 (It.), RCA FALP 111 La Voix de Son Maitre [2XAV.66-13N], RCA CT 7871, RCA 7871-2-RC(CD), BMG 61775, BMG 63025, Cascavelle 3048, RMG Records/Melodiya RMG-1445

Rheinlieder-Potpourri (arr.)
Edith Lorand Trio *3/21/24* Parlophon (unissued) [6759 and 6760]

Rimsky-Korsakov, Nikolai (1844–1908)
Song of India, from Sadko (arr. Kreisler). Karol Szreter, piano *6/10/27* Odeon O-2331 (A45365) [Be5832], Parlophone R679, Decca F2454, Odeon 165.164; Ralph Berkowitz, piano *10/24/45* Columbia M 684 [CO 35341-1A], 17413D, Columbia RL 3015 [CXLP 2637], Arleccchino A74

Rozsavolgyi, Mark (1789–1848)
Keserjoje, Edith Lorand Trio *2/10/23* Parlophon (unissued) [6200]

Rózsa, Miklós (1907–1995)
Tema con Variazioni, op. 29a, Jascha Heifetz, violin, Chamber Orchestra *10/7/63* RCA LM/LSC 2770 [PR-A5-4536], GD 87963, RCA 645.029 (Fr.), RCA 7963-2-RG(CD), BMG 61752

Rubinstein, Anton (1829–1894)
Melody, op. 3, no.1 (arr.). Karol Szreter, piano Dajos Béla, violin *3/8/27* Odeon O.6774 (AA 68034a) [WxxB 7641], Odeon A.170076; Karol Szreter, piano Dajos Béla, violin *2/23/28* Odeon O.6774B

[xxB 7641²]; Ralph Berkowitz, piano *12/43* V-Disc 133B VP418[D3-MC 484-1-C], Biddulph LAB 117; Ralph Berkowitz, piano *10/24/45* Columbia M 684 [CO 35354-1A], 17412D, Columbia RL 3015 [CXLP 2637], Arleccchino A74

Romance, op. 44, no.1 (arr. GP). Ralph Berkowitz, piano *1949* Concerts on Film Library/*Gregor Piatigorsky* Kultur (video)/DVD 1101; Ralph Berkowitz, piano *9/18/50* RCA LM 1187 [EO-RB-3779-1A], RCA Italianna LM 1187, HMV DA 2052 (10"), RCA WDM 1578 [49-3525B-2], RCA 45 rpm EP 3045, RCA ERA 122 [E3RW-2668 1S A1], Andromeda ANDRCD 5131 (Bel.)

Saint-Saëns, Camille (1835–1921)

Concerto no.1 in a, op. 33. Frederick Stock, Chicago Symphony Orchestra *3/6/40* Columbia MX 182 11442-43D [WXCO 26612-1, 26613-2, 26614 1, 26615 1], Columbia J55 and S3024-5 (Jap.), LX 25010-1, Sony MHK 62876, LYS103; Alexander Hilsberg, Philadelphia Orchestra *4/10/49* Columbia (unissued) [XCO 41145-50]; Fritz Reiner, RCA Symphony Orchestra *12/7/50, 6/1/51* (first mvt re-recorded) RCA LM 1187 [EO-RC 1961-2R1962-1, 1963-1,1964-1], RCA Italianna LM 1187, RCA WDM 1538[49-3339-40], RCA AVM 1-2020, Testament SBT1371, Naxos Classic 811 1069, Andromeda ANDRCD 5131 (Bel.)

The Swan (Le Cyne), from Le Carnaval des Animaux. Karol Szreter, piano *9/12/27* Odeon O-2411 (A45381) [WBe 6101], Decca 20043, Odeon193242 (Arg.), Parlophone R3543; Valentin Pavlovsky, piano *10/7/41* Columbia M/MM 501 [CO 31470-1], 17306-D, D 108, C10104 (Can.), Biddulph LAB 117; Ralph Berkowitz, piano (with spoken introduction by GP), *12/43* V-Disc 133A VP417 [D3-MC4831-A], Biddulph LAB 117; accompanied by harp *1946* United Artists film *Carnegie Hall* Bel Canto BCS DVD 791(PCM audio), BMG video 09026-60883-3 *Carnegie Hall at 100...* (excerpt), 790405 (Europe); Ralph Berkowitz, piano *9/18/50* RCA 09026-63861-2B [EO-RB-3784-1 "1"]; Ralph Berkowitz, piano *9/19/50* RCA LM 1187 [EO-RB-3784-1A], RCA Italianna LM 1187, RCA WDM 1578 [49-3525A-C1], RCA 60-0038-A (Arg.) [EO-RB 3784], RCA 45EP 3045, RCA ERA 122 [E3RW-2669 1S A2], Victor SF17 (25cm, 78 rpm) (Jap.), La Voix de Son Maitre EP45 RF 7 [229 M3-138777], RCA 63861, Andromeda ANDRCD 5131 (Bel.)

Saleski, Gdal (1889–1966)

Dedication, Karol Szreter, piano *9/12/27* Odeon 2454 [Be 5998], 193320 (Arg.), Columbia J5429 (Jap.), TLC-2587 private LP issue Thomas Clear

Sarasate, Pablo de (1844–1906)

Zapateado, op. 23, no.2 (arr.), Karol Szreter, piano *1924/25* Polyphon 50441(Kat.Nr.110048]) [552 az]

Schoolcraft, Luke (1847–1893)

Plantation Songs (arr. Maud Powell), Shine On Edith Lorand Trio *10/27/23* Parlophon P.1632 [6521 (6520 unissued)], Parlophone 10113, Odeon 3102

Schubert, Franz (1797–1828)

Adagio in G, D.178 (arr. GP), Ralph Berkowitz, piano *6/4/45* Columbia 72373D [XCO 34884 1], Columbia LX.1169

Am Meer (arr.), Edith Lorand Trio *11/14/23* Parlophon (unissued) [6555]

Du bist die Ruh (arr.), Edith Lorand Trio *11/14/23* Parlophon (unissued) [6556]

Frühlingslaube (arr.), Edith Lorand Trio *11/14/23* Parlophon (unissued) [6557]

Introduction, Theme and Variations in Bb, op. 82, no.2, D.603 (arr. GP). Ralph Berkowitz, piano *5/29/47* Columbia MM 808 [XCO 37828-1B, 37829-1A], Columbia 72768-69D, Columbia ML 4215 [XLP 1578], Cello Classics CC1006; *(abridged),* Ralph Berkowitz, piano *1949* Concerts on Film Library/*Gregor Piatigorsky* Kultur (video)/DVD 1101

Minuets(3), D.380 (arr. GP), Ralph Berkowitz, piano *6/4/45* Columbia 72373D [XCO 34885 1], Columbia LX.1169

Moment Musicale, op. 94, no.3, D.780 (arr. GP), Ralph Berkowitz, piano *9/18/50* RCA LM 1187 [EO-RB-3781-1], RCA Italianna LM 1187HMV DA 2052 (10"), RCA WDM 1578, RCA 60-0038-B (Arg.) [EO-RB 3781], RCA 45EP 3045, RCA ERA 122 [E3RW-2669 1S A2], Victor SF17 (25cm, 78 rpm) (Jap.), Andromeda ANDRCD 5131 (Bel.)

Octet, D803 (arr. Preghiera) (Adagio), Michael Raucheisen? piano Edith Lorand, violin *10/26/23* Parlophon (unissued) [6516]

Quintet in C, op. 163, D.956. Budapest Quartet, GP, cello I *10/14/60* Columbia (unissued) Library of Congress live; Jascha Heifetz, Israel Baker, violin William Primrose, viola Gabor Rejto, cello II *11/30/61, 12/1/61* RCA LM/LSC 2737 [M2-RB-3593-96], RCA LD/LDS 6159, GD 87964, RCA LSCSD 2737, RCA TP3-5022, Armed Forces Records RL-39-4, RCA 7964-2RG (CD), BMG 61768, RCA BVCC 37122 (Jap.)

Trio no.1 in Bb, op. 99, D.898. (Andante), Leonid Kreutzer, piano Joséf Wolfsthal, violin *5-6/25* Polydor 66214 [1952 as (?)]; *(Allegro moderato, abridged),* Arthur Rubinstein, piano Jascha Heifetz, violin *1949* Concerts on Film Library/*The Trio* Kultur (video)/DVD 1102

Trio no.2 in Eb, op. 100, D.929 (mvt IV abridged), Jacob Lateiner, piano Jascha Heifetz,violin *8/18,19/65* RCA/BMG 61769 [SR-A3-5872-5875]

Trio no.2 in Bb, D.581, Jascha Heifetz, violin William Primrose, viola *8/16,22/60* RCA LM/LSC/LSCSD 2563 [L2-RB-2501-04], RCA AGL1-4947, GD 87964, RCA FTC 2076(tape), RCA 7964-2-RG(CD), BMG 61768, RCA BVCC 37122 (Jap.)

Schumann, Robert (1810–1856)

Concerto in a, op. 129, John Barbirolli, London Philharmonic *5/34* HMV/Electrola DB 2244-46 [2B 6931-2, 6933-1, 6934-2, 6935-1, 6936-2, 6932-2, 6933-1], Disque "Gramophone" DB 2244, RCA M 247, Victor JD 353-5 (Jap.), RCA LCT 1119, WCT 1119 [E2RP-4270 (86113-18)], Melodiya M10-44841, Pavil CD 32-4592-97, Music & Arts CD 674, Pearl GEMM CD 9447, Testament SBT 1371, Naxos Classic 811 1069

Abendlied op. 85, no.12 (arr.Davidoff). Karol Szreter, piano *1/25, rel. 8/25* Vox 6259 [2699 B]; with organ accompaniment *9/3/29* Parlophone E11058 [(LW)xxB 8388], Decca 25139, Odeon 177625 (Arg.)

Fantasiestücke, op. 73. Ivor Newton, piano *1/17/40* Columbia 69836D [XCO 25684-1, 25685-1], Columbia S 3035, Columbia C 15219, Columbia 53035 (Jap.), Columbia 11-B (excerpt) [P28512 1-A], Biddulph LAB 117; Ralph Berkowitz, piano *5/29/47* Columbia M 808 [XCO 37830-1A, 37831-1F], 72770D, Columbia ML 4215 [XLP 1578]

Mondnacht, from Liederkreis op. 39, no.5 (arr.), Edith Lorand Trio *11/14/23* Parlophon (unissued) [6558]

Träumerei, from Kinderscenen, op. 15, no.7 (arr. Davidoff). Karol Szreter, piano *6/3/30* Odeon 2990 [Be 9020], Odeon 193582(Arg.), Parlophone R862, Decca 20019, Columbia J5521 (Jap.); Karol Szreter, piano *11/24/32* Odeon O-11756 "Odeon-Parade" [Be 10110-0-] (excerpt, promotional sampler); *(arr.)* Karol Szreter, piano Dajos Béla, violin *3/8/27* Odeon O-6774 [WxxB 7643], Odeon170076, 3249, Odeon A.6774A (AA 68034a), Parlophone E10573 (AA.212003); Karol Szreter, piano Dajos Béla, violin *2/23/28* Odeon O 6774A [xxB 7643-2]

Scriabin, Alexander (1872–1915)

Romance, op. posth. (arr. GP). Ivor, Newton, piano *12/7/33* HMV DB 2271[2B-4741-1], RCA 8419-A, Music & Arts CD644; Ralph Berkowitz, piano *9/20/50* RCA (unissued) [EO-RB-3786 1,1A]

Shostakovich, Dmitri (1906–1975)

Sonata, op. 40. Ivor Newton, piano *1/18/40* Columbia (unissued) [XCO 25802-07]; Ivor Newton, piano *10/25/40* Columbia (unissued) [XCO 25804]; Valentin Pavlovsky, piano *10/9/41* Columbia (unissued) [XCO 25804]; Valentin Pavlovsky, piano *1/7/42* Columbia M/MM 551 (71617-19D) [XCO 25802-2C, 25803-1C, 25804-2C, 25805-2C, 25806-2D, 25807-3C07], Columbia RL 3015 [CXLP 12039], Arlecchino A74, Biddulph LAB 117; Reginald Stewart, piano *3/21/47* Music & Arts CD644 (Library of Congress live)

Spendiarow, Aleksandr (1871–1928)

Berceuse, op. 3 no.2, Edith Lorand Trio *9/12/23* Parlophon P.1554 [6436]

Spohr, Ludwig (1784–1859)

Double Quartet in d, op. 65, Jascha Heifetz, Israel Baker, violin Milton Thomas, viola GP, cello Pierre Amoyal, Paul Rosenthal, violin Allan Harshman, viola

Laurence Lesser, cello *6/24,25/68* RCA LM/LSC/LSCSD 3068 [WR-A3-1504-07], GD 87870, RCA 7870-2-RG(CD), BMG 61756, BVCC-37123-4, RCA SRA-2600

Strauss, Johann (1825–1899)
Fantasie After the Opera, Der Zigeunerbaron Künstlerkapelle Tino Valeria (duet passages with Boris Kroyt, violin), *10/1925* Vox 01916 [2218-A/2219-A]

Strauss, Richard (1864–1949)
Don Quixote, op. 35. Fritz Fritz Reiner, Pittsburgh Symphony Orchestra *11/15/41* Columbia M 501 [XCO 31823-4/31824-3/31825-3/31826-1/31827-4/31828-4/31829-3/31830-1/31831-3/31832-4], Sony Classical MXX 62817 (Finale), LYS044/45, Biddulph Lab 83067, Documents 220983-202 (Ger.), Quadromania 222175-444/C; Charles Munch, Boston Symphony Orchestra *8/17/53* RCA LM 1781 [E3-RB-5322-23, E3-RB-5323-12S], HMV ALP 1211 RCA BC-3 (tape), RCA A 630206, BMG 09026-61485-2, BVCC-38457 (Jap.) K2 laser cutting
Sonata, op. 6, Leonard Pennario, piano *9/28/66* RCA LM/LSC/LSCSD 3021 [TR-A1-6084-86, SR-A3-8313-15, SR-RM 8319, SR-RS 8321], RCA SB 6785, Testamant SBT 1419

Stravinsky, Igor (1882–1971)
Suite Italienne. Lukas Foss, piano *6/2/58* RCA LM/LSC/LSCSD 2293 [J2PB-1213], AFRS C 1151, New Star Hall Classics CD SRC-1014, Shinseido Classics (Jap.), RCA Essential Collection SRC-1014 (74321-87294-2) (Jap.); *(arr. GP)*, Jascha Heifetz, violin *10/14/63, 11/12/63* Columbia M 33447, MP 38781 [BL-33447], Columbia 23558 and CBS 60.264 (Ger.), CBS 76421, RCA BVCC 37126 (Jap.), BMG 61762 [PR-A3-4562 & PR-A5-4539]

Sullivan, Jerry and **Harry Hosford**
Tripping Along, Karol Szreter? piano Georges Boulanger, violin *4-5/25* Vox 06280 [2292-A]

Tchaikovsky, Piotr Illyich (1840–1893)
Andante Cantabile, op. 11 (arr.); Michael Raucheisen? piano Edith Lorand, violin *10/29/23* Parlophon P-1571 [6525]; Michael Raucheisen? piano Edith Lorand, violin *10/29/23* Parlophon P-1571 [6526]
Barcarolle from the Seasons, op. 37a, no.6 (arr.). Michael Raucheisen, piano Edith Lorand, violin *10/29/23* Parlophon P-1572 [6524], Parlophone E 10459 [6524] (last side of Brahms' Violin Sonata no.2 (E 10457/9)), Odeon 3188a [2-6524]; Tino Valeria-Trio: Karol Szreter? piano Boris Kroyt, violin *1/26/24* Vox 06221
Herbstlied (Autumn Song) from the Seasons, op. 37a, no.10 (arr.). Michael Raucheisen? piano Edith Lorand, violin *10/29/23* Parlophon P-1572 [6527]; Karol Szreter, piano *1/24* Vox 06244 [1641]; Tino Valeria-Trio: Karol Szreter? piano Boris Kroyt, violin *1/27/24* Vox 0622][6]; Karol Szreter, piano Dajos Béla, violin *3/8/27* Parlophone E 10573 [xxB 7642], Odeon AA.68042 (AA.212003); Karol Szreter, piano Dajos Béla, violin *2/23/28* (issued?) [xxB 7642[2]]
Chanson Triste, op. 40, no.2 (arr. Popper), Ralph Berkowitz, piano *10/24/45* Columbia MM 684[CO 35353-1a], 17414D, Arleccchino A74, Columbia RL 3015 [CXLP 2637]
Douce Reverie, op. 9 no.1 (arr.), Michael Raucheisen? piano Edith Lorand, violin *10/27/23* Parlophon P-1573 [6522], Odeon 3188, Parlophone E 10121 [2-6522]
Mazurka di Salon in d, op. 9 no.3 (arr.), Michael Raucheisen? piano Edith Lorand, violin *10/27/23* Parlophon P-1573 [6523], Parlophone E 10121 [2-6523]
None but the Lonely Heart, op. 6, no.6 (arr. GP). Karol Szreter, piano *9/12/27* Odeon O-2454 [Be5999], Parlophone R679, Odeon (Arg.) 193242, Columbia J5429 (Jap.), Decca 20153, Music & Arts CD674; Ralph Berkowitz, piano *10/24/45* Columbia M684 [CO 35340-1A], 17414D, Arlecchino A74, Columbia RL 3015 [CXLP 2637]
Souvenir de Florence, op. 70. Budapest Quartet, Walter Trampler, viola I, GP, cello I *10/14/60* Columbia (unissued) Library of Congress live; Jascha Heifetz, Israel Baker, violin Milton Thomas, Paul Rosenthal, viola Laurence Lesser, cello II *6/26-28/68* RCA/BMG 61770 [WR-A3-1500-1503], RCA BVCC 37126 (Jap.)
Trio in a, op. 50. Arthur Rubinstein, piano Jascha Heifetz, violin *8/23,24/50* RCA DM-1488 [EO-REO370-2,71-1,72-1, 73-2,74-1AR,75-1,76-1, 72-1AR,78-1,79-2], RCA LM 1120, A 630639,

RCA WDM 1488, La Voix de Son Maitre FALP 166 [EO-LRC-1940], RCA 7768-2-RG(CD), RCA/BMG 61767, RCA CT 7768, BMG 63025, RCA R25C-1065, (Jap.), Andromeda ANDRCD 5131 (Bel.); *(Theme, Variations, Waltz)*, Kroyt-Trio: Karol Szreter, piano Boris Kroyt, violin *1924* Vox 06149 [1432A, 1522A]

Valse Sentimentale, op. 51, no.6 (arr. GP). Ivor Newton, piano *12/7/33* HMV DB 2271, RCA 8419A [2B 4741-1], Music & Arts CD644; Ralph Berkowitz, piano *1949* Concerts on Film Library/*Gregor Piatigorsky* Kultur (video)/DVD 1101; Ralph Berkowitz, piano *9/18/50* RCA LM 1187 [EO-RB-3780-1A], RCA Italianna LM 1187, RCA WDM 1578 [170349-3526A-B1A], RCA ERA 122 (45 rpm extended play) [E3RW-2669 1S A2], RCA 30.113 (South Africa), Andromeda ANDRCD 5131 (Bel.); Ralph Berkowitz, piano *9/18/50* RCA LM 2361 [EO-RB 3780-B1A(K2RP 4072)]

Variations on a Rococo Theme, op. 33 (abridged), Karol Szreter, Blüthner piano *4-5/25* Polydor DD 66168-69 (B28002/5) [1263av,1264av,1265av,1265 av], Schallplatte Grammophon 66168-69, Polydor 40016-17 (Jap.), Arlecchino A74

Tessarini, Carlo (1690–after 1766)

Sonata in F (Adagio and Presto), Valentin Pavlovsky, piano *10/22/36* RCA RL-14-a [VD 925] (Victor Record Lover's Society) (Jap.) [8584-1], Pearl GEMM CD9981-3

Thomé, Francis (1850–1909)

Simple Aveu, op. 25 (arr.Béla). Karol Szreter, piano Dajos Béla, violin *3/8/27* Parlophone E 10580 [WxxB 7644], Odeon 0-6625 (AA68042); Karol Szreter, piano Dajos Béla, violin *2/23/28* Odeon 0-6444 [WxxB 7644²], AA.212025, Odeon O.6625b

Toch, Ernst (1887–1964)

Divertimento, op. 37, no.2 (transc. GP), Jascha Heifetz, violin *4/16/65* RCA LM/LSC 3009 [SR-A3-1480], BMG 61766

Toselli, Enrico (1883–1926)

Serenade, op. 6 (Rimpianto no.1), Edith Lorand Trio *12/11/23* Parlophon [6598], Parlophone E-10134
Serenata, Edith Lorand with Orchestra Parlophon P 1468 [8716]

Tosti, Paolo (1846–1916)

Chanson de l'adieu, Karol Szreter? piano Georges Boulanger, violin *4-5/25* Vox 06246 [2164-A]
L'Idéale (arr.). Karol Szreter, piano Dajos Béla, violin *3/2/27* Parlophone E 10666 [xxB 7636], Odeon AA68035, 76612, Odeon O-6612AA, AA.212020, Odeon O-6608, Odeon U10014 (Jap.); Karol Szreter, piano Dajos Béla, violin *2/23/28* Odeon 0-6612B (AA68035b) [(W)xxB 7636², xxB 7636³], Odeon A.170102, Columbia G 50201-D

Turina, Joaquín (1882–1949)

Trio no.1, op. 35, Leonard Pennario, piano Jascha Heifetz, violin *11/6/63* RCA LM/LSC 2957 [PR-A5-5876-78], RCA AGL1-4931, BMG 61758

Valdez, Charles Robert

Gypsy Serenade, Michael Raucheisen? piano Edith Lorand, violin *10/26/23* Parlophon P-1583 [6514-2 (6412 unissued)], Parlophone E 10134

Valensin, Georges (18th c.)

Minuet (arr. GP), Karol Szreter, piano *1927* Odeon 2000 series, Odeon (Jap.)

Vivaldi, Antonio (1678–1741)

Concerto for Violin and Cello in Bb, F. IV, no.2, Jascha Heifetz, violin, Chamber Orchestra *10/10/63* RCA LM/LSC/LSCSD 2867 [PR-A5-4538], RCA SB 6661, BMG 61761

Walton, William (1902–1982)

Concerto. Charles Munch, Boston Symphony Orchestra *1/28,30/57* RCA LM/LSC 2109 [H2-RB-1204 (mvt I), 1205 (mvt II), 1206 (mvt III)], RCA AGL1-4086, RCA SB 6676, RB 16027, RCA LSB 4101, RCA 09026-61498-2(CD), RCA/BMG 74321, 29248, 925752, 92575, RCA/BMG

Classics 09026-61498-4 (cassette), Testament SBT1371, RCA SACD Hybrid Multichannell 82876663752, RCA Living Stereo CRCA 66375 SA (SACD Hybrid Multichannel); Sir Malcolm Sargent, Royal Philharmonic *2/13/57* BBC/ EMI Classics DVD DVA 4928419, Angel Records DVD 92841

Weber, Carl Maria von (1786–1826)
Adagio and Rondo, from op. 10b, Nos. 2 and 3 (J.100, 101)(arr. GP). Ivor Newton, piano *12/17/34* HMV DB 2539 [2EA-595-2], RCA 8995, Victor RL-8 (Jap.), TLC-2587 private LP issue Thomas Clear, Music & Arts CD 644, Testament SBT 2158; Joseph Benvenuti, piano *10/36* film *Andante [sic] et Rondo* Compagnie des Grands Artistes Internationaux (CGAI), Lyon; *1939* included in compilation film *First Film Concert* (CGAI), Lyon; *1948–1955* issued as *Andante [sic] et Rondo* Hoffberg Productions (U.S.), Official Filmusical series; Max Rudolf, Symphony of the Air *1/30/56* WRCA-TV (NBC) Festival of Music (*Producers Showcase* series), VAI DVD 4244; *(Rondo),* Ralph Berkowitz, piano *9/19/50* RCA LM 1187 [EORB-3785-1(E1-LRC-224)], RCA Italianna LM 1187, RCA WDM 1578[49-3526B-1A], Andromeda ANDRCD 5131 (Bel.)
Sonatina in A, from op. 10b, no.5 (J. 103) (arr. GP), Ivor Newton, piano *12/7/33, 5/15/34* HMV DB 2248 [2B 4738-5, 2B 4739-2], RCA 8453, Victor JD405 (Jap.), Pearl GEMM 9447, Music & Arts CD644, Pavil CD, Testament SBT 2158

Weber — arr. Hector Berlioz (1803–69)
Afforderung zum Tanz, op. 65, Oskar Fried, Vox Symphonie Orchester *7 or 8/23* Vox 01481 [1420A, 1421A]

Webern, Anton von (1883–1945)
Two Pieces (1899), Charles Rosen, piano *3/29/72* Columbia (unissued)
Sonata (1914), Charles Rosen, piano *3/29/72* Columbia (unissued)
Drei Kleine Stücke, op. 11, Charles Rosen, piano *3/29/72* Columbia M4-35193 [AL 35733], CBS S76775/8, CBS 79402, Sony SM3K 45845

Work, Henry Clay (1832–1884)
Plantation Songs (arr. Maud Powell) Kingdom Coming Edith Lorand Trio *10/27/23* Parlophon P.1632 [6521 (6520 unissued)], Parlophone 10113

Appendix B: Live Performances

Achron, Isidor (1892–1948)
Gavotte Satirique, op. 10, Valentin Pavlovsky, piano *3/7/43* WNYC 3 P.M. Frick Museum

Bach, J.S.
Suite no. 3 in C, BWV 1009, 7/9/50 CBS

Beethoven, Ludwig van (1770–1827)
Sonata no. 3 in A, op. 69, Ralph Berkowitz, piano *10/22/44* Frick Museum/Rhodes Collection G1206-10 via WNYC
Trio in G, op. 9, no.1, Itzhak Perlman, violin Pinchas Zuckerman, viola *7/8/74* City of London Festival BBC MX30 T36377
7 Variations in Eb on Mozart's Bei Männern welche Liebe fühlen from the Magic Flute, Wo046, Ralph Berkowitz, piano *12/3/50*
Rhodes Collection 16M 280A via WNYC

Beglarian, Grant (1927–2002)
Diversions for Viola, Cello and Orchestra, Milton Katims, viola Joseph Levine, Seattle Symphony *10/3/72* Private

Bloch, Ernest (1880–1959)
Schelomo. Sir Thomas Beecham, Royal Philharmonic *10/28/37* BBC, Queen's Hall; Howard Barlow, CBS Symphony *12/1/43* CBS *Invitation to Music* 11:45 P.M. (WTOP Washington, D.C.), Rhodes Collection G703-06, Library of Congress ItemA1391/D12-A1393/D12 [tape MT# 117]; Ernest Bloch, WOR Radio Orchestra *1944* WOR radio; Artur Rodzinski, New York Philharmonic *11/26/44* CBS, Library of Congress 16-P-527-28, 17-2430g2422, released on AS 631 (CD); rebroadcast of above [Rodzinski] *12/6/44* AFRS, *Concert Hall* H-33 no.55 (Introduction by Lionel Barrymore); Maurice Abravanel, Utah Symphony *1/24/51* Utah Symphony; Alfred Wallenstein, Los Angeles Philharmonic *1/13/55* Los Angeles Philharmonic Archives; Alfred Wallenstein, Los Angeles Philharmonic *1/23/55* NBC *Standard Hour* no.1437, San Diego; Zubin Mehta, Los Angeles Philharmonic *1/26/71* Los Angeles Philharmonic, private

Boccherini, Luigi (1843–1805)
Concerto in Bb, op. 34. Sir Thomas Beecham, Royal Philharmonic *10/28/37* BBC, Queen's Hall; José Iturbi, Rochester Philharmonic *1/11/40* WJZ 9:00 P.M.; Concert Orchestra *12/8/43* WABC 11:30 P.M.; Eugene Ormandy, Philadelphia Orchestra *3/26/43* Philadelphia Orchestra/Rhodes Collection; no conductor, WOR Radio Orchestra *1944* WOR radio
Sonata in C (arr. GP), Ralph Berkowitz, piano *mid 1940's* Library of Congress NCP 1312 *Great Artists* no.62 (Voice of America) Master no. DS-155
Quintet in C, G.310, Budapest Quartet, GP, cello I *10/14/60* Library of Congress LWO 3176
Quintet in Eb, G.266 (1771), Budapest Quartet, GP, cello I *10/6/60* Library of Congress LWO 3171
Quintet in E, G.275, Budapest Quartet, GP, cello I *10/21/60* Library of Congress LWO 3184, rebroadcast *1/19/90* WETA-FM (*Presto* only)

Brahms, Johannes (1833–1897)

Concerto in a for Violin and Cello, op. 102. Nathan Milstein, violin Hans Lange, New York Philharmonic *3/4/34* WABC [3 P.M., Major La Guardia, speaker] CBS; Erica Morini, violin Oswald Kabasta, Vienna Symphony Orchestra *4/13/37* Austrian Radio; Erica Morini, violin Boston Symphony, Serge Koussevitzky *8/4/46* CBS; Yehudi Menuhin, violin Sir Adrian Boult, BBC Orchestra *8/22,24/48* BBC Symphony, Usher Hall, Edinburgh Festival (rebroadcast 9/4/48); Efrem Zimbalist, violin Alexander Hilsberg, Curtis Symphony Orchestra *1/5/49* Library of Congress, Curtis Institute 3 16" acetates; Isaac Stern, violin Thomas Schippers, New York Philharmonic *7/29/53* WNYC 8:30, Lewisohn Stadium; Isaac Stern, violin Pierre Monteux, Boston Symphony Orchestra *7/31/55* Berkshire Festival, CBS *World Music Festivals*; Jascha Heifetz, violin Leonard Bernstein, New York Philharmonic *9/1/63* New York Philharmonic, Hollywood Bowl; Jascha Heifetz, violin (no conductor) *10/15/66* Private/(*Heifetz-Piatigorsky Concert*, Carnegie Hall)

Piano Quartet no.1 in g, op. 25, Daniel Barenboim, piano Itzhak Perlman, violin Pinchas Zukerman, viola *7/74* City of London Festival BBC MX30 T36377 broadcast *12/25/74*

Piano Quartet no.3 in c, op. 60, Daniel Barenboim, piano Itzhak Perlman, violin Pinchas Zukerman, viola *7/8/74* City of London Festival BBC MX30 T36377

Quintet no.2 in G, op. 111, Jascha Heifetz, Christiaan Bor, violin Yukiko Kamei, viola Sheila Rheinhold, viola *4/8/72* Private (*Heifetz-Piatigorsky Concert*/USC)

Sextet no.1 in Bb, op. 18, Budapest Quartet, Walter Trampler, viola I GP, cello I *10/6/60* Library of Congress LWO 3171

Sonata no.1 in e, op. 38. Valentin Pavlovsky, piano *3/7/43* WNYC 3 P.M. Frick Museum; Reginald Stewart, piano *3/21/47* Library of Congress LPO 1772F, LWO 1088 (2DF,2SF 16") (5232,11B2 x1088), — rebroadcast *1/19/90* WETA-FM, (released on Music & Arts CD 644); Ralph Berkowitz, piano *12/3/50* Rhodes Collection 16M 283A via WNYC; Daniel Barenboim, piano *7/5/74* City of London Festival BBC MX29 T36378

Sonata no.2 in F, op. 99, Reginald Stewart, piano *3/21/47* Library of Congress LPO 1772F, LWO 1088 (2DF,2SF 16") (5232,11B2 x1088), — rebroadcast *1/19/90* WETA-FM (first mvt)

Bruch, Max (1838–1920)

Kol Nidre, op. 47, Alfred Wallenstein, Los Angeles Philharmonic *12/16/51* NBC *Standard Hour*

Chopin, Frédéric (1810–1849)

Sonata in g, op. 65, Daniel Barenboim, piano *7/5/74* City of London Festival BBC MX29 T36378

Debussy, Claude (1862–1918)

Romance (arr. GP), Valentin Pavlovsky, piano *2/16/39* NBC *Kraft Music Hall*, Bing Crosby [KFI (Los Angeles) 7 P.M., WRC (Washington, D.C.), 10 P.M.]

Sonata no.1 in d. Ralph Berkowitz, piano *12/3/50* Rhodes Collection 16M 280B via WNYC; Daniel Barenboim, piano *7/5/74* City of London Festival BBC MX29 T36378

Dinicu, Grigoras (1889–1949)-Heifetz (1900–1987)

Hora Staccato, Valentin Pavlovsky, piano *2/16/39* NBC *Kraft Music Hall*, Bing Crosby [KFI (Los Angeles) 7 P.M., WRC (Washington, D.C.), 10 P.M.]

Dukelsky, Vladimir (1903–1969)

Concerto, Serge Koussevitzky, Boston Symphony Orchestra *1/9/46* CBS (Carl Fischer, Inc.) ending missing

Dvořák, Antonín (1841–1904)

Concerto in b, op. 104, — Nicolai Malko, Radio Symfoniorkestret (Allegro) *10/13/32* Danish Radio/ Danacord DACO 148-38, CD303; Eric Fogg, BBC Empire Orchestra *6/14/38* BBC MX40 T28027 (rebroadcast 11/29/38); Fritz Reiner, Pittsburgh Symphony Orchestra *11/15/41* private; Alexander Hilsberg, Philadelphia Orchestra *12/7/46* WCBS/Library of Congress P1833-M; Sir John Barbirolli, Halle Orchestra *9/1/48* BBC Edinburgh Festival; Eduard van Beinum, Concertgebouw Orchestra *9/4/48* BBC Edinburgh Festival (rebroadcasts, 12/2/48, 2/25/49, 3/3/49; Hans Schwieger, Kansas City Symphony *11/21/50* WHB Radio; Alfred Wallenstein, Hollywood

Bowl Symphony *7/26/51* AFRS; Eugene Ormandy, Philadelphia Orchestra *12/29/56* CBS; Erich Leinsdorf, Los Angeles Philharmonic *3/7/57* Los Angeles Philharmonic Archives; Richard Burgin, Boston Symphony Orchestra *2/5/60* Private; Richard Burgin, Boston Symphony Orchestra *2/6/60* Private/Library of Congress; Zubin Mehta, Los Angeles Philharmonic *1/26/71* Los Angeles Philharmonic; Pierre Boulez, New York Philharmonic *9/20/72* New York Philharmonic; Milton Katims, Seattle Symphony *10/3/72* Private; Maurice Abravanel, Utah Symphony *1/12/74* Utah Symphony/Private; Maurice Abravanel, Utah Symphony *3/31/76* Utah Symphony/Private

Quintet in A, op. 81, Jacob Lateiner, piano Jascha Heifetz, violin Israel Baker, violin Joseph de Pasquale, viola *1964* (*Heifetz-Piatigorsky Concert*, San Francisco/Private Edition XMS 964)

Elgar, Sir Edward (1857–1934)

Concerto in e, op. 85. Thomas Beecham, BBC Symphony Orchestra *11/22/33* BBC, Queen's Hall (rebroadcast *2/22/34*); Thomas Beecham, BBC Symphony Orchestra *12/9/39* BBC; John Barbirolli, New York Philharmonic *11/10/40* WABC 3 P.M. (Deems Taylor announcer)/CBS/Buchsbaum Collection

Fauré, Gabriel-Urbain (1845–1924)

Elégie, op. 24 (slightly abridged), Donald Voorhees, NBC Symphony *4/1/60* NBC-TV *Bell Telephone Hour* color, VAI DVD 4215

Francoeur, François (1698–1787)

Gavotte and Vivo (with piano), *1/19/36* WJSV *Ford Sunday Evening Hour* 9 P.M./WABC

Granados, Enrique (1867–1916)

Intermezzo (from Goyescas), Victor Kolar, Detroit Symphony *2/3/35* WABC 9 P.M. rebroadcast *2/5/35* 3 P.M.

Orientale, from Spanish Dances, op. 37, no.2 (arr. GP), Valentin Pavlovsky, piano *3/7/43* WNYC 3 P.M. Frick Museum

Handel, George Frideric (1685–1759)—arr. Johan Halvorsen (1864–1935)

Passacaglia, Jascha Heifetz, violin *9/1/63* Hollywood Bowl

Haydn, Joseph (1732–1809)

Concerto in D, op. 101. Bruno Walter, New York Philharmonic-Symphony *1/31/32* WABC 3:15 P.M. Brooklyn Academy of Music; Sir Henry Wood, BBC Empire Orchestra *9/28/35* BBC Promenade Concert; Victor Kolar, Ford Symphony Orchestra (Detroit Sym) *1/19/36* WABC; *(Adagio),* Victor Kolar, Ford Symphony Orchestra (Detroit Sym) *1/19/36* WJSV *Ford Sunday Evening Hour* 9 P.M.; Hyam Greenbaum, BBC Television Orchestra *5/28/37* BBC Television; Artur Rodzinski, New York Philharmonic *11/26/40* CBS; Artur Rodzinski, New York Philharmonic *11/23,24/44* Private; Boston Symphony, Charles Munch *7/15/51* CBS; Dimitri Mitropoulos, New York Philharmonic *11/1,2/51* Carnegie Hall; Richard Burgin, Boston Symphony Orchestra *11/9/51* Library of Congress LWO 9804 R44 B2; Richard Burgin, Boston Symphony Orchestra *11/9,10/51* Private, Rehearsals; no conductor *10/15/66* Private (*Heifetz-Piatigorsky Concert*, Carnegie Hall); Alexander Schneider, Casals Festival Orchestra *6/2/67* Voice of America (Casals Festival)

Divertimento (arr. GP), Ivor Newton, piano *10/6/54* BBC Television, *International Celebrity Recital* [Film: Tape33 TV 45-54 T13/123 T14]

Hindemith, Paul (1895–1963)

Concerto (1940). Eugene Ormandy, Philadelphia Orchestra *3/26/43* Philadelphia Orchestra/Buchsbaum Collection; Paul Hindemith, CBS Symphony *12/15/43* CBS *Invitation to Music* over WOR

Liadov, Anatol (1855–1914)

March-Variations (arr. GP), Ivor Newton, piano (?) *3/25/56* Film: BBC Tape 87 TV 55-64

Russian Dance (arr. GP), Victor Kolar, Detroit Symphony *2/3/35* WABC 9 P.M. rebroadcast *2/5/35* 3 P.M.

Marcello, Benedetto (1686–1739)

Sonata, Valentin Pavlovsky, piano *3/7/43* WNYC 3 P.M. Frick Museum

Martinů, Bohuslav (1890–1959)
Variations on a Rossini Theme, Valentin Pavlovsky, piano *3/7/43* WNYC 3 P.M. Frick Museum

Massenet, Jules (1842–1912)
Elégie (arr.), Jennie Tourel, soprano Donald Voorhees, NBC Symphony *10/16/44* WEAF/NBC *Bell Telephone Hour,* Library of Congress RWA 6594 A3-4, and LT-10 4058 acetate from WEAF

Mendelssohn, Felix (1809–1847)
Octet in Eb, op. 20, Jascha Heifetz et al. *4/4/65* Private (*Heifetz-Piatigorsky Concert,* USC, Los Angeles)
Sonata no.2 in D, op. 58 (Adagio), Daniel Barenboim, piano *7/5/74 City of London Festival* BBC MX29 T36378

Menotti, Gian Carlo (1911–2007)
Suite for 2 Cellos and Piano, Charles Wadsworth, piano Leslie Parnas, cello II *5/20/73* Private/Chamber Music Society, Lincoln Center

Milhaud, Darius (1892–1974)
Concerto no.1, John Barnett, Hollywood Bowl Symphony *8/25/53* Private/AFRS

Mozart, Wolfgang Amadeus (1756–1791)
Concerto for Horn in Eb, K (arr. Cassadó), Serge Koussevitzky, Boston Symphony Orchestra *3/25/33* Boston Symphony, NBC Blue network
Sonatina (arr. GP), Valentin Pavlovsky, piano *3/7/43* WNYC 3 P.M. Frick Museum
Piano Quartet in Eb, K.493, Daniel Barenboim, piano Itzhak Perlman, violin Pinchas Zuckerman, viola *7/8/74 City of London Festival* BBC MX30 T36377

Paganini, Niccolò (1782–1840)
La Campanella (arr. GP), Reginald Stewart, Toronto Promenade Symphony *7/4/40* WMAL, 9:15 (Washington, D.C.) [possibly with piano]

Piatigorsky, Gregor (1903–1976)
Prayer (Homage to Ernest Bloch). 12/74 Private; *5/17/76* Private/Grinnell College
Promenade (AKA Stroll or Procession), 5/17/76 Private/Grinnell College
Variations on a Theme of Paganini. Donald Voorhees, NBC Symphony (abridged) *10/15/45* NBC *Bell Telephone Hour,* AFRS *Concert Hall* no.226; RL 8685, 8686, RWA 7182 A2-3/LT-10 4077 Library of Congress, released by Pearl GEMM CD9981-3; Columbus Symphony *1946* Buchsbaum Collection; Pierre Monteux, San Francisco Symphony *1/26/47* NBC *Standard Hour* no.1031

Prokofiev, Sergey (1891–1953)
Masques, from Romeo and Juliet (arr. GP). Ralph Berkowitz, piano *mid 1940's* NCP 1312 *Great Artists* no.62 VOA Library of Congress; Valentin Pavlovsky, piano *3/7/43* WNYC 3 P.M. Frick Museum

Rachmaninoff, Sergey (1873–1943)
Sing Not to Me, Beautiful Maiden (arr. Kreisler from Romnasy, op. 4/4, orchestration by De Filippi), Jan Peerce, tenor, André Kostelanetz, CBS Symphony *4/4/43 Pause That Refreshes on the Air* (CBS), AFRS *Concert Hall* no.133/134 Prg #3, Prg #86, Library of Congress LWO 5855 r28A1/LTC 6830 from WABC radio, Buchsbaum Collection
When Night Descends in Silence (arr. from Romnasy, op. 4/3, orchestration by De Filippi), Jan Peerce, tenor, André Kostelanetz, CBS Symphony *2/28/43, 4/4/43* WABC 4:30 P.M. *Pause That Refreshes on the Air* (CBS), — rebroadcasts: AFRS *Concert Hall* no.133/134 Prg #86, Library of Congress, LWO 5855 r28A1, Universal WABC 1121 (78A) 78 rpm (Library of Congress)
Sonata in g, op. 19. Ralph Berkowitz, piano *10/22/44* Frick Museum/Rhodes Collection G1206-10 via WNYC; *(Andante)* Victor Babin, piano *6/3/70* Cleveland Institute of Music, Tape 1240; John Browning, piano *5/20/73* Private/Chamber Music Society, Lincoln Center

Ravel, Maurice (1875–1943)
Pièce en forme de Habanera, André Kostelanetz, CBS Symphony *4/4/43 Pause That Refreshes on the Air* (CBS), Library of Congress LWO 5855 r29A1/Buchsbaum Collection

Rimsky-Korsakov, Nikolai (1844–1908)

Flight of the Bumble Bee, Victor Kolar, Detroit Symphony *2/3/35* WABC 9 P.M. rebroadcast *2/5/35* 3 P.M.

Rubinstein, Anton (1829–1894)

Melody in F, op. 1, no.3. Ralph Berkowitz, piano *early 12/43* War Department, V-Disc 133-B, VP418-D3MC-484, Biddulph LAB 117; Donald Voorhees, NBC Symphony *6/18/51* NBC *Bell Telephone Hour* [Ct1039], RWA 7926 B3-4, and LT-10 8071 Library of Congress

Saint-Saëns, Camille (1835–1921)

Allegro Appassionato, op. 43. Donald Voorhees, NBC Symphony *10/16/44* WEAF/NBC *Bell Telephone Hour,* AFRS *Concert Hall* H33 no.77; Donald Voorhees, NBC Symphony *7/19/48* NBC *Bell Telephone Hour;* Alfred Wallenstein, Los Angeles Philharmonic *12/16/51* NBC *Standard Hour;* Ivor Newton, piano *10/6/54* BBC Television, *International Celebrity Recital* [Film: Tape33 TV 45-54 T13/123 T14]; Donald Voorhees, NBC Symphony *4/1/60* NBC-TV *Bell Telephone Hour* color, VAI DVD 4215

Concerto no.1 in a, op. 33. Hans Lange, NY Philharmonic-Symphony *2/9/36* WABC/WJSV, 3 P.M. (Washington, D.C.) KHJ (Los Angeles); Reginald Stewart, Toronto Promenade Symphony *7/4/40* WMAL, 9:30 (Washington, D.C.); *9/15/40* WJZ 10 P.M. (last concert of season); *9/19/40* WMAL, 9:15 (rebroadcast, Washington, D.C.); José Iturbi, Rochester Philharmonic *1/11/40* WJZ 9:00 P.M.; Donald Voorhees, NBC Symphony (abridged) *6/18/51* NBC *Bell Telephone Hour* [CT1039], RWA 7926 B3-4, and LT-10 8071 Library of Congress; Thomas Schippers, New York Philharmonic *7/29/53* WNYC 8:30 P.M. Lewisohn Stadium; John Barnett, Hollywood Bowl Symphony *8/25/53* Private/AFRS

The Swan (Le Cyne) from Le Carnaval des Animaux. with harp *1/19/36* WJSV *Ford Sunday Evening Hour* 9 P.M./WABC; André Kostelanetz, CBS Symphony (orchestration by David Terry) *1/31/43* WABC/WJSV 4:30 P.M. *The Pause That Refreshes on the Air* (CBS), Library of Congress, LWO 5855 r26B3-27A1; Ralph Berkowitz, piano *early 12/43* War Department, V-Disc 133-A [VP417-D3M3-483], Biddulph LAB 117; Donald Voorhees, NBC Symphony *10/16/44* WEAF/NBC *Bell Telephone Hour,* AFRS *Concert Hall* H33 no.77; Donald Voorhees, NBC Symphony *6/18/51* NBC *Bell Telephone Hour* [Ct1039], RWA 7926 B3-4, and LT-10 8071 Library of Congress; Ivor Newton, piano *10/6/54* BBC Television, *International Celebrity Recital* [Film: Tape33 TV 45-54 T13/123 T14]

Sarasate, Pablo de (1844–1906)

Zapateado, op. 23, no.2 (arr.). Victor Kolar, Detroit Symphony *2/3/35* WABC 9 P.M. rebroadcast *2/5/35* 3 P.M.; Valentin Pavlovsky, piano *12/3/36* NBC *Kraft Music Hall,* Bing Crosby[KFI (Los Angeles) 7 P.M.]

Schubert, Franz (1797–1828)

Allegro Grazioso (arr. Cassado), Valentin Pavlovsky, piano *3/7/43* WNYC 3 P.M. Frick Museum

Quintet in C, op. 163, D.956. Budapest Quartet, GP, cello I *10/21/60* Library of Congress LWO 3184, rebroadcast *1/19/90* WETA-FM; Alexander Schneider, Isidore Cohen, violin Milton Thomas, viola Pablo Casals, cello I *6/2/67* Voice of America (Casals Festival), Library of Congress LVH 1801 videocassette

Schumann, Robert (1810–1856)

Concerto in a, op. 129. Bruno Walter, New York Philharmonic-Symphony *1/31/32* WABC [3:15 P.M.]; Eugene Goosens, Cincinnati Symphony *12/18/36* WABC/WKRC (CBS), rebroadcast WJSV *4/13/37* [2:45-4:30]; Sir John Barbirolli, New York Philharmonic-Symphony *3/27/37* WABC 3 P.M. [Deems Taylor announcer]; Reginald Stewart, Toronto Philharmonic Orchestra *6/26/41*; Fritz Reiner, New York Philharmonic-Symphony *4/4/43* WTOP Washington, D.C., 3 P.M., Private/Rhodes Collection G395-400; via WABC (copy at NY Philharmonic Archives), Buchsbaum Collection; Boston Symphony, Serge Koussevitzky *8/8/46* CBS; Dimitri Mitropoulos, New York Philharmonic *11/4/51* Private, CBS; Pablo Casals, Casals Festival Orchestra *5/31/67* Voice of America, Library of Congress LVH 1817 videocassette

Fantasiestücke, op. 73, Daniel Barenboim, piano *7/5/74 City of London Festival* BBC MX29 T36378

Fünf Stücke im Volkston, op. 105 (Romanze), Valentin Pavlovsky, piano *3/7/43* WNYC 3 P.M. Frick Museum

Träumerei, op. 15, with piano *1/19/36* WJSV *Ford Sunday Evening Hour* 9 P.M./WABC

Shostakovich, Dmitri (1906–1975)

Sonata, op. 40. Valentin Pavlovsky, piano *6/28/42* WQXR 6 P.M. *Russian War Relief Concert,* Rhodes Collection 1607-09 (not located); Reginald Stewart, piano *3/21/47* Library of Congress LPO 1772F, LWO 1088 (2DF, 2SF 16")(5232,11B2 x1088), — rebroadcast *1/19/90* WETA, issued on Music & Arts CD 644

Strauss, Richard (1864–1949)

Don Quixote, op. 35. Serge Koussevitzky, Boston Symphony Orchestra, Jean Lefranc, viola *3/25/33* Boston Symphony, NBC Blue network; Eugene Goosens, Cincinnati Symphony, Vladimir Bakaleinikoff, viola *12/18/36* WABC/WKRC (CBS), rebroadcast WJSV*4/13/37* [2:45-4:30]; Fritz Reiner, NBC Symphony *3/10/42* NBC; Richard Burgin, Boston Symphony Orchestra *1/16/43* Buchsbaum Collection; Eugene Ormandy, Philadelphia Orchestra *1/4/45* Philadelphia Orchestra; Eugene Ormandy, Philadelphia Orchestra *2/24/45* Philadelphia Orchestra/Buchsbaum Collection; Richard Burgin, Boston Symphony Orchestra *11/9/51* Boston Symphony Orchestra; Richard Burgin, Boston Symphony Orchestra *11/9,10/51* Private, Rehearsals; Charles Munch, Boston Symphony Orchestra, Joseph de Pasquale, viola *8/9/53* Berkshire Festival, WCBS *World Music Festivals* 2:30; Alfred Wallenstein, Los Angeles Philharmonic *1/13/55* Los Angeles Philharmonic Archives; Eugene Ormandy, Philadelphia Orchestra *12/31/55* Philadelphia Orchestra; Zubin Mehta, Casals Festival Orchestra, Milton Thomas, viola *6/3/67* Voice of America (Casals Festival); Leonard Bernstein, New York Philharmonic *10/21,26/70* Private; Zubin Mehta, Los Angeles Philharmonic, Jan Hlinka, viola *1/26/71* Private

Stravinsky, Igor (1882–1971)

Suite Italienne (Adagio, Allegretto grazioso, Presto), Ralph Berkowitz, piano *12/3/50* Rhodes Collection 16M 280C via WNYC. *(Aria),* Victor Babin, piano *6/3/70* Cleveland Institute of Music, Tape 1240; *(Introduction and Finale) (arr. GP for 4 cellos),* GP, Stephen Kates, Nathaniel Rosen, Jeffrey Solow *5/18/73* WQXR-FM *Listening Room;* (complete) GP, Stephen Kates, Nathaniel Rosen, Jeffrey Solow *5/20/73* Private/Chamber Music Society, Lincoln Center; National Symphony Orchestra Cello Ensemble, Mark Evans Steven Honigsberg, James Lee, David Teie *10/3/01* Library of Congress Recording Library RGA 9985 RWE 5567-5568 preservation master (digital stereo); *(arr. GP for violin and cello),* Jascha Heifetz, violin *4/8/72* Private *(Heifetz-Piatigorsky Concert/ USC)*

Tchaikovsky, Piotr Illyich (1840–1893)

Andante Cantabile, op. 11 (orchestration by Julius Berger), André Kostelanetz, CBS Symphony *2/28/43* WABC 4:30 P.M. *Pause That Refreshes on the Air* (CBS), Library of Congress, LWO 5855 r28A1

Souvenir de Florence, op. 70, Budapest Quartet, Walter Trampler, viola I GP, cello *10/14/60* Library of Congress, LWO 3176

Trio in a, op. 50, Daniel Pollack, piano Jascha Heifetz, violin *4/8/72* Private/*(Heifetz-Piatigorsky Concert,* USC)

Valse Sentimentale, op. 51, no.6 (arr.). Valentin Pavlovsky, piano *12/3/36* NBC *Kraft Music Hall,* Bing Crosby [KFI (Los Angeles) 7 P.M.]; André Kostelanetz, CBS Symphony *2/28/43 Pause That Refreshes on the Air* (CBS), Library of Congress LWO 5855 r28A1

Variations on a Rococo Theme, Alfred Wallenstein, WOR Orchestra *10/3/41* WOR *America Preferred* series Deems Taylor, commentator, 9:30 P.M.

Toch, Ernst (1887–1964)

Divertimento, op. 37, no.2 (transc. GP), Jascha Heifetz, violin *4/4/65* Private *(Heifetz-Piatigorsky Concert,* USC, Los Angeles)

Valensin, Georges (18th c.)

Minuet (arr. GP). Valentin Pavlovsky, piano *2/16/39* NBC *Kraft Music Hall,* Bing Crosby [KFI (Los Angeles) 7 P.M., WRC Washington, D.C., 10 P.M.]; *(orchestration by Harold Byrns),* André Kostelanetz, CBS Symphony *2/4/43 Pause That Refreshes on the Air* (CBS), Library of Congress LWO 5855 r29A1/Buchsbaum Collection

Villa-Lobos, Heitor (1887–1959)
Bachianas Brasileiras no.5, Beverly Sills, soprano GP, Myung-Wa Chung, Stephen Kates, Laurence Lesser, Leslie Parnas, Nathaniel Rosen, Jeffrey Solow, Paul Tobias *5/20/73* Private/Chamber Music Society, Lincoln Center

Vivaldi, Antonio (1678–1741)
Concerto in Bb for Violin and Cello, F IV, no.2, Jascha Heifetz, violin, Chamber Orchestra *4/4/65* Private (*Heifetz-Piatigorsky Concert,* USC, Los Angeles)

Wagner, Richard (1813–1883)
The Evening Star (from Tannhäuser), Detroit Symphony, Victor Kolar(?) *1930s Ford Sunday Evening Hour*

Walton, Sir William (1902–1982)
Concerto. Charles Munch, Boston Symphony Orchestra *1/25/57* Private/Library of Congress WGB (5-281-286), LWO 7483, r15B2-16A-2, Voice of America (1782-87 VOA 198); Sir Malcolm Sargent, Royal Philharmonic *2/13/57* BBC Film: Tape 87 TV 55-64/EMI Classics DVD DVA 4928419, Angel Records DVD 92841; Dimitri Mitropoulos, New York Philharmonic *5/2,3/57* Private/Library of Congress RWD 8251 A1, Collector's no.139, Kostelanetz Collection

Weber, Carl Maria von (1786–1826)
Adagio and Rondo from op. 10b, Nos.2 and 3 (J100,101) (arr. GP). (Rondo only) with piano *1/19/36* WJSV *Ford Sunday Evening Hour* 9 P.M./WABC; André Kostelanetz, CBS Symphony *1/31/43 The Pause That Refreshes on the Air* (CBS), Library of Congress, LWO 5855 r26B3-27A1, [WJSV Washington, D.C. 4:30 P.M.]; Valentin Pavlovsky, piano *mid 1940s* War Department; Donald Voorhees, NBC Symphony *10/16/45* NBC *Bell Telephone Hour,* AFRS *Concert Hall* H-33 no.77, Library of Congress LT-10 4077; Max Rudolf, orchestra *1/30/56* VAI 4244 (DVD) WRCA-TV (NBC) Festival of Music (from Hurok's *Producers Showcase*)
Sonatina in A (Sicilenne and Variations)(arr. GP); Valentin Pavlovsky, piano *3/7/43* WNYC 3 P.M. Frick Museum; Ivor Newton, piano (?) *3/25/56* Film: BBC Tape 87 TV 55-64

Webern, Anton von (1883–1945)
Drei Kleine Stücke, op. 11, Victor Babin, piano *6/3/70* Cleveland Institute of Music, Tape 1240
Sonata (1914), Victor Babin, piano *6/3/70* Cleveland Institute of Music, Tape 1240
Two Pieces (1899), Victor Babin, piano *6/3/70* Cleveland Institute of Music, Tape 1240

Appendix C:
Performance Filmography

Bach: *Suite No.1 in G BWV 1007 (Minuets, abridged)*, 1975 *An Afternoon with Gregor Piatigorsky* Phoenix Films, Inc. (16mm color)/BFA Films and Videos *Suite No.3 in C BWV 1009 (Bourrée)*, 1949 *Gregor Piatigorsky* World Artists Inc. (16mm)/ Concerts on Film Library No.105/ Lesser Enterprises Recital 204/*Greatest Artists* TV series (Albert Goldberg, host)/Kultur (video), DVD 1101

Bruch: *Kol Nidre, op. 47 (abridged)*, Lillia Krauss, organ 10/3/73 *Choose Life* Jewish Chautauqua Society Film (16mm color)/Alden Films (video)

Chopin: *Sonata in g, op.65 (Largo)*, Ralph Berkowitz, piano 1949 *Gregor Piatigorsky* World Artists Inc. (16mm)/ Concerts on Film Library No.105/ Lesser Enterprises Recital 204/*Greatest Artists* TV series (Albert Goldberg, host)/Kultur (video), DVD 1101

Fauré: *Elégie, op.24 (slightly abridged)*, Donald Voorhees, NBC Symphony 4/1/60 NBC-TV *Bell Telephone Hour* (color video) Ralph Belamy, host

Haydn: *Divertimento in D [Hob XI:95,113] (arr. GP)*, Ivor Newton, piano 10/6/54 BBC-TV *International Celebrity Recital*

Mendelssohn: *Trio No.1 in d, op.49 (I abridged, II, III)*, Arthur Rubinstein, piano Jascha Heifetz, violin 1949 *The Trio* World Artists Inc. (16mm)/ Concerts on Film Library/*Meet the Masters* TV series Lee J. Cobb, narrator/Mills Picture Corp./Command Performance video/Classic Video Library WV055-35H (Japan) laser disc/Kultur video, DVD 1102

Piatigorsky: *Prayer (AKA Homage à Bloch) (excerpt)* 1975 *An Afternoon with Gregor Piatigorsky* Phoenix Films, Inc. (16mm color)/BFA Films and Videos

Prokofiev: *Masques, from Romeo and Juliet (arr. GP)*, Ralph Berkowitz, piano 1949 *Gregor Piatigorsky* World Artists Inc. (16mm)/ Concerts on Film Library No.105/ Lesser Enterprises Recital 204/ *Greatest Artists* TV series (Albert Goldberg, host)/Kultur (video), DVD 1101

Rubinstein: *Romance, op.44, No.1, (arr. GP)*, Ralph Berkowitz, piano 1949 *Gregor Piatigorsky* World Artists Inc. (16mm)/ Concerts on Film Library No.105/ Lesser Enterprises Recital 204/*Greatest Artists* TV series (Albert Goldberg, host)/Kultur (video), DVD 1101

Saint-Saëns: *Allegro Appassionato, op.43*. Ivor Newton, piano 10/6/54 BBC-TV *International Celebrity Recital;* Donald Voorhees, NBC Symphony 4/1/60 NBC-TV *Bell Telephone Hour* (video color) Ralph Belamy, host

The Swan. (with harp accompaniment) 1946 *Carnegie Hall* United Artists feature film/Federal Films/Bel Canto Society Video/Bel Canto Society DVD 791 (PCM audio)/*Carnegie Hall: A Place of Dreams* BMG video 0902660883-3 (excerpt)/Kino Video, DVD 1992; Ivor Newton, piano 10/6/54 BBC-TV *International Celebrity Recital*

Schubert: *Quintet in C, op.163, D.956,* Alexander Schneider, Isidore Cohen, violin Milton Thomas, viola Pablo Casals, violoncello I 6/2/67 Voice of America/Library of Congress Casals Festival video library

Introduction, Theme, and Variations in Bb, op.82, No.2, D.603 (arr. GP, abridged), Ralph Berkowitz, piano 1949 *Gregor Piatigorsky* World Artists Inc. (16mm)/ Concerts on Film Library No.105/ Lesser Enterprises Recital 204/*Greatest Artists* TV series (Albert Goldberg, host)/Kultur (video), DVD 1101

Trio No.1 in Bb, op.99, D.898, (Allegro moderato, abridged) Arthur Rubinstein, piano Jascha Heifetz, violin 1949 *The Trio* World Artists Inc. (16mm)/Concerts on Film Library/*Meet the Masters* TV series Lee J. Cobb, narrator/Mills Picture Corp./Command Performance video/Classic Video Library WV055-35H (Japan) laser disc/Kultur video, DVD 1102/

Schumann: *Concerto in A, op.129,* Pablo Casals, Casals Festival Orchestra 5/31/67 Voice of America/Library of Congress/Casals Festival video library

Tchaikovsky: *Valse Sentimentale, op.51, No.6 (arr. GP),* Ralph Berkowitz, piano 1949 *Gregor Piatigorsky* World Artists Inc. (16mm)/ Concerts on Film Library No.105/ Lesser Enterprises Recital 204/*Greatest Artists* TV series (Albert Goldberg, host)/Kultur (video), DVD 1101

Walton: *Concerto.* Sir Malcolm Sargent, Royal Philharmonic 2/13/57 BBC/EMI Classics DVD DVA 4928419, Angel Records DVD 92841; (cadenza excerpts) c.1966 *Gregor Piatigorsky* Tim Whelan Jr. film

Weber: *Adagio and Rondo, from op.10b, Nos. 2 and 3 (J100,101) (arr. Piatigorsky).* Joseph Benvenuti, piano 10/36 *Andante[sic] et Rondo* Compagnie des Grands Artistes Internationaux (CGAI); 1939 in compilation film *First Film Concert* (CGAI), Lyon; 1948-1955 *Andante et Rondo* Hoffberg Productions (U.S.), Official Filmusical series; Max Rudolf, Symphony of the Air 1/30/56 WRCA-TV (NBC) *Festival of Music* (*Producers Showcase* series) (Charles Laughton, host) VAI DVD 4244

Appendix D: Interviews and Miscellaneous Appearances on Radio and Television

Advertisement-Promotional 1940 Philco and Columbia Demonstration Records (10") 11-B [P28512 1-A] (radio)
Interview with Manuel Weisman 2/18/48 WOKZ (radio), Alton, IL
Address to Merembloom Junior Symphony 4/15/53 Private
Tex and Jinx Show (interview) 1/27/56 NBC-TV (audio only) from WCBS, NY
Sum and Substance, Herman Harvey, host 2/24/63 CBS Television (KNXT-TV), Los Angeles/rebroadcast
A Dialogue of Contemporary Values, Herman Harvey, host 2/24/63 Modern Learning Aids Records [LP] #R-5611 from CBS-TV series *The Sum and Substance*
The Virtuosi 4/16/63 WASH-FM, 9:15 P.M. (Washington, D.C.)
Toscanini: The Man Behind the Legend, Ben Grauer, host 5/7/63 Prg 9 Tape 4177, Library of Congress/BBC (rebroadcast 7/21/64) MY2 LP 30037
Personal Portrait, Lorin Peterson, interviewer 5/29,30/65 KABC (radio)
Creative Person 8/3/65 KCET TV series, Los Angeles video
Gregor Piatigorsky c.1966 16mm film produced by Tim Whelan Jr., also taped interviews (audio only)
CBC Tuesday Night, Larry Solway, host 6/21/66 CBC TV
An Hour with Gregor Piatigorsky, Tony Thomas, host 1966 CBC radio
Casals Festival, interview with Harold Boxer 5/67 Voice of America (radio)
Meet the Masters, Henri Temianka, host 2/16/68 UCLA Film and Television Archive, SLRF A4-154-13 [Database control#: 04-AAI-3022]
Fortsetzung Folgt reading and recollections from *Cellist* in German 1969 Rundfunk-Westdeutsches Fernsehen (7-hour TV series: FORTSETZUNG FOLGT)
Chaim Soutine 1970 RJM Productions (16mm color)
Gregor Piatigorsky: The Master and His Class 1972 KCET-TV (video, color) 2 60' programs
Interview with Hugh Downs 1/22/74 NBC-TV (audio only)
Entertainment Hall of Fame, Gene Kelly, host 3/21/74 NBC-TV (video color) GP accepts the posthumous *Hall of Fame* award for Igor Stravinsky
The Art of Piatigorsky, Natalie Wheen, host 7/5/74 BBC MX29 T36378 radio
In Conversation, with Ivor Newton 7/9/74 BBC MY2 LP36376-f01, rebroadcast 12/25/74 radio
The Art of Piatigorsky 7/11/74 BBC MY2 LP 36406 f01-b02 radio
The Art of Piatigorsky 7/23/74 BBC MY2 LP36341 b1-b02 radio
Composers and Colleagues, John Amis, host 9/27/74 BBC R3 1974, M 5313 W radio
Thoughts on Music and Musicians, Alan Blyth, host 11/26/74 BBC R3 1974, Tape 1+11(trk1), 2504BW (rebroadcast)
Panorama, Maury Povich, host 10/21/74 WTTG-TV-Washington, D.C. BBC R3 M5202R (rebroadcast12/25/74)
Through the Looking Glass, with Lenore Schulkrout and Steve Markham c.1974 KFAC (radio)

Panel discussion on music criticism with Martin Bernheimer and Grant Beglarian c.1974 KUSC (radio)

Memories of Berlin: Twilight of the Weimar Republic c.1974 Phoenix Films (color) CBC Documentary (color film)/Cantor Films. Piatigorsky recalls Schnabel, Flesch, Berg...

Zubin Mehta and His Masters: Rubinstein and Piatigorsky c.1975 Esmeralda Continuum (16mm color)/video

An Afternoon with Gregor Piatigorsky 1975 Phoenix Films, Inc., Steven Grumette Production

The Old Gray Myth, Joseph Benti, host 1976 CBS Television, Los Angeles (16mm color)

Interview with Abram Chasins 3/76 KUSC (radio)

Interview with Carl Princi 4/4/76 KFAC (radio)

Friends of Music 4/18/76 73rd birthday celebration (Voice of America no.517) LCCN: 89740902, LC: RWB 3077 A2-B2

Remarks at Concert 5/17/76 Grinnell College, Private

(Memorial Service) 8/12/76 KUSC, NPR radio Itzhak Perlman, Zubin Mehta, Grant Beglarian, Students...

(Kermit Murdock reads from *Cellist*) 1976 Canadian National Institute for the Blind 921 PIA

Piatigorsky Legacy 1977 KUSC (3 program radio series) Interviews, including students and colleagues, recordings

The Living Stereo Story: Music and Memories from Hi-Fi's Golden Age 1992 RCA Victor RCDJ 61909 with John Pfeiffer and Elliot Forrest: interviews and musical segments

Appendix E: Publications

(*) Works dedicated to GP
(+) Works edited, arranged, or transcribed by GP
(p) Year of publication
(All are for cello and piano unless stated otherwise.)

Achron, Isidor: *Gavotte Satirique*, op.10* (Carl Fischer P2291 ©1943) premiere 4/27/42
_____. *Sonnet*, op.5* (Carl Fischer B2511 © 1940) premiere 1/25/40

Bach[=Ernst][1]**–Piatigorsky**: *Concerto* No.1 (Schott 2405 ©1934/Int'l 852/MMP 1225) also with string orchestra (Int'l) +
_____.[2] *Concerto* No.1 State Music Edition (MZK), Moscow 1961 with additional editing by Alexander Stogorsky

Beglarian, Grant: Fables, Foibles and Fancies for cellist and narrator

Berezowski, Nicolai: *Concerto Lirico,* op.19* for cello and orchestra (Edition Russe de Musique RMV 591 piano reduction © 1935/Boosey & Hawkes)

Borodkin, Samuel: *Synco-Rhythmicon** (M. Witmark & Sons ©1956)

Cadman, Charles Wakefield: *A Mad Empress Remembers: Tone-Drama*, for cello and orchestra* (piano reduction Mills ©1944) Penn. St Bx1 fldr 10, bx3 fldr/bx6 fldr01,02/bx9 fldr 19–20

Cassado, Gaspar: *Partita** (Schott 2383 ©1935)

Castelnuovo-Tedesco, Mario: *Concerto** for cello and orchestra (piano reduction Ricordi 123248 ©1935)
_____, *Figaro** [Rossini] (Carl Fischer B2670 ©1945) +
_____, Mario: *Greeting Card: Valse on the name GREGOR PIATIGORSKY*, op.170/3* (General 658 ©1954) p'72
_____, *Toccata** [Introduzion, Aria e Finale] (Ricordi 123536 ©1935) p'36

Chopin–Piatigorsky: *Nocturne* in c#, op. posth.(B.49) (Schott 2407 ©1934/AMP/ Int'l 533/MMP 1246) +

Copland, Aaron: *Waltz and Celebration** from *Billy the Kid* (Boosey & Hawkes 17210 ©1952)

Debussy, Claude: *Intermezzo* (Elkan-Vogel ©1944) +

Debussy–Gretchaninoff: *Beau Soir* (Int'l 757 ©1946) +
_____, *Romance* (Int'l 666 ©1946) +

Dinicu–Heifetz: *Hora Staccato** (Carl Fischer B2288 ©1933) +

Dubois, P.M: *Concerto** for cello and orchestra (piano reduction Leduc AL 22723 ©1958)

Dukelsky, Vladimir: *Concerto** for cello and orchestra (piano reduction Carl Fischer 03305 ©1946)

de Falla–Markevitch: *Danse du Meunier** (Chester JWC 942 ©1951)

de Falla–Piatigorsky: *Danse de la Frayeur* [Dance of Terror] from *El Amor Brujo* (Chester JWC 934 ©1938) +

_____, *Danse Rituelle de Feu* [Ritual Fire Dance] from *El Amor Brujo* (Chester JWC 933 ©1938) + also with orchestration by Ernesto Halffter (Chester CH 61115)

Fine, Vivian: *Trio* for violin, cello, piano (1980) [mvt 1 *Passacaglia in memory of GP*] Gunmar Music, Inc.

Fitelberg, Jerzy (1903–51): *Sonata for Unaccompanied Cello** (Omega C1000 ©1948/Chester) + 10/45

_____, *Duo for Violin and Cello** (Omega/Chester) +

Foss, Lukas: *Capriccio** (Carl Fischer 41651C ©1948) +

_____, *Orpheus** for cello and orchestra (Salabert 17113 ©1972)

Golestan, Stan (1875–1956): *Concerto Moldave** for cello and orchestra (piano reduction Durand ©1937)

Granados–Piatigorsky: *Orientale* [Spanish Dance No.2] (Int'l 655 ©1945)+

Gronowetter, Freda: *In a Sacred Mood** (E.B. Marks 11790 ©1942/Presser) also with orchestra (Presser)

Hageman, Richard (1882–1966): *Recitative & Romance** (Schirmer ©)

Harsanyi, Tibor: *Rhapsodie** (Eschig 5996 ©1939)

Haydn–Piatigorsky: *Divertimento* (Elkan-Vogel ©1944) + also with orchestration by Ingolf Dahl, [also version for viola and strings by Lowell Liebermann, T. Presser ©1993]

Hindemith, Paul: *Concerto "1940"* [*] (piano reduction Schott 2838 ©1940) p'43 also with orchestra (study score Schott 4073 ©1940)

_____, *A Frog He Went a Courting* [*] (Schott 4276 ©1951)

_____, *Sonata "1948"* [*] (Schott 3839 ©1948)

Karjinsky, Nicolai: *Concert** pour 2 Cellos (no accompaniment) (Eschig 3997 ©1933)

_____, *Skázka** (Eschig 6501 ©1948)

Karjinsky–Piatigorsky: *Orientale** arr. de concert (Eschig 5883 ©1938) +

Korngold, Erich: *Concerto* in C, op.37 [*] in one movement for cello and orchestra (piano reduction Schott 4117 ©1946) p'50

Koutzen, Boris: *Sonata** for violin and cello (General Music 22 ©1952) +

_____, *Concert Piece** (Elkan-Vogel ©1940/Mercury) also with string quartet or string orchestra p'46

Kupferman, Meyer: *Evocation** (General 48 ©1951) p'61

Laderman, Ezra: *Parisot: Concerto for Multiple Cellos* [first mvt: "Piatigorsky"] (G Schirmer ©1996)

Liadov–Piatigorsky: *Pliaska, Danse russe* (Schott 2409 ©1935/MMP 1246) +

Lully–Piatigorsky: *Courante* (Schott BSS 33600 and 2283 ©1932/MMP 1246) +

Lutoslawski, Witold: *Bucolics* for viola and cello (Chester Music CH60920 ©1995)

Mainardi, Enrico: *Rhapsodia Italiana** in A (Ricordi 121874 ©1928) p'30

Martinů, Bohuslav: *Variations on a Theme of Rossini** (Boosey & Hawkes 16505 ©1942) + p'49

Mazzacurati, Benedetto: *Studio Fileuse*, op.9* for solo cello (Carisch 20476 ©1948) p'48

Menotti, Gian-Carlo: *Suite** for 2 Cellos and Piano (Schirmer 47325c ©1976) p'76

Milhaud, Darius: *Suite Cisalpine sur des airs populaires piédmontais*, op.332* for cello and orchestra (piano reduction Eschig 6745 ©1954) p'54

Moritz, Edvard: *Concerto* op.106* for cello and orchestra (piano reduction Maxwell Weaner ©1942) p'42

Mozart–Piatigorsky: *Divertimento* in C (Elkan-Vogel ©1947/also published for viola) + p'47
_____, *Sonatina* in A from *Divertimenti*, K. Anh. 229b (Elkan-Vogel ©1946/T. Presser) p'46+
_____, *Sonatina* in C from *Divertimenti*, K. Anh. 229b (Elkan-Vogel ©1944/also published for viola) + p'44
_____, *Sonatina* in D, from *Divertimenti*, K. Anh. 229b (Chester JWC 929 ©1938/MMP 2043) + p'38

Persichetti, Vincent: *Vocalise*, op. 27* (Elkan-Vogel ©1958) p'58

Piatigorsky: *Cadenza* to Schumann Cello Concerto, op.129 (Int'l 1992) [not credited] p'60
_____, *Pliaska* [after Liadov] (Schott 2409 ©1935/MMP) + p'35
_____, *Scherzo* (Chester JWC 935 ©1939) * '39
_____, *Stroll* for solo cello (Sovietskaya Muzyka 1978, no.4 [1 p.]) Ogareva 13, Moscow, USSR [also known as *Promenade*]
_____, *Variations on a Theme of Paganini* (Elkan-Vogel ©1944) p'46 + also with orchestration by Arthur Cohn

Prokofiev, Sergei: *Concerto*, op. 58 for cello and orchestra (piano reduction Boosey & Hawkes 17901 ©1954) p' 54

Prokofiev–Piatigorsky: *March* from *Music for Children* for solo cello (Int'l 762 ©1945 also by Detskaia muzyka) +p'45
_____, *Waltz* from *Music for Children* (Int'l 763 ©1945) + p'45

Prokofiev–Piatigorsky–Knushevitsky: *Waltz* from *The Tale of the Stone Flower*, op.118 (Russian edition]

Ravel — arr. Castelnuovo-Tedesco: *Alborada del Gracioso** concert transcription (Carl Fischer B 3268 ©1952) p'52
_____, *La Vallée des Cloches** (Carl Fischer B2802 ©1950) 7/25/50 p'50

Read, Gardner: *Concerto*, op.55* for cello and orchestra (piano reduction AMP as op.55a] 2/10/46

Rossini — arr. Castelnuovo-Tedesco, Mario: *Figaro** (Carl Fischer B2670 ©1945) + p'45

Rózsa, Miklós: *Sinfonia Concertante*, op.29* for violin, cello and orchestra (piano reduction Breitkopf EB6534 ©1969) (orchestral study score Breitkopf & Härtel 4769 ©1966) p'66
_____, *Tema con Variazioni*, op.29a * for violin, cello and piano (Breitkopf EB6452 ©1965) p'65 also with orchestra
_____, *Toccata capricciosa*, op.36* for solo cello (Breitkopf 8062 ©1979) p'79

Saleski, Gdal: *Dedication (A Nocturne)** (Schirmer 32691c ©1926) p'26, ded. '38

Schifrin, Lalo: *Sinfonia Concertante** for violin, cello, and orchestra (piano reduction MMB R00783) p'98

Saminsky, Lazare: *Meditation*, op. 24/2* from Chasidic Suite, op. 24 (Carl Fischer B2425 ©1937) p'37

Schnabel, Artur: *Sonata*[*] for solo cello (Boosey & Hawkes B.S.I.84 ©1961) p'61 c'

Schubert–Piatigorsky: *Adagio* (Elkan-Vogel ©1946) +p'46
_____, *Three Minuets*, D600, D336, D380 (Elkan-Vogel ©1946) +p'46
_____, *Introduction, Theme & Variations*, op. 82/2 (Elkan-Vogel ©1949) + p'49
_____, *Waltzes* (Elkan-Vogel) +

Scriabin–Piatigorsky: *Etude*, op. 8/11 (Schott BSS 33636 and 2284 ©1933/Int'l 611/MMP 1246) + p'33
_____, *Poem*, op.32/1 (Schott 2408 ©1934/Int'l 605/MMP 1246) + p'34

Shostakovich, Dimitri: *Sonata* (Anglo-Soviet Music Press, Ltd ASMP 50 ©1947/Leeds/Boosey & Hawkes) +p'47

Shuk, Lajos: *Csárdás** (Schirmer 42537C ©1951) p'51

Stravinsky, Igor: *Suite Italienne** (Edition Russe de Musique, London ©1934/Boosey & Hawkes 16350)/Muzyka 5623, revision M. Shpanova 2004 + p'34

Tansman, Alexandre: *Fantasie** for cello and orchestra (piano reduction Eschig 4962 ©1936) p'36

Tcherepnin, Alexander: *Songs & Dances*, op.84* (Balïeff 3476/Boosey & Hawkes ©1953) p'55 [Georgian Song, Tartar Dance, Russian Song, Kazakh Dance]

Toch, Ernst: *Three Impromptus*, op.90c* for solo cello (Mills ©1963) p'65 inscribed "For Gregor Piatigorsky The Friend and Grand Master of his instrument on his 60th birthday, Santa Monica 4/20/63" originally titled "*Improvisation in 3 mvts*" Andante cantabile, Allegretto grazioso, Adagio con espressione, quasi "der letze Kampf" ["The Last Struggle"]

Valensin-Piatigorsky: *Minuet* (Chester JWC 930 ©1937) + p'37

Vierne, Louis: *Poissons Chinois** from *Soirs Étrangers, Cinq Pieces*, op.56/5 (Henry Lemoine 23,031.H ©1928) p'38 [Grenada, On Lake Léman, Venice, Canadian Steppe, Goldfish]

Walton, William: *Concerto** for cello and orchestra (piano reduction Oxford University Press ©1957) + p'57

Waxman, Franz: *Auld Lang Syne Variations* for piano quartet (Fidelio Music ©1947) p' also for string orchestra and piano
_____ (arranged and developed by Angela Morley), *Ruth: Elegy* from *The Story of Ruth* (Fidelio Music ©1960)/1998 p'05 also for cello and orchestra

Weber–Piatigorsky: *Adagio & Rondo* (Schott 2284 ©1932/AMP/Int'l 534/Kalmus 4448/MMP 1225/Alfred Publishing/Goz.Muz.Ixd-vo, Moscow) +
_____, *Sonata* in A (Schott BSS 33601 and 2282 ©1932/AMP and MMP 1205) +
_____, *Sonata* in C (Schott 2281 n.d. and MMP 1205) +

Webern, Anton von: *Sonata* (1914) (Carl Fischer 04860 ©1976) p'76
_____, *Two Pieces* (1899) (Carl Fischer 04949 ©1975) p'75

Zeisl, Eric (1905–59): *Sonata** (Doblinger ©1951) c'51

COMPILATIONS OF CONCERT TRANSCRIPTIONS
(Music Masters Publications, MMP)

Concert Transcriptions Book 1 Weber: *Sonatas* in A and C (MMP 1205)
Concert Transcriptions Book 2 Bach: *Concerto*, Weber: *Adagio & Rondo* (MMP 1225)
Concert Transcriptions Book 3 Scriabin: *Etude* and *Poem*, Liadov: *Pliaska*, Lully: *Courante*, Chopin: *Nocturne* (MMP 1246)

A SCHUBERT ALBUM (Elkan-Vogel ©1988) p'88

Adagio
Three Minuets
Introduction, Theme & Variations op.82/2

DE FALLA ALBUM (Chester)

Dance of Terror [Danse de la Frayeur], and
Ritual Dance of Fire [Danse Rituelle de Feu] from *El Amor Brujo*

TRANSCRIPTIONS FOR VIOLA (Elkan-Vogel)

Haydn: *Divertimento*
Mozart: *Sonatina* in A

Mozart: *Sonatina* in C
Mozart: *Divertimento* in C
Schubert: *Adagio*
Schubert: *Three Minuets*
Debussy-Gretchaninoff: *Beau Soir* (International)

Transcription for Contrabass

Scriabin-Piatigorsky: *Poem*, op.32/1 (Music Masters Publications M1777 by Lucas Drew)

New Piatigorsky Editions (King)

Bach, J.S: *Adagio* from BWV 1024 [Pisendel?]

Boccherini–Piatigorsky: *Sonata* in C

Chopin–Piatigorsky: *Introduction and Polonaise Brillante*, op.3

Debussy–Piatigorsky: *Prelude/Intermezzo*

Fauré–Piatigorsky: *Tarantelle*, op. 10/2

Paganini–Piatigorsky: *Divertimento (Divertissement)*
_____, *La Campanella (La Clochette)*

Piatigorsky: Four Pieces for Solo Cello: *Prelude, Prayer, Syrinx, Stroll*
_____, cadenzas to concertos by Boccherini in G, Haydn in D, Herbert No.2, Schumann, Volkmann, and Vivaldi Concerto for Two Cellos

Prokofiev–Piatigorsky: *Masques* from *Romeo & Juliet*
_____, *Regrets* from *Music for Children*

Scriabin–Piatigorsky: *Romance*

Stravinsky–Piatigorsky: *Suite Italienne* arr. for violin and cello and for 4 cellos

Szymanowski–Piatigorsky: *Etude* op.4/3

Unpublished in Manuscripts

Anonymous–Piatigorsky: Sonata (Chester contract) +

Ari, Paul (née Jacqueline Piatigorsky): Chorals (6/13/37)*

Bach — arr. Castelnuovo-Tedesco, Mario: Suite No.6 for cello and string orchestra (1940) * 7/13/40 given '43

Bach–Piatigorsky: Adagio, BWV 1024 (Chester contract) perhaps by Pisendal +

Beglarian, Grant: Diversions for Viola and Cello and Orchestra*
_____, Elegy for Solo Cello
_____, Wraggle-Taggle Gypsies, O' for soprano and cello*

Castelnuovo-Tedesco, Mario: Kol Nidre, also with orchestra * 10/21/41

Mozart — arr. Castelnuovo-Tedesco, Mario: Serenade from *Don Giovanni* (concert transcription, 1944)*

Lieberson, Goddard: Inscriptions*

Piatigorsky–Beglarian: Variations on a Theme by Paganini for 3 cellos *'75

Shulman, Alan: Duos for violin and cello*

Zeisl, Eric: Concerto Grosso, with orchestra, amplified cello, ad lib. *c'55–56

The Gregor Piatigorsky Collection at the Library of Congress: a checklist: manuscript and printed music, correspondence, and other items owned by or associated with Gregor Piatigorsky/compiled by Raymond A. White, 1986. Microfilm 86/20,244 (ML136.U5 W5 1986)

Appendix F: Piatigorsky's Original Compositions, Arrangements and Transcriptions Recorded by Other Cellists

Bach: *Concerto in G, BWV 592*
Antonio Janigro, cello I Solisti di Zagreb RCA LSC 2365 *c. 1964*

Boccherini: *Sonata in C*
Stephen Kates, cello Samuel Sanders, piano RCA LSC 2940 *1966*

Chopin: *Nocturne in C#*
Radu Aldulescu, cello Electrecord ECD 35
Ofra Harnoy, cello Helena Bowkun, piano Carlton Classics 6600672 *c.1997* Masters of the Bow WRC1-1740, Discopaedia MBS 2011
Antonio Janigro, cello Antonio Beltrami, piano Vanguard VCS 10018 *c.1967*
Stephen Kates, cello Brooks Smith, piano Sonic Arts LS 13 *1978*
Stephen Kates, cello Samuel Saunders, piano RCA LSC 2940 *1966*
Maria Kliegel, cello Bernd Glemser, piano Naxos 553159, NAX967842C *1996*
Laurence Lesser, cello Evgeniya Dyachenko, piano Melodiya D 19179
Edgar Lustgarten, cello Anthony Newman, piano Art Center in La Jolla SSR 6662 *1962* Crystal S-303
Enrico Mainardi, cello Michael Raucheisen, piano Deutsche Grammophon LV 36108 (10") *c.1938*
Therese Motard, cello Louise-Andree Baril, piano Analektov FL 23142 *2001*
Leonard Rose, cello Frank Iogha, piano VAI VAIA 1261-2 *2007*
Pieter Wispelwey, cello Dejan Lazic, piano Channel Classics CCS 16298 *2003*

Debussy: *Romance (ed.)*
Nathaniel Rosen, cello Doris Stevenson, piano John Marks Records JMR 10 *1996*

Debussy: *Beau soir*
Leonid Gorokhov, cello Irina Nikitina, piano Melodiya A10 00311D, Melodiya CD SU10 304 *1984*
Nathaniel Rosen, cello Doris Stevenson, piano North Star Records NS 0027 *1990*

de Falla: *Danse Rituelle de Feu*
Alban Gerhardt, cello Rina Dokshinsky, piano EMI Classics 73164 *1998*
Ofra Harnoy, cello William Aide, piano RCA 68369 *1996*
Ofra Harnoy, cello Catherine Wilson, piano Mastersound *1993*
Maria Kliegel, cello Bernd Glemser, piano Naxos 55075 *1995*
Aleth Lamasse, cello Daria Hovora, piano Floretti Classics/Forlane *2005*
Zara Nelsova, cello W. Parry, piano Decca 2088 *1940s*
Nathaniel Rosen, cello Doris Stevenson, piano North Star Records NS 0027 *1990*
Mstislav Rostropovich, cello Alexander Dedyukhin, piano EMI 7243 5 72294 2 5, EMI 7243 5 72017 2 8 *1960*

Milos Sadlo, cello Alfred Holecek, piano Supraphon SUA 10919
Heinrich Schiff, cello Samuel Sanders, piano Philips 4424092
Felix Schmidt, cello Annette Cole, piano IMP (Pickwick) PCD 891, Camelot CAMCD 1019 *1987*
Daniel Shafran, celloNina Musinian, piano Bruno Records BR 14015, Melodiya D 28163 *c.1954*
Daniel Shafran, cello Nina Musinian, piano Vanguard VRS 6028
Janos Starker, cello Leon Pommers, piano Contrepoint 20054 *c.1954* Everest 3222, Period SPL 584, Nixa 584
Janos Starker, cello Shigeo Neriki, piano Columbia OX 7140 *1978* Star XO 6, Denon OX 7140-ND, Denon C37-7812, Denon 8118 (CD)
Tsutoshi Tsutsumi, cello Uta-Mamiya, piano CBS-SONY SONIC 12 *1972*
Julian Lloyd Webber, cello Charles Gerhardt, National Philharmonic Orchestra 1LP0190680 2 RCA (British Library) *1981*

de Falla: *Danse de la Frayeur*
Evgeny Altman, cello R. Branovskaya, piano Melodiya D 20331
Nathaniel Rosen, cello Doris Stevenson, piano North Star Records NS 0027 *1990*
Felix Schmidt, cello Annette Cole, piano IMP (Pickwick) PCD 891,Camelot CAMCD 1019 *1987*

Granados: *Orientale (Spanish Dance No.2)*
Kate Dillingham, cello Linda Kessler-Ferri, piano MusicMinusOne CD3704 *2000*
Evan Drachman, cello Richard Dowling, piano Piatigorsky Foundation PF 2901 *1998*
Ofra Harnoy, cello Michael Dussek, piano RCA *1990*
Stephen Kates, cello Samuel Sanders, piano RCA LSC 2940 *1966*
Aleth Lamasse, cello Daria Hovora, piano Floretti Classics/Forlane *2005*
Nathaniel Rosen, cello Doris Stevenson, piano North Star Records NS 0027 *1990*
Milos Sadlo, cello Alfred Holecek, piano Supraphon SUA ST 50919

Haydn: *Divertimento*
Jeff Bradetich, bass Judi Rockey Bradetich, piano Klavier 11100
Denis Brott, cello Samuel Sanders, piano Analekta: Fleir de Lys FL 2 3035 *1989*
Marin Cazacu, cello Dans Dimitrescu, piano Electrecord DG-ECE 4037
Hamilton Cheifetz, cello Bryan Johanson, piano Gagliano 929
Evan Drachman, cello Richard Dowling, piano Piatigorsky Foundation PF 2901 *1998*
Karine Georgian, cello Nanse Gum, Moscow Chamber Orchestra Cantabile SRCD-1040 Philips
Leonid Gorokhov, cello Irina Nikitina, piano Melodiya A10 00311D, Melodiya CD SU10 304 *1984*
Emanuel Gruber, cello Herut Israeli, piano CDI (Israel) *2006*
Alexandra Gutu, cello Electrecord ST-ECE 1408
Stephen Kates, cello Brooks Smith, piano Sonic Arts LS 13 *1978*
Vasily Popov, cello Pavel Bubelnikov St Petersburg Chamber Orchestra High Definition Classics
William Primrose, viola David Stimer, piano RCA 12-0689 [D7-RC-8244/5] *1947* Biddulph 80147
Nathaniel Rosen, cello Doris Stevenson, piano North Star Records NS 0027 *1990*
Daniel Shafran, cello Nina Musinyan, piano Vanguard Classics 1026, VRS 6028
Janos Starker, cello Shuku Iwashaki, piano Columbia OX 7041 *1975* Denon OX 7041-ND, 8117 3/16-17, Denon C37-7302 (CD), Star X 5 (CD)
Yuli Turovsky, cello and conductor I Musici de Montreal Chandos CHAN 8768 *1988*
Mihaly Virizlay, cello Rebecca Pennys, piano Orion ORS 73103
Christina Walevska, cello Robert Parris, piano Academia Santa Cecilia Discos ASC 1016
Velitchka Yotcheva, cello Patrice Laré, piano Xxi-21 Canada

Lully: *Courante*
Mischa Miasky, cello Pavel Giliov, piano Polygram 431544 *1991*

Mozart: *Sonatina in A*
Tamás Varga, cello Christopher Hinterhuber, piano Gesellshaft der Musikfreunde *Remembering Piatigorsky, 2003*

Piatigorsky: *Prayer*
Evan Drachman, cello Piatigorsky Foundation PF 2901 *1998*
Terry King, cello Music & Arts CD 1076 *1995*

Piatigorsky: *Preludio*
Terry King, cello Music & Arts CD 1076 *1995*

Piatigorsky: *Procession (AKA Stroll or Promenade)*
Denis Brott, cello Analekta: Fleir de Lys FL 2 3035 *1989*
Evan Drachman, cello Piatigorsky Foundation PF 2901 *1998*
Terry King, cello Music & Arts CD 1076 *1995*

Piatigorsky: *Scherzo*
Evan Drachman, cello Richard Dowling, piano Piatigorsky Foundation PF 2901 *1998*

Piatigorsky: *Syrinx*
Denis Brott, cello Analekta: Fleir de Lys FL 2 3035 *1989*
Evan Drachman, cello Piatigorsky Foundation PF 2901 *1998*
Terry King, cello Music & Arts CD 1076 *1995*
Nathaniel Rosen, cello North Star Records NS 0027 *1990*

Piatigorsky: *Variations on a Paganini Theme*
Julie Albers, cello Orion Weiss, piano Artek Recordings *2005*
Nicolas Anderson, cello Jeffrey Anderson, piano Meteora Records *1996*
Denis Brott, cello Samuel Sanders, piano Analekta: Fleir de Lys FL 2 3035 *1989*
Stephen Kates, cello Brooks Smith, piano Sonic Arts LS 13 *1978*
Tamás Varga, cello Christopher Hinterhuber, piano Gesellschaft der Musikfreunde *Remembering Piatigorsky, 2003*
Windy Warner, cello Eileen Buck, piano Cedille CDR 90000 111, *2009*

Prokofiev: *March (Music for Children)*
Mirei Iancovici, cello Electrecord ST-ECE 1349
Laurence Lesser, cello Melodiya LP D 19179
Heinrich Schiff, cello Philips 4424092 *1989*
Heinrich Schiff, celloKoch Schwann 480 0316 *2007*
Nathaniel Rosen, cello North Star Records NS 0027 *1990*
Mark Varshavsky, cello Duraphon LP HD 257
Rafael Wallfisch, cello Black Box 1027 *2000*

Prokofiev: *Masques (Romeo and Juliet)*
Evan Drachman, cello Richard Dowling, piano Piatigorsky Foundation PF 2901 *1998*

Prokofiev: *Waltz (Music for Children) (also used in The Tale of the Stone Flower op.118)*
Frederique Fontanarosa, cello Renaud Fontanarosa, piano ILD 642119 *1992*
Mischa Maisky, cello pianist unknown Russian Disc RDCD 00378

Prokofiev: *Waltz (The Tale of the Stone Flower op.118)*
Mischa Maisky, cello Martha Argerich, piano Deutsche Grammophon 4775323/4777442 *2005/07*
Rafael Wallfisch, cello John York, piano Black Box 1027 *2000*

Schubert: *Introduction, Theme and Variations, Op82/2*
Denis Brott, cello Rebecca Pennys, piano CBC SM 185
Evan Drachman, cello Richard Dowling, piano Piatigorsky Foundation PF 2901 *1998*
Tamás Merei, cello Peter Koczor, piano Hungaroton 31926 *2000*
Nathaniel Rosen, cello Doris Stevenson, piano North Star Records NS 0027 *1990*

Scriabin: *Etude, Op.8 No.11*
Valentin Feigin, cello E. Seidel, piano Melodiya D 11189
Mstislav Rostropovich, cello Vladimir Yampolsky, piano EMI 7243 5 72294 2 5, EMI 7243 5 72017 2 8
Mstislav Rostropovich, cello (pianist unknown) Testament 1101 *released1997*
Julian Lloyd Webber, cello John Lenehan, piano Philips 434 917-2 *1992*

Scriabin: *Poème, Op. 32/1*
Mats Lidstrom, cello Bengt Forsberg, piano Hyperion 67184 *2001*

Weber: *Adagio and Rondo*
Evan Drachman, cello Richard Dowling, piano Piatigorsky Foundation PF 2901 *1998*
Pierre Fournier, cello Lamar Crowson, piano DGG 135132(LP), CD 453 667-2GFS *1969*
Pierre Fournier, cello Gerald Moore, piano Columbia 33CX 1606, Angel 35599 *1957*
Leonid Gorokhov, cello Bobby Chen, pianoCello Classics CC1002 *2001*
Yuhuda Hanani, cello Michele Levin, piano Eroica Classical Recordings 3072 *1991*
Simca Heled, cello Jonathan Feldman, piano Classico 153 *1996*
Stephen Kates, cello Brooks Smith, piano Sonic Arts LS 13 *1978*
Joel Krosnick, cello Cameron Grant, piano Orion ORS 73103 *1972*
Samuel Mayes, cello pianist unknown Pearl 9981 *released1993*
Lorne Munroe, cello Ormandy, Philadelphia Orchestra, *First Chair* Columbia ML 4629 *c.1955*
Andrea Noferini, cello Sergio La Stella, piano Bongiovanni 5073 *2000*
Arto Noras, cello Tapani Vista, piano Finlandia 95883 *1994*
Aldo Parisot, cello Robert Shalka, piano Phonodisc Luxo 0.33-501-002 *1978*
Michael Rudiakov, cello Ron Levy, piano Centaur CRC 2192 *1993*
Janos Starker, cello Shuku Iwashaki, piano Columbia OX 7041,Denon OX7041-ND, Denon C37-7302, Denon 8117 and 17389 and 17372 (CD), Star X 5 *3/1975*
Paul Tortelier, cello Maria de la Pau, piano EMI HMV ASD 3283 *1970s*
Paul Tortelier, cello Maria de la Pau, piano 1CL072835 (British Library live) *1975*
Christine Walevska, cello Bruce Gaston, piano Owl Records ORLP 14 *1970s*

Weber: *Sonatina in A (Sonates Progressives No.5)*
Enrico Mainardi, cello Sergio Lorenzi, piano DGG 68287 *1942*
Jeffrey Solow, cello Doris Stevenson, piano ABC Classics AB-67014, COMS-9006 *1974*
Paul Tortelier, cello Tasso Janopoulo, piano La Voix de Son Maitre SK-103, Disques Pierre Verany 705101 *1995*

Weber: *Sonatina in C (Sonates Progressives No.6 Polaca)*[1]
Pierre Fournier, cello Tasso Janopoulo, piano La Voix de Son Maitre HMV (France) DA 4955 *1943*

Chapter Notes

Part I : Chapter 1

1. Isaac Abramovich Piatigorsky (1876–1962) and Basya [Maria] Amshislavska (1883–1956) were married in 1898. Their children were Nadezha [Nadia] (b.1898), Leonid (b.1902), Grigorii [Gregor] (b.1903), Polina [Paulina] (b.1905), Alexander [Shura] (b.1910) and Anatoli (b.1919). Gregor was born on April 17.
2. Alexander Stogorsky, "In Love with the Cello," *Soviet Music, no. 4* (1978): 116–127. To make it easier for people to distinguish between the brothers, Alexander changed his last name to Stogorsky.
3. Early unpublished draft for *Cellist* herein cited as "Unpublished draft."
4. Culled from Gregor Piatigorsky, "My Cello and I," *Atlantic Monthly*, 1962, p. 41, and Gregor Piatigorsky, *Cellist* (Garden City: Doubleday 1965), 8.
5. Yampolsky (1879–1951) was a student of Fyodor Vilgelmovich Mulert, himself a student of Karl Davidov, the father of the Russian school of cello playing.
6. Gubarev (1870–1942) studied in Saint Petersburg and in 1901 became the director of the Yekaterinoslav Conservatory (now the Dnipropetrovs'k Conservatory).
7. Decree issued by Czar Nicholas in December 1904, abbreviation and translation by Jan Guerny.
8. Piatigorsky dramatically recalls hiding in the cellar during one of the pogroms as a very young child in *Cellist* (p. 5): "It was there in the cellar that I learned to hear the beating of my own heart and to really feel the fear of others."
9. Jacqueline Rebecca de Rothschild, *Jump in the Waves: A Memoir* (New York: St. Martin's, 1988), 160.
10. Piatigorsky, *Cellist* (Garden City: Doubleday, 1965), 69, hereafter cited as Piatigorsky, *Cellist*.
11. Biographical material from Henry Holt, Ltd., Piatigorsky's British concert management.
12. Apparently his improvisational skills were already in evidence at this early age. Cellist Sergei Shirinsky (future cellist in the famed Beethoven Quartet) took over the job at the coliseum when Gregor (Grisha) left: "I was anxious to do the same things everyone told me Grisha did at the Theatre. Much to my horror, I found that Grisha never wrote down anything he played, only parts for the rest of the players!" (Roman Suchecki, *Wiolonczela od A od Z*, trans. Magdalena Richter (Krakow: Polskie Wydawnictwo Muzyczne, 1982), 148).
13. May 26, 1913, performing Goltermann's Concerto no.1.
14. Ippolitov-Ivanov (1859–1935) prominent composer and conductor. Gregor may have met Ippolitov-Ivanov during the spring semester of 1912 at the Yekaterinoslav conservatory when he performed the composer's Piano Quartet, op. 9, in a concert honoring the composer. Gregor also performed the work in Moscow on June 3, 1912, in the hall of the State Duma, celebrating the annual concert of Yekaterinoslav's branch of the Imperial Russian Music Society. Gregor would later record the *Danse d'aoule* from his most famous work, *Caucasian Sketches*, in Berlin. Again, his ease with reading orchestra parts is evident as he plays both the viola and clarinet solos on the recording.
15. Von Glehn (1858–1927), a prize-winning student of Karl Davidov, father of the Russian school of cello playing. Glehn's concert success led to his appointment as solo cellist of the Berlin Philharmonic (1883–85) as he had played under Brahms, Joachim, Dvořák, von Bülow, and Anton Rubinstein. Soloists during his tenure included pianist Clara Schumann, cellists Robert Hausmann and David Popper, and violinist Pablo de Sarasate. Von Glehn replaced Wilhelm Fitzenhagen at the Moscow Conservatory and remained there for thirty years (1890–1920).
16. Interview *CBC Tuesday Night*, Larry Solway, host, June 21, 1966.
17. Alexander Fyodorovich Gedike (1877–1957) composer and pianist. Gregor premiered his *Three Improvisations* for cello and piano in 1919. Composer Fyodor Fyodorovich Koenemann [Kineman] (1873–1937) was also pianist for basso Fyodor Chaliapin.
18. E. Rivkind was especially known for his quartet class. For a time Gregor was a member of the Moscow Conservatory Quartet and may have been under Rivkind's tutelage. Faculty, including von Glehn, sometimes joined the ensemble as well.
19. Hotel Metropol, nicknamed "Tower of Babylon," was completed in 1905 and took seven years to build. Located next to the Bolshoi Theatre near Red Square, it had electric elevators, hot water, refrigeration, and a special ventilation system. The cream of society stayed there and concerts were given.
20. Unpublished draft.
21. From the opera by Leon Minkus, once quite popular.
22. Unpublished draft.
23. Piatigorsky, *Cellist*, 32.
24. Unpublished draft.
25. Brandukov (1856–1930) was a student of Bernhard Cossmann and Wilhelm Fitzenhagen and a friend and colleague of Tchaikovsky, Arensky, Saint-Saëns, Liszt, and Rachmaninoff. He taught at Moscow's Philharmonic School and succeeded von Glehn at the Moscow Conser-

vatory. Von Glehn's appointment to succeed Fitzenhagen was not met with universal approval; many, including Tchaikovsky, considered Brandukov the superior candidate.

26. Inna Marinel, "The Last Word," *Music Journal* 35, no. 6 (July 1977): 62. Gregor visited the Marinel home from the age of fourteen. They shared the house with Professor von Glehn and all three sisters were harpists attending the conservatory.

27. "It was the same when I played for Richard Strauss. In *Don Quixote* there is an aria in one of the variations — I thought of Chaliapin and his suggestion 'to talk,' for Strauss also wanted 'talk' from the cello!" Samuel and Sada Applebaum, *The Way They Play* (Neptune City, NJ: Paganiniana, 1972), 305–6.

28. Gregor's younger brother Alexander (Shura) Stogorsky claimed that Chaliapin and Gregor performed Massenet's *Elegie* and *Romance* by Glinka and made a recording in Moscow of the *Elegie*. Stogorsky wrote that he heard this recording; however, none has been found (Alexander Stogorsky letter, Glinka Museum, St. Petersburg).

29. H.G. Wells, *Russia in the Shadows* (New York: George H. Doran, 1921), 24–25.

30. Boris Schwarz, *Music and Musical Life in Soviet Russia, 1917–1981* (Bloomington: Indiana University Press, 1983), 1.

31. Lenin to Maxim Gorky, cited in Amy Nelson, *Music for the Revolution: Musicians and Power in Early Soviet Russia* (University Park: Penn State Press, 2004), 1.

32. Wells, *Shadows*, 53.

33. Marinel, *Last Word*, 62.

34. Zeitlin, Lev Moiseyevitch (1881–1952): concertmaster of Zimin Opera and Koussevitzky's orchestra. He taught at the Music School of the Moscow Philharmonic Society and the Moscow Conservatory, and created the celebrated conductorless orchestra, Persimfons. After Gregor's success, he also arranged for Pavel and Leonid Piatigorsky to play in the Zimin Opera Orchestra in its remaining weeks before disbanding. Soon afterward, the Piatigorsky family returned to Yekaterinoslav.

35. Vassily Podgorny, in April 1918.

36. Konstantin G. Mostras, cited in *Chronicle-Documents and Materials. Musical Life of Moscow during the First Years after October 1917* (Moscow, 1972), 42–43, translated by Anya Morozkina.

37. Mostras (1886–1965) was a pupil of Auer and taught at School of the Moscow Philharmonic Society and the Moscow Conservatory. He taught Ivan Galamian and wrote many works and books on the violin.

38. Pulver (1883–1970), a student of Sevcik and Liadov and founding member of the Stradivari Quartet, became a conductor, as did Krisch.

39. The quartet would also occasionally split up to reach small venues as well as expand others. Piatigorsky recalled a series of programs he did with a poet, alternating solos with recitation, and musical improvisation in storytelling.

40. Mostras, *Chronicle-Documents and Materials*, 135, translated by Frank Bacon and Anya Morozkina.

41. Lenin was an avid chess player.

42. Piatigorsky, *Cellist*, 48–50.

43. Bekman-Shcherbina (1881–1951) studied with Pavel Pabst, Nikolai Zerev (a student of Tchaikovsky who also taught Rachmaninoff and Scriabin), and Vasily Safronov. Goldenweiser (1875–1961) studied with Pabst, Siloti, Arensky, Taneyev and Ippolitov-Ivanov. He headed the concert organizing commission under Lunacharsky and arranged works for workers and people of meager means. These largely unknowledgeable audiences were treated to easily comprehensible programs preceded by introductory lectures. Folkloric Russian classical music was especially popular. Igumnov (1873–1948) studied with Zerev, Siloti and Pabst, taught at the Moscow Conservatory, and was renowned for his piano method.

44. Nezhdanova (1873–1950).

45. Suk (1861–1933) was one of the Bolshoi's principal conductors from 1906 to 1932. Safonov (1852–1918) toured with Davidov and succeeded Taneyev as director of the Moscow Conservatory and was the first modern conductor to dispense with the baton.

46. Schwarz, *Music*, 12, 17–18.

47. Piatigorsky, *Cellist*, 42.

48. Probably Koussevitzky's first opera performance, Tchaikovsky's *Queen of Spades*, assisted by the composer's brother, Modest Tchaikovsky. Modest was the librettist and dramatist for several Tchaikovsky operas.

49. Piatigorsky, *Cellist*, 44–45.

50. Composer Vladimir Vlasov in *Sovietskaya Musika*, vol. 7, 1962. Written upon Piatigorsky's first return to Moscow in 1962 to judge the Tchaikovsky Competition.

51. Kubatzky was the lover of the Bolshoi Theatre's director, Elena Malinovskaya, which may explain the decision. He later joined the Stradivari Quartet, became a close colleague of Shostakovich and toured with him, premiering his cello sonata.

52. Marinel, "Last Word," 62.

Part I : Chapter 2

1. H.G. Wells, *Russia in the Shadows* (New York: George H. Doran, 1921), 45.

2. Originally Michail Isaakevich Fishberg before immigrating to the U.S. Mischakoff, eight years older than Piatigorsky, would become the most celebrated concertmaster of the twentieth century.

3. Marinel, Inna, "The Last Word," *Music Journal* 35, no. 6 (July 1977): 62.

4. Also spelled Vesilovsky, (1885–1964). Made his career in Italy and performed with Toscanini.

5. This group included the distinguished solo violinist Naoum Blinder, future concertmaster of the San Francisco Symphony.

6. Piatigorsky to Zeitlin, June 18, 1923, file 12#341 Glinka Museum, Moscow. Herein cited as Zeitlin.

7. Piatigorsky, *Cellist*, 52.

8. CBC Interview, *CBC Tuesday Night*, Larry Soloway, host, June 21, 1966.

9. Cited from *London Daily Telegraph* [ca. 1930], reprinted in *The Strad*, July 1939, p. 102.

10. Piatigorsky, *Cellist*, 51, 195.

11. CBC interview, *CBC Tuesday Night*, Larry Soloway, host, June 21, 1966.

12. Anne Heiles Mischakoff, *Mischa Mischakoff: Journeys of a Concertmaster* (Sterling Heights: Harmonie Park: Detroit Monographs in Musicology/Studies in Music, No. 46, 2006), 38–39 [General information from Heiles is gleaned to p. 41].

13. A cellist in the Centennial Orchestra in Denver, Colorado, Marcia Whitcomb studied with Polish pianist Wiktor Łabu ski (1895–1974), who was married to Mlynarski's older daughter, Wanda. She heard this story more than once from her teacher and retold it to Joseph A. Herter, who included it in his article Mischa Mischa-

koff—Concertmaster of the Warsaw Philharmonic Orchestra, published online January-February 2004 by University of Southern California at the Polish Music Center, *http://www.usc.edu/dept/polish_music/news/jan04.html and /feb04.html*. Herter published the same article in Polish as "Misza Miszakow, koncertmistrz Filharmonii Warszawskiej," *Dwutygodnik Ruch Muzyczny* 49, no. 1 (January 2005): 34–8.

14. Piatigorsky shared the position with the principal solo cellist, Eli Kochanski (1885–1940, Holocaust victim), brother of violinist Paul Kochanski (1887–1934), who at age 14 was the orchestra's first concertmaster before beginning his international career.

15. Zeitlin.

16. Unpublished draft.

17. Piatigorsky, *Cellist*, 57–58.

18. They revisited the Handel-Halvorsen *Passacaglia* when Mischakoff was concertmaster and Piatigorsky was soloist with the Chicago Symphony Orchestra, marking the fifteenth anniversary of their escape. They repeated the Handel-Halvorsen and the Brahms Double Concerto on their final concert together in 1968, upon the violinist's retirement from the Detroit Symphony.

19. *Felicjan Szap, Kourier Warszawski*, October 2, 1921, translated by Magdalena Richter.

20. *Golebiewski, Kourier Warszawski*, March 9, 1922, translated by Magdalena Richter.

21. Zeitlin.

22. Before immigrating to the U.S., Mischakoff altered his name variously to Fibère, Fiber, Fieber, and perhaps others, to conceal his Jewish identity.

23. Anne Heiles Mischakoff, *Mischa Mischakoff: Journeys of a Concertmaster* (Sterling Heights: Harmonie Park Press: Detroit Monographs in Musicology/Studies in Music, No. 46, 2006), 46.

24. Kostelanetz (1901–1980) became an important and popular conductor in the U.S. Another pianist-conductor, Artur Rodzinski (1892–1958), was already a regular conductor with the orchestra and fondly remembered his celebrated principal players, Piatigorsky and Mischakoff.

25. Soon to be called Leningrad and today St. Petersburg, its original name.

26. André Kostelanetz and G. Hammond, *Echoes: Memoirs of André Kostelanetz* (New York: Harcourt Brace Jovanovich, 1981), 46.

27. Hugo Becker, a former student of Piatti and Grützmacher, taught at the Berlin Hochschule and delved deep into physiology and anatomy in an effort to make a science of cello playing. Many, including Piatigorsky and Raya Garbousova, considered him to be rigid and dictatorial. However, a loyal Becker student, Josef (Joseph) Schuster, was offended whenever Piatigorsky voiced his negative opinion of him. Other students included Arnold Földesy, Boris Hambourg, Ludwig Hoelscher, Enrico Mainardi, Beatrice Harrison and Herbert Walenn.

28. Zeitlin.

29. Piatigorsky, *Cellist*, 61–64.

30. Letter from Becker to Flesch, July 13, 1933. Carl F. Flesch, ... *und spielst Du auch Geige?*, translated by Melinda Fort (Zurich: Atlantis Musikbuch-Verlag AG, 1990), 277.

31. Unpublished draft.

32. Julius Klengel (1859–1933) came from a musical family. His grandfather played violin with the Gewandhaus Orchestra for fifty years without missing a single concert, a feat his grandson repeated as principal cellist of the same orchestra from 1881 to 1924. Klengel was a member of Brahms' circle of performers; and as a teacher, he mentored many famous students, including Feuermann, Suggia, Eisenberg, Stutschewsky, Edmund Kurtz, Wallenstein, Grümmer, and Pleeth.

Pleeth observed that Klengel "had a fantastic, Paganini-like technique. He had a sincerity and innocence that was a hallmark of the German School at the time. His greatest strength lay in the flexibility of his teaching, which allowed you to discover your own personality" (Elizabeth Wilson, *Jacqueline du Pré: Her Life, Her Music, Her Legend* (New York: Arcade, 1999), 34). By the turn of the century Klengel's technique was considered outdated. Recordings made in 1927 when he was 68 years old are ample proof, as are the recordings of Becker.

33. Zeitlin.

34. Piatigorsky, *Cellist*, 70.

35. Zeitlin.

36. Piatigorsky, *Cellist*, 76.

37. Zeitlin.

38. 1924 was Klengel's final season as solo cellist with the Gewanthaus.

39. Piatigorsky did perform in the 1924-25 season with the Gewandhaus in October and the Berlin Philharmonic Orchestra in January.

40. Anatoly Lunacharsky (1875–1933), Piatigorsky's acquaintance in Moscow did not prevent the cellist from defecting. The NKID (Narodnïy Komissariat Inostrannïkh Del, the People's Commissariat for Foreign Affairs) intended to court Prokofiev, Koussevitzky, Nikolai Malko and Piatigorsky to moving to the Soviet Union as late as 1932 (Simon Morrison, *The People's Artist: Prokofiev's Soviet Years* (New York: Oxford University Press, 2009), 16, 17).

41. Zeitlin.

42. Unpublished draft.

43. Future cellist of the Budapest Quartet.

44. Future accompanist for major artists, especially Isaac Stern.

45. Koretzki and Piatigorsky played at least two chamber concerts in December 1922. A pupil of Auer, he later joined the New York Philharmonic and founded the Doran String Quartet, changing his name to Cores.

46. Koutzen was one of the Bolshoi's concertmasters and studied with Lev Zeitlin and composition with Glière at the conservatory. He played in Koussevitzky's Moscow Symphony, joined the Philadelphia Orchestra (1923) and the NBC Symphony (1937), and increasingly devoted his life to composition and teaching.

47. Mittman later became one of the most important accompanists of his era, especially in the U.S.

48. The Pozniak Trio had other prominent cellists during this period: Gaspar Cassadó, Joseph Schuster, and Jascha Bernstein. Piatigorsky was preceded by Hugo Dechert (1860–1923), a student of Robert Hausmann, who was a member of the Halir and Joachim quartets and solo cellist for the Hofkapelle Berlin. De Kresz had been concertmaster of the Berlin Philharmonic (1917–21).

49. Ostdeutsche Konzertdirektion Richard Hoppe of Breslau represented Kreisler, Szigeti and most of the artists concertizing in the region.

50. Austrian composer (1891–1959), future professor at the Vienna Academy and deputy director of the Mozarteum in Salzburg.

51. Zeitlin.

52. Gesellschaft für Jüdische Musik in Moskau and Jibneh Verlag, Abteilung für Musik.

53. Kroyt (1897–1969), Szreter (1898–1933). For these concerts and perhaps others, Piatigorsky was also billed as a member of the Kroyt String Quartet.

54. Szreter's wife was a former girlfriend of Kroyt's, and his brother Zigmunt [Schreter] (1886–1977) was a

well-known post impressionist painter. The duo's friendship was deep; when news of Szreter's death reached Piatigorsky, he was "devastated and wept for days" (quote from Lida Antik, via her son, Jean-Pierre Fonda (Fournier), telephone interview, July 1, 2001).

55. Prominent conductor and student of Wagner's disciple Humperdinck.
56. Zeitlin.
57. Berlin at that time had a population of 100,000 Russian immigrants.
58. Zeitlin.
59. Berlin State Opera (Staatsoper Berlin).
60. Zeitlin.
61. Mária Kresz and Péter Király, *Géza de Kresz and Norah Drewett: Their Life and Music on Two Continents* (Toronto: Canadian Stage and Arts, 1989), 24.

Part I : Chapter 3

1. Dobrowen, Mischakoff and Piatigorsky performed as a trio in Moscow. It was Dobrowen's playing of the *Appassionata* that prompted Lenin's famous letter to Gorky (see chapter 1).
2. By 1939, Berlin organizations grew to 81 orchestras, 200 chamber ensembles and over 600 choral groups. Berlin's first radio orchestra was established in 1925.
3. Very sweet candies with chocolate inside.
4. Lev Aronson, "My Remembrance of Gregor Piatigorsky" (unpublished).
5. A fictitious name (along with Pietro Garassi and Rene Valesco) created by the Vox company for Boris Kroyt as conductor and violin soloist on more than ninety 78 rpm sides recorded from 1923 to1927. Berlin thrived on foreign names, and Vox competed with other labels for the same market. Piatigorsky served, along with members of the Staatsper Orchestra, as solo cellist in Kroyt's orchestras (see chapter on recordings).
6. With pianist Szreter and Piatigorsky.
7. With pianist Michael Raucheisen and Piatigorsky, they recorded trio movements by Mendelssohn, Haydn and Goldmark, for example.
8. Unpublished draft.
9. César Saerchinger, *My Life and Music* (New York: St. Martin's, 1964), 79.
10. Piatigorsky, *Cellist*, 103.
11. *Ibid.*
12. Hans Heinz Stuckenschmidt, *Schoenberg: His Life, World and Work* (London: John Calder, 1977), 217. "The most brilliant performance from the public point of view took place on 5 January 1924 with Gutheil-Schoder in the Berlin Singakademie, which was filled to capacity."
13. And charter member of the orchestra from 1882.
14. Solo cellist only during the 1915-16 season; his laissez-faire attitude probably prevented further orchestral posts, but he appeared subsequently as a soloist.
15. The celebrated Hungarian cellist and pedagogue David Popper (1843–1913).
16. Rudolf Kastner, *Berliner Morgenpost*, January 1925.
17. A DVD which contains the entire film evidence of the conductor is available through the Société Furtwängler.
18. Piatigorsky, *Cellist*, 126–27.
19. "Toscanini: The Man Behind the Legend," BBC interview, Ben Grauer, host, July 31, 1963.
20. Piatigorsky, *Cellist*, 201. "Furtwängler told the story of common dancing lessons with pleasure. I very much doubt that they learned a lot" (the conductor's widow, Elisabeth Furtwängler, in a fax to the author, July 5, 2000).
21. Violinist Nathan Milstein recalled that she was one of the most beautiful women in Europe.
22. Angela Hughes, *Pierre Fournier: Cellist in a Landscape with Figures* (Hants: Ashgate, 1998), 29.
23. The companies he worked for included Parlophon, Polydor, Vox, and Tri-Ergon.
24. Letter from Lida Antik to Alexander Glazunov, April 26, 1925, from Berlin (Russian National Library, Department of Manuscripts, A.K. Glazunov's Archive, No. 1020). Glazunov eventually wrote a solo work, *Concerto Ballata*, completed in 1931 (see chapter 4).
25. Piatigorsky, *Cellist*, 124–25.
26. In the fall of 1928, Emanuel Feuermann briefly took Piatigorsky's place, but the trio did not work well together and disbanded.
27. Wolfsthal and Piatigorsky also played the Brahms Double Concerto with the Philharmonic.
28. Other students included Erno Balogh, Artur Balsam, Franz Reisenstein, Fujiko Hemming, Yashiro Akio, Lily Dumont, Karl Ulrich Schnabel, and composers Franz Grothe and Pantcho Vladiguerov. In 1934 Kreutzer returned to Moscow where he became the venerable professor of piano at the Moscow Conservatory.
29. The Strauss-Wolfsthal collaboration is preserved on their Staatsoper Berlin recordings of *Ein Heldenleben* and *Le Bourgeois Gentilhomme*.
30. Another trio with conductor-pianist Bruno Walter, Sigmund and Emanuel Feuermann had been "unfavorably compared" to the Kreutzer-Wolfsthal-Piatigorsky ensemble. The latter were "of a totally different caliber. It is a sheer joy to listen to the playing of these splendid artists full of genuine musicianship performing with understanding and love" (Annette Morreau, *Emanuel Feuermann* (New Haven: Yale University Press, 2002), 31).
31. In spite of his twelve-tone compositional style, Krenek (1900–1990) was at that time a favorite with opera audiences for the first boxing opera, *Jonny spielt auf*, which also contained jazz elements.
32. Krenek withheld the work from further performances (letter to author October 21, 1985).
33. Schnabel wrote a difficult sonata for solo cello for Piatigorsky. The cellist complained that he needed at least ten fingers on his left hand to play it. He never performed it, and it may have strained their relationship. Stravinsky thought it "probably the unlovliest lucubration I have ever heard."
34. Carl F. Flesch, *And Do You Also Play the Violin?* (London: Toccata, 1990), 240.
35. Schnabel to Flesch, May 1, 1930. Items of correspondence from the Schnabel-Flesch-Piatigorsky trio are through the courtesy of Carl F. Flesch. Schnabel could also aim a joke at himself. Two that Piatigorsky liked to share follow: When someone asked Schnabel how his recital programs were different from others, he quipped, "My programs are boring also after the intermission." And when the pianist was aware that he was dominating conversation at an after-concert reception, he would say, "Well, enough about me." And then he would begin again: "So, what do *you* think of my playing?"
36. Future principal cellist of the Berlin Philharmonic and the New York Philharmonic.
37. Feuermann first appeared with the Berlin Philharmonic in 1916 and began recording a few years later.
38. Quote from Lida Fournier (Piatigorsky) to her son, Jean-Pierre Fonda (Fournier) as interviewed by the author.
39. As witnessed by Jascha Bernstein.
40. Morreau, *Feuermann*, 50, 165, 337. Cologne story

also told to author by Sophie Feuermann in New York in 2000.

41. Starting on December 1, 1925. Other faculty included Daniel Karpilowski (Guarneri Quartet), Harry Son (Budapest Quartet), Kroyt and Szreter.

42. Aronson, "Remembrance."

43. Joseph Schuster formally replaced Piatigorsky in November 1929. It is assumed by this time that Piatigorsky had already given up teaching at the Russian Conservatory.

44. Aronson, "Remembrance."

45. Piatigorsky, *Cellist*, 115.

46. Among the more historic premieres were Stravinsky's Piano Concerto with the composer as soloist, Respighi's *Pines of Rome*, Hindemith's *Concerto for Orchestra*, and Bartok's *Tanzsuite*.

47. The concert bureau was started in 1880 by her future husband, Hermann, and lasted until 1935 when the Nazis closed it down.

48. Piatigorsky to Koutzen, September 15, 1927 (Library of Congress Special Collections: Boris Koutzen).

49. About $250 to $350 adjusted to today's dollar.

50. It was during a performance of the cello solo in Mahler's 9th Symphony at about this time that Piatigorsky made the decision to become strictly a soloist.

51. Piatigorsky, *Cellist*, 163–64.

52. Piatigorsky and Flesch also premiered Haydn's Symphony No. 6 "Le Matin," which features solo violin and cello, in Krekfeld.

53. Zakin was Gregor Fitelberg's nephew and one of Piatigorsky's first friends in Berlin. Piatigorsky also knew Zakin's father, an assistant conductor and violinist with the Warsaw Philharmonic. They played several recitals, one of which was on the Volksbühne series at the Theatre am Bülowplatz. These concerts were aimed at the working class where membership was only 50 pfennig.

54. *Schelomo* on March 17, 1927, Webern in a 1926 recital (see chapter on recordings).

55. Henry Prunières, *La Revue Musicale*, numéro 9 (July 1927): 9. Also compared Horowitz with Busoni.

56. Henri Temianka, in conversation with Gregor Piatigorsky, Milton Thomas and Sidney Harth, "Pablo Casals," *The Instrumentalist* 27, no. 5 (December 1973): 34.

57. Quote from Lida Fournier (Piatigorsky) to her son, Jean-Pierre Fonda (Fournier) to the author in July 2000.

58. Piatigorsky, *Cellist*, 156.

59. Joseph Szigeti, "ce bougre de Duo," *With Strings Attached: Reminiscences and Reflections* (New York: Knopf, 1967), 139.

60. Piatigorsky, *Cellist*, 156.

61. Robert Schmitt Scheubel, Hamburg, October 1928.

62. "Furtwängler spoke often about Piatigorsky. His words always were full of respect and his memories very positive. He regretted very much when Piatigorsky had to leave his desk at the Celli" (Elisabeth Furtwängler fax to author, July 5, 2000).

Part I : Chapter 4

1. Piatigorsky, *Cellist*, 180.

2. In just two months, September and October, the stock market had lost 40 percent of its value. By the end of November, investors had lost $100 billion in assets. The stock market would continue to fall until bottoming out in July 1932.

3. Piatigorsky, *Cellist*, 180–1, 171.

4. Glenn Plaskin, *Horowitz* (New York: William Morrow, 1983), 144.

5. Piatigorsky, *Cellist*, 168.

6. *Neue Freie Press* (Vienna), November 11, 1933. Amusingly, after playing *Flight of the Bumble Bee*, Piatigorsky spoke of a lady who told him that her favorite instrument was the cello because it was closest to the *human* voice.

7. Reporter Charles "Brick" Garrigues of the *Los Angeles Daily Illustrated News*, to a correspondent, Fanny Strassman, December 8, 1929.

8. *Public Ledger*, Philadelphia, November 9, 1929. It was at this concert during Tchaikovsky's Fourth Symphony that Stokowski chastised the audience not to applaud in between movements, earning headlines in many newspapers. Claiming the custom as medieval, "I rebuke nobody. But I want you to think this over and later in the season decide whether you want to show your appreciation by clapping hands," whereupon the audience greeted his remarks "with loud applause" (*New York Times*, November 9, 1929).

9. Then known as the New York Philharmonic-Symphony.

10. Unpublished draft.

11. *Margaret Campbell*, "Professor and Populariser," *The Strad*, April 1993, p. 355.

12. October 19, 1930. Mengelberg and Piatigorsky reprised the Dvořák Concerto with the Concertgebouw in the 1930s. A broadcast of the work with Maurice Gendron from January 1, 1944, shows the conductor to be a sensible partner.

13. Campbell, "Professor," 355.

14. "Another artist who wants to become a conductor is Gregor Piatigorsky, the Russian cellist. He does not practice scores before a mirror (as does Iturbi), but he is working very hard" (*New York Times*, September 28, 1930). The quote may have been a publicity ploy generated by Merovitch.

15. Nathan Milstein and Solomon Volkov, *From Russia to the West: The Musical Memoirs and Reminiscences of Nathan Milstein* (London: Barrie & Jenkins, 1990), 155.

16. Unpublished draft.

17. November 24, 1929.

18. Unpublished draft. They met one last time in Paris shortly before his death: "Glazunov, a poor, sick helpless old man felt embarrassed during his meeting with me—my heart was full of pity for him. I wanted to say something optimistic to him, but this did not happen—I was silent, and with a feeling of deep respect towards him which has never left me, I shook his hand."

19. Piatigorsky to Berezowski, December 15, 1929: "In America I am still communicating mostly with my hands on stage as well as in real life."

20. One wonders whether this experimental treatment exacerbated his final illness.

21. Prominent Boston music supporters, Steinert was a notable composer, and developed a retail piano company that is still in existence.

22. Spalding to his wife, January 26, 1932.

23. Unpublished draft.

24. Flesch to Schnabel, May 24, 1930.

25. Piatigorsky to Schnabel, September 9, 1930.

26. *Musical Record*, November 1, 1930.

27. For the thousands of Russian refugees who fled to the West after the October Revolution, crossing borders became traumatic. The Red Cross proposed the creation of a special passport for the now stateless refugees, and the League of Nations approved the idea in 1922. Fridtjof Nansen was appointed its first High Commissioner for

Refugees, and the "Nansen" passport became very sought after and enabled such Russian artists as Stravinsky, Rachmaninov, Chagall and Pavlova to begin new lives in the West.

28. Carl F. Flesch, *And Do You Also Play the Violin?* (London: Toccata, 1990), 60. An entry from Flesch's diary, probably on September 7, 1931.

29. Piatigorsky, *Cellist*, 150–151.

30. Author of *Paganini, the Genoese* (Norman: University of Oklahoma Press, 1957); reprint by Da Capo, 1977.

31. Edith Stargardt-Wolff, *Wegbereiter Grosser Musiker* (Wiesbaden: Bote & Bock, 1954), 178.

32. Piatigorsky, *Cellist*, 151.

33. Stargardt-Wolff, *Musiker*, 178.

34. Piatigorsky, *Cellist*, 151.

35. Milstein, *From Russia*, 116.

36. Piatigorsky, *Cellist*, 151–52.

37. Milstein, *From Russia*, 123–24.

38. Ivor Newton, *At the Piano: The World of an Accompanist* (London: Hamish Hamilton, 1966), 155–56.

39. May 23, 1931.

40. Plaskin, *Horowitz*, 143.

41. Piatigorsky, *Cellist*, 171.

42. Piatigorsky, *Cellist*, 199.

43. Milstein, *From Russia*, 182–83. Rachmaninoff no doubt was referring to both his respect of and disappointment with Brahms, that craft was not balanced with heart or inspiration. Tchaikovsky also shared this belief about Brahms.

44. Herbert Howells, *New York Times*, March 31, 1932, p. 24, cited in Plaskin, *Horowitz*, 146-7.

45. Arthur Rubinstein, *My Many Years* (New York: Knopf, 1980), 303.

46. The strained relationship with Furtwängler and Strauss notwithstanding.

47. Piatigorsky, *Cellist*, 145–146.

48. An observation that the conductor Sir Thomas Beecham made with typical humor: "It is not known in this country that the most accomplished conductor since Nikisch was Strauss — when he was in the right mood" (*Beecham Stories*, compiled by Harold Atkins and Archie Newman (London: Robson, 1978), 60).

49. Just before Variation VI.

50. Translated by Wolfdieter Jordan.

51. Strauss's fondness for skat stemmed from his student years when he managed to make a good living at it.

52. October 19 or 20, 1932.

53. Strauss, however, may have not resisted the Reich in order to protect certain Jewish relatives.

54. Also at Café de la Paix, Paris, and the Pierre Hotel, NY.

55. From album notes by Piatigorsky, RCA LSC 2293.

56. Milstein, *From Russia*, 142–3.

57. Music Library Association Notes, June 1984.

58. Though this amusingly complex explanation may seem manipulative or mercenary, a 5 percent royalty is standard for the transcriber of a work by a living composer.

59. Promotional materials, Hurok Concerts, Inc.

60. One recalls Mark Twain's comment to a correspondent: "I didn't have time to write a short letter, so I wrote a long one instead" (paraphrased).

Part I : Chapter 5

1. And would appear in each administration up through Eisenhower.

2. Interview, *CBC Tuesday Night*, Larry Soloway, host, June 21, 1966.

3. Piatigorsky, *Cellist*, 129.

4. Completed in May 1932 aboard the SS *Winchester Castle*. Published by Carl Fischer, Inc., edited by Piatigorsky.

5. As Piatigorsky told violinist Roman Totenberg circa 1930 (from recorded conversations with Totenberg March 27, 2007). It is all the more curious in that Heifetz's staccato is so different from Piatigorsky's; the violinist tended to use a sticky, almost heavy approach, while Piatigorsky favored a smoother style.

6. Robert Kraft, ed. *Stravinsky Selected Correspondence*, vol. 2 (New York: Knopf, 1984), 298.

7. Piatigorsky, *Cellist*, 144–5.

8. Flesch to Schnabel, January 2, 1933. Flesch had decided to begin a limited retirement, emphasizing chamber music over solo appearances.

9. Schnabel to Flesch, February 25, 1933.

10. César Saerchinger, *My Life and Music* (New York: St. Martin's, 1964), 105–06.

11. He stayed there even after being fired from the Hochschule on September 30, 1934, and did not move to London until June 1935.

12. Piatigorsky to Flesch, August 15, 1933, from Sils Maria, Switzerland.

13. Flesch to Piatigorsky, August 20, 1933. Flesch's son, Carl F. Flesch, also repeated his father's disappointment with Piatigorsky in conversations with the author.

14. Piatigorsky to Koutzen, undated, 1927. Library of Congress Special Collection: Boris Koutzen.

15. Lida and Piatigorsky continued to live with each other through the winter.

16. Piatigorsky to Koussevitzky, October 1933. Letters to and from Koussevitzky reprinted by permission of the Koussevitzky Music Foundation, copyright owner.

17. "She could be critical of Pierre's playing in the early days. He needed to let himself let go and be less cautious. Once, he was taken aback when he began a crescendo. 'Go on!' Lida shouted from the next room. 'Right through to the end of it ... like Grisha!'" (Angela Hughes, *Pierre Fournier: Cellist in a Landscape With Figures* (Hants: Ashgate, 1998), 36).

18. Inna Marinel, "The Last Word," *Music Journal* 35, no. 6 (July, 1977): 62.

19. Letter to Ibbs & Tillet, April 13, 1933, cited in Christopher Fifield, *The Rise and Fall of a Musical Empire* (London: Ashgate, 2006), 202.

20. Harold C. Schonberg, *Horowitz: His Life and Music* (New York: Simon & Schuster, 1992), 100.

21. Glenn Plaskin, *Horowitz* (New York: William Morrow, 1983), 171.

22. Merovitch occasionally arranged single concerts for individual artists such as Chaliapin and Stravinsky and represented conductors Vladimir Golschmann, Guido Cantelli and younger artists such as violinists Oscar Shumsky and Ruth Posselt.

23. Ella Brailowsky, cited in Plaskin, *Horowitz*, 171.

24. See chapter on recordings.

25. Schonberg, *Life and Music*, 137.

26. Though he had been the de facto dictator from March 24 when the German Parliament passed the Enabling Act, giving him unlimited powers.

27. Between Aryans and Jews.

28. This helps explain how concertmaster Szymon Goldberg and principal cellists Nikolai Graudan and Josef Schuster remained until 1934. Nonetheless, Goldberg had a difficult time leaving without incident. By 1934 the orchestra had become the Reich's official orchestra.

29. In 1938 Goebbels banned all recordings that featured non–Aryans.
30. Nationalsozialistische Deutsche Arbeiterpartei (National Socialist German Workers' Party), i.e., the Nazi Party.
31. After the war he and others in the organization were not punished, and their careers were unharmed by their active participation in the confiscation of musicalia from Jewish owners.
32. For instance, the play and film *Taking Sides* addresses the polemics between Furtwängler and an American military inquisitor. Furtwängler's explanation for remaining in Germany is explained in chapter 9. Piatigorsky thought that Furtwängler and Strauss were of very weak character.
33. *Musical Times*, October 1933, p. 943.
34. Commemorating the birth of Brahms, 1833–1933. Austria had not yet been annexed.
35. Furtwängler to Huberman, June 30, 1933.
36. Letters to this effect were confiscated from Piatigorsky's Paris apartment in 1941 by Sonderstab Musik, the Reich's clandestine unit charged with eliminating all traces of Jewish musical life.
37. *Manchester Guardian*, March 7, 1936.
38. *New York Times*, January 5, 1934, p. 10. Menuhin performed with the conductor after World War II.
39. Berlin,12th October [19]34/To the Members of my Berlin Philharmonic Orchestra/Gentlemen!/We worked effectively together for fifteen years. As you have yours, so have I given my best efforts to you and your work. I considered the establishment of the Philharmonic Orchestra as my life's mission. Together we experienced unrivaled artistic successes in all the European countries; our work has been considered exemplary in our homeland Germany. Through years and years of combined work did we accomplish the high level of musical-artistic cooperation that accounted for our fame and continuously justified it./It is not easy to leave behind such a work, created and welded together of almost two decades. I am not ever going to forget the time we were allowed to work together./Wilhelm Furtwängler (courtesy of the Berlin Philharmonic, translated by Melinda Fort).
40. Piatigorsky to Koussevitzky, December 16, 1934. Furtwängler's resignation was only temporary; he was reappointed the following year, whereupon a good deal of the world presses applauded his return to his post. Letters to and from Koussevitzky reprinted by permission of the Koussevitzky Music Foundation, Inc., copyright owner.
41. Unpublished draft.

Part I : Chapter 6

1. Boccherini, Haydn, Tartini, and Bach.
2. Piatigorsky to Koussevitzky, December 12, 1934. Letters to and from Koussevitzky reprinted by permission of the Koussevitzky Music Foundation, Inc., copyright owner.
3. James Westby, ed., *Una vita di musica* (Fiesole: Cadmo, 2005), 56 [1932–35].
4. Castelnuovo-Tedesco, *New York Times*, October 29, 1939, p. X7.
5. Castelnuovo-Tedesco to Nick Rossi, August 5, 1963, Mario Castelnuovo-Tedesco Collection, University of Southern Carolina Music Library.
6. Castelnuovo-Tedesco is quoted: "Composition for a cello concerto is a very difficult problem because of the difficulty of making the solo instrument come through, especially with a large orchestra as I had used; and it was also one of the rare occasions in which I retouched one of my scores, which generally I never correct, following the precious advice of Toscanini" (*New York Times*, October 29, 1939, p. X7).
7. Columbia Concerts publicity materials.
8. Piatigorsky, *Cellist*, 138, 225–6.
9. Columbia Concerts publicity materials.
10. Each letter of the alphabet is assigned a pitch.
11. Premiered during the 1936-37 season, published by Ricordi.
12. His wife and partner in the renowned two-piano team, Luboshutz and Nemenoff.
13. Then conductor of the Cleveland Orchestra. They met in Warsaw when Rodzinski was an opera accompanist and just starting his conducting career with the Warsaw Philharmonic.
14. Piatigorsky, *Cellist*, 218–21.
15. "Mr. Piatigorsky was in rare form last night ... warmth, a singing tone and a grasp of the spirit of the music.... [T]he cellist made it clear that his instrument was an element in a chamber work" (*New York Times*, March 12, 1935).
16. Alice Berezowsky, *Duet with Nicky* (Philadelphia: J.B. Lippincott, 1943), 65–7.
17. One of his first successes was his violin concerto, which was premiered in Dresden by Carl Flesch, composer conducting, April 29, 1930. Later, he also wrote a viola concerto for William Primrose and a clarinet concerto for Artie Shaw.
18. Piatigorsky to Koussevitzky, November 4, 1934. Letters to and from Koussevitzky reprinted by permission of the Koussevitzky Music Foundation, Inc., copyright owner.
19. Parisian publisher.
20. The letter continues: "before February 22. (Pittsburgh)— Athens: November 9,10,11,12; Antwerp: November 16 and 17; London: 19 and 21; Brussels: 24 and 25; Newcastle: 28; Glasgow: 29; Dundee: 30; Edinburgh: December 1; Aberdeen: 3; Birmingham: 5; Liverpool: 6; Sheffield (?): 7; London: 8; Bristol: 9; London: 10; Middlesboro: 11; Leicester: 12; London: 14; Manchester: 15; Bordeaux 17; Paris: 18; Marseille: 20; Barcelona: 23; Madrid: 25; Lisbon: 27 and 28; Madrid: 31; Balboa: January 2 and 3; Valencia: 5; Monte Carlo: 8; Neapol: 10; Rome: 12; Zurich: 14; Bonn (?): 15; Strasbourg: 16; Geneva: 17; Vevey! 18; New York (Toscanini): January 31 and February 1."
21. Koussevitzky to Piatigorsky, undated, 1935. Letters to and from Koussevitzky reprinted by permission of the Koussevitzky Music Foundation, Inc., copyright owner.
22. Piatigorsky, *Cellist*, 229–30.
23. The concerto is in one movement, beginning with a slow introduction, leading to a passacaglia with six variations, cadenza and coda.
24. Olin Downes, *New York Times*, March 3, 1935, p. N4.
25. With Hitler as Führer in August 1934 aggressions rapidly escalated.
26. Piatigorsky to Koussevitzky, November 12, 1935, from Stockholm. Letters to and from Koussevitzky reprinted by permission of the Koussevitzky Music Foundation, Inc., copyright owner.
27. Margie A. McLeod, *Musical America*, April 10, 1936. The month of their escape was actually May 1921.
28. April 3, 1936.
29. BBC interview on 10th anniversary of Furtwängler's death, 1964.

30. Unpublished draft.
31. *Musical Times*, London, November 1937, p. 989, regarding the concert on October 28, 1937.
32. Premiered February 13, 1938, in New York.
33. There is a photo of them picnicking at MGM together.
34. David Ewen, *Men and Women Who Make Music* (New York: Readers, 1946), 195.
35. Vuillermoz was the foremost French critic of music and film. A former student of Fauré, he also wrote the composer's biography as well as those for Debussy and his classmate Ravel, and championed their music as well as Stravinsky, Honegger and Schmitt.
36. Referred to as Société des Artistes Internationaux distributed through World Pictures, Inc.
37. The correct title should be, Weber-Piatigorsky: *Adagio & Rondo*.
38. All but *Andante et Rondo* were directed by Max Ophüls. Cortot's film won a Special Recommendation Award at the Venice Film Festival in 1936. Serge Lifar also directed the *corps de ballet* of the Paris Opera in their short film *Ballerina*.
39. Vitaphones covered all entertainment from vaudeville to classical and opera.
40. Frank S. Nugent, *New York Times*, November 2, 1939, p. 31. The film's failure necessitated a return to the individual shorts format and was eventually sold in the 16mm educational film market.
41. R.L.C., *Washington Post*, May 30, 1940, p. 6.
42. Completed in 1927. The violinist referred to the Duo as "ce bougre de Duo" ("this devil of a Duo").
43. BBC interview, "The Art of Piatigorsky: Composers and Colleagues," John Amis, host, July 11, 1974.
44. Piatigorsky, *Cellist*, 250.
45. Junnosuke Chiba, ed., *Haru no Umi* (Tokyo: Iwanami Shoten, 2002), 133–38, translated by Anne Prescott.
46. The work was originally written for koto and shakuhachi (bamboo flute) and is heard especially during the New Year holiday.
47. One disc was recorded by the RCA Victor Music Lovers Society (see discography).
48. Unpublished draft.
49. George D. Oakley, *Honolulu Star-Bulletin*, November 15, 1936.
50. Gary Giddins, *Bing Crosby: A Pocketful of Dreams: The Early Years* (Boston: Little, Brown, 2001), 399, 401–02.
51. Unpublished draft.
52. In this case, two gas pipes and a whisky funnel.
53. Zapateado is literally tap dance. The script is from the NBC broadcast of December 3, 1936.
54. Piatigorsky, *Cellist*, 231. In 1937 roughly only 2000 television sets were in use.
55. *Ibid.*, 223–25.
56. Norah Drewett, *Chesterian*, September-October 1938, cited in *Geza de Kresz and Norah Drewett: Their Life on Two Continents* (Toronto: Canadian Stage and Arts, 1987) ,140.
57. Aladár Tóth, *Válogatott Zenekritikái, 1934–1939* (Budapest: Zenemükiadó, 1968), 366–367, translated by Lilla Kulsar.

Part I : Chapter 7

1. Jacqueline Rebecca de Rothschild, *Jump in the Waves: A Memoir* (New York: St. Martin's, 1988) 123, 5.

2. Jacqueline represented the U.S. in the Woman's Chess Olympiad.
3. Rothschild, *Jump*, 119.
4. *Ibid.*, 121.
5. *Ibid.*, 121, 123.
6. Arthur Rubinstein, *My Many Years* (New York: Knopf, 1980), 303.
7. de Rothschild, 126. They were married on January 26, 1937.
8. Bethsabée de Rothschild in conversation with author, August 1976.
9. As with Jacqueline, he helped her find joy in self-accomplishment. With his urging, though she had little musical training, Germaine went on to become an expert in the life of composer Luigi Boccherini. She not only wrote his biography (Oxford University Press, 1962), but also sponsored a 700-page catalog of his works compiled by the French musicologist Yves Gérard. Consequently, Boccherini's works are now identified with the letter G designating Gérard's catalog.
10. Rothschild, *Jump*, 162.
11. March 28, 1939.
12. Unpublished draft.
13. Violinist-composer from the Bolshoi and an important ally in Berlin.
14. Oversold by at least 400. The 1777 passengers included conductor Vladimir Golschmann, Grand Duchess Marie of Russia and former U.S. ambassador Walter E. Edge.
15. de Rothschild, *Jump*, 129–30.
16. Niall Ferguson, *The House of Rothschild: The World's Banker 1849–1999* (New York: Viking, 1999), 477.
17. According to a handwritten itemization from the Amt Musik (music department) from February 1942: "Only 6 of the 23 crates from Gregor Piatigorsky, MR 1, 3, 4, 5, 12, and 15 (containing books, sheet music, gramophone records, and pictures) were delivered to the Amt Musik [in Berlin]. All crates and suitcases containing his prized possessions, such as gold and silver, ivory, ceramics, paintings, valuable books, and other belongings, apparently reached a different destination" (Willem de Vries, *Sonderstab Musik: Music Confiscations by the Einsatzstab Reichsleiter Rosenberg under the Nazi Occupation of Western Europe* (Amsterdam: Amsterdam University Press, 1996), 232).
18. One of the founders of the Israel Philharmonic and president of the Robin Hood Dell Concerts of the Philadelphia Orchestra.
19. Galamian's position was 6th chair, second violin.
20. Galamian had been a member of the Capet Quartet and was a disciple of Lucian Capet. He synthesized the Capet method with the French-Belgian and Russian schools to create what is referred to as the "Galamian" technique. Meadowmount was modeled after Piotr Stoliarski's violin school in Odessa.
21. The arrest is on public record: *Chateaugay Record*, December 27, 1940.
22. Unpublished draft.

Part I : Chapter 8

1. Piatigorsky, *Cellist*, 236–37.
2. Sergey Prokof'yev, *Dnevniki*, 2 vols. (Paris: Serge Prokofiev Estate, 2002), 2:799, translated by Simon Morrison.
3. Israel V. Nestyev, *Prokofiev*, translated by Florence Jonas (Stanford: Stanford University Press, 1960), 297.

4. Harlow Robinson, *Sergei Prokofiev: A Biography* (New York: Viking Press, 1987), 292. However, the actual manuscript bears the date September 18, 1938.

5. Piatigorsky, *Cellist*, 237.

6. Some passages bear a resemblance to Piatigorsky's style: the four-string figure 6 before No. 32, the double strokes (performed as a down-bow staccato) after No. 71, the ricochet variation at No. 89, and the three-string figure at No. 92.

7. Ivor Newton, *At the Piano: the World of an Accompanist* (London: Hamish Hamilton, 1966), 127.

8. Piatigorsky to Koussevitzky, August 18, 1939, from Paris. But two weeks later, Germany invaded Czechoslovakia and the onset of World War II prevented Piatigorsky from further European tours. The Koussevitzky correspondence is reprinted by permission of the Koussevitzky Music Foundation, Inc., copyright owner.

9. Piatigorsky, *Cellist*, 237.

10. Sviatoslav Richter, *Richter in His Own Words*, translated by Stewart Spencer (Princeton: Princeton University Press, 2001), 70–71.

11. Elizabeth Wilson, *Rostropovich* (Chicago: Ivan R. Dee, 2007), 67.

12. Nestyev, *Prokofiev*, 297.

13. Piatigorsky, *Cellist*, 237–38.

14. Warren Story Smith, "Muck Tribute by Symphony," *Boston Post*, March 9, 1940. The premiere of the concerto was part of a concert dedicated to the German conductor Karl Muck, who died on March 3, 1940. Muck led the Boston Symphony from 1912 to 1918, resigning following his arrest in the U.S. as an enemy alien. Piatigorsky soloed with him several times, most notably in Hamburg.

15. Wilson, *Rostropovich*, 67.

16. Piatigorsky, *Cellist*, 238.

17. Prokofiev's revision (op. 125) further attests to the original's excessive finale where the composer eliminated the two *Interludios* and the *Reminiscenza* (a lengthy reprise of the first movement). These substantial sections diffused the movement's theme and variation form, causing the concerto to ramble—becoming as long as the first two movements combined. An alternative revision of the original might follow Prokofiev's lead with the elimination of the *Interludios* and *Reminiscenza* and a few small cuts elsewhere balancing the movement and preserving the material retained in op. 125.

18. Piatigorsky, *Cellist*, 237.

19. Later Piatigorsky sometimes called it *Stroll* and added the descriptive subtitle "Prokofiev meets Shostakovich in Moscow," in which the two composers exchange greetings and sarcastic witticisms as they take a walk.

20. Unpublished draft.

21. Samuel Thaviu, violinist (1934–37), interviewed by Jon Bentz, September 11, 1990, Rosenthal Archives of the Chicago Symphony Orchestra, Oral History Collection. Archive Number: OHP-A.

22. One arrangement was his orchestration of Tchaikovsky's Piano Trio, op. 50.

23. Edward Barry, *Chicago Daily Tribune*, April 5, 1940, p. 29.

24. Their performances of the Hindemith (February 26 and 27, 1942) were their last, for Stock died a few months later.

25. Peter Yates, "Visit to an Untyped Cellist, Gregor Piatigorsky," *High Fidelity* (February 1961), 45–47, 104.

26. Hindemith to Gertrude Hindemith, Lenox, July 28, 1940. Letter excerpts regarding the Cello Concerto are taken from *Hindemith: Complete Works*, vol. III, no. 6, p. ix–x, Musikverlag Schott Musik International, Mainz, 1984, edited by Magda Marx-Weber and Hans Joachim Marx.

27. The composer Paul Dessau. He immigrated to the United States in 1933, and, in need of work, accepted assignments from AMP such as the cello concerto.

28. May 30, 1941.

29. John Cage, "South Winds in Chicago," *Modern Music* 19 (1942), 68.

30. Letter excerpts regarding the Variations and Sonata are taken from *Hindemith: Complete Works*, vol. V, no. 7, Musikverlag Schott Musik International, Mainz, 1992, edited by Dorothea Baumann.

31. Piatigorsky was not clear in his touring as to the very first presentation of a new work, but listed for instance, his Chicago recital in Orchestra Hall for March 24, 1945, as its Chicago premiere as part of the 1945-46 season.

32. Piatigorsky to Koussevitzky, February 16, 1948. Letters to and from Koussevitzky reprinted by permission of the Koussevitzky Music Foundation, Inc., copyright owner.

33. Cellist Aldo Parisot played the Cello Concerto for Hindemith in 1959, being careful to play it exactly as written. When he finished, the composer "kept his head down, still looking at the score.... 'Is that the way you feel my music?'" He then asked the cellist to come back in a few days "and play it the way you really want to" (interview with Aldo Parisot by Tim Janof, Internet Cello Society, May 1, 2001).

34. Hindemith to Walton July 29, 1963. Geoffrey Skelton, *Paul Hindemith: The Man Behind the Music* (London: Victor Gollancz, 1977), 292.

35. Salmond had been at Curtis for many years and resigned after Feuermann was hired without his knowledge or consultation.

36. Lorne Munroe interview, June 4, 2002.

37. Gordon Epperson interview with Tim Janof, Internet Cello Society, July 31 1995.

38. "Cellist II," an unpublished sequel.

39. The yearly salary was $3,600, teaching a maximum of four hours a week.

40. Roy Milan, *Efrem Zimbalist: A Life* (Pompton Plains, NY: Amadeus, 2004), 260.

41. A recording of the concert is at the Library of Congress.

Part I : Chapter 9

1. The latter also in conjunction with the National War Fund's Defense Recreation Committee.

2. Under the auspices of Mayor La Guardia and the War Services Section Music Unit, the concerts were presented for the U.S. Treasury Department to promote and sell war bonds and stamps.

3. Piatigorsky to Stogorsky, July 1, 1944.

4. Hurok Attractions biographical and publicity materials (Piatigorsky stood at over six feet three inches).

5. *Ibid.*

6. *Ibid.*

7. Elizabeth A.H. Green, with Judith Galamian and Josef Gingold, *Miraculous Teacher: Ivan Galamian and the Meadowmount Experience* (Elizabeth A.H. Green, 1993), 38.

8. Antal Dorati, *Notes of Seven Decades* (Detroit: Wayne State University Press, 1981), 171.

9. October 1940 issue.

10. This work may have been the Concerto No. 2 from 1945, premiered by Fournier.

11. The composer and cellist recorded it in 1958.

12. While organizing Piatigorsky's music collection for deposit at the Library of Congress, the author came across pencil sketches of Foss's *Early Song, Dedication*, and *Composer's Holiday* arranged for cello. These pieces were originally written for violin and later transcribed for flute as *Three American Pieces*. Foss wrote to the author stating that these works were also a projected suite for Piatigorsky. The suite would have begun with the *Capriccio*, followed by *Early Song, Dedication*, and *Composer's Holiday* in that order. Foss later wrote a work for cello and orchestra for the cellist entitled *Orpheus* (1968).

13. The composer wrote to the author explaining that he could not remember the exact date of the arrangement. Piatigorsky performed it in the 1949-50 season. It was published in 1952.

14. Vernon Duke to Koussevitzky, January 24, 1946. Letters to and from Koussevitzky reprinted by permission of the Koussevitzky Music Foundation, Inc., copyright owner.

15. Robert A. Simon, *New Yorker*, January 19, 1946.

16. Alexander Williams, *Boston Herald*, January 5, 1946.

17. *Brooklyn (NY) Eagle*, January 10, 1946.

18. Gena Bennett, *New York Journal American*, January 10, 1946.

19. Cyril Durgin, *Boston Daily Globe*, January 5, 1946.

20. Vernon Duke, *Passport to Paris* (Boston: Little, Brown, 1955), 435.

21. Piatigorsky, *Cellist*, 244.

22. First orchestrated by Ralph Berkowitz and in 1946 by Arthur Cohen.

23. "Cellist II," an unpublished sequel.

24. March 22, 1945.

25. To author. Postwar conflicts were mentioned in Furtwängler's *Notebooks, 1924–54* (London: Quartet Books, 1989), 190–91. He wanted Jews to know that "I was the one artist that remained in Germany and emphatically intervened on behalf of Jews until the very end. Then I see Herr Brailowsky and Herr Isaac Stern. Have those two condescended to play, in the past year, at the celebration concerts in Lucerne, although they must have known that I am definitely employed here [Lucerne] as a conductor? When they are in Europe, do they have a different conscience from the one they have in America, which permits them to do in Lucerne what they would have to refuse in Chicago? Then I see my old friend Gregor Piatigorsky, the long-haired solo cellist of the Berlin Philharmonic. I watched the beginnings of his rise with my own eyes, and even shortly before the war, when it had been long clear that I was staying in Germany, we associated in a most friendly manner in Paris."

26. Elisabeth Furtwängler's fax to author, July 5, 2000.

27. *New York Times*, January 7, 1949, p. 19.

28. Nathan Milstein and Solomon Volkov, *From Russia to the West* (London: Barrie & Jenkins, 1990), 150–151.

29. Claudia Cassidy, *Chicago Tribune*, March 25, 1965.

30. "It is true that Furtwängler was sad and offended when he read in the newspapers that Piatigorsky apparently joined other musicians in the 'Chicago Affair.' After a while, however, he was convinced that this was only (American) propaganda. At that time, we unfortunately were used to this kind of lies.... Deep in his heart, Furtwängler knew that Piatigorsky appreciated him as much as he appreciated Piatigorsky. In 1971 Piatigorsky explained the truth to me" (Elisabeth Furtwängler's fax to author, July 5, 2000).

31. Daniel Gillis, *Furtwängler and America* (New York: Manyland, 1970), 125–126.

32. Claudia Cassidy, *Chicago Tribune*, September 4, 1949, p. F6, from a breakfast meeting with the conductor in Salzburg that summer.

33. Hollywood producer, director and actor who is famously quoted: "I speak Russian, French and German. I murder Italian; English I only manslaughter." The quote is equally appropriate for Piatigorsky.

34. Unpublished draft.

35. *Chicago Tribune*, April 13, 1949, p. G2.

36. Hurok Attractions publicity materials.

37. Unpublished draft.

38. Some years later he began its sequel ("Cellist II"), but it did not amount to much more than what is quoted here.

39. Harry Ellis Dickson, *Beating Time: A Musician's Memoir* (Boston: Northeastern University Press, 1995), 120.

40. Polk graduated from the Hochschule für Musik in Berlin, where he studied with Henri Marteau. He performed many times with the Berlin Philharmonic in the early twenties and toured with Chaliapin (and his longtime pianist Fyodor Koenemann) in the U.S.; he also made a few recordings of violin tidbits.

41. He and Heifetz stopped working together on a regular basis after the violinist's 1939 film, *They Shall Have Music*, where Polk served as a music supervisor. Polk still maintained a relationship with the violinist and was helpful in drawing composer Erich Korngold and Heifetz together in the commission of Korngold's Violin Concerto.

42. In later years he was assistant musical director at Columbia Pictures and musical director for Enterprise Studios. He also occasionally represented Vladimir Horowitz and José Iturbi.

43. Perhaps the most familiar is Wayman Adams's large portrait of the cellist in performance. Painted in 1942, the work won several prizes and was shown at the Metropolitan Museum of Art in New York City.

44. Dorle J. Soria, *High Fidelity-Musical America*, December 1970, p. MA-6.

45. Hurok Attractions publicity materials.

46. Boris Morros, *My Ten Years as a Counterspy* (New York: Dell, 1959), 12–13.

47. Piatigorsky, *Cellist*, 233. His embarrassment did not prevent him joining Walter Damrosch, Bruno Walter, Enzio Pinza, Artur Rodzinski and other members of the cast in attending Polk's son's wedding in New York (March 3, 1947).

48. Arthur Rubinstein, *My Many Years* (New York: Knopf, 1980), 529.

49. Polk was much more successful as a producer for the *Superman* television series of the 1950s.

50. Artur Weschler-Vered, *Jascha Heifetz* (London: Robert Hale, 1986), 177. In any case, Heifetz and Piatigorsky helped fund the posthumous Rudolph Polk Scholarship at the Claremont Colleges.

51. Mendelssohn movements, 1–3 (abridged), and the first movement (abridged) of Schubert. Unfortunately they did not commercially record the Schubert trio.

52. In spite of superb directors Jules Dassin and Robert Aldrich.

53. Ralph Berkowitz.

54. Art Ryon, "Jam Session," *Los Angeles Times*, December 23, 1961.

55. Conversation with Jean Pierre Fonda (Fournier) and author.

56. Carl Fischer, Inc., published the cello arrangement in 1933.

57. "Cellist II," an unpublished sequel.
58. *Time*, August 22, 1949.
59. Piatigorsky left Columbia Records in 1949 and joined RCA in March 1950. (Simultaneously, Columbia announced their exclusive contract for Casals in March 1950.)
60. Ivor Newton, *At the Piano: the World of an Accompanist* (London: Hamish Hamilton, 1966), 152–3. Violist Joseph de Pasquale recalled their sessions from the 1960s: "On playbacks Heifetz would say, 'a little more viola there,' 'a little less viola there,' and 'I want to hear more of myself' ... things like that — he would balance it very well, but he liked to be the prima donna" (taped conversation with the author, June 2, 2003).
61. Weschler-Vered, *Heifetz*, 179.
62. Arthur Rubinstein, *My Many Years* (New York: Knopf, 1980), 237.
63. Herbert Axelrod, *Heifetz* (Neptune City, NJ: Paganiniana, 1990), 615.
64. Piatigorsky, "Cellist II."
65. Harry Ellis Dickson, *Beating Time: A Musician's Memoir* (Boston: Northeastern University Press, 1995), 172–3.

Part I : Chapter 10

1. Piatigorsky, "Cellist II," an unpublished sequel.
2. *Time*, February 13, 1956.
3. The three programs mentioned are available on DVD (see Filmography).
4. "Toscanini: The Man Behind the Legend," Ben Grauer, host, July 31, 1963, BBC.
5. *Time*, June 4, 1965.
6. Rather than interested only in his solos (Harald Eggebrecht, *Sergiu Celibidache*, Luebbe, 2001).
7. Thomas Schippers (1930–1977).
8. Piatigorsky, "Cellist II."
9. Loren Glickman, comp., *Don't Sqveeze de Bow! Reminiscences about Alexander Schneider* (Norwich: Terra Nova, 1996), 11–12.
10. In this case, much more than a figurehead advisor; he was a vital presence at the academy.
11. *A Tanglewood Dream*, a booklet published by the Koussevitzky Music Foundation.
12. Piatigorsky to Koussevitzky, May 1, 1951. Letters to and from Koussevitzky reprinted by permission of the Koussevitzky Music Foundation, Inc., copyright owner.
13. Howard Taubman, *New York Times*, January 3, 1949: Little Orchestra Society, Thomas Scherman, Town Hall, New York: "Mr. Piatigorsky played the solo part with a rich, singing tone and with a complete command of all the composer's requirements."
14. Piatigorsky joked about the amazingly prolific composer, saying, "Don't let Milhaud take any music paper with him to the bathroom; he'll come out with a new piece."
15. By unanimous decision of the jury — she later became professor at the Ecole Normale de Musique, Paris, and taught in Tokyo, Basel, and Lyon.
16. Morely fashioned a one-movement work, *Ruth: Elegy*, in 1998 using only the sketches, and tied it together with a short cadenza. (Morely had shaped similar projects commissioned by John Williams, both for himself and Alex North.) An earlier request from Piatigorsky (in 1941) was to create a symphonic poem for cello and orchestra based on the main theme from Waxman's film *Rebecca*. The project was not completed.
17. Mozart ("Eine Kleine Nichtmusik"), Beethoven ("Moonlight Concerto"), Bach ("Chaconne à Son Goût"), Shostakovich and Prokofiev ("Homage to Shostakofiev").
18. Malcolm S. Cole and Barbara Barclay, *Armseelchen: The Life and Music of Eric Zeisl* (Westport: Greenwood, 1984).
19. Interviews with Gertrude Zeisl from September 9, 18 and 23, 1975, Malcolm S. Cole interviewer (Zeisl Archive, UCLA).
20. *Ibid*.
21. *Ibid*.
22. The premiere, which took place shortly after the composer's sudden death on November 23, 1959, was left to another cellist, George Neikrug; Piatigorsky attended the concert.
23. A down payment of one half of the commission, $1,500, was and cashed. The commission was never resolved or adjusted, straining their relationship.
24. Chairman and managing director of Harold Holt, Ltd.
25. Ivor Newton, *At the Piano: The World of an Accompanist* (London: Hamish Hamilton, 1966), 128–9. The commission was $3,000. Unlike British currency, the American dollar was not taxed at that time.
26. Michael Kennedy, *Portrait of Walton* (Oxford: Oxford University Press, 1990), 197.
27. It was publicly announced in the press on October 10, 1955, in the *New York Times*.
28. Kennedy, *Portrait*, 197.
29. Susana Walton, *William Walton: Behind the Façade* (Oxford: Oxford University Press, 1988), 163.
30. Hurok Attractions publicity materials, also printed in *Time*, November 1, 1956.
31. Piatigorsky to Walton, May 17, 1956, Los Angeles.
32. Piatigorsky to Walton, July 22, 1956, Los Angeles.
33. Piatigorsky to Walton, August 2, 1956, Los Angeles.
34. Piatigorsky to Walton, September 4, 1956, Saigon. Surely the codas referred to by Hindemith, Schumann and Prokofiev are meant for emphasis, as they are not particularly short.
35. Malcolm Hayes, ed., *The Selected Letters of William Walton* (London: Faber and Faber, 2002), 278. Actual date of completion was October 25.
36. Piatigorsky to Walton, October 22 1956, Los Angeles.
37. Kennedy, *Portrait*, 197.
38. Piatigorsky to Walton, November 9, 1956, Los Angeles.
39. Walton, *Walton*, 164.
40. Piatigorsky to Walton, December 12, 1956, Los Angeles.
41. Piatigorsky to Walton, January 7, 1957, Denver.
42. Piatigorsky to Walton, January 26, 1957, Boston.
43. EMI Classics DVD DVA 4928419 and Angel Records DVD 92841.
44. Kennedy, *Portrait*, 198.
45. Piatigorsky to Walton, April 5, 1957, Los Angeles.
46. Walton, *Walton*, 166.
47. Kennedy, *Portrait*, 198. Critics Peter Heyworth and Donald Mitchell, who were dismissive about the concerto.
48. Quoting Piatigorsky in "A Portrait of William Walton," BBC RADIO3, broadcast June 4, 1977 (taken from conversations in 1974).
49. Piatigorsky to Ian Hunter, December 1, 1954.
50. Kennedy, *Portrait*, 198, 197.
51. Hayes, ed., *Letters*, 296.

52. *Ibid.*, 308.
53. Piatigorsky to Walton, February 1, 1967, Los Angeles.
54. Piatigorsky to Walton, August 2, 1967, Los Angeles.
55. Kennedy, *Portrait*, 237.
56. Hayes, ed., *Letters*, 413, July 24, 1974.
57. Piatigorsky to Walton, September 20, 1974, Los Angeles.
58. Hayes, ed., *Letters*, 413.
59. Piatigorsky to Walton, September 9, 1974, Los Angeles.
60. Piatigorsky to Walton, December 3, 1974, Los Angeles. The ending starting five bars before rehearsal cue 19 on p.112 of the printed score.
61. Piatigorsky to Walton, February 1975, Los Angeles.
62. Kennedy, *Portrait*, 198–99.
63. Hurok Attractions publicity materials, also reprinted in *Time*.
64. The tenth anniversary celebrations of the founding of Israel when he was scheduled to play Bloch's *Schelomo* and the Brahms Double Concerto with Isaac Stern.
65. October 26, 1959.
66. Other cellists appearing at the White House included Casals and Beatrice Harrison.

Part I : Chapter 11

1. Unpublished draft.
2. *Time*, February 2, 1962.
3. "The Big Two," *Time*, October 2, 1964.
4. *Time*, February 2, 1962.
5. See CDs: RCA 630459 and BMG 61741.
6. Schwann-1 Record & Tape Guide, December 1974, p. 185.
7. William Primrose, *Walk On The North Side: Memoirs of a Violist* (Provo: Brigham Young University Press, 1978), 147, 144, 139–40.
8. As a bonus in the video series of the Heifetz Master Classes (Kultur International Video, 1990), the violinist does one of his famous imitations of a bad violinist, something he had perfected from childhood. The imitation is all the more impressive as it causes one to wonder whether perhaps the violinist has some hidden talent buried beneath the glaring mistakes.
9. *Newsweek*, August 21, 1961, p. 80.
10. Leon Fleisher taped conversation with the author, November 27, 2004.
11. Lateiner taped conversation with the author, December 4, 2003.
12. Heifetz had nothing to prove. Only once did Heifetz actually seek an edit "dishonestly"—in the Fuga of the A Minor Solo Sonata of Bach. At measure 239 the sequence naturally follows to low F, out of the violin's range. Heifetz decided to dub in the F by lowering the tuning of the G-string by one step. One has to really know the score to notice it (courtesy violinist Arturo Delmoni).
13. Miklós Rózsa, *Double Life* (New York: Wynwood, 1982), 185.
14. They also led their respective sections in a Heifetz-Piatigorsky Concert, October 1, 1964, in Carnegie Hall.
15. *Divertimento*, op. 37, no.1, for violin and cello and op. 37, no. 2, for violin and viola.
16. Elsewhere, slight rhythmical errors still remain. Similarly, in a solo violin session, Heifetz, exasperated with a recurring fluffed note exclaimed, "Out, damned spot!"
17. RCA recording engineer and producer Jon Samuels.
18. Primrose, *Walk*, 147.
19. *Ibid.*, 148.
20. RCA/BMG CD 09026-61770-2, The Heifetz Collection, volume 39.
21. "But I still practice and play, and it doesn't stop me from demonstrating things to students." He added: "I can still be of service. I still have some time." Quoted in the *New York Times*, December 12, 1987, p. 111.
22. To wit, the Dvořák Piano Quintet performance from San Francisco in 1964 and the Tchaikovsky Trio from 1972. Hopefully these performances will become available.
23. See Ayke Agus, *Heifetz As I Knew Him* (Portland: Amadeus, 2001).
24. Rózsa, *Double Life*, 230.
25. Alexander Schneider, unpublished autobiography.
26. *Time*.
27. Martin Bookspan, *Time*.
28. Fortunately the video of the Schubert Quintet and the Schumann Concerto are preserved at both the Casals Museum and the Library of Congress. Violinist Louis Kaufman recalled a chamber music evening with Heifetz, Sascha Jacobson, himself, and cellists Piatigorsky and Marie Roemaet-Rosanoff: "We were about to play Schubert's Quintet.... Marie Roemaet-Rosanoff sat down at the first cello stand, remarking to Piatigorsky, 'I don't know the second part.' With typical Russian directness, he playfully pushed her off the chair and seated himself before the first stand, saying firmly, 'Neither do I!'" (Louis Kaufman, *A Fiddler's Tale*, 2003), 84.
29. Yehudi Menuhin, *Unfinished Journey* (New York: Knopf, 1977), 186–87.
30. Gregory Piatigorsky's nephew (son of Anatoly Piatigorsky) in conversation with the author, June 12, 2002; Mischa Boguslavsky, member of the Moscow Radio under Leonid, interview with author in June 1993.
31. Hurok publicity materials, also quoted in the *Los Angeles Times*, January 16, 1954, p. 4.
32. Also known as *Stroll*.
33. Apparently Shostakovich held no ill will toward Piatigorsky. While at Oxford University to receive an honorary doctorate degree in 1958, Shostakovich attended a private house concert that included the composer's cello sonata as played by Rohan de Saram. The composer was complimentary to de Saram but complained that he played two passages incorrectly. Embarrassed, the cellist provided him with the published score as edited by Piatigorsky—which revealed no mistake by de Saram—but Piatigorsky's unapproved alterations. Shostakovich took a pencil and angrily crossed out Piatigorsky's fabrication and restored his original passages (paraphrased from Isaiah Berlin, "Shostakovich at Oxford" *New York Review of Books*, vol. 56, no. 12, July 16, 2009, from an extract of Berlin's *Enlightening: Letters 1946–1960*).
34. *Sovietskaya Muzyka*, 1978, no. 4 [1 p.], Ogareva 13, Moscow.
35. Piatigorsky to Stogorsky.
36. "Measure of True Art," *Izvestiya*, April 17, 1962.
37. Daniil Shafran, "Memorable Encounters," *Soviet Music* 4 (1978) commemorating Piatigorsky's 75th birthday.
38. "Measure of True Art," *Izvestiya*, April 17, 1962.
39. Tim Janof, "Conversation with Stephen Kates," Internet Cello Society, September 1, 2002.
40. *Three Impromptus*, Op. 90c (Mills ©1963), inscribed "For Gregor Piatigorsky The Friend and Grand Master of his instrument on his 60th birthday, Santa

Monica 4/20/63," originally titled *Improvisation in Three Movements* (Andante cantabile, Allegretto grazioso, Adagio con espressione, quasi "der letze Kampf" ("The Last Struggle").

41. Art Seidenbaum, "Piatigorsky's Concerto of Cello and Charity," *Los Angeles Times*, November 17, 1963, p. B3.

42. Janos Starker, *The World of Music According to Starker* (Bloomington: Indiana University Press, 2004), 230.

43. Rózsa, *Double Life*, 184–85, 168, 214–16.

44. Fax to author, June 23, 1995. The work was premiered on March 5 and 6, 1999, with the author and violinist Laura Bossert, and the Lubbock Symphony, Albert-George Schram, conductor. "Schifrin's Double Concerto, especially, was a triumph, driven by magnificent performances by the team of Terry King and Laura Bossert. The word team is not used lightly here — the unspoken communication between cellist and violinist consistently elevated the performance ... as captivating as it was joyous. And again, King and Bossert delivered a double dose of adrenaline ... obviously enraptured by the very music they were creating. A standing ovation lured Schifrin back on stage" (*Lubbock Avalanche Journal*, March 7 1999).

Part I : Chapter 12

1. The same orchestra featured with Heifetz in the film *They Shall Have Music* (1939).

2. Other Advisors were composer Darius Milhaud, soprano Lotte Lehmann, conductors Richard Lert, Alexander Hilsberg and Fritz Zweig, pianist Gyorgy Sandor and violinist Sascha Jacobsen.

3. Leopold Auer, *My Long Life in Music* (New York: Frederick A. Stokes, 1923).

4. The center's concert hall was named after Dorothy Chandler.

5. Quotes following are from two interviews with Grant Beglarian and the author, January 2001.

6. $2,500 per month.

7. Key trustees included Virginia and Simon Ramo (the R in TRW), and Anna Bing.

8. Piatigorsky to Adele Siegal.

9. Heifetz sued many times.

10. (1870–1965), American financier, stock market speculator, statesman and presidential adviser.

11. Beglarian explained: "We had a huge house with mortgage and everything else with children growing up."

12. Heifetz was a founder of the American Guild of Musical Artists (AGMA).

13. *The School Musician & Teacher* (April 1975), 28.

14. USC materials dedicating the Piatigorsky Chair in Violoncello.

15. Hope's daughter-in-law also attended Wellesley.

16. See chapter 10 on Walton.

17. Violinist Kenneth Goldsmith, pianist John Jensen and the author.

Part II : Recalling Piatigorsky

Accompanists

1. Piatigorsky, *Cellist*, 215.

2. Ivor Newton, *At the Piano* (London: Hamish Hamilton, 1966), 123–128.

3. "Accompanying the Immortals: Mr. Ivor Newton Looks Back," *London Times*, December 10, 1962.

4. Newton, *Piano*, 132–133.

5. Ivor Newton, *Music & Musicians* (November 1976), 8, 10.

6. Interview with Ralph Berkowitz, August 1998.

Friends and Colleagues

7. In alphabetical order.

8. Jascha Bernstein was a fellow cello student of Alfred von Glehn at the Moscow Conservatory with Piatigorsky. Bernstein later arranged the initial meeting to study with Julius Klengel in Leipzig. After studying with Klengel, Piatigorsky was adrift in Germany: "Grisha always thought of this period as being perhaps the most difficult, the most trying time in his entire life" (spoken as part of a memorial to Piatigorsky sponsored by the Violoncello Society of New York, December 6, 1976, at the Kosciuszko Foundation).

9. Interview with Stephen Wadsworth, 1981. Galamian was a member of the Bolshoi Theatre with Piatigorsky. They were lifelong friends and were also colleagues at the Curtis Institute of Music. When Piatigorsky settled in Elizabethtown, New York, he persuaded Galamian that Elizabethtown was a perfect place for a music school, the future Meadowmount.

10. Excerpts from "A Tribute to Gregor Piatigorsky," in acceptance of the First Piatigorsky Chair position at USC.

11. Taped conversation with author, June 6 2002.

12. Culled from interview on December 4, 2003, conversations with Vera Lateiner in 2003, and album notes to RCA/BMG 61761.

13. Culled from the Friends of Music birthday celebration honoring Piatigorsky, April 17, 1976, and *Los Angeles Times*, August 15, 1976, p. 70.

14. Interview with Tim Janof, Internet Cello Society, June 2, 2000.

15. Joseph de Pasquale was principal violist with the Boston Symphony and later with the Philadelphia Orchestra. He has taught at the leading schools of music and currently teaches at the Curtis Institute. He was a student of William Primrose (taped conversation with author, June 4, 2002).

16. Taped conversation with author, June 4, 2002.

17. Spoken as president emeritus of the Violoncello Society (NY) at a concert given in memory of Piatigorsky at Caspary Auditorium, Rockefeller University, New York City, November 21, 1976.

18. Daniil Shafran, "Memorable Encounters," *Soviet Music* 4 (1978), commemorating Piatigorsky's 75th birthday.

19. Isaac Stern and Chaim Potok, *My First 79 Years* (New York: Knopf, 1999), 231–32.

The Students Remember

20. In alphabetical order, and by no means complete.

21. Letter to the Friends of Music Piatigorsky Celebration, March 2, 1976.

22. Article by Myung-Wa Chung for the author.

23. Article by Gary Hoffman for the author.

24. Article by Steven Isserlis for the author.

25. Culled from interview with Tim Janof, Internet Cello Society, September 1, 2002.

26. Culled from interviews with the author, May

2006, and Tim Janof, Internet Cello Society, October 10, 2005.
27. At that time Gerald Robbins and Doris Stevenson.
28. Article by John Koenig for the author.
29. Telephone interview with the author, June 6, 2002.
30. Richard Dyer, *Boston Globe*, April 24, 1983, p. N1.
31. Culled from a Soviet interview, "To Give the Audience the Best You Have," [Muzykal Na I A Akademi I A., "Otdavit' Publike Vse Lucsee" Moscow: Kompozitor, 1994, 120–23] and interview with Tim Janof, Internet Cello Society, May 27, 2007.
32. Culled from conversations with author and interview with Tim Janof, Internet Cello Society, February 17, 1999.
33. Article by Jeffrey Solow for the author.
34. Article by Paul Tobias for the author.
35. "The first rehearsal was a disaster because he couldn't even be bothered to tune his violin and didn't know when to come in. Piatigorsky got very cross and said, "How can you play so ugly, Jascha?" Everybody was very uncomfortable with the situation. However, he practiced by the time of the concert and it was an incredible thrill to be on the same stage with these two musical giants" (interview with Tim Janof, Internet Cello Society, July 10, 2004).
36. Article by Raphael Wallfisch for the author.

Part III : "Philosophies and Advices"

Musician, Teacher and Servant of Art

1. Included among these are Georg Faust (Berlin), William Stokking (Philadelphia), Lorne Munroe (New York, Philadelphia), Jules Eskin (Boston), John Martin (Washington, D.C.), Robert Sayre (San Francisco), Shirley Trepel (Houston), and Robert LaMarchina (Los Angeles, Chicago).
2. Henri Temianka, in conversation with Gregor Piatigorsky, Milton Thomas and Sidney Harth, "Pablo Casals," *The Instrumentalist* 27, no. 5 (December 1973): 34.
3. *An Afternoon with Gregor Piatigorsky*, dir. Steve and Elizabeth Grumette, Phoenix Films, 1974.
4. Culled from author's recollections, interview with Hugh Downs, NBC, 1974; Leroy V. Brant, *Etude* (July 1955): 20–1; Gregor Piatigorsky "Measurement of True Art," *Izvestiya (News)*, June 18, 1966; *Baltimore Sunday Sun*, June 3, 1973; Deena and Bernard Rosenberg, San Francisco Symphony magazine, November 1976; Marshall Berges, *Los Angeles Times*, Home Section, November 25, 1969; Henri Temianka, "An Interview with Gregor Piatigorsky," *The Instrumentalist* (February 1968); Peter Yates, "Visit to an Untyped Cellist," *High Fidelity* (February 1961), 45-7.

Musical "Advices"

5. He once asked me why the students laughed at one point during a master class. I replied, "You said that his turds [thirds] were out of tune." "So," he said, "they were!" I was forced to explain, which made him livid.

6. Culled from author's recollections; Lewis Segal, "Gregor Piatigorsky," *Los Angeles Times*, Home Section, November 25, 1969, p. 13, 50; interview with Hugh Downs, NBC, 1974; Deena and Bernard Rosenberg, "Gregor Piatigorsky," *High Fidelity/Musical America* (November 1976), MA-15, MA-37; Digby Diehl, *Los Angeles Times West* (magazine), June 4, 1972, pp. 47, 51; Art Seidenbaum, "Piatigorsky's Concerto of Cello and Charity," *Los Angeles Times*, November 17, 1963, p. B3.
7. The Berlin premiere of Webern's *Drei Kleine Stücke*, op. 11.
8. This was in his last season with the Berlin Philharmonic in a performance of Bach's *Saint Matthew Passion*, Bruno Kittel Choir, Georg Schumann, conducting. Schumann subsequently forbade Piatigorsky to be in the orchestra when he conducted.
9. Isaac Kashdan, ed., *The Piatigorsky Cup* (New York: Dover, 1978), introduction.
10. *Ibid.*

Cello "Advices"

11. Culled from the author's recollections; Piatigorsky's unpublished drafts; and interviews with Tony Thomas, "An Hour with Gregor Piatigorsky," CBC radio, 1966; interview with Hugh Downs, NBC, 1974; Samuel Applebaum, ed., "The Heart of the 'Cello," *Etude* (August 1947): 425–6; Samuel and Sada Applebaum, ed., *The Way They Play* (Neptune City, NJ: Paganiniana, 1972), 305–19; Peter Yates, "Visit to an Untyped Cellist," *High Fidelity* (February 1961), 45–47, 104; *An Afternoon with Gregor Piatigorsky*, a film by Steven Grumette, 1974; *The Piatigorsky Master Classes*, a film for KCET television, 1972; interview, *CBC Tuesday Night*, Larry Solway, host, June 21, 1966.

Part IV : Writings

Cellos

1. Unpublished draft.
2. Probably the *Seligman* Amati. Fine instruments acquire nicknames as identifiers, usually the name of an illustrious owner.
3. Described as from the "Amatese" (early) period.
4. The following is taken from publicity materials by Harold Holt, Ltd.
5. The cello's size was still not standardized, and most were slightly larger than a modern cello. The instruments were commonly cut down to adhere to the standard size established in the 19th century.
6. "It was like a story of Haroun Al Raschid and it wasn't until I actually played my new cello in concert that I realized that it was really mine." Many of the tales in the Arabian Nights take place in the caliphate of Haroun-al-Raschid, who is also a patron of the arts. In one called "Sleeper Awakened," the hero, Abou Hassan, sleeps as he is taken to Haroun-al-Raschid's palace. The attendants are ordered to do everything they can to make him believe he is the caliph. Hassan can't believe his sudden fortune. He subsequently becomes Haroun-al-Raschid's favorite subject.
7. It has since been in the possessions of Aldo Parisot, Orlando Cole and Heinrich Schiff.

8. Unpublished draft.

9. His first performance with the instrument was with Erica Morini in the Brahms Concerto, August 4, 1946, at Tanglewood. By November 1946 he confided to Koussevitzky, "I am happy sometimes with the new cello, but never with myself." Letters to and from Koussevitzky reprinted by permission of the Koussevitzky Music Foundation, Inc., copyright owner.

10. It was in the possession of Janos Starker for a number of years.

11. The career of Charles Baudiot (1773–1849) was impressive as a performer and professor at the Paris Conservatory, as he had written a cello method adopted by the conservatory. But he will always be remembered for a concert that took place in 1807 when he was to perform his own *Fantasie* on a theme by Haydn with orchestra. Before his appearance, the orchestra began with a Haydn symphony, the Andante movement of which Baudiot used as the theme in his *Fantasie*. Unaware that the symphony had just been performed, he was called to enter the stage. As he began, the audience began to snicker, assuming the performance was a joke. As the laughter continued it unnerved him and he played increasingly worse until he stopped, completely undone. A fellow colleague helped usher the dazed Baudiot off the stage.

12. Piatigorsky to Koussevitzky, February 1948: "My concerts are going very well, and my new Stradivari brings me tremendous joy. This cello really is peerless in all respects." Letters to and from Koussevitzky reprinted by permission of the Koussevitzky Music Foundation, Inc., copyright owner.

13. Piatigorsky, *Cellist*, 257–58.

14. October 1955. First played in a recital given at Stanford University on January 13, 1956.

15. *The Strad*, April 2005, p. 39.

CRITICS

16. James Vrhel, Donald Evans and Warren Benfield (CSO members) interview for the *Rosenthal Archives of the Chicago Symphony Orchestra, Oral History Collection*, Archives Number: OHP-A, ca. 1986.

17. Portraying Olin Downes of the *New York Times*.

18. Unpublished draft.

19. Portraying Claudia Cassidy of the *Chicago Tribune*.

20. Unpublished draft.

21. *London Times*, January 1937.

22. *London News Chronicle*, December 1936.

23. Interview with Ivor Newton, July 1974.

24. Hubert Saal, *Newsweek*, November 9, 1970, p. 87.

25. *Ibid*.

26. Piatigorsky, "Cellist II," an unpublished sequel.

27. *Chicago Tribune*, April 3, 1949, p. G2.

THE RELUCTANT JUDGE

28. *Los Angeles Times*, November 18, 1990, p. 6.

29. "Orange v. Bicycle," *Time*, July 5, 1954, vol. 64, p. 67.

30. Culled from Hurok Attractions materials.

31. "Measure of True Art," *Izvestiya*, April 17, 1962.

GERONTOLOGY

32. *Washington Post*, December 22, 1992, p. D11.

33. Culled from conversations with author and excerpts from Digby Diehl, *Super-Talk*, (Garden City: Doubleday, 1974); Marshall Berges, *Los Angeles Times*, Home Section, November 25, 1973, pp. 47, 51.

34. July 12, 1973, p. 43.

Part V : The Recordings

1. The early period could not have been written without the untiring detective work of Wolfdieter Jordan of Hamburg. It was Jordan who discovered the link between Piatigorsky and Boulanger and the earliest solo and salon recordings.

2. Lorand (1898–1960) was an extremely popular gypsy and salon soloist and made approximately two thousand recordings for Parlophon, averaging about 166 discs per year — the most prolific recording artist of the era in Germany. Lorand held the unusual position of conductor, a rarity for a woman in the 1920s and early 1930s. A Hungarian Jew, Lorand escaped Nazi Germany at the height of her career in 1934 and eventually emigrated to the U.S. There she toured with both an all-men as well as an all-women Hungarian orchestra, but she never regained the status she had in Europe.

3. Raucheisen (1889–1984) was one of the most popular accompanists in Europe, appearing with Fritz Kreisler and many other great artists. Piatigorsky and Raucheisen also performed recitals together in Berlin. Raucheisen married soprano Maria Ivogün, one of the era's most well known singers, for whom Piatigorsky had very high regard. Later, Raucheisen's pro-Nazi views dismayed the cellist. Raucheisen recalled his fond association with Piatigorsky in a letter to the author, June 6 ,1976.

4. Boulanger (1893–1956) was born in Romania and studied with Auer in Dresden and St. Petersburg. In 1910 Auer presented him with a violin that Boulanger used all his life. He developed his unique gypsy–Balkan folkloric–Viennese style entertaining the Russian aristocracy both in St Petersburg and Berlin.

5. Boulanger: *Vox Boston*, Vox 06166.

6. Boulanger: *Potpourri Russischer Lieder*, Vox 06167.

7. Kroyt (1897–1969) was known as a concert violinist throughout the twenties and, though he had soloed with the Berlin Philharmonic six times, was struggling in Berlin. For a time Kroyt wanted to become a conductor and had his first opportunity with Vox. Later, after performing with Richard Strauss, the composer asked Kroyt to lead his new orchestra, the Vienna Opera, after its celebrated concertmaster Arnold Rosé would retire. Kroyt, however, declined the flattering offer for personal reasons. Kroyt switched to viola and is now remembered primarily as violist of the famed Budapest Quartet.

8. However, famed conductors Oskar Fried and Erich Kleiber recorded with Vox, but with "pick up" orchestras. Piatigorsky can be heard in the Weber-Berlioz recording of *Invitation to the Dance* with Fried conducting the Vox Orchestra (Vox 01481) from August 1923.

9. Though Szreter and Piatigorsky are not identified on the label, the Vox catalog lists them as members of the trio. Kroyt himself also mentions them as his trio personnel in an interview with Nate Brandt, August 27, 1964, *American Music Series*, tape 5, part 1, Yale University.

10. Béla (1897–1978) was actually a Russian-Jewish émigré from Kiev by the name of Leonid Golzman and was deemed in Berlin "The Second Kreisler" as a violinist and "The German Paul Whiteman" as a bandleader. He found his calling as an ersatz gypsy-styled Hungarian bandleader, performing in the best hotels in Berlin. As

Dajos Béla (and other aliases), he became enormously popular and recorded over one thousand discs.

11. Interview with Max Rostal by Peter Tschupp in 1985. "Twenty years ago I asked Max Rostal who the performers of the Tri-Ergon Trio were. He answered: It is Karol Szreter, Gregor Piatigorsky and myself. We are young and needed money. But we didn't like to use our name, because the records were light classical music (*Salonmusik*)" (Letter to author December 22, 2005). Actually very few discs of the Tri-Ergon Trio with the Szreter-Rostal-Piatigorsky assemblage were released; most were with other performers.

12. Ivor Newton, *At the Piano: The World of an Accompanist* (London: Hamish Hamilton, 1966), 125–126.

13. *Schwann-1 Record & Tape Guide*, December 1974, p. 184.

14. Léon Goossens and Edwin Roxburgh, *Oboe: Yehudi Menuhin Music Guides* (New York: Schirmer, 1977), 162.

15. Letter to Alexander Stogorsky, November 18, 1957. The cadenza is published anonymously in the international edition of the concerto (Leonard Rose, editor). All of Piatigorsky's manuscripts and possessions were looted by the Nazis and were duly documented (by Sonderstab Musik) on February 19, 1941.

16. Milstein letter to Piatigorsky, March 3, 1976, and in *From Russia to the West.*

17. Gaby Casadesus and J. Muller, *Our Musical Marriage*, translated by P. Dussaux, Cleveland, Ohio: Hagley, 1993.

18. Comment to the author, July 1976.

19. Interview with Ralph Berkowitz, 1996.

20. To Adele Siegal, October 10, 1954.

21. Her interference was so complete that he was not able to correct the pianist's ornamental turn in measure 54 of the last movement in the Sonata in A Major, op. 69.

22. Berkowitz.

23. *Time,* February 25, 1966.

24. Philip Hart, *Fritz Reiner*, 86.

25. Jack Pfeiffer, RCA CD 61739.

26. Kapell to Piatigorsky, April 3, 1953.

27. Miklós Rózsa, *Double Life* (New York: Wynwood, 1989), 209–10.

Part VI : Appendix A

1. Possibly Nikolay Romanovich Bakaleinikov (1881–1957), who also wrote *Habe Mitlied mit mir...*

2. "The lacquer masters for this and all other Minneapolis Symphony Columbia recordings made from 12/6/41 forward were destroyed in 1990. All that is known to survive of this recording is the first movement, which is preserved on a 16-inch pressing in the YMW series located at Sony Music Archives in New York" (*ARSC Journal* 34, no.2 (Fall 2003): 169).

3. Takes Be 8456 and 8456-2 were issued but later destroyed.

4. Stamped as 193414.

5. Music published as *Sonatina in D*.

6. A test pressing *Herbstlied* with the matrix number 188A from 9/26/24 lists violinist Max Rostal.

Appendix E

1. Actually by Johann Ernst, Duke of Weimar (1696–1710).

2. *Ibid.*

Appendix F

1. A recording with cellist Diran Alexanian has been mentioned but not found.

Bibliography

Adaskin, Harry. *A Fiddler's World: Memoirs to 1938*. Vancouver: November House, 1977.

Agus, Ayke. *Heifetz as I Knew Him*. Portland, OR: Amadeus, 2001.

Alford, Kenneth D. *Nazi Plunder: Great Treasure Stories of World War II*. Cambridge Center: Da Capo, 2001.

Andrews, Frank, comp. *Parlophone Records 12 inch E Series 1923–1956*. Norfolk, UK: City of London Phonograph and Gramophone Society, 2000.

Applebaum, Samuel, and Sada Applebaum. *The Way They Play*. Neptune City, NJ: Paganiniana, 1972.

Atkins, Harold, and Archie Newman, comp. *Beecham Stories*. London, Robson, 1978.

Auer, Leopold. *My Long Life in Music*. New York: Frederick A. Stokes, 1923.

Axelrod, Herbert. *Heifetz*. Neptune City, NJ: Paganiniana, 1990.

Brant, Nat. *Con Brio: Four Russians Called the Budapest String Quartet*. New York: Oxford University Press, 1993.

Brinkmann, Reinhold, and Christoph Wolff, eds. *Driven into Paradise*. Berkeley: University of California Press, 1999.

Carpozi, George Jr. *Nazi Gold: The Real Story of How the World Plundered Jewish Treasures*. Far Hills: New Horizon, 1999.

Casadesus, Gaby, and J. Muller. *Our Musical Marriage*. Translated by P. Dussaux. Cleveland, Ohio: Hagley, 1993.

Chiba, Junnosuke, ed. *Haru no Umi*. Tokyo: Iwanami Shoten, 2002.

Dickson, Harry Ellis. *Beating Time: A Musician's Memoir*. Boston: Northeastern University Press, 1995.

Dickson, Harry Ellis. *"Gentlemen, More Dolce Please!"* Boston: Beacon, 1969.

Diehl, Digby. *Super-Talk*. Garden City NJ: Doubleday, 1974.

Dorati, Antal. *Notes of Seven Decades*. Detroit: Wayne State University Press, 1981.

Drobatschewsky, Dimitri. *My Father's Son: A Memoir*. Phoenix: Bridgewood, 2003.

Duke, Vernon. *Passport to Paris*. Boston: Little, Brown, 1955.

Ewen, David. *Men and Women Who Make Music*. New York: Readers, 1946.

Ferguson, Niall. *The House of Rothschild: The World's Banker, 1849–1999*. New York: Viking, 1999.

Fifield, Christopher. *The Rise and Fall of a Musical Empire*. London: Ashgate, 2006.

Fitzlyon, Kyril, and Tatiana Browning. *Before the Revolution: Russia and Its People under the Czar*. Woodstock: Overlook, 1978.

Flesch, Carl. *The Memoirs of Carl Flesch*. Translated and edited by Hans Keller. Salisbury Square: Rockliff, 1957.

Flesch, Carl F. *And Do You Also Play the Violin?* London: Toccata, 1990.

———. *...und spielst Du auch Geige?* Zurich: Atlantis Musikbuch-Verlag, 1990.

Furtwängler, Wilhelm. *Notebooks 1924–54*. Translated by Shaun Whiteside. London: Quartet, 1989.

Gaisberg, Fred. *The Music Goes Round*. New York: Macmillan, 1942.

Gay, Peter. *Freud, Jews and Other Germans: Masters and Victims in Modernist Culture*. New York: Oxford University Press, 1979.

Geissmar, Berta. *The Baton and the Jackboot*. London: Columbus, 1988.

Giddins, Gary. *Bing Crosby: A Pocketful of Dreams: The Early Years*. Boston: Little, Brown, 2001.

Gillis, Daniel. *Furtwängler and America*. New York: Manyland, 1970.

Ginsburg, Lev. *History of the Violoncello*. Translated by Tanya Tchistyakova. Neptune City, NJ: Paganiniana, 1983.

Glickman, Loren, comp. *Don't Squeeze de Bow! Reminiscences About Alexander Schneider*. Norwich: Terra Nova, 1996.

Golebiowski, Marian. *Filharmonia W Warszawie, 1901–1976*. Warsaw: Polskie Wydawnictowo Muzyczne, 1976.

Goossens, Léon, and Roxburgh, Edwin. *Oboe*. Yehudi Menuhin Music Guides, New York: Schirmer, 1977.

Green, Elizabeth A.H., with Judith Galamian and Josef Gingold. *Miraculous Teacher Ivan Galamian and the Meadowmount Experience*. Elizabeth A.H. Green, 1993.

Hart, Philip. *Fritz Reiner: A Biography*. Evanston: Northwestern University Press, 1994.

Hartnack, Joachim W. *Grosse Geiger Unserer Zeit*. Zürich: Atlantis Musikbuch-Verlag, 1983.

Hayes, Malcolm, ed. *The Selected Letters of William Walton*. London: Faber and Faber, 2002.
Hindemith, Paul. *Complete Works*, vol. 3, no. 6. Magda Marx-Weber and Hans Joachim Marx, eds. Mainz: Musikverlag Schott Musik International, 1984.
———. *Complete Works*, vol. 5, no. 7. Dorothea Baumann, ed. Mainz: Musikverlag Schott Musik International, 1992.
Horowitz, Joseph. *Classical Music in America: A History of Its Rise and Fall*. New York: W.W. Norton, 2005.
Hughes, Angela. *Pierre Fournier: Cellist in a Landscape with Figures*. Aldershot, Hants, England; Brookfield, VT: Ashgate, 1998.
Itzkoff, Seymour W. *Emanuel Feuermann, Virtuoso: A Biography*. Tuscaloosa: University of Alabama Press, 1979.
Jezic, Diane Peacock. *The Musical Migration of Ernst Toch*. Ames: Iowa State University Press, 1989.
Kashdan, Isaac, ed. *The Piatigorsky Cup*. New York: Dover, 1978.
Kater, Michael H. *Composers of the Nazi Era: Eight Portraits*. New York: Oxford University Press, 2000.
———. *The Twisted Muse: Musicians and Their Music in the Third Reich*. New York: Oxford University Press, 1997.
Kaufman, Louis, and Annette Kaufman. *A Fiddler's Tale: How Hollywood and Vivaldi Discovered Me*. Madison: University of Wisconsin Press, 2003.
Kennedy, Michael. *Portrait of Walton*. Oxford: Oxford University Press, 1990.
Kirk, Elise K. *Music at the White House: A History of the American Spirit*. Chicago: University of Chicago Press, 1986.
Kostelanetz, André, and G. Hammond. *Echoes: Memoirs of André Kostelanetz*. New York: Harcourt Brace Jovanovich, 1981.
Kraft, Robert, ed. *Stravinsky Selected Correspondence*, vol. 2. New York: Knopf, 1984.
Kresz, Mária, and Peter Király. *Géza de Kresz, and Norah Drewett: Their Life on Two Continents*. Toronto: Canadian Stage and Arts, 1987.
Leichtentritt, Hugo. *Das Konservatorium Der Musik Klindworth-Scharwenka Berlin, 1881–1931*. Festschrift aus Anlass des Fünfzigjährigen Bestehens.
Liebman, Roy. *Vitaphone Films*. Jefferson, NC: McFarland, 2003.
Malan, Roy. *Efrem Zimbalist: A Life*. Pompton Plains, NJ: Amadeus, 2004.
Menuhin, Yehudi. *Unfinished Journey*. New York: Knopf, 1977.
Milstein, Nathan, and Solomon Volkov. *From Russia to the West: The Musical Memoirs and Reminiscences of Nathan Milstein*. London: Barrie & Jenkins, 1990.
Mischakoff, Anne Heiles. *Mischa Mischakoff: Journeys of a Concertmaster*. Sterling Heights: Harmonie Park, Detroit Monographs in Musicology/Studies in Music, No. 46, 2006.
Morreau, Annette. *Emanuel Feuermann*. New Haven: Yale University Press, 2002.
Morrison, Simon. *The People's Artist: Prokofiev's Soviet Years*. New York: Oxford University Press, 2009.
Morros, Boris. *My Ten Years as a Counterspy*. New York: Dell, 1959.
Moscow Conservatory, 1866–1966. Moscow: 1966.
Muck, Peter. *Einhundert Jahre Berliner Philharmonisches Orchester*. Band 1–3. Tutzing: Hans Schneider, 1982.
Nestyev, Israel V. *Prokofiev*. Translated by Florence Jonas. Stanford: Stanford University Press, 1960.
O'Connell, Charles. *The Other Side of the Record*. New York: Knopf, 1947.
Piatigorsky, Gregor. *Cellist*. Garden City, NY: Doubleday, 1965.
Plaskin, Glenn. *Horowitz*. New York: William Morrow, 1983.
Potter, Pamela M. *Most German of the Arts: Musicology and Society from the Weimar Republic to the End of Hitler's Reich*. New Haven/London: Yale University Press, 1998.
Prieberg, Fred. *Trial of Strength: Furtwängler and the Third Reich*. London: Quartet, 1991.
Primrose, William. *Walk on the North Side: Memoirs of a Violist*. Provo, UT: Brigham Young University Press, 1978.
Richter, Sviatislav. *Richter in His Own Words*. Translated by Stewart Spencer. Princeton: Princeton University Press, 2001.
Robinson, Harlow. *Sergei Prokofiev: A Biography*. New York: Viking, 1987.
Rodzinski, Halina. *Our Two Lives*. New York: Scribner's, 1976.
Rosen, Charles. *Piano Notes: The World of the Pianist*. New York: Free Press, 2002.
Rosenberg, Deena, and Bernard Rosenberg. *The Music Makers*. New York: Columbia University Press, 1979.
Roth, Henry. *Violin Virtuosos from Paganini to the 21st Century*. Los Angeles: California Classics, 1977.
Rothschild, Jacqueline Rebecca de. *Jump in the Waves: A Memoir*. New York: St. Martin's, 1988.
Rózsa, Miklós. *Double Life*. New York: Wynwood, 1982.
Rubinstein, Arthur. *My Many Years*. New York: Knopf, 1980.
Saerchinger, César. *Artur Schnabel: A Biography*. New York: Dodd, Mead, 1957.
Saleski, Gdal. *Famous Musicians of a Wondering Race*. New York: Bloch, 1927.
Schnabel, Artur. *My Life and Music*. New York: St. Martin's, 1963.
Schwarz, Boris. *Great Masters of the Violin*. New York: Simon & Schuster, 1983.
———. *Music and Musical Life in Soviet Russia, 1917–1981*. Bloomington: Indiana University Press, 1983.
Shirakawa, Sam H. *The Devil's Music Master: The Controversial Life and Career of Wilhem Furtwängler*. New York: Oxford University Press, 1992.
Sieben, Hansfried. *Parlophon: Die Matrizen-Nummern der akustischen Aufnahmen 30 cm, Band I: 254 bis 8859 (1910–1926)*. Düsseldorf: Hansfried Sieben, 1990.
———. *Parlophon: Die Matrizen-Nummern der elektrischen Aufnahmen 30 cm, Band II: (1926–1933)*. Düsseldorf: Hansfried Sieben, 1990.

Skelton, Geoffrey. *Paul Hindemith: The Man Behind the Music*. London: Gollancz, 1975.

———. *Selected Letters of Paul Hindemith*. London: Yale University Press, 1995.

Stargardt-Wolff, Edith. *Wegbereiter Grosser Musiker*. Berlin: Bote & Bock, 1954.

Starker, Janos. *The World of Music According to Starker*. Bloomington: Indiana University Press, 2004.

Stuckenschmidt, Hans Heinz. *Schoenberg: His Life, World and Work*. London: John Calder, 1977.

Suchecki, Roman. *Wiolonczela od A od Z*. Krakow: Polskie Wydawnictwo Muzyczne, 1982.

Temianka, Henri. *Facing the Music: An Irreverent Close-up of the Real Concert World*. New York: David McKay, 1973.

Tóth, Aladár. *Válogatott Zenekritikái, 1934–1939*. Budapest: Zeneműkiadó, 1968.

Vries, Willem de. *Organisierte Plündererungen in Westeuropa 1940–45*. Köln: Dittrich, 1998.

———. *Sonderstab Musik: Music Confiscations by the Einstatzstab Reichsleiter Rosenberg under the Nazi Occupation of Western Europe*. Amsterdam: Amsterdam University Press, 1996.

Walton, Susana. *William Walton: Behind the Façade*. Oxford: Oxford University Press, 1988.

Wells, H.G. *Russia in the Shadows*. New York: George H. Doran, 1921.

Weschler-Vered, Artur. *Jascha Heifetz*. London: Robert Hale, 1986.

Wilson, Elizabeth. *Jacqueline du Pré: Her Life, Her Music, Her Legend*. New York: Arcade, 1999.

———. *Rostropovich*. Chicago: Ivan R. Dee, 2007.

Wordsworth, William, ed. *Jacqueline du Pré: Impressions*. New York: Vanguard, 1983.

Index

Numbers in ***bold italics*** indicate pages with photographs.

Abravanel, Maurice 172
Achron, Isidor 105
Adams, Wayman 147, 342
Adlon Hotel 40
Afternoon with Gregor Piatigorsky 162
Agranoff, Julia *11*
Agranoff, Leonid 9, *11*
Aitay, Victor 204
Akio, Yashiro 336
Aldrich, Robert 342
Alexanian, Diran 348
Alice Tully Hall 211
Allied Relief Fund 145
Amati, Nicolá 54, 266, 346
America Israel Cultural Foundation 200
American Fund for Palestinian Institutions 170
American Russian Committee for Medical Aid to USSR 146
Amoyal, Pierre 188
Amshislavska, Basya 5, 7, *11*, 333; *see also* Piatigorsky, Maria
Amt Musik 340
Andante et Rondo *97*, 107, 340
Anderson, Marian 289
Andrus Gerontological Center 275, 276
Antik, Lida [Lyda] 48, 50, *60*, 61, 67, 86, 87, *90*, 115, 336, 338
Applebaum, Sada 346
Applebaum, Samuel 346
Arensky, Anton 333
Armed Forces Radio Service [AFRS] 146
Arnold, Anna Bing 213
Aspen Festival *156*, 166
Atovmyan, Levon 127
Auber, Stephan 32
Auer, Leopold 7, 123, 206, 334, 335, 347

Babin, Victor 211, 291
Bach, Johann Sebastian 10, 346
Bachianas Brasilieras No. 5 (Villa Lobos) 214

Bakaleinikoff, Konstantin 160
Bakaleinikoff, Vladimir 288
Baker, Israel 188
Balogh, Erno 336
Balsam, Artur 336
Barber, Samuel 217, 288
Barbirolli, Sir John 90, 286
Barenboim, Daniel 184, *204*, *205*, 211
Bartók, Béla 54, *105*, 113, 114, 123, 337
Batta (Stradivari) 178, 188, 268, 269
Baudiot (Stradivari) 166, 268, 347
Bauldoff, Herbert 32, 33
Bay, Emanuel 215
BBC Symphony 80
BBC Television *104*, 112
Beare, Charles 269
Beck, Gilbert 157
Becker, Hugo 28, 51, 335
Beecham, Sir Thomas 103, 103, 105, 338
Beethoven Centenniary Festival 83
Beethoven Quartet 196
Beethoven Trios 186, 189, 285
Beglarian, Grant 207, 210, 213, 214, 345
Bekman Shcherbina, Yelena A. 18, 107, 334
Béla, Dajos 284, 285, 347
Bell Telephone Hour 146, 153, 162, 169
La Belle Blonde (Stradivari) 268
Belnick, Arnold 188
Belousov, Yevsei 127
Bengtsson, Erling 142, *204*, 228
Benny, Jack *179*, 200, 211
Benvenuti, Joseph *97*
Berezovsky, Leonid 129
Berezowski, Nicolai [Koyla, Nicky] 96, 100, 337
Berges, Marshall 346, 347
Bergonzi 19, 196
Berkowitz, Ralph 138, 144, 162, *180*, 215, 217, 219, 288, 290, 342
Berkshire Music Center 218

Berlin Philharmonic 34, 40, 43, 45, 47, 54, 58, 59, 91, 127, 133, 218, 271, 333, 336, 342, 346
Berlin Singakademie 336
Bernstein, Jascha 31, 32, 219, 335, 336, 345
Bernstein, Leonard 140, 202
Birnbaum, Zdislaw 27
Blech, Leo 38
Blinder, Naoum 334
Bloch, Ernst 58
Boccherini, Luigi 194, 200, 340
Boguslavsky, Mikhail 344
Bolshoi Theatre 18, *22*, 100, 196, 340, 345
Bor, Christiaan 188
Bose, Paul *41*, 43, 45
Bossert, Laura 345
Boston Symphony 151, 152, 168, 174, 177, 206, 224, 266, 335, 337, 341, 345
Boston University 174
Boucher, François 122
Boulanger, Georges 41, 283, 284, 347
Boult, Sir Adrian 154
Bradbury, Ray 202
Brahms, Johannes *26*, *31*, *57*, 54, 69, 72, 188, 190, 194, 218, 333, 338
Brahms Centenniary Festival 83, 84, 133
Brailowski, Alexander 107, 154
Brandt, Nate 347
Brandukov, Anatoly 13, *13*, 333
Brant, Leroy V. 346
Bronson, Carl (*Los Angeles Herald*) 63
Brott, Denis 249
Browning, John 211, 274
Brückner, Hans 92
Budapest Quartet 171, 194, 335, 336, 347
Bunin, Ivan 173
Burgin, Richard *151*
Burns, Bob 112
Busoni, Ferruccio 43, 337

353

Cage, John 137
California Youth Symphony 206
La Campanella (Paganini Piatigorsky) 108, 217, 287
Canadian customs 149
Cantelli, Guido 338
Capet, Lucian 340
Carini, Professor 99
Carnegie Hall 161
Carpenter, John Alden 176
Casadesus, Robert 287
Casals, Pablo 27, 58, 59, 68, 84, 105, 163, 189, 194, **201**, 202, 216, 250, 261, 263, 272, 342, 344
Casals Festival 194, 344
Casella, Alfredo 54
Cassadó, Gaspar 96, 103, **198**, 335
Cassidy, Claudia 157, 271
Castelnuovo Tedesco, Mario 96, 98, 100, 101, 174, 339
Celibidache, Sergiu 170
Chagall, Marc 338
Chaliapin, Fyodor 13, 103, 110, 112, 154, 333, 334, 338, 342
Chamber Music Society of Lincoln Center 211
Chandler, Dorothy "Buffy" 207
Chandler, Ralph 207
Chant du Minestrel 67
Chausson (*Poème*) 184
Cheifetz, Hamilton 210
Chester Publications 106
Chicago Symphony 142, 154, 158, 269, 289, 292, 341, 342
Choose Life 162
Chotzinoff, Samuel (New York World) 63
Chung, Kyung Wa 228
Chung, Myung Wa 228, 229
Church, Senator Frank 275, 276
City of London Festival 211
Clark House 207, 208
Cleveland Institute 211, 291
Cliff, Windy 121
Cohen, Arthur 342
Cohen, Isidore 195
Cole, Orlando 66, 346
Columbia Records 287, 342, 348
Columbia University 211
Community Concerts 64, 96
Compagnie des Grands Artistes Internationaux (CGAI) 107
Compinsky, Manuel 205
Concertgebouw Orchestra 67
Congressional Record 275, 281
Cooley, Carlton 289
Copland, Aaron 140, 152, 273
Cores, Alexander *see* Koretzki, Alexander
Cortot, Alfred 58, 107, 163, 261, 340
Cossmann, Bernhard 333
Courtauld Sargent concert series 69
Crawford, Joan 107
Crosby, Bing 111–112
Curtis Institute 54, 141, 144, 151, **164**, 217, 221, 237, 241, 345

Dahl, Ingolf 190
D'Albert, Eugen **31**, 284
Damrosch, Walter 342
Dane, Ernest B. 266
Dassin, Jules 342
Davidov, Karl [Carl] 12, 333, 334
Davidsbündler 116
Davydov, Karl *see* Davidov, Karl
Debussy 105, 177
Dechert, Hugo 335
De Courcy, Geraldine 74
De Falla 107, 109
de Kresz, Géza 36, 39, 335, 336
Delius, Frederick 103, 105
Delmoni, Arturo 344
Denver Symphony **139**, 153
De Pasquale, Joseph 188, 191, 223, 224, 343, 345
De Rosa, William 210, 249
De Rothschild, Bethsabée 213, 340
De Rothschild, Edouard [Baron] 115, 121, 122, **125**
De Rothschild, Germaine [Baroness] 117, **125**, 200, 218, 340
De Saram, Rohan 344
Dessau, Paul 134, 341
Detroit Symphony 67, 146, 335
Dickson, Harry Ellis 160, 168
Diehl, Digby 346, 347
Dixon, Dean 145
Dobrowen, Issay 40, 336
Dohnanyi, Ernst von 103
Don Quixote 20, 78, 79, 103, 132, 195, 222, 223, 272, 288, 334
Dorati, Antal 150
Dorfmann, Anja 115
Douglas, Roy 182
Downes, Olin 339, 347
Downs, Hugh 346
Drobatchevsky, Henry 36
Duchamp, Marcel 257
Dukelsky, Vladmir [Vernon Duke] 152
Dumas, Alexander 53
Dumont, Lily 336
Duntley, Leonard 123
Duport (Stradivari) 268
du Pré, Jacqueline **205**, 211
Dushkin, Samuel 83
Dvořák, Antonín 190, 333

Edge, Walter E. 340
Einstein, Albert 170, 279
Eisenberg, Maurice **32**, 335
Eisenhower, Dwight 82, 185
Eisenstein, Sergei 128
Elfentanz 53
Elman, Mischa 163
Enesco, Georges 145
Epperson, Gordon 141
Eskin, Jules 346
Eugen Onegin 9
Eyle, Felix 100

Farrar, Geraldine 62
Faust, Georg 142, 346
Ferrières, Château de 117
Feuermann, Emanuel [Munio] 30, 36, 51, 53, 96, 134, 141, 163, 167, 335, 336, 341
Feuermann, Sigmund 336
Feuermann, Sophie 52, 337
Fiameta 11, 12
Fiber, Michal [Mischa Mischakoff] **26**
Fifth Party Congress 19
Fine, Irving 273
First Film Concert 107
Fischer, Bobby 258
Fischer, Edwin 49, 163
Fishberg, Mischa 22, 334; *see also* Mischakoff, Mischa
Fishberg, Tevia 25
Fisher, Marjorie (*San Francisco News*) 63
Fitelberg, Grzegorz 20, 337
Fitzenhagen, Wilhelm 333
Flachot, Reine 174
Fleck, G. Peter 213
Fleisher, Leon 188, 189, 344
Flesch, Carl 30, 51, 54, **57**, 58, 69, 73, 83, 86, 145, 336, 339; *see also* Schnabel-Flesch-Piatigorsky Trio
Flesch, Carl F. [son] 336, 338
Flight of the Bumblebee 65, 337
Földesy, Arnold 47, 51, 52, 122, 266, 267, 284, 335
Fonda (Fournier), Jean Pierre 336, 337, 342
Ford Evening Hour 146
Foss, Lukas 97, 151, 152, 290, 342
Fournier, Pierre 88, **198**, 341
Frank, Alan 182
Fried, Oskar 347
Friedberg, Carl 51, 86
Friedberg-Flesch-Piatigorsky Trio 51, **64**
Fritsch, Theodor 92
Furtwängler, Elisabeth 154, 336, 337, 342
Furtwängler, Wilhelm 45, 48, **46**, 49, **50**, **52**, 54, **57**, 59, 61, 68, **72**, 73, 84, 86, 92, 93, 94, 133, 154, 258, 271, 337, 339, 342

Gabrilowitsch, Ossip 48, 67
Gaisberg, Fred 285, 292
Galamian, Ivan 123, **136**, 219, 334, 340, 345
Garbusova, Raya 142, 287, 335
Garrigues, Charles "Brick" 65
Gedike, Alexander Fyodorovich [Goedicke] 10, 29, 333
Gendron, Maurice 130
George, King VI 112
Gérard, Yves 200, 340
Gerigk, Herbert 92, 122
Gewandhaus Orchestra 34, 335
Gieseking, Walter 103, 163
Gigli, Beniamino 217
Gillis, Don 157
Gitlis, Ivry 87, 145
Glazunov, Alexander 6, 15, 16, 48, 49, 67, 68, 336, 337
Glehn, Alfred von 9, 12, **13**, 53, 333, 334, 345

Gluckmann, Grigori 49
Goebbels, Joseph 92, 285, 339
Goedicke 29; *see also* Gedike, Alexander Fyodorovich
Goldberg, Albert 273
Goldberg, Szymon 338
Goldenweiser, Alexander 18, 334
Goldsmith, Kenneth 345
Goldwyn, Samuel 160
Golschmann, Vladimir 338, 340
Goltermann, Georg 99, 333
Golzman, Leonid 347, 348
Goossens, Leon 286
Göring, Reichsmarschall Hermann 91, 122
Gorky, Maxim 14, 40, 336
Gould, Glenn 186, 273
Grammy 146, 192, 290
Gramophone Company, Ltd. (HMV) 90, 285
Graudan, Nikolai *52*, 338
Greene, Patterson (*Los Angeles Examiner*) 63
Greenhouse, Bernard 202
Greiner, Alexander 89
Griffith, Anthony 285
Grinnell College 3, 4, 211
Gromyko, Andrei 146
Grothe, Franz 336
Grotrian Hall 103
Gruber, Emanuel 249
Grumette, Steven 162, 346
Grümmer, Paul 335
Grünfeld, Heinrich 92, 284
Grützmacher, Friedrich 99, 335
Guarneri Quartet 337
Gubarev, Dimitri Petrovich 6, *13*, 333
Gutheil Schoder, Marie *41*, 43, 336
Gutman, Natalia *197*, 275

Hageman, Richard 174
Halir Quartet 335
Hals, Frans 122
Hambourg, Boris 335
Harrell, Lynn 210, 219, 220
Harris, Roy 176
Harrison, Beatrice 335, 344
Harsanyi, Tibor 105
Harshman, Alan 220
Harth, Sidney 337
Harty, Sir Hamilton 103
Hausmann, Robert 333, 335
Havemeyer, Horace 268
Hawks, Howard 160
Haydn Divertimento 190
Haydn Symphony no. 6 "Le Matin" 337, 346
Heermann, Emil 266
Heifetz, Benar 32
Heifetz, Jascha 48, 49, 54, 78, 82, 154, 161, 163, 167, 168, 173, 176, 180, 184, 186, *191*, *193*, 202, 210, *209*, 262, 292, 342, 345
Held, Adolph 28, 33, 34
Hemming, Fujiko 336
Herz, Gerhard 171
Herz, Otto 215

HIAS (Hebrew Immigrant Aid Society) 25, 28
Hill, Alfred 266, 267, 269
Hill & Sons 268
Hilsberg, Alexander 345
Hindemith, Gertrude 134
Hindemith, Paul 54, 83, 84, 86, 93, 94, 133, 141, *134*, *135*, 290, 337
Hitler, Adolf 48, 84, 91, 94, 339
Hochschule [Berlin] 29, 48, 335, 338
Hoelscher, Ludwig 335
Hoffman, Gary *212*, 229
Hofkapell Berlin 335
Hollywood Bowl 174
Holst, Henry *52*, 58
Holt, Henry Ltd. 333, 346
Honegger, Arthur 54
Honegger, Henri 32
Hoogeveen, Gottfried 249
Hooper, Johnny 123
Hoover, Herbert 82, 185
Hope, Bob 211, 345
Hoppe, Richard 36, 335
Hora Staccato 82, 163
Horowitz, Vladimir 48, *55*, 58, 61, 84, 86, 88, 90, 94, 154, 186, 292, 337, 342
Horowitz Milstein Piatigorsky Trio 75, *77*, *84*, *90*
Houston Symphony 142
Hubbard, John 210
Huberman, Bronislaw 27, 51, 58, 83, 84, 86, 93, 94, 133, 292, 339 *see* Schnabel-Huberman-Piatigorsky Trio
Humperdinck, Engelbert 336
Hunter, Ian 182
Hurok, Sol 167, 169, 165, 186, 288, 289
Huxley, Aldous 159, 256

Ibbs and Tillet 88, 89
Igumnov, Konstantin 18
Ikerman, Ruth C. 280
Ile de France 121
Imperial Russian Musical Society 6, 16
Indiana University 201
Institute for Special Musical Studies 206
Invitation to Music 146
Invitation to the Dance (Weber/Berlioz) 347
Ippolitov-Ivanov, Mikhail 9, 12, 333, 334
Israel Philharmonic 340
Isserlis, Stephen 210, *212*, 230
Iturbi, José 342
Ivogün, Maria 347
Izvestiya 16, 199, 274, 346

Jacobs, Arthur 184
Jacobsen, Sascha 172, 345
Jensen, John 345
Jewish Chatauqua Society 162
Jewish Council for Russian War Relief 146

Joachim, Joseph 333
Joachim Quartet 335
Jordan, Wolfdieter 347
Joyce, James 159
Judd, William 189
Judson, Arthur 54, 62, *71*, 88, 89, 163

Kabalevsky, Dimitri 196
Kabasta, Oswald 112
Kachouk, Mikhail 154
Kaiserhof Hotel 40
Kamei, Yukiko 313
Kandinsky, Wassily 40, 49
Kapell, William 292, 348
Karpilowski, Daniel 337
Kates, Stephen 196, 228, 230, 233, 253, 254
Katz, Paul 233, 234
Kaufman, Louis 344
Kaye, Danny 160
Keena, Leo 28
Kendall, Raymond 207
Kennedy Center 211
Kerensky, Alexander 15
Khachaturian, Aram 196
Khrennikov, Tikhon 196
Kineman *see* Koenemann, Fyodor
King, Terry 234, 235, 345, 346
Kinkulkin, Alexei 7, *32*
Kirchner, Wassily 49
Kittel, Bruno 346
Kiwanis Club 123
Kleiber, Erich 67, 347
Klein, Herbert (*Los Angeles Record*) 63
Klemperer, Otto 67, 91, 124
Klengel, Julius 7, 31, *31*, *32*, 53, 54, 205, 335, 345
Klindworth Scharwenka Conservatory 53
Knushevitsky, Sviatoslav 196
Kochanski, Eli 335
Kochanski, Paul 335
Kodaly, Zoltan 59, 188
Koenemann, Fyodor [Kineman] 10, 333, 342
Koenig, John 235, 237
Koodlach, Benjamin 1
Koretzki, Alexander [Alexander Cores] 35, *37*, 335
Kornauth, Egon 36, 335
Korngold, Erich 54, 174, *175*, 284, 342
Kostelanetz, André 27, 154, 335
Koussevitzky, Serge 20, 68, 87, 94, 96, 101, 102, 129, 131, 133, 135, 136, *143*, 150, 152, 158, 172, 173, 218, 219, 266, 273, 335, 346
Koussevitzky Music Foundation 173, 338, 346
Koutzen, Boris 35, 36, 39, 50, 54, 87, 117, 335, 337, 338
Kraft Music Hall 110
Kreisler, Fritz 163, 287, 335
Krenek, Ernst 51, 154, 336
Kreutzer, Leonid 48, 336; *see also* Kreutzer-Wolfsthal-Piatigorsky Trio

Kreutzer-Wolfsthal-Piatigorsky Trio *44*, 50, 284, 336
Krisch, Ferdinand 16
Kroyt, Boris 36, 41, *41*, 44, 45, 283, 284, 335, 337, 347
Kubatzky, Viktor 21, 334
Kulenkampf, Georg 58, 163
Kulturbund, Jewish 91, 110
Kuni, Prince Asaakira 108
Kurtz, Edmond 335

Lalo, Eduard 80
LaMarchina, Robert 142, 237, 238, 346
Landecker Loge 43, 45
Landowska, Wanda 122
Lateiner, Jacob 188, 221
Lateiner, Vera 345
Legge, Robert (*Daily Telegraph*) 67
Legge, Walter 178
Legion of Honor 170
Lehmann, Lotte 172, 345
Leipzig University 33
Lenin, Vladimir Ilyich 14, 17, 334, 336
Lenin Quartet (First State String Quartet) 15, 18, *16*
Leonard, Ronald 210
Lert, Richard 172, 345
Lesser, Laurence 188, 192, 238, 239, 249
Levitski, Mischa 112
Lexicon der juden in der Musik *119*
Lhevinne, Josef 112
Liadov, Anatol 334
Lieberson, Goddard 288, 292
Lifar, Serge 107, 340
Lincer, William 289
Lipatti, Dinu 215
Liszt, Franz 333
Locatelli, Pietro 40
London Philharmonic 80, 90, 154, 286
London Symphony 67, 69
Lorand, Edith 41, 283, 347
Lord Aylesford (Stradivari) 267
Los Angeles Philharmonic 65, 213, 221, 222
Louisville Chamber Society 171
Luboshutz, Pierre, Genia 100, 339
Ludlow, Lady 217
Lunacharsky, Anatoly 14, 16, 19, 34, 127, 334, 335

Magnin, Rabbi Edgar F. 213
Mahler, Gustav 43, 337
Mainardi, Enrico 53, 106, 163, 335
Maisky, Mischa 239, 241
Malinovskaya, Elena 334
Malko, Nikolai 335
Manicini, Henry 97
Mann, Fredric 123, *179*
Mann, Thomas 162
Marc, Franz 49
Marie, Grand Duchess 340
Marinel, Inna Elizabeth 22, 88, 334
Markevitch, Dimitry 232, 241
Martin, John 142, 346
Martinon, Jean 204

Martinu, Bohuslav 150, *151*, 190
Massenet (*Meditation*) 285
Master and His Class 162
Maxfield, J.P. 291
Mayes, Samuel 142, 174, 206
McCarthy, Joseph 196
McCormick, Ken 159
Meadowmount 123, 340, 345
Mehlich, Ernst 85
Mehta, Zubin 184, 195, 202, *202*, 207, 211, 213, 221, 223
Meir, Prime Minister Golda *203*, 211
Meistersinger 51
Melik-Pashayev, Alexandr 129
Melos *41*, 44
Mendelssohn, Felix 190
Mengelberg, Willem 66, 67, 337
Menotti, Gian Carlo 142, 211, 217
Menuhin, Yehudi 86, 94, 150, 154, 195
Merovitch, Alexander (Sasha) 54, 58, 61, *70*, *71*, *84*, 88, 90, 337
Metropol Hotel 11, 12, 67, 333
MGM 340
Miaskovsky, Nikolai 127
Milhaud, Darius 54, 97, 122, 174, 343, 345
Miller, Frank *148*, 202, 289
Milstein, Nathan 54, 58, 61, 65, 74, 76, *85*, 86, 88, 89, 154, *156*, 166, 212, 213, *212*, 275, 287, 289, 292, 336, 337
Minkus, Leon 333
Mirecourt Trio 213
Mischakoff, Anne Heiles 334
Mischakoff, Mischa 22, 36, 103, 335, 336; *see also* Fishberg, Mischa
Mr. Blok 158, 160
Mitropoulos, Dimitri 137, 154, *156*, 177
Mittman, Bronislaw 36
Mittman, Leopold 36, 335
Miyagi, Michio 108, 110, *108*
Mlynarski, Emil 25, 26
Mohr, Richard *171*
Moldenauer, Hans 211, 291
Molinari, Bernardo *90*
Monday Morning Musicals 145
Monn, Georg 173
Monteux, Pierre 170
Moore, Edward (*Chicago Tribune*) 63
Moore, Grace 82
Morely, Angela 175, 343
Morini, Erika [Erica] 58, *93*, 103, 266, 346
Morros, Boris 161
Moscow Conservatory 9, 10, 12, 13, 15; *Quartet* 333, 345
Mostras, Konstantin Georgievich 15, 17, 196, 334
Mozart, W.A. 107, 190
Muck, Karl *56*, 341
Mulert, Fridrich Vilgelmovich 333
Müller, Otto 45
Munch, Charles 177
Munroe, Lorne 141, 142, 346

Music Academy of the West 172, 206
Musical America *113*
Musicians Benevolent Fund 216, 217
Musicians Emergency Fund [Aid] *77*, 145
Mussolini, Benito 94
MUZO 16

Nabokov, Vladimir 40
Nansen passport 73, 337
NARKOMPROS [Narodnïy Komissariat Prosveshcheniya] 16
National Symphony 142
National War Fund Drive 145
Neikrug, George 343
Nelsova, Zara 106, 223
Neue Streichquartet 91
Nevsky, Alexander 128
New York Art Foundation 176
New York Philharmonic Symphony [New York Philharmonic] 25, 62, 67, 142, 145, 146, 174, 177, 287, 335, 337
Newton, Ernest 272
Newton, Ivor 75, 105, 128, *155*, 177, 215, 217, 285, 286
Nezhdanova, Antonina 18, 334
NHK Symphony 110
Niessen, Mathias 122
Nixon, Marni 202
NKID (Narodnïy Komissariat Inostrannïkh Del, the People's Commissariat for Foreign Affairs) 335

Ochi Albi, Nicolas 29, 65
Odeon *72*, 285
Oistrakh, David 170, *198*
Olevsky, Paul 142
Ophüls, Max 340
Orloff, Nikolai 18
Ormandy, Eugene 153, 288, 289, 292
Ostdeutsche Konzertdirektion Richard Hoppe 335

Pabst, Pavel 334
Paganini/Piatigorsky (*La Campanella*) 108, 217, 287
Paganini Quartet 186
Paganini Variations (Piatigorsky) 153
Paichadze, Gavriil 101
Painlevé, Paul 59
Parisot, Aldo 202, 341, 346
Parlophon recording company 41, 347
Parnas, Leslie *197*, 249
Partos Quartet 91
Passacaglia (Handel/Halvorsen) 23, 103, 192, 335
Pathétique (Tchaikovsky) 47
Pause That Refreshes on the Air 146
Pavlova, Anna 338
Pavlovsky, Valentin 62, 108, 123, 213, 287
Peabody Institute 174

Peck, Gregory 202
Peerce, Jan 161, 162
Pennario, Leonard 188, 220, 224, 290, 292, 293
Performing Arts Academy of the Music Center 207
Perlman, Itzhak 96, 184, **204**, 211, 213
Persinger, Louis 123
Peters, C.F. 92
Petri, Egon 36
Peyser, H.F. (*N.Y. Telegram*) 62
Pfeiffer, Jack 187, **191**, 292
Pfitzner, Hans 36
Philadelphia Orchestra 54, 146, 288, 292, 340, 345
Piastro brothers 53
Piatigorsky, Abram 7
Piatigorsky, Alexander [Shura] 5, **11**, 52, 146, 158; *see also* Stogorsky, Alexander
Piatigorsky, Gregory [cousin] 344
Piatigorsky, Isaac Abramovich 5, 10, **11**, 333, 334; *see also* Piatigorsky, Pavel [Paul] Ivanovich
Piatigorsky, Jacqueline Rebecca de Rothschild 115, 126, **125**, **210**
Piatigorsky, Jephta 117, 123, **125**, **210**
Piatigorsky, Joram 123, **125**, **210**
Piatigorsky, Leonid 5, 9, **11**, 196, 333, 334, 344
Piatigorsky, Lida *see* Antik, Lida
Piatigorsky, Maria 5, 7, **11**, 333; *see also* Amshislavska, Basya
Piatigorsky, Nadezha [Nadja] 5, 10, **11**, 333
Piatigorsky, Pavel [Paul] Ivanovich 5, 10, **11**, 333, 334; *see also* Piatigorsky, Isaac Abramovich
Piatigorsky, Polina [Paulina] 5, 333
Piatigorsky Chair in Violoncello at USC 210, 345
Piatigorsky Cup 258
Piatigorsky Memorial Scholarship 123
Piatigorsky Prize 174, 210
Piatigorsky Seminar for Cellists at USC 210
Piatti (Stradivari) 266
Piatti, Alfredo 335
Pilgrimage Theatre 188
Pinza, Enzio 342
Pittsburgh Symphony 288
Pleeth, William 335
Podgorny, Vasily 334
Polanski, Roman 50
Polk, Rudolph 160, 162, 342
Polydor 284
Polyphon 284
Pons, Lily 154, 161, 163
Popper, David 47, 214, 333, 336
Posselt, Ruth 152, 338
Pozniak Trio 36, 335
Prayer in Homage Ernst Bloch (Piatigorsky) 211
Previn, Andre 97
Primrose, William 143, 150, 176, 186, 191, 206, 216, 224, 345

Producer's Showcase 146, 162, 169
Prokofiev, Sergei 15, 127, 133, **131**, 335, 341
Prokofiev Meets Shostakovich in Moscow [Promenade or Stroll] (Piatigorsky) 132, 196, 341
Prunières, Henry 58
Pulver, Lev Milchaylovich 16, 334

Raccoon 124
Rachmaninoff, Sergei 15, 73–78, 214, 292, 333, 334, 338
Radiolympia 113
Rastelli, Enrico 65
Ratoff, Gregor 158, 342
Raucheisen, Michael 58, 163, 283, 336, 347
Ravel, Maurice 59, 88, 107, 108
Ravinia 161, 165, 167
RCA 288, 343
Reger, Max 61
Reiner, Fritz **142**, 161, 170, 287, 289
Reisenstein, Franz 336
Rejto, Gabor 188
Rembrandt van Rijn 122
Reshevsky, Sammy 258
Respighi, Ottorino 54, 337
Rethberg, Elisabeth 292
Das Rheingold 38
Richter, Sviatoslav 129
Riddle, Nelson 97
Rivkind, E. 10, 333
Robbins, Gerald 346
Robin Hood Dell 289, 340
Rococo Variations (Tchaikovsky) 34, 174, 284
Rodzinski, Artur 100, 123, 161, 335, 339, 342
Roemaet Rosanoff, Marie 344
Romberg, Bernhard 99
Ronald, Sir Landon 103
Rose, Leonrad 348
Rosen, Charles 290, 291
Rosen, Nathaniel 205, 241, 243
Rosenberg, Bernard 346
Rosenberg, Deena 346
Rosenstock, Joseph 110
Rosenthal, Paul 188
Rosowsky, Solomon 176
Rostal, Max 36, 285, 347
Rostropovich, Mstislav 130, **198**
Rothmuller, Daniel 214
Royal Philharmonic 181, 182, **181**
Rózsa, Miklos 174, 189, 192, 202, 205, 292, 293
Rubinstein, Anton 333
Rubinstein, Arthur 78, 117, 122, 152, 154, 161, 162, 166, 168, **201**, 274, 287, 290
Rubinstein-Heifetz-Piatigorsky Trio 161, 162, 165, 167, **171**
Rupp, Franz 289
Ruscho Café 35, 36
Russian War Relief 146

Sacher, Paul 150
Safonov, Vasily 18, 334
Saint Louis Symphony 142

Saint-Saëns, Camille 333
Saks, Toby 275
Salmond, Felix 141, 218, 341
Sandor, Arpad 215
Sandor, Gyorgy 172, 345
Sarasate, Pablo de 333
Sargent, Malcolm 69, 80, 181, **181**
Sayre, Robert 142, 346
La Scala 170
Scheherazade (Rimsky Korsakov) 27
Schelomo (Bloch) 58, 105, 337; *see also* Bloch, Ernest
Scherchen, Hermann 44
Scherzo (Piatigorsky) 107
Scheubel, Robert Schmitt 337
Schiff, Heinrich 346
Schifrin, Lalo 205, 345
Schippers, Thomas 171, 343
Schnabel, Artur **41**, 43, 45, 51, 58, 69, 71, 73, 83, 84, 86, 93, 94, 154, 163, 285, 286, 292, 336, 338
Schnabel, Karl Ulrich 336
Schnabel-Flesch-Piatigorsky Trio 50, **63**, 68, 72, 159
Schnabel-Huberman-Piatigorsky Trio 51
Schneider, Alexander 194, 195
Schneider, Mischa **32**, 35, 194, 195
Scholz, Janos 224, 225
Schön Rosmarin (Kreisler) 23
Schonbach, Sanford 188
Schonberg, Arnold **41**, 43, 45, 54, 162, 173, 271
Schott 105
Schram, Albert George 345
Schumann, Clara 333
Schumann, Elisabeth 107, 143
Schumann, Georg 346
Schumann, Robert (*Concerto*) 286, 287
Schuster, Joseph 51, 335, 337, 338
Schweitzer, Albert **157**
Scriabin, Alexander 334
Segal, Lewis 346
Segovia, Andres 98, 97, 100, 162, 202
Seidenbaum, Art 346
Serachevsky 41
Serenade Espagnole (Glazunov) 67
Serkin, Rudolf 58, 163
Sevcik 334
Sevizky, Fabien [Koussevitzky] 53
Shafran, Daniil **198**, 225, 227
Shakovskaya, Natalia **197**, 275
Shalyapin, Fyodor Ivanovich *see* Chaliapin, Fyodor
Shazar, Pres. Zalman 211
Sherman, Russell 273
Shirinsky, Sergei 196, 333
Shostakovich 103, 196, 199, 334, 344
Shumsky, Oscar 338
Shutkin, [Gaspar] 10, 11
Sicilienne (Faure) 58
Siegal, Adele 345, 348
Sills, Beverly 211
Siloti, Alexander 334

Sinatra, Frank 147
Sink, Charles A. 117
Skat 80
Sleeping Beauty (Montagnana) 266, 267
Smith, Warren Story 130, 341
Sokoloff, Vladimir 144
Solomon, Cutner 169, 289, 348
Solow, Jeffrey 214, 243, 245
Solway, Larry 346
Son, Harry 337
Sonderstab Musik **120**, 121, 122, 339
Soria, Dorle 160
Soutine, Chaim 49, 258
Souvenir de Spa (Servais) 13
Spalding, Albert 68, **143**, 163, 337
Spohr (*Double Quartet*) 220
Staatsoper Unter den Linden [formerly Königliche Kapelle (Royal Opera Theatre)] 336
Stack, Robert 202
Stanislavski, Constantin 19, 40
Stanislavski Theatre 18
Starker, Janos 289, 346
Stegman, Evel 43
Steinert, Alexander, Sylvia 68, 337
Stengel, Theo 92
Stern, Isaac 202, 212, 227, 228, 335
Stevenson, Doris **202**, 214, 346
Stewart, Reginald 194
Stiedry, Fritz **41**, 43, 44, 134
Still, William Grant 274
Stock, Frederick 103, 132, 133, 292
Stogorsky, Alexander 53, 196, 197, **198**, 261, 287, 333, 334, 348; *see also* Piatigorsky, Alexander
Stokking, William 142, 346
Stokowski, Leopold 65, 161, 292, 337
Stoliarski, Piotr 340
Stradivari, Antonio 122, 266
Stradivari Quartet 334
Strauss, Richard 78, **79**, 272, 290, 334, 336, 338, 339, 347
Stravinsky, Igor 54, 80, 98, 99, 162, 254, 273, 336, 337, 338
Strecker, Willy 136
Stroll (Piatigorsky) 341; *see also Prokofiev Meets Shostakovich in Moscow*
Stutschewsky, Joachim 335
Suchov, Ivan 40
Suggia, Guilhermina 335
Suk, Václav 18, 334
Super Sensitive String Company 146
Susskind, Walter 130
Szell, George 174
Szigeti, Josef 27, 59, 163, 292, 335, 337, 340
Szpilman, Wladyslaw 50
Szreter, Karol 36, 41, **44**, 73, 74, 163, 284, 285, 335, 337, 347, 348

Tanglewood 133, **165**, 218
Taneyev, Sergei 334
Tansman, Alexander 97
Taube, Michael 91
Taubman, Howard 343
Tchaikovsky, Modest 334
Tchaikovsky, Piotr 192, 194, 333, 334, 337, 338, 341
Tchaikovsky Competition 195, 200, 226, 227, 261, 274, 275
Tcherepnine, Alexandre 97, 174
Temianka, Henri 186, 202, 288, 337, 346
Thaviu, Samuel 341
Thibaud, Jacques 107, 145, 163, 261
Thomas, Michael Tilson 172, 244
Thomas, Milton 190, 195, 337
Thomas, Tony 346
Tobias, Paul 245, 246
Toch, Ernst 54, 97, 190, 200, 344, 345
Topping, Norman 207
Tortelier, Paul 106
Toscanini, Arturo 67, **90**, 90, 94, 98, 99, 169
Toscanini, Wally 169
Toscanini, Wanda 90, **90**
Totenberg, Roman 338
Trepel, Shirley 142, 346
Tri Ergon 285, 348
Triple Concerto (Beethoven) 50, 72
Tschupp, Peter 248

U.S. Junior Chess Championship 258
U.S. Navy Department **148**, **149**
U.S. State Department 177, 178
USO **147**
University of California, Los Angeles [UCLA] 206
University of Chicago 174
University of Southern California [USC] 191, 192, 206
Ussher, David Bruno (*Los Angeles Express*) 63

Valensin, Georges 107
Valeria, Tino *see* Kroyt, Boris
Vallin, Ninon 107
Van Beinum 154
Van der Pas, Theo 215
Varga, Laszlo 289
Veis, D. 10
Vengerova, Isabelle 144
Vermeer, Johannes 122
Vesselovsky, Alexander 22
Victory Disc [V Disc] 146
Vierne, Louis 105
Violoncello Society 225, 345
Vishau, B. 10
Vitaphone 340
Vladiguerov, Pantcho 336
Vlasov, Vladimir 20, 334
Vocalise (Rachmaninoff) 74, 214
Voice of America 146
Voigt, Ernest 134, 136
Volkbühne Konzerts 337
Volkskonzerts 45
Von Bülow, Gert 249
Von Bülow, Hans 333
Von Hindenburg, Pres. Paul 83, 91
Von Sauer, Emil 284

Von Vecsey, Franz 284
Vox recording company 41, 45, 284, 336, 347
Vuillaume 267
Vuillermoz, Emile 107, 340

Wadsworth, Stephen 345
Walenn, Herbert 335
Wallace, Henry A. 147
Wallenstein, Alfred 174, 188, 335
Wallfisch, Ralphael 230, 246, 247, 346
Walter, Bruno 47, 67, 161, 162, 174, 336
Walton, William 141, 162, 177, 185, 343, 344
War Department 146
Warner, Jack 207
Warren, Robert Penn 159
Warsaw Conservatory 26, 27, **26**
Warsaw Philharmonic 25, 28, **26**, 337, 339
Waxman, Franz 175, 176, 343
Weber, C.M. von 106, 107
Webern, Anton von 58, 211, 290, 291, 346
Weingartner, Felix 83
Wellesley College 211, 345
Wells, H.G. 14, 15, 22
Westby, James 97
Western Electric 291
Whalen, Tim, Jr. 162
Wilde, Oscar 180
Wilder, Billy 160
William, Alexander 130
Windisch, Fritz-Fridolin 44
Wolff, Louise 54, 73, 74
Wolff & Sachs concert bureau **37**, **46**, 54, **72**
Wolfsthal, Joseph 50, 163, 336; *see also* Kreutzer Wolfsthal Piatigorsky Trio
Women's Chess Olympiad 132
Wood, Sir Henry 103
Works Progress Administration [WPA] 145
Wurlitzer, Rembert 268

Yampolsky, Abram Ilyich 16
Yampolsky, Mark Ilyich 6, **13**, 333
Yates, Peter 346
Yekaterinoslav Conservatory 6
Young Musician's Foundation [YMF] 172, 206

Zakin, Alexander 35, 185, 227, 337
Zeisl, Eric 97, 176
Zeitlin, Lev Moiseyevitch 15, 17, 23, 38, 39, 334, 335
Zerev, Nikolai 334
Zigeunerweisen (Sarasate) 45
Zimbalist, Efrem 141, 143, 144
Zimin Opera Company 15, 334
Zirato, Bruno 124
Ziring, Vladimir 10
Zorich, S. 23
Zukerman, Pinchas 184, **204**, 211
Zweig, Fritz 172, 345
Zweig, Stefan 122

www.ingramcontent.com/pod-product-compliance
Lightning Source LLC
Chambersburg PA
CBHW081536300426
44116CB00015B/2648